BRET HARTE

TALES
OF THE
WEST

BRET HARTE

TALES OF THE WEST

EDITED BY **MARY ATKINS**

AVENEL BOOKS
NEW YORK

Introduction and compilation copyright © 1991 by Outlet Book
Company, Inc.

First published in 1991 by Avenel Books, distributed by Outlet Book
Company, Inc., a Random House Company, 225 Park Avenue South,
New York, New York 10003.

Printed and bound in the United States of America

Library of Congress Cataloging-in-Publication Data

Harte, Bret, 1836–1902.
    Tales of the West/Bret Harte: edited by Mary Atkins.
      p.   cm.
    ISBN 0-517-05289-X
    1. Western stories. I. Atkins, Mary, 1956– . II. Title.
PS1822.A85   1991
813′.4—dc20   90-47811
                                        CIP

8 7 6 5 4 3 2 1

CONTENTS

INTRODUCTION

TALES OF THE WEST presents the best of the short stories and novellas of Bret Harte, who captured the wild spirit and romance of the West during the era of the California Gold Rush. Harte was a masterful and entertaining storyteller who created a new and powerful literature of Western America. The colorful local characters and exotic landscapes in his Pacific tales are as fresh and compelling today as when they were first written.

Journalist, novelist, poet, playwright, and diplomat, Harte was a brilliant craftsman, but frequently a failure personally and financially. His close friendship with Mark Twain, for example, ended with a legendary and lasting enmity on both sides.

As an expatriate in Europe at the end of his long career, Harte was widely hailed as the true voice of American literature—the embodiment of one element of pioneer America. In some ways his public life was as meticulously crafted as his writing, although his private life was often awry and his difficult muses were known to be best inspired by late hours and a plentiful supply of whiskey.

To understand the genesis of Harte's California stories it is necessary to know something about the man himself. The following biographical extract from Harte's obituary appeared in *The New York Times* of May 7, 1902:

Several months ago, when a false report of his death was circulated in America, a correspondent called at Mr. Harte's rooms. He then appeared to be perfectly well. He laughed heartily, and quoted Mark Twain's old saying about the report being greatly exaggerated. "Except for a little cold," said Mr. Harte, "I have no ailments or complaints. While I am getting to be a pretty old man"—pointing to his snow-white hair—"there is life in the old dog yet," and thereupon he lighted a cigar so large that it would have done credit to any of his Poker Flat friends. . . .

Bret Harte was born at Albany, N.Y., and his family is still remembered by some people there. His father had been a professor in the Albany Female College, but died when comparatively young and left his family in very moderate circumstances. Bret Harte was born on Aug. 25, 1839, and received a common school education. Upon the death of his father the family decided in 1854 to migrate to California, and the journey was made via Panama. Soon after reaching San Francisco, Bret Harte set out for Sonora in search of work. He left his mother at San

Francisco and walked all the way to Sonora. There he taught school for
a time, but soon gave it up and commenced a wandering life among the
mining camps in the mountains. He was, at various times, a miner, a
mounted express agent, and a compositor. In the last-named capacity
he worked on a small paper at Eureka and began his literary career by
putting small sketches of his own into type and printing them in the
paper without consulting the editor. The latter, however, encouraged
him, and when he left the town for a time he put Harte in charge of the
journal. No sooner had the editor left than the leading citizens indulged
in a quiet little massacre of a band of Indians who had been bothering
them. Harte condemned these proceedings in a strong editorial and the
people of the town nearly wrecked the newspaper office in consequence.
He was obliged to leave in a hurry, and he made his way back to San
Francisco, reaching there in 1857. There, he went to work as a compositor on *The Golden Era,* but the editor encouraged his literary ambitions
and put him on the staff. By writing a series of San Francisco sketches
he acquired a local reputation. His one idea at this time was to write
something indigenous that would, as he said, "form the beginning of a
peculiarly characteristic Western American literature." His first important order was from *The Atlantic Monthly* in 1863, when he was twenty-
four years of age, and he turned out "The Society of the Stanislaus," the
first of his original and humorous dialect poems.

    Between 1860 and 1865 Harte wrote poems and lyrics of the war for
San Francisco papers, and in the latter year published his first volume, a
book of verses called "The Lost Galleon." His real fame, however, came
when he was made editor of *The Overland Monthly,* the second number
of which, published in August, 1868, contained "The Luck of Roaring
Camp." His next tale did not appear until the following January, when
he published "The Outcasts of Poker Flat." His literary reputation was
now established and the publication of the verses called "The Heathen
Chinee" in September, 1870, added greatly to his fame. Next to "The
Luck of Roaring Camp," his most celebrated production probably was
"The Heathen Chinee." He was for a time connected with *The Atlantic
Monthly,* which in one year is said to have paid him $10,000 for twelve
articles. He also won great success by lecturing on "The Argonauts of
'49." He took up his residence in New York, where he lived for several
years. He dramatized "The Two Men of Sandy Bar," which won a
moderate success. In 1878 he was appointed United States Consul at
Krefeld, Germany; and two years later was transferred to the Consulate
at Glasgow, but he resigned this position in 1885. He was heartily
received in English and Scotch literary circles, and at public banquets,
frequently responded to the toast "American Literature."

Harte's best and most enduring works are his short stories describing pioneer life on the Pacific coast—a lifestyle that within a decade of his brief experiences in the California gold mines had largely passed away. His voice is powerful and original, and was often considered in his time to be controversially racy. "The Luck of Roaring Camp" won him his literary reputation, but almost terminated his career at *The Overland Monthly* after a young female proofreader and the magazine's printer informed the publisher that Harte's writing was indecent, irreligious, and improper.

As the originator of a new genre in literature, Harte was able to create his own distinctive style. He also wrote his own criticism, using frequent lecture tours to air his views, as well as composing the introductions to the many editions of his collected works published in his lifetime. In the *Introduction* to the *Writings of Bret Harte* (Houghton, Mifflin, 1886), Harte described his working characterization of the Argonaut of '49:

> As a general thing the Argonauts were not burthened with sentiment, and were utterly free from its more dangerous ally, sentimentalism. They took a sardonic delight in stripping all meretricious finery from the speech; they had a sarcastic fashion of eliminating everything but the facts from poetic or imaginative narrative. With all that terrible directness of statement which was habitual to them, when they indulged in innuendo it was significantly cruel and striking. . . . Their humor was frequent, although never exuberant or spontaneous, and always contained a certain percentage of rude justice or morality under its sardonic exterior.

Vivid physical description, finely drawn characterization, and an acute ear and imagination for local dialect combined with meticulous craftsmanship make Harte's stories sensual, passionate, and eminently believable. At the beginning of "Flip," Harte's unusual description of the surrounding land introduces the emotion appropriate for his tragic tale:

> The heated air was filled and stinging with resinous exhalations. The delirious spices of balm, bay, spruce, juniper, *yerba buena,* wild syringa, and strange aromatic herbs as yet unclassified, distilled and evaporated in that mighty heat, seemed to fire with a midsummer madness all who breathed their fumes.

In this harsh land where character ruled, the strongest man (or woman) was not always the best. Harte's "A Drift from Redwood Camp" opens with one of his typical mood characterizations:

They had all known him as a shiftless, worthless creature. From the time he first entered Redwood Camp, carrying his entire effects in a red handkerchief on the end of a long-handled shovel, until he lazily drifted out of it on a plank in the terrible inundation of 1856, they never expected anything better of him. In a community of strong men with sullen virtues and dangerously fascinating vices, he was tolerated as possessing neither—not even rising by any dominant human weakness or ludicrous quality of the importance of a butt.

Finally, Harte's accurate ear for the humor inherent in local dialect brings a startling realism and another original dimension to his writing. This particularly delightful example comes from "The Man on the Beach":

"Look yer," he said finally, "I don't know ez it's your fault you don't know this kentry ez well ez you do Yurup; so I'll drag this yer team over to Robinson's on the river, give the horses a bite, and then meander down this yer ridge, and wait for ye. . . ."

The twenty-eight stories in *Tales of the West* are all drawn from *The Complete Works of Bret Harte,* a seven-volume collection revised by the author, and published by Chatto and Windus (London) in 1888. This modern anthology preserves the old-fashioned spelling and punctuation of the original volumes.

To read Harte's magnificent stories is to be moved not only with a nostalgia for the simpler times of the past, but with the immediacy of harsh sunlight beating down on the fragrant land where the pulse and emotion rushing through the stories ultimately becomes our own. To transcend time and space in this way, with such immediacy so many years later, is the signature of a master storyteller. But nothing less should be expected from the man who, as *The (London) Times* wrote, "revealed to the dull civilized world of the East that rough, new Western world, with its passions, problems, comedy, tragedy, pathos, and humour."

MARY ATKINS

New York
1991

The Luck of
Roaring Camp

THERE WAS COMMOTION in Roaring Camp. It could not have been a fight, for in 1850 that was not novel enough to have called together the entire settlement. The ditches and claims were not only deserted, but "Tuttle's grocery" had contributed its gamblers, who, it will be remembered, calmly continued their game the day that French Pete and Kanaka Joe shot each other to death over the bar in the front room. The whole camp was collected before a rude cabin on the outer edge of the clearing. Conversation was carried on in a low tone, but the name of a woman was frequently repeated. It was a name familiar enough in the camp,—"Cherokee Sal."

Perhaps the less said of her the better. She was a coarse, and, it is to be feared, a very sinful woman. But at that time she was the only woman in Roaring Camp, and was just then lying in sore extremity, when she most needed the ministration of her own sex. Dissolute, abandoned, and irreclaimable, she was yet suffering a martyrdom hard enough to bear even when veiled by sympathising womanhood, but now terrible in her loneliness. The primal curse had come to her in that original isolation which must have made the punishment of the first transgression so dreadful. It was, perhaps, part of the expiation of

1

her sin, that, at a moment when she most lacked her sex's intuitive tenderness and care, she met only the half-contemptuous faces of her masculine associates. Yet a few of the spectators were, I think, touched by her sufferings. Sandy Tipton thought it was "rough on Sal," and, in the contemplation of her condition, for a moment rose superior to the fact that he had an ace and two bowers in his sleeve.

It will be seen, also, that the situation was novel. Deaths were by no means uncommon in Roaring Camp, but a birth was a new thing. People had been dismissed the camp effectively, finally, and with no possibility of return; but this was the first time that anybody had been introduced *ab initio*. Hence the excitement.

"You go in there, Stumpy," said a prominent citizen known as "Kentuck," addressing one of the loungers. "Go in there, and see what you kin do. You've had experience in them things."

Perhaps there was a fitness in the selection. Stumpy, in other climes, had been the putative head of two families; in fact, it was owing to some legal informality in these proceedings that Roaring Camp—a city of refuge—was indebted to his company. The crowd approved the choice, and Stumpy was wise enough to bow to the majority. The door closed on the extempore surgeon and midwife, and Roaring Camp sat down outside, smoked its pipe, and awaited the issue.

The assemblage numbered about a hundred men. One or two of these were actual fugitives from justice, some were criminal, and all were reckless. Physically, they exhibited no indication of their past lives and character. The greatest scamp had a Raphael face, with a profusion of blonde hair; Oakhurst, a gambler, had the melancholy air and intellectual abstraction of a Hamlet; the coolest and most courageous man was scarcely over five feet in height, with a soft voice and an embarrassed, timid manner. The term "roughs" applied to them was a distinction rather than a definition. Perhaps in the minor details of fingers, toes, ears, &c., the camp may have been deficient, but these slight omissions did not detract from their aggregate force. The strongest man had but three fingers on his right hand; the best shot had but one eye.

Such was the physical aspect of the men that were dispersed around the cabin. The camp lay in a triangular valley between two hills and a river. The only outlet was a steep trail over the summit of a hill that faced the cabin, now illuminated by the rising moon. The suffering woman might have seen it from the rude bunk whereon she lay,—seen it winding like a silver thread until it was lost in the stars above.

A fire of withered pine-boughs added sociability to the gathering. By degrees the natural levity of Roaring Camp returned. Bets were freely offered and taken regarding the result. Three to five that "Sal would get through with it;" even that the child would survive; side bets as to the sex and complexion of the coming stranger. In the midst of an excited discussion an exclamation came from those nearest the door, and the camp stopped to listen. Above the swaying and moaning of the pines, the swift rush of the river, and the crackling of the fire rose a sharp, querulous cry,—a cry unlike anything heard before in the camp. The pines stopped moaning, the river ceased to rush, and the fire to crackle. It seemed as if Nature had stopped to listen too.

The camp rose to its feet as one man! It was proposed to explode a barrel of gunpowder, but, in consideration of the situation of the mother, better counsels prevailed, and only a few revolvers were discharged; for, whether owing to the rude surgery of the camp, or some other reason, Cherokee Sal was sinking fast. Within an hour she had climbed, as it were, that rugged road that led to the stars, and so passed out of Roaring Camp, its sin and shame, for ever. I do not think that the announcement disturbed them much, except in speculation as to the fate of the child. "Can he live now?" was asked of Stumpy. The answer was doubtful. The only other being of Cherokee Sal's sex and maternal condition in the settlement was an ass. There was some conjecture as to fitness, but the experiment was tried. It was less problematical than the ancient treatment of Romulus and Remus, and apparently as successful.

When these details were completed, which exhausted another hour, the door was opened, and the anxious crowd of men, who had already formed themselves into a queue, entered in single file. Beside the low bunk or shelf, on which the figure of the mother was starkly outlined below the blankets, stood a pine table. On this a candle-box was placed, and within it, swathed in staring red flannel, lay the last arrival at Roaring Camp. Beside the candle-box was placed a hat. Its use was soon indicated. "Gentlemen," said Stumpy, with a singular mixture of authority and *ex officio* complacency,—"Gentlemen will please pass in at the front door, round the table, and out at the back door. Them as wishes to contribute anything toward the orphan will find a hat handy." The first man entered with his hat on; he uncovered, however, as he looked about him, and so unconsciously set an example to the next. In such communities good and bad actions are catching. As the procession filed in comments were audible,—criticisms addressed perhaps rather to Stumpy in the character of showman:—"Is that him?" "Mighty small specimen;" "Hasn't mor'n got the colour;" "Ain't bigger nor a derringer." The contributions were as characteristic:—A silver tobacco box; a doubloon; a navy revolver, silver mounted; a gold specimen; a very beautifully embroidered lady's handkerchief (from Oakhurst the gambler); a diamond breastpin; a diamond ring (suggested by the pin, with the remark from the giver that he "saw that pin and went two diamonds better"); a slung shot; a Bible (contributor not detected); a golden spur; a silver teaspoon (the initials, I regret to say, were not the giver's); a pair of surgeon's shears; a lancet; a Bank of England note for £5; and about $200 in loose gold and silver coin. During these proceedings Stumpy maintained a silence as impassive as the dead on his left, a gravity as inscrutable as that of the newly-born on his right. Only one incident occurred to break the monotony of the curious procession. As Kentuck bent over the candle-box half curiously, the child turned, and, in a spasm of pain, caught at his groping finger, and held it fast for a moment. Kentuck looked foolish and embarrassed. Something like a blush tried to assert itself in his weather-beaten cheek. "The d—d little cuss!" he said, as he extricated his finger, with perhaps more tenderness and care than he might have been deemed capable of showing. He held that finger a little apart from its fellows as he went out, and examined it curiously. The examination provoked the same original remark in regard to the child. In fact, he seemed to enjoy repeating it. "He rastled with my finger," he remarked to Tipton, holding up the member, "the d—d little cuss!"

It was four o'clock before the camp sought repose. A light burnt in the cabin where the watchers sat, for Stumpy did not go to bed that night. Nor did Kentuck. He drank quite freely, and related with great gusto his experience, invariably ending with his characteristic condemnation of the newcomer. It seemed to relieve him of any unjust implication of sentiment, and Kentuck had the weaknesses of the nobler sex. When everybody else had gone to bed, he walked down to the river and whistled reflectingly. Then he walked up the gulch past the cabin, still whistling with demonstrative unconcern. At a large redwood tree he paused and retraced his steps, and again passed the cabin. Half-way down to the river's bank he again paused, and then returned and knocked at the door. It was opened by Stumpy. "How goes it?" said Kentuck, looking past Stumpy toward the candle-box. "All serene!" replied Stumpy. "Anything up?" "Nothing." There was a pause—an embarrassing one—Stumpy still holding the door. Then Kentuck had recourse to his finger, which he held up to Stumpy. "Rastled with it,—the d—d little cuss," he said, and retired.

The next day Cherokee Sal had such rude sepulture as Roaring Camp afforded. After her body had been committed to the hillside, there was a formal meeting of the camp to discuss what should be done with her infant. A resolution to adopt it was unanimous and enthusiastic. But an animated discussion in regard to the manner and feasibility of providing for its wants at once sprang up. It was remarkable that the argument partook of none of those fierce personalities with which discussions were usually conducted at Roaring Camp. Tipton proposed that they should send the child to Red Dog,—a distance of forty miles,—where female attention could be procured. But the unlucky suggestion met with fierce and unanimous opposition. It was evident that no plan which entailed parting from their new acquisition would for a moment be entertained. "Besides," said Tom Ryder, "them fellows at Red Dog would swap it, and ring in somebody else on us." A disbelief in the honesty of other camps prevailed at Roaring Camp, as in other places.

The introduction of a female nurse in the camp also met with objection. It was argued that no decent woman could be prevailed to accept Roaring Camp as her home, and the speaker urged that "they didn't want any more of the other kind." This unkind allusion to the defunct mother, harsh as it may seem, was the first spasm of propriety,—the first symptom of the camp's regeneration. Stumpy advanced nothing. Perhaps he felt a certain delicacy in interfering with the selection of a possible successor in office. But, when questioned, he averred stoutly that he and "Jinny"—the mammal before alluded to—could manage to rear the child. There was something original, independent, and heroic about the plan that pleased the camp. Stumpy was retained. Certain articles were sent for to Sacramento. "Mind," said the treasurer, as he pressed a bag of gold-dust into the expressman's hand, "the best that can be got,—lace, you know, and filigree-work and frills,—d—n the cost!"

Strange to say, the child thrived. Perhaps the invigorating climate of the mountain camp was compensation for material deficiencies. Nature took the foundling to her broader breast. In that rare atmosphere of the Sierra foothills,—that air pungent with balsamic odour, that ethereal cordial at once bracing and exhilarating,—he may have found food and nourishment, or a subtle chemistry that transmuted ass's milk to lime and phosphorus. Stumpy inclined to the belief that it was the latter and good nursing. "Me and that ass," he would say, "has been father and mother to him! Don't you," he would add, apostrophising the helpless bundle before him, "never go back on us."

By the time he was a month old the necessity of giving him a name became apparent. He had generally been known as "The Kid," "Stumpy's Boy," "The Coyote" (an allusion to his vocal powers), and even by Kentuck's endearing diminutive of "The d—d little cuss." But these were felt to be vague and unsatisfactory, and were at last dismissed under another influence. Gamblers and adventurers are generally superstitious, and Oakhurst one day declared that the baby had brought "the luck" to Roaring Camp. It was certain that of late they had been successful. "Luck" was the name agreed upon, with the prefix of Tommy for greater convenience. No allusion was made to the mother, and the father was unknown. "It's better," said the philosophical Oakhurst, "to take a fresh deal all round. Call him Luck, and start him fair." A day was accordingly set apart for the christening. What was meant by this ceremony the reader may imagine who has already gathered some idea of the reckless irreverence of Roaring Camp. The master of ceremonies was one "Boston," a noted wag, and the occasion seemed to promise the greatest facetiousness. This ingenious satirist had spent two days in preparing a burlesque of the Church service, with pointed local allusions. The choir was properly trained, and Sandy Tipton was to stand godfather. But after the procession had marched to the grove with music and banners, and the child had been deposited before a mock altar, Stumpy stepped before the expectant crowd. "It ain't my style to spoil fun, boys," said the little man, stoutly eyeing the faces around him, "but it strikes me that this thing ain't exactly on the squar. It's playing it pretty low down on this yer baby to ring in fun on him that he ain't goin' to understand. And ef there's goin' to be any godfathers round, I'd like to see who's got any better rights than me." A silence followed Stumpy's speech. To the credit of all humourists be it said that the first man to acknowledge its justice was the satirist thus stopped of his fun. "But," said Stumpy, quickly following up his advantage, "we're here for a christening, and we'll have it. I proclaim you Thomas Luck, according to the laws of the United States and the State of California, so help me God." It was the first time that the name of the Deity had been otherwise uttered than profanely in the camp. The form of christening was perhaps even more ludicrous than the satirist had conceived; but, strangely enough, nobody saw it and nobody laughed. "Tommy" was christened as seriously as he would have been under a Christian roof, and cried and was comforted in as orthodox fashion.

And so the work of regeneration began in Roaring Camp. Almost imperceptibly a change came over the settlement. The cabin assigned to "Tommy Luck"—or "The Luck," as he was more frequently called —first showed signs of improvement. It was kept scrupulously clean and whitewashed. Then it was boarded, clothed, and papered. The rosewood cradle, packed eighty miles by mule, had, in Stumpy's way of putting it, "sorter killed the rest of the furniture." So the rehabilitation of the cabin became a necessity. The men who were in the habit of lounging in at Stumpy's to see "how 'The Luck' got on" seemed to appreciate the change, and, in self-defence, the rival establishment of "Tuttle's grocery" bestirred itself and imported a carpet and mirrors. The reflections of the latter on the appearance of Roaring Camp tended to produce stricter habits of personal cleanliness. Again,

Stumpy imposed a kind of quarantine upon those who aspired to the honour and privilege of holding The Luck. It was a cruel mortification to Kentuck—who, in the carelessness of a large nature and the habits of frontier life, had begun to regard all garments as a second cuticle, which, like a snake's, only sloughed off through decay—to be debarred this privilege from certain prudential reasons. Yet such was the subtle influence of innovation that he thereafter appeared regularly every afternoon in a clean shirt and face still shining from his ablutions. Nor were moral and social sanitary laws neglected. "Tommy," who was supposed to spend his whole existence in a persistent attempt to repose, must not be disturbed by noise. The shouting and yelling which had gained the camp its infelicitous title were not permitted within hearing distance of Stumpy's. The men conversed in whispers or smoked with Indian gravity. Profanity was tacitly given up in these sacred precincts, and throughout the camp a popular form of expletive, known as "D—n the luck!" and "Curse the luck!" was abandoned, as having a new personal bearing. Vocal music was not interdicted, being supposed to have a soothing, tranquillising quality, and one song, sung by "Man-o'-War Jack," an English sailor from her Majesty's Australian colonies, was quite popular as a lullaby. It was a lugubrious recital of the exploits of "the Arethusa, Seventy-four," in a muffled minor, ending with a prolonged dying fall at the burden of each verse, "On b-oo-o-ard of the Arethusa." It was a fine sight to see Jack holding The Luck, rocking from side to side as if with the motion of a ship, and crooning forth this naval ditty. Either through the peculiar rocking of Jack or the length of his song—it contained ninety stanzas, and was continued with conscientious deliberation to the bitter end,—the lullaby generally had the desired effect. At such times the men would lie at full length under the trees in the soft summer twilight, smoking their pipes and drinking in the melodious utterances. An indistinct idea that this was pastoral happiness pervaded the camp. "This 'ere kind o' think," said the Cockney Simmons, meditatively reclining on his elbow, "is 'evingly." It reminded him of Greenwich.

On the long summer days The Luck was usually carried to the gulch from whence the golden store of Roaring Camp was taken. There, on a blanket spread over pine-boughs, he would lie while the men were working in the ditches below. Latterly there was a rude attempt to decorate this bower with flowers and sweet-smelling shrubs, and generally some one would bring him a cluster of wild honeysuckles, azaleas, or the painted blossoms of Las Mariposas. The men had suddenly awakened to the fact that there were beauty and significance in these trifles, which they had so long trodden carelessly beneath their feet. A flake of glittering mica, a fragment of variegated quartz, a bright pebble from the bed of the creek, became beautiful to eyes thus cleared and strengthened, and were invariably put aside for The Luck. It was wonderful how many treasures the woods and hill-sides yielded that "would do for Tommy." Surrounded by playthings such as never child out of fairyland had before, it is to be hoped that Tommy was content. He appeared to be serenely happy, albeit there was an infantine gravity about him, a contemplative light in his round grey eyes, that sometimes worried Stumpy. He was always tractable and quiet, and it is recorded that once, having crept beyond his "cor-ral,"—a hedge of tesselated pine-boughs, which surrounded his bed,—he dropped over the bank on his head in the soft earth, and remained with his mottled legs in the air in that position for at least five minutes with unflinching gravity. He was extricated without a murmur. I hesi-tate to record the many other instances of his sagacity, which rest, unfortunately, upon the statements of prejudiced friends. Some of them were not without a tinge of superstition. "I crep' up the bank just now," said Kentuck one day, in a breathless state of excitement, "and dern my skin if he wasn't a talking to a jaybird as was a sittin' on his lap. There they was, just as free and sociable as anything you please, a jawin' at each other just like to cherrybums." Howbeit, whether creep-ing over the pine-boughs or lying lazily on his back blinking at the leaves above him, to him the birds sang, the squirrels chattered, and the flowers bloomed. Nature was his nurse and playfellow. For him she would let slip between the leaves golden shafts of sunlight that fell just within his grasp; she would send wandering breezes to visit him with the balm of bay and resinous gum; to him the tall redwoods nodded familiarly and sleepily, the bumble-bees buzzed, and the rooks cawed a slumbrous accompaniment.

Such was the golden summer of Roaring Camp. They were "flush times," and the luck was with them. The claims had yielded enor-mously. The camp was jealous of its privileges and looked suspiciously on strangers. No encouragement was given to immigration, and, to make their seclusion more perfect, the land on either side of the moun-tain wall that surrounded the camp they duly pre-empted. This, and a reputation for singular proficiency with the revolver, kept the reserve of Roaring Camp inviolate. The expressman—their only connecting link with the surrounding world—sometimes told wonderful stories of the camp. He would say, "They've a street up there in 'Roaring' that would lay over any street in Red Dog. They've got vines and flowers round their houses, and they wash themselves twice a day. But they're mighty rough on strangers, and they worship an Ingin baby."

With the prosperity of the camp came a desire for further

improvement. It was proposed to build a hotel in the following spring, and to invite one or two decent families to reside there for the sake of The Luck, who might perhaps profit by female companionship. The sacrifice that this concession to the sex cost these men, who were fiercely sceptical in regard to its general virtue and usefulness, can only be accounted for by their affection for Tommy. A few still held out. But the resolve could not be carried into effect for three months, and the minority meekly yielded in the hope that something might turn up to prevent it. And it did.

The winter of 1851 will long be remembered in the foothills. The snow lay deep on the Sierras, and every mountain creek became a river, and every river a lake. Each gorge and gulch was transformed into a tumultuous watercourse that descended the hillsides, tearing down giant trees and scattering its drift and débris along the plain. Red Dog had been twice under water, and Roaring Camp had been forewarned. "Water put the gold into them gulches," said Stumpy. "It's been here once and will be here again!" And that night the North Fork suddenly leaped over its banks and swept up the triangular valley of Roaring Camp.

In the confusion of rushing water, crashing trees, and crackling timber, and the darkness which seemed to flow with the water and blot out the fair valley, but little could be done to collect the scattered camp. When the morning broke, the cabin of Stumpy, nearest the river-bank, was gone. Higher up the gulch they found the body of its unlucky owner; but the pride, the hope, the joy, The Luck, of Roaring Camp had disappeared. They were returning with sad hearts when a shout from the bank recalled them.

It was a relief-boat from down the river. They had picked up, they said, a man and an infant, nearly exhausted, about two miles below. Did anybody know them, and did they belong here?

It needed but a glance to show them Kentuck lying there, cruelly crushed and bruised, but still holding The Luck of Roaring Camp in his arms. As they bent over the strangely assorted pair, they saw that the child was cold and pulseless. "He is dead," said one. Kentuck opened his eyes. "Dead?" he repeated feebly. "Yes, my man, and you are dying too." A smile lit the eyes of the expiring Kentuck. "Dying!" he repeated; "he's a taking me with him. Tell the boys I've got The Luck with me now;" and the strong man, clinging to the frail babe as a drowning man is said to cling to a straw, drifted away into the shadowy river that flows forever to the unknown sea.

The Outcasts of
Poker Flat

As Mr. John Oakhurst, gambler, stepped into the main street of Poker Flat on the morning of the 23d of November 1850, he was conscious of a change in its moral atmosphere since the preceding night. Two or three men, conversing earnestly together, ceased as he approached, and exchanged significant glances. There was a Sabbath lull in the air, which, in a settlement unused to Sabbath influences, looked ominous.

Mr. Oakhurst's calm handsome face betrayed small concern in these indications. Whether he was conscious of any predisposing cause was another question. "I reckon they're after somebody," he reflected; "likely it's me." He returned to his pocket the handkerchief with which he had been whipping away the red dust of Poker Flat from his neat boots, and quietly discharged his mind of any further conjecture.

In point of fact, Poker Flat was "after somebody." It had lately suffered the loss of several thousand dollars, two valuable horses, and a prominent citizen. It was experiencing a spasm of virtuous reaction, quite as lawless and ungovernable as any of the acts that had provoked it. A secret committee had determined to rid the town of all improper persons. This was done permanently in regard of two men who were then hanging from the boughs of a sycamore in the gulch, and temporarily in the banishment of certain other objectionable characters. I regret to say that some of these were ladies. It is but due to the sex, however, to state that their impropriety was professional, and it was only in such easily established standards of evil that Poker Flat ventured to sit in judgment.

Mr. Oakhurst was right in supposing that he was included in this category. A few of the committee had urged hanging him as a possible example and a sure method of reimbursing themselves from his pockets of the sums he had won from them. "It's agin justice," said Jim Wheeler, "to let this yer young man from Roaring Camp—an entire stranger—carry away our money." But a crude sentiment of equity residing in the breasts of those who had been fortunate enough to win from Mr. Oakhurst overruled this narrower local prejudice.

Mr. Oakhurst received his sentence with philosophic calmness, none the less coolly that he was aware of the hesitation of his judges. He was too much of a gambler not to accept fate. With him life was at best an uncertain game, and he recognised the usual percentage in favour of the dealer.

A body of armed men accompanied the deported wickedness of Poker Flat to the outskirts of the settlement. Besides Mr. Oakhurst, who was known to be a coolly desperate man, and for whose intimidation the armed escort was intended, the expatriated party consisted of a young woman familiarly known as "The Duchess;" another who had won the title of "Mother Shipton;" and "Uncle Billy," a suspected sluice-robber and confirmed drunkard. The cavalcade provoked no comments from the spectators, nor was any word uttered by the escort. Only when the gulch which marked the uttermost limit of Poker Flat was reached, the leader spoke briefly and to the point. The exiles were forbidden to return at the peril of their lives.

As the escort disappeared, their pent-up feelings found vent in a few hysterical tears from the Duchess, some bad language from Mother Shipton, and a Parthian volley of expletives from Uncle Billy. The philosophic Oakhurst alone remained silent. He listened calmly to Mother Shipton's desire to cut somebody's heart out, to the repeated statements of the Duchess that she would die in the road, and to the alarming oaths that seemed to be bumped out of Uncle Billy as he rode forward. With the easy good-humour characteristic of his class, he insisted upon exchanging his own riding-horse, "Five Spot," for the sorry mule which the Duchess rode. But even this act did not draw the party into any closer sympathy. The young woman readjusted her somewhat draggled plumes with a feeble, faded coquetry; Mother

Shipton eyed the possessor of "Five Spot" with malevolence, and Uncle Billy included the whole party in one sweeping anathema.

The road to Sandy Bar—a camp that, not having as yet experienced the regenerating influences of Poker Flat, consequently seemed to offer some invitation to the emigrants—lay over a steep mountain range. It was distant a day's severe travel. In that advanced season the party soon passed out of the moist, temperate regions of the foot-hills into the dry, cold, bracing air of the Sierras. The trail was narrow and difficult. At noon the Duchess, rolling out of her saddle upon the ground, declared her intention of going no farther, and the party halted.

The spot was singularly wild and impressive. A wooded amphitheatre, surrounded on three sides by precipitous cliffs of naked granite, sloped gently toward the crest of another precipice that overlooked the valley. It was, undoubtedly, the most suitable spot for a camp, had camping been advisable. But Mr. Oakhurst knew that scarcely half the journey to Sandy Bar was accomplished, and the party were not equipped or provisioned for delay. This fact he pointed out to his companions curtly, with a philosophic commentary on the folly of "throwing up their hand before the game was played out." But they were furnished with liquor, which in this emergency stood them in place of food, fuel, rest, and prescience. In spite of his remonstrances, it was not long before they were more or less under its influence. Uncle Billy passed rapidly from a bellicose state into one of stupor, the Duchess became maudlin, and Mother Shipton snored. Mr. Oakhurst alone remained erect, leaning against a rock, calmly surveying them.

Mr. Oakhurst did not drink. It interfered with a profession which required coolness, impassiveness, and presence of mind, and, in his own language, he "couldn't afford it." As he gazed at his recumbent fellow-exiles, the loneliness begotten of his pariah-trade, his habits of life, his very vices, for the first time seriously oppressed him. He bestirred himself in dusting his black clothes, washing his hands and face, and other acts characteristic of his studiously neat habits, and for a moment forgot his annoyance. The thought of deserting his weaker and more pitiable companions never perhaps occurred to him. Yet he could not help feeling the want of that excitement which, singularly enough, was most conducive to that calm equanimity for which he was notorious. He looked at the gloomy walls that rose a thousand feet sheer above the circling pines around him, at the sky ominously clouded, at the valley below, already deepening into shadow; and, doing so, suddenly he heard his own name called.

A horseman slowly ascended the trail. In the fresh, open face of the newcomer Mr. Oakhurst recognised Tom Simson, otherwise known as "The Innocent," of Sandy Bar. He had met him some months before over a "little game," and had, with perfect equanimity, won the entire fortune—amounting to some forty dollars—of that guileless youth. After the game was finished, Mr. Oakhurst drew the youthful speculator behind the door and thus addressed him: "Tommy, you're a good little man, but you can't gamble worth a cent. Don't try it over again." He then handed him his money back, pushed him gently from the room, and so made a devoted slave of Tom Simson.

There was a remembrance of this in his boyish and enthusiastic greeting of Mr. Oakhurst. He had started, he said, to go to Poker Flat to seek his fortune. "Alone?" No, not exactly alone; in fact (a giggle), he had run away with Piney Woods. Didn't Mr. Oakhurst remember Piney? She that used to wait on the table at the Temperance House? They had been engaged a long time, but old Jake Woods had objected, and so they had run away, and were going to Poker Flat to be married, and here they were. And they were tired out, and how lucky it was they had found a place to camp and company. All this the Innocent delivered rapidly, while Piney, a stout, comely damsel of fifteen, emerged from behind the pine-tree, where she had been blushing unseen, and rode to the side of her lover.

Mr. Oakhurst seldom troubled himself with sentiment, still less with propriety; but he had a vague idea that the situation was not fortunate. He retained, however, his presence of mind sufficiently to kick Uncle Billy, who was about to say something, and Uncle Billy was sober enough to recognize in Mr. Oakhurst's kick a superior power that would not bear trifling. He then endeavoured to dissuade Tom Simson from delaying further, but in vain. He even pointed out the fact that there was no provision, nor means of making a camp. But, unluckily, the Innocent met this objection by assuring the party that he was provided with an extra mule loaded with provisions, and by the discovery of a rude attempt at a loghouse near the trail. "Piney can stay with Mrs. Oakhurst," said the Innocent, pointing to the Duchess, "and I can shift for myself."

Nothing but Mr. Oakhurst's admonishing foot saved Uncle Billy from bursting into a roar of laughter. As it was, he felt compelled to retire up the cañon until he could recover his gravity. There he confided the joke to the tall pine trees, with many slaps of his leg, contortions of his face, and the usual profanity. But when he returned to the party, he found them seated by a fire—for the air had grown strangely chill and the sky overcast—in apparently amicable conversation.

Piney was actually talking in an impulsive girlish fashion to the Duchess, who was listening with an interest and animation she had not shown for many days. The Innocent was holding forth, apparently with equal effect, to Mr. Oakhurst and Mother Shipton, who was actually relaxing into amiability. "Is this yer a d—d picnic?" said Uncle Billy, with inward scorn, as he surveyed the sylvan group, the glancing firelight, and the tethered animals in the foreground. Suddenly an idea mingled with the alcoholic fumes that disturbed his brain. It was apparently of a jocular nature, for he felt impelled to slap his leg again and cram his fist into his mouth.

As the shadows crept slowly up the mountain, a slight breeze rocked the tops of the pine-trees and moaned through their long and gloomy aisles. The ruined cabin, patched and covered with pine-boughs, was set apart for the ladies. As the lovers parted, they unaffectedly exchanged a kiss, so honest and sincere that it might have been heard above the swaying pines. The frail Duchess and the malevolent Mother Shipton were probably too stunned to remark upon this last evidence of simplicity, and so turned without a word to the hut. The fire was replenished, the men lay down before the door, and in a few minutes were asleep.

Mr. Oakhurst was a light sleeper. Toward morning he awoke benumbed and cold. As he stirred the dying fire, the wind, which was now blowing strongly, brought to his cheek that which caused the blood to leave it,—snow!

He started to his feet with the intention of awakening the sleepers, for there was no time to lose. But turning to where Uncle Billy had been lying, he found him gone. A suspicion leaped to his brain and a curse to his lips. He ran to the spot where the mules had been tethered; they were no longer there. The tracks were already rapidly disappearing in the snow.

The momentary excitement brought Mr. Oakhurst back to the fire with his usual calm. He did not waken the sleepers. The Innocent slumbered peacefully, with a smile on his good-humoured, freckled face; the virgin Piney slept beside her frailer sisters as sweetly as though attended by celestial guardians, and Mr. Oakhurst, drawing his blanket over his shoulders, stroked his mustaches and waited for the dawn. It came slowly in a whirling mist of snowflakes that dazzled and confused the eye. What could be seen of the landscape appeared magically changed. He looked over the valley and summed up the present and future in two words,—"Snowed in!"

A careful inventory of the provisions, which, fortunately for the party, had been stored within the hut, and so escaped the felonious fingers of Uncle Billy, disclosed the fact that with care and prudence they might last ten days longer. "That is," said Mr. Oakhurst, *sotto voce* to the Innocent, "if you're willing to board us. If you ain't—and perhaps you'd better not—you can wait till Uncle Billy gets back with provisions." For some occult reason, Mr. Oakhurst could not bring himself to disclose Uncle Billy's rascality, and so offered the hypothesis that he had wandered from the camp and had accidentally stampeded the animals. He dropped a warning to the Duchess and Mother Shipton, who of course knew the facts of their associate's defection. "They'll find out the truth about us *all* when they find out anything," he added significantly, "and there's no good frightening them now."

Tom Simson not only put all his worldly store at the disposal of Mr. Oakhurst, but seemed to enjoy the prospect of their enforced seclusion. "We'll have a good camp for a week, and then the snow'll melt, and we'll all go back together." The cheerful gaiety of the young man and Mr. Oakhurst's calm infected the others. The Innocent, with the aid of pine-boughs, extemporised a thatch for the roofless cabin, and the Duchess directed Piney in the rearrangement of the interior with a taste and tact that opened the blue eyes of that provincial maiden to their fullest extent. "I reckon now you're used to fine things at Poker Flat," said Piney. The Duchess turned away sharply to conceal something that reddened her cheeks through their professional tint, and Mother Shipton requested Piney not to "chatter." But when Mr. Oakhurst returned from a weary search for the trail, he heard the sound of happy laughter echoed from the rocks. He stopped in some alarm, and his thoughts first naturally reverted to the whisky, which he had prudently *cachéd*. "And yet it don't somehow sound like whisky," said the gambler. It was not until he caught sight of the blazing fire through the still blinding storm and the group around it that he settled to the conviction that it was "square fun."

Whether Mr. Oakhurst had *cachéd* his cards with the whisky as something debarred the free access of the community, I cannot say. It was certain that, in Mother Shipton's words, he "didn't say cards once" during that evening. Haply the time was beguiled by an accordion, produced somewhat ostentatiously by Tom Simson from his pack. Notwithstanding some difficulties attending the manipulation of this instrument, Piney Woods managed to pluck several reluctant melodies from its keys, to an accompaniment by the Innocent on a pair of bone castanets. But the crowning festivity of the evening was reached in a rude camp-meeting hymn, which the lovers, joining hands, sang with great earnestness and vociferation. I fear that a certain defiant tone and Covenanter's swing to its chorus, rather than any devotional quality, caused it speedily to infect the others, who at last joined in the refrain:—

"I'm proud to live in the service of the Lord,
And I'm bound to die in His army."

The pines rocked, the storm eddied and whirled above the miserable group, and the flames of their altar leaped heavenward, as if in token of the vow.

At midnight the storm abated, the rolling clouds parted, and the stars glittered keenly above the sleeping camp. Mr. Oakhurst, whose professional habits had enabled him to live on the smallest possible amount of sleep, in dividing the watch with Tom Simson somehow managed to take upon himself the greater part of that duty. He excused himself to the Innocent by saying that he had "often been a week without sleep." "Doing what?" asked Tom. "Poker!" replied Oakhurst sententiously. "When a man gets a streak of luck,—nigger-luck,—he don't get tired. The luck gives in first. Luck," continued the gambler, reflectively, "is a mighty queer thing. All you know about it for certain is that it's bound to change. And it's finding out when it's going to change that makes you. We've had a streak of bad luck since we left Poker Flat,—you come along, and slap you get into it, too. If you can hold your cards right along you're all right. For," added the gambler, with cheerful irrelevance—

" 'I'm proud to live in the service of the Lord,
And I'm bound to die in His army.' "

The third day came, and the sun, looking through the white-curtained valley, saw the outcasts divide their slowly decreasing store of provisions for the morning meal. It was one of the peculiarities of that mountain climate that its rays diffused a kindly warmth over the wintry landscape, as if in regretful commiseration of the past. But it revealed drift on drift of snow piled high around the hut,—a hopeless, uncharted, trackless sea of white lying below the rocky shores to which the castaways still clung. Through the marvellously clear air the smoke of the pastoral village of Poker Flat rose miles away. Mother Shipton saw it, and from a remote pinnacle of her rocky fastness hurled in that direction a final malediction. It was her last vituperative attempt, and perhaps for that reason was invested with a certain degree of sublimity. It did her good, she privately informed the Duchess. "Just you go out there and cuss, and see." She then set herself to the task of amusing "the child," as she and the Duchess were pleased to call Piney. Piney was no chicken, but it was a soothing and original theory of the pair thus to account for the fact that she didn't swear and wasn't improper.

When night crept up again through the gorges, the reedy notes of the accordion rose and fell in fitful spasms and long-drawn gasps by the flickering camp-fire. But music failed to fill entirely the aching void left by insufficient food, and a new diversion was proposed by Piney,—storytelling. Neither Mr. Oakhurst nor his female companions caring to relate their personal experiences, this plan would have failed too, but for the Innocent. Some months before he had chanced upon a stray copy of Mr. Pope's ingenious translation of the "Iliad." He now proposed to narrate the principal incidents of that poem—having thoroughly mastered the argument and fairly forgotten the words—in the current vernacular of Sandy Bar. And so for the rest of that night the Homeric demigods again walked the earth. Trojan bully and wily Greek wrestled in the winds, and the great pines in the cañon seemed to bow to the wrath of the son of Peleus. Mr. Oakhurst listened with quiet satisfaction. Most especially was he interested in the fate of "Ash-heels," as the Innocent persisted in denominating the "swift-footed Achilles."

So, with small food and much of Homer and the accordion, a week passed over the heads of the outcasts. The sun again forsook them, and again from leaden skies the snowflakes were sifted over the land. Day by day closer around them drew the snowy circle, until at last they looked from their prison over drifted walls of dazzling white, that towered twenty feet above their heads. It became more and more difficult to replenish their fires, even from the fallen trees beside them, now half hidden in the drifts. And yet no one complained. The lovers turned from the dreary prospect and looked into each other's eyes and were happy. Mr. Oakhurst settled himself coolly to the losing game before him. The Duchess, more cheerful than she had been, assumed the care of Piney. Only Mother Shipton—once the strongest of the party—seemed to sicken and fade. At midnight on the tenth day she called Oakhurst to her side. "I'm going," she said, in a voice of querulous weakness, "but don't say anything about it. Don't waken the kids. Take the bundle from under my head and open it." Mr. Oakhurst did so. It contained Mother Shipton's rations for the last week, untouched. "Give 'em to the child," she said, pointing to the sleeping Piney. "You've starved yourself," said the gambler. "That's what they call it," said the woman querulously, as she lay down again, and, turning her face to the wall, passed quietly away.

The accordion and the bones were put aside that day, and Homer was forgotten. When the body of Mother Shipton had been committed to the snow, Mr. Oakhurst took the Innocent aside, and showed him a pair of snowshoes, which he had fashioned from the old pack-saddle.

"There's one chance in a hundred to save her yet," he said, pointing to Piney; "but it's there," he added, pointing toward Poker Flat. "If you can reach there in two days she's safe." "And you?" asked Tom Simson. "I'll stay here," was the curt reply.

The lovers parted with a long embrace. "You are not going, too?" said the Duchess, as she saw Mr. Oakhurst apparently waiting to accompany him. "As far as the cañon," he replied. He turned suddenly and kissed the Duchess, leaving her pallid face aflame, and her trembling limbs rigid with amazement.

Night came, but not Mr. Oakhurst. It brought the storm again and the whirling snow. Then the Duchess, feeding the fire, found that some one had quietly piled beside the hut enough fuel to last a few days longer. The tears rose to her eyes, but she hid them from Piney.

The women slept but little. In the morning, looking into each other's faces, they read their fate. Neither spoke, but Piney, accepting the position of the stronger, drew near and placed her arm around the Duchess's waist. They kept this attitude for the rest of the day. That night the storm reached its greatest fury, and, rending asunder the protecting pines, invaded the very hut.

Toward morning they found themselves unable to feed the fire, which gradually died away. As the embers slowly blackened, the Duchess crept closer to Piney, and broke the silence of many hours: "Piney, can you pray?" "No, dear," said Piney, simply. The Duchess, without knowing exactly why, felt relieved, and, putting her head upon Piney's shoulder, spoke no more. And so reclining, the younger and purer pillowing the head of her soiled sister upon her virgin breast, they fell asleep.

The wind lulled as if it feared to waken them. Feathery drifts of snow, shaken from the long pine-boughs, flew like white-winged birds, and settled about them as they slept. The moon through the rifted clouds looked down upon what had been the camp. But all human stain, all trace of earthly travail, was hidden beneath the spotless mantle mercifully flung from above.

They slept all that day and the next, nor did they waken when voices and footsteps broke the silence of the camp. And when pitying fingers brushed the snow from their wan faces, you could scarcely have told from the equal peace that dwelt upon them which was she that had sinned. Even the law of Poker Flat recognised this, and turned away, leaving them still locked in each other's arms.

But at the head of the gulch, on one of the largest pine trees, they found the deuce of clubs pinned to the bark with a bowie-knife. It bore the following, written in pencil in a firm hand:—

†
BENEATH THIS TREE
LIES THE BODY
OF
JOHN OAKHURST,
WHO STRUCK A STREAK OF BAD LUCK
ON THE 23D OF NOVEMBER 1850,
AND
HANDED IN HIS CHECKS
ON THE 7TH DECEMBER 1850.
⸸

And pulseless and cold, with a Derringer by his side and a bullet in his heart, though still calm as in life, beneath the snow lay he who was at once the strongest and yet the weakest of the outcasts of Poker Flat.

The Idyl of Red Gulch

SANDY WAS VERY DRUNK. He was lying under an azalea bush, in pretty much the same attitude in which he had fallen some hours before. How long he had been lying there he could not tell, and didn't care; how long he should lie there was a matter equally indefinite and unconsidered. A tranquil philosophy, born of his physical condition, suffused and saturated his moral being.

The spectacle of a drunken man, and of this drunken man in particular, was not, I grieve to say, of sufficient novelty in Red Gulch to attract attention. Earlier in the day some local satirist had erected a temporary tombstone at Sandy's head, bearing the inscription, "Effects of McCorkle's whisky,—kills at forty rods," with a hand pointing to McCorkle's saloon. But this, I imagine, was, like most local satire, personal; and was a reflection upon the unfairness of the process rather than a commentary upon the impropriety of the result. With this facetious exception, Sandy had been undisturbed. A wandering mule, released from his pack, had cropped the scant herbage beside him, and sniffed curiously at the prostrate man; a vagabond dog, with that deep sympathy which the species have for drunken men, had licked his dusty boots and curled himself up at his feet, and lay there, blinking one eye in the sunlight, with a simulation of dissipation that was ingenious and dog-like in its implied flattery of the unconscious man beside him.

Meanwhile the shadows of the pine trees had slowly swung around until they crossed the road, and their trunks barred the open meadow with gigantic parallels of black and yellow. Little puffs of red dust, lifted by the plunging hoofs of passing teams, dispersed in a grimy shower upon the recumbent man. The sun sank lower and lower, and still Sandy stirred not. And then the repose of this philosopher was disturbed, as other philosophers have been, by the intrusion of an unphilosophical sex.

"Miss Mary," as she was known to the little flock that she had just dismissed from the log schoolhouse beyond the pines, was taking her afternoon walk. Observing an unusually fine cluster of blossoms on the azalea bush opposite, she crossed the road to pluck it, picking her way through the red dust, not without certain fierce little shivers of disgust and some feline circumlocution. And then she came suddenly upon Sandy!

Of course she uttered the little *staccato* cry of her sex. But when she had paid that tribute to her physical weakness she became overbold and halted for a moment,—at least six feet from this prostrate monster,—with her white skirts gathered in her hand, ready for flight. But neither sound nor motion came from the bush. With one little foot she then overturned the satirical headboard, and muttered "Beasts!"—an epithet which probably, at that moment, conveniently classified in her mind the entire male population of Red Gulch. For Miss Mary being possessed of certain rigid notions of her own, had not, perhaps, properly appreciated the demonstrative gallantry for which the Californian has been so justly celebrated by his brother Californians, and had, as a newcomer, perhaps fairly earned the reputation of being "stuck up."

As she stood there she noticed, also, that the slant sunbeams were heating Sandy's head to what she judged to be an unhealthy temperature, and that his hat was lying uselessly at his side. To pick it up and to place it over his face was a work requiring some courage, particularly as his eyes were open. Yet she did it and made good her retreat. But she was somewhat concerned, on looking back, to see that the hat was removed, and that Sandy was sitting up and saying something.

The truth was, that in the calm depths of Sandy's mind he was satisfied that the rays of the sun were beneficial and healthful; that from childhood he had objected to lying down in a hat; that no people but condemned fools, past redemption, ever wore hats; and that his right to dispense with them when he pleased was inalienable. This was the statement of his inner consciousness. Unfortunately, its outward expression was vague, being limited to a repetition of the following formula:—"Su'shine all ri'! Wasser maär, eh? Wass up, su'shine?"

Miss Mary stopped, and, taking fresh courage from her vantage of distance, asked him if there was anything that he wanted.

"Wass up? Wasser maär?" continued Sandy, in a very high key.

"Get up, you horrid man!" said Miss Mary, now thoroughly incensed; "get up and go home."

Sandy staggered to his feet. He was six feet high, and Miss Mary trembled. He started forward a few paces and then stopped.

"Wass I go home for?" he suddenly asked, with great gravity.

"Go and take a bath," replied Miss Mary, eying his grimy person with great disfavour.

To her infinite dismay, Sandy suddenly pulled off his coat and vest, threw them on the ground, kicked off his boots, and, plunging wildly forward, darted headlong over the hill in the direction of the river.

"Goodness Heavens! the man will be drowned!" said Miss Mary; and then, with feminine inconsistency, she ran back to the schoolhouse and locked herself in.

That night, while seated at supper with her hostess, the blacksmith's wife, it came to Miss Mary to ask, demurely, if her husband ever got drunk. "Abner," responded Mrs. Stidger reflectively, "let's see! Abner hasn't been tight since last 'lection." Miss Mary would have liked to ask if he preferred lying in the sun on these occasions, and if a cold bath would have hurt him; but this would have involved an explanation, which she did not then care to give. So she contented herself with opening her grey eyes widely at the red-cheeked Mrs. Stidger,—a fine specimen of South-Western efflorescence,—and then dismissed the subject altogether. The next day she wrote to her dearest friend in Boston: "I think I find the intoxicated portion of this community the least objectionable. I refer, my dear, to the men, of course. I do not know anything that could make the women tolerable."

In less than a week Miss Mary had forgotten this episode, except that her afternoon walks took thereafter, almost unconsciously, another direction. She noticed, however, that every morning a fresh cluster of azalea blossoms appeared among the flowers on her desk. This was not strange, as her little flock were aware of her fondness for flowers, and invariably kept her desk bright with anemones, syringas, and lupines; but, on questioning them, they one and all professed ignorance of the azaleas. A few days later, Master Johnny Stidger, whose desk was nearest to the window, was suddenly taken with spasms of apparently gratuitous laughter, that threatened the discipline of the school. All that Miss Mary could get from him was, that some one had been "looking in the winder." Irate and indignant, she sallied from her hive to do battle with the intruder. As she turned the corner of the schoolhouse she came plump upon the quondam drunkard, now perfectly sober, and inexpressibly sheepish and guilty-looking.

These facts Miss Mary was not slow to take a feminine advantage of, in her present humour. But it was somewhat confusing to observe, also, that the beast, despite some faint signs of past dissipation, was amiable looking,—in fact, a kind of blonde Samson, whose corn-coloured silken beard apparently had never yet known the touch of barber's razor or Delilah's shears. So that the cutting speech which quivered on her ready tongue died upon her lips, and she contented herself with receiving his stammering apology with supercilious eyelids and the gathered skirts of uncontamination. When she re-entered the schoolroom, her eyes fell upon the azaleas with a new sense of revelation; and then she laughed, and the little people all laughed, and they were all unconsciously very happy.

It was on a hot day—and not long after this—that two short-legged boys came to grief on the threshold of the school with a pail of water, which they had laboriously brought from the spring, and that Miss Mary compassionately seized the pail and started for the spring herself. At the foot of the hill a shadow crossed her path, and a blue-shirted arm dexterously but gently relieved her of her burden. Miss Mary was both embarrassed and angry. "If you carried more of that for yourself," she said spitefully to the blue arm, without deigning to raise her lashes to its owner, "you'd do better." In the submissive silence that followed she regretted the speech, and thanked him so sweetly at the door that he stumbled. Which caused the children to laugh again,—a laugh in which Miss Mary joined, until the colour came faintly into her pale cheek. The next day a barrel was mysteriously placed beside the door, and as mysteriously filled with fresh spring-water every morning.

Nor was this superior young person without other quiet attentions. "Profane Bill," driver of the Slumgullion Stage, widely known in the newspapers for his "gallantry" in invariably offering the box-seat to the fair sex, had excepted Miss Mary from this attention, on the ground that he had a habit of "cussin' on up grades," and gave her half the coach to herself. Jack Hamlin, a gambler, having once silently ridden with her in the same coach, afterward threw a decanter at the head of a confederate for mentioning her name in a bar-room. The over-dressed mother of a pupil whose paternity was doubtful had often lingered near this astute Vestal's temple, never daring to enter its sacred precincts, but content to worship the priestess from afar.

With such unconscious intervals the monotonous procession of blue skies, glittering sunshine, brief twilights, and starlit nights passed over

Red Gulch. Miss Mary grew fond of walking in the sedate and proper woods. Perhaps she believed, with Mrs. Stidger, that the balsamic odours of the firs "did her chest good," for certainly her slight cough was less frequent and her step was firmer; perhaps she had learned the unending lesson which the patient pines are never weary of repeating to heedful or listless ears. And so one day she planned a picnic on Buckeye Hill, and took the children with her. Away from the dusty road, the straggling shanties, the yellow ditches, the clamour of restless engines, the cheap finery of shop-windows, the deeper glitter of paint and coloured glass, and the thin veneering which barbarism takes upon itself in such localities, what infinite relief was theirs! The last heap of ragged rock and clay passed, the last unsightly chasm crossed,—how the waiting woods opened their long files to receive them! How the children—perhaps because they had not yet grown quite away from the breast of the bounteous Mother—threw themselves face downward on her brown bosom with uncouth caresses, filling the air with their laughter; and how Miss Mary herself—felinely fastidious and intrenched as she was in the purity of spotless skirts, collar, and cuffs—forgot all, and ran like a crested quail at the head of her brood, until, romping, laughing, and panting, with a loosened braid of brown hair, a hat hanging by a knotted ribbon from her throat, she came suddenly and violently, in the heart of the forest, upon the luckless Sandy!

The explanations, apologies, and not overwise conversation that ensued need not be indicated here. It would seem, however, that Miss Mary had already established some acquaintance with this ex-drunkard. Enough that he was soon accepted as one of the party; that the children, with that quick intelligence which Providence gives the helpless, recognised a friend, and played with his blonde beard and long silken mustache, and took other liberties,—as the helpless are apt to do. And when he had built a fire against a tree, and had shown them other mysteries of woodcraft, their admiration knew no bounds. At the close of two such foolish, idle, happy hours he found himself lying at the feet of the schoolmistress, gazing dreamily in her face as she sat upon the sloping hillside weaving wreaths of laurel and syringa, in very much the same attitude as he had lain when first they met. Nor was the similitude greatly forced. The weakness of an easy, sensuous nature, that had found a dreamy exaltation in liquor, it is to be feared was now finding an equal intoxication in love.

I think that Sandy was dimly conscious of this himself. I know that he longed to be doing something,—slaying a grizzly, scalping a savage, or sacrificing himself in some way for the sake of this sallow-faced, grey-eyed schoolmistress. As I should like to present him in a heroic attitude, I stay my hand with great difficulty at this moment, being only withheld from introducing such an episode by a strong conviction that it does not usually occur at such times. And I trust that my fairest reader, who remembers that, in a real crisis, it is always some uninteresting stranger or unromantic policeman, and not Adolphus, who rescues, will forgive the omission.

So they sat there undisturbed,—the woodpeckers chattering overhead and the voices of the children coming pleasantly from the hollow below. What they said matters little. What they thought—which might have been interesting—did not transpire. The woodpeckers only learned how Miss Mary was an orphan; how she left her uncle's house to come to California for the sake of health and independence; how Sandy was an orphan too; how he came to California for excitement; how he had lived a wild life, and how he was trying to reform; and other details, which, from a woodpecker's view-point, undoubtedly must have seemed stupid and a waste of time. But even in such trifles was the afternoon spent; and when the children were again gathered, and Sandy, with a delicacy which the schoolmistress well understood, took leave of them quietly at the outskirts of the settlement, it had seemed the shortest day of her weary life.

As the long, dry summer withered to its roots, the school term of Red Gulch—to use a local euphuism—"dried up" also. In another day Miss Mary would be free, and for a season, at least, Red Gulch would know her no more. She was seated alone in the schoolhouse, her cheek resting on her hand, her eyes half closed in one of those day-dreams in which Miss Mary, I fear, to the danger of school discipline, was lately in the habit of indulging. Her lap was full of mosses, ferns, and other woodland memories. She was so preoccupied with these and her own thoughts that a gentle tapping at the door passed unheard, or translated itself into the remembrance of far-off woodpeckers. When at last it asserted itself more distinctly, she started up with a flushed cheek and opened the door. On the threshold stood a woman, the self-assertion and audacity of whose dress were in singular contrast to her timid, irresolute bearing.

Miss Mary recognised at a glance the dubious mother of her anonymous pupil. Perhaps she was disappointed, perhaps she was only fastidious; but as she coldly invited her to enter, she half-unconsciously settled her white cuffs and collar, and gathered closer her own chaste skirts. It was, perhaps, for this reason that the embarrassed stranger, after a moment's hesitation, left her gorgeous parasol open and sticking in the dust beside the door, and then sat down at the farther end of a long bench. Her voice was husky as she began—

"I heerd tell that you were goin' down to the Bay tomorrow, and I couldn't let you go until I came to thank you for your kindness to my Tommy."

Tommy, Miss Mary said, was a good boy, and deserved more than the poor attention she could give him.

"Thank you, miss; thank ye!" cried the stranger, brightening even through the colour which Red Gulch knew facetiously as her "war paint," and striving, in her embarrassment, to drag the long bench nearer the schoolmistress. "I thank you, miss, for that; and if I am his mother, there ain't a sweeter, dearer, better boy lives than him. And if I ain't much as says it, thar ain't a sweeter, dearer, angeler teacher lives than he's got."

Miss Mary, sitting primly behind her desk, with a ruler over her shoulder, opened her grey eyes widely at this, but said nothing.

"It ain't for you to be complimented by the like of me, I know," she went on hurriedly. "It ain't for me to be comin' here, in broad day, to do it, either; but I come to ask a favour,—not for me, miss,—not for me, but for the darling boy."

Encouraged by a look in the young schoolmistress's eye, and putting her lilac-gloved hands together, the fingers downward, between her knees, she went on, in a low voice—

"You see, miss, there's no one the boy has any claim on but me, and I ain't the proper person to bring him up. I thought some, last year, of sending him away to 'Frisco to school, but when they talked of bringing a schoolma'am here, I waited till I saw you, and then I knew it was all right, and I could keep my boy a little longer. And oh! miss, he loves you so much; and if you could hear him talk about you in his pretty way, and if he could ask you what I ask you now, you couldn't refuse him.

"It is natural," she went on, rapidly, in a voice that trembled strangely between pride and humility,—"it's natural that he should take to you, miss, for his father, when I first knew him, was a gentleman,—and the boy must forget me, sooner or later,—and so I ain't a goin' to cry about that. For I come to ask you to take my Tommy,—God bless him for the bestest, sweetest boy that lives,—to—to—take him with you."

She had risen and caught the young girl's hand in her own, and had fallen on her knees beside her.

"I've money plenty, and it's all yours and his. Put him in some good school, where you can go and see him, and help him to—to—to forget his mother. Do with him what you like. The worst you can do will be kindness to what he will learn with me. Only take him out of this wicked life, this cruel place, this home of shame and sorrow. You will! I know you will,—won't you? You will,—you must not, you cannot say no! You will make him as pure, as gentle as yourself; and when he has grown up, you will tell him his father's name,—the name that hasn't passed my lips for years,—the name of Alexander Morton, whom they call here Sandy! Miss Mary!—do not take your hand away! Miss Mary, speak to me! You will take my boy? Do not put your face from me. I know it ought not to look on such as me. Miss Mary!—my God, be merciful!—she is leaving me!"

Miss Mary had risen, and, in the gathering twilight, had felt her way to the open window. She stood there, leaning against the casement, her eyes fixed on the last rosy tints that were fading from the western sky. There was still some of its light on her pure young forehead, on her white collar, on her clasped white hands, but all fading slowly away. The suppliant had dragged herself, still on her knees, beside her.

"I know it takes time to consider. I will wait here all night; but I cannot go until you speak. Do not deny me now. You will!—I see it in your sweet face,—such a face as I have seen in my dreams. I see it in your eyes, Miss Mary!—you will take my boy!"

The last red beam crept higher, suffused Miss Mary's eyes with something of its glory, flickered, and faded, and went out. The sun had set on Red Gulch. In the twilight and silence Miss Mary's voice sounded pleasantly.

"I will take the boy. Send him to me to-night."

The happy mother raised the hem of Miss Mary's skirts to her lips. She would have buried her hot face in its virgin folds, but she dared not. She rose to her feet.

"Does—this man—know of your intention?" asked Miss Mary suddenly.

"No, nor cares. He has never even seen the child to know it."

"Go to him at once—to-night—now! Tell him what you have done. Tell him I have taken his child, and tell him—he must never see—see —the child again. Wherever it may be, he must not come; wherever I may take it, he must not follow! There, go now, please,—I'm weary, and—have much yet to do!"

They walked together to the door. On the threshold the woman turned.

"Good-night!"

She would have fallen at Miss Mary's feet. But at the same moment the young girl reached out her arms, caught the sinful woman to her own pure breast for one brief moment, and then closed and locked the door.

It was with a sudden sense of great responsibility that Profane Bill took the reins of the Slumgullion Stage the next morning, for the schoolmistress was one of his passengers. As he entered the highroad, in obedience to a pleasant voice from the "inside," he suddenly reined up his horses and respectfully waited, as "Tommy" hopped out at the command of Miss Mary.

"Not that bush, Tommy,—the next."

Tommy whipped out his new pocket-knife, and cutting a branch from a tall azalea bush, returned with it to Miss Mary.

"All right now?"

"All right!"

And the stage-door closed on the Idyl of Red Gulch.

A Lonely Ride

AS I STEPPED into the Slumgullion stage I saw that it was a dark night, a lonely road, and that I was the only passenger. Let me assure the reader that I have no ulterior design in making this assertion. A long course of light reading has forewarned me what every experienced intelligence must confidently look for from such a statement. The storyteller who wilfully tempts fate by such obvious beginnings, who is to the expectant reader in danger of being robbed or half-murdered, or frightened by an escaped lunatic, or introduced to his lady-love for the first time, deserves to be detected. I am relieved to say that none of these things occurred to me. The road from Wingdam to Slumgullion knew no other banditti than the regularly licensed hotel-keepers; lunatics had not yet reached such depth of imbecility as to ride of their own free will in Californian stages; and my Laura, amiable and long-suffering as she always is, could not, I fear, have borne up against these depressing circumstances long enough to have made the slightest impression on me.

I stood with my shawl and carpet-bag in hand, gazing doubtingly on the vehicle. Even in the darkness the red dust of Wingdam was visible on its roof and sides, and the red slime of Slumgullion clung tenaciously to its wheels. I opened the door; the stage creaked uneasily, and in the gloomy abyss the swaying straps beckoned me, like ghostly hands, to come in now, and have my sufferings out at once.

I must not omit to mention the occurrence of a circumstance which struck me as appalling and mysterious. A lounger on the steps of the hotel, whom I had reason to suppose was not in any way connected with the stage company, gravely descended, and, walking toward the conveyance, tried the handle of the door, opened it, expectorated in the carriage, and returned to the hotel with a serious demeanour. Hardly had he resumed his position, when another individual, equally disinterested, impassively walked down the steps, proceeded to the back of the stage, lifted it, expectorated carefully on the axle, and returned slowly and pensively to the hotel. A third spectator wearily disengaged himself from one of the Ionic columns of the portico and walked to the box, remained for a moment in serious and expectorative contemplation of the boot, and then returned to his column. There was something so weird in this baptism that I grew quite nervous.

Perhaps I was out of spirits. A number of infinitesimal annoyances, winding up with the resolute persistency of the clerk at the stage-office to enter my name misspelt on the waybill, had not predisposed me to cheerfulness. The inmates of the Eureka House, from a social viewpoint, were not attractive. There was the prevailing opinion—so common to many honest people—that a serious style of deportment and conduct toward a stranger indicates high gentility and elevated station. Obeying this principle, all hilarity ceased on my entrance to supper, and general remark merged into the safer and uncompromising chronicle of several bad cases of diphtheria, then epidemic at Wingdam. When I left the dining-room, with an odd feeling that I had been supping exclusively on mustard and tea leaves, I stopped a moment at the parlour door. A piano, harmoniously related to the dinner-bell, tinkled responsive to a diffident and uncertain touch. On the white wall the shadow of an old and sharp profile was bending over several symmetrical and shadowy curls. "I sez to Mariar, Mariar, sez I, 'Praise to the face is open disgrace.' " I heard no more. Dreading some susceptibility to sincere expression on the subject of female loveliness, I walked away, checking the compliment that otherwise might have risen unbidden to my lips, and have brought shame and sorrow to the household.

It was with the memory of these experiences resting heavily upon me that I stood hesitatingly before the stage door. The driver, about to mount, was for a moment illuminated by the open door of the hotel. He had the wearied look which was the distinguishing expression of Wingdam. Satisfied that I was properly way-billed and receipted for, he took no further notice of me. I looked longingly at the box-seat, but he did not respond to the appeal. I flung my carpet-bag into the chasm, dived recklessly after it, and—before I was fairly seated—with a great sigh, a creaking of unwilling springs, complaining bolts, and harshly expostulating axle, we moved away. Rather the hotel door slipped behind, the sound of the piano sank to rest, and the night and its shadows moved solemnly upon us.

To say it was dark expressed but faintly the pitchy obscurity that encompassed the vehicle. The roadside trees were scarcely distinguishable as deeper masses of shadow; I knew them only by the peculiar sodden odour that from time to time sluggishly flowed in at the open window as we rolled by. We proceeded slowly; so leisurely that, leaning from the carriage, I more than once detected the fragrant sigh of some astonished cow, whose ruminating repose upon the highway we had ruthlessly disturbed. But in the darkness our progress, more the guidance of some mysterious instinct than any apparent volition of our own, gave an indefinable charm of security to our journey, that a moment's hesitation or indecision on the part of the driver would have destroyed.

I had indulged a hope that in the empty vehicle I might obtain that rest so often denied me in its crowded condition. It was a weak delusion. When I stretched out my limbs it was only to find that the ordinary conveniences for making several people distinctly uncomfortable were distributed throughout my individual frame. At last, resting my arms on the straps, by dint of much gymnastic effort I became sufficiently composed to be aware of a more refined species of torture. The springs of the stage, rising and falling regularly, produced a rhythmical beat, which began to painfully absorb my attention. Slowly this thumping merged into a senseless echo of the mysterious female of the hotel parlour, and shaped itself into this awful and benumbing axiom:—"Praise-to-the-face-is-open-disgrace. Praise-to-the-face-is-open-disgrace." Inequalities of the road only quickened its utterance or drawled it to an exasperating length.

It was of no use to seriously consider the statement. It was of no use to except to it indignantly. It was of no use to recall the many instances where praise to the face had redounded to the everlasting honour of praiser and bepraised; of no use to dwell sentimentally on modest genius and courage lifted up and strengthened by open commendation; of no use to except to the mysterious female,—to picture her as rearing a thin-blooded generation on selfish and mechanically-repeated axioms,—all this failed to counteract the monotonous repetition of this sentence. There was nothing to do but to give in, and I was about to accept it weakly, as we too often treat other illusions of darkness and necessity, for the time being, when I became aware of some other annoyance that had been forcing itself upon me for the last few moments. How quiet the driver was!

Was there any driver? Had I any reason to suppose that he was not lying gagged and bound on the roadside, and the highwayman, with blackened face, who did the thing so quietly, driving me—whither? The thing is perfectly feasible. And what is this fancy now being jolted out of me? A story? It's of no use to keep it back, particularly in this abyssmal vehicle, and here it comes:—I am a Marquis—a French Marquis; French, because the peerage is not so well known, and the country is better adapted to romantic incident—a Marquis, because the democratic reader delights in the nobility. My name is something *ligny*. I am coming from Paris to my country-seat at St. Germain. It is a dark night, and I fall asleep and tell my honest coachman, André, not to disturb me, and dream of an angel. The carriage at last stops at the château. It is so dark that, when I alight, I do not recognise the face of the footman who holds the carriage-door. But what of that?— *peste!* I am heavy with sleep. The same obscurity also hides the old familiar indecencies of the statues on the terrace; but there is a door, and it opens and shuts behind me smartly. Then I find myself in a trap, in the presence of the brigand who has quietly gagged poor André and conducted the carriage thither. There is nothing for me to do, as a gallant French Marquis, but to say, *"Parbleu!"* draw my rapier, and die valorously! I am found, a week or two after, outside a deserted *cabaret* near the barrier, with a hole through my ruffled linen, and my pockets stripped. No; on second thoughts, I am rescued,—rescued by the angel I have been dreaming of, who is the assumed daughter of the brigand, but the real daughter of an intimate friend.

Looking from the window again, in the vain hope of distinguishing the driver, I found my eyes were growing accustomed to the darkness. I could see the distant horizon, defined by India-inky woods relieving a lighter sky. A few stars, widely spaced in this picture, glimmering sadly. I noticed again the infinite depth of patient sorrow in their serene faces; and I hope that the Vandal who first applied the flippant "twinkle" to them may not be driven melancholy mad by their reproachful eyes. I noticed again the mystic charm of space, that imparts a sense of individual solitude to each integer of the densest constellation, involving the smallest star with immeasurable loneliness. Something of this calm and solitude crept over me, and I dozed in my gloomy cavern. When I awoke the full moon was rising. Seen from my window, it had an indescribably unreal and theatrical effect. It was the full moon of *Norma*—that remarkable celestial phenomenon which rises so palpably to a hushed audience and a sublime *andante* chorus, until the *Casta Diva* is sung—the "inconstant moon" that then and thereafter remains fixed in the heavens as though it were a part of the solar system inaugurated by Joshua. Again the white-robed Druids filed past me, again I saw that improbable mistletoe cut from that impossible oak, and again cold chills ran down my back with the first strain of the recitative. The thumping springs essayed to beat time, and the private box-like obscurity of the vehicle lent a cheap enchantment to the view. But it was a vast improvement upon my past experience, and I hugged the fond delusion.

My fears for the driver were dissipated with the rising moon. A familiar sound had assured me of his presence in the full possession of at least one of his most important functions. Frequent and full expectoration convinced me that his lips were as yet not sealed by the gag of highwaymen, and soothed my anxious ear. With this load lifted from my mind, and assisted by the mild presence of Diana, who left, as when she visited Endymion, much of her splendour outside my cavern —I looked around the empty vehicle. On the forward seat lay a woman's hairpin. I picked it up with an interest that, however, soon abated. There was no scent of the roses to cling to it still, not even of hair-oil. No bent or twist in its rigid angles betrayed any trait of its wearer's character. I tried to think that it might have been "Mariar's." I tried to imagine that, confining the symmetrical curls of that girl, it might have heard the soft compliments whispered in her ears which provoked the wrath of the aged female. But in vain. It was reticent and unswerving in its upright fidelity, and at last slipped listlessly through my fingers.

I had dozed repeatedly,—waked on the threshold of oblivion by contact with some of the angles of the coach, and feeling that I was unconsciously assuming, in imitation of a humble insect of my childish recollection, that spherical shape which could best resist those impressions, when I perceived that the moon, riding high in the heavens, had begun to separate the formless masses of the shadowy landscape. Trees isolated, in clumps, and assemblages, changed places before my window. The sharp outlines of the distant hills came back as in daylight, but little softened in the dry, cold, dewless air of a California summer night. I was wondering how late it was, and thinking that if the horses of the night travelled as slowly as the team before us, Faustus might have been spared his agonising prayer, when a sudden spasm of activity attacked my driver. A succession of whip-snappings, like a pack of Chinese crackers, broke from the box before me. The stage leaped forward, and when I could pick myself from under the seat, a long white building had in some mysterious way rolled before my window. It must be Slumgullion! As I descended from the stage I addressed the driver:—

"I thought you changed horses on the road?"

"So we did. Two hours ago."

"That's odd. I didn't notice it."

"Must have been asleep, sir. Hope you had a pleasant nap. Bully place for a nice quiet snooze, empty stage, sir!"

Flip

Chapter I

JUST WHERE THE red track of the *Los Gatos* road streams on and upward, like the sinuous trail of a fiery rocket, until it is extinguished in the blue shadows of the coast range, there is an embayed terrace near the summit hedged by dwarf firs. At every bend of the heat-laden road the eye rests upon it wistfully; all along the flank of the mountain, which seemed to pant and quiver in the oven-like air; through rising dust, the slow creaking of dragging wheels, the monotonous cry of tired springs and the muffled beat of plunging hoofs, it held out a promise of sheltered coolness and green silences beyond. Sunburned and anxious faces yearned towards it from the dizzy, swaying tops of stagecoaches, from lagging teams far below, from the blinding white canvas covers of "mountain schooners," and from scorching saddles that seemed to weigh down the scrambling, sweating animals beneath. But it would seem that the hope was vain, the promise illusive. When the terrace was reached it appeared not only to have caught and gathered all the heat of the valley below, but to have evolved a fire of its own from some hidden crater-like source unknown. Nevertheless, instead of prostrating and enervating man and beast, it was said to have induced the wildest exaltation. The heated air was filled and stifling

35

with resinous exhalations. The delirious spices of balm, bay, spruce, juniper, *yerba buena,* wild syringa, and strange aromatic herbs as yet unclassified, distilled and evaporated in that mighty heat, seemed to fire with a midsummer madness all who breathed their fumes. They stung, smarted, stimulated, intoxicated. It was said that the most jaded and footsore horses became furious and ungovernable under their influence; wearied teamsters and muleteers, who had exhausted their profanity in the ascent, drank fresh draughts of inspiration in this fiery air, extended their vocabulary, and created new and startling forms of objurgation. It is recorded that one bibulous stage-driver exhausted description and condensed its virtues in a single phrase—"Gin and Ginger." This felicitous epithet, flung out in a generous comparison with his favourite drink, "Rum and Gum," clung to it ever after.

Such was the current comment on this vale of spices. Like most human criticism, it was hasty and superficial. No one yet had been known to have penetrated deeply its mysterious recesses. It was still far below the summit and its wayside inn. It had escaped the intruding foot of hunter and prospector, and the inquisitive patrol of the County Surveyor had only skirted its boundary. It remained for Mr. Lance Harriott to complete its exploration. His reasons for so doing were simple. He had made the journey thither underneath the stage-coach and clinging to its axle. He had chosen this hazardous mode of conveyance at night as the coach crept by his place of concealment in the wayside brush, to elude the Sheriff of Monterey County and his *posse,* who were after him. He had not made himself known to his fellow-passengers, as they already knew him as a gambler, an outlaw, and a desperado; he deemed it unwise to present himself in his newer reputation of a man who had just slain a brother-gambler in a quarrel, and for whom a reward was offered. He slipped from the axle as the stage-coach swirled past the brushing branches of fir, and for an instant lay unnoticed, a scarcely-distinguishable mound of dust in the broken furrows of the road. Then, more like a beast than man, he crept on his hands and knees into the steaming underbrush. Here he lay still, until the clatter of harness and the sound of voices faded in the distance. Had he been followed it would have been difficult to detect in that inert mass of rags any semblance to a known form or figure. A hideous reddish mask of dust and clay obliterated his face; his hands were shapeless stumps exaggerated in his trailing sleeves. And when he rose, staggering like a drunken man, and plunged wildly into the recesses of the wood, a cloud of dust followed him, and pieces and patches of his frayed and rotten garments clung to the impeding branches. Twice he fell, but, maddened and upheld by the smarting spices and stimulating aroma of the air, he kept on his course.

Gradually the heat became less oppressive; once when he stopped and leaned exhaustedly against a sapling, he fancied he saw the zephyr he could not yet feel in the glittering and trembling of leaves in the distance before him. Again the deep stillness was moved with a faint sighing rustle, and he knew he must be nearing the edge of the thicket. The spell of silence thus broken was followed by a fainter, more musical interruption—the glassy tinkle of water! A step farther his foot trembled on the verge of a slight ravine still closely canopied by the interlacing boughs overhead. A tiny stream that he could have dammed with his hand yet lingered in this parched red gash in the hillside and trickled into a deep, irregular, well-like cavity, that again overflowed and sent its light surplus on. It had been the luxurious retreat of many a spotted trout; it was to be the bath of Lance Harriott. Without a moment's hesitation, without removing a single garment, he slipped cautiously into it, as if fearful of losing a single drop. His head disappeared from the level of the bank; the solitude was again unbroken. Only two objects remained upon the edge of the ravine—his revolver and tobacco-pouch.

A few minutes elapsed. A fearless blue jay alighted on the bank and made a prospecting peck at the tobacco-pouch. It yielded in favour of a gopher, who endeavoured to draw it towards his hole, but in turn gave way to a red squirrel, whose attention was divided, however, between the pouch and the revolver, which he regarded with mischievous fascination. Then there was a splash, a grunt, a sudden dispersion of animated nature, and the head of Mr. Lance Harriott appeared above the bank. It was a startling transformation. Not only that he had, by this wholesale process, washed himself and his light "drill" garments entirely clean, but that he had, apparently by the same operation, morally cleansed *himself,* and left every stain and ugly blot of his late misdeeds and reputation in his bath. His face, albeit scratched here and there, was rosy, round, shining with irrepressible good-humour and youthful levity. His large blue eyes were infantine in their innocent surprise and thoughtlessness. Dripping yet with water, and panting, he rested his elbows lazily on the bank, and became instantly absorbed with a boy's delight in the movements of the gopher, who after the first alarm returned cautiously to abduct the tobacco-pouch. If any familiar had failed to detect Lance Harriott in his hideous masquerade of dust and grime and tatters, still less would any passing stranger have recognised in this blonde faun the possible outcast and murderer. And when with a swirl of his spattering sleeve he drove back the gopher in a shower of spray, and leaped to the bank, he seemed to have accepted his felonious hiding-place as a mere picnicking bower.

A slight breeze was unmistakedly permeating the wood from the west. Looking in that direction, Lance imagined that the shadow was less dark, and although the undergrowth was denser, he struck off carelessly towards it. As he went on, the wood became lighter and lighter; branches, and presently leaves, were painted against the vivid blue of the sky. He knew he must be near the summit, stopped, felt for his revolver, and then lightly put the few remaining branches aside.

The full glare of the noonday sun at first blinded him. When he could see more clearly he found himself on the open western slope of the mountain, which in the coast range was seldom wooded. The spiced thicket stretched between him and the summit, and again between him and the stage-road that plunged from the terrace like forked lightning into the valley below. He could command all the approaches without being seen. Not that this seemed to occupy his thoughts or cause him any anxiety. His first act was to disencumber himself of his tattered coat; he then filled and lighted his pipe, and stretched himself full-length on the open hillside, as if to bleach in the fierce sun. While smoking he carelessly perused the fragment of a newspaper which had enveloped his tobacco, and being struck with some amusing paragraph, read it half aloud again to some imaginary auditor, emphasising its humour with a hilarious slap upon his leg.

Possibly from the relaxation of fatigue and the bath, which had become a vapour one as he alternately rolled and dried himself in the baking grass, his eyes closed dreamily. He was awakened by the sound of voices. They were distant, they were vague, they approached no nearer. He rolled himself to the verge of the first precipitous grassy descent. There was another bank or plateau below him, and then a confused depth of olive shadows, pierced here and there by the spiked helmets of pines. There was no trace of habitation. Yet the voices were those of some monotonous occupation, and Lance distinctly heard through them the click of crockery and the ring of some household utensil. It appeared to be the interjectional, half listless, half perfunctory domestic dialogue of an old man and a girl, of which the words were unintelligible. Their voices indicated the solitude of the mountain but without sadness, they were mysterious without being awe-inspiring, they might have uttered the dreariest commonplaces, but in their vast isolation they seemed musical and eloquent. Lance drew his first sigh—they had suggested dinner.

Careless as his nature was, he was too cautious to risk detection in broad daylight. He contented himself for the present with endeavouring to locate that particular part of the depths from which the voices seemed to rise. It was more difficult, however, to select some other way of penetrating it than by the stage-road. "They're bound to have a fire or show a light when it's dark," he reasoned, and satisfied with that reflection, lay down again. Presently he began to amuse himself by tossing some silver coins in the air. Then his attention was directed to a spur of the coast range which had been sharply silhouetted against the cloudless western sky. Something intensely white, something so small that it was scarcely larger than the silver coin he held in his hand, was appearing in a slight cleft of the range.

While he looked it gradually filled and obliterated the cleft. In another moment the whole serrated line of mountain had disappeared. The dense, dazzling, white, encompassing host began to pour over and down every ravine and pass of the coast. Lance recognized the sea-fog, and knew that scarcely twenty miles away lay the ocean—and safety! The drooping sun was now caught and hidden in its soft embraces. A sudden chill breathed over the mountain. He shivered, rose, and plunged again for very warmth into the spice-laden thicket. The heated balsamic air began to affect him like a powerful sedative; his hunger was forgotten in the languor of fatigue; he slumbered. When he awoke it was dark. He groped his way through the thicket. A few stars were shining directly above him, but beyond and below everything was lost in the soft, white, fleecy veil of fog. Whatever light or fire might have betokened human habitation was hidden. To have pushed on blindly was madness; he could only wait for morning. It suited the outcast's lazy philosophy; he crept back again to his bed in the hollow and slept. In that profound silence and shadow, shut out from human association and sympathy by the ghostly fog, what torturing visions conjured up by remorse and fear should have pursued him? what spirit passed before him or slowly shaped itself out of the infinite blackness of the wood? None. As he slipped gently into that blackness he remembered with a slight regret some biscuits that were dropped from the coach by a careless luncheon-consuming passenger. That pang over, he slept as sweetly, as profoundly, as divinely as a child.

Chapter II

He awoke with the aroma of the woods still steeping his senses. His first instinct was that of all young animals; he seized a few of the young, tender green leaves of the *yerba buena* vine that crept over his mossy pillow and ate them, being rewarded by a half berry-like flavour that seemed to soothe the cravings of his appetite. The languor of sleep being still upon him, he lazily watched the quivering of a sunbeam that was caught in the canopying boughs above. Then he dozed again. Hovering between sleeping and waking, he became conscious of a slight movement among the dead leaves on the bank beside the hollow in which he lay. The movement appeared to be intelligent, and directed towards his revolver, which glittered on the bank. Amused at this evident return of his larcenous friend of the previous day, he lay perfectly still. The movement and rustle continued, but it now seemed long and undulating. Lance's eyes suddenly became set; he was intensely, keenly awake. It was not a snake, but the hand of a human arm half hidden in the moss, groping for the weapon. In that flash of perception he saw that it was small, bare, and deeply freckled. In an instant he grasped it firmly, and rose to his feet, dragging to his own level as he did so the struggling figure of a young girl.

"Leave me go," she said, more ashamed than frightened.

Lance looked at her. She was scarcely more than fifteen, slight and lithe, with a boyish flatness of breast and back. Her flushed face and bare throat were absolutely peppered with minute brown freckles, like grains of spent gunpowder. Her eyes, which were large and grey, presented the singular spectacle of being also freckled—at least they were shot through in pupil and cornea with tiny spots like powdered allspice. Her hair was even more remarkable in its tawny, deer-skin colour, full of lighter shades, and bleached to the faintest of blondes on the crown of her head, as if by the action of the sun. She had evidently outgrown her dress, which was made for a smaller child, and the too brief skirt disclosed a bare, freckled, and sandy desert of shapely limb, for which the darned stockings were equally too scant. Lance let his grasp slip from her thin wrist to her hand, and then with a good-humoured gesture tossed it lightly back to her.

She did not retreat, but continued looking at him in half-surly embarrassment.

"I ain't a bit frightened," she said. "I'm not going to run away— don't you fear."

"Glad to hear it," said Lance, with unmistakable satisfaction; "but why did you go for my revolver?"

She flushed again, and was silent. Presently she began to kick the earth at the roots of the tree, and said, as if confidentially to her foot, "I wanted to get hold of it before you did."

"You did! and why?"

"Oh, you know why."

Every tooth in Lance's head showed that he did perfectly. But he was discreetly silent.

"I didn't know what you were hiding there for," she went on, still addressing the tree, "and," looking at him sideways under her white lashes, "I didn't see your face."

This subtle compliment was the first suggestion of her artful sex. It actually sent the blood into the careless rascal's face, and for a moment confused him. He coughed. "So you thought you'd freeze on to that six-shooter of mine until you saw my hand?"

She nodded. Then she picked up a broken hazel branch, fitted it into the small of her back, threw her tanned bare arms over the ends of it, and expanded her chest and her biceps at the same moment. This simple action was supposed to convey an impression at once of ease and muscular force.

"Perhaps you'd like to take it now," said Lance, handing her the pistol.

"I've seen six-shooters before now," said the girl, cleverly evading the proffered weapon and its suggestions. "Dad has one, and my brother had two derringers before he was half as big as me."

She stopped to observe in her companion the effect of this capacity of her family to bear arms. Lance only regarded her amusedly. Presently she again spoke abruptly—

"What made you eat that grass just now?"

"Grass!" echoed Lance.

"Yes, there," pointing to the *yerba buena.*

Lance laughed. "I was hungry. Look," he said, gaily tossing some silver into the air. "Do you think you could get me some breakfast for that, and have enough left to buy something for yourself?"

The girl eyed the money and the man with half-bashful curiosity.

"I reckon Dad might give ye suthing if he had a mind ter, though ez a rule he's down on tramps ever since they run off his chickens. Ye might try."

"But I want *you* to try. You can bring it to me here."

The girl retreated a step, dropped her eyes, and with a smile that was a charming hesitation between bashfulness and impudence, said— "So you *are* hidin', are ye?"

"That's just it. Your head's level. I am," laughed Lance unconcernedly.

"Yur ain't one o' the M'Carty gang—are ye?"

Mr. Lance Harriott felt a momentary moral exaltation in declaring truthfully that he was not one of a notorious band of mountain freebooters known in the district under that name.

"Nor ye ain't one of them chicken-lifters that raided Henderson's ranch? We don't go much on that kind o' cattle yer."

"No," said Lance cheerfully.

"Nor ye ain't that chap ez beat his wife unto death at Santa Clara?"

Lance honestly scorned the imputation. Such conjugal ill-treatment as he had indulged in had not been physical, and had been with other men's wives.

There was a moment's further hesitation on the part of the girl. Then she said shortly—

"Well, then, I reckon you kin come along with me."

"Where?" asked Lance.

"To the ranch," she replied simply.

"Then you won't bring me anything to eat here?"

"What for? You kin get it down there." Lance hesitated. "I tell you it's all right," continued the girl, "I'll make it all right with Dad."

"But suppose I reckon I'd rather stay here," persisted Lance, with a perfect consciousness, however, of affectation in his caution.

"Stay away, then," said the girl coolly; "only as Dad perempted this yer woods"——

"*Pre*-empted," suggested Lance.

"Per-empted or prem-emp-ted, as you like," continued the girl scornfully, "ez he's got a holt on this yer woods, ye might ez well see him down thar ez here. For here he's like to come any minit. You can bet your life on that."

She must have read Lance's amusement in his eyes, for she again dropped her own, with a frown of brusque embarrassment. "Come along, then; I'm your man," said Lance gaily, extending his hand.

She would not accept it, eyeing it, however, furtively, like a horse about to shy. "Hand me your pistol first," she said.

He handed it to her with an assumption of gaiety. She received it on her part with unfeigned seriousness, and threw it over her shoulder like a gun. This combined action of the child and heroine, it is quite unnecessary to say, afforded Lance undiluted joy.

"You go first," she said.

Lance stepped promptly out, with a broad grin. "Looks kinder as if I was a prisoner, don't it?" he suggested.

"Go on, and don't fool," she replied.

The two fared onward through the wood. For one wild moment he entertained the facetious idea of appearing to rush frantically away, "just to see what the girl would do," but abandoned it. "It's an even thing if she wouldn't spot me the first pop," he reflected admiringly.

When they had reached the open hillside Lance stopped inquiringly. "This way," she said, pointing toward the summit, and in quite an opposite direction to the valley where he had heard the voices, one of which he now recognised as hers. They skirted the thicket for a few moments, and then turned sharply into a trail which began to dip towards a ravine leading to the valley. "Why do you have to go all the way round?" he asked.

"*We* don't," the girl replied with an emphasis; "there's a shorter cut."

"Where?"

"That's telling," she answered shortly.

"What's your name?" asked Lance, after a steep scramble and a drop into the ravine.

"Flip."

"What?"

"Flip."

"I mean your first name—your front name."

"Flip."

"Flip! Oh, short for Felipa?"

"It ain't Flipper—it's Flip." And she relapsed into silence.

"You don't ask me mine?" suggested Lance.

She did not vouchsafe a reply.

"Then you don't want to know?"

"Maybe Dad will. You can lie to *him.*"

This direct answer apparently sustained the agreeable homicide for some moments. He moved onward, silently exuding admiration. "Only," added Flip, with a sudden caution, "you'ld better agree with me."

The trail here turned away abruptly and re-entered the cañon. Lance looked up and noticed they were almost directly beneath the bay thicket and the plateau that towered far above them. The trail here showed signs of clearing, and the way was marked by felled trees and stumps of pines.

"What does your father do here?" he finally asked. Flip remained silent, swinging the revolver in her hand. Lance repeated his question.

"Burns charcoal and makes diamonds," said Flip, looking at him out of the corners of her eyes.

"Makes diamonds?" echoed Lance.

Flip nodded her head.

"Many of 'em?" he continued carelessly.

"Lots. But they're not big," she returned with a sidelong glance.

"Oh, they're not big, then," said Lance gravely.

They had by this time reached a small staked enclosure, whence the sudden fluttering and cackle of poultry welcomed the return of the evident mistress of this sylvan retreat. It was scarcely imposing. Farther on, a cooking stove under a tree, a saddle and bridle, a few household implements scattered about, indicated the "ranch." Like most pioneer clearings, it was simply a disorganised raid upon Nature that had left behind a desolate battlefield strewn with waste and decay. The fallen trees, the crushed thicket, the splintered limbs, the rudely torn-up soil, were made hideous by their grotesque juxtaposition with the wrecked fragments of civilisation, in empty cans, broken bottles, battered hats, soleless boots, frayed stockings, cast-off rags, and the crowning absurdity of the twisted wire skeleton of a hooped skirt hanging from a branch. The wildest defile, the densest thicket, the most virgin solitude was less dreary and forlorn than this first foot-print of man. The only redeeming feature of this prolonged bivouac was the cabin itself. Built of the half-cylindrical strips of pine bark, and thatched with the same material, it had a certain picturesque rusticity. But this was an accident of economy rather than taste, for which Flip apologised by saying that the bark of the pine was "no good" for charcoal.

"I reckon Dad's in the woods," she added, pausing before the open door of the cabin. "O Dad!" Her voice, clear and high, seemed to fill the whole long cañon, and echoed from the green plateau above. The monotonous strokes of an axe were suddenly pretermitted, and some-where from the depths of the close-set pines a returning voice an-swered "Flip." There was a pause of a few moments, with some mut-tering, stumbling, and crackling in the underbrush, and then the sudden appearance of "Dad."

Had Lance first met him in the thicket he would have been puzzled to assign his race to Mongolian, Indian, or Ethiopian origin. Perfunc-tory but incomplete washings of his hands and face, after charcoal burning, had gradually ground into his skin a greyish slate-pencil pal-lor, grotesquely relieved at the edges where the washing had left off with a border of a darker colour. He looked like an over-worked Christy Minstrel with the briefest of intervals between his perfor-mances. There were black rims in the orbits of his eyes, as if he gazed feebly out of unglazed spectacles, which heightened his simian resem-blance, already grotesquely exaggerated by what appeared to be re-peated and spasmodic experiments in dying his grey hair. Without the slightest notice of Lance, he inflicted his protesting and querulous presence entirely on his daughter.

"Well! what's up now? Yer ye are calling me from work an hour before noon. Dog my skin—ef I ever get fairly limbered up afore it's 'Dad!' and 'O Dad!' "

To Lance's intense satisfaction the girl received this harangue with an air of supreme indifference, and when "Dad" had finally relapsed into an unintelligible, and, as it seemed to Lance, a half-frightened muttering, she said coolly—

"Ye'd better drop that axe and scoot round gettin' this stranger some breakfast and some grub to take with him. He's one of them San Francisco sports out here trout-fishing in the Branch. He's got adrift from his party, has lost his rod and fixins, and had to camp out last night in the Gin and Ginger Woods."

"That's just it; it's allers suthin like that," screamed the old man, dashing his fist on his leg in a feeble, impotent passion, but without looking at Lance. "Why in blazes don't he go up to that there blamed hotel on the summit? Why in thunder?"——But here he caught his daughter's large freckled eyes full in his own. He blinked feebly, his voice fell into a tone of whining entreaty. "Now, look yer, Flip, it's playing it rather low down on the old man, this yer running in o' tramps, and desarted emigrants, and castashore sailors, and forlorn widders, and ravin' lunatics on this yer ranch. I put it to you, Mister," he said abruptly, turning to Lance for the first time, but as if he had already taken an active part in the conversation—"I put it as a gentleman yourself, and a far-minded sportin' man, if this is the square thing?"

Before Lance could reply, Flip had already began. "That's just it! D'ye reckon, being a sportin' man and an AI feller, he's goin' to waltz down inter that hotel, rigged out ez he is? D'ye reckon he's goin' to let his partners get the laugh outer him? Do ye reckon he's goin' to show his head outer this yer ranch till he can do it square? Not much! Go 'long. Dad, you're talking silly!"

The old man weakened. He feebly trailed his axe between his legs to a stump and sat down, wiping his forehead with his sleeve, and imparting to it the appearance of a slate with a difficult sum partly rubbed out. He looked despairingly at Lance. "In course," he said, with a deep sigh, "you naterally ain't got any money. In course you left your pocket-book, containing fifty dollars, under a stone and can't find it. In course," he continued, as he observed Lance put his hand to his pocket, "you've only got a blank cheque on Wells, Farge & Co. for a hundred dollars, and you'ld like me to give you the difference?"

Amused as Lance evidently was at this, his absolute admiration for Flip absorbed everything else. With his eyes still fixed upon the girl, he briefly assured the old man that he would pay for everything he wanted. He did this with a manner quite different from the careless, easy attitude he had assumed towards Flip; at least the quickwitted girl noticed it, and wondered if he was angry. It was quite true that ever since his eye had fallen upon another of his own sex its glance had been less frank and careless. Certain traits of possible impatience which might develop into man-slaying were coming to the fore. Yet a word or a gesture of Flip's was sufficient to change that manner, and when she had, with the fretful assistance of her father, prepared a somewhat sketchy and primitive repast, he questioned the old man about diamond-making. The eye of Dad kindled.

"I want ter know how ye knew I was making diamonds," he asked, with a certain bashful pettishness not unlike his daughter's.

"Heard it in 'Frisco," replied Lance, with glib mendacity glancing at the girl.

"I reckon they're gettin' sort of skeert down there—them jewellers," chuckled Dad; "yet it's in nater that their figgers will have to come down. It's only a question of the price of charcoal. I suppose they didn't tell you how I made the discovery?"

At any other time Lance would have stopped the old man's narrative by saying that he knew the story, but he wished to see how far Flip lent herself to her father's delusion.

"Ye see one night about two years ago I had a pit o' charcoal burning out there, and tho' it had been a smouldering and a smoking and a blazing for nigh unto a month, somehow it didn't charcoal worth a cent. And yet, dog my skin, but the heat o' that er pit was suthin' hidyus and frightful; ye couldn't stand within a hundred yards of it, and they could feel it on the stage road three miles over yon—t'other side the mountain. There was nights when me and Flip had to take our blankets up the ravine and camp out all night, and the back of this yer hut shrivelled up like that bacon. It was about as nigh on to hell as any sample ye kin get here. Now, mebbee you think I built that air fire? Mebbee you'll allow the heat was just the nat'ral burning of that pit?"

"Certainly," said Lance, trying to see Flip's eyes, which were resolutely averted.

"Thet's whar you'ld be lying! That yar heat kem out of the bowels of the yearth—kem up like out of a chimbley or a blast, and kep up that yar fire. And when she cools down a month after, and I got to strip her, there was a hole in the yearth and a spring o' bilin' scaldin' water pourin' out of it ez big as your waist. And right in the middle of it was this yer." He rose with the instinct of a skilful *raconteur,* and whisked from under his bunk a chamois-leather bag, which he emptied on the table before them. It contained a small fragment of native rock-crystal, half fused upon a petrified bit of pine. It was so glaringly truthful, so really what it purported to be, that the most unscientific woodman or pioneer would have understood it at a glance. Lance raised his mirthful eyes to Flip. "It was cooled suddint—stunted by the water," said the girl eagerly. She stopped, and as abruptly turned away her eyes and her reddened face.

"That's it—that's just it," continued the old man. "Thar's Flip, thar —knows it—she ain't no fool!"

Lance did not speak, but turned a hard, unsympathising look upon the old man, and rose almost roughly. The old man clutched his coat. "That's it, ye see. The carbon's just turning to di'mens. And stunted. And why? 'Cos the heat wasn't kep up long enough. Mebbee yer think I stopped thar? That ain't me. Thar's a pit out yar in the woods ez hez

been burning six months; it hain't, in course, got the advantages o' the
old one, for it's nat'ral heat. But I'm keeping that heat up. I've got a
hole where I kin watch it every four hours. When the time comes I'm
thar! Don't you see? That's me! that's David Fairley—that's the old
man—you bet!"

"That's so," said Lance curtly; "and now, Mr. Fairley, if you'll
hand me over a coat or a jacket till I can get past these fogs on the
Monterey Road, I won't keep you from your diamond pit." He threw
down a handful of silver on the table.

"Ther's a deerskin jacket yer," said the old man, "that one o' them
Vaqueros left for the price of a bottle of whisky."

"I reckon it wouldn't suit the stranger," said Flip, dubiously producing a much-worn, slashed, and braided Vaquero's jacket. But it did
suit Lance, who found it warm, and also had suddenly found a certain
satisfaction in opposing Flip. When he had put it on, and nodded
coldly to the old man and carelessly to Flip, he walked to the door.

"If you're going to take the Monterey Road, I can show you a short
cut to it," said Flip, with a certain kind of shy civility. The paternal
Fairley groaned. "That's it; let the chickens and the ranch go to thunder as long as there's a stranger to trapse round with; go on!"

Lance would have made some savage reply, but Flip interrupted.
"You know yourself, Dad, it's a blind trail, and as that 'ere constable
that kem out here hunting French Pete couldn't find it, and had to go
round by the cañon, like ez not the stranger would lose his way, and
have to come back!" This dangerous prospect silenced the old man,
and Flip and Lance stepped into the road together. They walked on
for some moments without speaking. Suddenly Lance turned upon his
companion.

"You didn't swallow all that rot about the diamond, did you?" he
asked crossly.

Flip ran a little ahead, as if to avoid a reply.

"You don't mean to say that's the sort of hog-wash the old man
serves out to you regularly?" continued Lance, becoming more slangy
in his ill-temper.

"I don't know that it's any consarn o' yours what I think," replied
Flip, hopping from boulder to boulder, as they crossed the bed of a dry
watercourse.

"And I suppose you've piloted round and dry-nussed every tramp
and dead-beat you've met since you came here?" continued Lance,
with unmistakable ill-humour. "How many have you helped over this
road?"

"It's a year since there was a Chinaman chased by some Irishman
from the Crossing into the brush about yer, and he was too afeered to

come out, and nigh most starved to death in thar. I had to drag him out and start him on the mountain, for you couldn't get him back to the road. He was the last one but *you.*"

"Do you reckon it the right thing for a girl like you to run about with trash of this kind, and mix herself up with all sorts of roughs and bad company?" said Lance.

Flip stopped short. "Look! if you're goin' to talk like Dad I'll go back."

The ridiculousness of such a resemblance struck him more keenly than a consciousness of his own ingratitude. He hastened to assure Flip that he was joking. When he had made his peace they fell into talk again, Lance becoming unselfish enough to inquire into one or two facts concerning her life which did not immediately affect him. Her mother had died on the plains when she was a baby, and her brother had run away from home at twelve. She fully expected to see him again, and thought he might sometime stray into their cañon. "That is why, then, you take so much stock in tramps," said Lance. "You expect to recognise *him?*"

"Well," replied Flip gravely, "there is suthing in *that,* and there's suthing in *this:* some o' these chaps might run across brother and do him a good turn for the sake of me."

"Like me, for instance?" suggested Lance.

"Like you. You'ld do him a good turn, wouldn't you?"

"You bet!" said Lance, with a sudden emotion that quite startled him; "only don't *you* go throwing yourselves round promiscuously." He was half-conscious of an irritating sense of jealousy, as he asked if any of her *protégés* had ever returned.

"No," said Flip, "no one ever did. It shows," she added with sublime simplicity, "I had done 'em good, and they could get on alone. Don't it?"

"It does," responded Lance grimly. "Have you any other friends that come?"

"Only the Postmaster at the Crossing."

"The Postmaster?"

"Yes; he's reckonin' to marry me next year if I'm big enough."

"And what do *you* reckon?" asked Lance earnestly. Flip began a series of distortions with her shoulders, ran on ahead, picked up a few pebbles and threw them into the wood, glanced back at Lance with swimming mottled eyes, that seemed a piquant incarnation of everything suggestive and tantalising, and said, "That's telling."

They had by this time reached the spot where they were to separate. "Look," said Flip, pointing to a faint deflection of their path, which seemed, however, to lose itself in the underbrush a dozen yards away, "there's your trail. It gets plainer and broader the farther you get on, but you must use your eyes here, and get to know it well afore you get into the fog. Good-bye."

"Good-bye." Lance took her hand and drew her beside him. She was still redolent of the spices of the thicket, and to the young man's excited fancy seemed at that moment to personify the perfume and intoxication of her native woods. Half laughingly, half earnestly, he tried to kiss her; she struggled for some time strongly, but at the last moment yielded with a slight return, and the exchange of a subtle fire that thrilled him and left him standing confused and astounded as she ran away. He watched her lithe, nymph-like figure disappear in the chequered shadows of the wood, and then he turned briskly down the half hidden trail. His eyesight was keen, he made good progress, and was soon well on his way towards the distant ridge.

But Flip's return had not been as rapid. When she reached the wood she crept to its beetling verge and looking across the cañon watched Lance's figure as it vanished and reappeared in the shadows and sinuosities of the ascent. When he reached the ridge the outlying fog crept across the summit, caught him in its embrace, and wrapped him from her gaze. Flip sighed, raised herself, put her alternate foot on a stump, and took a long pull at her too-brief stockings. When she had pulled down her skirt, and endeavoured once more to renew the intimacy that had existed in previous years between the edge of her petticoat and the top of her stockings, she sighed again, and went home.

Chapter III

For six months the sea fogs monotonously came and went along the Monterey coast; for six months they beleagured the Coast Range with afternoon sorties of white hosts, that regularly swept over the mountain crest and were as regularly beaten back again by the levelled lances of the morning sun. For six months that white veil which had once hidden Lance Harriott in its folds returned without him. For that amiable outlaw no longer needed disguise or hiding-place. The swift wave of pursuit that had dashed him on the summit had fallen back, and the next day was broken and scattered. Before the week had passed a regular judicial inquiry relieved his crime of premeditation, and showed it to be a rude duel of two armed and equally desperate men. From a secure vantage in a sea-coast town, Lance challenged a trial by his peers, and, as an already prejudged man escaping from his executioners, obtained a change of venue. Regular justice, seated by the calm Pacific, found the action of an interior, irregular jury rash and hasty. Lance was liberated on bail.

The Postmaster at Fisher's Crossing had just received the weekly mail and express from San Francisco, and was engaged in examining them. They consisted of five letters and two parcels. Of these, three of the letters and the two parcels were directed to Flip. It was not the first time during the last six months that this extraordinary event had occurred, and the curiosity of the Crossing was duly excited. As Flip had never called personally for the letters or parcels, but had sent one of her wild, irregular scouts or henchmen to bring them, and as she was seldom seen at the Crossing or on the stage-road, that curiosity was never satisfied. The disappointment to the Postmaster—a man past the middle age—partook of a sentimental nature. He looked at the letters and parcels, he looked at his watch; it was yet early, he could return by noon. He again examined the addresses; they were in the same handwriting of the previous letters. His mind was made up, he would deliver them himself. The poetic, soulful side of his mission was delicately indicated by a pale blue necktie, a clean shirt, and a small package of "ginger nuts," of which Flip was extravagantly fond.

The common road to Fairley's Rancho was by the stage turnpike to a point below the Gin and Ginger Woods, where the prudent horseman usually left his beast and followed the intersecting trail afoot. It was here that the Postmaster suddenly observed on the edge of the wood the figure of an elegantly-dressed woman; she was walking slowly and apparently at her ease, one hand held her skirts lightly gathered between her gloved fingers, the other slowly swung a riding-whip. Was it a picnic of some people from Monterey or Santa Cruz? The spectacle was novel enough to justify his coming nearer. Suddenly she withdrew in the wood; he lost sight of her; she was gone. He remembered, however, that he had still to call on Flip, and as the steep trail was beginning to tax all his energies, he was fain to hurry forward. The sun was nearly vertical when he turned into the cañon, and saw the bark roof of the cabin beyond. At almost the same moment Flip appeared, flushed and panting, in the road before him.

"You've got something for me," she said, pointing to the parcel and letter.

Completely taken by surprise, the Postmaster mechanically yielded them up and as instantly regretted it.

"They're paid for?" continued Flip, observing his hesitation.

"That's so," stammered the official of the Crossing, seeing his last chance of knowing the contents of the parcel vanish; "but I thought ez it's a valooable package, maybe ye might want to examine it to see that it was all right afore ye receipted for it."

"I'll risk it," said Flip coolly, "and if it ain't right I'll let ye know."

As the girl seemed inclined to retire with her property, the Postmaster was driven to other conversation. "We ain't had the pleasure of seeing you down at the Crossing for a month o' Sundays," he began, with airy yet pronounced gallantry. "Some folks let on you was keepin' company with some feller like Bijah Brown, and you were getting a little too set up for the Crossing." The individual here mentioned being the county butcher, and supposed to exhibit his hopeless affection for Flip by making a long and useless divergence from his weekly route to enter the cañon "for orders," Flip did not deem it necessary to reply. "Then I allowed ez how you might have company," he continued; "I reckon there's some City folks up at the Summit. I saw a mighty smart fash'n'ble gal cavorting round. Hed no end o' style and fancy fixin's. That's my kind, I tell you. I just weaken on that sort o' gal," he continued, in the firm belief that he had awakened Flip's jealousy, as he glanced at her well-worn homespun frock, and found her eyes suddenly fixed on his own.

"Strange I ain't got to see her yet," she replied coolly, shouldering her parcel, and quite ignoring any sense of obligation to him for his extra-official act.

"But you might get to see her at the edge of the Gin and Ginger Woods," he persisted feebly, in a last effort to detain her, "if you'll take a *pasear* there with me."

Flip's only response was to walk on towards the cabin, whence, with a vague complimentary suggestion of "droppin' in to pass the time o' day" with her father, the Postmaster meekly followed.

The paternal Fairley, once convinced that his daughter's new companion required no pecuniary or material assistance from his hands, relaxed to the extent of entering into a querulous confidence with him, during which Flip took the opportunity of slipping away. As Fairley had that infelicitous tendency of most weak natures to unconsciously exaggerate unimportant details in their talk, the Postmaster presently became convinced that the butcher was a constant and assiduous suitor of Flip's. The absurdity of his sending parcels and letters by post, when he might bring them himself, did not strike the official. On the contrary, he believed it to be a master-stroke of cunning. Fired by jealousy and Flip's indifference, he "deemed it his duty"—using that facile form of cowardly offensiveness—to betray Flip.

Of which she was happily oblivious. Once away from the cabin she plunged into the woods, with the parcel swung behind her like a knapsack. Leaving the trail, she presently struck off in a straight line through cover and underbrush with the unerring instinct of an animal, climbing hand-over-hand the steepest ascent, or fluttering like a bird

from branch to branch down the deepest declivity. She soon reached
that part of the trail where the susceptible Postmaster had seen the
fascinating unknown. Assuring herself she was not followed, she crept
through the thicket until she reached a little waterfall and basin that
had served the fugitive Lance for a bath. The spot bore signs of later
and more frequent occupancy, and when Flip carefully removed some
bark and brushwood from a cavity in the rock and drew forth various
folded garments, it was evident she had used it as a sylvan dressing-
room! Here she opened the parcel; it contained a small and delicate
shawl of yellow China crêpe. Flip instantly threw it over her shoulders
and stepped hurriedly towards the edge of the wood. Then she began
to pass backwards and forwards before the trunk of a tree. At first
nothing was visible on the tree, but a closer inspection showed a large
pane of ordinary window glass stuck in the fork of the branches. It was
placed at such a cunning angle against the darkness of the forest opening that it made a soft and mysterious mirror, not unlike a Claude
Lorraine glass, wherein not only the passing figure of the young girl
was seen, but the dazzling green and gold of the hillside, and the far-
off silhouetted crests of the Coast Range.

But this was evidently only a prelude to a severer rehearsal. When
she returned to the waterfall, she unearthed from her stores a large
piece of yellow soap and some yards of rough cotton "sheeting." These
she deposited beside the basin, and again crept to the edge of the wood
to assure herself that she was alone. Satisfied that no intruding foot
had invaded that virgin bower, she returned to her bath, and began to
undress. A slight wind followed her, and seemed to whisper to the
circumjacent trees. It appeared to waken her sister naïads and
nymphs, who, joining their leafy fingers, softly drew around her a
gently-moving band of trembling lights and shadows, of flecked sprays
and inextricably mingled branches, and involved her in a chaste sylvan
obscurity, veiled alike from pursuing god or stumbling shepherd.
Within these hallowed precincts was the musical ripple of laughter
and falling water, and at times the glimpse of a lithe briar-caught limb,
or a ray of sunlight trembling over bright flanks or the white, austere
outline of a childish bosom.

When she drew again the leafy curtain, and once more stepped out
of the wood, she was completely transformed. It was the figure that
had appeared to the Postmaster; the slight, erect, graceful form of a
young woman modishly attired. It was Flip, but Flip made taller by
the lengthened skirt and clinging habiliments of fashion. Flip freckled,
but, through the cunning of a relief of yellow colour in her gown, her
piquant brown-shot face and eyes brightened and intensified until she
seemed like a spicy odour made visible. I cannot affirm that the

judgment of Flip's mysterious *modiste* was infallible, or that the taste of Mr. Lance Harriott, her patron, was fastidious; enough that it was picturesque, and perhaps not more glaring and extravagant than the colour in which Spring herself had once clothed the sere hillside where Flip was now seated. The phantom mirror in the tree fork caught and held her with the sky, the green leaves, the sunlight, and all the graciousness of her surroundings, and the wind gently tossed her hair and the gay ribbons of her gipsy hat. Suddenly she started. Some remote sound in the trail below, inaudible to any ear less fine than her own, arrested her breathing. She rose swiftly and darted into cover.

Ten minutes passed. The sun was declining; the white fog was beginning to creep over the Coast Range. And then from the edge of the wood Cinderella appeared, disenchanted, and in her homespun garments. The clock had struck, the spell was past. As she disappeared down the trail even the magic mirror, moved by the wind, slipped from the tree top to the ground and became a piece of common glass.

Chapter IV

The events of the day had produced a remarkable impression on the facial aspect of the charcoal-burning Fairley. Extraordinary processes of thought, indicated by repeated rubbing of his forehead, had produced a high light in the middle and a corresponding deepening of shadow at the sides, until it bore the appearance of a perfect sphere. It was this forehead that confronted Flip reproachfully as became a deceived comrade, menacingly as became an outraged parent in the presence of a third party and—a Postmaster!

"Fine doin's this, yer receivin' clandecent bundles and letters, eh?" he began.

Flip sent one swift, withering look of contempt at the Postmaster, who at once becoming invertebrate and grovelling, mumbled that he must "get on" to the Crossing, and rose to go. But the old man, who had counted on his presence for moral support, and was clearly beginning to hate him for precipitating this scene with his daughter, whom he feared, violently protested.

"Sit down, can't ye? Don't you see you're a witness?" he screamed hysterically.

It was a fatal suggestion. "Witness!" repeated Flip scornfully.

"Yes, a witness! He gave ye letters and bundles."

"Weren't they directed to me?" asked Flip.

"Yes," said the Postmaster hesitatingly; "in course, yes."

"Do *you* lay claim to them?" she said, turning to her father.

"No," responded the old man.

"Do you?" sharply, to the Postmaster.

"No," he replied.

"Then," said Flip coolly, "if you're not claimin' 'em for yourself, and you hear father say they ain't his, I reckon the less you have to say about 'em the better."

"Thar's suthin' in that," said the old man, shamelessly abandoning the Postmaster.

"Then why don't she say who sent 'em, and what they are like," said the Postmaster, "if there's nothin' in it?"

"Yes," echoed Dad feebly. "Flip, why don't you?"

Without answering the direct question, Flip turned upon her father. "Maybe you forget how you used to row and tear round here because tramps and such like came to the ranch for suthin', and I gave it to 'em? Maybe you'll quit tearin' round and letting yourself be made a fool of now by that man, just because one of those tramps gets up and sends us some presents back in return?"

" 'Twasn't me, Flip," said the old man deprecatingly, but glaring at the astonished Postmaster. "Twasn't my doin'. I allus said if you cast your bread on the waters it would come back to you by return mail. The fact is the Gov'ment is gettin' too high-handed! Some o' these bloated officials had better climb down before next leckshen."

"Maybe," continued Flip to her father, without looking at their discomfited visitor, "ye'd better find out whether one of those officials comes up to this yer ranch to steal away a gal about my own size, or to get points about diamond-making; I reckon he don't travel round to find out who writes all the letters that goes through the postoffice."

The Postmaster had seemingly miscalculated the old man's infirm temper, and the daughter's skilful use of it. He was unprepared for Flip's boldness and audacity, and when he saw that both barrels of the accusation had taken effect on the charcoal-burner, who was rising with epileptic rage, he fairly turned and fled. The old man would have followed him with objurgation beyond the door but for the restraining hand of Flip.

Baffled and beaten, nevertheless Fate was not wholly unkind to the retreating suitor. Near the Gin and Ginger Woods he picked up a letter which had fallen from the pocket of Flip. He recognised the writing, and did not scruple to read it. It was not a love epistle—at least, not such a one as *he* would have written; it did not give the address nor the name of the correspondent; but he read the following with greedy eyes—

"Perhaps it's just as well that you don't rig yourself out for the benefit of those dead-beats at the Crossing, or any tramp that might hang round the ranch. Keep all your style for me when I come. I can't tell you when—it's mighty uncertain before the rainy season. But I'm coming soon. Don't go back on your promise about lettin' up on the tramps and being a little more high-toned. And don't you give 'em so much. It's true I sent you hats *twice*. I clean forgot all about the first; but *I* wouldn't have given a ten-dollar hat to a nigger woman who had a sick baby because I had an extra hat. I'd have let that baby slide. I forgot to ask whether the skirt is worn separately; I must see that dressmaking sharp about it; but I think you'll want something on besides a jacket and skirt, at least it looks like it up here. I don't think you could manage a piano down there without the old man knowing it, and raisin' the devil generally. I promised you I'd let up on him. Mind you keep all your promises to me. I'm glad you're gettin' on with the six-shooter; tin cans are good at fifteen yards, but try it on sunthin' that *moves!* I forgot to say that I am on the track of your big brother. It's a three years' old track, and he was in Arizona. The friend who told me didn't expatiate much on what he did there, but I reckon they had a high old time. If he's above the earth I'll find him, you bet. The *yerba buena* and the southern-wood came all right—they smelt like you. Say, Flip, do you remember the *last*—the *very last* thing that happened when you said 'Good-bye' on the trail. Don't let me ever find out that you've let anybody else kiss"——But here the virtuous indignation of the Postmaster found vent in an oath. He threw the letter away. He retained of it only two facts—Flip *had* a brother who was missing; she had a lover present in the flesh.

How much of the substance of this and previous letters Flip had confided to her father I cannot say. If she suppressed anything it was probably that which affected Lance's secret alone, and it was doubtful how much of that she herself knew. In her own affairs she was frank without being communicative, and never lost her shy obstinacy even with her father. Governing the old man as completely as she did, she appeared most embarrassed when she was most dominant; she had her own way without lifting her voice or her eyes, she seemed oppressed by *mauvaise honte* when she was most triumphant; she would end a discussion with a shy murmur addressed to herself, or a single gesture of self-consciousness.

The disclosure of her strange relations with an unknown man, and the exchange of presents and confidences, seemed to suddenly awake Fairley to a vague uneasy sense of some unfulfilled duties as a parent. The first effect of this on his weak nature was a peevish antagonism to the cause of it. He had long fretful monologues on the vanity of dia-mond-making, if accompanied with "pestering" by "interlopers," on the wickedness of concealment and conspiracy, and their effects on charcoal-burning, on the nurturing of spies and "adders" in the family circle, and on the seditiousness of dark and mysterious councils in which a grey-haired father was left out. It was true that a word or a look from Flip generally brought these monologues to an inglorious and abrupt termination, but they were none the less lugubrious as long as they lasted. In time they were succeeded by an affectation of contrite apology and self-depreciation. "Don't go out o' the way to ask the old man," he would say, referring to the quantity of bacon to be ordered; "it's nat'ral a young gal should have her own advisers." The state of the flour-barrel would also produce a like self-abasement. "Unless ye're already in correspondence about more flour ye might take the opinion o' the first tramp ye meet ez whether Santa Cruz Mills is a good brand, but don't ask the old man." If Flip was in conversation with the butcher, Fairley would obtrusively and markedly retire with the hope "he wasn't intrudin' on their secrets."

These phases of her father's weakness were not frequent enough to excite her alarm, but she could not help noticing they were accompanied with a seriousness unusual to him. He began to be tremulously watchful of her, returning often from work at an earlier hour, and lingering by the cabin in the morning. He brought absurd and useless presents for her, and presented them with a nervous anxiety, poorly concealed by an assumption of careless, paternal generosity. "Suthin' I picked up at the Crossing for ye to-day," he would say airily, and retire to watch the effect of a pair of shoes two sizes too large, or a fur cap in September. He would have hired a cheap parlour-organ for her, but for the apparently unexpected revelation that she couldn't play. He had received the news of a clue to his long-lost son without emotion, but lately he seemed to look upon it as a foregone conclusion, and one that necessarily solved the question of companionship for Flip. "In course, when you've got your own flesh and blood with ye, ye can't go foolin' around with strangers." These autumnal blossoms of affection, I fear, came too late for any effect upon Flip, precociously matured by her father's indifference and selfishness. But she was good-humoured, and seeing him seriously concerned, gave him more of her time, even visited him in the sacred seclusion of the "diamond pit" and listened with far-off eyes to his fitful indictment of all things outside his grimy laboratory. Much of this patient indifference came with a capricious change in her own habits; she no longer indulged in the rehearsal of dress, she packed away her most treasured garments, and her leafy boudoir knew her no more. She sometimes walked on the hillside, and often followed the trail which she had taken with Lance, when she led him to the rancho. She once or twice extended her walk to the spot where she had parted from him, and as often came shyly away, her eyes downcast and her face warm with colour. Perhaps because these experiences and some mysterious instinct of maturing womanhood had left a story in her eyes, which her two adorers, the Postmaster and the butcher, read with passion, she became famous without knowing it. Extravagant stories of her fascinations brought strangers into the valley. The effect upon her father may be imagined. Lance could not have desired a more effective guardian than he proved to be in this emergency. Those who had been told of this hidden pearl were surprised to find it so jealously protected.

Chapter V

The long parched summer had drawn to its dusty close. Much of it was already blown abroad and dissipated on trail and turnpike, or crackled in harsh, unelastic fibres on hillside and meadow. Some of it had disappeared in the palpable smoke by day and fiery crests by night of burning forests. The besieging fogs on the Coast Range daily thinned their hosts, and at last vanished. The wind changed from north-west to south-west. The salt breath of the sea was on the summit. And then one day, the staring, unchanged sky was faintly touched with remote mysterious clouds, and grew tremulous in expression. The next morning dawned upon a newer face in the heavens, on changed woods, on altered outlines, on vanished crests, on forgotten distances. It was raining!

Four weeks of this change, with broken spaces of sunlight, and intense blue aërial islands, and then a storm set in. All day the summit pines and redwoods rocked in the blast. At times the onset of the rain seemed to be held back by the fury of the gale, or was visibly seen in sharp waves on the hillside. Unknown and concealed watercourses suddenly overflowed the trails, pools became lakes, and brooks rivers. Hidden from the storm, the sylvan silence of sheltered valleys was broken by the impetuous rush of waters; even the tiny streamlet that traversed Flip's retreat in the Gin and Ginger Woods became a cascade.

The storm drove Fairley from his couch early. The falling of a large tree across the trail, and the sudden overflow of a small stream beside it, hastened his steps. But he was doomed to encounter what was to him a more disagreeable object—a human figure. By the bedraggled drapery that flapped and fluttered in the wind, by the long, unkempt hair that hid the face and eyes, and by the grotesquely-misplaced bonnet, the old man recognised one of his old trespassers—an Indian squaw.

"Clear out 'er that! Come, make tracks, will ye?" the old man screamed; but here the wind stopped his voice, and drove him against a hazel bush.

"Me heap sick," answered the squaw, shivering through her muddy shawl.

"I'll make ye a heap sicker if ye don't vamose the ranch," continued Fairley, advancing.

"Me wantee Wangee girl. Wangee girl give me heap grub," said the squaw, without moving.

"You bet your life," groaned the old man to himself. Nevertheless an idea struck him. "Ye ain't brought no presents, hev ye!" he asked cautiously. "Ye ain't got no pootey things for poor Wangee girl?" he continued insinuatingly.

"Me got heap *cache* nuts and berries," said the squaw.

"Oh, in course! in course! That's just it," screamed Fairley; "you've got 'em *cached* only two mile from yer, and you'll go and get 'em for a half-dollar, cash down."

"Me bring Wangee girl to *cache,*" replied the Indian, pointing to the wood; "honest Injin."

Another bright idea struck Mr. Fairley. But it required some cautious elaboration. Hurrying the squaw with him through the pelting rain, he reached the shelter of the corral. Vainly the shivering aborigine drew her tightly-bandaged papoose closer to her square flat breast and looked longingly towards the cabin; the old man backed her against the palisade. Here he cautiously imparted his dark intentions to employ her to keep watch and ward over the rancho, and especially over its young mistress—"Clear out all the tramps 'ceptin' yourself, and I'll keep ye in grub and rum." Many and deliberate repetitions of this offer in various forms at last seem to affect the squaw; she nodded violently, and echoed the last word "rum." "Now," she added. The old man hesitated; she was in possession of his secret; he groaned, and promising an immediate instalment of liquor, led her to the cabin.

The door was so securely fastened against the impact of the storm, that some moments elapsed before the bar was drawn, and the old man had become impatient and profane. When it was partly opened by Flip, he hastily slipped in, dragging the squaw after him, and cast one single, suspicious glance around the rude apartment which served as a sitting-room. Flip had apparently been writing. A small inkstand was still on the board table, but her paper had evidently been concealed before she allowed them to enter. The squaw instantly squatted before the adobe hearth, warmed her bundled baby, and left the ceremony of introduction to her companion. Flip regarded the two with calm preoccupation and indifference. The only thing that touched her interest was the old squaw's draggled skirt and limp neckerchief. They were Flip's own, long since abandoned and cast off in the Gin and Ginger Woods. "Secrets again," whined the paternal Fairley, still eying Flip furtively. "Secrets again, in course—in course—jiss so. Secrets that must be kep from the ole man! Dark doin's by one's own flesh and blood. Go on! go on! Don't mind me." Flip did not reply; she had even lost the interest in her old dress; perhaps it had only touched some note in unison with her reverie.

"Can't ye get the poor critter some whisky!" he queried fretfully. "Ye used to be peart enuff before." As Flip turned to the corner to lift the demijohn, Fairley took occasion to kick the squaw with his foot, and indicate by extravagant pantomine that the bargain was not to be alluded to before the girl. Flip poured out some whisky in a tin cup, and, approaching the squaw, handed it to her. "It's like ez not," continued Fairley to his daughter, but looking at the squaw, "that she'll be hauntin' the woods off and on, and kinder looking after the last pit near the *Madroños;* ye'll give her grub and licker ez she likes. Well, d'ye hear, Flip? Are ye moonin' agin with yer secrets? What's gone with ye?"

If the child were dreaming, it was a delicious dream. Her magnetic eyes were suffused by a strange light, as though the eye itself had blushed; her full pulse showed itself more in the rounding outline of her cheek than in any deepening of colour; indeed, if there was any heightening of tint, it was in her freckles, which fairly glistened like tiny spangles. Her eyes were downcast, her shoulders slightly bent, but her voice was low and clear and thoughtful as ever.

"One o' the big pines above the *Madroño* pit has blown over into the run," she said quietly. "It's choked up the water, and it's risin' fast. Like ez not it's pourin' over into the pit by this time."

The old man rose with a fretful cry. "And why in blazes didn't you say so first?" he screamed, catching up his axe, and rushing to the door.

"Ye didn't give me a chance," said Flip, raising her eyes for the first time. With an impatient imprecation Fairley darted by her and rushed into the wood. In an instant she had shut the door and bolted it; in the same instant the squaw arose, dashed the long hair not only from her eyes but from her head, tore away her shawl and blanket, and revealed the square shoulders of Lance Harriott! Flip remained leaning against the door; but the young man in rising dropped the bandaged papoose, which rolled from his lap into the fire. Flip, with a cry, sprang towards it; but Lance caught her by the waist with one arm, as with the other he dragged the bundle from the flames. "Don't be alarmed," he said gaily; "it's only"——

"What?" said Flip, trying to disengage herself.

"My coat and trousers."

Flip laughed, which encouraged Lance to another attempt to kiss her. She evaded it by diving her head into his waistcoat and saying, "There's father."

"But he's gone to clear away that tree?" suggested Lance.

One of Flip's significant silences followed.

"Oh, I see," he laughed. "That was a plant to get him away! Ah!" She had released herself.

"Why did you come like that?" she said, pointing to his wig and blanket.

"To see if you'd know me," he responded.

"No," said Flip, dropping her eyes, "it was to keep other people from knowing you. You're hidin' agin."

"I am," returned Lance; "but," he interrupted gaily, "it's only the same old thing."

"But you wrote from Monterey that it was all over," she persisted.

"So it would have been," he said gloomily, "but for some dog down here who is hunting up an old scent. I'll spot him yet, and"——he stopped suddenly, with such utter abstraction of hatred in his fixed and glittering eyes that she almost feared him. She laid her hand quite unconsciously on his arm. He grasped it—his face changed.

"I couldn't wait any longer to see you, Flip, so I came here anyway," he went on gaily. "I thought to hang round and get a chance to speak to you first, when I fell afoul of the old man. He didn't know me, and tumbled right in my little game. Why; do you believe he wants to hire me for my grub and liquor, to act as a sort of sentry over you and the rancho?" And here he related with great gusto the substance of his interview. "I reckon as he's that suspicious," he concluded, "I'd better play it out now as I've begun, only it's mighty hard I can't see you here before the fire in your fancy toggery, Flip, but must dodge in and out of the wet underbrush in these yer duds of yours that I picked up in the old place in the Gin and Ginger Woods."

"Then you came here just to see me?" added Flip.

"I did."

"For only that?"

"Only that."

Flip dropped her eyes. Lance had got his other arm around her waist, but her resisting little hand was still potent.

"Listen," she said at last, without looking up, but apparently talking to the intruding arm, "when Dad comes I'll get him to send you to watch the diamond pit. It isn't far; it's warm, and"——

"What?"

"I'll come after a bit and see you. Quit foolin' now. If you'd only have come here like yourself—like—like—a white man."

"The old man," interrupted Lance, "would have just passed me on to the summit. I couldn't have played the lost fisherman on him at this time of year."

"Ye could have been stopped at the Crossing by high water, you silly," said the girl. "It was." This grammatical obscurity referred to the stage-coach.

"Yes, but I might have been tracked to this cabin. And look here, Flip," he said, suddenly straightening himself, and lifting the girl's face to a level with his own, "I don't want you to lie any more for me. It ain't right."

"All right. Ye needn't go to the pit, then, and I won't come."

"Flip!"

"And here's Dad coming. Quick!"

Lance chose to put his own interpretation on this last adjuration. The resisting little hand was now lying quite limp on his shoulder. He drew her brown, bright face near his own, felt her spiced breath on his lips, his cheeks, his hot eyelids, his swimming eyes, kissed her, hurriedly replaced his wig and blanket, and dropped beside the fire with the tremulous laugh of youth and innocent first passion. Flip had withdrawn to the window, and was looking out upon the rocking pines.

"He don't seem to be coming," said Lance, with a half shy laugh.

"No," responded Flip demurely, pressing her hot oval cheek against the wet panes; "I reckon I was mistaken. You're sure," she added, looking resolutely another way, but still trembling like a magnetic needle towards Lance, as he moved slightly before the fire, "you're *sure* you'd like me to come to you?"

"Sure, Flip?"

"Hush!" said Flip, as this re-assuring query of reproachful astonishment appeared about to be emphasised by a forward amatory dash of Lance's; "hush! he's coming this time, sure."

It was indeed Fairley, exceedingly wet, exceedingly bedraggled, exceedingly sponged out as to colour, and exceedingly profane. It appeared that there was, indeed, a tree that had fallen in the "run," but that, far from diverting the overflow into the pit, it had established "back water," which had forced another outlet. All this might have been detected at once by any human intellect not distracted by correspondence with strangers, and enfeebled by habitually scorning the intellect of its own progenitor. This reckless selfishness had further only resulted in giving "rheumatics" to that progenitor, who now required the external administration of opodeldoc to his limbs, and the internal administration of whisky. Having thus spoken, Mr. Fairley, with great promptitude and infantine simplicity, at once bared two legs of entirely different colours, and mutely waited for his daughter to rub them. If Flip did this all unconsciously, and with the mechanical dexterity of previous habit, it was because she did not quite understand the savage eyes and impatient gestures of Lance in his encompassing wig and blanket, and because it helped her to voice her thought.

"Ye'll never be able to take your reg'lar watch at the diamond pit tonight, Dad," she said; "and I've been reck'nin' you might set the squaw there instead. I can show her what to do."

But to Flip's momentary discomfiture, her father promptly objected. "Mebbee I've got suthin' else for her to do. Mebbee I may have *my* secrets too—eh?" he said, with dark significance, at the same time administering a significant nudge to Lance, which kept up the young man's exasperation. "No, she'll rest yer a bit just now. I'll set her to watchin' suthin' else, like as not, when I want her." Flip fell into one of her suggestive silences. Lance watched her earnestly, mollified by a single furtive glance from her significant eyes; the rain dashed against the windows, and occasionally spattered and hissed in the hearth of the broad chimney, and Mr. David Fairley, somewhat assuaged by the internal administration of whisky, grew more loquacious. The genius of incongruity and inconsistency which generally ruled his conduct came out with freshened vigour under the gentle stimulation of spirit. "On an evening like this," he began, comfortably settling himself on the floor beside the chimney, "ye might rig yerself out in them new duds and fancy fixin's that that Sacramento shrimp sent ye, and let your own flesh and blood see ye. If that's too much to do for your ole Dad, ye might do it to please that digger squaw as a Christian act." Whether in the hidden depths of the old man's consciousness there was a feeling of paternal vanity in showing this wretched aborigine the value and importance of the treasure she was about to guard I cannot say. Flip darted an interrogatory look at Lance, who nodded a quiet assent, and she flew into the inner room. She did not linger on the details of her toilet, but reappeared almost the next moment in her new finery, buttoning the neck of her gown as she entered the room, and chastely stopping at the window to characteristically pull up her stocking. The peculiarity of her situation increased her usual shyness; she played with the black and gold beads of a handsome necklace— Lance's last gift—as the merest child might; her unbuckled shoe gave the squaw a natural opportunity of showing her admiration and devotion by insisting upon buckling it, and gave Lance under that disguise an opportunity of covertly kissing the little foot and ankle in the shadow of the chimney; an event which provoked slight hysterical symptoms in Flip, and caused her to sit suddenly down in spite of the remonstrance of her parent. "Ef you can't quit gigglin' and squirmin' like an Injin baby yourself, ye'd better git rid o' them duds," he ejaculated with peevish scorn.

Yet even under this perfunctory rebuke his weak vanity could not be hidden, and he enjoyed the evident admiration of a creature whom he believed to be half-witted and degraded, all the more keenly because it did not make him jealous. She could not take Flip from him. Rendered garrulous by liquor, he went to voice his contempt for those who might attempt it. Taking advantage of his daughter's absence to resume her homely garments, he whispered confidentially to Lance—

"Ye see these yer fine dresses, ye might think is presents. P'r'aps Flip lets on they are? P'r'aps she don't know any better. But they ain't presents. They're only samples o' dressmaking and jewellery that a vain, conceited shrimp of a feller up in Sacramento sends down here to get customers for. In course I'm to pay for 'em. In course he reckons I'm to do it. In course I calkilate to do it: but he needn't try to play 'em off as presents. He talks suthin' o' coming down here, sportin' hisself off on Flip as a fancy buck! Not ez long ez the old man's here— you bet." Thoroughly carried away by his fancied wrongs, it was perhaps fortunate that he did not observe the flashing eyes of Lance behind his lank and lustreless wig; but seeing only the figure of Lance as he had conjured him, he went on. "That's why I want you to hang around her. Hang around her until my boy—him that's comin' home on a visit—gets here, and I reckon he'll clear out that yar Sacramento counterjumper. Only let me get a sight o' him afore Flip does. Eh? D'ye hear? Dog my skin if I don't believe the d——d Injin's drunk." It was fortunate that at that moment Flip reappeared, and dropping on the hearth between her father and the infuriated Lance, let her hand slip in his with a warning pressure. The light touch momentarily recalled him to himself and her, but not until the quickwitted girl had had revealed to her in one startled wave of consciousness the full extent of Lance's infirmity of temper. With the instinct of awakened tenderness came a sense of responsibility and a vague premonition of danger. The coy blossom of her heart was scarce unfolded before it was chilled by approaching shadows. Fearful of she knew not what, she hesitated. Every moment of Lance's stay was imperilled by a single word that might spring from his suppressed white lips; beyond and above the suspicions his sudden withdrawal might awaken in her father's breast, she was dimly conscious of some mysterious terror without that awaited him. She listened to the furious onslaught of the wind upon the sycamores beside their cabin, and thought she heard it there;

she listened to the sharp fusilade of rain upon roof and pane, and the turbulent roar and rush of leaping mountain torrents at their very feet, and fancied it was there. She suddenly sprang to the window, and pressing her eyes to the pane saw through the misty turmoil of tossing boughs and swaying branches the scintillating intermittent flames of torches moving on the trail above, and *knew* it was there!

In an instant she was collected and calm. "Dad," she said, in her ordinary indifferent tone, "there's torches movin' up toward the diamond pit. Likely it's tramps. I'll take the squaw and see." And before the old man could stagger to his feet she had dragged Lance with her into the road.

Chapter VI

The wind charged down upon them, slamming the door at their backs, extinguishing the broad shaft of light that had momentarily shot out into the darkness, and swept them a dozen yards away. Gaining the lee of a madroño tree, Lance opened his blanketed arms, enfolded the girl, and felt her for one brief moment tremble and nestle in his bosom like some frightened animal.

"Well," he said, gaily, "what next?"

Flip recovered herself. "You're safe now anywhere outside the house. But did you expect them to-night?"

Lance shrugged his shoulders. "Why not?"

"Hush!" returned the girl; "they're coming this way."

The four flickering, scattered lights presently dropped into line. The trail had been found; they were coming nearer. Flip breathed quickly; the spiced aroma of her presence filled the blanket as he drew her tightly beside him. He had forgotten the storm that raged around them, the mysterious foe that was approaching, until Flip caught his sleeve with a slight laugh.

"Why, it's Kennedy and Bijah."

"Who's Kennedy and Bijah?" asked Lance curtly.

"Kennedy's the Postmaster, and Bijah's the butcher."

"What do they want?" continued Lance.

"Me," said Flip coyly.

"You?"

"Yes; let's run away."

Half leading, half dragging her friend, Flip made her way with unerring woodcraft down the ravine. The sound of voices and even the tumult of the storm became fainter, an acrid smell of burning greenwood smarted Lance's lips and eyes; in the midst of the profound darkness beneath him gradually a faint, gigantic nimbus like a lurid eye glowed and sank, quivered and faded with the spent breath of the gale as it penetrated their retreat. "The pit," whispered Flip; "it's safe on the other side," she added, cautiously skirting the orbit of the great eye, and leading him to a sheltered nest of bark and sawdust. It was warm and odorous. Nevertheless, they both deemed it necessary to enwrap themselves in the single blanket. The eye beamed fitfully upon them, occasionally a wave of lambent tremulousness passed across it; its weirdness was an excuse for their drawing nearer each other in playful terror.

"Flip."

"Well?"

"What did the other two want? To see you *too?*"

"Likely," said Flip, without the least trace of coquetry. "There's been a lot of strangers yer, off and on."

"Perhaps you'd like to go back and see them?"

"Do you want me to?"

Lance's reply was a kiss. Nevertheless he was vaguely uneasy. "Looks a little as if I were running away, don't it?" he suggested.

"No," said Flip, "they think you're only a squaw; it's me they're after."

Lance smarted a little at this infelicitous speech. A strange and irritating sensation had been creeping over him—it was his first experience of shame and remorse. "I reckon I'll go back and see," he said, rising abruptly.

Flip was silent. She was thinking. Believing that the men were seeking her only, she knew that their attention would be directed from her companion when it was found out he was no longer with her, and she dreaded to meet them in his irritable presence.

"Go," she said, "tell Dad something's gone wrong in the diamond pit, and say I'm watching it for him here."

"And you?"

"I'll go there and wait for him. If he can't get rid of them, and they follow him there, I'll come back here and meet you. Anyhow, I'll manage to have Dad wait there a spell."

She took his hand and led him back by a different path to the trail. He was surprised to find that the cabin, its window glowing from the fire, was only a hundred yards away. "Go in the back way, by the shed. Don't go in the room, nor near the light if you can. Don't talk inside, but call or beckon to Dad. Remember," she said with a laugh, "you're keeping watch of me for him. Pull your hair down on your eyes, so." This operation, like most feminine embellishments of the masculine toilette, was attended by a kiss, and Flip, stepping back into the shadow, vanished in the storm.

Lance's first movements were inconsistent with his assumed sex. He picked up his draggled skirt, and drew a bowie-knife from his boot. From his bosom he took a revolver, turning the chambers noiselessly as he felt the caps. He then crept towards the cabin softly and gained the shed. It was quite dark but for a pencil of light piercing a crack of the rude ill-fitting door that opened on the sitting-room. A single voice not unfamiliar to him, raised in half brutal triumph, greeted his ears. A name was mentioned—his own? His angry hand was on the latch. One moment more and he would have burst the door, but in that instant another name was uttered—a name that dropped his hand from the latch and the blood from his cheeks. He staggered backward, passed his hand swiftly across his forehead, recovered himself with a gesture of mingled rage and despair, and sinking on his knees beside the door pressed his hot temples against the crack.

"Do I know Lance Harriott?" said the voice. "Do I know the d——d ruffian? Didn't I hunt him a year ago into the brush three miles from the Crossing? Didn't we lose sight of him the very day he turned up yer at this ranche, and got smuggled over into Monterey? Ain't it the same man as killed Arkansaw Bob—Bob Ridley—the name he went by in Sonora? And who was Bob Ridley, eh? Who? Why, you d——d old fool, it was Bob Fairley—YOUR SON!"

The old man's voice rose querulous and indistinct.

"What are ye talkin' about?" interrupted the first speaker. "I tell you I *know*. Look at these pictures, I found 'em on his body. Look at 'em. Pictures of you and your girl. P'r'aps you'll deny them. P'r'aps you'll tell me I lie when I tell you *he* told me he was your son; told me how he ran away from you, how you were livin' somewhere in the mountains makin' gold or suthin' else outer charcoal. He told me who he was as a secret. He never let on he told it to any one else. And when I found that the man who killed him, Lance Harriott, had been hidin' here, had been sendin' spies all around to find out all about your son, had been foolin' you and tryin' to ruin your gal as he had killed your boy, I know that *he* knew it too."

"LIAR!"

The door fell in with a crash. There was the sudden apparition of a demoniac face, still half-hidden by the long trailing black locks of hair that curled like Medusa's around it. A cry of terror filled the room. Three of the men dashed from the door and fled precipitately. The man who had spoken sprang towards his rifle in the chimney corner. But the movement was his last; a blinding flash and shattering report interposed between him and his weapon. The impulse carried him forward headlong into the fire, that hissed and spluttered with his blood, and Lance Harriott, with his smoking pistol, strode past him to the door. Already far down the trail there were hurried voices, the crash and crackling of impeding branches growing fainter and fainter in the distance. Lance turned back to the solitary living figure—the old man.

Yet he might have been dead too, he sat so rigid and motionless, his fixed eyes staring vacantly at the body on the hearth. Before him on the table lay two cheap photographs, one evidently of himself, taken in some remote epoch of complexion, one of a child which Lance recognised as Flip.

"Tell me," said Lance hoarsely, laying his quivering hand on the table, "was Bob Ridley your son?"

"My son!" echoed the old man, in a strange, far-off voice, without turning his eyes from the corpse—"My son—is—is—is there!" pointing to the dead man. "Hush! Didn't he tell you so? Didn't you hear him say it? Dead—dead—shot—shot!"

"Silence! are you crazy, man?" repeated Lance tremblingly; "that is not Bob Ridley, but a dog, a coward, a liar gone to his reckoning. Hear me! If your son *was* Bob Ridley, I swear to God I never knew it, now or—or—*then*. Do you hear me? Tell me! Do you believe me? Speak! You shall speak."

He laid his hand almost menacingly on the old man's shoulder. Fairley slowly raised his head. Lance fell back with a groan of horror. The weak lips were wreathed with a feeble imploring smile, but the eyes wherein the fretful, peevish, suspicious spirit had dwelt were blank and tenantless; the flickering intellect that had lit them was blown out and vanished.

Lance walked towards the door and remained motionless for a moment, gazing into the night. When he turned back again towards the fire his face was as colourless as the dead man's on the hearth; the fire of passion was gone from his beaten eyes; his step was hesitating and slow. He went up to the table.

"I say, old man," he said, with a strange smile and an odd, premature suggestion of the infinite weariness of death in his voice, "you wouldn't mind giving me this, would you?" and he took up the picture of Flip.

The old man nodded repeatedly.

"Thank you," said Lance. He went to the door, paused a moment, and returned. "Good-bye, old man," he said, holding out his hand.

Fairley took it, with a childish smile. "He's dead," said the old man softly, holding Lance's hand, but pointing to the hearth.

"Yes," said Lance, with the faintest of smiles on the palest of faces.

"You feel sorry for any one that's dead, don't you?" Fairley nodded again. Lance looked at him with eyes as remote as his own, shook his hand, and turned away. When he reached the door he laid his revolver carefully, and, indeed, somewhat ostentatiously, upon a chair. But when he stepped from the threshold he stopped a moment in the light of the open door to examine the lock of a small derringer which he drew from his pocket. He then shut the door carefully, and with the same slow, hesitating step, felt his way into the night.

He had but one idea in his mind—to find some lonely spot; some spot where the footsteps of man would never penetrate, some spot that would yield him rest, sleep, obliteration, forgetfulness—and, above all, where *he* would be forgotten. He had seen such places—surely there were many—where bones were picked up of dead men who had faded from the earth and had left no other record. If he could only keep his senses now he might find such a spot, but he must be careful, for her little feet went everywhere, and she must never see him again alive or dead. And in the midst of his thoughts, and the darkness, and the storm, he heard a voice at his side—"Lance, how long you have been!"

Left to himself, the old man again fell into a vacant contemplation of the dead body before him, until a stronger blast swept down like an avalanche upon the cabin, burst through the ill-fastened door and broken chimney, and dashing the ashes and living embers over the floor, filled the room with smoke and flame. Fairley rose with a feeble cry, and then, as if acted upon by some dominant memory, groped under the bed until he found his buckskin bag and his precious crystal, and fled precipitantly from the room. Lifted by this second shock from his apathy, he returned to the fixed idea of his life—the discovery and creation of the diamond—and forgot all else. The feeble grasp that his shaken intellect kept of the events of the night relaxed, the disguised Lance, the story of his son, the murder, slipped into nothingness; there remained only the one idea—his nightly watch by the diamond pit. The instinct of long habit was stronger than the darkness or the onset of the storm, and he kept his tottering way over stream and fallen timber until he reached the spot. A sudden tremor seemed to shake the lambent flame that had lured him on. He thought he heard the sound of voices; there were signs of recent disturbance—footprints in the sawdust! With a cry of rage and suspicion, Fairley slipped into the pit and sprang towards the nearest opening. To his frenzied fancy it had been tampered with, his secret discovered, the fruit of his long labours stolen from him that very night. With superhuman strength he began to open the pit, scattering the half-charred logs right and left, and giving free vent to the suffocating gases that rose from the now

incandescent charcoal. At times the fury of the gale would drive it
back and hold it against the sides of the pit, leaving the opening free;
at times, following the blind instinct of habit, the demented man
would fall upon his face and bury his nose and mouth in the wet bark
and sawdust. At last, the paroxysm past, he sank back again in his old
apathetic attitude of watching, the attitude he had so often kept beside
his sylvan crucible. In this attitude and in silence he waited for the
dawn.

It came with a hush in the storm; it came with blue openings in the
broken-up and tumbled heavens; it came with stars that glistened first
and then paled, and at last sank drowning in those deep cerulean
lakes; it came with those cerulean lakes broadening into vaster seas,
whose shores expanded at last into one illimitable ocean, cerulean no
more, but flecked with crimson and opal dyes; it came with the lightly-
lifted misty curtain of the day, torn and rent on crag and pine top, but
always lifting, lifting. It came with the sparkle of emerald in the young
grasses, and the flash of diamonds in every spray, with a whisper in the
awakening woods, and voices in the travelled roads and trails.

The sound of these voices stopped before the pit, and seemed to
interrogate the old man. He came, and putting his finger on his lips,
made a sign of caution. When three or four men had descended he
bade them follow him, saying, weakly and disjointedly, but persistently, "My boy . . . my son Robert . . . came home . . . came
home at last . . . here with Flip . . . both of them . . . Come and
see!"

He had reached a little niche or nest in the hillside, and stopped and
suddenly drew aside a blanket. Beneath it, side by side, lay Flip and
Lance, dead, with their cold hands clasped in each other's.

"Suffocated!" said two or three, turning with horror toward the
broken-up and still smouldering pit.

"Asleep!" said the old man. "Asleep! I've seen 'em lying that way
when they were babies together. Don't tell me! Don't say I don't know
my own flesh and blood! So! so! So, my pretty ones!" He stooped and
kissed them. Then drawing the blanket over them gently he rose and
said softly, "Good night!"

A Waif of the Plains

Chapter I

A LONG LEVEL of dull grey that further away became a faint blue, with here and there darker patches that looked like water. At times an open space, blackened and burnt in an irregular circle, with a shred of newspaper, an old rag, or broken tin can lying in the ashes. Beyond these always a low dark line that seemed to sink into the ground at night, and rose again in the morning with the first light, but never otherwise changed its height and distance. A sense of always moving with some indefinite purpose, but of always returning at night to the same place—with the same surroundings, the same people, the same bedclothes, and the same awful black canopy dropped down from above. A chalky taste of dust on the mouth and lips, a gritty sense of earth on the fingers, and an all-pervading heat and smell of cattle.

This was "The Great Plains" as they seemed to two children from the hooded depth of an emigrant waggon above the swaying heads of toiling oxen, in the summer of 1852.

It had appeared so to them for two weeks, always the same, and always without the least sense to them of wonder or monotony. When they viewed it from the road, walking beside the waggon, there was only the team itself added to the unvarying picture. One of the waggons bore on its canvas hood the inscription, in large black letters, "Off to California!" on the other "Root Hog, or Die," but neither of them awoke in the minds of the children the faintest idea of playfulness or jocularity. Perhaps it was difficult to connect the serious men, who occasionally walked beside them and seemed to grow more taciturn and depressed as the day wore on, with this past effusive pleasantry.

Yet the impressions of the two children differed slightly. The eldest, a boy of eleven, was apparently new to the domestic habits and customs of a life to which the younger, a girl of seven, was evidently native and familiar. The food was coarse, and less skilfully prepared than that to which he had been accustomed. There was a certain freedom and roughness in their intercourse; a simplicity that bordered almost on rudeness in their domestic arrangements, and a speech that was at times almost untranslatable to him. He slept in his clothes, wrapped up in blankets; he was conscious that in the matter of cleanliness he was left to himself to overcome the difficulties of finding water and towels. But it is doubtful if in his youthfulness it affected him more than a novelty. He ate and slept well, and found his life amusing. Only at times the rudeness of his companions, or, worse, an indifference that made him feel his dependency upon them, awoke a vague sense of some wrong that had been done to him which, while it was voiceless to all others, and even uneasily put aside by himself, was still always slumbering in his childish consciousness.

To the party he was known as an orphan put on the train at "St. Jo." by some relative of his stepmother, to be delivered to another relative at Sacramento. As his stepmother had not even taken leave of him, but had entrusted his departure to the relative with whom he had been lately living, it was considered as an act of "riddance," and accepted as such by her party, and even vaguely acquiesced in by the boy himself. What consideration had been offered for his passage he did not know; he only remembered that he had been told "to make himself handy." This he had done cheerfully, if at times with the unskilfulness of a novice; but it was not a peculiar or a menial task in a company where all took part in manual labour, and where existence seemed to him to bear the charm of a prolonged picnic. Neither was he subjected to any difference of affection or treatment from Mrs. Silsbee, the mother of his little companion, and the wife of the leader of the train. Prematurely old, of ill-health, and harassed with cares, she had no time to waste in discriminating maternal tenderness for her daughter, but treated the children with equal and unbiassed querulousness.

The rear waggon creaked, swayed, and rolled on slowly and heavily. The hoofs of the draught oxen, occasionally striking in the dust with a dull report, sent little puffs like smoke on either side of the track. Within, the children were playing "keeping store." The little girl, as an opulent and extravagant customer, was purchasing of the boy, who sat behind a counter improvised from a nail keg and the front seat, most of the available contents of the waggon, either under their own names or an imaginary one as the moment suggested, and paying for them in the easy and liberal currency of dried beans and bits of paper. Change was given by the expeditious method of tearing the paper into smaller fragments. The diminution of stock was remedied by buying the same article over again under a different name. Nevertheless, in spite of these favourable commercial conditions, the market seemed dull.

"I can show you a fine quality of sheeting at four cents a yard, double width," said the boy, rising and leaning on his fingers on the counter as he had seen the shopmen do. "All wool, and will wash," he added with easy gravity.

"I can buy it cheaper at Jackson's," said the girl, with the intuitive duplicity of her bargaining sex.

"Very well," said the boy. "I won't play any more."

"Who cares?" said the girl indifferently.

The boy here promptly upset the counter; the rolled-up blanket, which had deceitfully represented the desirable sheeting, falling on the waggon floor. It apparently suggested a new idea to the former sales-man. "I say! let's play 'damaged stock.' See, I'll tumble all the things down here right on top o' the others, and sell 'em for less than cost."

The girl looked up. The suggestion was bold, bad, and momentarily attractive. But she only said "No," apparently from habit, picked up her doll, and the boy clambered to the front of the waggon. The in-complete episode terminated at once with that perfect forgetfulness, indifference, and irresponsibility common to all young animals. If ei-ther could have flown away or bounded off finally at that moment, they would have done so with no more concern for preliminary detail than a bird or squirrel. The waggon rolled steadily on. The boy could see that one of their teamsters had climbed up on the tail-board of the preceding vehicle. The other seemed to be walking in a dusty sleep.

"Kla'uns," said the girl.

The boy, without turning his head, responded "Susy."

"Wot are you going to be?" said the girl.

"Goin' to be?" repeated Clarence.

"When you is growed," exclaimed Susy.

Clarence hesitated. His settled determination had been to become a pirate, merciless yet discriminating. But reading in a bethumbed "Guide to the Plains" that morning of Fort Laramie and Kit Carson, he had decided upon the career of a "scout," as being more accessible and requiring less water. Yet, out of compassion for Susy's possible ignorance, he said neither, and responded with the American boy's modest conventionality, "President." It was safe, required no embarrassing description, and had been approved by benevolent old gentlemen with their hands on his head.

"I'm goin' to be a parson's wife," said Susy, "and keep hens, and have things giv' to me. Baby clothes, and apples, and apple sass—and melasses! and more baby clothes! and pork when you kill."

She had thrown herself at the bottom of the waggon with her back towards him and her doll in her lap. He could see the curve of her curly head, and beyond her bare dimpled knees which were raised, and over which she was trying to fold the hem of her brief skirt. "I wouldn't be a President's wife," she said presently.

"You couldn't!"

"Could if I wanted to!"

"Couldn't!"

"Could now!"

"Couldn't!"

"Why?"

Finding it difficult to explain his convictions of her ineligibility, Clarence thought it equally crushing not to give any. There was a long silence. It was very hot and dusty. The waggon scarcely seemed to move. Clarence gazed at the vignette of the track behind them formed by the hood of the rear. Presently he rose and walked past her to the tail-board. "Goin' to get down," he said, putting his legs over.

"Maw says 'No,' " said Susy.

Clarence did not reply, but dropped to the ground beside the slowly turning wheels. Without quickening his pace he could easily keep his hand on the tail-board.

"Kla'uns."

He looked up.

"Take me."

She had already clapped on her sun-bonnet, and was standing at the edge of the tail-board, her little arms extended in such perfect confidence of being caught that the boy could not resist. He caught her cleverly. They halted a moment and let the lumbering vehicle move away from them as it swayed from side to side as if labouring in a heavy sea. They remained motionless until it had reached nearly a hundred yards, and then with a sudden half real, half assumed, but altogether delightful trepidation, ran forward and caught up with it again. This they repeated two or three times until both themselves and the excitement were exhausted, and they again plodded on hand in hand. Presently Clarence uttered a cry.

"My! Susy—look there!"

The rear waggon had once more slipped away from them a considerable distance. Between it and them, crossing its track, a most extraordinary creature had halted.

At first glance it seemed a dog—a discomfited, shameless, ownerless, outcast of streets and byways, rather than an honest estray of some drover's train. It was so gaunt, so dusty, so greasy, so slouching and so lazy! But as they looked at it more intently they saw that the greyish hair of its back had a bristly ridge, and there were great poisonous-looking dark blotches on its flanks, and that the slouch of its haunches was a peculiarity of its figure, and not the cowering of fear. As it lifted its suspicious head towards them they could see that its thin lips, too short to cover its white teeth, were curled in a perpetual sneer.

"Here, doggie!" said Clarence excitedly. "Good dog! Come."

Susy burst into a triumphant laugh. "Et taint no dog, silly; it's er coyote."

Clarence blushed. It wasn't the first time the pioneer's daughter had shown her superior knowledge. He said quickly, to hide his discomfiture, "I'll ketch him anyway, he's nothin' mor'n a ki yi."

"Ye kant, tho," said Susy, shaking her sun-bonnet. "He's faster nor a hoss!"

Nevertheless Clarence ran towards him, followed by Susy. When they had come within twenty feet of him, the lazy creature, without apparently the least effort, took two or three limping bounds to one side and remained at the same distance as before. They repeated this onset three or four times with more or less excitement and hilarity, the animal evading them to one side, but never actually retreating before them. Finally, it occurred to them both that although they were not catching him they were not driving him away. The consequences of that thought were put into shape by Susy with round-eyed significance.

"Kla'uns, he bites."

Clarence picked up a hard sun-baked clod, and, running forward, threw it at the coyote. It was a clever shot, and struck him on his slouching haunches. He snapped and gave a short snarling yelp and vanished. Clarence returned with a victorious air to his companion. But she was gazing intently in the opposite direction, and for the first time he discovered that the coyote had been leading them half round a circle.

"Kla'uns," says Susy, with an hysterical little laugh.

"Well?"

"The waggon's gone."

Clarence started. It was true. Not only their waggon, but the whole train of oxen and teamsters had utterly disappeared, vanishing as completely as if they had been caught up in a whirlwind or engulfed in the earth. Even the low cloud of dust that usually marked their distant course by day was nowhere to be seen. The long level plain stretched before them to the setting sun, without a sign or trace of moving life or animation. That great blue crystal bowl, filled with dust and fire by day, with stars and darkness by night, which had always seemed to drop its rim round them everywhere and shut them in, seemed to them now to have been lifted to let the train pass out, and then closed down upon them for ever.

Chapter II

Their first sensation was one of purely animal freedom!

They looked at each other with sparkling eyes and long silent breaths. But this spontaneous outburst of savage nature soon passed. Susy's little hand presently reached forward and clutched Clarence's jacket. The boy understood it, and said quickly—"They ain't gone far, and they'll stop as soon as they find us gone."

They trotted on a little faster; the sun they had followed every day and the fresh waggon-tracks being their unfailing guides; the keen cool air of the plains, taking the place of that all-pervading dust and smell of the perspiring oxen, invigorating them with its breath.

"We ain't skeered a bit, are we?" said Susy.

"What's there to be afraid of?" said Clarence scornfully. He said this none the less strongly because he suddenly remembered that they had been often left alone in the waggon for hours without being looked after, and that their absence might not be noticed until the train stopped to encamp at dusk, two hours later.

They were not running very fast, yet either they were more tired than they knew, or the air was thinner, for they both seemed to breathe quickly. Suddenly Clarence stopped. "There they are now."

He was pointing to a light cloud of dust in the far-off horizon, from which the black hulk of a waggon emerged for a moment and was lost. But even as they gazed the cloud seemed to sink like a fairy mirage to the earth again, the whole train disappeared, and only the empty stretching track returned. They did not know that this seemingly flat and level plain was really undulatory, and that the vanished train had simply dipped below their view on some further slope even as it had once before. But they knew they were disappointed, and that disappointment revealed to them the fact that they had concealed it from each other. The girl was the first to succumb, and burst into a quick spasm of angry tears. That single act of weakness called out the boy's pride and strength. There was no longer an equality of suffering; he had become her protector; he felt himself responsible for both. Considering her no longer his equal, he was no longer frank with her.

"There's nothin' to boo-hoo for," he said, with a half-affected brusqueness. "So quit now! They'll stop in a minit and send some one back for us. Shouldn't wonder if they're doin' it now."

But Susy, with feminine discrimination detecting the hollow ring in his voice, here threw herself upon him and began to beat him violently with her little fists. "They ain't! They ain't! They ain't! You know it! How dare you?" Then, exhausted with her struggles, she suddenly threw herself flat on the dry grass, shut her eyes tightly, and clutched at the stubble.

"Get up," said the boy, with a pale, determined face that seemed to have got much older.

"You leave me be!" said Susy.

"Do you want me to go away and leave you?" asked the boy.

Susy opened one blue eye furtively in the secure depths of her sunbonnet and gazed at his changed face.

"Ye-e-s."

He pretended to turn away, but really to look at the height of the sinking sun.

"Kla'uns!"

"Well?"

"Take me."

She was holding up her hands. He lifted her gently in his arms, dropping her head over his shoulder. "Now," he said cheerfully, "you keep a good look-out that way, and I this, and we'll soon be there."

The idea seemed to please her. After Clarence had stumbled on for a few moments, she said, "Do you see anything, Kla'uns?"

"Not yet."

"No more don't I." This equality of perception apparently satisfied her. Presently she lay more limp in his arms. She was asleep.

The sun was sinking lower; it had already touched the edge of the horizon, and was level with his dazzled and straining eyes. At times it seemed to impede his eager search and task his vision. Haze and black spots floated across the horizon, and round wafers, like duplicates of the sun, glittered back from the dull surface of the plains. Then he resolved to look no more until he had counted fifty, a hundred—but always with the same result, the return of the empty, unending plains; the disc growing redder as it neared the horizon, the fire it seemed to kindle as it sank, but nothing more!

Staggering under his burden, he tried to distract himself by fancying how the discovery of their absence would be made. He heard the listless, half-querulous discussion about the locality that regularly pervaded the nightly camp. He heard the discontented voice of Jake Silsbee as he halted beside their waggon and said, "Come, out o' that now, you two, and mighty quick about it." He heard the command harshly repeated. He saw the look of irritation on Silsbee's dusky-bearded face that followed his hurried glance into the empty waggon. He heard the query "What's gone o' them limbs now?" handed from waggon to waggon. He heard a few oaths; Mrs. Silsbee's high, rasping voice, abuse of himself, the hurried and discontented detachment of a search party, Silsbee and one of the hired men, and vociferation and blame. Blame always for himself, the elder, who might have "known better!" A little fear, perhaps, but he could not fancy either pity or commiseration. Perhaps the thought upheld his pride; under the prospect of sympathy he might have broken down.

At last he stumbled, and stopped to keep himself from falling forward on his face. He could go no further; his breath was spent; he was dripping with perspiration; his legs were trembling under him; there was a roaring in his ears; round red discs of the sun were scattered everywhere around him like spots of blood. To the right of the trail there seemed to be a slight mound where he could rest awhile and yet keep his watchful survey of the horizon. But on reaching it he found that it was only a tangle of taller mesquite grass, into which he sank with his burden. Nevertheless, if useless as a point of vantage, it afforded a soft couch for Susy, who seemed to have fallen quite naturally into her usual afternoon siesta, and in a measure it shielded her from a cold breeze that had sprung up from the west. Utterly exhausted himself, but not daring to yield to the torpor that seemed to be creeping over him, Clarence half sat, half knelt down beside her, supporting himself with one hand, and, partly hidden in the long grass, kept his straining eyes fixed on the lonely track.

The red disc was sinking lower. It seemed to have already crumbled away a part of the distance with its eating fires. As it sank still lower, it shot out long luminous rays, diverging fan-like across the plain as if, in the boy's excited fancy, it too were searching, with parted and extended fingers, for the lost estrays. And as one long beam seemed to linger over his hiding-place, he even thought that it might serve as a guide to Silsbee and the other seekers, and was constrained to stagger to his feet, erect in its light. But it soon sank, and with it Clarence dropped back again to his crouching watch. Yet he knew that the daylight was still good for an hour, and with the withdrawal of that mystic sunset glory, objects became even more distinct and sharply defined than at any other time. And with the merciful sheathing of that flaming sword which seemed to have waved between him and the vanished train, his eyes already felt a blessed relief.

Chapter III

With the setting of the sun an ominous silence fell. He could hear the low breathing of Susy, and even fancied he could detect the beating of his own heart in that oppressive hush of all nature. For the day's march had always been accompanied by the monotonous creaking of wheels and axles, and even the quiet of the night encampment had been always more or less broken by the movement of unquiet sleepers on the waggon-beds, or the breathing of the cattle. But here there was neither sound nor motion. Susy's prattle, and even the sound of his own voice, would have broken the benumbing spell. But it was part of his growing self-denial now that he refrained from waking her even by a whisper. She would awaken soon enough to thirst and hunger, perhaps; and then what was he to do? If that looked-for help would only come now—while she still slept. For it was part of his boyish fancy that if he could deliver her asleep, and undemonstrative of fear and suffering, he would be less blameful, and she less mindful, of her trouble. If it did not come—but he would not think of that yet. If she was thirsty meantime—well, it might rain, and there was always the dew which they used to brush off the morning grass—he would take off his shirt and catch it in that, like a shipwrecked mariner. It would be funny, and make her laugh. For himself he would not laugh, he felt he was getting very old and grown-up in this loneliness.

It was getting darker—they should be looking into the waggons now. A new doubt began to assail him. Ought he not, now that he was rested, make the most of the remaining moments of daylight, and before the glow faded from the west, when he would no longer have any bearings to guide him? But there was always the risk of waking her!—to what? The fear of being confronted again with *her* fear, and of being unable to pacify her, at last decided him to remain. But he crept softly through the grass, and in the dust of the track traced the four points of the compass, as he would still determine them by the sunset light, with a large printed W to indicate the west! This boyish contrivance particularly pleased him. If he had only a pole, a stick, or even a twig, on which to tie his handkerchief and erect it above the clump of mesquite as a signal to the searchers in case he should be overcome by fatigue or sleep, he would have been happy. But the plain was barren of brush or timber; he did not dream that this omission and the very unobtrusiveness of his hiding-place would be his salvation from a greater danger.

With the coming darkness the wind arose and swept the plain with a long-drawn sigh. This increased to a murmur, till presently the whole expanse—before sunk in awful silence—seemed to awake with vague complaints, incessant sounds, and low moanings. At times he thought he heard the hollowing of distant voices, at times it seemed as a whisper in his own ear. In the silence that followed each blast he fancied he could detect the creaking of the waggon, the dull thud of the oxen's hoofs, or broken fragments of speech, blown and scattered even as he strained his ears to listen by the next gust. This tension of the ear began to confuse his brain, as his eyes had been previously dazzled by the sunlight, and a strange torpor began to steal over his faculties. Once or twice his head dropped.

He awoke with a start. A moving figure had suddenly uplifted itself between him and the horizon! It was not twenty yards away, so clearly outlined against the still luminous sky that it seemed even nearer. A human figure, but so dishevelled, so fantastic, and yet so mean and puerile in its extravagance, that it seemed the outcome of a childish dream. It was a mounted figure, but so ludicrously disproportionate to the pony it bestrode, whose slim legs were stiffly buried in the dust in a breathless halt, that it might have been a straggler from some vulgar wandering circus. A tall hat, crownless and brimless, a castaway of civilisation, surmounted by a turkey's feather, was on its head; over its shoulders hung a dirty tattered blanket that scarcely covered the two painted legs, which seemed clothed in soiled yellow hose. In one hand it held a gun; the other was bent above its eyes in eager scrutiny of some distant point beyond and east of the spot where the children lay concealed. Presently, with a dozen quick noiseless strides of the pony's legs, the apparition moved to the right, its gaze still fixed on that mysterious part of the horizon. There was no mistaking it now! The painted Hebraic face, the large curved nose, the bony cheek, the broad mouth, the shadowed eyes, the straight long matted locks: it was an Indian! Not the picturesque creature of Clarence's imagination, but still an Indian! The boy was uneasy, suspicious, antagonistic; but not afraid. He looked at the heavy animal face with the superiority of intelligence, at the half-naked figure with the conscious supremacy of dress, at the lower individuality with the contempt of a higher race. Yet a moment after, when the figure wheeled and disappeared towards the undulating west, a strange chill crept over him. Yet he did not know that in this puerile phantom and painted pigmy the awful majesty of death had passed him by.

"Mamma!"

It was Susy's voice, struggling into consciousness. Perhaps she had been instinctively conscious of the boy's sudden fears.

"Hush!"

He had just turned to the objective point of the Indian's gaze. There *was* something! A dark line was moving along with the gathering darkness. For a moment he hardly dared to voice his thoughts even to himself. It was a following train overtaking them from the rear! And from the rapidity of its movements a train with horses, hurrying forward to evening camp. He had never dreamt of help from that quarter. And this was what the Indian's keener eyes had been watching, and why he had so precipitately fled.

The strange train was now coming up at a round trot. It was evidently well appointed, with five or six large waggons and several outriders. In half-an-hour it would be here. Yet he restrained from waking Susy, who had fallen asleep again; his old superstition of securing her safety first being still uppermost. He took off his jacket to cover her shoulders, and rearranged her nest. Then he glanced again at the coming train. But for some unaccountable reason it had changed its direction, and instead of following the track that should have brought it to his side, it had turned off to the left! In ten minutes it would pass abreast of him a mile and a half away! If he woke Susy now he knew she would be helpless in her terror, and he could not carry her half that distance. He might rush to the train himself and return with help, but he would never leave her alone—in the darkness. Never! If she woke she would die of fright perhaps, or wander blindly and aimlessly away. No! The train would pass, and with it that hope of rescue. Something was in his throat, but he gulped it down and was quiet again, albeit he shivered in the night wind.

The train was nearly abreast of him now. He ran out of the tall grass, waving his straw hat above his head in the faint hope of attracting attention. But he did not go far, for he found, to his alarm, that when he turned back again the clump of mesquite was scarcely distinguishable from the rest of the plain. This settled all question of his going. Even if he reached the train and returned with some one, how would he ever find her again in this desolate expanse?

He watched the train slowly pass, still mechanically—almost hopelessly—waving his hat as he ran up and down before the mesquite as if he were waving a last farewell to his departing hope. Suddenly it appeared to him that three of the outriders who were preceding the first waggon had changed their shape. They were no longer sharp, oblong, black blocks against the horizon, but had become at first blurred and indistinct, then taller and narrower, until at last they stood out like exclamation points against the sky. He continued to wave his hat, they continued to grow taller and narrower. He understood it now—the three transformed blocks were the outriders coming towards him.

This is what he had seen—

■ ■ ■

This is what he saw now—

! ! !

He ran back to Susy to see if she still slept, for his foolish desire to have her saved unconsciously was stronger than ever now that safety seemed so near. She was still sleeping, although she had moved slightly. He ran to the front again.

The outriders had apparently halted. What were they doing? Why wouldn't they come on?

Suddenly a blinding flash of light seemed to burst from one of them. Away over his head something whistled like a rushing bird, and sped off invisible. They had fired a gun; they were signalling to him, Clarence, like a grown-up man! He would have given his life at that moment to have had a gun. But he could only wave his hat frantically.

One of the figures here bore away and impetuously darted forward again. He was coming nearer, powerful, gigantic, formidable as he loomed through the darkness. All at once he threw up his arm with a wild gesture to the others; and his voice, manly, frank, and assuring, came ringing before him.

"Hold up! Don't fire! It's no Injin—it's a child!"

In another moment he had reined up beside Clarence and leaned over him, bearded, handsome, all-encompassing and protecting.

"Hallo! What's all this? What are you doing here?"

"Lost from Mr. Silsbee's train," said Clarence, pointing to the now darkened west.

"Lost! How long?"

"About three hours. I thought they'd come back for us," said Clarence apologetically to this big kindly man.

"And you kalkilated to wait here for 'em?"

"Yes, yes—I did—till I saw you."

"Then why in thunder didn't you light out straight for us, instead of hanging round here and drawing us out?"

The boy hung his head. He knew his reasons were unchanged, but all at once they seemed very foolish and unmanly to speak out.

"Only that we were on the keen jump for Injins," continued the stranger, "we wouldn't have seen you at all, and might hev shot you when we did. What possessed you to stay here?"

The boy was still silent. "Kla'uns," said a faint, sleepy voice from the mesquite, "take me." The rifle shot had awakened Susy.

The stranger turned quickly towards the sound. Clarence started and recalled himself.

"There," he said bitterly, "you've done it now, you've wakened her! *That's* why I stayed. I couldn't carry her over there to you! I couldn't let her walk, for she'd be frightened. I wouldn't wake her up, for she'd be frightened, and I mightn't find her again. There!" He had made up his mind to be abused, but he was reckless now that she was safe.

The men glanced at each other. "Then," said the spokesman quietly, "you didn't strike out for us on account of your sister?"

"She ain't my sister," said Clarence quickly. "She's a little girl. She's Mrs. Silsbee's little girl. We were in the waggon and got down. It's my fault. I helped her down."

The three men reined their horses closely round him, leaning forward from their saddles, with their hands on their knees, and their heads on one side. "Then," said the spokesman gravely, "you just reckoned to stay here, old man, and take your chances *with her* rather than run the risk of frightening or leaving her—though it was your one chance of life!"

"Yes," said the boy, a little weary of this feeble, grown-up repetition.

"Come here."

The boy came doggedly forward. The man pushed back the well-worn straw hat from Clarence's forehead and looked into his lowering face. With his hand still on the boy's head he turned him round to the others, and said quietly—

"Suthin' of a pup, eh?"

"You bet," they responded.

The voice was not unkindly, although the speaker had thrown his lower jaw forward as to pronounce the word "pup" with a humorous suggestion of a mastiff. Before Clarence could make up his mind if the epithet was insulting or not, the man put out his stirruped foot, and, with a gesture of invitation, said, "Jump up."

"But Susy," said Clarence, drawing back.

"Look; she's making up to Phil already."

Clarence looked. Susy had crawled out of the mesquite, and with her sun-bonnet hanging down her back, her curls tossed around her face still flushed with sleep, and Clarence's jacket over her shoulders, was gazing up with grave satisfaction in the laughing eyes of one of the men who was, with outstretched hands, bending over her. Could he believe his senses? The terror-stricken, wilful, unmanageable Susy, whom he would have translated unconsciously to safety without this terrible ordeal of being awakened to the loss of her home and parents, at any sacrifice to himself—this ingenuous infant was absolutely throwing herself, with every appearance of forgetfulness, into the arms of the first new-comer! Yet his perception of this fact was accompanied by no sense of ingratitude. For her sake he felt relieved, and with a boyish smile of satisfaction and encouragement vaulted into the saddle before the stranger.

Chapter IV

The dash forward to the train, securely held in the saddle by the arms of their deliverers, was a secret joy to the children that seemed only too quickly over. The resistless gallop of the fiery mustangs, the rush of the night wind, the gathering darkness in which the distant waggons, now halted and facing them, looked like domed huts in the horizon—all then seemed but a delightful and fitting climax to the events of the day. In the sublime forgetfulness of youth, all they had gone through had left no embarrassing record behind it; they were willing to repeat their experiences, on the morrow, confident of some equally happy end. And when Clarence, timidly reaching his hand towards the horse-hair reins lightly held by his companion, had them playfully yielded up to him by that bold and confident rider, the boy felt himself indeed a man.

But a greater surprise was in store for them. As they neared the waggons, now formed into a circle with a certain degree of military formality, they could see that the appointments of the strange party were larger and more liberal than their own, or, indeed, anything they had ever known of the kind. Forty or fifty horses were tethered within the circle, and the camp fires were already blazing. Before one of them a large tent was erected, and through the parted flaps could be seen a table actually spread with a white cloth. Was it a school-feast, or was this their ordinary household arrangements? Clarence and Susy thought of their own dinners usually laid on bare boards beneath the sky, or under the low hood of the waggon in rainy weather, and marvelled. And when they finally halted and were lifted from their horses, and passed one waggon fitted up as a bedroom and another as a kitchen, they could only nudge each other with silent appreciation. But here again the difference already noted in the quality of the sensations of the two children was observable. Both were equally and agreeably surprised. But Susy's wonder was merely the sense of novelty and inexperience, and a slight disbelief in the actual necessity of what she saw; while Clarence, whether from some previous general experience or peculiar temperament, had the conviction that what he saw here was the usual custom, and what he had known with the

Silsbees was the novelty. The feeling was attended with a slight sense of wounded pride for Susy, as if her enthusiasm had exposed her to ridicule.

The man who had carried him, and seemed to be the head of the party, had already preceded them to the tent, and presently re-appeared with a lady with whom he had exchanged a dozen hurried words. They seemed to refer to him and Susy; but Clarence was too much preoccupied with the fact that the lady was pretty, that her clothes were neat and thoroughly clean, that her hair was tidy and not rumpled, and that although she wore an apron it was as clean as her gown, and even had ribbons on it, to listen to what was said. And when she ran eagerly forward, and with a fascinating smile lifted the astonished Susy in her arms, Clarence, in his delight for his young charge, quite forgot that she had not noticed him. The bearded man, who seemed to be the lady's husband, evidently pointed out the omission, with some additions that Clarence could not catch, for after saying, with a pretty pout, "Well, why shouldn't he?" she came forward with the same dazzling smile, and laid her small and clean white hand upon his shoulder.

"And so you took good care of the dear little thing? She's such an angel, isn't she? and you must love her very much."

Clarence coloured with delight. It was true it had never occurred to him to look at Susy in the light of a celestial visitant, and I fear he was just then more struck with the fair complimenter than the compliment to his companion, but he was pleased for her sake. He was not yet old enough to be conscious of the sex's belief in its irresistible domination over mankind at all ages—that "Johnny" in his check apron would be always a hopeless conquest of "Jeannette" in her pinafore, and that he ought to have been in love with Susy.

Howbeit, the lady suddenly whisked her away to the recesses of her own waggon, to reappear later, washed, curled, and beribboned like a new doll, and Clarence was left alone with the husband and another of the party.

"Well, my boy, you haven't told me your name yet."

"Clarence, sir."

"So Susy calls you—but what else?"

"Clarence Brant."

"Any relation to Colonel Brant?" asked the second man carelessly.

"He was my father," said the boy, brightening under this faint prospect of recognition in his loneliness.

The two men glanced at each other. The leader looked at the boy curiously and said—

"Are you the son of Colonel Brant of Louisville?"

"Yes, sir," said the boy, with a dim stirring of uneasiness in his heart. "But he's dead now," he added finally.

"Ah, when did he die?" said the man quickly.

"Oh, a long time ago. I don't remember him much. I was very little," said the boy, half apologetically.

"Ah, you don't remember him?"

"No," said Clarence shortly. He was beginning to fall back upon that certain dogged repetition which in sensitive children arises from their hopeless inability to express their deeper feelings. He also had an instinctive consciousness that this want of a knowledge of his father was part of that vague wrong that had been done him. It did not help his uneasiness that he could see that one of the two men who turned away with a half laugh misunderstood or did not believe him.

"How did you come with the Silsbees?" asked the first man.

Clarence repeated mechanically, with a child's distaste of practical details, how he had lived with an aunt of St. Jo., how his stepmother had procured his passage with the Silsbees to California, where he was to meet his cousin. All this with a lack of interest and abstraction that he was miserably conscious told against him, but he was yet helpless to resist.

The first man remained thoughtful, and then glanced at Clarence's sunburnt hands. Presently his large good-humoured smile returned.

"Well, I suppose you are hungry?"

"Yes," said Clarence shyly. "But"——

"But what?"

"I should like to wash myself a little," he returned hesitatingly, thinking of the clean tent, the clean lady, and Susy's ribbons.

"Certainly," said his friend with a pleased look. "Come with me." Instead of leading Clarence to the battered tin basin and bar of yellow soap which had formed the toilet service of the Silsbee party, he brought the boy into one of the waggons, where there was a wash-stand, a china basin, and a cake of scented soap. Standing beside Clarence, he watched him perform his ablutions with an approving air which rather embarrassed his *protégé*. Presently he said, almost abruptly—

"Do you remember your father's house at Louisville?"

"Yes, sir; but it was a long time ago."

Clarence remembered it as being very different from his home at St. Joseph's, but from some innate feeling of diffidence he would have shrunk from describing it in that way. He, however, said he thought it was a large house. Yet the modest answer only made his new friend look at him the more keenly.

"Your father was Colonel Hamilton Brant of Louisville, wasn't he?" he said half confidentially.

"Yes," said Clarence hopelessly.

"Well," said his friend cheerfully, as if dismissing an abstruse problem from his mind, "let's go to supper."

When they reached the tent again, Clarence noticed that the supper was laid only for his host and wife and the second man—who was familiarly called "Harry," but who spoke of the former always as "Mr. and Mrs. Peyton"—while the remainder of the party, a dozen men, were at the second camp-fire, and evidently enjoying themselves in a picturesque fashion. Had the boy been allowed to choose he would have joined them, partly because it seemed more "manly," and partly that he dreaded a renewal of the questioning. But here Susy, sitting bolt upright on an extemporised high stool, happily diverted his attention by pointing to the empty chair beside her.

"Kla'uns," she said suddenly, with her usual clear and appalling frankness, "they is chickens and hamanaigs and hot biksquits, and lasses, and Mister Peyton says I kin have 'em all."

Clarence, who had begun suddenly to feel that he was responsible for Susy's deportment, and was balefully conscious that she was holding her plated fork in her chubby fist by its middle, and, from his previous knowledge of her, was likely at any moment to plunge it into a dish before her, said softly—

"Hush!"

"Yes, you shall, dear," said Mrs. Peyton, with tenderly-beaming assurance to Susy, and a half-reproachful glance at the boy. "Eat what you like, darling."

"It's a fork," whispered the still uneasy Clarence, as Susy now seemed inclined to stir her bowl of milk with it.

"Tain't now, Kla'uns, it's only a split spoon," said Susy.

But Mrs. Peyton, in her rapt admiration, took small note of these irregularities, plying the child with food, forgetting her own meal, and only stopping at times to lift back the forward straying curls on Susy's shoulders. Mr. Peyton looked on gravely and contentedly. Suddenly the eyes of husband and wife met.

"She'd have been nearly as old as this, John," said Mrs. Peyton, in a faint voice.

John Peyton nodded without speaking, and turned his eyes away into the gathering darkness. The man "Harry" also looked abstractedly at his plate as if he was saying grace. Clarence wondered who "she" was, and why two little tears dropped from Mrs. Peyton's lashes into Susy's milk, and whether Susy might not violently object to it. He never knew until later that the Peytons had lost their only child, and Susy comfortably drained this mingled cup of a mother's grief and tenderness without suspicion.

"I suppose we'll come up with their train early tomorrow, if some of them don't find us to-night," said Mrs. Peyton with a long sigh and a regretful glance at Susy. "Perhaps we might travel together for a little while," she added timidly. Harry laughed, and Mr. Peyton replied gravely, "I am afraid we wouldn't travel with them, even for company's sake; and," he added in a lower and graver voice, "it's rather odd the search party hasn't come upon us yet, though I'm keeping Pete and Hank patrolling the trail to meet them."

"It's heartless—so it is"——said Mrs. Peyton, with sudden indignation. "It would be all very well if it was only this boy—who can take care of himself—but to be so careless of a mere baby like this, it's shameful!"

For the first time Clarence tasted the cruelty of discrimination. All the more keenly that he was beginning to worship—after his boyish fashion—this sweet-faced, clean, and tender-hearted woman. Perhaps Mr. Peyton noticed it, for he came quietly to his aid.

"Maybe they know better than we in what careful hands they had left her," he said, with a cheerful nod towards Clarence. "And, again, they may have been fooled as we were by Injin signs and left the straight road."

This suggestion instantly recalled to Clarence his vision in the mesquite. Should he dare tell them? Would they believe him, or would they laugh at him before her? He hesitated, and at last resolved to tell it privately to the husband. When the meal was ended, and he was made happy by Mrs. Peyton's laughing acceptance of his offer to help her clear the table and wash the dishes, they all gathered comfortably in front of the tent before the large camp-fire. At the other fire the rest of the party were playing cards and laughing, but Clarence no longer cared to join them. He was quite tranquil in the maternal propinquity of his hostess, albeit a little uneasy as to his reticence about the Indian.

"Kla'uns," said Susy, relieving a momentary pause, in her highest voice, "knows how to speak. Speak, Kla'uns!"

It appearing from Clarence's blushing explanation that this gift was not the ordinary faculty of speech, but a capacity to recite verse, he was politely pressed by the company for a performance.

"Speak 'em, Kla'uns—the boy what stood unto the burnin' deck and said, 'the boy, oh, where was he?'" said Susy, comfortably lying down on Mrs. Peyton's lap and contemplating her bare knees in the air. "It's 'bout a boy," she added confidently to Mrs. Peyton, "whose father wouldn't never, never stay with him on a burnin' ship, though he said 'Stay, father, stay,' ever so much."

With this clear, lucid, and perfectly satisfactory explanation of Mrs. Hemans's "Casabianca," Clarence began. Unfortunately his actual rendering of this popular school performance was more an effort of memory than anything else, and was illustrated by those wooden gestures which a Western schoolmaster had taught him. He described the flames that "roared around him," by indicating with his hand a perfect circle of which he was the axis: he adjured his father, the late Admiral Casabianca, by clasping his hands before his chin, as if wanting to be manacled in an attitude which he was miserably conscious was unlike anything to himself he had ever felt or seen before; he described that father "faint in death below," and "the flag on high," with one single motion. Yet something that the verses had kindled in his active imagination, rather perhaps than an illustration of the verses themselves, at times brightened his grey eyes, became tremulous in his youthful voice, and I fear occasionally incoherent on his lips. At times, when not conscious of his affected art, the plain and all upon it seemed to him to slip away into the night, the blazing camp-fire at his feet to wrap him in a fateful glory, and a vague devotion to something—he knew not what—so possessed him that he communicated it, and probably some of his own youthful delight in extravagant voice, to his hearers, until when he ceased, with a glowing face, he was surprised to find that the card-players had deserted their camp-fires and gathered round the tent.

Chapter V

"You didn't say 'stay, father, stay,' enough, Kla'uns," said Susy critically. Then suddenly starting upright in Mrs. Peyton's lap, she continued rapidly: "I kin dance. And sing. I kin dance High Jambooree."

"What's High Jambooree, dear?" asked Mrs. Peyton.

"You'll see. Lemme down." And Susy slipped to the ground.

The dance of High Jambooree, evidently of remote mystical African origin, appeared to consist of three small skips to the right and then to the left, accompanied by the holding up of very short skirts, incessant "teetering" on the toes of small feet, the exhibition of much bare knee and stocking, and a gurgling accompaniment of childish laughter. Vehemently applauded, it left the little performer breathless, but invincible and ready for fresh conquest.

"I kin sing too," she gasped hurriedly, as if unwilling that the applause should lapse. "I kin sing. Oh dear! Kla'uns" (piteously), *"what* is it I sing?"

" 'Ben Bolt,' " suggested Clarence.

"Oh, yes. 'Oh, don't you remember sweet Alers Ben Bolt?' " began Susy, in the same breath and the wrong key. " 'Sweet Alers, with hair so brown, who wept with delight when you giv'd her a smile, and' " ——with knitted brows and appealing recitative, "what's er rest of it, Kla'uns?"

" 'Who trembled with fear at my frown?' " prompted Clarence.

" 'Who trembled with fear at my frown?' " shrilled Susy. "I forget er rest. Wait! I kin sing"——

" 'Praise God,' " suggested Clarence.

"Yes." Here Susy, a regular attendant in camp and prayer-meetings, was on firmer ground.

Promptly lifting her high treble, yet with a certain acquired deliberation, she began, "Praise God, from whom all blessings flow." At the end of the second line the whispering and laughing ceased. A deep voice to the right, that of the champion poker-player, suddenly rose on the swell of the third line. He was instantly followed by a dozen ringing voices, and by the time the last line was reached it was given with a full chorus, in which the dull chant of teamsters and drivers mingled with the soprano of Mrs. Peyton and Susy's childish treble. Again and again it was repeated, with forgetful eyes and abstracted faces, rising and falling with the night wind and the leap and gleam of the campfires, and fading again like them in the immeasurable mystery of the darkened plain.

In the deep and embarrassing silence that followed at last, the party hesitatingly broke up, Mrs. Peyton retiring with Susy after offering the child to Clarence for a perfunctory "good-night" kiss, an unusual proceeding, which somewhat astonished them both, and Clarence found himself near Mr. Peyton.

"I think," said Clarence timidly, "I saw an Injin today."

Mr. Peyton bent down towards him. "An Injin—where?" he asked quickly, with the same look of doubting interrogatory with which he had received Clarence's name and parentage.

The boy for a moment regretted having spoken. But with his old doggedness he particularised his statement. Fortunately, being gifted with a keen perception, he was able to describe the stranger accurately, and to impart with his description that contempt for its subject which he had felt, and which to his frontier auditor established its truthfulness. Peyton turned abruptly away, but presently returned with Harry and another man.

"You are sure of this?" said Peyton, half encouragingly.

"Yes, sir."

"As sure as you are that your father is Colonel Brant and is dead?" said Harry, with a light laugh.

Tears sprang into the boy's lowering eyes. "I don't lie," he said doggedly.

"I believe you, Clarence," said Peyton quietly. "But why didn't you say it before?"

"I didn't like to say it before Susy and—her!" stammered the boy.

"Her?"

"Yes—sir—Mrs. Peyton"——said Clarence blushingly.

"Oh," said Harry sarcastically, "how blessed polite we are!"

"That'll do. Let up on him, will you," said Peyton roughly, to his subordinate; "the boy knows what he's about. But," he continued, addressing Clarence, "how was it the Injin didn't see you?"

"I was very still on account of not waking Susy," said Clarence, "and"——He hesitated.

"And what?"

"He seemed more keen watching what *you* were doing," said the boy boldly.

"That's so," broke in the second man, who happened to be experienced; "and as he was to wind'ard o' the boy he was off *his* scent and bearings. He was one of their rear scouts; the rest o' them's ahead crossing our track to cut us off. Ye didn't see anything else?"

"I saw a coyote first," said Clarence, greatly encouraged.

"Hold on!" said the expert, as Harry turned away with a sneer. "That's a sign, too. Wolf don't go where wolf hez been, and coyote don't foller Injins—there's no pickins! How long afore did you see the coyote?"

"Just after we left the waggon," said Clarence.

"That's it," said the man thoughtfully. "He was driven on ahead, or hanging on their flanks. These Injins are betwixt us and that ar train, or following it."

Peyton made a hurried gesture of warning, as if reminding the speaker of Clarence's presence—a gesture which the boy noticed and wondered at. Then the conversation of the three men took a lower tone, although Clarence as distinctly heard the concluding opinion of the expert.

"It ain't no good now, Mr. Peyton, and you'd be only exposing yourself on their ground by breakin' camp agin to-night. And you don't know that it ain't *us* they're watchin'. You see, if we hadn't turned off the straight road when we got that first scare from these yer lost children, we might hev gone on and walked plump into some cursed trap of those devils. To my mind, we're just in nigger luck, and with a good watch and my patrol we're all right to be fixed where we be till daylight."

Mr. Peyton presently turned away, taking Clarence with him. "As we'll be up early and on the track of your train to-morrow, my boy, you had better turn in now. I've put you up in my waggon, and as I expect to be in the saddle most of the night, I reckon I won't trouble you much." He led the way to a second waggon—drawn up beside the one where Susy and Mrs. Peyton had retired—which Clarence was surprised to find fitted with a writing-table and desk, a chair, and even a book shelf containing some volumes. A long locker, fitted like a lounge, had been made up as a couch for him, with the unwonted luxury of clean white sheets and pillow-cases. A soft matting covered the floor of the heavy waggon bed, which, Mr. Peyton explained, was hung on centre springs to prevent jarring. The sides and roof of the vehicle were of lightly-panelled wood, instead of the usual hooked canvas frame of the ordinary emigrant waggon, and fitted with a glazed door and movable window for light and air. Clarence wondered why the big, powerful man, who seemed at home on horseback, should ever care to sit in this office like a merchant or a lawyer; and if this train sold things to the other trains, or took goods, like the pedlars, to towns on the route—but there seemed to be nothing to sell, and the other waggons were filled with only the goods required by the party. He would have liked to ask Mr. Peyton who *he* was, and have questioned *him* as freely as he himself had been questioned. But as the average adult man never takes into consideration the injustice of denying to the natural and even necessary curiosity of childhood that questioning which he himself is so apt to assume without right, and almost always without delicacy, Clarence had no recourse. Yet the boy, like all children, was conscious that if he had been afterwards questioned about *this* inexplicable experience, he would have been blamed for his ignorance concerning it. Left to himself presently, and ensconced between the sheets, he lay for some moments staring about him. The unwonted comfort of his couch, so different from the stuffy blanket in the hard waggon bed which he had shared with one of the teamsters, and the novelty, order, and cleanliness of his surroundings, while they were grateful to his instincts, began in some vague way to depress him. To his loyal nature it seemed a tacit infidelity to his former rough companions to be lying here; he had a dim idea that he had lost that independence which equal discomfort and equal pleasure among them had given him. There seemed a sense of servitude in accepting this luxury which was not his. This set him endeavouring to remember something of his father's house, of the large rooms, draughty staircases, and far-off ceilings, and the cold formality of a life that seemed made up of strange faces; some stranger—his parents; some kinder— the servants; particularly the black nurse who had him in charge. Why did Mr. Peyton ask him about it? Why, if it were so important to strangers, had not his mother told him more of it? And why was she not like this good woman with the gentle voice who was so kind to—to Susy? And what did they mean by making *him* so miserable? Something rose in his throat, but with an effort he choked it back, and, creeping from the lounge, went softly to the window, opened it to see if it "would work," and looked out. The shrouded camp-fires, the stars that glittered but gave no light, the dim moving bulk of a patrol beyond the circle, all seemed to intensify the darkness, and changed the current of his thoughts. He remembered what Mr. Peyton had said of him when they first met. "Suthin of a pup, ain't he?" Surely that meant something that was not bad! He crept back to the couch again.

Lying there, still awake, he reflected that he wouldn't be a scout when he grew up, but would be something like Mr. Peyton, and have a train like this, and invite the Silsbees and Susy to accompany him. For this purpose he and Susy, early to-morrow morning, would get permission to come in here and play at that game. This would familiarise him with the details, so that he would be able at any time to take charge of it. He was already an authority on the subject of Indians! He had once been fired at—as an Indian. He would always carry a rifle like that hanging from the hooks at the end of the waggon before him, and would eventually slay many Indians and keep an account of them in a big book like that on the desk. Susy would help him, having grown up a lady, and they would both together issue provisions and rations from the door of the waggon to the gathered crowds. He would be known as the "White Chief," his Indian name being "Suthin of a pup." He would have a circus van attached to the train, in which he would occasionally perform. He would also have artillery for protection. There would be a terrific engagement, and he would rush into the waggon, heated and blackened with gunpowder, and Susy would put down an account of it in a book, and Mrs. Peyton—for she would be there in some vague capacity—would say, "Really, now, I don't see but what we were very lucky in having such a boy as Clarence with us. I begin to understand him better." And Harry, who, for purposes of vague poetical retaliation, would also drop in at that moment, would mutter and say, "He is certainly the son of Colonel Brant; dear me!" and apologise. And his mother would come in also, in her coldest and most indifferent manner, in a white ball dress, and start and say, "Good gracious, how that boy has grown! I am sorry I did not see more of him when he was young." Yet even in the midst of this came a confusing numbness, and then the side of the waggon seemed to melt away, and he drifted out again alone into the empty desolate plain from which even the sleeping Susy had vanished, and he was left deserted and forgotten. Then all was quiet in the waggon, and only the night wind moving round it. But lo! the lashes of the sleeping White Chief—the dauntless leader, the ruthless destroyer of Indians—were wet with glittering tears!

Yet it seemed only a moment afterwards that he awoke with a faint consciousness of some arrested motion. To his utter consternation, the sun, three hours high, was shining in the waggon, already hot and stifling in its beams. There was the familiar smell and taste of the dirty road in the air about him. There was a faint creeking of boards and springs, a slight oscillation, and beyond the audible rattle of harness as if the train had been under way, the waggon moving, and then there had been a sudden halt. They had probably come up with the Silsbee train; in a few moments the change would be effected and all of his strange experience would be over. He must get up now. Yet, with the morning laziness of the healthy young animal, he curled up a moment longer in his luxurious couch.

How quiet it was! There were far-off voices, but they seemed suppressed and hurried. Through the window he saw one of the teamsters run rapidly past him with a strange, breathless, preoccupied face, halt a moment at one of the following waggons, and then run back again to the front. Then two of the voices came nearer, with the dull beating of hoofs in the dust.

"Rout out the boy and ask him," said a half-suppressed, impatient voice, which Clarence at once recognised as the man Harry's.

"Hold on till Peyton comes up," said the second voice, in a low tone; "leave it to him."

"Better find out what they were like, at once," grumbled Harry.

"Wait—stand back," said Peyton's voice, joining the others; "*I'll* ask him."

Clarence looked wonderingly at the door. It opened on Mr. Peyton, dusty and dismounted, with a strange, abstracted look in his face.

"How many waggons are in your train, Clarence?"

"Three, sir."

"Any marks on them?"

"Yes, sir," said Clarence eagerly; " 'Off to California,' and 'Root, Hog, or Die.' "

Mr. Peyton's eye seemed to leap up and hold Clarence's with a sudden, strange significance, and then looked down.

"How many were you in all?" he continued.

"Five, and there was Mrs. Silsbee."

"No other woman?"

"No."

"Get up and dress yourself," he said gravely, "and wait here till I come back. Keep cool and have your wits about you." He dropped his voice slightly. "Perhaps something's happened that you'll have to show yourself a little man again for, Clarence!"

The door closed, and the boy heard the same muffled hoofs and voices die away towards the front. He began to dress himself mechanically, almost vacantly, yet conscious always of a vague undercurrent of thrilling excitement. When he had finished he waited almost breathlessly, feeling the same beating of his heart that he had felt when he was following the vanished train the day before. At last he could stand the suspense no longer, and opened the door. Everything was still in the motionless caravan, except—it struck him oddly even then—the unconcerned prattling voice of Susy from one of the nearer waggons. Perhaps a sudden feeling that this was something that concerned *her,* perhaps an irresistible impulse overcame him, but the next moment he had leaped to the ground, faced about, and was running feverishly to the front.

The first thing that met his eyes was the helpless and desolate bulk of one of the Silsbee waggons a hundred rods away, bereft of oxen and pole, standing alone and motionless against the dazzling sky! Near it was the broken frame of another waggon, its fore-wheels and axles gone, pitched forward on its knees like an ox under the butcher's sledge. Not far away there were the burnt and blackened ruins of a third, around which the whole party on foot and horseback seemed to be gathered. As the boy ran violently on, the group opened to make way for two men carrying some helpless but awful object between them. A terrible instinct made Clarence swerve from it in his headlong course, but he was at the same moment discovered by the others, and a cry arose of "Go back!" "Stop!" "Keep him back." Heeding it no more than the wind that whistled by him, Clarence made directly for the foremost waggon—the one in which he and Susy had played. A powerful hand caught his shoulder; it was Mr. Peyton's.

"Mrs. Silsbee's waggon," said the boy, with white lips, pointing to it. "Where is she?"

"She's missing," said Peyton, "and one other—the rest are dead."

"She must be there," said the boy, struggling, and pointing to the waggon, "let me go."

"Clarence," said Peyton sternly, accenting his grasp upon the boy's arm, "be a man! Look around you. Try and tell us who these are."

There seemed to be one or two heaps of old clothes lying on the ground, and further on, where the men at a command from Peyton had laid down their burden, another. In those ragged dusty heaps of clothes, from which all the majesty of life seemed to have been ruthlessly stamped out, only what was ignoble and grotesque appeared to be left. There was nothing terrible in this! The boy moved slowly

towards them; and, incredible even to himself, the overpowering fear
of them that a moment before had overcome him left him as suddenly.
He walked from the one to the other, recognising them by certain
marks and signs, and mentioning name after name. The groups gazed
at him curiously; he was conscious that he scarcely understood himself, still less the same quiet purpose that now made him turn towards
the furthest waggon.

"There's nothing there," said Peyton; "we've searched it." But the
boy, without replying, continued his way, and the crowd followed
him.

The deserted waggon, more rude, disorderly, and slovenly than it
had ever seemed to him before, was now heaped and tumbled with
broken bones, cans, scattered provisions, pots, pans, blankets, and
clothing in the foul confusion of a dust-heap. But in this heterogeneous
mingling the boy's quick eye caught sight of a draggled edge of calico.

"That's Mrs. Silsbee's dress," he cried, and leapt into the waggon.

At first the men stared at each other, but an instant later a dozen
hands were helping him, nervously digging and clearing away the rubbish. Then one man uttered a sudden cry, and fell back with frantic
but furious eyes uplifted against the pitiless, smiling sky above him.

"Great God! Look here!"

It was the yellowish, waxen face of Mrs. Silsbee that had been uncovered. But to the fancy of the boy it had changed; the old familiar
lines of worry, care, and querulousness had given way to a look of
remote peace and statue-like repose. He had often vexed her in her
aggressive life; he was touched with remorse at her cold, passionless
apathy now, and pressed timidly forward. Even as he did so, the man,
with a quick but warning gesture, hurriedly threw his handkerchief
over the matted locks, as if to shut out something awful from his view.
Clarence felt himself drawn back; but not before the white lips of a
bystander had whispered a single word—

"Scalped, too! by God!"

Chapter VI

Then followed days and weeks that seemed to Clarence as a dream. At
first an interval of hushed and awed restraint, when he and Susy were
kept apart—a strange and artificial interest taken little note of by him,
but afterwards remembered when others had forgotten it; the burial of
Mrs. Silsbee beneath a cairn of stones, with some ceremonies that,
simple though they were, seemed to usurp the sacred rights of grief
from him and Susy, and leave them cold and frightened; days of

frequent and incoherent childish outbursts from Susy—growing fainter and rarer as time went on, until they ceased, he knew not when; the haunting by night of that morning vision of the three or four heaps of ragged clothes upon the ground, and a half regret that he had not examined them more closely; a recollection of the awful loneliness and desolation of the broken and abandoned waggon left behind on its knees as if praying mutely when the train went on and left it; the trundling behind of the fateful waggon in which Mrs. Silsbee's body had been found—superstitiously shunned by every one—and when at last turned over to the authorities at an outpost garrison, seeming to drop the last link from the dragging chain of the past. The revelation to the children of a new experience in that brief glimpse of the frontier garrison; the handsome officer in uniform and belted sword—an heroic, vengeful figure to be admired and imitated hereafter; the sudden importance and respect given to Susy and himself as "survivors;" the sympathetic questioning and kindly exaggerations of their experiences —quickly accepted by Susy—all these, looking back upon them afterwards, seemed to have passed in a dream.

No less strange and visionary to them seemed the real transitions they noted from the moving train. How one morning they missed the changeless, motionless, low dark line along the horizon, and before noon found themselves among rocks and trees and a swiftly-rushing river. How there suddenly appeared beside them a few days later a great grey cloud-covered ridge of mountains that they were convinced was that same dark line that they had seen so often. How the men laughed at them, and said that for the last three days they had been *crossing* that dark line, and that it was *higher* than the great grey-clouded range before them, which it had always hidden from their view. How Susy firmly believed that these changes took place in her sleep, when she always "kinder felt they were crawlin' up," and how Clarence, in the happy depreciation of extreme youth, expressed his conviction that they "weren't a bit high after all." How the weather became cold, though it was already summer, and at night the camp-fire was a necessity, and there was a stove in the tent with Susy; and yet how all this faded away, and they were again upon a dazzling, burnt, and sun-dried plain. But always as in a dream!

More real were the persons who composed the party—whom they seemed to have always known—and who, in the innocent caprice of children, had become to them more actual than the dead had ever been. There was Mr. Peyton, who, they now knew, owned the train, and who was so rich that he "needn't go to California if he didn't want to, and was going to buy a great deal of it if he liked it," and who was also a lawyer and "policeman"—which was Susy's rendering of "politician"—and was called "Squire" and Judge at the frontier out-post, and could order anybody to be "took up if he wanted to," and who knew everybody by their Christian names; and Mrs. Peyton, who had been delicate, and was ordered by the doctor to live in the open air for six months, and "never go into a house or a town agin," and who was going to adopt Susy as soon as her husband could arrange with Susy's relatives and draw up the papers! How "Harry" was Henry Benham, Mrs. Peyton's brother, and a kind of partner of Mr. Peyton. And how the scout's name was Gus Gildersleeve, or the "White Crow;" and how, through his recognised intrepidity, an attack upon their train was no doubt averted. Then there was "Bill," the stockherder, and "Texas Jim," the *vaquero*—the latter marvellous and unprecedented in horsemanship. Such were their companions, as appeared through the gossip of the train and their own inexperienced consciousness. To them they were all astounding and important personages. But, either from boyish curiosity or some sense of being misunderstood, Clarence was more attracted by the two individuals of the party who were least kind to him—namely, Mrs. Peyton and her brother Harry. I fear that, after the fashion of most children, and some grown-up people, he thought less of the steady kindness of Mr. Peyton and the others than of the rare tolerance of Harry or the polite conces-sions of his sister. Miserably conscious of this at times, he quite convinced himself that if he could only win a word of approbation from Harry, or a smile from Mrs. Peyton, he would afterwards revenge himself by "running away." Whether he would or not I cannot say. I am writing of a foolish, growing, impressionable boy of eleven, of whose sentiments nothing could be safely predicted but uncertainty.

It was at this time that he became fascinated by another member of the party, whose position had been too humble and unimportant to be included in the group already noted. Of the same appearance as the other teamsters in size, habits, and apparel, he had not at first exhib-ited to Clarence any claim to sympathy. But it appeared that he was actually a youth of only sixteen—a hopeless incorrigible of St. Joseph, whose parents had prevailed on Peyton to allow him to join the party by way of removing him from evil associations and as a method of reform. Of this Clarence was at first ignorant, not from any want of frankness on the part of the youth, for that ingenious young gentleman later informed him that he had killed three men in St. Louis, two in St. Jo., and that the officers of justice were after him. But it was evident that to precocious habits of drinking, smoking, chewing, and card-playing this overgrown youth added a strong tendency to exaggeration of statement. Indeed, he was known as "Lying Jim Hooker," and his various qualities presented a problem to Clarence that was attractive

and inspiring, doubtful, but always fascinating. With the hoarse voice
of early wickedness and a contempt for ordinary courtesy, he had a
round, perfectly good-humoured face, and a disposition that, when not
called upon to act up to his self-imposed *rôle* of reckless wickedness,
was not unkindly.

It was only a few days after the massacre, and while the children
were still wrapped in the gloomy interest and frightened reticence
which followed it, that "Jim Hooker" first characteristically flashed
upon Clarence's perceptions. Hanging half on and half off the saddle
of an Indian pony, the lank Jim suddenly made his appearance, dashing violently up and down the track and around the waggon in which
Clarence was sitting, tugging desperately at the reins, with every indication of being furiously run away with, and retaining his seat only
with the most dauntless courage and skill. Round and round they
went, the helpless rider at times hanging by a single stirrup near the
ground, and again recovering himself by—as it seemed to Clarence—
almost superhuman effort. Clarence sat open-mouthed with anxiety
and excitement, and yet a few of the other teamsters laughed. Then the
voice of Mr. Peyton, from the window of his car, said quietly—

"There, that will do, Jim. Quit it!"

The furious horse and rider instantly disappeared. A few moments
after, the bewildered Clarence saw the redoubtable horseman trotting
along quietly in the dust of the rear on the same fiery steed, who in
that prosaic light bore an astounding resemblance to an ordinary team
horse. Later in the day he sought an explanation from the rider.

"You see," answered Jim gloomily, "thar ain't a galoot in this yer
crowd ez knows jist *what's* in that hoss! And them ez suspecks daren't
say! It wouldn't do for to hev it let out that the Judge hez a Morgan-
Mexican plug that's killed two men afore he got him, and is bound to
kill another afore he gets through! Why, ony the week afore we kem
up to you that thar hoss bolted with me at camping! Bucked and
throwd me, but I kept my holt o' the stirrups with my foot—so!
Dragged me a matter of two miles, head down, and me keepin' away
rocks with my hand—so!"

"Why didn't you loose your foot and let go?" asked Clarence
breathlessly.

"*You* might," said Jim, with deep scorn; "that ain't *my* style. I just
laid low till we kem to a steep-pitched hill, and goin' down, when the
hoss was, so to speak, kinder *below* me, I just turned a hand spring so,
and that landed me onter his back again."

This action, though vividly illustrated by Jim's throwing his hands
down like feet beneath him and indicating the parabola of a spring in

the air, proving altogether too much for Clarence's mind to grasp, he timidly turned to a less difficult detail.

"What made the horse bolt first, Mr. Hooker?"

"Smelt Injins!" said Jim, carelessly expectorating tobacco-juice in a curving jet from the side of his mouth—a singularly fascinating accomplishment, peculiarly his own. " 'n likely *your* Injins."

"But," argued Clarence hesitatingly, "you said it was a week before —and"——

"Er Mexican plug can smell Injins fifty, yes, a hundred miles away," said Jim, with scornful deliberation; " 'n if Judge Peyton had took my advice, and hadn't been so mighty feared about the character of his hoss gettin' out, he'd hev played roots on them Injins afore they tetched ye. But," he added, with gloomy dejection, "thar ain't no sand in this yer crowd, thar ain't no vim; thar ain't nothin'; and thar kant be ez long ez thar's women and babies, and women and baby fixins mixed up with it. I'd hev cut the whole blamed gang ef et weren't for one or two things," he added darkly.

Clarence, impressed by Jim's mysterious manner, for the moment forgot his contemptuous allusion to Mr. Peyton, and the evident implication of Susy and himself, and asked hurriedly, "What things?"

Jim, as if forgetful of the boy's presence in his fitful mood, abstractedly half drew a glittering bowie-knife from his boot-leg, and then slowly put it back again. "Thar's one or two old scores," he continued, in a low voice, although no one was in hearing distance of them; "one or two private accounts," he went on tragically, averting his eyes as if watched by some one, "that hev to be wiped out with blood afore *I* leave. Thar's one or two men *too many* alive and breathin' in this yer crowd. Mebbee it's Gus Gildersleeve; mebbee it's Harry Benham; mebbee," he added, with dark, yet noble disinterestedness, "it's *me.*"

"Oh, no," said Clarence, with polite deprecation.

Far from placating the gloomy Jim, this seemed only to awaken his suspicions. "Mebbee," he said, dancing suddenly away from Clarence, "mebbee you think I'm lyin'. Mebbee you think because you're Colonel Brant's son yer kin run *me* with this yer train. Mebbee," he continued, dancing violently back again, "ye kalkilate because ye run off'n stampeded a baby, ye kin tote me round too, sonny. Mebbee," he went on, executing a double shuffle in the dust, and alternately striking his hands on the sides of his boots, "mebbee you're spyin' round and reportin' to the Judge."

Firmly convinced that Jim was working himself up by an Indian war-dance to some desperate assault on himself, but resenting the last unjust accusation, Clarence had recourse to one of his old dogged silences. Happily, at this moment, an authoritative voice called out, "Now then, you Jim Hooker!" and the desperate Hooker, as usual, vanished instantly. Nevertheless, he appeared an hour or two later beside the waggon in which Susy and Clarence were seated with an expression of satiated vengeance and remorseful bloodguiltiness in his face, and his hair combed Indian fashion over his eyes. As he generously contented himself with only passing a gloomy and disparaging criticism on the game of cards that the children were playing, it struck Clarence for the first time that a great deal of his real wickedness resided in his hair. This set him to thinking that it was strange that Mr. Peyton did not try to reform him with a pair of scissors, but not until Clarence himself had for at least four days attempted to imitate Jim by combing his own hair in that fashion.

A few days later Jim again casually favoured him with a confidential interview. Clarence had been allowed to bestride one of the team-leaders postillion-wise, and was correspondingly elevated when Jim joined him on the Mexican plug, which appeared—no doubt a part of its wicked art—heavily docile, and even slightly lame.

"How much," said Jim, in a tone of gloomy confidence, "how much did you reckon to make by stealin' that gal-baby, sonny?"

"Nothing," replied Clarence, with a smile. Perhaps it was an evidence of the marked influence that Jim was beginning to exert over him that he already did not attempt to resent this fascinating implication of grown-up guilt.

"It orter bin a good job if it warn't revenge," continued Jim moodily.

"No, it wasn't revenge," said Clarence hurriedly.

"Then ye kalkilated ter get er hundred dollars reward ef the old man and old woman hadn't bin skelped afore ye got up to 'em?" said Jim. "That's your blamed dodgasted luck, eh! Enyhow, you'll make Mrs. Peyton plank down suthin' if she adopts the babby. Look yer, young feller," he said, starting suddenly and throwing his face forward, glaring fiendishly through his matted sidelocks, "d'ye meanter tell me it wasn't a plant—a skin game—the hull thing?"

"A what?" said Clarence.

"D'ye mean to say"—it was wonderful how gratuitously husky his voice became at this moment—"d'ye mean ter tell *me* ye didn't set on them Injins to wipe out the Silsbees, so that ye could hev an out-an-out gal *orfen* on hand fer Mrs. Peyton to adopt—eh?"

But here Clarence was forced to protest, and strongly, although Jim contemptuously ignored it. "Don't lie ter me," he repeated mysteriously; "I'm fly. I'm dark, young fel. We're cahoots in this thing?" and with this artful suggestion of being in possession of Clarence's guilty secret, he departed in time to elude the usual objurgation of his superior, "Phil," the head teamster.

Nor was his baleful fascination exercised entirely on Clarence. In spite of Mrs. Peyton's jealously affectionate care, Clarence's frequent companionship, and the little circle of admiring courtiers that always surrounded Susy, it became evident that this small Eve had been secretly approached and tempted by the satanic Jim. She was found one day to have a few heron's feathers in her possession with which she adorned her curls, and at another time was discovered to have rubbed her face and arms with yellow and red ochre, confessedly the free gift of Jim Hooker. It was to Clarence alone that she admitted the significance and purport of these offerings. "Jim gave 'em to me," she said, "and Jim's a kind of Injin hisself that won't hurt me, and when bad Injins come they'll think I'm his Injin baby and run away. And Jim said if I'd just told the Injins when they came to kill papa and mamma that I b'longed to him they'd hev runned away."

"But," said the practical Clarence, "you could not; you know you were with Mrs. Peyton all the time."

"Kla'uns," said Susy, shaking her head and fixing her round blue eyes with calm mendacity on the boy, "don't you tell me. *I was there!*"

Clarence started back and nearly fell over the waggon in hopeless dismay at this dreadful revelation of Susy's powers of exaggeration. "But," he gasped, "you know, Susy, you and me left before"——

"Kla'uns," said Susy calmly, making a little pleat in the skirt of her dress with her small thumb and fingers, "don't you talk to me. I was there. I'se a *seriver!* The men at the fort said so! The *serivers* is allus, allus there, and allus, allus knows everythin'."

Clarence was too dumbfounded to reply. He had a vague recollection of having noticed before that Susy was very much fascinated by the reputation given to her at Fort Ridge as a "survivor," and was trying in an infantile way to live up to it. This the wicked Jim had evidently encouraged. For a day or two Clarence felt a little afraid of her, and more lonely than ever.

It was in this state, and while he was doggedly conscious that his association with Jim did not prepossess Mrs. Peyton or her brother in his favour, and that the former even believed him responsible for Susy's unhallowed acquaintance with Jim, that he drifted into one of those youthful escapades on which elders are apt to sit in severe but not always considerate judgment. Believing, like many other children, that nobody cared particularly for him, except to *restrain* him; discovering, as children do, much sooner than we complacently imagine, that love and preference have no logical connection with desert or character, Clarence became boyishly reckless. But when one day it was rumoured that a herd of buffalo was in the vicinity, and that the train would be delayed the next morning in order that a hunt might be organised by Gildersleeve, Benham, and a few others, Clarence listened willingly to Jim's proposition that they should secretly follow it.

To effect their unhallowed purpose required boldness and duplicity. It was arranged that shortly after the departure of the hunting-party Clarence should ask permission to mount and exercise one of the team horses—a favour that had been frequently granted him. That in the outskirts of the camp he should pretend that the horse ran away with him, and Jim would start in pursuit. The absence of the shooting-party with so large a contingent of horses and men would preclude any further detachment from the camp to assist them. Once clear, they would follow the track of the hunters, and, if discovered by them, would offer the same excuse, with the addition that they had lost their way to the camp. The plan was successful. The details were carried out with almost too perfect effect; as it appeared that Jim, in order to give dramatic intensity to the fractiousness of Clarence's horse, had inserted a thorn-apple under the neck of his saddle, which Clarence only discovered in time to prevent himself from being unseated. Urged forward by ostentatious "Whoas!" and surreptitious cuts in the rear from Jim, pursuer and pursued presently found themselves safely beyond the half-dry stream and fringe of alder-bushes that skirted the camp. They were not followed. Whether the teamsters suspected and winked at this design or believing that the boys could take care of themselves, and ran no risk of being lost in the proximity of the hunting-party, there was no general alarm.

Thus reassured, and having a general idea of the direction of the hunt, the boys pushed hilariously forward. Before them opened a vast expanse of bottom-land, slightly sloping on the right to a distant half-filled lagoon formed by the main river overflow, on whose tributary they had encamped. The lagoon was partly hidden by straggling timber and "brush," and beyond that again stretched the unlimitable plains—the pasture of their mighty game. Hither Jim hoarsely informed his companion the buffaloes came to water. A few rods further on, he started dramatically, and alighting, proceeded to slowly examine the round. It seemed to be scattered over with half-circular patches, which he pointed out mysteriously as "buffalo chip." To Clarence's inexperienced perception the plain bore a singular resemblance to the surface of an ordinary unromantic cattle pasture that somewhat chilled his heroic fancy. However, the two companions halted and professionally examined their arms and equipments.

These, I grieve to say, though varied, were scarcely full or satisfactory. The necessities of their flight had restricted Jim to an old double-barrelled fowling-piece, which he usually carried slung across his shoulders; an old-fashioned "six-shooter"—whose barrels revolved occasionally and unexpectedly—known as "Allen's Pepper Box," on account of its culinary resemblance, and a bowie-knife! Clarence carried an Indian bow and arrow with which he had been exercising, and a hatchet which he had concealed under the flanks of his saddle. To this Jim generously added the six-shooter, taking the hatchet in exchange —a transfer that at first delighted Clarence, until, seeing the warlike and picturesque effect of the hatchet in Jim's belt, he regretted the transfer. The gun, Jim meantime explained, "extry charged," "chuck up" to the middle, with slugs and revolver bullets, could only be fired by himself, and even then, he darkly added, not without danger. This poverty of equipment was, however, compensated by the opposite statements from Jim of the extraordinary results obtained by these simple weapons from "fellers I knew." How *he* himself had once brought down a "bull" by a bold shot with a revolver through its open bellowing mouth that pierced its "innards." How a friend of his—an intimate in fact—now in jail at Louisville for killing a sheriff's deputy —had once found himself alone and dismounted, with a simple clasp knife and a lariat, among a herd of buffaloes; how, leaping calmly upon the shaggy shoulders of the biggest bull, he lashed himself with the lariat firmly to his horns, goading it onward with his clasp-knife, and subsisting for days upon the flesh cut from its living body, until, abandoned by its fellows, and exhausted by loss of blood, it finally succumbed to its victor at the very outskirts of the camp to which he had artfully driven it! It must be confessed that this recital somewhat took away Clarence's breath, and he would have liked to ask a few questions. But they were alone on the prairie, they were linked by a common transgression; the glorious sun was coming up victoriously, the pure, crisp air was intoxicating their nerves—in the bright forecast of youth everything *was* possible!

The surface of the bottom-land that they were crossing was here and there broken up by fissures and "pot holes," and some circumspection in their progress became necessary. In one of these halts, Clarence was struck by a dull, monotonous jarring, that sounded like the heavy, regular fall of water over a dam. Each time they slackened their pace the sound would become more audible, and was at last accompanied by that slight but unmistakable tremor of the earth that betrayed the vicinity of a waterfall. Hesitating over this phenomenon, which seemed to imply that their topography was wrong and that they had blundered from the track, they were presently startled by the fact that the sound was actually *approaching* them! With a sudden instinct they both galloped towards the lagoon. As the timber opened before them Jim uttered a long ecstatic shout. "Why, it's *them!*"

At a first glance it seemed to Clarence as if the whole plain beyond was broken up and rolling in tumbling waves or furrows towards them. A second glance showed the tossing fronts of a vast herd of buffaloes, and here and there, darting in and out and among them, or emerging from the cloud of dust behind, wild figures and flashes of fire. With the idea of water still in his mind, it seemed as if some tumultuous tidal wave were sweeping unseen towards the lagoon, carrying everything before it. He turned with eager eyes in speechless expectancy to his companion.

Alack! that redoubtable hero and mighty hunter was, to all appearances, equally speechless and astonished! It was true that he remained rooted to the saddle, a lank, still, heroic figure, alternately grasping his hatchet and gun with a kind of spasmodic regularity! How long he would have continued this could never be known, for the next moment, with a deafening crash, the herd broke through the brush and, swerving at the right of the lagoon, bore down directly upon them. All further doubt or hesitation on their part was stopped. The far-seeing, sagacious Mexican plug, with a terrific snort, wheeled and fled furiously with his rider. Moved no doubt by touching fidelity, Clarence's humbler team-horse instantly followed. In a few moments those devoted animals struggled neck to neck in noble emulation.

"What are we goin' off this way for?" gasped the simple Clarence.

"Peyton and Gildersleeve are back there—and they'll see us," gasped Jim in reply.

It struck Clarence that the buffaloes were much nearer them than the hunting-party, and that the tramping hoofs of a dozen bulls were close behind them, but with another gasp he shouted—"When are we going to hunt 'em?"

"Hunt *them,*" screamed Jim, with an hysterical outburst of truth; "why, they're huntin' *us*—dash it."

Indeed, there was no doubt that their frenzied horses were flying before the equally frenzied herd behind them. They gained a momentary advantage by riding into one of the fissures, and out again on the other side, while their pursuers were obliged to make a detour. But in a few minutes they were overtaken by that part of the herd who had taken the other and nearer side of the lagoon, and were now fairly in the midst of them. The ground shook with their trampling hoofs; their steaming breath, mingling with the stinging dust that filled the air, half choked and blinded Clarence. He was dimly conscious that Jim had wildly thrown his hatchet at a cow-buffalo pressing close upon his flanks. As they swept down into another gully he saw him raise his fateful gun in utter desperation. Clarence crouched low on his horse's outstretched neck. There was a blinding flash; a single, stunning report from both barrels; Jim reeled in one way half out of the saddle, while the smoking gun seemed to leap in another over his head, and then rider and horse vanished in a choking cloud of dust and gunpowder. A moment after Clarence's horse stopped with a sudden check, and the boy felt himself hurled over its head into the gully, alighting on something that seemed to be a bounding cushion of curled and twisted hair. It was the shaggy shoulder of an enormous buffalo! For Jim's desperate random shot and double charge had taken effect on the near hind leg of a preceding bull, tearing away the flesh and ham-stringing the animal, who had dropped in the gully just in front of Clarence's horse.

Dazed, but unhurt, the boy rolled from the lifted forequarters of the struggling brute to the ground. Then he staggered to his feet again; not only his horse was gone, but the whole herd of buffaloes seemed to have passed too, and he could hear the shouts of unseen hunters now ahead of him. They had evidently overlooked his fall, and the gully had concealed him. The sides before him were too steep for his aching limbs to climb; the slope by which he and the bull descended when the collision occurred was behind the wounded animal. Clarence was staggering towards it, when the bull, by a supreme effort, lifted itself on three legs, half turned, and faced him.

These events had passed too quickly for the inexperienced boy to have felt any active fear, or indeed anything but wild excitement and confusion. But the spectacle of that shaggy and enormous front, that seemed to fill the whole gully, rising with awful deliberation between him and escape, sent a thrill of terror through his frame. The great, dull, bloodshot eyes glared at him with a dumb, wondering fury; the large wet nostrils were so near that their first snort of inarticulate rage made him reel backwards as from a blow. The gully was only a narrow and short fissure or subsidence of the plain; a few paces more of retreat and he would be at its end, against an almost perpendicular bank fifteen feet high. If he attempted to climb its crumbling sides, and fell, there would be those short but terrible horns waiting to impale him! It seemed too terrible, too cruel! He was so small beside this overgrown monster. It wasn't fair! The tears started to his eyes, and then, in a rage at the injustice of Fate, he stood doggedly still with clenched fists. He fixed his gaze with half hysterical, childish fury on those lurid eyes; he did not know that, owing to the strange magnifying power of the bull's convex pupils, he, Clarence, appeared much bigger than he really was to the brute's heavy consciousness, the distance from him most deceptive, and that it was to this fact that hunters so often owed their escape. He only thought of some desperate means of attack. Ah!

the six-shooter. It was still in his pocket. He drew it nervously, hope-lessly—it looked so small compared with his large enemy!

He presented it with flashing eyes, and pulled the trigger. A feeble click followed—another, and again! Even *this* had mocked him. He pulled the trigger once more wildly; there was a sudden explosion, and another. He stepped back; the balls had apparently flattened them-selves harmlessly on the bull's forehead. He pulled again hopelessly; there was another report, a sudden furious bellow, and the enormous brute threw his head savagely to one side, burying his left horn deep in the crumbling bank beside him. Again and again he charged the bank, driving his left horn home, and bringing down the stones and earth in showers. It was some seconds before Clarence saw, in a single glimpse of that wildly tossing crest, the reason of this fury. The blood was pouring from his left eye, penetrated by the last bullet; the bull was blinded! A terrible revulsion of feeling, a sudden sense of remorse that was for the moment more awful than even his previous fear, overcame him. *He* had done *that thing!* As much to fly from the dreadful specta-cle as any instinct of self-preservation, he took advantage of the next mad paroxysm of pain and blindness that always impelled the suffer-ing beast towards the left, to slip past him on the right, reach the incline, and scramble wildly up to the plain again. Here he ran confus-edly forward—not knowing whither—only caring to escape that agonised bellowing, to shut out for ever the accusing look of that huge, blood-weltering eye.

Suddenly he heard a distant angry shout. To his first hurried glance the plain had seemed empty, but looking up he saw two horsemen rapidly advancing with a led horse behind them—his own. With the blessed sense of relief that overtook him now came the fevered desire for sympathy, and to tell them all. But as they came nearer he saw that they were Gildersleeve the scout and Henry Benham, and that, far from sharing any delight in his deliverance, their faces only exhibited irascible impatience. Overcome by this new defeat the boy stopped, again dumb and dogged.

"Now then, blank it all, *will* you get up and come along, or do you reckon to keep the train waiting another hour over your blanked fool-ishness?" said Gildersleeve savagely.

The boy hesitated, and then mounted mechanically, without a word.

" 'Twould have served 'em right to have gone and left 'em," mut-tered Benham vindictively.

For one wild instant Clarence thought of throwing himself from his horse and bidding them go on and leave him. But before he could put this thought into action, the two men were galloping forward, with his horse led by a lariat fastened to the horn of Gildersleeve's saddle.

In two hours more they had overtaken the train, already on the march, and were in the midst of the group of outriders. Judge Peyton's face, albeit a trifle perplexed, turned towards Clarence with a kindly, half-tolerant look of welcome. The boy's heart instantly melted with forgiveness.

"Well, my boy, let's hear *your* story. What happened?"

Clarence cast a hurried glance around, and saw Jim, with face averted, riding gloomily behind. Then, nervously and hurriedly, he told how he had been thrown into the gully on the back of the wounded buffalo, and the manner of his escape. An audible titter ran through the cavalcade. Mr. Peyton regarded him gravely. "But how did the buffalo get so conveniently into the gully?" he asked.

"Jim Hooker lamed him with a shot-gun, and he fell over," said Clarence timidly.

A roar of Homeric laughter went up from the party. Clarence looked up, stung and startled, but caught a single glimpse of Jim Hooker's face that made him forget his own mortification. In its hopeless, heart-sick, and utterly beaten dejection—the first and only real expression he had seen on it—he read the dreadful truth! Jim's *reputation* had ruined him! The one genuine and striking episode of his life— the one trustworthy account he had given of it—had been unanimously accepted as the biggest and most consummate lie of his record!

Chapter VII

With this incident of the hunt closed, to Clarence, the last remembered episode of his journey. But he did not know until long after that it had also closed to him what might have been the opening of a new career. For it had been Judge Peyton's intention in adopting Susy to include a certain guardianship and protection of the boy, provided he could get the consent of that vague relation to whom he was consigned. But it had been pointed out by Mrs. Peyton and her brother that Clarence's association with Jim Hooker had made him a doubtful companion for Susy, and even the Judge himself was forced to admit that the boy's apparent taste for evil company was inconsistent with his alleged birth and breeding. Unfortunately, Clarence, in the conviction of being hopelessly misunderstood, and that dogged acquiescence to fate which was one of his characteristics, was too proud to correct the impression by any of the hypocrisies of childhood. He had also a cloudy instinct of loyalty to Jim in his disgrace, without, however, experiencing either the sympathy of an equal or the zeal of a partisan, but rather—if it could be said of a boy of his years—with the patronage and protection of a superior. So he accepted without demur the intimation that when the train reached California he would be forwarded from Stockton with an outfit and a letter of explanation to Sacramento—it being understood that in the event of not finding his relative he would return to the Peytons in one of the Southern valleys, where they elected to purchase a tract of land.

With this outlook, and the prospect of change, independence, and all the rich possibilities that, to the imagination of youth, are included in them, Clarence had found the days dragging. The halt at Salt Lake, the transit of the dreary Alkali desert, even the wild passage of the Sierras, were but a blurred picture in his memory. The sight of eternal snows, and the rolling of endless ranks of pines; the first glimpse of a hillside of wild oats, the spectacle of a rushing yellow river, that to his fancy seemed tinged with gold, were momentary excitements, quickly forgotten. But when one morning, halting at the outskirts of a struggling settlement, he found the entire party eagerly gathered around a passing stranger, who had taken from his saddlebags a small buckskin pouch to show them a double handful of shining scales of metal, Clarence felt the first feverish and overmastering thrill of the gold-seekers. Breathlessly he followed the breathless questions and careless replies. The gold had been dug out of a *placer* only thirty miles away—it might be worth, say, a hundred and fifty dollars—it was only *his* share of a week's work with two partners. It was not much—"the country was getting played out with fresh arrivals and greenhorns." All this falling carelessly from the unshaven lips of a dusty, roughly-dressed man, with a long-handled shovel and pickaxe strapped on his back, and a frying-pan depending from his saddle. But no panoplied or armed knight ever seemed so heroic or independent a figure to Clarence. What could be finer than the noble scorn conveyed in his critical survey of the train, with its comfortable covered waggons and appliances of civilisation? "Ye'll hev to get rid of them ther fixins if yer goin' in for *placer* diggin'!" What a corroboration of Clarence's real thoughts! What a picture of independence was this! The picturesque scout, the all-powerful Judge Peyton, the daring young officer, all crumbled on their clayey pedestals before this hero in a red flannel shirt and high-topped boots! To stroll around in the open air all day, and pick up those shining bits of metal, without study, without method or routine—this was really life—to some day come upon that large nugget "you couldn't lift"—that was worth as much as the train and horses—such a one as the stranger said was found the other day at Sawyer's Bar—this was worth giving up everything for. That rough man, with his smile of careless superiority, was the living link between

Clarence and the Thousand and One Nights; in him were Aladdin and Sinbad incarnate.

Two days later they reached Stockton. Here Clarence, whose single suit of clothes had been reinforced by patching, odds and ends from Peyton's stores, and an extraordinary costume of army cloth, got up by the regimental tailor of Fort Ridge, was taken to be refitted at a general furnishing "emporium." But alas! in the selection of the clothing for that adult locality scant provision seemed to have been made for a boy of Clarence's years, and he was with difficulty fitted from an old condemned Government stores with "a boy's" seaman suit and a brass-button pea-jacket. To this outfit Mr. Peyton added a small sum of money for his expenses, and a letter of explanation to his cousin. The stage-coach was to start at noon. It only remained for Clarence to take leave of the party. The final parting with Susy had been discounted on the two previous days with some tears, small frights and clingings, and the expressed determination on the child's part "to go with him;" but in the excitement of the arrival at Stockton it was still further mitigated, and under the influence of a little present from Clarence—his first disbursement of his small capital—had at last taken the form and promise of merely temporary separation. Nevertheless, when the boy's scanty pack was deposited under the stage-coach seat, and he had been left alone, he ran rapidly back to the train for one moment more with Susy. Panting and a little frightened, he reached Mrs. Peyton's car.

"Goodness! You're not gone yet," said Mrs. Peyton sharply. "Do you want to lose the stage?"

An instant before, in his loneliness, he might have answered "Yes." But under the cruel sting of Mrs. Peyton's evident annoyance at his reappearance he felt his legs suddenly tremble, and his voice left him. He did not dare to look at Susy. But her voice rose comfortably from the depths of the waggon where she was sitting.

"The stage will be goned away, Kla'uns."

She, too! Shame at his foolish weakness sent the yearning blood that had settled round his heart flying back into his face.

"I was looking for—for—for Jim, ma'am," he said at last boldly.

He saw the look of disgust pass over Mrs. Peyton's face, and felt a malicious satisfaction as he turned and ran back to the stage. But here, to his surprise, he actually found Jim, whom he really hadn't thought of, darkly watching the last strapping of luggage. With a manner calculated to convey the impression to the other passengers that he was parting from a brother criminal, probably on his way to a State prison, Jim shook hands gloomily with Clarence, and eyed the other passengers furtively between his matted locks.

"Ef ye hear o' anythin' happenin', ye'll know what's up," he said, in a low, hoarse, but perfectly audible whisper. "Me and them's bound to part kompany afore long. Tell the fellows at Deadman's Gulch to look out for me at any time."

Although Clarence was not going to Deadman's Gulch, knew nothing of it, and had a faint suspicion that Jim was equally ignorant, yet as one or two of the passengers glanced anxiously at the demure, grey-eyed boy who seemed booked for such a baleful destination, he really felt the half-delighted, half-frightened consciousness that he was starting in life under fascinating, immoral pretences. But the forward spring of the fine-spirited horses, the quickened motion, the glittering sunlight, and the thought that he really was leaving behind him all the shackles of dependence and custom, and plunging into a life of freedom, drove all else from his mind. He turned at last from this hopeful, blissful future, and began to examine his fellow-passengers with boyish curiosity. Wedged in between two silent men on the front seat, one of whom seemed a farmer, and the other, by his black attire, a professional man, Clarence was finally attracted by a black-mantled, dark-haired, bonnetless woman on the back seat, whose attention seemed to be monopolised by the jocular gallantries of her companions and the two men before her in the middle seat. From her position he could see little more than her dark eyes, which occasionally seemed to meet his frank curiosity in an amused sort of way, but he was chiefly struck by the pretty foreign sound of her musical voice, which was unlike anything he had ever heard before, and—alas! for the inconstancy of youth—much finer than Mrs. Peyton's. Presently his farmer companion, casting a patronising glance on Clarence's pea-jacket and brass buttons, said cheerily—

"Jest off a voyage, sonny?"

"No, sir," stammered Clarence; "I came across the plains."

"Then I reckon that's the rig-out for the crew of a prairie schooner, eh?" There was a laugh at this which perplexed Clarence. Observing it, the humourist kindly condescended to explain that "prairie schooner" was the current slang for an emigrant waggon.

"I couldn't," explained Clarence, naïvely looking at the dark eyes on the back seat, "get any clothes at Stockton but these; I suppose the folks didn't think there'd ever be boys in California."

The simplicity of this speech evidently impressed the others, for the two men in the middle seats turned at a whisper from the lady and regarded him curiously. Clarence blushed slightly and became silent. Presently the vehicle began to slacken its speed. They were ascending a hill; on either bank grew huge cottonwoods, from which occasionally depended a beautiful scarlet vine.

"Ah! eet ees pretty," said the lady, nodding her black veiled head towards it. "Eet is good in ze hair."

One of the men made an awkward attempt to clutch a spray from the window. A brilliant inspiration flashed upon Clarence. When the stage began the ascent of the next hill, following the example of an outside passenger, he jumped down to walk. At the top of the hill he rejoined the stage, flushed and panting, but carrying a small branch of the vine in his scratched hands. Handing it to the man on the middle seat, he said, with grave, boyish politeness—"Please—for the lady."

A slight smile passed over the face of Clarence's neighbours. The bonnetless woman nodded a pleasant acknowledgment, and coquettishly wound the vine in her glossy hair. The dark man at his side, who hadn't spoken yet, turned to Clarence drily—

"If you're goin' to keep up this gait, sonny, I reckon ye won't find much trouble gettin' a man's suit to fit you by the time you reach Sacramento."

Clarence didn't quite understand him, but noticed that a singular gravity seemed to overtake the two jocular men on the middle seat, and the lady looked out of the window. He came to the conclusion that he had made a mistake about alluding to his clothes and his size. He must try and behave more manly. That opportunity seemed to be offered two hours later, when the stage stopped at a wayside hotel or restaurant.

Two or three passengers had got down to refresh themselves at the bar. His right and left hand neighbours were, however, engaged in a drawling conversation on the comparative merits of San Francisco sand-hill and water lots; the jocular occupants of the middle seats were still engrossed with the lady. Clarence slipped out of the stage and entered the bar-room with some ostentation. The complete ignoring of his person by the bar-keeper and his customers, however, somewhat disconcerted him. He hesitated a moment, and then returned gravely to the stage door and opened it.

"Would you mind taking a drink with me, sir?" said Clarence politely, addressing the farmer-looking passenger, who had been most civil to him. A dead silence followed. The two men on the middle seat faced entirely around to gaze at him.

"The Commodore asks if you'll take a drink with him," explained one of the men to Clarence's friend with the greatest seriousness.

"Eh? Oh, yes, certainly," returned that gentleman, changing his astonished expression to one of the deepest gravity, "seeing it's the Commodore."

"And perhaps you and your friend will join too?" said Clarence timidly to the passenger who had explained; "and you too, sir?" he added to the dark man.

"Really, gentlemen, I don't see how we can refuse," said the latter, rising with the greatest formality, and appealing to the others. "A compliment of this kind from our distinguished friend is not to be taken lightly."

"I have observed, sir, that the Commodore's head is level," returned the other man with equal gravity.

Clarence could have wished they had not treated his first hospitable effort quite so formally, but as they stepped from the coach with unbending faces he led them, a little frightened, into the bar-room. Here, unfortunately, as he was barely able to reach over the counter, the barkeeper would have again overlooked him, but for a quick glance from the dark man, which seemed to change even the bar-keeper's perfunctory smiling face into supernatural gravity.

"The Commodore is standing treat," said the dark man, with unbroken seriousness, indicating Clarence, and leaning back with an air of respectful formality. "*I* will take straight whisky. The Commodore, on account of just changing climate, will, I believe, for the present content himself with lemon soda."

Clarence had previously resolved to take whisky like the others, but a little doubtful of the politeness of countermanding his guest's order, and perhaps slightly embarrassed by the fact that all the other customers seemed to have gathered round him and his party with equally immovable faces, he said hurriedly, "Lemon soda for me, please."

"The Commodore," said the bar-keeper, with impassive features, as he bent forward and wiped the counter with professional deliberation, "is right. No matter how much a man may be accustomed all his life to liquor, when he is changing climate, gentlemen, he says 'lemon soda for me' all the time."

"Perhaps," said Clarence, brightening, "*you* will join too?"

"I shall be proud on this occasion, sir."

"I think," said the tall man, still as ceremoniously unbending as before, "that there can be but one toast here, gentlemen. I give you the health of the Commodore. May his shadow never be less!"

The health was drunk solemnly. Clarence felt his cheeks tingle, and in his excitement drank his own health with the others. Yet he was disappointed that there was not more joviality, he wondered if men always drank together so stiffly. And it occurred to him that it would be expensive. Nevertheless, he had his purse all ready ostentatiously in his hand; in fact, the paying for it out of his own money was not the least manly and independent pleasure he had promised himself. "How much?" he asked, with an affectation of carelessness. The bar-keeper cast his eye professionally over the bar-room. "I think you said treats for the crowd; call it twenty dollars to make even change."

Clarence's heart sank. He had heard already of the exaggeration of California prices. Twenty dollars! It was half his fortune. Nevertheless, with an heroic effort, he controlled himself, and with slightly nervous fingers counted out the money. It struck him, however, as curious, not to say ungentlemanly, that the bystanders craned their necks over his shoulder to look at the contents of his purse, although some slight explanation was offered by the tall man.

"The Commodore's purse, gentlemen, is really a singular one. Permit me," he said, taking it from Clarence's hand with great politeness. "It is one of the new pattern, you observe, quite worthy of inspection." He handed it to a man behind him, who in turn handed it to another, while a chorus of "suthin' quite new," "the latest style," followed it in its passage round the room, and indicated to Clarence its whereabouts. It was presently handed back to the bar-keeper, who had begged also to inspect it, and who, with an air of scrupulous ceremony, insisted upon placing it himself in Clarence's side pocket, as if it were an important part of his function. The driver here called "all aboard." The passengers hurriedly re-seated themselves, and the episode abruptly ended. For, to Clarence's surprise, these attentive friends of a moment ago at once became interested in the views of a new passenger concerning the local politics of San Francisco, and he found himself utterly forgotten. The bonnetless woman had changed her position, and her head was no longer visible. The disillusion and depression that overcame him suddenly were as complete as his previous expectations and hopefulness had been extravagant. For the first time his utter unimportance in the world and his inadequacy to this new life around him came upon him crushingly.

The heat and jolting of the stage caused him to fall into a slight slumber, and when he awoke he found his two neighbours had just got out at a wayside station. They had evidently not cared to waken him to say "Good-bye." From the conversation of the other passengers he learned that the tall man was a well-known gambler, and the one who looked like a farmer was a ship captain who had become a wealthy merchant. Clarence thought he understood now why the latter had asked him if he came off a voyage, and that the nickname of "Commodore" given to him, Clarence, was some joke intended for the captain's understanding. He missed them, for he wanted to talk to them about his relative at Sacramento whom he was now so soon to see. At last, between sleeping and waking, the end of his journey was unexpectedly reached. It was dark, but, being "steamer night," the shops and business places were still open, and Mr. Peyton had arranged that the stage driver should deliver Clarence at the address of his relative in "J. Street," an address which Clarence had luckily remembered. But the boy was somewhat discomfited to find that it was a large office or banking-house. He, however, descended from the stage, and, with his small pack in his hand, entered the building as the stage drove off, and addressing one of the busy clerks, asked for "Mr. Jackson Brant."

There was no such person in the office. There never had been any such person. The bank had always occupied that building. Was there not some mistake in the number?

No! the name, number, and street had been deeply engrafted in the boy's recollection. Stop! it might be the name of a customer who had given his address at the bank. The clerk who made this suggestion disappeared promptly to make inquiries in the counting-room. Clarence, with a rapidly-beating heart, awaited him. The clerk returned. There was no such name on the books. Jackson Brant was utterly unknown to every one in the establishment.

For an instant the counter against which the boy was leaning seemed to yield with his weight; he was obliged to steady himself with both hands to keep from falling. It was not his disappointment— which was terrible; it was not a thought of his future—which seemed hopeless; it was not his injured pride at appearing to have wilfully deceived Mr. Peyton—which was more dreadful than all these—but it was the sudden, sickening sense that *he* himself had been deceived, tricked, and fooled! For it flashed upon him for the first time that the vague sense of wrong which had always haunted him was this—that this was the vile culmination of a plan to *get rid of him,* and that he had been deliberately lost and led astray by his relatives as helplessly and completely as a useless cat or dog!

Perhaps there was something of this in his face, for the clerk, staring at him, bade him sit down for a moment, and again vanished into the mysterious interior. Clarence had no conception how long he was absent, or indeed of anything but his own breathless thoughts, for he was conscious of wondering afterwards why the clerk was leading him through a door in the counter into an inner room of many desks, and again through a glass door into a smaller office where a preternaturally busy-looking man sat writing at a desk. Without looking up, but pausing only to apply a blotting-pad to the paper before him, the man said crisply—

"So you've been consigned to some one who don't seem to turn up, and can't be found, eh? Never mind that," as Clarence laid Peyton's letter before him. "Can't read it now. Well, I suppose you want to be shipped back to Stockton?"

"No!" said the boy, recovering his voice with an effort.

"Eh, that's business though. Know anybody here?"

"Not a living soul; that's why they sent me," said the boy, in sudden reckless desperation. He was the more furious that he knew the tears were standing in his eyes.

The idea seemed to strike the man amusingly. "Looks a little like it, don't it?" he said, smiling grimly at the paper before him. "Got any money?"

"A little."

"How much?"

"About twenty dollars," said Clarence hesitatingly.

The man opened a small drawer at his side, mechanically, for he did not raise his eyes, and took out two ten-dollar gold pieces. "I'll go twenty better," he said, laying them down on the desk. "That'll give you a chance to look around. Come back here, if you don't see your way clear." He dipped his pen into the ink with a significant gesture as if closing the interview.

Clarence pushed back the coin. "I'm not a beggar," he said doggedly.

The man this time raised his head and surveyed the boy with two keen eyes. "You're not, hey? Well, do I look like one?"

"No," stammered Clarence, as he glanced into the man's haughty eyes.

"Yet, if I were in your fix, I'd take that money and be glad to get it."

"If you'll let me pay you back again," said Clarence, a little ashamed, and considerably frightened at his implied accusation of the man before him.

"You can," said the man, bending over his desk again.

Clarence took up the money and awkwardly drew out his purse. But it was the first time he had touched it since it was returned to him in the bar-room, and it struck him that it was heavy and full—indeed, so full that on opening it a few coins rolled out on to the floor. The man looked up abruptly.

"I thought you said you had only twenty dollars?" he remarked grimly.

"Mr. Peyton gave me forty," returned Clarence, stupefied and blushing. "I spent twenty dollars for drinks at the bar—and," he stammered, "I—I—I don't know how the rest came here."

"You spent twenty dollars for *drinks?*" said the man, laying down his pen and leaning back in his chair to gaze at the boy.

"Yes—that is—I treated some gentlemen of the stage, sir, at Davidson's Crossing."

"Did you treat the whole stage company?"

"No, sir, only about four or five—and the bar-keeper. But everything's so dear in California. *I* know that."

"Evidently. But it don't seem to make much difference with *you,*" said the man, glancing at the purse.

"They wanted my purse to look at," said Clarence hurriedly, "and that's how the thing happened. Somebody put *his own money* back into *my* purse by accident."

"Of course," said the man grimly.

"Yes, that's the reason," said Clarence, a little relieved, but somewhat embarrassed by the man's persistent eyes.

"Then, of course," said the other quietly, "you don't require my twenty dollars now."

"But," returned Clarence hesitatingly, "this isn't *my* money. I must find out who it belongs to, and give it back again. Perhaps," he added timidly, "I might leave it here with you, and call for it when I find the man, and send him here."

With the greatest gravity he here separated the surplus from what was left of Peyton's gift and the twenty dollars he had just received. The balance unaccounted for was forty dollars. He laid it on the desk before the man, who, still looking at him, rose and opened the door.

"Mr. Reed."

The clerk who had shown Clarence in appeared.

"Open an account with"——He stopped and turned interrogatively to Clarence.

"Clarence Brant," said Clarence, colouring with excitement.

"With Clarence Brant. Take that deposit," pointing to the money, "and give him a receipt." He paused, as the clerk retired with a wondering gaze at the money, looked again at Clarence, said, "I think *you'll* do," and re-entered the private office, closing the door behind him.

I hope it will not be deemed inconceivable that Clarence, only a few moments before crushed with bitter disappointment and the hopeless revelations of his abandonment by his relatives, now felt himself lifted up suddenly into an imaginary height of independence and manhood! He was leaving the bank in which he stood a minute before a friendless boy—not as a successful beggar, for this important man had disclaimed the idea, but absolutely as a customer! a depositor! a business man like the grown-up clients who were thronging the outer office, and before the eyes of the clerk who had pitied him! And he, Clarence, had been spoken to by this man, whose name he now recognized as the one that was on the door of the building—a man of whom his fellow-passengers had spoken of with admiring envy—a banker famous in all California! Will it be deemed incredible that this imaginative and hopeful boy, forgetting all else, the object of his visit, and even the fact that he considered this money was not his own, actually put his hat a little on one side as he strolled out on his way to the streets and perspective fortune?

Two hours later the banker had another visitor. It chanced to be the farmer-looking man who had been Clarence's fellow-passenger. Evidently a privileged person, he was at once ushered as "Captain Stevens" into the presence of the banker. At the end of a familiar business interview the captain asked carelessly—

"Any letters for me?"

The busy banker pointed with his pen to the letter "S" in a row of alphabetically labelled pigeon-holes against the wall. The captain, having selected his correspondence, paused with a letter in his hand.

"Look here, Carden, there are letters here for some chap called 'John Silsbee.' They were here when I called—ten weeks ago."

"Well?"

"That's the name of that Pike County man who was killed by Injins in the plains. The 'Frisco papers had all the particulars last night; may be it's for that fellow. It hasn't got a postmark. Who left it here?"

Mr. Carden summoned a clerk. It appeared that the letter had been left by a certain Brant Fanquier to be called for.

Captain Stevens smiled. "Brant's been too busy dealin' faro to think of 'em agin, and since that shootin' affair at Angels' I hear he's skipped to the southern coast somewhere. Cal Johnson, his old chum, was in the up-stage from Stockton this afternoon."

"Did you come by the up-stage from Stockton this afternoon?" said Carden, looking up.

"Yes, as far as Ten-mile Station—rode the rest of the way here."

"Did you notice a queer little old-fashioned kid—about so high—like a runaway schoolboy?"

"Did I? By G—d, sir, he treated me to drinks."

Carden jumped from his chair. "Then he wasn't lying!"

"No! We let him do it—but we made it good for the little chap afterwards. Hello! What's up?"

But Mr. Carden was already in the outer office beside the clerk who had admitted Clarence.

"You remember that boy Brant who was here?"

"Yes, sir."

"Where did he go?"

"Don't know, sir."

"Go and find him somewhere and somehow. Go to all the hotels, restaurants, and gin-mills near here, and hunt him up. Take some one with you—if you can't do it alone. Bring him back here, quick!"

It was nearly midnight when the clerk fruitlessly returned. It was the fierce high noon of "steamer night;" lights flashed brilliantly from shops, counting-houses, drinking-saloons, and gambling-hells. The streets were yet full of eager, hurrying feet, swift to fortune, ambition, pleasure, or crime. But from among these deeper, harsher footfalls, the echo of the homeless boy's light, innocent tread seemed to have died out for ever.

Chapter VIII

When Clarence was once more in the busy street before the bank, it seemed clear to his boyish mind that, being now cast adrift upon the world and responsible to no one, there was no reason why he should not at once proceed to the nearest gold-mines! The idea of returning to Mr. Peyton and Susy, as a disowned and abandoned outcast, was not to be thought of. He would purchase some kind of an outfit, such as he had seen the miners carry, and start off as soon as he had got his supper. But although one of his most delightful anticipations had been the unfettered freedom of ordering a meal at a restaurant, on entering the first one he found himself the object of so much curiosity, partly from his size and partly from his dress, which the unfortunate boy was beginning to suspect was really preposterous, that he turned away with a stammered excuse, and did not try another. Further on he found a baker's shop, where he refreshed himself with some gingerbread and lemon soda. At an adjacent grocery he purchased some herrings, smoked beef, and biscuits, as future provisions for his "pack" or kit. Then began his real quest for an outfit. In an hour he had secured— ostensibly for some friend, to avoid curious inquiry—a pan, a blanket, a shovel and pick, all of which he deposited at the baker's—his unostentatious headquarters—with the exception of a pair of disguising high boots that half hid his sailor trousers, which he kept to put on at the last. Even to his inexperience the cost of these articles seemed enormous; when his purchases were complete, of his entire capital scarcely four dollars remained! Yet in the fond illusions of boyhood these rude appointments seemed possessed of far more value than the gold he had given in exchange for them, and he had enjoyed a child's delight in testing the transforming magic of money.

Meanwhile the feverish contact of the crowded street had, strange to say, increased his loneliness, while the ruder joviality of its dissipations began to fill him with a vague uneasiness; the passing glimpse of dancing halls and gaudily whirling figures that seemed only feminine in their apparel; the shouts and boisterous choruses from concert rooms; the groups of drunken roysterers that congregated around the doors of saloons or hilariously charging down the streets, elbowed him against the wall, or humorously insisted on his company, discomposed and frightened him. He had known rude companionship before, but it was serious, practical, and under control. There was something in this vulgar degradation of intellect and power—qualities that Clarence had always boyishly worshipped—which sickened and disillusioned him. Later on a pistol shot in a crowd beyond, the rush of eager men past him, the disclosure of a limp and helpless figure against the wall, the closing of the crowd again around it, although it stirred him with a fearful curiosity, actually shocked him less hopelessly than their brutish enjoyments and abandonment.

It was in one of these rushes that he had been crushed against a swinging door, which, giving way to his pressure, disclosed to his wondering eyes a long, glitteringly-adorned, and brightly-lit room, densely filled with a silent, attentive throng in attitudes of decorous abstraction and preoccupation, that even the shouts and tumult at its very doors could not disturb. Men of all ranks and conditions, plainly or elaborately clad, were grouped together under this magic spell of silence and attention. The tables before them were covered with cards and loose heaps of gold and silver. A clicking, the rattling of an ivory ball, and the frequent, formal, lazy reiteration of some unintelligible sentence was all that he heard. But by a sudden instinct he *understood* it all. It was a gambling saloon!

Encouraged by the decorous stillness, and the fact that everybody appeared too much engaged to notice him, the boy drew timidly beside one of the tables. It was covered with a number of cards, on which were placed certain sums of money. Looking down, Clarence saw that he was standing before a card that as yet had nothing on it. A single player at his side looked up, glanced at Clarence curiously, and then placed half-a-dozen gold pieces on the vacant card. Absorbed in the general aspect of the room and the players, Clarence did not notice that his neighbour won twice, and even *thrice,* upon that card. Becoming aware, however, that the player, while gathering in his gains, was smilingly regarding him, he moved in some embarrassment to the other end of the table where there seemed another gap in the crowd. It so chanced that here was also another vacant card. The previous neighbour of Clarence instantly shoved a sum of money across the table on the vacant card and won. At this the other players began to regard Clarence singularly, one or two of the spectators smiled, and the boy, colouring, moved awkwardly away. But his sleeve was caught by the successful player, who, detaining him gently, put three gold pieces into his hand.

"That's *your* share, sonny," he whispered.

"Share—for what?" stammered the astounded Clarence.

"For bringing me 'the luck,'" said the man.

Clarence stared. "Am I—to—to play with it?" he said, glancing at the coins and then at the table, in ignorance of the stranger's meaning.

"No, no!" said the man hurriedly, "don't do that. You'll lose it, sonny, sure! Don't you see *you bring the luck to others,* not to yourself. Keep it, old man, and run home!"

"I don't want it! I won't have it!" said Clarence, with a swift recollection of the manipulation of his purse that morning, and a sudden distrust of all mankind.

"There!" He turned back to the table and laid the money on the first vacant card he saw. In another moment, as it seemed to him, it was raked away by the dealer. A sense of relief came over him.

"There," said the man with an awed voice, and a strange fatuous look in his eye. "What did I tell you? You see, it's allus so! Now," he added roughly, "get up and get out o' this, afore you lose the boots and shirt off ye."

Clarence did not wait for a second command. With another glance round the room, he began to make his way through the crowd towards the front. But in that parting glance he caught a glimpse of a woman presiding over a "wheel of fortune" in a corner, whose face seemed familiar. He looked again timidly. In spite of an extraordinary headdress or crown that she wore as the "Goddess of Fortune," he recognised, twisted in its tinsel, a certain scarlet vine which he had seen before; in spite of the hoarse formula which she was continually repeating, he recognised the foreign accent. It was the woman of the stage-coach! With a sudden dread that she might recognise him, and likewise demand his services "for luck," he turned and fled.

Once more in the open air, there came upon him a vague loathing and horror of the restless madness and feverish distraction of this half-civilised city. It was the more powerful that it was vague, and the outcome of some inward instinct. He found himself longing for the pure air and sympathetic loneliness of the plains and wilderness; he began to yearn for the companionship of his humble associates—the teamster, the scout Gildersleeve, and even Jim Hooker. But above all, and before all, was the wild desire to get away from these maddening streets and their bewildering occupants. He ran back to the baker's, gathered his purchases together, took advantage of a friendly doorway to strap them on his boyish shoulders, slipped into a side street, and struck out at once for the outskirts.

It had been his first intention to take stage to the nearest mining district, but the diminution of his small capital forbade that outlay, and he decided to walk there by the highroad, of whose general direction he had informed himself. In half-an-hour the lights of the flat, struggling city, and their reflection in the shallow turbid river before it, had sunk well behind him. The air was cool and soft; a yellow moon swam in the slight haze that rose above the *tules*, in the distance a few scattered cottonwoods and sycamores marked like sentinels the road. When he had walked some distance he sat down beneath one of them, made a frugal supper from the dry rations in his pack, but in the absence of any spring he was forced to quench his thirst with a glass of water in a wayside tavern. Here he was good-humouredly offered something stronger, which he declined, and replied to certain curious interrogations by saying that he expected to overtake his friends in a waggon further on. A new distrust of mankind had begun to make the boy an adept in innocent falsehood, the more deceptive as his careless, cheerful manner, the result of his relief at leaving the city, and his perfect ease in the loving companionship of night and nature, certainly gave no indication of his homelessness and poverty.

It was long past midnight when, weary in body, but still hopeful and happy in mind, he turned off the dusty road into a vast rolling expanse of wild oats, with the same sense of security of rest as a traveller to his inn. Here, completely screened from view by the tall stalks of grain that rose thickly around him to the height of a man's shoulder, he beat down a few of them for a bed on which he deposited his blanket. Placing his pack for a pillow, he curled himself up in his blanket, and speedily fell asleep.

He awoke at sunrise refreshed, invigorated, and hungry. But he was forced to defer his first self-prepared breakfast until he had reached water, and a less dangerous place than the wild oat field to build his first camp-fire. This he found a mile further on, near some dwarf willows on the bank of a half-dry stream. Of his various efforts to prepare his first meal, the fire was the most successful; the coffee was somewhat too substantially thick, and the bacon and herring lacked definiteness of quality from having been cooked in the same vessel. In this boyish picnic he missed Susy, and recalled, perhaps a little bitterly, her coldness at parting. But the novelty of his situation, the brilliant sunshine, and sense of freedom, and the road already awakening to dusty life with passing teams, dismissed anything but the future from his mind. Readjusting his pack, he stepped on cheerily. At noon he was overtaken by a teamster, who in return for a match to light his pipe gave him a lift of a dozen miles. It is to be feared that Clarence's account of himself was equally fanciful with his previous story, and that the teamster parted from him with a genuine regret, and a hope that he would soon be overtaken by his friends along the road. "And mind that you ain't such a fool agin to let 'em make you tote their dodd—blasted tools fur them!" he added unsuspectingly, pointing to Clarence's mining outfit. Thus saved the heaviest part of the day's journey, for the road was continually rising from the plains during the last six miles, Clarence was able yet to cover a considerable distance on foot before he halted for supper. Here he was again fortunate. An empty lumber team watering at the same spring, its driver offered to take Clarence's purchases—for the boy had profited by his late friend's suggestion to personally detach himself from his equipment—to Buck-eye Mills for a dollar, which would also include a "shakedown pas-sage" for himself on the floor of the waggon. "I reckon you've been foolin' away in Sacramento the money yer parents give yer fur return stage fare, eh? Don't lie, sonny," he added grimly, as the now artful Clarence smiled diplomatically. "I've been thar myself!" Luckily the excuse that he was "tired and sleepy" prevented further dangerous questioning, and the boy was soon really in deep slumber on the wag-gon floor.

He awoke betimes to find himself already in the mountains. Buckeye Mills was a straggling settlement, and Clarence prudently stopped any embarrassing inquiry from his friend by dropping off the waggon with his equipment as they entered it, and hurriedly saying "Good-bye" from a cross-road through the woods. He had learned that the nearest mining-camp was five miles away, and its direction was indicated by a long wooden "flume" or water-way that alternately appeared and dis-appeared on the flank of the mountain opposite. The cooler and drier air, the grateful shadow of pine and bay, and the spicy balsamic odours that everywhere greeted him, thrilled and exhilarated him. The trail plunging sometimes into an undisturbed forest, he started the birds before him like a flight of arrows through its dim recesses; at times he hung breathlessly over the blue depths of cañons where the same forests were repeated a thousand feet below. Towards noon he struck into a rude road—evidently the thoroughfare of the locality— and was surprised to find that it—as well as the adjacent soil wherever disturbed—was a deep Indian red! Everywhere; along its sides, powdering the banks and boles of trees with its ruddy stain, in mounds and hillocks of piled dirt on the road, or in liquid paint-like pools, when a trickling stream had formed a gutter across it, there was al-ways the same deep sanguinary colour. Once or twice it became more vivid in contact with the white teeth of quartz that peeped through it from the hillside or crossed the road in crumbled strata. One of those pieces Clarence picked up with a quickened pulse. It was veined and streaked with shining mica and tiny glittering cubes of mineral that *looked* like gold!

The road now began to descend towards a winding stream, shrunken by drought and ditching, that glared dazzlingly in the sunlight from its white bars of sand, or glistened in shining sheets and channels. Along its banks, and even encroaching upon its bed, were scattered a few mud cabins, strange-looking wooden troughs and gutters, and here and there, glancing through the leaves, the white canvas of tents. The stumps of felled trees and blackened spaces, as of recent fires, marked the stream on either side. A sudden sense of disappointment overcame Clarence. It looked vulgar, common, and worse than all—*familiar*. It was like the unlovely outskirts of a dozen other prosaic settlements he had seen in less romantic localities. In that muddy red stream, pouring out of a wooden gutter, in which three or four bearded, slouching, half-naked figures were raking like *chiffoniers,* there was nothing to suggest the royal metal. Yet he was so absorbed in gazing at the scene, and had walked so rapidly during the past few minutes, that he was startled on turning a sharp corner of the road to come abruptly upon an outlying dwelling.

It was a nondescript building, half canvas and half boards. The interior, seen through the open door, was fitted up with side shelves, a counter carelessly piled with provisions, groceries, clothing, and hardware—with no attempt at display or even ordinary selection—and a table on which stood a demijohn and three or four dirty glasses. Two roughly-dressed men, whose long matted beards and hair left only their eyes and lips visible in the tangled hirsute wilderness below their slouched hats, were leaning against the opposite sides of the doorway smoking. Almost thrown against them in the rapid momentum of his descent, Clarence halted violently.

"Well, sonny, you needn't capsize the shanty," said the first man, without taking his pipe from his lips.

"If yer looking fur yer ma, she and yer Aunt Jane hev jest gone over to Parson Doolittle's to take tea," observed the second man lazily. "She allowed that you'ld wait."

"I'm—I'm—going to—to the mines," explained Clarence, with some hesitation. "I suppose this is the way."

The two men took their pipes from their lips, looked at each other, completely wiped every vestige of expression from their faces with the back of their hands, turned their eyes into the interior of the cabin, and said "Will yer come yer, now *will* yer?" Thus adjured, half-a-dozen men, also bearded and carrying pipes in their mouths, straggled out of the shanty, and, filing in front of it, squatted down with their backs against the boards and gazed comfortably at the boy. Clarence began to feel uneasy.

"I'll give," said one, taking out his pipe and grimly eyeing Clarence, "a hundred dollars for him as he stands."

"And seein' as he's got that bran-new rig-out o' tools," said another, "I'll give a hundred and fifty—and the drinks. I've been," he added apologetically, "wantin' suthin' like this a long time."

"Well, gen'lemen," said the man who had first spoken to him, "lookin' at him by and large; takin' in, so to speak, the gin'ral gait of him in single harness, bearin' in mind the perfect freshness of him, and the coolness and size of his cheek—the easy downyness, previousness, and utter don't-care-a-damnativeness of his coming yer, I think two hundred ain't too much for him, and we'll call it a bargain."

Clarence's previous experience of this grim, smileless Californian chaff was not calculated to restore his confidence. He drew away from the cabin and repeated doggedly, "I asked you if this was the way to the mines."

"It *are* the mines, and these yere are the miners," said the first speaker gravely. "Permit me to interdoose 'em. This yere's Shasta Jim, this yere's Shortcard Billy, this is Nasty Bob, and this Slumgullion Dick. This yere's the Dook o' Chatham Street, the Livin' Skeleton, and me!"

"May we ask, fair young sir," said the Living Skeleton, who, however, seemed in fairly robust condition, "whence came ye on the wings of the morning, and whose Marble Halls ye hev left desolate?"

"I came across the plains, and got into Stockton two days ago on Mr. Peyton's train," said Clarence indignantly, seeing no reason now to conceal anything. "I came to Sacramento to find my cousin, who isn' living there any more. I don't see anything funny in *that!* I came here to the mines to dig gold—because—because Mr. Silsbee, the man who was to bring me here and might have found my cousin for me, was killed by Indians."

"Hold up, sonny. Let me help ye," said the first speaker, rising to his feet. "*You* didn't get killed by Injins because you got lost out of a train with Silsbee's infant darter. Peyton picked you up while you was takin' care of her, and two days arter you kem up to the broken-down Silsbee waggons, with all the folks lyin' there slartered."

"Yes, sir," said Clarence, breathless with astonishment.

"And," continued the man, putting his hand gravely to his head as if to assist his memory, "when you was all alone on the plains with that little child, you saw one of those redskins, as near to you as I be, watchin' the train, and you didn't breathe or move while he was there?"

"Yes, sir," said Clarence eagerly.

"And you was shot at by Peyton, he thinkin' you was an Injin in the mesquite grass? And you once shot a buffalo that had been pitched with you down a gully—all by yourself?"

"Yes," said Clarence, crimson with wonder and pleasure. "You know me, then?"

"Well, ye-e-es," said the man gravely, parting his moustache with his fingers. "You see, *you've been here before.*"

"Before! Me?" repeated the astounded Clarence.

"Yes, before. Last night. You was taller then, and hadn't cut your hair. You cursed a good deal more than you do now. You drank a man's share of whisky, and you borrowed fifty dollars to get to Sacramento with. I reckon you haven't got it about you now, eh?"

Clarence's brain reeled in utter confusion and hopeless terror.

Was he going crazy, or had these cruel men learned his story from his faithless friends, and this was a part of the plot? He staggered forward, but the men had risen and quickly encircled him, as if to prevent his escape. In vague and helpless desperation he gasped—

"What place is this?"

"Folks call it Deadman's Gulch."

Deadman's Gulch! A flash of intelligence lit up the boy's blind confusion. Deadman's Gulch! Could it have been Jim Hooker who had really run away, and had taken his name? He turned half-imploringly to the first speaker.

"Wasn't he older than me and bigger? Didn't he have a smooth, round face, and little eyes? Didn't he talk hoarse? Didn't he"——he stopped hopelessly.

"Yes; oh, he wasn't a bit like you," said the man musingly. "Ye see, that's the h-ll of it! You're altogether *too many* and *too various* fur this camp."

"I don't know who's been here before, or what they have said," said Clarence desperately—yet even in that desperation retaining the dogged loyalty to his old playmate which was part of his nature. "I don't know, and I don't care—there! I'm Clarence Brant, of Kentucky; I started in Silsbee's train from St. Jo., and I'm going to the mines, and you can't stop me!"

The man who had first spoken started, looked keenly at Clarence, and then turned to the others. The gentleman known as the Living Skeleton had obtruded his huge bulk in front of the boy, and, gazing at him, said reflectively, "Darned if it don't look like one of Brant's pups—sure!"

"Air ye any relation to Kernel Hamilton Brant, of Looeyville?" asked the first speaker.

Again that old question! Poor Clarence hesitated despairingly. Was he to go through the same cross-examination he had undergone with the Peytons? "Yes," he said doggedly, "I am—but he's dead. And you know it."

"Dead—of course." "Sartin." "He's dead." "The Kernel's planted," said the men in chorus.

"Well, yes," reflected the Living Skeleton ostentatiously, as one who spoke from experience. "Ham Brant's about as bony now as they make 'em." "You bet! About the dustiest, deadest corpse you kin turn out," corroborated Slumgullion Dick, nodding his head gloomily to the others; "in point o' fack, es a corpse, about the last one I should keer to go huntin' fur."

"The Kernel's tech 'ud be cold and clammy!" concluded the Duke of Chatham Street, who had not yet spoken, "sure. But what did yer mammy say about it? Is she gettin' married agin? Did *she* send ye here?"

It seemed to Clarence that the Duke of Chatham Street here received a kick from his companions; but the boy repeated doggedly—

"I came to Sacramento to find my cousin, Jackson Brant; but he wasn't there."

"Jackson Brant!" echoed the first speaker, glancing at the others. "Did your mother say he was your cousin?"

"Yes," said Clarence wearily. "Good-bye."

"Hullo, sonny, where are you going?"

"To dig gold," said the boy. "And you know you can't prevent me, if it isn't on your claim. I know the law." He had heard Mr. Peyton discuss it at Stockton, and he fancied that the men, who were whispering among themselves, looked kinder than before, and as if they were no longer "acting" to him. The first speaker laid his hand on his shoulder and said, "All right, come with me, and I'll show you where to dig."

"Who are you?" said Clarence. "You call yourself only 'me.' "

"Well, you can call me Flynn—Tom Flynn."

"And you'll show me where I can dig—myself?"

"I will."

"Do you know," said Clarence timidly, yet with a half-conscious smile, "that I—I kinder bring luck?"

The man looked down upon him, and said gravely, but, as it struck Clarence, with a new kind of grávity, "I believe you."

"Yes," said Clarence eagerly, as they walked along together, "I brought luck to a man in Sacramento the other day." And he related with great earnestness his experience in the gambling-saloon. Not content with that—the sealed fountains of his childish deep being broken up by some mysterious sympathy—he spoke of his hospitable exploit with the passengers at the wayside bar, of the finding of his Fortunatus purse, and his deposit at the bank. Whether that characteristic old-fashioned reticence which had been such an important factor for good or ill in his future had suddenly deserted him, or whether some extraordinary prepossession in his companion had affected him, he did not know: but by the time the pair had reached the hillside, Flynn was in possession of all the boy's history. On one point only was his reserve unshaken. Conscious although he was of Jim Hooker's duplicity, he affected to treat it as a comrade's joke.

They halted at last in the middle of an apparently fertile hillside. Clarence shifted his shovel from his shoulders, unslung his pan, and looked at Flynn. "Dig anywhere here, where you like," said his companion carelessly, "and you'll be sure to find the colour. Fill your pan with the dirt, go to that sluice, and let the water run in on the top of the pan—workin' it round so"—he added, illustrating a rotary motion with the vessel. "Keep doing that until all the soil is washed out of it, and you have only the black sand at the bottom. Then work that the same way until you see the colour. Don't be afraid of washing the gold out of the pan—you couldn't do it if you tried. There, I'll leave you here, and you wait till I come back." With another grave nod and something like a smile in the only visible part of his bearded face—his eyes—he strode rapidly away.

Clarence did not lose time. Selecting a spot where the grass was less thick he broke through the soil and turned up two or three spadefuls of red soil. When he had filled the pan and raised it to his shoulder he was astounded at its weight. He did not know that it was due to the red precipitate of iron that gave it its colour. Staggering along with his burden to the running sluice—which looked like an open wooden gutter—at the foot of the hill be began to carefully carry out Flynn's direction. The first dip of the pan in the running water carried off half the contents of the pan in liquid paint-like ooze. For a moment he gave way to boyish satisfaction in the sight and touch of this unctuous solution, and dabbled his fingers in it. A few moments more of rinsing and he came to the sediment of fine black sand that was beneath it. Another plunge and swilling of water in the pan, and—could he believe his eyes!—a few yellow tiny scales, scarcely larger than pins' heads, glittered among the sand. He poured it off. But his companion was right; the lighter sand shifted from side to side with the water, but the glittering points remained adhering by their own tiny specific gravity to the smooth surface of the bottom. It was "the colour"—Gold!

Clarence's heart seemed to give a great leap within him. A vision of wealth, of independence, of power, sprang before his dazzled eyes, and —a hand lightly touched him on the shoulder.

He started! In his complete preoccupation and excitement he had not heard the clatter of horse-hoofs, and to his amazement Flynn was already beside him, mounted, and leading a second horse.

"You kin ride," he said shortly.

"Yes," stammered Clarence; "but"——

"*But*—we've only got two hours to reach Buckeye Mills in time to catch the down stage. Drop all that, jump up, and come with me!"

"But I've just found gold," said the boy excitedly.

"And I've just found your—cousin. Come!"

He spurred his horse across Clarence's scattered implements, half helped, half lifted the boy into the saddle of the second horse, and with a cut of his riata over the animal's haunches, the next moment they were both galloping furiously away.

Chapter IX

Torn suddenly from his prospective future, but too much dominated by the man beside him to protest, Clarence was silent until a rise in the road a few minutes later partly abated their headlong speed, and gave him chance to recover his breath and courage.

"Where is my cousin?" he asked.

"In the southern county, two hundred miles from here."

"Are we going to him?"

"Yes."

They rode furiously forward again. It was nearly half-an-hour before they came to a longer ascent. Clarence could see that Flynn was from time to time examining him curiously under his slouched hat. This somewhat embarrassed him, but in his singular confidence in the man no distrust mingled with it.

"Ye never saw your—cousin?" he asked.

"No," said Clarence; "nor he me. I don't think he knew me much, anyway."

"How old mout ye be, Clarence?"

"Twelve."

"Well, as you're suthin' of a pup"—Clarence started, and recalled Peyton's first criticism of him—"I reckon to tell ye suthin'! Ye aint goin' to be skeert, or afeard, or lose yer sand, I kalkilate, for skunkin' aint in your breed. Well, wot ef I told ye that thish yer—thish yer—*cousin* o' yours was the biggest devil onhung!—that he'd just killed a man, and had to lite out elsewhere? And *thet's* why he didn't show up in Sacramento! What if I told you that?"

Clarence felt that this was somehow a little too much! He was perfectly truthful, and therefore lifting his frank eyes to Flynn, he said—

"I should think you were talking a good deal like Jim Hooker!"

His companion stared, and suddenly reined up his horse, then bursting into a shout of laughter he galloped ahead, from time to time shaking his head, slapping his legs, and making the dim woods ring with his boisterous mirth. Then as suddenly becoming thoughtful again he rode off rapidly for half-an-hour, only speaking to Clarence to urge him forward, and assisting his progress by lashing the haunches of his horse. Luckily the boy was a good rider—a fact which Flynn seemed to thoroughly appreciate—or he would have been unseated a dozen times.

At last the straggling sheds of Buckeye Mills came into softer purple view on the opposite mountain. Then laying his hand on Clarence's shoulder as he reined in at his side, Flynn broke the silence.

"There, boy," he said, wiping the mirthful tears from his eyes. "I was only foolin'—only trying yer grit! This yer cousin I'm taking you to ez as quiet and soft-spoken and as old-fashioned ez you be. Why, he's that wrapped up in books and study that he lives alone in a big *adobe rancherie* among a lot o' Spanish, and he don't keer to see his own countrymen! Why, he's even changed his name, and calls himself Don Juan Robinson! But he's very rich; he owns three leagues of land and heaps of cattle and horses, and," glancing approvingly at Clarence's seat in the saddle, "I reckon you'll hev plenty of fun thar."

"But," hesitated Clarence—to whom this proposal seemed only a repetition of Peyton's charitable offer—"I think I'd better stay here and dig gold—*with you.*"

"And I think you'd better not," said the man, with a gravity that was very like a settled determination.

"But my cousin never came for me to Sacramento—nor sent, nor even wrote," persisted Clarence indignantly.

"Not to *you,* boy; but he wrote to the man whom he reckoned would bring you there—Jack Silsbee—and left it in the care of the bank. And Silsbee, being dead, didn't come for the letter; and as you didn't ask for it when you came, and didn't even mention Silsbee's name, that same letter was sent back to your cousin through me, because the bank thought we knew his whereabouts. It came to the gulch by an express rider, whilst you were prospecting, on the hillside. Rememberin' your story I took the liberty of opening it, and found out that your cousin had told Silsbee to bring you straight to him. So, I'm only doin' now what Silsbee would have done."

Any momentary doubt or suspicion that might have arisen in Clarence's mind vanished as he met his companion's steady and masterful eye. Even his disappointment was forgotten in the charm of this new-found friendship and protection. And as its outset had been marked by an unusual burst of confidence on Clarence's part, the boy in his gratitude now felt something of the timid shyness of a deeper feeling, and once more became reticent.

They were in time to snatch a hasty meal at Buckeye Mills before the stage arrived, and Clarence noticed that his friend, despite his rough dress and lawless aspect, provoked a marked degree of respect from those he met—in which, perhaps, a wholesome fear was mingled. It is certain that the two best places in the stage were given up to them without protest, and that a careless, almost supercilious, invitation to drink from Flynn was responded to with singular alacrity by all—including even two fastidiously-dressed and previously-reserved passengers. I am afraid that Clarence enjoyed this proof of his friend's singular dominance with a boyish pride, and, conscious of the curious eyes of the passengers, directed occasionally to himself, was somewhat ostentatious in his familiarity with this bearded autocrat.

At noon the next day they left the stage at a wayside ride station, and Flynn briefly informed Clarence that they must again take horses. This at first seemed difficult in that out-of-the-way settlement, where they alone had stopped, but a whisper from the driver in the ear of the station-master produced a couple of fiery mustangs with the same accompaniment of cautious awe and mystery. For the next two days they travelled on horseback, resting by night at the lodgings of one or other of Flynn's friends in the outskirts of a large town, where they arrived in the darkness, and left before day. To any one more experienced than the simple-minded boy it would have been evident that Flynn was purposely avoiding the more travelled roads and conveyances; and when they changed horses again the next day's ride was through an apparently unbroken wilderness of scattered wood and rolling plain. Yet to Clarence, with his Pantheistic reliance and joyous sympathy with nature, the change was filled with exhilarating pleasure. The vast seas of tossing wild oats, the hillside still variegated with strange flowers, the virgin freshness of untrodden woods and leafy aisles, whose floors of moss or bark were undisturbed by human footprint, were a keen delight and novelty. More than this, his quick eye, trained perceptions, and frontier knowledge now stood him in good stead. His intuitive sense of distance, instincts of woodcraft, and his unerring detection of those signs, landmarks, and guide-posts of nature, undistinguishable to aught but birds and beasts and some children, were now of the greatest service to his less favoured companion. In this part of their strange pilgrimage it was the boy who took the lead. Flynn, who during the past two days seemed to have fallen into a mood of watchful reserve, nodded his approbation. "This sort of thing's yer best holt, boy," he said. "Men and cities ain't your little game."

At the next stopping-place Clarence had a surprise. They had again entered a town at nightfall, and lodged with another friend of Flynn's in rooms which from vague sounds appeared to be over a gambling-saloon. Clarence woke late in the morning, and descending into the street to mount for the day's journey, was startled to find that Flynn was not on the other horse, but that a well-dressed and handsome stranger had taken his place. But a laugh, and the familiar command, "Jump up, boy," made him look again. It *was* Flynn, but completely shaven of beard and moustache, closely clipped of hair, and in a fastidiously cut suit of black!

"Then you didn't know me?" said Flynn.

"Not till you spoke," replied Clarence.

"So much the better," said his friend sententiously, as he put spurs to his horse. But as they cantered through the street, Clarence, who had already become accustomed to the stranger's hirsute adornment, felt a little more awe of him. The profile of the mouth and chin now exposed to his sidelong glance was hard and stern, and slightly saturnine. Although unable at the time to identify it with anybody he had ever known, it seemed to the imaginative boy to be vaguely connected with some sad experience. But the eyes were thoughtful and kindly, and the boy later believed that if he had been more familiar with the face he would have loved it better. For it was the last and only day he was to see it—as, late that afternoon, after a dusty ride along more travelled highways, they reached their journey's end.

It was a low-walled house, with red-tiled roofs showing against the dark green of venerable pear and fig trees, and a square courtyard in the centre where they had dismounted. A few words in Spanish from Flynn to one of the lounging peons admitted them to a wooden corridor, and thence to a long low room, which to Clarence's eyes seemed literally piled with books and engravings. Here Flynn hurriedly bade him stay while he sought the host in another part of the building. But Clarence did not miss him; indeed, it may be feared, he forgot even the object of their journey in the new sensations that suddenly thronged upon him, and the boyish vista of the future that they seemed to open. He was dazed and intoxicated. He had never seen so many books before; he had never conceived of such lovely pictures. And yet in some vague way he thought he must have dreamt of them at some time. He had mounted a chair, and was gazing spell-bound at an engraving of a sea-fight, when he heard Flynn's voice.

His friend had quietly re-entered the room, in company with an oldish, half-foreign-looking man—evidently his relation. With no helping recollection, with no means of comparison beyond a vague idea that his cousin might look like himself, Clarence stood hopelessly before him. He had already made up his mind that he would have to go through the usual cross-questioning in regard to his father and family; he had even forlornly thought of inventing some innocent details to fill out his imperfect and unsatisfactory recollection. But, glancing up, he was surprised to find that his elderly cousin was as embarrassed as he was. Flynn, as usual, masterfully interposed—

"Of course, ye don't remember each other, and thar ain't much that either of you knows about family matters, I reckon," he said grimly; "and as your cousin calls himself Don Juan Robinson," he added to Clarence, "it's just as well that you let 'Jackson Brant' slide. I know him better than you, but you'll get used to him and he to you soon enough. At least, you'd better," he concluded, with his occasional singular gravity.

As he turned as if to leave the room with Clarence's embarrassed relative—much to that gentleman's apparent relief—the boy looked up at the latter and said timidly—

"May I look at those books?"

His cousin stopped and glanced at him with the first expression of interest he had shown.

"Ah, you read; you like books?"

"Yes," said Clarence. As his cousin remained still looking at him thoughtfully, he added, "My hands are pretty clean, but I can wash them first if you like."

"You may look at them," said Don Juan smilingly; "and as they are old books you can wash your hands afterwards." And, turning to Flynn suddenly with an air of relief, "I tell you what I'll do, I'll teach him Spanish!"

They left the room together, and Clarence turned eagerly to the shelves. They were old books, some indeed very old, queerly bound, and worm-eaten. Some were in foreign languages, but others in clear bold English type, with quaint woodcuts and illustrations. One seemed to be a chronicle of battles and sieges, with pictured representations of combatants spitted with arrows, cleanly lopped off in limb, or toppled over distinctly by visible cannon-shot. He was deep in its perusal when he heard the clatter of horses' hoofs in the courtyard and the voice of Flynn. He ran to the window, and was astonished to see his friend already on horseback taking leave of his host.

For one instant Clarence felt one of those sudden revulsions of feeling common to his age, but which he had always timidly hidden under dogged demeanour. Flynn, his only friend! Flynn, his only boyish confidant! Flynn, his latest hero, was going away and forsaking him without a word of parting! It was true that he had only agreed to take him to his guardian, but still Flynn need not have left him without a word of hope or encouragement! With any one else Clarence would probably have taken refuge in his usual Indian stoicism, but the same feeling that had impelled him to offer Flynn his boyish confidences on their first meeting now overpowered him. He dropped his book, ran out into the corridor, and made his way to the courtyard, just as Flynn galloped out from the arch.

But the boy uttered a despairing shout that reached the rider. He drew rein, wheeled, halted, and sat facing Clarence impatiently. To add to Clarence's embarrassment his cousin had lingered in the corridor, attracted by the interruption, and a peon, lounging in the archway, obsequiously approached Flynn's bridle rein. But the rider waved him off, and, turning sternly to Clarence, said—

"What's the matter now?"

"Nothing," said Clarence, striving to keep back the hot tears that rose in his eyes. "But you were going away without saying 'good-bye.' You've been very kind to me, and—and—I want to thank you!"

A deep flush crossed Flynn's face. Then glancing suspiciously towards the corridor, he said hurriedly—

"Did *he* send you?"

"No, I came myself! I heard you going."

"All right. Good-bye." He leaned forward as if about to take Clarence's outstretched hand, checked himself suddenly with a grim smile, and taking from his pocket a gold coin handed it to the boy.

Clarence took it, tossed it with a proud gesture to the waiting peon, who caught it thankfully, drew back a step from Flynn, and saying, with white cheeks, "I only wanted to say good-bye," dropped his hot eyes to the ground. But it did not seem to be his own voice that had spoken, nor his own self that had prompted the act.

There was a quick interchange of glances between the departing guest and his late host, in which Flynn's eyes flashed with an odd admiring fire, but when Clarence raised his head again he was gone. And as the boy turned back with a broken heart towards the corridor, his cousin laid his hand upon his shoulder.

"*Muy hidalgamente,* Clarence," he said pleasantly. "Yes, we shall make something of you!"

Chapter X

Then followed to Clarence three uneventful years. During that interval he learnt that Jackson Brant, or Don Juan Robinson—for the tie of kinship was the least factor in their relations to each other, and after the departure of Flynn was tacitly ignored by both—was more Spanish than American. An early residence in Lower California, marriage with a rich Mexican widow, who dying childless left him sole heir, and some strange restraining idiosyncrasy of temperament, had quite denationalised him. A bookish recluse, somewhat superfastidious towards his own countrymen, the more Clarence knew him the more singular appeared his acquaintance with Flynn, but as he did not exhibit more communicativeness on this point than upon their own kinship, Clarence finally concluded that it was due to the dominant character of his former friend, and thought no more about it. He entered upon the new life at El Refugio with no disturbing past. Quickly adapting himself to the lazy freedom of this *hacienda* existence, he spent the mornings on horseback ranging the hills among his cousin's cattle, and the afternoons and evenings busied among his cousin's books with equally lawless and undisciplined independence. The easygoing Don Juan, it is true, attempted to make good his rash promise to teach the boy Spanish, and actually set him a few tasks; but in a few weeks the quickwitted Clarence acquired such a colloquial proficiency from his casual acquaintance with vaqueros and small traders that he was glad to leave the matter in his young kinsman's hands. Again, by one of those illogical sequences which make a lifelong reputation depend upon a single trivial act, Clarence's social status was settled for ever at El Refugio Rancho by his picturesque diversion of Flynn's parting gift. The grateful peon, to whom the boy had scornfully tossed the coin, repeated the act, gesture, and spirit of the scene to his companion, and Don Juan's unknown and youthful relation was at once recognised as *hijo de la familia,* and undeniably a hidalgo born and bred. But in the more vivid imagination of feminine El Refugio the incident reached its highest poetic form. "It is true, Mother of God," said Chucha of the Mill; "it was Domingo who himself relates it as it were the Creed. When the American escort has arrived with the young gentleman, this escort, look you, being not of the same quality, he is departing again without a word of permission. Comes to him at this moment my little hidalgo. 'You have yourself forgotten to take from me your demission,' he said. This escort, thinking to make his peace with a mere *muchacho,* gives to him a gold piece of 20 pesos. The little hidalgo has taken it *so,* and with the words, 'Ah! you would make of me your almoner to my cousin's people,' has given it at the moment to Domingo, and with a grace and fire admirable." But it is certain that

134

Clarence's singular simplicity and truthfulness, a faculty of being picturesquely indolent in a way that suggested a dreamy abstraction of mind, rather than any vulgar tendency to bodily ease and comfort, and possibly the fact that he was a good horseman, made him a popular hero at El Refugio. At the end of three years Don Juan found that this inexperienced and apparently idle boy of fourteen knew more of the practical ruling of the ranche than he did himself. Also that this unlettered young rustic had devoured nearly all the books in his library with boyish recklessness of digestion. He found, too, that in spite of his singular independence of action, Clarence was possessed of an invincible loyalty of principle, and that, asking no sentimental affection, and indeed yielding none, he was, without presuming on his relationship, devoted to his cousin's interest. It seemed that from being a glancing ray of sunshine in the house, evasive but never obtrusive, he had become a daily necessity of comfort and security to his benefactor.

Clarence was, however, astonished when one morning, Don Juan, with the same embarrassed manner he had shown at their first meeting, suddenly asked him "what business he expected to follow." It seemed the more singular, as the speaker, like most abstracted men, had hitherto always studiously ignored the future in their daily intercourse. Yet this might have been either the habit of security or the caution of doubt. Whatever it was, it was some sudden disturbance of Don Juan's equanimity, as disconcerting to himself as it was to Clarence. So conscious was the boy of this, that without replying to his cousin's question, but striving in vain to recall some delinquency of his own, he asked with his usual boyish directness—

"Has anything happened? Have I done anything wrong?"

"No, no," returned Don Juan hurriedly. "But, you see, it's time that you should think of your future—or at least prepare for it. I mean you ought to have some more regular education. You will have to go to school. It's too bad," he added fretfully, with a certain impatient forgetfulness of Clarence's presence, and as if following his one thought. "Just as you are becoming of service to me, and justifying your ridiculous position here—and all this d——d nonsense that's gone before—I mean, of course, Clarence," he interrupted himself, catching sight of the boy's whitening cheek and darkening eye, "I mean, you know—this ridiculousness of my keeping you from school at your age, and trying to teach you myself—don't you see."

"You think it is—ridiculous," repeated Clarence with dogged persistency.

"I mean *I* am ridiculous," said Don Juan hastily—"There! there!—let's say no more about it. To-morrow we'll ride over to San José and see the Father Secretary at the Jesuits' College about your entering at once. It's a good school, and you'll always be near the rancho!" And so the interview ended.

I am afraid that Clarence's first idea was to run away. There are few experiences more crushing to an ingenuous nature than the sudden revelation of the aspect in which it is regarded by others. The unfortunate Clarence, conscious only of his loyalty to his cousin's interest, and what he believed were the duties of his position, awoke to find that position "ridiculous." In an afternoon's gloomy ride through the lonely hills, and later in the sleepless solitude of his room at night, he concluded that his cousin was right. He would go to school—he would study hard—so hard that in a little—a very little while—he could make a living for himself. He awoke contented. It was the blessing of youth that this resolve and execution seemed as one and the same thing.

The next day found him installed as a pupil and boarder in the college. Don Juan's position and Spanish predilections naturally made his relation acceptable to the faculty; but Clarence could not help perceiving that Father Sobriente, the Principal, regarded him at times with a thoughtful curiosity that made him suspect that his cousin had especially bespoken that attention, and that he occasionally questioned him on his antecedents in a way that made him dread a renewal of the old questioning about his progenitor. For the rest, he was a polished, cultivated man; yet, in the characteristic, material criticism of youth, I am afraid that Clarence chiefly identified him as a priest with large hands, whose soft palms seemed to be cushioned with kindness, and whose equally large feet, encased in extraordinary shapeless shoes of undyed leather, seemed to tread down noiselessly—rather than to ostentatiously crush—the obstacles that beset the path of the young student. In the cloistered galleries of the courtyard Clarence sometimes felt himself borne down by the protecting weight of this paternal hand; in the midnight silence of the dormitory he fancied he was often conscious of the soft browsing tread and snuffly muffled breathing of his elephantine-footed mentor.

His relations with his schoolfellows, however, were at first far from pleasant. Whether they suspected favouritism; whether they resented that old and unsympathetic manner which sprang from his habits of association with his elders, or whether they rested their objections on the broader grounds of his being a stranger, I do not know, but they presently passed from cruel sneers to physical opposition. It was then found that this gentle and reserved youth had retained certain objectionable, rude, direct, rustic qualities of fist and foot, and that violating all rules and disdaining the pomp and circumstance of schoolboy warfare, of which he knew nothing—he simply thrashed a few of his equals out of hand, with or without ceremony, as the occasion or the insult happened. In this emergency one of the seniors was selected to teach this youthful savage his proper position. A challenge was given and accepted by Clarence with a feverish alacrity that surprised himself as much as his adversary. This was a youth of eighteen, his superior in size and skill. The first blow bathed Clarence's face in his own blood. But the sanguinary chrism, to the alarm of the spectators, effected an instantaneous and unhallowed change in the boy. Instantly closing with his adversary, he sprang at his throat like an animal, and locking his arm around his neck began to strangle him. Blind to the blows that rained upon him, he eventually bore his staggering enemy by sheer onset and surprise to the earth. Amidst the general alarm the strength of half-a-dozen hastily-summoned teachers was necessary to unlock his hold. Even then he struggled to renew the conflict. But his adversary had disappeared, and from that day forward Clarence was never again molested!

Seated before Father Sobriente, in the infirmary, with swollen and bandaged face, and eyes that still seemed to see everything in the murky light of his own blood, Clarence felt the soft weight of the father's hand upon his knee.

"My son," said the priest gently, "you are not of our religion, or I should claim as a right to ask a question of your own heart at this moment. But as to a good friend, Claro, a good friend," he continued, patting the boy's knee, "you will tell me, old Father Sobriente, frankly and truthfully as is your habit, one little thing. Were you not afraid?"

"No," said Clarence doggedly, "I'll lick him again tomorrow."

"Softly, my son! It was not of *him* I speak, but of something more terrible and awful. Were you not afraid of—of"—he paused, and suddenly darting his clear eyes into the very depths of Clarence's soul, added—"of *yourself!*"

The boy started, shuddered, and burst into tears. "So, so," said the priest gently, "we have found our real enemy. Good! Now, by the grace of God, my little warrior, we shall fight *him* and conquer."

Whether Clarence profited by this lesson, or whether this brief exhibition of his quality prevented any repetition of the cause, the episode was soon forgotten. As his schoolfellows had never been his associates or confidants it mattered little to him whether they feared, respected him, or were hypocritically obsequious after the fashion of the weaker. His studies, at all events, profited by this lack of distraction. Already his two years of desultory and omnivorous reading had given him a facile familiarity with many things, which left him utterly free of the timidity, awkwardness, or non-interest of a beginner. His usually reserved manner, which had been lack of expression rather than of conviction, had deceived his tutors. The audacity of a mind that had never been dominated by others, and owed no allegiance to precedent, made his merely superficial progress something marvellous.

At the end of the first year he was a phenomenal scholar, who seemed capable of anything. Nevertheless, Father Sobriente had an interview with Don Juan, and as a result Clarence was slightly kept back in his studies, a little more freedom from the rules was conceded to him, and he was even encouraged to take some diversion. Of such was the privilege to visit the neighbouring town of Santa Clara un-restricted and unattended. He had always been liberally furnished with pocket-money, for which in his companionless state and Spartan hab-its he had a singular and unboyish contempt. Nevertheless, he always appeared dressed with scrupulous neatness, and was rather distin-guished-looking in his older reserve and melancholy self-reliance.

Lounging one afternoon along the Alameda, a leafy avenue set out by the early Mission Fathers between the village of San José and the convent of Santa Clara, he saw a double file of young girls from the convent approaching on their usual promenade. A view of this proces-sion being the fondest ambition of the San José collegian, and espe-cially interdicted and circumvented by the good Fathers attending the college excursions, Clarence felt for it the profound indifference of a boy who, in the intermediate temperate zone of fifteen years, thinks that he is no longer young and romantic! He was passing them with a careless glance, when a pair of deep violet eyes caught his own under the broad shade of a coquettishly beribboned hat, even as it had once looked at him from the depths of a calico sun-bonnet. Susy! He started and would have spoken, but with a quick little gesture of caution and a meaning glance at the two nuns who walked at the head and foot of the file, she indicated him to follow. He did so at a respectful distance —albeit wondering. A little further on Susy dropped her handkerchief, and was obliged to dart out and run back to the end of the file to recover it. But she gave another swift glance of her blue eyes as she snatched it up and demurely ran back to her place. The procession passed on, but when Clarence reached the spot where she had paused he saw a three-cornered bit of paper lying in the grass. He was too discreet to pick it up while the girls were still in sight, but continued on; returning to it later. It contained a few words in a school-girl's hand hastily scrawled in pencil, "Come to the south wall near the big pear-tree at six."

Delighted as Clarence felt, he was at the same time embarrassed. He could not understand the necessity of this mysterious rendezvous. He knew that if she was a scholar, she was under certain conventual restraints; but with the privileges of his position and friendship with his teachers, he believed that Father Sobriente would easily procure him an interview with this old playfellow, of whom he had often spoken, and who was, with himself, the sole survivor of his tragical past. And trusted as he was by Sobriente, there was something in this clan-, destine though innocent rendezvous that went against his loyalty. Nevertheless he kept the appointment, and at the stated time was at the south wall of the convent, over which the gnarled boughs of the distinguishing pear tree hung. Hard by in the wall was a grated wicket door that seemed unused.

Would she appear among the boughs or on the edge of the wall? Either would be like the old Susy! But to his surprise he heard the sound of the key turning in the lock. The grated door suddenly turned on its hinges, and Susy slipped out. Grasping his hand she said, "Let's run, Clarence," and before he could reply, she started off with him at a rapid pace. Down the lane they flew—very much, as it seemed to Clarence's fancy, as they had flown from the old emigrant waggon on the prairie four years before. He glanced at the fluttering, fairy-like figure beside him. She had grown taller and more graceful; she was dressed in exquisite taste, with a minuteness of luxurious detail that bespoke the spoilt child—but there was the same prodigal outburst of rippling, golden hair down her back and shoulders, violet eyes, capricious little mouth, and the same delicate hands and feet he had remembered. He would have preferred a more deliberate survey, but with a shake of her head and an hysteric little laugh she only said, "Run, Clarence, run," and again darted forward. Arriving at the cross street they turned the corner and halted breathlessly.

"But you're not running away from school, Susy, are you?" said Clarence anxiously.

"Only a little bit. Just enough to get ahead of the other girls," she said, re-arranging her brown curls and tilted hat. "You see, Clarence," she condescended to explain, with a sudden assumption of older superiority, "mother's here at the hotel all this week, and I'm allowed to go home every night, like a day scholar. Only there's three or four other girls that go out at the same time with me and one of the Sisters—and to-day I got ahead of 'em just to see *you*."

"But"—began Clarence.

"Oh, it's all right; the other girls knew it, and helped me. They don't start out for half-an-hour yet, and they'll say I've just run ahead, and when they and the Sister get to the hotel I'll be there already—don't you see?"

"Yes," said Clarence dubiously.

"And we'll go to an ice-cream saloon now, shan't we? There's a nice one near the hotel. I've got some money," she added quickly, as Clarence looked embarrassed.

"So have I," said Clarence, with a faint accession of colour. "Let's go!" She had relinquished his hand to smooth out her frock, and they were walking side by side at a more moderate pace. "But," he continued, clinging to his first idea with masculine persistence, and anxious to assure his companion of his power, of his position, "I'm in the college, and Father Sobriente, who knows your lady superior, is a good friend of mine, and gives me privileges; and—and—when he knows that you and I used to play together—why, he'll fix it that we may see each other whenever we want."

"Oh, you silly," said Susy, "*what!*—when you're"——

"When I'm *what?*"

The young girl shot a violet blue ray from under her broad hat. "Why—when we're grown up now?" Then with a certain precision, "Why, they're *very* particular about young gentlemen! Why, Clarence, if they suspected that you and I were"——another violet ray from under the hat completed this unfinished sentence.

Pleased and yet confused, Clarence looked straight ahead with deepening colour. "Why," continued Susy, "Mary Rogers, that was walking with me, thought you were ever so old—and a distinguished Spaniard! And I," she said abruptly, "haven't I grown? Tell me, Clarence," with her old appealing impatience, "haven't I grown? Do tell me!"

"Very much," said Clarence.

"And isn't this frock pretty—it's only my second best—but I've a prettier one with lace all down in front; but isn't this one pretty, Clarence, tell me?"

Clarence thought the frock and its fair owner perfection, and said so. Whereat Susy, as if suddenly aware of the presence of passers-by, assumed an air of severe propriety, dropped her hands on her side, and with an affected conscientiousness walked on, a little further from Clarence's side, until they reached the ice-cream saloon.

"Get a table near the back, Clarence," she said, in a confidential whisper, "where they can't see us—and strawberry, you know, for the lemon and vanilla here is just horrid!"

They took their seats in a kind of rustic arbour in the rear of the shop, which gave them the appearance of two youthful, but somewhat over-dressed and over-conscious shepherds. There was an interval of slight awkwardness, which Susy endeavoured to displace. "There has been," she remarked, with easy conversational lightness, "quite an excitement about our French teacher being changed. The girls—in our class—think it most disgraceful."

And this was all she could say after a separation of four years!

Clarence was desperate—but as yet idealess and voiceless. At last, with an effort, over his spoon, he gasped a floating recollection—"Do you still like flap-jacks, Susy?"

"Oh, yes," with a laugh, "but we don't have them now."

"And 'Mose' " (a black pointer, who used to yelp when Susy sang), "does he still sing with you?"

"Oh, *he's* been lost ever so long," said Susy composedly; "but I've got a Newfoundland and a spaniel and a black pony," and here, with a rapid inventory of her other personal effects, she drifted into some desultory details of the devotion of her adopted parents, whom she now readily spoke of as "papa" and "mamma," with evidently no disturbing recollection of the dead. From which it appeared that the Peytons were very rich, and, in addition to their possessions in the lower country, owned a ranche in Santa Clara and a house in San Francisco. Like all children, her strongest impressions were the most recent. In the vain hope to lead her back to this material yesterday, he said—

"You remember Jim Hooker?"

"Oh, *he* ran away—when you left! But just think of it! The other day, when papa and I went into a big restaurant in San Francisco, who should be there *waiting* on the table—yes, Clarence—a real waiter—but Jim Hooker! Papa spoke to him; but, of course," with a slight elevation of her pretty chin, "*I* couldn't, you know; fancy—a waiter."

The story of how Jim Hooker had personated him stopped short upon Clarence's lips. He could not bring himself now to add that revelation to the contempt of his small companion, which, in spite of its *naïveté,* somewhat grated on his sensibilities.

"Clarence," she said, suddenly turning towards him mysteriously, and indicating the shopman and his assistants, "I really believe these people suspect us."

"Of what?" said the practical Clarence.

"Don't be silly! Don't you see how they are staring?"

Clarence was really unable to detect the least curiosity on the part of the shopman, or that any one exhibited the slightest concern in him or his companion. But he felt a return of the embarrassed pleasure he was conscious of a moment before.

"Then you're living with your father?" said Susy, changing the subject.

"You mean my *cousin,*" said Clarence, smiling; "you knew my father died long before I ever knew you."

"Yes; that's what *you* used to say, Clarence, but papa says it isn't so." But seeing the boy's wondering eyes fixed on her with a troubled expression, she added quickly, "Oh, then, he *is* your cousin!"

"Well, I think I ought to know," said Clarence, with a smile, that was, however, far from comfortable, and a quick return of his old unpleasant recollections of the Peytons. "Why, I was brought to him by one of his friends." And Clarence gave a rapid boyish summary of his journey from Sacramento, and Flynn's discovery of the letter addressed to Silsbee. But before he had concluded, he was conscious that Susy was by no means interested in these details, nor in the least affected by the passing allusion to her dead father and his relation to Clarence's misadventures. With her rounded chin in her hand, she was slowly examining his face, with a certain mischievous, yet demure abstraction. "I tell you what, Clarence," she said, when he had finished, "you ought to make your cousin get you one of those *sombreros,* and a nice gold-braided *serape.* They'd just suit you! And then—then, you could ride up and down the Alameda when we are going by."

"But I'm coming to see you at—at your house, and at the Convent," he said eagerly; "Father Sobriente and my cousin will fix it all right."

But Susy shook her head with superior wisdom. "No; they must never know our secret!—neither papa nor mamma, especially mamma. And they mustn't know that we've met again—*after these years!*" It is impossible to describe the deep significance which Susy's blue eyes gave to this expression. After a pause she went on—

"No! We must never meet again, Clarence, unless Mary Rogers helps. She is my best—my *onliest* friend, and older than I; having had trouble herself, and being expressly forbidden to see him again. You can speak to her about Suzette—that's my name now; I was re-christened Suzette Alexandra Peyton by mamma. And now, Clarence," dropping her voice and glancing shyly around the saloon, "you may kiss me just once under my hat, for good-bye." She adroitly slanted her broad-brimmed hat towards the front of the shop, and in its shadow advanced her fresh young cheek to Clarence.

Colouring and laughing, the boy pressed his lips to it twice. Then Susy arose with the faintest affectation of a sigh, shook out her skirt, drew on her gloves with the greatest gravity, and saying, "Don't follow me further than the door—they're coming now," walked with supercilious dignity past the preoccupied proprietor and waiters to the entrance. Here she said, with marked civility, "Good afternoon, Mr. Brant," and tripped away towards the hotel. Clarence lingered for a moment to look after the lithe and elegant little figure, with its shining undulations of hair that fell over the back and shoulders of her white frock like a golden mantle, and then turned away in the opposite direction.

He walked home in a state, as it seemed to him, of absurd perplexity! There were many reasons why his encounter with Susy should have been of unmixed pleasure. She had remembered him of her own free will, and, in spite of the change in her fortune, had made the first advances. Her doubts about her future interviews had affected him but little; still less, I fear, did he think of the other changes in her character and disposition, for he was of that age when they added only a piquancy and fascination to her—as of one who, in spite of her weakness of nature, was still devoted to him! But he was painfully conscious that this meeting had revived in him all the fears, vague uneasiness, and sense of wrong that had haunted his first boyhood, and which he thought he had buried at El Refugio four years ago. Susy's allusion to his father and the reiteration of Peyton's scepticism awoke in his older intellect the first feeling of suspicion that was compatible with his open nature. Was this recurring reticence and mystery due to any act of his father's? But, looking back upon it in after years, he concluded that the incident of that day was a premonition rather than a recollection.

Chapter XI

When he reached the college the Angelus had long since rung. In the corridor he met one of the Fathers, who, instead of questioning him, returned his salutation with a grave gentleness that struck him. He had turned into Father Sobriente's quiet study with the intention of reporting himself, when he was disturbed to find him in consultation with three or four of the faculty, who seemed to be thrown into some slight confusion by his entrance. Clarence was about to retire hurriedly when Father Sobriente, breaking up the council with a significant glance at the others, called him back. Confused and embarrassed, with a dread of something impending, the boy tried to avert it by a hurried account of his meeting with Susy, and his hopes of Father Sobriente's counsel and assistance. Taking upon himself the idea of suggesting Susy's escapade, he confessed the fault. The old man gazed into his frank eyes with a thoughtful, half-compassionate smile. "I was just thinking of giving you a holiday with—with Don Juan Robinson." The unusual substitution of this final title for the habitual "your cousin" struck Clarence uneasily. "But we will speak of that later. Sit down, my son, I am not busy. We shall talk a little. Father Pedro says you are getting on fluently with your translations. That is excellent, my son, excellent."

Clarence's face beamed with relief and pleasure. His vague fears began to dissipate.

"And you translate even from dictation! Good! We have an hour to spare, and you shall give to me a specimen of your skill. Eh? Good! I will walk here and dictate to you in my poor English, and you shall sit there and render it to me in your good Spanish. Eh? So we shall amuse and instruct ourselves."

Clarence smiled. These sporadic moments of instruction and admonitions were not unusual to the good father. He cheerfully seated himself at the Padre's table before a blank sheet of paper with a pen in his hand. Father Sobriente paced the apartment with his usual heavy but noiseless tread. To his surprise the good priest, after an exhaustive pinch of snuff, blew his nose, and began, in his most lugubrious style of pulpit exhortation—

"It has been written that the sins of the father shall be visited upon the children, and the unthinking and worldly have sought refuge from this law by declaring it harsh and cruel! Miserable and blind! For do we not see that the wicked man, who in the pride of his power and vainglory is willing to risk punishment to *himself*— and believes it to be courage—must pause before the awful mandate that condemns an equal suffering to those he loves—which he cannot withhold or suffer for. In the spectacle of these innocents struggling against disgrace, perhaps disease, poverty, or desertions, what avails his haughty, all-defying spirit? Let us imagine, Clarence."

"Sir," said the literal Clarence, pausing in his exercise.

"I mean," continued the priest, with a slight cough, "let the thoughtful man picture a father! A desperate, self-willed man who scorned the laws of God and society—keeping only faith with a miserable subterfuge he called 'honour'—and relying only on his own courage and his knowledge of human weakness! Imagine him cruel and bloody—a gambler by profession, an outlaw among men, an outcast from the Church, voluntarily abandoning friends and family, the wife he should have cherished, the son he should have reared and educated —for the gratification of his deadly passions. Yet imagine that man, suddenly confronted with the thought of that heritage of shame and disgust which he had brought upon his innocent offspring—to whom he cannot give even his own desperate recklessness to sustain its vicarious suffering. What must be the feelings of a parent"——

"Father Sobriente," said Clarence softly.

To the boy's surprise, scarcely had he spoken when the soft protecting palm of the priest was already upon his shoulder, and the snuffy, but kindly upper lip, trembling with some strange emotion, close beside his cheek.

"What is it, Clarence?" he said hurriedly. "Speak, my son, without fear! you would ask"——

"I only wanted to know if 'padre' takes a masculine verb here," said Clarence naïvely.

Father Sobriente blew his nose violently. "Truly—though used for either gender, by the context masculine," he responded gravely. "Ah," he added, leaning over Clarence, and scanning his work hastily. "Good, very good! And now, possibly," he continued, passing his hand like a damp sponge over his heated brow, "we shall reverse our exercise. I shall deliver to you, in Spanish, what you shall render back in English, eh? And—let us consider—we shall make something more familiar and narrative, eh?"

To this Clarence, somewhat bored by these present solemn abstractions, assented gladly, and took up his pen. Father Sobriente, resuming his noiseless pacing, began—

"On the fertile plains of Guadalajara lived a certain caballero, possessed of flocks and lands, and a wife and son. But, being also possessed of a fiery and roving nature, he did not value them as he did perilous adventure, feats of arms, and sanguinary encounters. To this may be added riotous excesses, gambling, and drunkenness, which in time decreased his patrimony, even as his rebellious and quarrelsome spirit had alienated his family and neighbours. His wife, borne down by shame and sorrow, died while her son was still an infant. In a fit of equal remorse and recklessness the caballero married again within the year. But the new wife was of a temper and bearing as bitter as her consort. Violent quarrels ensued between them, ending in the husband abandoning his wife and son, and leaving St. Louis—I should say Guadalajara—for ever. Joining some adventurers in a foreign land, under an assumed name, he pursued his reckless course until, by one or two acts of outlawry, he made his return to civilisation impossible. The deserted wife and stepmother of his child coldly accepted the situation, forbidding his name to be spoken again in her presence, announced that he was dead, and kept the knowledge of his existence from his own son, whom she placed under the charge of her sister. But the sister managed to secretly communicate with the outlawed father, and, under a pretext, arranged between them, of sending the boy to another relation, actually despatched the innocent child to his unworthy parent. Perhaps stirred by remorse the infamous man"——

"Stop," said Clarence suddenly.

He had thrown down his pen, and was standing erect and rigid before the father.

"You are trying to tell me something, Father Sobriente," he said, with an effort. "Speak out, I implore you. I can stand anything but this mystery. I am no longer a child, I have a right to know all. This that you are telling me is no fable—I see it in your face, Father Sobriente; it is the story of—of"——

"Your father, Clarence," said the priest, in a trembling voice.

The boy drew back with a white face. "My father!" he repeated. "Living or dead?"

"Living—when you first left your home," said the old man hurriedly, seizing Clarence's hand, "for it was he who in the name of your cousin sent for you. Living! yes, while you were here—for it was he who for the past three years stood in the shadow of this assumed cousin Don Juan, and at last sent you to this school. Living, Clarence, yes; but living under a name and reputation that would have blasted you! And now *dead*—dead in Mexico, shot as an insurgent and in a still desperate career! May God have mercy on his soul!"

"Dead!" repeated Clarence, trembling, "only now!"

"The news of the insurrection and his fate came only an hour since," continued the Padre quickly; "his complicity with it and his identity were known only to Don Juan. He would have spared you any knowledge of the truth, even as this dead man would. But I and my brothers thought otherwise. I have broken it to you badly, my son, but forgive me?"

An hysterical laugh broke from Clarence, and the priest recoiled before him. "Forgive *you!* What was this man to me?" he said, with boyish vehemence. "He never *loved* me! He deserted me; he made my life a lie. He never sought me, came near me, or stretched a hand to me that I could take?"

"Hush! hush!" said the priest, with a horrified look, laying his huge hand upon the boy's shoulder and bearing him down to his seat. "You know not what you say. Think—think, Clarence! was there none of all those who have befriended you—who were kind to you in your wanderings—to whom your heart turned unconsciously? Think, Clarence, you yourself have spoken to me of such a one. Let your heart speak again, for his sake—for the sake of the dead."

A gentler light suffused the boy's eyes, and he started. Catching convulsively at his companion's sleeve, he said in an eager boyish whisper, "There was one, a wicked desperate man, whom they all feared—Flynn, who brought me from the mines. Yes, I thought that he was my cousin's loyal friend—more than all the rest; and I told him everything—all, that I never told the man I thought my cousin, or any one, or even you; and I think, I think, Father, I liked him best of all. I thought since it was wrong," he continued with a trembling smile, "for I was foolishly fond even of the way the others feared him—he that I feared not, and who was so kind to me. Yet he, too, left me without a word, and when I would have followed him"—but the boy broke down and buried his face in his hands.

"No, no," said Father Sobriente, with eager persistence, "that was his foolish pride to spare you the knowledge of your kinship with one so feared, and part of the blind and mistaken penance he had laid upon himself. For even at that moment of your boyish indignation he never was so fond of you as then. Yes, my poor boy, this man, to whom God led your wandering feet at Deadman's Gulch—the man who brought you here, and by some secret hold—I know not what—on Don Juan's past, persuaded him to assume to be your relation—this man Flynn, this Jackson Brant the gambler, this Hamilton Brant the outlaw—*was your father!* Ah, yes! Weep on, my son; each tear of love and forgiveness from thee hath vicarious power to wash away his sin."

With a single sweep of his protecting hand he drew Clarence towards his breast, until the boy slowly sank upon his knees at his feet. Then lifting his eyes towards the ceiling, he said softly in an older tongue, "And *thou,* too, unhappy and perturbed spirit, rest!"

It was nearly dawn when the good padre wiped the last tears from Clarence's clearer eyes. "And now, my son," he said, with a gentle smile, as he rose to his feet, "let us not forget the living. Although your stepmother has, through her own act, no legal claim upon you, far be it from me to indicate your attitude towards her. Enough that *you* are independent." He turned, and, opening a drawer in his secretaire, took out a bank-book, and placed it in the hands of the wondering boy.

"It was *his* wish, Clarence, that even after his death you should never have to prove your kinship to claim your rights. Taking advantage of the boyish deposit you had left with Mr. Carden at the bank, with his connivance and in your name he added to it, month by month and year by year; Mr. Carden cheerfully accepting the trust and management of the fund. The seed thus sown has produced a thousandfold, Clarence, beyond all expectations. You are not only free, my son, but of yourself and in whatever name you choose—your own master."

"I shall keep my father's name," said the boy simply.

"Amen!" said Father Sobriente.

Here closes the chronicle of Clarence Brant's boyhood. How he sustained his name and independence in after years, and who, of those already mentioned in these pages, helped him to make or mar it, may be a matter for future record.

A Phyllis of the Sierras

PART I

Chapter I

WHERE THE GREAT highway of the Sierras nears the summit, and the pines begin to show sterile reaches of rock and waste in their drawn-up files, there are signs of occasional departures from the main road, as if the weary traveller had at times succumbed to the long ascent, and turned aside for rest and breath again. The tired eyes of many a dusty passenger on the old overland coach have gazed wistfully on those sylvan openings, and imagined recesses of primeval shade and virgin wilderness in their dim perspectives. Had he descended, however, and followed one of these diverging paths, he would have come upon some rude waggon track, or "logslide," leading from a clearing on the slope, or the ominous saw-mill, half hidden in the forest it was slowly decimating. The woodland hush might have been broken by the sound of water passing over some unseen dam in the hollow, or the hiss of escaping steam and throb of an invisible engine in the covert.

Such, at least, was the experience of a young fellow of five-and-twenty, who, knapsack on back and stick in hand, had turned aside from the highway and entered the woods one pleasant afternoon in

July. But he was evidently a deliberate pedestrian, and not a recent deposit of the proceeding stage-coach; and, although his stout walking-shoes were covered with dust, he had neither the habitual slouch and slovenliness of the tramp, nor the hurried fatigue and growing negligence of an involuntary wayfarer. His clothes, which were strong and serviceable, were better fitted for their present usage than the ordinary garments of the Californian travellers, which were too apt to be either above or below their requirements. But perhaps the stranger's greatest claim to originality was the absence of any weapon in his equipment. He carried neither rifle nor gun in his hand, and his narrow leathern belt was empty of either knife or revolver.

A half-mile from the main road, which seemed to him to have dropped out of sight the moment he had left it, he came upon a half-cleared area, where the hastily cut stumps of pines, of irregular height, bore an odd resemblance to the broken columns of some vast and ruined temple. A few fallen shafts, denuded of their bark and tessellated branches, sawn into symmetrical cylinders, lay beside the stumps, and lent themselves to the illusion. But the freshly cut chips, so damp that they still clung in layers to each other as they had fallen from the axe, and the stumps themselves, still wet and viscous from their drained life-blood, were redolent of an odour of youth and freshness.

The young man seated himself on one of the logs, and deeply inhaled the sharp balsamic fragrance—albeit with a slight cough and a later hurried respiration. This, and a certain drawn look about his upper lip, seemed to indicate, in spite of his strength and colour, some pulmonary weakness. He, however, rose after a moment's rest with undiminished energy and cheerfulness, readjusted his knapsack, and began to lightly pick his way across the fallen timber. A few paces on, the muffled whirr of machinery became more audible, with the lazy, monotonous command of "Gee thar," from some unseen ox-driver. Presently, the slow, deliberately swaying heads of a team of oxen emerged from the bushes, followed by the clanking chain of the "skids" of sawn planks, which they were ponderously dragging, with that ostentatious submissiveness peculiar to their species. They had nearly passed him when there was a sudden hitch in the procession. From where he stood he could see that a projecting plank had struck a pile of chips and become partly imbedded in it. To run to the obstruction and, with a few dexterous strokes and the leverage of his stout stick, dislodge the plank was the work, not only of the moment, but of an evidently energetic hand. The teamster looked back and merely nodded his appreciation, and with a "Gee up! Out of that, now!" the skids moved on.

"Much obliged, there!" said a hearty voice, as if supplementing the teamster's imperfect acknowledgment.

The stranger looked up. The voice came from the open, sashless, shutterless window of a rude building—a mere shell of boards and beams half hidden in the still leafy covert before him. He had completely overlooked it in his approach, even as he had ignored the nearer throbbing of the machinery, which was so violent as to impart a decided tremor to the slight edifice, and to shake the speaker so strongly that he was obliged while speaking to steady himself by the sashless frame of the window at which he stood. He had a face of good-natured and alert intelligence, a master's independence and authority of manner, in spite of his blue jean overalls and flannel shirt.

"Don't mention it," said the traveller, smiling with equal but more deliberate good-humour. Then, seeing that his interlocutor still lingered a hospitable moment in spite of his quick eyes and the jarring impatience of the machinery, he added hesitatingly, "I fancy I've wandered off the track a bit. Do you know a Mr. Bradley—somewhere here?"

His hesitation seemed to be more from some habitual conscientiousness of statement than awkwardness. The man in the window replied, "I'm Bradley."

"Ah! Thank you: I've a letter for you—somewhere. Here it is." He produced a note from his breast-pocket. Bradley stooped to a sitting posture in the window. "Pitch it up." It was thrown and caught cleverly. Bradley opened it, read it hastily, smiled and nodded, glanced behind him as if to implore further delay from the impatient machinery, leaned perilously from the window, and said—

"Look here! Do you see that silver-fir straight ahead?"

"Yes."

"A little to the left there's a trail. Follow it and skirt along the edge of the canyon until you see my house. Ask for my wife—that's Mrs. Bradley—and give her your letter. Stop!" He drew a carpenter's pencil from his pocket, scrawled two or three words across the open sheet, and tossed it back to the stranger. "See you at tea! Excuse me, Mr. Mainwaring;—we're short-handed—and—the engine"——But here he disappeared suddenly.

Without glancing at the note again, the stranger quietly replaced it in his pocket, and struck out across the fallen trunks towards the silver-fir. He quickly found the trail indicated by Bradley, although it was faint and apparently worn by a single pair of feet, as a shorter and private cut from some more travelled path. It was well for the stranger that he had a keen eye or he would have lost it; it was equally fortunate that he had a mountaineering instinct, for a sudden profound deepening of the blue mist seen dimly through the leaves before him caused him to slacken his steps. The trail bent abruptly to the right; a gulf fully two thousand feet deep was at his feet! It was the Great Canyon.

At the first glance it seemed so narrow that a rifle-shot could have crossed its tranquil depths; but a second look at the comparative size of the trees on the opposite mountain convinced him of his error. A nearer survey of the abyss also showed him that, instead of its walls being perpendicular, they were made of successive ledges or terraces to the valley below. Yet the air was so still, and the outlines so clearly cut, that they might have been only the reflections of the mountains around him cast upon the placid mirror of a lake. The spectacle arrested him, as it arrested all men, by some occult power beyond the mere attraction of beauty or magnitude; even the teamster never passed it without the tribute of a stone or broken twig tossed into its immeasurable profundity.

Reluctantly leaving the spot, the stranger turned with the trail that now began to skirt its edge. This was no easy matter, as the undergrowth was very thick, and the foliage dense, to the perilous brink of the precipice. He walked on, however, wondering why Bradley had chosen so circuitous and dangerous a route to his house, which naturally would be some distance back from the canyon. At the end of ten minutes' struggling through the "brush," the trail became vague, and, to all appearance, ended. Had he arrived? The thicket was as dense as before; through the interstices of leaf and spray he could see the blue void of the canyon at his side, and he even fancied that the foliage ahead of him was more symmetrical and less irregular, and was touched here and there with faint bits of colour. To complete his utter mystification, a woman's voice, very fresh, very youthful, and by no means unmusical, rose apparently from the circumambient air. He looked hurriedly to the right and left, and even hopelessly into the trees above him.

"Yes," said the voice, as if renewing a suspended conversation; "it was too funny for anything. There were the two Missouri girls from Skinner's, with their auburn hair ringleted, my dear, like the old 'Books of Beauty'—in white frocks and sashes of an unripe greenish yellow, that puckered up your mouth like persimmons. One of them was speechless from good behaviour, and the other—well! the other was so energetic she called out the figures before the fiddler did, and shrieked to my *vis-à-vis* to dance up to the entire stranger—meaning *me*, if you please."

The voice appeared to come from the foliage that overhung the canyon, and the stranger even fancied he could detect through the shimmering leafy veil something that moved monotonously to and fro. Mystified and impatient, he made a hurried stride forward, his foot struck a wooden step, and the next moment the mystery was made clear. He had almost stumbled upon the end of a long verandah that projected over the abyss, before a low, modern dwelling, till then invisible, nestling on its very brink. The symmetrically-trimmed foliage he had noticed were the luxuriant Madeira vines that hid the rude pillars of the verandah; the moving object was a rocking-chair, with its back towards the intruder, that disclosed only the brown hair above, and the white skirts and small slippered feet below, of a seated female figure. In the meantime a second voice from the interior of the house had replied to the figure in the chair, who was evidently the first speaker—

"It must have been very funny; but as long as Jim is always bringing somebody over from the mill, I don't see how *I* can go to those places. You were lucky, my dear, to escape from the new Division Superintendent last night. He was insufferable to Jim, with his talk of his friend the San Francisco millionaire, and to me with his cheap society airs. I do hate a provincial fine gentleman."

The situation was becoming embarrassing to the intruder. At the apparition of the woman, the unaffected and simple directness he had previously shown in his equally abrupt contact with Bradley had fled utterly. Confused by the awkwardness of his arrival, and shocked at the idea of overhearing a private conversation, he stepped hurriedly on the verandah.

"Well? Go on!" said the second voice impatiently. "Well, who else was there? *What* did you say? I don't hear you. What's the matter?"

The seated figure had risen from her chair, and turned a young and pretty face somewhat superciliously towards the stranger, as she said in a low tone to her unseen auditor, "Hush! there is somebody here!"

The young man came forward with an awkwardness that was more boyish than rustic. His embarrassment was not lessened by the simultaneous entrance from the open door of a second woman, apparently as young as and prettier than the first.

"I trust you'll excuse me for—for—being so wretchedly stupid," he stammered, "but I really thought, you know, that—that—I was following the trail to—to—the front of the house, when I stumbled in—in here."

Long before he had finished, both women, by some simple feminine intuition, were relieved, and even prepossessed, by his voice and manner. They smiled graciously. The later comer pointed to the empty chair. But, with his habit of pertinacious conscientiousness, the stranger continued: "It was regularly stupid, wasn't it?—and I ought to have known better. I should have turned back and gone away when I found out what an ass I was likely to be; but I was—afraid—you know, of alarming you by the noise."

"Won't you sit down?" said the second lady pleasantly.

"Oh, thanks. I've a letter here—I"——He transferred his stick and hat to his left hand as he felt in his breast-pocket with his right. But the action was so awkward that the stick dropped on the verandah. Both women made a movement to restore it to its embarrassed owner, who, however, quickly anticipated them. "Pray don't mind it," he continued, with accelerated breath and heightened colour. "Ah, here's the letter!" He produced the letter Bradley had returned to him. "It's mine, in fact—that is, I brought it to Mr. Bradley. He said I was to give it to—to—to—Mrs. Bradley." He paused, glancing embarrassedly from the one to the other.

"I'm Mrs. Bradley," said the prettiest one, with a laugh. He handed her the letter. It ran as follows—

Dear Bradley,—Put Mr. Mainwaring through as far as he wants to go, or hang him up at The Lookout, just as he likes. The Bank's behind him, and his hat's chalked all over the Road. But he don't care much about being on velvet. That ain't his style—and you'll like him. He's somebody's son in England.   B.

Mrs. Bradley glanced simply at the first sentence. "Pray sit down, Mr. Mainwaring," she said gently; "or, rather, let me first introduce my cousin—Miss Macy."

"Thanks," said Mainwaring, with a bow to Miss Macy, "but I—I—I—think," he added conscientiously, "you did not notice that your husband had written something across the paper."

Mrs. Bradley smiled, and glanced at her husband's endorsement— "All right. Wade in." "It's nothing but Jim's slang," she said, with a laugh and a slightly heightened colour. "He ought not to have sent you by that short cut; it's a bother, and even dangerous for a stranger. If you had come directly to *us* by the road, without making your first call at the mill," she added, with a touch of coquetry, "you would have had a pleasanter walk, and seen *us* sooner. I suppose, however, you got off the stage at the mill?"

"I was not on the coach," said Mainwaring, unfastening the strap of his knapsack. "I walked over from Lone Pine Flat."

"Walked!" echoed both women in simultaneous astonishment.

"Yes," returned Mainwaring simply, laying aside his burden and taking the proffered seat. "It's a very fine bit of country."

"Why, it's fifteen miles," said Mrs. Bradley, glancing horror-stricken at her cousin. "How dreadful! And to think Jim could have sent you a horse to Lone Pine. Why, you must be dead!"

"Thanks, I'm all right! I rather enjoyed it, you know."

"But," said Miss Macy, glancing wonderingly at his knapsack, "you must want something, a change—or some refreshment—after fifteen miles."

"Pray don't disturb yourself," said Mainwaring, rising hastily, but not quickly enough to prevent the young girl from slipping past him into the house, whence she rapidly returned with a decanter and glasses.

"Perhaps Mr. Mainwaring would prefer to go into Jim's room and wash his hands and put on a pair of slippers?" said Mrs. Bradley, with gentle concern.

"Thanks, no. I really am not tired. I sent some luggage yesterday by the coach to the Summit Hotel," he said, observing the women's eyes still fixed upon his knapsack. "I dare say I can get them if I want them. I've got a change here," he continued, lifting the knapsack as if with a sudden sense of its incongruity with its surroundings, and depositing it on the end of the verandah.

"Do let it remain where it is," said Mrs. Bradley, greatly amused, "and pray sit still and take some refreshment. You'll make yourself ill after your exertions," she added, with a charming assumption of matronly solicitude.

"But I'm not at all deserving of your sympathy," said Mainwaring, with a laugh. "I'm awfully fond of walking, and my usual constitutional isn't much under this."

"Perhaps you were stronger than you are now," said Mrs. Bradley, gazing at him with a frank curiosity that, however, brought a faint deepening of colour to his cheek.

"I dare say you're right," he said suddenly, with an apologetic smile. "I quite forgot that I'm a sort of an invalid, you know, travelling for my health. I'm not very strong here," he added, lightly tapping his chest, that now, relieved of the bands of his knapsack, appeared somewhat thin and hollow in spite of his broad shoulders. His voice, too, had become less clear and distinct.

Mrs. Bradley, who was still watching him, here rose potentially. "You ought to take more care of yourself," she said. "You should begin by eating this biscuit, drinking that glass of whisky, and making yourself more comfortable in Jim's room until we can get the spare room fixed a little."

"But I am not to be sent to bed—am I?" asked Mainwaring, in half-real, half-amused consternation.

"I'm not so sure of that," said Mrs. Bradley, with playful precision.

"But for the present we'll let you off with a good wash and a nap afterwards in that rocking-chair, while my cousin and I make some little domestic preparations. You see," she added with a certain proud humility, "we've got only one servant—a Chinaman, and there are many things we can't leave to him."

The colour again rose on Mainwaring's cheek, but he had tact enough to reflect that any protest or hesitation on his part at that moment would only increase the difficulties of his gentle entertainers. He allowed himself to be ushered into the house by Mrs. Bradley, and shown to her husband's room, without perceiving that Miss Macy had availed herself of his absence to run to the end of the verandah, mischievously try to lift the discarded knapsack to her own pretty shoulder, but, failing, heroically stagger with it into the passage and softly deposit it at his door. This done, she pantingly rejoined her cousin in the kitchen.

"Well," said Mrs. Bradley emphatically. "*Did* you ever? Walking fifteen miles for pleasure—and with such lungs!"

"And that knapsack!" added Louise Macy, pointing to the mark in her little palm where the strap had imbedded itself in the soft flesh.

"He's nice, though; isn't he?" said Mrs. Bradley tentatively.

"Yes," said Miss Macy; "he isn't, certainly, one of those provincial fine gentlemen you object to. But *did* you see his shoes? I suppose they make the miles go quickly, or seem to measure less by comparison."

"They're probably more serviceable than those high-heeled things that Captain Greyson hops about in."

"But the Captain always rides—and rides very well—you know," said Louise reflectively. There was a moment's pause.

"I suppose Jim will tell us all about him," said Mrs. Bradley, dismissing the subject, as she turned her sleeves back over her white arms, preparatory to grappling certain culinary difficulties.

"Jim," observed Miss Macy shortly, "in my opinion, knows nothing more than his note says. That's like Jim."

"There's nothing more to know, really," said Mrs. Bradley, with a superior air. "He's undoubtedly the son of some Englishman of fortune, sent out here for his health."

"Hush!"

Miss Macy had heard a step in the passage. It halted at last, half irresolutely, before the open door of the kitchen, and the stranger appeared with an embarrassed air. But in his brief absence he seemed to have completely groomed himself, and stood there, the impersonation of close-cropped, clean, and wholesome English young manhood. The two women appreciated it with cat-like fastidiousness.

"I beg your pardon; but really you're going to let a fellow do something for you," he said, "just to keep him from looking like a fool. I really can do no end of things, you know, if you'll try me. I've done some camping-out, and can cook as well as the next man."

The two women made a movement of smiling remonstrance, half coquettish, and half superior, until Mrs. Bradley, becoming conscious of her bare arms and the stranger's wandering eyes, coloured faintly, and said with more decision—

"Certainly not. You'd only be in the way. Besides, you need rest more than we do. Put yourself in the rocking-chair, in the verandah, and go to sleep until Mr. Bradley comes."

Mainwaring saw that she was serious, and withdrew, a little ashamed at the familiarity into which his boyishness had betrayed him. But he had scarcely seated himself in the rocking-chair before Miss Macy appeared, carrying with both hands a large tin basin of unshelled peas.

"There," she said pantingly, placing her burden in his lap, "if you really want to help, there's something to do that isn't very fatiguing. You may shell these peas."

"*Shell* them—I beg pardon, but how?" he asked, with smiling earnestness.

"How? Why, I'll show you—look."

She frankly stepped beside him, so close that her full-skirted dress half encompassed him and the basin in a delicious confusion, and, leaning over his lap, with her left hand picked up a pea-pod, which, with a single movement of her charming little right thumb, she broke at the end, and stripped the green shallow of its tiny treasures.

He watched her with smiling eyes; her own, looking down on him, were very bright and luminous. "There; that's easy enough," she said, and turned away.

"But—one moment, Miss—Miss?"——

"Macy," said Louise.

"Where am I to put the shells?"

"Oh! throw them down there—there's room enough."

She was pointing to the canyon below. The verandah actually projected over its brink, and seemed to hang in mid-air above it. Mainwaring almost mechanically threw his arm out to catch the incautious girl, who had stepped heedlessly to its extreme edge.

"How odd! Don't you find it rather dangerous here?" he could not help saying. "I mean—you might have had a railing that wouldn't intercept the view, and yet be safe?"

"It's a fancy of Mr. Bradley's," returned the young girl carelessly. "It's all like this. The house was built on a ledge against the side of the precipice, and the road suddenly drops down to it."

"It's tremendously pretty, all the same, you know," said the young man thoughtfully, gazing, however, at the girl's rounded chin above him.

"Yes," she replied curtly. "But this isn't working. I must go back to Jenny. You can shell the peas until Mr. Bradley comes home. He won't be long."

She turned away, and re-entered the house. Without knowing why, he thought her withdrawal abrupt, and he was again feeling his ready colour rise with the suspicion of either having been betrayed by the young girl's innocent fearlessness into some unpardonable familiarity, which she had quietly resented, or of feeling an ease and freedom in the company of these two women that were inconsistent with respect, and should be restrained.

He, however, began to apply himself to the task given to him with his usual conscientiousness of duty, and presently acquired a certain manual dexterity in the operation. It was "good fun" to throw the cast-off husks into the mighty unfathomable void before him and watch them linger with suspended gravity in mid-air for a moment— apparently motionless—until they either lost themselves, a mere vanishing black spot in the thin ether, or slid suddenly at a sharp angle into unknown shadow. How deuced odd for him to be sitting here in this fashion! It would be something to talk of hereafter, and yet—he stopped—it was not at all in the line of that characteristic adventure, uncivilised novelty, and barbarous freedom which for the last month he had sought and experienced. It was not at all like his meeting with the grizzly last week while wandering in a lonely canyon; not a bit in the line of his chance acquaintance with that notorious ruffian, Spanish Jack, or his witnessing with his own eyes that actual lynching affair at Angels. No! Nor was it at all characteristic, according to his previous ideas of frontier rural seclusion—as for instance the Pike County cabin of the family where he stayed one night, and where the handsome daughter asked him what his Christian name was. No! These two young women were very unlike her; they seemed really quite the equals of his family and friends in England—perhaps more attractive —and yet, yes it was this very attractiveness that alarmed his inbred social conservatism regarding women. With a man it was very different; that alert, active, intelligent husband, instinct with the throbbing life of his saw-mill, creator and worker in one, challenged his unqualified trust and admiration.

He had become conscious for the last minute or two of thinking rapidly and becoming feverishly excited; of breathing with greater difficulty, and a renewed tendency to cough. The tendency increased until he instinctively put aside the pan from his lap and half rose. But even that slight exertion brought on an accession of coughing. He put his handkerchief to his lips, partly to keep the sound from disturbing the women in the kitchen, partly because of a certain significant taste in his mouth which he unpleasantly remembered. When he removed the handkerchief it was, as he expected, spotted with blood. He turned quickly and re-entered the house softly, regaining the bedroom without attracting attention. An increasing faintness here obliged him to lie down on the bed until it should pass.

Everything was quiet. He hoped they would not discover his absence from the verandah until he was better; it was deucedly awkward that he should have had this attack just now—and after he had made so light of his previous exertions. They would think him an effeminate fraud, these two bright, active women and that alert, energetic man. A faint colour came into his cheek at the idea, and an uneasy sense that he had been in some way foolishly imprudent about his health. Again, they might be alarmed at missing him from the verandah; perhaps he had better have remained there; perhaps he ought to tell them that he had concluded to take their advice and lie down. He tried to rise, but the deep blue chasm before the window seemed to be swelling up to meet him, the bed slowly sinking into its oblivious profundity. He knew no more.

He came to with the smell and taste of some powerful volatile spirit, and the vague vision of Mr. Bradley still standing at the window of the mill and vibrating with the machinery; this changed presently to a pleasant lassitude and lazy curiosity as he perceived Mr. Bradley smile and apparently slip from the window of the mill to his bedside.

"You're all right now," said Bradley cheerfully.

He was feeling Mainwaring's pulse. Had he really been ill, and was Bradley a doctor?

Bradley evidently saw what was passing in his mind. "Don't be alarmed," he said gaily. "I'm not a doctor, but I practise a little medicine and surgery on account of the men at the mill, and accidents, you know. You're all right now; you've lost a little blood; but in a couple of weeks in this air we'll have that tubercle healed, and you'll be as right as a trivet."

"In a couple of weeks!" echoed Mainwaring, in faint astonishment. "Why, I leave here to-morrow."

"You'll do nothing of the kind," said Mrs. Bradley, with smiling peremptoriness, suddenly slipping out from behind her husband. "Everything is all perfectly arranged. Jim has sent off messengers to your friends, so that if you can't come to them they can come to you. You see, you can't help yourself? If you *will* walk fifteen miles with such lungs, and then frighten people to death, you must abide by the consequences."

"You see, the old lady has fixed you," said Bradley, smiling, "and she's the master here. Come, Mainwaring, you can send any other message you like, and have who and what you want here; but *here* you must stop for awhile."

"But did I frighten you really?" stammered Mainwaring faintly to Mrs. Bradley.

"Frighten us!" said Mrs. Bradley. "Well, look there!"

She pointed to the window, which commanded a view of the verandah. Miss Macy had dropped into the vacant chair, with her little feet stretched out before her, her cheeks burning with heat and fire, her eyes partly closed, her straw hat hanging by a ribbon round her neck, her brown hair clinging to her ears and forehead in damp tendrils, and an enormous palm-leaf fan in each hand violently playing upon this charming picture of exhaustion and abandonment.

"She came tearing down to the mill, barebacked on our half-broken mustang, about half-an-hour ago, to call me 'to help you,' " explained Bradley. "Heaven knows how she managed to do it!"

Chapter II

The medication of the woods was not over-estimated by Bradley. There was surely some occult healing property in that vast reservoir of balmy and resinous odours over which The Lookout beetled and clung, and from which at times the pure exhalations of the terraced valley seemed to rise. Under its remedial influence and a conscientious adherence to the rules of absolute rest and repose laid down for him, Mainwaring had no return of the haemorrhage. The nearest professional medical authority, hastily summoned, saw no reason for changing or for supplementing Bradley's intelligent and simple treatment, although astounded that the patient had been under no more radical or systematic cure than travel and exercise. The women especially were amazed that Mainwaring had taken "nothing for it," in their habitual experience of an unfettered pill-and-elixir consuming democracy. In their knowledge of the thousand "panaceas" that filled the shelves of the General Store, this singular abstention of their guest seemed to indicate a national peculiarity.

His bed was moved beside the low window, from which he could not only view the verandah, but converse at times with its occupants, and even listen to the book which Miss Macy, seated without, read aloud to him. In the evening, Bradley would linger by his couch until

late, beguiling the tedium of his convalescence with characteristic stories and information which he thought might please the invalid. For
Mainwaring, who had been early struck with Bradley's ready and
cultivated intelligence, ended by shyly avoiding the discussion of more
serious topics, partly because Bradley impressed him with a suspicion
of his own inferiority, and partly because Mainwaring questioned the
taste of Bradley's apparent exhibition of his manifest superiority. He
learned accidentally that this millowner and back-woodsman was a
college-bred man; but the practical application of that education to the
ordinary affairs of life was new to the young Englishman's traditions,
and grated a little harshly on his feelings. He would have been quite
content if Bradley had, like himself and fellows he knew, undervalued
his training, and kept his gifts conservatively impractical. The knowledge also that his host's education naturally came from some provincial institution unlike Oxford and Cambridge, may have unconsciously
affected his general estimate. I say unconsciously, for his strict conscientiousness would have rejected any such formal proposition.

Another trifle annoyed him. He could not help noticing also that,
although Bradley's manner and sympathy were confidential and almost brotherly, he never made any allusion to Mainwaring's own family or connections, and, in fact, gave no indication of what he believed
was the national curiosity in regard to strangers. Somewhat embarrassed by this indifference, Mainwaring made the occasion of writing
some letters home an opportunity for laughingly alluding to the fact
that he had made his mother and his sisters fully aware of the great
debt they owed the household of The Lookout.

"They'll probably all send you a round robin of thanks, except,
perhaps, my next brother, Bob." Bradley contented himself with a
gesture of general deprecation, and did not ask *why* Mainwaring's
young brother should contemplate his death with satisfaction. Nevertheless, some time afterwards Miss Macy remarked that it seemed
hard that the happiness of one member of a family should depend
upon a calamity to another. "As for instance?" asked Mainwaring,
who had already forgotten the circumstance. "Why, if you had died,
and your younger brother succeeded to the baronetcy, and become Sir
Robert Mainwaring," responded Miss Macy, with precision. This was
the first and only allusion to his family and prospective rank. On the
other hand he had—through naïve and boyish inquiries, which seemed
to amuse his entertainers—acquired, as he believed, a full knowledge
of the history and antecedents of the Bradley household. He knew how
Bradley had brought his young wife and her cousin to California, and
abandoned a lucrative law practice in San Francisco to take possession

of this mountain mill and woodland, which he had acquired through some professional service.

"Then you are a barrister, really?" said Mainwaring gravely.

Bradley laughed. "I'm afraid I've had more practice—though not as lucrative a one—as surgeon or doctor."

"But you're regularly on the rolls, you know; you're entered as counsel, and all that sort of thing?" continued Mainwaring, with great seriousness.

"Well, yes," replied Bradley, much amused. "I'm afraid I must plead guilty to that."

"It's not a bad sort of thing," said Mainwaring naïvely, ignoring Bradley's amusement. "I've got a cousin who's gone in for the law. Got out of the army to do it—too. He's a sharp fellow."

"Then you *do* allow a man to try many trades—over there," said Miss Macy demurely.

"Yes, sometimes," said Mainwaring graciously, but by no means certain that the case was at all analogous.

Nevertheless, as if relieved of certain doubts of the conventional quality of his host's attainments, he now gave himself up to a very hearty and honest admiration of Bradley. "You know it's awfully kind of him to talk to a fellow like me, who just pulled through, and never got any prizes at Oxford, and don't understand the half of these things," he remarked confidentially to Mrs. Bradley. "He knows more about the things we used to go in for at Oxford than lots of our men, and he's never been there. He's uncommonly clever."

"Jim was always very brilliant," returned Mrs. Bradley indifferently, and with more than even conventionally polite wifely deprecation; "I wish he were more practical."

"Practical! Oh, I say, Mrs. Bradley! Why, a fellow that can go in among a lot of workmen and tell them just what to do—an all-round chap that can be independent of his valet, his doctor, and his—banker! By Jove—*that's* practical!"

"I mean," said Mrs. Bradley coldly, "that there are some things that a gentleman ought not to be practical about nor independent of. Mr. Bradley would have done better to have used his talents in some more legitimate and established way."

Mainwaring looked at her in genuine surprise. To his inexperienced observation Bradley's intelligent energy, and, above all, his originality, ought to have been priceless in the eyes of his wife—the American female of his species. He felt that slight shock which most loyal or logical men feel when first brought face to face with the easy disloyalty and incomprehensible logic of the feminine affections. Here was a fellow, by Jove, that any woman ought to be proud of, and—and—he stopped blankly. He wondered if Miss Macy sympathised with her cousin.

Howbeit, this did not affect the charm of their idyllic life at The Lookout. The precipice over which they hung was as charming as ever in its poetic illusions of space and depth and colour; the isolation of their comfortable existence in the tasteful yet audacious habitation, the pleasant routine of daily tasks and amusements, all tended to make the enforced quiet and inaction of his convalescence a lazy recreation. He was really improving; more than that, he was conscious of a certain satisfaction in this passive observation of novelty that was healthier and perhaps *truer* than his previous passion for adventure and that febrile desire for change and excitement which he now felt was a part of his disease. Nor were incident and variety entirely absent from this tranquil experience. He was one day astonished at being presented by Bradley with copies of the latest English newspapers, procured from Sacramento, and he equally astonished his host, after profusely thanking him, by only listlessly glancing at their columns. He stopped a proposed visit from one of his influential countrymen; in the absence of his fair entertainers at their domestic duties, he extracted infinite satisfaction from Foo-Yup, the Chinese servant, who was particularly detached for his service. From his invalid coign of vantage at the window he was observant of all that passed upon the verandah, that *alfresco* audience-room of The Lookout, and he was good-humouredly conscious that a great many eccentric and peculiar visitors were invariably dragged thither by Miss Macy, and goaded into characteristic exhibition within sight and hearing of her guest, with a too evident view, under the ostentatious excuse of extending his knowledge of national character, of mischievously shocking him. "When you are strong enough to stand Captain Gashweiler's opinions of the Established Church and Chinamen," said Miss Macy, after one of those revelations, "I'll get Jim to bring him here, for really he swears so outrageously that even in the broadest interests of international understanding and goodwill neither Mrs. Bradley nor myself could be present."

On another occasion she provokingly lingered before his window for a moment with a rifle slung jauntily over her shoulder. "If you hear a shot or two don't excite yourself, and believe we're having a lynching case in the woods. It will be only me. There's some creature—confess, you expected me to say 'critter'—hanging round the barn. It may be a bear. Good-bye." She missed the creature—which happened to be really a bear—much to Mainwaring's illogical satisfaction. "I wonder why," he reflected, with vague uneasiness, "she doesn't leave all that sort of thing to girls like that tow-headed girl at the blacksmith's."

It chanced, however, that this blacksmith's tow-headed daughter, who, it may be incidentally remarked, had the additional eccentricities of large black eyes and large white teeth, came to the fore in quite another fashion. It was when, Mainwaring being able to leave his room and join the family board, Mrs. Bradley found it necessary to enlarge her domestic service, and arranged with their nearest neighbour, the blacksmith, to allow his daughter to come to The Lookout for a few days to "do the chores" and assist in the housekeeping, as she had on previous occasions. The day of her advent Bradley entered Mainwaring's room, and, closing the door mysteriously, fixed his blue eyes, kindling with mischief, on the young Englishman.

"You are aware, my dear boy," he began with affected gravity, "that you are now living in a land of liberty where mere artificial distinctions are not known, and where Freedom from her mountain heights generally levels all social positions. I think you have graciously admitted that fact."

"I know I've been taking a tremendous lot of freedom with you and yours, old man, and it's a deuced shame," interrupted Mainwaring, with a faint smile.

"And that nowhere," continued Bradley, with immovable features, "does equality exist as perfectly as above yonder unfathomable abyss, where you have also, doubtless, observed the American eagle proudly soars and screams defiance."

"Then that was the fellow that kept me awake this morning, and made me wonder if I was strong enough to hold a gun again."

"That wouldn't have settled the matter," continued Bradley imperturbably. "The case is simply this: Miss Minty Sharpe, that blacksmith's daughter, has once or twice consented, for a slight emolument, to assist in our domestic service for a day or two, and she comes back again to-day. Now, under the aegis of that noble bird whom your national instincts tempt you to destroy, she has on all previous occasions taken her meals with us, at the same table, on terms of perfect equality. She will naturally expect to do the same now. Mrs. Bradley thought it proper, therefore, to warn you, that, in case your health was not quite equal to this democratic simplicity, you could still dine in your room."

"It would be great fun—if Miss Sharpe won't object to my presence."

"But it must not be 'great fun,'" returned Bradley, more seriously; "for Miss Minty's perception of humour is probably as keen as yours, and she would be quick to notice it. And, so far from having any objection to you, I am inclined to think that we owe her consent to come to her desire of making your acquaintance."

"She will find my conduct most exemplary," said Mainwaring earnestly.

"Let us hope so," concluded Bradley, with unabated gravity. "And, now that you have consented, let me add, from my own experience, that Miss Minty's lemon-pies alone are worthy of any concession."

The dinner-hour came. Mainwaring, a little pale and interesting, leaning on the arm of Bradley, crossed the hall, and for the first time entered the dining-room of the house where he had lodged for three weeks. It was a bright, cheerful apartment, giving upon the laurels of the rocky hillside, and permeated, like the rest of the house, with the wholesome spice of the valley—an odour that, in its pure desiccating property, seemed to obliterate all flavour of alien human habitation, and even to dominate and etherealise the appetising smell of the viands before them. The bare, shining, planed, boarded walls appeared to resent any decoration that might have savoured of dust, decay, or moisture. The four large windows and long, open door, set in scanty strips of the plainest, spotless muslin, framed in themselves pictures of woods and rock and sky of limitless depth, colour, and distance, that made all other adornment impertinent. Nature, invading the room at every opening, had banished Art from those neutral walls.

"It's like a picnic, with comfort," said Mainwaring, glancing round him with boyish appreciation. Miss Minty was not yet there; the Chinaman was alone in attendance. Mainwaring could not help whispering, half mischievously, to Louise, "You draw the line at Chinamen, I suppose?"

"*We* don't, but *he* does," answered the young girl. "He considers us his social inferiors. But—hush!"

Minty Sharpe had just entered the room, and was advancing with smiling confidence towards the table. Mainwaring was a little startled; he had seen Minty in a holland sun-bonnet and turned-up skirt crossing the verandah only a moment before; in the brief instant between the dishing-up of dinner and its actual announcement she had managed to change her dress, put on a clean collar, cuffs, and a large jet brooch, and apply some odorous unguent to her rebellious hair. Her face, guiltless of powder or cold cream, was still shining with the healthy perspiration of her last labours as she promptly took the vacant chair beside Mainwaring.

"Don't mind me, folks," she said cheerfully, resting her plump elbow on the table, and addressing the company generally, but gazing with frank curiosity into the face of the young man at her side. "It was a keen jump, I tell yer, to get out of my old duds inter these, and look decent inside o' five minutes. But I reckon I ain't kept yer waitin' long —least of all this yer sick stranger. But you're looking pearter than you did. You're wonderin' like ez not where I ever saw ye before?" she continued, laughing. "Well, I'll tell you. Last week! I'd kem over yer on a chance of seein' Jenny Bradley, and while I was meanderin' down the verandah I saw you lyin' back in your chair by the window drowned in sleep, like a baby. Lordy! I mout hev won a pair o' gloves, but I reckoned you were Loo's game, and not mine."

The slightly-constrained laugh which went round the table after Miss Minty's speech was due quite as much to the faint flush that had accented Mainwaring's own smile as to the embarrassing remark itself. Mrs. Bradley and Miss Macy exchanged rapid glances. Bradley, who alone retained his composure, with a slight flicker of amusement in the corner of his eye and nostril, said quickly: "You see, Mainwaring, how Nature stands ready to help your convalescence at every turn. If Miss Minty had only followed up her healing opportunity, your cure would have been complete."

"Ye mout hev left some o' that pretty talk for *him* to say," said Minty, taking up her knife and fork with a slight shrug, "and you needn't call me *Miss* Minty either, jest because there's kempeny present."

"I hope you won't look upon me as company, Minty, or I shall be obliged to call you 'Miss' too," said Mainwaring, unexpectedly regaining his usual frankness.

Bradley's face brightened; Miss Minty raised her black eyes from her plate with still broader appreciation.

"There's nothin' mean about that," she said, showing her white teeth. "Well, what's *your* first name?"

"Not as pretty as yours, I'm afraid. It's Frank."

"No, it ain't, it's Francis! You reckon to be Sir Francis some day," she said gravely. "You can't play any Frank off on me; you wouldn't do it on *her,*" she added, indicating Louise with her elbow.

A momentous silence followed. The particular form that Minty's vulgarity had taken had not been anticipated by the two other women. They had not unreasonably expected some original audacity or *gaucherie* from the blacksmith's daughter, which might astonish yet amuse their guest, and condone for the situation forced upon them. But they were not prepared for a playfulness that involved themselves in a ridiculous indiscretion. Mrs. Bradley's eyes sought her husband's meaningly; Louise's pretty mouth hardened. Luckily, the cheerful cause of it suddenly jumped up from the table, and saying that the stranger was starving, insisted upon bringing a dish from the other side, and helping him herself plentifully. Mainwaring rose gallantly to take the dish from her hand, a slight scuffle ensued, which ended in the young man being forced down in his chair by the pressure of Minty's strong plump hand on his shoulder. "There," she said, "ye kin mind your dinner now, and I reckon we'll give the others a chance to chip into the conversation," and at once applied herself to the plate before her.

The conversation presently became general, with the exception that Minty, more or less engrossed by professional anxiety in the quality of the dinner, and occasional hurried visits to the kitchen, briefly answered the few polite remarks which Mainwaring felt called upon to address to her. Nevertheless he was conscious, *malgré* her rallying allusion to Miss Macy, that he felt none of the vague yet half-pleasant anxiety with which Louise was beginning to inspire him. He felt at ease in Minty's presence, and believed, rightly or wrongly, that she understood him as well as he understood her. And there were certainly points in common between his two hostesses and their humbler though proud dependent. The social evolution of Mrs. Bradley and Louise Macy from some previous Minty was neither remote nor complete; the self-sufficient independence, ease, and quiet self-assertion were alike in each. The superior position was still too recent and accidental for either to resent or criticise qualities that were common to both. At least, this was what he thought when not abandoning himself to the gratification of a convalescent appetite; to the presence of two pretty women, the sympathy of a genial friend, the healthy intoxication of the white sunlight that glanced upon the pine walls, the views that mirrored themselves in the open windows, and the pure atmosphere in which The Lookout seemed to swim. Wandering breezes of balm and spice lightly stirred the flowers on the table, and seemed to fan his hair and forehead with softly healing breath. Looking up in an interval of silence, he caught Bradley's grey eyes fixed upon him with a subdued light of amusement and affection, as of an elder brother regarding a schoolboy's boisterous appetite at some feast. Mainwaring laid down his knife and fork with a laughing colour, touched equally by Bradley's fraternal kindliness and the consciousness of his gastronomical powers.

"Hang it, Bradley, look here! I know my appetite's disgraceful; but what can a fellow do? In such air, with such viands and such company! It's like the bees getting drunk on Hybla and Hymettus, you know. I'm not responsible!"

"It's the first square meal I believe you've really eaten in six months," said Bradley gravely. "I can't understand why your doctor allowed you to run down so dreadfully."

"I reckon you aint as keerful of yourself, you Britishers, ez us," said Minty. "Lordy! Why there's Pop invests in more patent medicines in one day than you have in two weeks, and he'd make two of you. Mebbe your folks don't look after you enough."

"I'm a splendid advertisement of what *your* care and your medicines have done," said Mainwaring, gratefully, to Mrs. Bradley; "and if you ever want to set up a 'Cure' here, I'm ready with a ten-page testimonial."

"Have a care, Mainwaring," said Bradley, laughing, "that the ladies don't take you at your word. Louise and Jenny have been doing their best for the last year to get me to accept a flattering offer from a Sacramento firm to put up an Hotel for Tourists on the site of The Lookout. Why, I believe that they have already secretly in their hearts concocted a flaming prospectus of 'Unrivalled Scenery' and 'Health-giving Air,' and are looking forward to Saturday night hops on the piazza."

"Have you really though?" said Mainwaring, gazing from the one to the other.

"We should certainly see more company than we do now, and feel a little less out of the world," said Louise candidly. "There are no neighbours here—I mean the people at the Summit are not," she added, with a slight glance towards Minty.

"And Mr. Bradley would find it more profitable—not to say more suitable to a man of his position—than this wretched saw-mill and timber business," said Mrs. Bradley decidedly.

Mainwaring was astounded; was it possible they considered it more dignified for a lawyer to keep an hotel than a saw-mill? Bradley, as if answering what was passing in his mind, said mischievously, "I'm not sure, exactly, what my position is, my dear, and I'm afraid I've declined the hotel on business principles. But, by the way, Mainwaring, I found a letter at the mill this morning from Mr. Richardson. He is about to pay us the distinguished honour of visiting The Lookout, solely on your account, my dear fellow."

"But I wrote him that I was much better, and it wasn't necessary for him to come," said Mainwaring.

"He makes an excuse of some law business with me. I suppose he considers the mere fact of his taking the trouble to come here, all the way from San Francisco, a sufficient honour to justify any absence of formal invitation," said Bradley, smiling.

"But he's only—I mean he's my father's banker," said Mainwaring, correcting himself, "and you don't keep an hotel."

"Not yet," returned Bradley, with a mischievous glance at the two women, "but The Lookout is elastic, and I dare say we can manage to put him up."

A silence ensued. It seemed as if some shadow, or momentary

darkening of the brilliant atmosphere; some film across the mirror-like expanse of the open windows, or misty dimming of their wholesome light, had arisen to their elevation. Mainwaring felt that he was look-ing forward with unreasoning indignation and uneasiness to this im-pending interruption of their idyllic life; Mrs. Bradley and Louise, who had become a little more constrained and formal under Minty's freedom, were less sympathetic; even the irrepressible Minty appeared absorbed in the responsibilities of the dinner.

Bradley alone preserved his usual patient good-humour. "We'll take our coffee on the verandah, and the ladies will join us by-and-by, Mainwaring; besides, I don't know that I can allow you, as an invalid, to go entirely through Minty's bountiful *menu* at present. You shall have the sweets another time."

When they were alone on the verandah, he said, between the puffs of his black briarwood pipe—a pet aversion of Mrs. Bradley—"I wonder how Richardson will accept Minty!"

"If *I* can, I think he *must,*" returned Mainwaring drily. "By Jove, it will be great fun to see him; but"—he stopped and hesitated—"I don't know about the ladies. I don't think, you know, that they'll stand Minty again before another stranger."

Bradley glanced quickly at the young man; their eyes met, and they both joined in a superior and, I fear, disloyal smile. After a pause Bradley, as if in a spirit of further confidence, took his pipe from his mouth and pointed to the blue abyss before them.

"Look at that profundity, Mainwaring, and think of it ever being bullied and over-awed by a long verandah-load of gaping, patronising tourists, and the idiotic flirting females of their species. Think of a lot of over-dressed creatures flouting those severe outlines and deep-toned distances with frippery and garishness. You know how you have been lulled to sleep by that delicious indefinite far-off murmur of the canyon at night—think of it being broken by a crazy waltz or a monotonous German—by the clatter of waiters and the pop of champagne corks. And yet, by thunder, those women are capable of liking both and finding no discord in them!"

"Dancing ain't half bad, you know," said Mainwaring conscien-tiously, "if a chap's got the wind to do it; and all Americans, especially the women, dance better than we do. But I say, Bradley, to hear you talk, a fellow wouldn't suspect you were as big a Vandal as anybody, with a beastly howling saw-mill in the heart of the primeval forest. By Jove, you quite bowled me over that first day we met, when you popped your head out of that *delirium tremens* shaking mill, like the very genius of destructive improvement."

"But that was *fighting* Nature, not patronising her; and it's a business that pays. That reminds me that I must go back to it," said Bradley, rising and knocking the ashes from his pipe.

"Not *after* dinner, surely!" said Mainwaring, in surprise. "Come now, that's too much like the bolting Yankee of the travellers' books."

"There's a heavy run to get through to-night. We're working against time," returned Bradley. Even while speaking he had vanished within the house, returned quickly—having replaced his dark suit by jean trousers tucked in heavy boots, and a red flannel shirt over his starched white one—and, nodding gaily to Mainwaring, stepped from the lower end of the verandah. "The beggar actually looks pleased to go," said Mainwaring to himself in wonderment.

"Oh! Jim," said Mrs. Bradley, appearing at the door.

"Yes," said Bradley, faintly, from the bushes.

"Minty's ready. You might take her home."

"All right. I'll wait."

"I hope I haven't frightened Miss Sharpe away," said Mainwaring. "She isn't going, surely?"

"Only to get some better clothes, on account of company. I'm afraid you are giving her a good deal of trouble, Mr. Mainwaring," said Mrs. Bradley, laughing.

"She wished me to say good-bye to you for her, as she couldn't come on the verandah in her old shawl and sunbonnet," added Louise, who had joined them. "What do you really think of her, Mr. Mainwaring? I call her quite pretty, at times. Don't you?"

Mainwaring knew not what to say. He could not understand why they could have any special interest in the girl, or care to know what he, a perfect stranger, thought of her. He avoided a direct reply, however, by playfully wondering how Mrs. Bradley could subject her husband to Miss Minty's undivided fascinations.

"Oh, Jim always takes her home—if it's in the evening. He get's along with these people better than we do," returned Mrs. Bradley drily. "But," she added, with a return of her piquant Quaker-like coquettishness, "Jim says we are to devote ourselves to you to-night— in retaliation, I suppose. We are to amuse you, and not let you get excited; and you are to be sent to bed early."

It is to be feared that these latter wise precautions—invaluable for all defenceless and enfeebled humanity—were not carried out; and it was late when Mainwaring eventually retired, with brightened eyes and a somewhat accelerated pulse. For the ladies, who had quite regained that kindly equanimity which Minty had rudely interrupted, had also added a delicate and confidential sympathy in their relations with Mainwaring—as of people who had suffered in common—and he experienced these tender attentions at their hands which any two

women are emboldened by each other's saving presence to show any
single member of our sex. Indeed, he hardly knew if his satisfaction
was the more complete when Mrs. Bradley, withdrawing for a few
moments, left him alone on the verandah with Louise and the vast,
omnipotent Night.

For awhile they sat silent, in the midst of the profound and mea-
sureless calm. Looking down upon the dim moonlit abyss at their feet,
they themselves seemed a part of this night that arched above it; the
half-risen moon appeared to linger long enough at their side to enwrap
and suffuse them with its glory; a few bright stars quietly ringed themselves around them, and looked wonderingly into the level of their
own shining eyes. For some vague yearning to humanity seemed to
draw this dark and passionless void towards them. The vast protecting
maternity of Nature leant hushed and breathless over this solitude.
Warm currents of air rose occasionally from the valley, which one
might have believed were sighs from its full and overflowing breast, or
a grateful coolness swept their cheeks and air when the tranquil
heights around them were moved to slowly respond. Odours from
invisible bay and laurel sometimes filled the air; the incense of some
rare and remoter cultivated meadow beyond their ken, or the strong
germinating breath of leagues of wild oats, that had yellowed the upland by day. In the silence and shadow, their voices took upon themselves, almost without their volition, a far-off confidential murmur,
with intervals of meaning silence—rather as if their thoughts had spoken for themselves, and they had stopped wonderingly to listen. They
talked at first vaguely to this discreet audience of space and darkness,
and then, growing bolder, spoke to each other and of themselves.
Invested by the infinite gravity of Nature, they had no fear of human
ridicule to restrain their youthful conceit or the extravagance of their
unimportant confessions. They talked of their tastes, of their habits, of
their friends and acquaintances. They settled some points of doctrine,
duty, and etiquette, with the sweet seriousness of youth and its all-
powerful convictions. The listening vines would have recognised no
flirtation or love-making in their animated but important confidences;
yet when Mrs. Bradley reappeared to warn the invalid that it was time
to seek his couch, they both coughed slightly in the nervous consciousness of some unaccustomed quality in their voices, and a sense of
interruption far beyond their own or the innocent intruder's ken.

"Well?" said Mrs. Bradley, in the sitting-room, as Mainwaring's
steps retreated down the passage to his room.

"Well," said Louise with a slight yawn, leaning her pretty shoulders
languidly against the door-post, as she shaded her moonlight-accus-
tomed eyes from the vulgar brilliancy of Mrs. Bradley's bedroom

candle. "Well—oh, he talked a great deal about 'his people' as he called them, and I talked about us. He's very nice. You know, in some things he's really like a boy."

"He looks much better."

"Yes; but he is far from strong, yet."

Meantime, Mainwaring had no other confidant of his impressions than his own thoughts. Mingled with his exaltation, which was the more seductive that it had no well-defined foundation for existing, and implied no future responsibility, was a recurrence of his uneasiness at the impending visit of Richardson the next day. Strangely enough, it had increased under the stimulus of the evening. Just as he was really getting on with the family, he felt sure that this visitor would import some foreign element into their familiarity as Minty had done. It was very possible they would not like him; now he remembered there was really something ostentatiously British and insular about this Richardson—something they would likely resent. Why couldn't this fellow have come later—or even before? Before what? But here he fell asleep, and almost instantly slipped from this verandah in the Sierras, six thousand miles away, to an ancient terrace, overgrown with moss and tradition, that overlooked the sedate glory of an English park. Here he found himself, restricted painfully by his inconsistent night-clothes, endeavouring to impress his mother and sisters with the singular virtues and excellences of his American host and hostesses—virtues and excellences that he himself was beginning to feel conscious had become more or less apocryphal in that atmosphere. He heard his mother's voice saying severely, "When you learn, Francis, to respect the opinions and prejudices of your family enough to prevent your appearing before them in this uncivilised aboriginal costume, we will listen to what you have to say of the friends whose habits you seem to have adopted;" and he was frantically indignant that his efforts to convince them that his negligence was a personal oversight, and not a Californian custom, were utterly futile. But even then this vision was brushed away by the bewildering sweep of Louise's pretty skirt across the dreamy picture, and her delicate features and softly-fringed eyes remained the last to slip from his fading consciousness.

The moon rose higher and higher above the sleeping house and softly breathing canyon. There was nothing to mar the idyllic repose of the landscape; only the growing light of the last two hours had brought out in the far eastern horizon a dim white peak, that gleamed faintly among the stars, like a bridal couch spread between the hills ringed with fading nuptial torches. No one would have believed that behind that impenetrable shadow to the west, in the heart of the forest, the throbbing saw-mill of James Bradley was even at that moment eating its destructive way through the conserved growth of Nature and centuries, and that the refined proprietor of house and greenwood, with the glow of his furnace fires on his red shirt, and his alert, intelligent eyes, was the genie of that devastation, and the toiling leader of the shadowy toiling figures around him.

Chapter III

Amid the beauty of the most uncultivated and untrodden wilderness there are certain localities where the meaner and more common processes of Nature take upon themselves a degrading likeness to the slovenly, wasteful, and improvident processes of man. The unrecorded landslip, disintegrating a whole hillside, will not only lay bare the delicate framework of strata and deposit to the vulgar eye, but hurl into the valley a debris so monstrous and unlovely as to shame even the hideous ruins left by dynamite, hydraulic, or pick and shovel; an overflown and forgotten woodland torrent will leave in some remote hollow a disturbed and ungraceful chaos of inextricable logs, branches, rock, and soil, that will rival the unsavoury details of some wrecked or abandoned settlement. Of lesser magnitude and importance, there are certain natural dust-heaps, sinks, and cesspools, where the elements have collected the cast-off, broken, and frayed disjecta of wood and field—the sweepings of the sylvan household. It was remarkable that Nature, so kindly considerate of mere human ruins, made no attempt to cover up or disguise these monuments of her own mortality: no grass grew over the unsightly landslides, no moss or ivy clothed the stripped and bleached skeletons of overthrown branch and tree; the dead leaves and withered husks rotted in their open grave, uncrossed by vine or creeper. Even the animals, except the lower organisations, shunned those haunts of decay and ruin.

It was scarcely a hundred yards from one of those dreary receptacles that Mr. Bradley had taken leave of Miss Minty Sharpe. The cabin occupied by her father, herself, and a younger brother, stood, in fact, on the very edge of the little hollow, which was partly filled with decayed wood, leaves, and displacements of the crumbling bank, with the coal dust and ashes which Mr. Sharpe had added from his forge, that stood a few paces distant at the corner of a cross-road. The occupants of the cabin had also contributed to the hollow the refuse of their household in broken boxes, earthenware, tin cans, and cast-off clothing; and it is not improbable that the site of the cabin was chosen with reference to this convenient disposal of useless and encumbering impediments. It was true that the locality offered little choice in the way of beauty. An outcrop of brown granite—a portent of higher altitudes—extended a quarter of a mile from the nearest fringe of dwarf laurel and "brush" in one direction; in the other an advanced file of Bradley's woods had suffered from some long-forgotten fire, and still raised its blackened masts and broken stumps over the scorched and arid soil, swept of older underbrush and verdure. On the other side of the road a dark ravine, tangled with briars and haunted at night by owls and wild cats, struggled wearily on, until blundering at last upon the edge of the Great Canyon, it slipped and lost itself for ever in a single furrow of those mighty flanks. When Bradley had once asked Sharpe why he had not built his house in the ravine, the blacksmith had replied: "That until the Lord had appointed his time, he reckoned to keep his head above ground and the foundations thereof." Howbeit the ravine or the "run," as it was locally known, was Minty's only Saturday-afternoon resort for recreation or berries. "It was," she had explained, "pow'ful soothin', and solitary."

She entered the house—a rude, square building of unpainted boards —containing a sitting-room, a kitchen, and two bedrooms. A glance at these rooms, which were plainly furnished, and whose canvas-coloured walls were adorned with gorgeous agricultural implement circulars, patent medicine calendars, with poly-tinted chromos and cheaply illuminated scriptural texts, showed her that a certain neatness and order had been preserved during her absence; and, finding the house empty, she crossed the barren and blackened intervening space between the back door and her father's forge, and entered the open shed. The light was fading from the sky; but the glow of the forge lit up the dusty road before it, and accented the blackness of the rocky ledge beyond. A small curly-headed boy, bearing a singular likeness to a smudged and blackened crayon drawing of Minty, was mechanically blowing the bellows, and obviously intent upon something else; while her father—a powerfully-built man, with a quaintly dissatisfied expression of countenance—was with equal want of interest mechanically hammering at a horseshoe. Without noticing Minty's advent, he lazily broke into a querulous drawling chaunt of some vague religious character:

> "O tur-ren, sinner; tur-ren.
> For the Lord bids you turn—ah!
> O tur-ren, sinner; tur-ren.
> Why will you die?"

The musical accent adapted itself to the monotonous fall of the sledge-hammer; and at every repetition of the word "turn," he suited the action to the word by turning the horse-shoe with the iron in his left hand. A slight grunt at the end of every stroke, and the simultaneous repetition of "turn," seemed to offer him amusement and relief. Minty, without speaking, crossed the shop, and administered a sound box on her brother's ear. "Take that, and let me ketch you agen layin' low when my back's turned, to put on your store pants."

"The others had fetched away in the laig," said the boy, opposing a knee and elbow at acute angle to further attack.

"You jest get and change 'em," said Minty.

The sudden collapse of the bellows broke in upon the soothing refrain of Mr. Sharpe, and caused him to turn also.

"It's Minty," he said, replacing the horse-shoe on the coals, and setting his powerful arms and the sledge on the anvil with an exaggerated expression of weariness.

"Yes; it's me," said Minty, "and Creation knows it's time I *did* come, to keep that boy from ruinin' us with his airs and conceits."

"Did ye bring over any o' that fever mixter?"

"No. Bradley sez you're loading yerself up with so much o' that bitter bark—kuinine they call it over there—that you'll lift the ruff off your head next. He allows ye ain't got no ague; it's jest wind and dyspepsy. He sez yer's strong ez a hoss."

"Bradley," said Sharpe, laying aside his sledge with an aggrieved manner, which was, however, as complacent as his fatigue and discontent, "ez one of them nat'ral born finikin skunks ez I despise. I reckon he began to give p'ints to his parents when he was about knee-high to Richelieu there. He's on them confidential terms with hisself and the Almighty that he reckons he ken run a saw-mill and a man's insides at the same time with one hand tied behind him. And his finikin is up to his conceit: he wanted to tell me that that yer handy brush dump outside our shanty was unhealthy. Give a man with frills like that his own way and he'd be a sprinkling odor Cologne and peppermint all over the country."

"He set your shoulder as well as any doctor," said Minty.

"That's bone-settin', and a nat'ral gift," returned Sharpe, as triumphantly as his habitual depression would admit; "it ain't conceit and finikin got out o' books! Well," he added, after a pause, "wot's happened?"

Minty's face slightly changed. "Nothin'; I kem back to get some things," she said shortly, moving away.

"And ye saw *him?*"

"Ye-e-s," drawled Minty carelessly, still retreating.

"Bixby was along here about noon. He says the stranger was suthin' high and mighty in his own country, and them 'Frisco millionaires are quite sweet on him. Where are ye goin'?"

"In the house."

"Well, look yer, Minty. Now that you're here, ye might get up a batch o' hot biscuit for supper. Dinner was that promiscous and experimental to-day, along o' Richelieu's nat'ral foolin', that I think I could git outside of a little suthin' now, if only to prop up a kind of innard sinkin' that takes me. Ye ken tell me the news at supper."

Later, however, when Mr. Sharpe had quitted his forge for the night, and, seated at his domestic board, was, with a dismal presentiment of future indigestion, voraciously absorbing his favourite meal of hot saleratus biscuits swimming in butter, he had apparently forgotten his curiosity concerning Mainwaring and settled himself to a complaining chronicle of the day's mishaps. "Nat'rally, havin' an extra lot o' work on hand and no time for foolin', what does that ornery Richelieu get up and do this mornin'? Ye know them ridiklus specimens that he's been chippin' outer that ledge that the yearth slipped from down the run, and litterin' up the whole shanty with 'em. Well, darn my skin! if he didn't run a heap of 'em, mixed up with coal, unbeknownd to me, in the forge, to make what he called a 'fire essay' of 'em. Nat'rally I couldn't get a blessed iron hot, and didn't know what had gone of the fire, or the coal either, for two hours, till I stopped work and raked out the coal. That comes from his hangin' round that sawmill in the woods, and listenin' to Bradley's high-falutin' talk about rocks and strata and sich."

"But Bradley don't go a cent on minin', Pop," said Minty. "He sez the woods is good enough for him; and there's millions to be made when the railroad comes along, and timber's wanted."

"But until then he's got to keep hisself, to pay wages, and keep the mill runnin'. Onless it's, ez Bixby says, that he hopes to get that Englishman to rope in some o' them 'Frisco friends of his to take a hand. Ye didn't have any o' that kind o' talk, did ye?"

"No; not *that* kind o' talk," said Minty.

"Not *that* kind o' talk!" repeated her father with aggrieved curiosity. "Wot kind, then?"

"Well," said Minty, lifting her black eyes to her father's; "I ain't no account, and you ain't no account either; you ain't got no college education, ain't got no friends in 'Frisco, and ain't got no high-toned style; I can't play the pianner, jabber French, nor get French dresses; we ain't got no fancy 'Shallet,' as they call it, with a first-class view of nothing; we've only a shanty on dry rock! But, afore *I'd* take advantage of a lazy, gawky boy—for it ain't anything else, though he's good meanin' enough—that happened to fall sick in *my* house, and coax and cosset him, and wrap him in white cotton, and mother him, and sister him, and Aunt Sukey him, and almost dry-nuss him gin'rally, jist to get him sweet on me and on mine, and take the inside track of others —*I'd* be an Injin! And if you'd allow it, Pop, you'd be wuss nor a nigger."

"Sho!" said her father, kindling with that intense gratification with which the male receives any intimation of alien feminine weakness. "It ain't that, Minty, I wanter know!"

"It's jist that, Pop; and I ez good ez let 'em know I seed it. I ain't a fool, if some folk do drop their eyes and pertend to wipe the laugh out of their noses with a handkerchief when I let out to speak. I mayn't be good enough kempany"——

"Look yer, Minty," interrupted the blacksmith sternly, half rising from his seat with every trace of his former weakness vanished from his hard-set face; "do you mean to say that they put on airs to ye—to *my* darter?"

"No," said Minty quickly; "the men didn't, and don't you, a man, mix yourself up with women's meannesses. I ken manage 'em, Pop, with one hand."

Mr. Sharpe looked at his daughter's flashing black eyes. Perhaps an uneasy recollection of the late Mrs. Sharpe's remarkable capacity in that respect checked his further rage.

"No. Wot I was sayin'," resumed Minty, "ez that I mayn't be thought by others good enough to keep kempany with baronetts ez is to be—though baronetts mightn't object—but I ain't mean enough to try to steal away some old woman's darling boy in England, or snatch some likely young English girl's big brother outer the family without sayin' by your leave. How'd you like it if Richelieu was growed up, and went to sea—and it would be like his peartness—and he fell sick in some foreign land, and some princess or other skyugled *him* underhand away from us?"

Probably owing to the affair of the specimens, the elder Sharpe did not seem to regard the possible mesalliance of Richelieu with extraordinary disfavour. "That boy is conceited enough with hair ile and fine clothes for anything," he said plaintively. "But didn't that Louie Macy hev a feller already—that Captain Greyson? Wot's gone o' him?"

"That's it," said Minty; "he kin go out in the woods and whistle now. But all the same, she could hitch him in again at any time if the other stranger kicked over the traces. That's the style over there at The Lookout. There ain't ez much heart in them two women put together ez would make a green gal flush up playin' forfeits. It's all in their breed, Pop. Love ain't going to spile their appetites and complexions, give 'em nose-bleed, nor put a drop o' water into their eyes in all their natural born days. That's wot makes me mad. Ef I thought that Loo cared a bit for that child I wouldn't mind; I'd just advise her to make him get up and get—pack his duds out o' camp, and go home and not come back until he had a written permit from his mother, or the other baronet in office."

"Looks sorter ef some one orter interfere," said the blacksmith reflectively. "Tain't exakly a case for a vigilance committee, tho' it's agin public morals this sorter kidnappin' o' strangers. Looks ez if it might bring the county into discredit in England."

"Well, don't *you* go and interfere and havin' folks say ez my nose was put out o' jint over there," said Minty curtly. "There's another Englishman comin' up from 'Frisco to see him to-morrow. Ef he ain't scooped up by Jenny Bradley he'll guess there's a nigger in the fence somewhere. But there, Pop, let it drop. It's a bad aig, anyway," she concluded, rising from the table, and passing her hands down her frock and her shapely hips as if to wipe off further contamination of the subject. "Where's Richelieu agin?"

"Said he didn't want supper, and like ez not he's gone over to see that fammerly at the Summit. There's a little girl thar he's sparkin', about his own age."

"His own age!" said Minty indignantly. "Why, she's double that, if she's a day. Well—if he ain't the triflinest, conceitednest little limb that ever grew! I'd like to know where he got it from—it wasn't mar's style."

Mr. Sharpe smiled darkly. Richelieu's precocious gallantry evidently was not considered as gratuitous as his experimental metallurgy. But as his eyes followed his daughter's wholesome, Phyllis-like figure, a new idea took possession of him; needless to say, however, it was in the line of another personal aggrievement, albeit it took the form of religious reflection.

"It's curious, Minty, wot's fore-ordained, and wot ain't. Now, yer's one of them high and mighty fellows, after the Lord, ez comes meanderin' around here, and drops off—ez fur ez I kin hear—in a kind o' faint at the first house he kems to, and is taken in and lodged and sumptuously fed; and nat'rally, they gets their reward for it. Now wot's to hev kept that young feller from coming *here* and droppin' down in my forge, or in this very room, and *you* a tendin' him, and jist layin' over them folks at The Lookout?"

"Wot's got hold o' ye, Pop! Don't I tell ye he had a letter to Jim Bradley?" said Minty quickly, with an angry flash of colour in her cheek.

"That ain't it," said Sharpe confidently; "it's cos he *walked*. Nat'rally you'd think he'd *ride*, being high and mighty, and that's where,

ez the parson will tell ye, wot's merely fi-nite and human wisdom errs!
Ef that feller had ridden he'd have had to come by this yer road, and
by this yer forge, and stop a spell like any other. But it was fore-
ordained that he should walk, jest cos it wasn't generally kalkilated
and reckoned on. So *you* had no show."

For a moment Minty seemed struck with her father's original theory. But with a vigorous shake of her shoulders she threw it off. Her
eyes darkened.

"I reckon you ain't thinking, Pop"—she began.

"I was only sayin' it was curous," he rejoined quietly. Nevertheless,
after a pause, he rose, coughed, and going up to the young girl, as she
leaned over the dresser, bent his powerful arm around her, and drawing her and the plate she was holding against his breast, laid his
bearded cheek for an instant softly upon her rebellious head. "It's all
right, Minty," he said; "ain't it, pet?" Minty's eyelids closed gently
under the familiar pressure. "Wot's that in your hair, Minty?" he said
tactfully, breaking an embarrassing pause.

"Bar's grease, father," murmured Minty in a child's voice—the
grown-up woman, under that magic touch, having lapsed again into
her father's motherless charge of ten years before.

"It's pow'ful soothin', and pretty," said her father.

"I made it myself—do you want some?" asked Minty.

"Not now, girl!" For a moment they slightly rocked each other in
that attitude—the man dexterously, the woman with infinite tenderness—and then they separated.

Late that night, after Richelieu had returned, and her father wrestled in his fitful sleep with the remorse of his guilty indulgence at
supper, Minty remained alone in her room, hard at work, surrounded
by the contents of one of her mother's trunks and the fragments of
certain ripped-up and newly-turned dresses. For Minty had conceived
the bold idea of altering one of her mother's gowns to the fashion of a
certain fascinating frock worn by Louise Macy. It was late when her
self-imposed task was completed. With a nervous trepidation that was
novel to her, Minty began to disrobe herself preparatory to trying on
her new creation. The light of a tallow candle and a large swinging
lantern, borrowed from her father's forge, fell shyly on her milky neck
and shoulders, and shone in her sparkling eyes, as she stood before her
largest mirror—the long glazed door of a kitchen clock which she had
placed upon her chest of drawers. Had poor Minty been content with
the full, free, and goddess—like outlines that it reflected, she would
have been spared her impending disappointment. For, alas! the dress of
her model had been framed upon a symmetrically attenuated French
corset, and the unfortunate Minty's fuller and ampler curves had

under her simple country stays known no more restraining cincture than knew the Venus of Milo. The alteration was a hideous failure; it was neither Minty's statuesque outline nor Louise Macy's graceful contour. Minty was no fool, and the revelation of this slow education of the figure and training of outline—whether fair or false in art— struck her quick intelligence with all its full and hopeless significance. A bitter light sprang to her eyes; she tore the wretched sham from her shoulders, and then wrapping a shawl around her, threw herself heavily and sullenly on the bed. But inaction was not a characteristic of Minty's emotion; she presently rose again, and, taking an old work-box from her trunk, began to rummage in its recesses. It was an old shell-encrusted affair, and the apparent receptacle of such cheap odds and ends of jewellery as she possessed: a hideous cameo ring, the property of the late Mrs. Sharpe, was missing. She again rapidly explored the contents of the box, and then an inspiration seized her, and she darted into her brother's bedroom.

That precocious and gallant Lovelace of ten, despite all sentiment, had basely succumbed to the gross materialism of youthful slumber. On a cot in the corner, half hidden under the wreck of his own careless and hurried disrobing, with one arm hanging out of the coverlid, Richelieu lay supremely unconscious. On the forefinger of his small but dirty hand the missing cameo was still glittering guiltily. With a swift movement of indignation Minty rushed with uplifted palm towards the tempting expanse of youthful cheek that lay invitingly exposed upon the pillow. Then she stopped suddenly.

She had seen him lying thus a hundred times before. On the pillow near him an undistinguishable mass of golden fur—the helpless bulk of a squirrel chained to the leg of his cot; at his feet a wall-eyed cat, who had followed his tyrannous caprices with the long-suffering devotion of her sex; on the shelf above him a loathsome collection of flies and tarantulas in dull green bottles; a slab of ginger-bread for light nocturnal refection, and her own pot of bear's grease. Perhaps it was the piteous defencelessness of youthful sleep, perhaps it was some lingering memory of her father's caress; but as she gazed at him with troubled eyes, the juvenile reprobate slipped back into the baby-boy that she had carried in her own childish arms such a short time ago, when the maternal responsibility had descended with the dead mother's ill-fitting dresses upon her lank girlish figure and scant virgin breast—and her hand fell listlessly at her side.

The sleeper stirred slightly and awoke. At the same moment, by some mysterious sympathy, a pair of beady bright eyes appeared in the bulk of fur near his curls, the cat stretched herself, and even a vague agitation was heard in the bottles on the shelf. Richelieu's blinking eyes wandered from the candle to his sister, and then the guilty hand was suddenly withdrawn under the bedclothes.

"No matter, dear," said Minty; "it's mar's, and you kin wear it when you like, if you'll only ask for it."

Richelieu wondered if he was dreaming! This unexpected mildness —this inexplicable tremor in his sister's voice: it must be some occult influence of the night season on the sisterly mind, possibly akin to a fear of ghosts! He made a mental note of it in view of future favours, yet for the moment he felt embarrassedly gratified. "Ye ain't wantin' anything, Minty," he said affectionately; "a pail o' cold water from the far spring—no, nothin'?" He made an ostentatious movement as if to rise, yet sufficiently protracted to prevent any hasty acceptance of his prodigal offer.

"No, dear," she said, still gazing at him with an absorbed look in her dark eyes.

Richelieu felt a slight creepy sensation under that lovely far-off gaze. "Your eyes look awful big at night, Minty," he said. He would have added "and pretty," but she was his sister, and he had the lofty fraternal conviction of his duty in repressing the inordinate vanity of the sex. "Ye're sure ye ain't wantin' nothin'?"

"Not now, dear." She paused a moment, and then said deliberately: "But you wouldn't mind turnin' out after sunup and runnin' an errand for me over to The Lookout?"

Richelieu's eyes sparkled so suddenly that even in her absorption Minty noticed the change. "But ye're not goin' to tarry over there, ner gossip—you hear? Yer to take this yer message. Yer to say, 'that it will be onpossible for me to come back there, on account—on account of' ?"——

"Important business," suggested Richelieu; "that's the perlite style."

"Ef you like." She leaned over the bed and put her lips to his forehead, still damp with the dews of sleep, and then to his long-lashed lids. "Mind Nip!"—the squirrel—he practically suggested. For an instant their blonde curls mingled on the pillow. "Now go to sleep," she said curtly.

But Richelieu had taken her white neck in the short strangulatory hug of the small boy, and held her fast. "Ye'll let me put on my best pants?"

"Yes."

"And wear that ring?"

"Yes"—a little sadly.

"Then yer kin count me in, Minty; and see here"—his voice sank to a confidential whisper—"mebbee some day ye'll be beholden to *me* for a lot o' real jewellery."

She returned slowly to her room, and, opening the window, looked out upon the night. The same moon that had lent such supererogatory grace to the natural beauty of The Lookout, here seemed to have failed, as Minty had, in disguising the relentless limitations of Nature or the cruel bonds of custom. The black plain of granite, under its rays, appeared only to extend its poverty to some remoter barrier; the blackened stumps of the burnt forest stood bleaker against the sky, like broken and twisted pillars of iron. The cavity of the broken ledge where Richelieu had prospected was a hideous chasm of bluish blackness, over which a purple vapour seemed to hover; the "brush dump" beside the house showed a cavern of writhing and distorted objects stiffened into dark rigidity. She had often looked upon the prospect: it had never seemed so hard and changeless; yet she accepted it, as she had accepted it before.

She turned away, undressed herself mechanically, and went to bed. She had an idea that she had been very foolish; that her escape from being still more foolish was something miraculous, and in some measure connected with Providence, her father, her little brother, and her dead mother, whose dress she had recklessly spoiled. But that she had even so slightly touched the bitterness and glory of renunciation—as written of heroines and fine ladies by novelists and poets—never entered the foolish head of Minty Sharpe, the blacksmith's daughter.

Chapter IV

It was a little after daybreak next morning that Mainwaring awoke from the first unrefreshing night he had passed at The Lookout. He was so feverish and restless that he dressed himself at sunrise, and cautiously stepped out upon the still silent verandah. The chairs which he and Louise Macy had occupied were still, it seemed to him, conspicuously confidential with each other, and he separated them; but as he looked down into the Great Canyon at his feet he was conscious of some undefinable change in the prospect. A slight mist was rising from the valley, as if it were the last of last night's illusions; the first level sunbeams were obtrusively searching, and the keen morning air had a dryly practical insistance which irritated him, until a light footstep on the further end of the verandah caused him to turn sharply.

It was the singular apparition of a small boy, bearing a surprising resemblance to Minty Sharpe, and dressed in a unique fashion. On a tumbled sea of blonde curls a "chip" sailor hat, with a broad red ribbon, rode jauntily. But here the nautical suggestion changed, as had the desire of becoming a pirate which induced it. A red shirt, with a white collar, and a yellow plaid ribbon tie, that also recalled Minty Sharpe, lightly turned the suggestion of his costume to mining. Short black velvet trousers, coming to his knee, and ostentatiously new short-legged boots, with visible straps like curling ears, completed the entirely original character of his lower limbs.

Mainwaring, always easily gentle and familiar with children and his inferiors, looked at him with an encouraging smile. Richelieu—for it was he—advanced gravely and held out his hand, with the cameo ring apparent. Mainwaring, with equal gravity, shook it warmly, and removed his hat. Richelieu, keenly observant, did the same.

"Is Jim Bradley out yet?" asked Richelieu carelessly.

"No; I think not. But I'm Frank Mainwaring. Will I do?"

Richelieu smiled. The dimples, the white teeth, the dark, laughing eyes, were surely Minty's?

"I'm Richelieu," he rejoined with equal candour.

"Richelieu?"

"Yes. That Frenchman—the Lord Cardinal—you know. Mar saw Forrest do him out in St. Louis."

"Do him?"

"Yes, in the theayter."

With a confused misconception of his meaning, Mainwaring tried to recall the historical dress of the great Cardinal and fit it to the masquerader—if such he were—before him. But Richelieu relieved him by adding—

"Richelieu Sharpe."

"Oh, that's your *name!*" said Mainwaring cheerfully. "Then you're Miss Minty's brother. I know her. How jolly lucky!"

They both shook hands again. Richelieu, eager to get rid of the burden of his sister's message, which he felt was in the way of free-and-easy intercourse with this charming stranger, looked uneasily towards the house.

"I say," said Mainwaring, "if you're in a hurry, you'd better go in there and knock. I hear some one stirring in the kitchen."

Richelieu nodded, but first went back to the steps of the verandah, picked up a small blue knotted handkerchief, apparently containing some heavy objects, and repassed Mainwaring.

"What! have you cut it, Richelieu, with your valuables? What have you got there?"

"Specimens," said Richelieu shortly, and vanished.

He returned presently. "Well, Cardinal, did you see anybody?" asked Mainwaring.

"Mrs. Bradley; but Jim's over to the mill. I'm goin' there."

"Did you see Miss Macy?" continued Mainwaring carelessly.

"Loo?"

"Loo!—well; yes."

"No. She's philanderin' with Captain Greyson."

"Philandering with Greyson?" echoed Mainwaring, in wonder.

"Yes; on horseback on the ridge."

"You mean she's riding out with Mr. —with Captain Greyson?"

"Yes; ridin' *and* philanderin'," persisted Richelieu.

"And what do you call philandering?"

"Well; I reckon you and she oughter know," returned Richelieu, with a precocious air.

"Certainly," said Mainwaring with a faint smile. Richelieu really was like Minty.

There was a long silence. This young Englishman was becoming exceedingly uninteresting. Richelieu felt that he was gaining neither profit nor amusement, and losing time. "I'm going," he said.

"Good morning," said Mainwaring, without looking up.

Richelieu picked up his specimens, thoroughly convinced of the stranger's glittering deceitfulness, and vanished.

It was nearly eight o'clock when Mrs. Bradley came from the house. She apologised, with a slightly distrait smile, for the tardiness of the household. "Mr. Bradley stayed at the mill all night, and will not be here until breakfast, when he brings your friend Mr. Richardson with him"—Mainwaring scarcely repressed a movement of impatience—"who arrives early. It's unfortunate that Miss Sharpe can't come to-day."

In his abstraction Mainwaring did not notice that Mrs. Bradley slightly accented Minty's formal appellation, and said carelessly—

"Oh, that's why her brother came over here so early!"

"Did *you* see him?" asked Mrs. Bradley, almost abruptly.

"Yes. He is an amusing little beggar; but I think he shares his sister's preference for Mr. Bradley. He deserted me here in the verandah for him at the mill."

"Louise will keep you company as soon as she has changed her dress," continued Mrs. Bradley. "She was out riding early this morning with a friend. She's very fond of early morning rides."

"*And* philandering," repeated Mainwaring to himself. It was quite natural for Miss Macy to ride out in the morning, after the fashion of the country, with an escort; but why had the cub insisted on the "philandering?" He had said, "*and* philandering," distinctly. It was a nasty thing for him to say. Any other fellow but he, Mainwaring, might misunderstand the whole thing. Perhaps he ought to warn her

—but no! he could not repeat the gossip of a child, and that child the brother of one of her inferiors. But was Minty an inferior? Did she and Minty talk together about this fellow Greyson? At all events, it would only revive the awkwardness of the preceding day, and he resolved to say nothing.

He was rewarded by a half-inquiring, half-confiding look in Louise's bright eyes, when she presently greeted him on the verandah. "She had quite forgotten," she said, "to tell him last night of her morning's engagement; indeed, she had half forgotten *it*. It used to be a favourite practice of hers, with Captain Greyson; but she had lately given it up. She believed she had not ridden since—since"——

"Since when?" asked Mainwaring.

"Well, since you were ill," she said frankly.

A quick pleasure shone in Mainwaring's cheek and eye; but Louise's pretty lips did not drop, nor her faint quiet bloom deepen. Breakfast was already waiting when Mr. Richardson arrived alone. He explained that Mr. Bradley had some important and unexpected business which had delayed him, but which, he added, "Mr. Bradley says may prove interesting enough to you to excuse his absence this morning." Mainwaring was not displeased that his critical and observant host was not present at their meeting. Louise Macy was, however, as demurely conscious of the different bearing of the two compatriots. Richardson's somewhat self-important patronage of the two ladies, and that Californian familiarity he had acquired, changed to a certain uneasy deference towards Mainwaring; while the younger Englishman's slightly stiff and deliberate cordiality was, nevertheless, mingled with a mysterious understanding that appeared innate and unconscious. Louise was quick to see that these two men, more widely divergent in quality than any two of her own countrymen, were yet more subtly connected by some unknown sympathy than the most equal of Americans. Minty's prophetic belief of the effect of the two women upon Richardson was certainly true as regarded Mrs. Bradley. The banker—a large material nature—was quickly fascinated by the demure, puritanic graces of that lady, and was inclined to exhibit a somewhat broad and ostentatious gallantry that annoyed Mainwaring. When they were seated alone on the verandah, which the ladies had discreetly left to them, Richardson said—

"Odd I didn't hear of Bradley's wife before. She seems a spicy, pretty, comfortable creature. Regularly thrown away with him up here."

Mainwaring replied coldly that she was "an admirable helpmeet of a very admirable man," not, however, without an uneasy recollection of her previous confidences respecting her husband. "They have been most thoroughly good and kind to me; my own brother and sister could not have done more. And certainly not with better taste or delicacy," he added markedly.

"Certainly, certainly," said Richardson hurriedly. "I wrote to Lady Mainwaring that you were taken capital care of by some very honest people, and that"——

"Lady Mainwaring already knows what I think of them, and what she owes to their kindness," said Mainwaring drily.

"True, true," said Richardson apologetically. "Of course you must have seen a good deal of them. I only know Bradley in a business way. He's been trying to get the Bank to help him put up some new mills here; but we didn't see it. I dare say he is good company—rather amusing—eh?"

Mainwaring had the gift of his class of snubbing by the polite and forgiving oblivion of silence. Richardson shifted uneasily in his chair, but continued with assumed carelessness.

"No; I only knew of this cousin, Miss Macy. I heard of her when she was visiting some friends in Menlo Park last year. Rather an attractive girl. They say Colonel Johnson, of Sacramento, took quite a fancy to her—it would have been a good match, I dare say, for he is very rich; but the thing fell through in some way. Then they say *she* wanted to marry that Spaniard, young Pico, of the Amador Ranche; but his family wouldn't hear of it. Somehow she's deuced unlucky. I suppose she'll make a mess of it with that Captain Greyson she was out riding with this morning."

"Didn't the Bank think Bradley's mills a good investment?" asked Mainwaring quietly, when Richardson paused.

"Not with him in it; he is not a business man, you know."

"I thought he was. He seems to me an energetic man, who knows his work, and is not afraid to look after it himself."

"That's just it. He has got absurd ideas of co-operating with his workmen, you know, and doing everything slowly, and on a limited scale. The only thing to be done is to buy up all the land on this ridge, run off the settlers, freeze out all the other mills, and put it into a big San Francisco company on shares. That's the only way we would look at it."

"But you don't consider the investment bad, even from *his* point of view?"

"Perhaps not."

"And you only decline it because it isn't big enough for the Bank?"

"Exactly."

"Richardson," said Mainwaring, slowly rising, putting his hands in his trouser pockets and suddenly looking down upon the banker from the easy level of habitual superiority, "I wish you'd attend to this thing for me. I desire to make some return to Mr. Bradley for his kindness. I wish to give him what help he wants—in his own way—you understand. I wish it, and I believe my father wishes it too. If you'd like him to write to you to that effect"——

"By no means; it's not at all necessary," said Richardson, dropping with equal suddenness into his old-world obsequiousness. "I shall certainly do as you wish. It is not a bad investment, Mr. Mainwaring, and, as you suggest, a very proper return for their kindness. And, being here, it will come quite naturally for me to take up the affair again."

"And—I say, Richardson."

"Yes, sir?"

"As these ladies are rather short-handed in their domestic service, you know, perhaps you'd better *not* stay to luncheon or dinner, but go on to the Summit House—it's only a mile or two further—and come back here this evening. I shan't want you until then."

"Certainly!" stammered Richardson. "I'll just take leave of the ladies!"

"It's not at all necessary," said Mainwaring quietly; "you would only disturb them in their household duties. I'll tell them what I've done with you if they ask. You'll find your stick and hat in the passage, and you can leave the verandah by these steps. By the way, you had better manage at the Summit to get some one to bring my traps from here to be forwarded to Sacramento to-morrow. I'll want a conveyance, or a horse of some kind, myself, for I've given up walking for a while; but we can settle about that to-night. Come early. Good morning!"

He accompanied his thoroughly subjugated countryman—who, however, far from attempting to reassert himself, actually seemed easier and more cheerful in his submission—to the end of the verandah, and watched him depart. As he turned back he saw the pretty figure of Louise Macy leaning against the doorway. How graceful and refined she looked in that simple morning dress! What wonder that she was admired by Greyson, by Johnson, and by that Spaniard!—no, by Jove, it was *she* that wanted to marry him!

"What have you sent away Mr. Richardson for?" asked the young girl, with a half-reproachful, half-mischievous look in her bright eyes.

"I packed him off because I thought it was a little too hard on you and Mrs. Bradley to entertain him without help."

"But as he was *our* guest, you might have left that to us," said Miss Macy.

"By Jove! I never thought of that," said Mainwaring, colouring in consternation. "Pray forgive me, Miss Macy—but, you see, I knew the man, and could say it, and you couldn't."

"Well, I forgive you, for you look really so cut up," said Louise, laughing. "But I don't know what Jenny will say of your disposing of her conquest so summarily." She stopped and regarded him more attentively. "Has he brought you any bad news? if so, it's a pity you didn't send him away before. He's quite spoiling our cure."

Mainwaring thought bitterly that he had. "But it's a cure for all that, Miss Macy," he said, with an attempt at cheerfulness; "and being a cure, you see, there's no longer an excuse for my staying here. I have been making arrangements for leaving here to-morrow."

"So soon?"

"Do you think it soon, Miss Macy?" asked Mainwaring, turning pale in spite of himself.

"I quite forgot—that you were here as an invalid only, and that we owe our pleasure to the accident of your pain."

She spoke a little artificially, he thought, yet her cheeks had not lost their pink bloom, nor her eyes their tranquillity. Had he heard Minty's criticism he might have believed that the organic omission noticed by her was a fact.

"And now that your good work as Sister of Charity is completed, you'll be able to enter the world of gaiety again with a clear conscience," said Mainwaring, with a smile that he inwardly felt was a miserable failure. "You'll be able to resume your morning rides, you know, which the wretched invalid interrupted."

Louise raised her clear eyes to his, without reproach, indignation, or even wonder. He felt as if he had attempted an insult and failed.

"Does my cousin know you are going so soon?" she asked finally.

"No, I did not know myself until to-day. You see," he added hastily, while his honest blood blazoned the lie in his cheek, "I've heard of some miserable business affairs that will bring me back to England sooner than I expected."

"I think you should consider your health more important than any mere business," said Louise. "I don't mean that you should remain *here,*" she added, with a hasty laugh, "but it would be a pity, now that you have reaped the benefit of rest and taking care of yourself, that you should not make it your only business to seek it elsewhere."

Mainwaring longed to say that within the last half-hour, living or dying had become of little moment to him; but he doubted the truth or efficacy of this time-worn heroic of passion. He felt, too, that anything he said was a mere subterfuge for the real reason of his sudden departure. And how was he to question her as to that reason? In escaping from these subterfuges, he was compelled to lie again. With an assumption of changing the subject, he said carelessly, "Richardson thought he had met you before—in Menlo Park, I think."

Amazed at the evident irrelevance of the remark, Louise said coldly that she did not remember having seen him before.

"I think it was at a Mr. Johnson's—or *with* a Mr. Johnson—or perhaps at one of those Spanish Ranches—I think he mentioned some name like Pico!"

Louise looked at him wonderingly for an instant and then gave way to a frank, irrepressible laugh, which lent her delicate but rather set little face all the colour he had missed. Partially relieved by her uncon- cern, and yet mortified that he had only provoked her sense of the ludicrous, he tried to laugh also.

"Then, to be quite plain," said Louise, wiping her now humid eyes, "you want me to understand that you really didn't pay sufficient atten- tion to hear correctly! Thank you; that's a pretty English compliment, I suppose."

"I dare say you wouldn't call it 'philandering?' "

"I certainly shouldn't, for I don't know what 'philandering' means."

Mainwaring could not reply with Richelieu, "You ought to know;" nor did he dare explain what he thought it meant, and how he knew it. Louise, however, innocently solved the difficulty.

"There's a country song I've heard Minty sing," she said. "It runs—

> Come, Philander, let us be a-marchin',
> Every one for his true love a-sarchin';
> Choose your true love now or never. . . .

Have you been listening to her also?"

"No," said Mainwaring, with a sudden incomprehensible, but ut- terly irrepressible resolution; "but *I'm* 'a-marchin',' you know, and perhaps I must 'choose my true love now or never.' Will you help me, Miss Macy?"

He drew gently near her. He had become quite white, but also very manly, and it struck her, more deeply, thoroughly, and conscien- tiously sincere than any man who had before addressed her. She moved slightly away, as if to rest herself by laying both hands upon the back of the chair.

"Where do you expect to begin your 'sarchin'?' " she said, leaning on the chair and tilting it before her; "or are you as vague as usual as to locality? Is it at some 'Mr. Johnson' or 'Mr. Pico,' or"——

"Here," he interrupted boldly.

"I really think you ought to first tell my cousin that you are going away to-morrow," she said, with a faint smile: "it's such short notice.

She's just in there." She nodded her pretty head, without raising her eyes, towards the hall.

"But it may not be so soon," said Mainwaring.

"Oh, then the 'sarchin'' is not so important?" said Louise, raising her head, and looking towards the hall with some uneasy but indefinable feminine instinct.

She was right; the sitting-room door opened, and Mrs. Bradley made her smiling appearance.

"Mr. Mainwaring was just looking for you," said Louise, for the first time raising her eyes to him. "He's not only sent off Mr. Richardson, but he's going away himself tomorrow."

Mrs. Bradley looked from the one to the other in mute wonder. Mainwaring cast an imploring glance at Louise, which had the desired effect. Much more seriously, and in a quaint, business-like way, the young girl took it upon herself to explain to Mrs. Bradley that Richardson had brought the invalid some important news that would, unfortunately, not only shorten his stay in America, but even compel him to leave The Lookout sooner than he expected—perhaps to-morrow. Mainwaring thanked her with his eyes, and then turned to Mrs. Bradley.

"Whether I go to-morrow or next day," he said with simple and earnest directness, "I intend, you know, to see you soon again, either here or in my own home in England. I do not know," he added with marked gravity, "that I have succeeded in convincing you that I have made your family already well known to my people, and that"—he fixed his eyes with a meaning look on Louise—"no matter when, or in what way, you come to them, your place is made ready for you. You may not like them, you know; the governor is getting to be an old man —perhaps too old for young Americans—but *they* will like *you,* and you must put up with that. My mother and sisters know Miss Macy as well as I do, and will make her one of the family."

The conscientious earnestness with which these apparent conventionalities were uttered, and some occult quality of quiet conviction in the young man's manner, brought a pleasant sparkle to the eyes of Mrs. Bradley and Louise.

"But," said Mrs. Bradley gaily, "our going to England is quite beyond our present wildest dreams; nothing but a windfall, an unexpected rise in timber, or even the tabooed hotel speculation, could make it possible."

"But *I* shall take the liberty of trying to present it to Mr. Bradley tonight in some practical way that may convince even his critical judgment," said Mainwaring, still seriously. "It will be," he added more lightly, "the famous testimonial of my cure which I promised you."

"And you will find Mr. Bradley so sceptical that you will be obliged
to defer your going," said Mrs. Bradley triumphantly. "Come, Louise,
we must not forget that we have still Mr. Mainwaring's present comfort to look after; that Minty has basely deserted us, and that we
ourselves must see that the last days of our guest beneath our roof are
not remembered for their privation."

She led Louise away with a half-mischievous suggestion of maternal
propriety, and left Mainwaring once more alone on the verandah.

He had done it! Certainly she must have understood his meaning,
and there was nothing left for him now but to acquaint Bradley with
his intentions to-night, and press her for a final answer in the morning.
There would be no indelicacy then in asking her for an interview more
free from interruption than this public verandah. Without conceit he
did not doubt what the answer would be. His indecision, his sudden
resolution to leave her, had been all based upon the uncertainty of *his*
own feelings, the propriety of *his* declaration, the possibility of some
previous experience of hers that might compromise *him*. Convinced by
her unembarrassed manner of her innocence, or rather satisfied of her
indifference to Richardson's gossip, he had been hurried by his feelings
into an unexpected avowal. Brought up in the perfect security of his
own social position and familiarly conscious—without vanity—of its
importance and power in such a situation, he believed, without under-
valuing Louise's charms or independence, that he had no one else than
himself to consult. Even the slight uneasiness that still pursued him
was more due to his habitual conscientiousness of his own intention
than to any fear that she would not fully respond to it. Indeed, with
his conservative ideas of proper feminine self-restraint, Louise's calm
passivity and undemonstrative attitude were a proof of her superiority;
had she blushed over-much, cried, or thrown herself into his arms, he
would have doubted the wisdom of so easy a selection. It was true he
had known her scarcely three weeks; if he chose to be content with
that his own accessible record of three centuries should be sufficient
for her, and condone any irregularity.

Nevertheless, as an hour slipped away and Louise did not make her
appearance—either on the verandah or in the little sitting-room of the
hall—Mainwaring became more uneasy as to the incompleteness of
their interview. Perhaps a faint suspicion of the inadequacy of her
response began to trouble him; but he still fatuously regarded it rather
as owing to his own hurried and unfinished declaration. It was true
that he hadn't said half what he intended to say; it was true that she
might have misunderstood it as the conventional gallantry of the situation, as—terrible thought!—the light banter of the habitual love-
making American, to which she had been accustomed; perhaps even

now she relegated him to the level of Greyson, and this accounted for her singular impassiveness—an impassiveness that certainly was singular now he reflected upon it—that might have been even contempt! The last thought pricked his deep conscientiousness; he walked hurriedly up and down the verandah, and then suddenly re-entering his room, took up a sheet of note-paper and began to write to her:—

Can you grant me a few moments' interview alone? I cannot bear you should think that what I was trying to tell you when we were interrupted was prompted by anything but the deepest sincerity and conviction, or that I am willing it should be passed over lightly by you or be forgotten. Pray give me a chance of proving it by saying you will see me.   F.M.

But how should he convey this to her? His delicacy revolted against handing it to her behind Mrs. Bradley's back, or the prestidigitation of slipping it into her lap or under her plate before them at luncheon; he thought for an instant of the Chinaman, but gentlemen—except in that "mirror of nature," the stage—usually hesitate to suborn other people's servants, or entrust a woman's secret to her inferiors. He remembered that Louise's room was at the further end of the house, and its low window gave upon the verandah, and was guarded at night by a film of white and blue curtains that were parted during the day to allow a triangular revelation of a pale blue and white draped interior. Mainwaring reflected that the low inside windowledge was easily accessible from the verandah, would afford a capital lodgment for the note, and be quickly seen by the fair occupant of the room on entering. He sauntered slowly past the window; the room was empty, the moment propitious. A slight breeze was stirring the blue ribbons of the curtain; it would be necessary to secure the note with something; he returned along the verandah to the steps, where he had noticed a small irregular stone lying, which had evidently escaped from Richelieu's bag of treasure specimens, and had been overlooked by that ingenuous child. It was of a pretty peacock-blue colour, and, besides securing a paper, would be sure to attract her attention. He placed his note on the inside ledge and the blue stone atop, and went away with a sense of relief.

Another half-hour passed without incident. He could hear the voices of the two women in the kitchen and dining-room. After a while they appeared to cease, and he heard the sound of an opening door. It then occurred to him that the verandah was still too exposed for a confidential interview, and he resolved to descend the steps, pass before the windows of the kitchen, where Louise might see him, and penetrate the shrubbery, where she might be induced to follow him. They would not be interrupted nor overheard there.

But he had barely left the verandah before the figure of Richelieu, who had been patiently waiting for Mainwaring's disappearance, emerged stealthily from the shrubbery. He had discovered his loss on handing his "fire assays" to the good-humoured Bradley for later examination, and he had retraced his way, step by step, looking everywhere for his missing stone with the unbounded hopefulness, lazy persistency, and lofty disregard for time and occupation known only to the genuine boy. He remembered to have placed his knotted bag upon the verandah, and, slipping off his stiff boots, slowly and softly slid along against the wall of the house, looking carefully on the floor, and yet preserving a studied negligence of demeanour, with one hand in his pocket and his small mouth contracted into a singularly soothing and almost voiceless whistle—Richelieu's own peculiar accomplishment. But no stone appeared. Like most of his genus he was superstitious, and repeated to himself the cabalistic formula: "Losin's seekin's, findin's keepin's"—presumed to be of great efficacy in such cases—with religious fervour. He had laboriously reached the end of the verandah when he noticed the open window of Louise's room, and stopped as a perfunctory duty to look in. And then Richelieu Sharpe stood for an instant utterly confounded and aghast at this crowning proof of the absolute infamy and sickening enormity of Man.

There was *his* stone—*his, Richelieu's, own specimen,* carefully gathered by himself and none other—and now stolen, abstracted, "sky-ugled," "smouged," "hooked" by this "rotten, skunkified, long-legged, splay-footed, hoss-laughin', nigger-toothed, or'nary despot!" And, worse than all, actually made to do infamous duty as a love token!— a "candy-gift"!—a "philanderin' box"! to *his,* Richelieu's, girl—for Louise belonged to that innocent and vague outside seraglio of Richelieu's boyish dreams—and put atop of a letter to her! and Providence permitted such an outrage! "Wot was he, Richelieu, sent to school for, and organised wickedness in the shape of gorilla Injins like this allowed to ride high horses rampant over Californey!" He looked at the heavens in mute appeal. And then—Providence not immediately interfering—he thrust his own small arm into the window, regained his priceless treasure, and fled swiftly.

A fateful silence ensued. The wind slightly moved the curtain outward, as if in a playful attempt to follow him, and then subsided. A moment later, apparently reinforced by other winds, or sympathising with Richelieu, it lightly lifted the unlucky missive and cast it softly from the window. But here another wind, lying in wait, caught it cleverly, and tossed it, in a long curve, into the abyss. For an instant it seemed to float lazily, as on the mirrored surface of a lake, until, turning upon its side, it suddenly darted into utter oblivion.

When Mainwaring returned from the shrubbery, he went softly to the window. The disappearance of the letter and stone satisfied him of the success of his stratagem, and for the space of three hours relieved his anxiety. But at the end of that time, finding no response from Louise, his former uneasiness returned. Was she offended, or—the first doubt of her acceptance of him crossed his mind! A sudden and inexplicable sense of shame came upon him. At the same moment, he heard his name called from the steps, turned—and beheld Minty.

Her dark eyes were shining with a pleasant light, and her lips parted on her white teeth with a frank, happy smile. She advanced and held out her hand. He took it with a mingling of disappointment and embarrassment.

"You're wondering why I kem on here, arter I sent word this morning that I kelkilated not to come. Well, 'twixt then and now suthin's happened. We've had fine doin's over at our house, you bet! Pop don't know which end he's standin' on; and I reckon that for about ten minutes I didn't know my own name. But ez soon ez I got fairly hold o' the hull thing, and had it put straight in my mind, I sez to myself, Minty Sharpe, sez I, the first thing for you to do now, is to put on yer bonnet and shawl, and trapse over to Jim Bradley's, and help them two women-folks get dinner for themselves and that sick stranger. And," continued Minty, throwing herself into a chair and fanning her glowing face with her apron, "yer I am!"

"But you have not told me *what* has happened," said Mainwaring, with a constrained smile, and an uneasy glance towards the house.

"That's so," said Minty, with a brilliant laugh. "I clean forgot the hull gist of the thing. Well, we're rich folks now—over thar on Barren Ledge! That onery brother of mine, Richelieu, hez taken some of his specimens over to Jim Bradley to be tested. And Bradley, just to please that child, takes 'em; and not an hour ago Bradley comes running, likety switch, over to Pop to tell him to put up his notices, for the hull of that ledge where the forge stands is a mine o' silver and copper. Afore ye knew it, Lordy! half the folks outer the Summit and the mill was scattered down thar all over it. Richardson—that stranger ez knows you—kem thar too with Jim, and he allows, ef Bradley's essay is right, it's worth more than a hundred thousand dollars ez it stands!"

"I suppose I must congratulate you, Miss Sharpe," said Mainwaring with an attempt at interest, but his attention still preoccupied with the open doorway.

"Oh, *they* know all about it!" said Minty, following the direction of his abstracted eyes with a slight darkening of her own, "I jest kem out o' the kitchen the other way, and Jim sent 'em a note; but I allowed I'd tell *you* myself. Specially ez you was going away to-morrow."

"Who said I was going away to-morrow?" asked Mainwaring uneasily.

"Loo Macy!"

"Ah—she did? But I may change my mind, you know!" he continued, with a faint smile.

Minty shook her curls decisively. "I reckon *she* knows," she said drily, "she's got law and gospel for wot she says. But yer she comes. Ask her! Look yer, Loo," she added, as the two women appeared at the doorway, with a certain exaggeration of congratulatory manner that struck Mainwaring as being as artificial and disturbed as his own; "didn't Sir Francis yer say he was going to-morrow?"

"That's what I understood!" returned Louise, with cold astonishment, letting her clear indifferent eyes fall upon Mainwaring. "I do not know that he has changed his mind."

"Unless, as Miss Sharpe is a great capitalist now, she is willing to use her powers of persuasion," added Mrs. Bradley, with a slight acidulous pointing of her usual prim playfulness.

"I reckon Minty Sharpe's the same ez she allus wos, unless more so," returned Minty, with an honest egotism that carried so much conviction to the hearer as to condone its vanity. "But I kem yer to do a day's work, gals, and I allow to pitch in and do it, and not sit yer swoppin' compliments and keeping *him* from packin' his duds. Onless," she stopped, and looked around at the uneasy, unsympathetic circle with a faint tremulousness of lip that belied the brave black eyes above it, "onless I'm in yer way."

The two women sprang forward with a feminine bewildering excess of protestation; and Mainwaring, suddenly pierced through his outer selfish embarrassment to his more honest depths, stammered quickly—

"Look here, Miss Sharpe, if you think of running away again, after having come all the way here to make us share the knowledge of your good fortune and your better heart, by Jove! I'll go back with you."

But here the two women effusively hurried her away from the dangerous proximity of such sympathetic honesty, and a moment later Mainwaring heard her laughing voice, as of old, ringing in the kitchen. And then, as if unconsciously responding to the significant commonsense that lay in her last allusion to him, he went to his room and grimly began his packing.

He did not again see Louise alone. At their informal luncheon the conversation turned upon the more absorbing topic of the Sharpes' discovery, its extent, and its probable effect upon the fortunes of the locality. He noticed, abstractedly, that both Mrs. Bradley and her cousin showed a real or assumed scepticism of its value. This did not disturb him greatly, except for its intended check upon Minty's enthusiasm. He was more conscious, perhaps—with a faint touch of mortified vanity—that his own contemplated departure was of lesser importance than this local excitement. Yet, in his growing conviction that all was over—if, indeed, it had ever begun—between himself and Louise, he was grateful to this natural diversion of incident which spared them both an interval of embarrassing commonplaces. And, with the suspicion of some indefinable insincerity—either of his own or Louise's—haunting him, Minty's frank heartiness and outspoken loyalty gave him a strange relief. It seemed to him as if the clear cool breath of the forest had entered with her homely garments, and the steadfast truths of Nature were incarnate in her shining eyes. How far this poetic fancy would have been consistent or even co-existent with any gleam of tenderness or self-forgetfulness in Louise's equally pretty orbs, I leave the satirical feminine reader to determine.

It was late when Bradley at last returned, bringing further and more complete corroboration of the truth of Sharpe's good fortune. Two experts had arrived, one from Pine Flat and another from the Summit, and upon this statement Richardson had offered to purchase an interest in the discovery that would at once enable the blacksmith to develop his mine. "I shouldn't wonder, Mainwaring," he added cheerfully, "if he'd put you into it, too, and make your eternal fortune."

"With larks falling from the skies all round you, it's a pity *you* couldn't get put into something," said Mrs. Bradley, straightening her pretty brows.

"I'm not a gold-miner, my dear," said Bradley pleasantly.

"Nor a gold-finder," returned his wife, with a cruel little depression of her pink nostrils; "but you can work all night in that stupid mill, and then," she added in a low voice, to escape Minty's attention, "spend the whole of the next day examining and following up a boy's discovery that his own relations had been too lazy and too ignorant to understand and profit by. I suppose that next you will be hunting up a site on the *other side* of the Canyon where somebody else can put up an hotel and ruin your own prospects."

A sensitive shadow of pain quickly dimmed Bradley's glance—not the first or last time, evidently, for it was gradually bringing out a background of sadness in his intelligent eyes. But the next moment he turned kindly to Mainwaring, and began to deplore the necessity of his early departure, which Richardson had already made known to him with practical and satisfying reasons.

"I hope you won't forget, my dear fellow, that your most really urgent business is to look after your health; and if, hereafter, you'll only remember the old Lookout enough to impress that fact upon you, I shall feel that any poor service I have rendered you has been amply repaid."

Mainwaring, notwithstanding that he winced slightly at this fateful echo of Louise's advice, returned the grasp of his friend's hand with an honest pressure equal to his own. He longed now only for the coming of Richardson, to complete his scheme of grateful benefaction to his host.

The banker came, fortunately, as the conversation began to flag; and Mrs. Bradley's half-coquettish ill-humour of a pretty woman, and Louise's abstracted indifference, were becoming so noticeable as to even impress Minty into a thoughtful taciturnity. The graciousness of his reception by Mrs. Bradley somewhat restored his former ostentatious gallantry, and his self-satisfied, domineering manner had enough masculine power in it to favourably affect the three women, who, it must be confessed, were a little bored by the finer abstractions of Bradley and Mainwaring. After a few moments, Mainwaring rose, and, with a significant glance at Richardson to remind him of his proposed conference with Bradley, turned to leave the room. He was obliged to pass Louise, who was sitting by the table. His attention was suddenly arrested by something in her hand with which she was listlessly playing. It was the stone which he had put on his letter to her.

As he had not been present when Bradley arrived, he did not know that this fateful object had been brought home by his host, who, after receiving it from Richelieu, had put it in his pocket to illustrate his story of the discovery. On the contrary, it seemed that Louise's careless exposure of his foolish stratagem was gratuitously and purposely cruel. Nevertheless, he stopped and looked at her.

"That's a queer stone you have there," he said, in a tone which she recognised as coldly and ostentatiously civil.

"Yes," she replied, without looking up; "it's the outcrop of that mine." She handed it to him as if to obviate any further remark. "I thought you had seen it before."

"The outcrop," he repeated drily. "That is—it—it—it is the indication or sign of something important that's below it—isn't it?"

Louise shrugged her shoulders sceptically. "It don't follow. It's just as likely to cover rubbish, after you've taken the trouble to look."

"Thanks," he said, with measured gentleness, and passed quietly out of the room.

The moon had already risen when Bradley, with his briar-wood pipe, preceded Richardson upon the verandah. The latter threw his large frame into Louise's rocking-chair near the edge of the abyss;

Bradley, with his own chair tilted against the side of the house after the national fashion, waited for him to speak. The absence of Mainwaring and the stimulus of Mrs. Bradley's graciousness had given the banker a certain condescending familiarity, which Bradley received with amused and ironical tolerance that his twinkling eyes made partly visible in the darkness.

"One of the things I wanted to talk to you about, Bradley, was that old affair of the advance you asked for from the Bank. We did not quite see our way to it then, and, speaking as a business man, it isn't really a matter of business now; but it has lately been put to me in a light that would make the doing of it possible—you understand? The fact of the matter is this: Sir Robert Mainwaring, the father of the young fellow you've got in your house, is one of our directors and largest shareholders, and I can tell you—if you don't suspect it already —you've been lucky, Bradley—deucedly lucky—to have had him in your house, and to have rendered him a service. He's the heir to one of the largest landed estates in his county, one of the oldest county families, and will step into the title some day. But, ahem!" he coughed patronisingly, "you knew all that! No? Well, that charming wife of yours, at least, does; for she's been talking about it. Gad, Bradley, it takes those women to find out anything of that kind, eh?"

The light in Bradley's eyes and his pipe went slowly out together.

"Then we'll say that affair of the advance is as good as settled. It's Sir Robert's wish, you understand—and this young fellow's wish—and if you'll come down to the Bank next week we'll arrange it for you; I think you'll admit they're doing the handsome thing to you and yours. And therefore," he lowered his voice confidentially, "you'll see, Bradley, that it will only be the honourable thing in you, you know, to look upon the affair as finished, and, in fact, to do all you can"—he drew his chair closer—"to—to—to drop this other foolishness."

"I don't think I quite understand you," said Bradley slowly.

"But your wife does, if you don't," returned Richardson bluntly; "I mean this foolish flirtation between Louise Macy and Mainwaring, which is utterly preposterous. Why, man, it can't possibly come to anything, and it couldn't be allowed for a moment. Look at his position and hers. I should think, as a practical man, it would strike you"——

"Only one thing strikes me, Richardson," interrupted Bradley in a singularly distinct whisper, rising, and moving nearer the speaker; "it is that you're sitting perilously near the edge of this verandah. For, by the living God, if you don't take yourself out of that chair and out of this house, I won't be answerable for the consequences!"

"Hold on there a minute, will you?" said Mainwaring's voice from the window.

Both men turned towards it. A long leg was protruding from Mainwaring's window; it was quickly followed by the other leg and body of the occupant, and the next moment Mainwaring came towards the two men, with his hands in his pockets.

"Not so loud," he said, looking towards the house.

"Let that man go," said Bradley, in a repressed voice. "You and I, Mainwaring, can speak together afterwards."

"That man must stay until he hears what I have got to say," said Mainwaring, stepping between them. He was very white and grave in the moonlight, but very quiet; and he did not take his hands from his pockets. "I've listened to what he said because he came here on *my* business, which was simply to offer to do you a service. That was all, Bradley, that *I* told him to do. This rot about what he expects of you in return is his own impertinence. If you'd punched his head when he began it, it would have been all right. But since he has begun it, before he goes I think he ought to hear me tell you that I have already *offered* myself to Miss Macy, and she has *refused* me! If she had given me the least encouragement, I should have told you before. Further, I want to say that, in spite of that man's insinuations, I firmly believe that no one is aware of the circumstance except Miss Macy and myself."

"I had no idea of intimating that anything had happened that was not highly honourable and creditable to you and the young lady," began Richardson hurriedly.

"I don't know that it was necessary for you to have any ideas on the subject at all," said Mainwaring sternly; "nor that, having been shown how you have insulted this gentleman and myself, you need trouble us an instant longer with your company. You need not come back. I will manage my other affairs myself."

"Very well, Mr. Mainwaring—but—you may be sure that I shall certainly take the first opportunity to explain myself to Sir Robert," returned Richardson, as, with an attempt at dignity, he strode away.

There was an interval of silence.

"Don't be too hard upon a fellow, Bradley," said Mainwaring, as Bradley remained dark and motionless in the shadow. "It is a poor return I'm making you for your kindness, but I swear I never thought of anything like—like—this."

"Nor did I," said Bradley bitterly.

"I know it, and that's what makes it so infernally bad for me. Forgive me, won't you? Think of me, old fellow, as the wretchedest ass you ever met, but not such a cad as this would make me!" As

Mainwaring stepped out from the moonlight towards him with extended hand, Bradley finally grasped it.

"Thanks—there—thanks, old fellow! And, Bradley—I say—don't
say anything to your wife, for I don't think she knows it. And, Bradley
—look here—I didn't like to be anything but plain before that fellow;
but I don't mind telling *you,* now that it's all over, that I really think
Louise—Miss Macy—didn't altogether understand me either."

With another shake of the hand they separated for the night. For a
long time after Mainwaring had gone, Bradley remained gazing
thoughtfully into the Great Canyon. He thought of the time when he
had first come there, full of life and enthusiasm, making an ideal world
of his pure and wholesome eyrie on the ledge. What else he thought
will, probably, never be known until the misunderstanding of honourable and chivalrous men by a charming and illogical sex shall be
analysed and explained by some more daring romancer.

When he returned to the house, he said kindly to his wife, "I have
been thinking to-day about your hotel scheme, and I shall write to
Sacramento to-night to accept that capitalist's offer."

PART II

Chapter I

The sun was just rising. In two years of mutation and change it had
seen the little cottage, clinging like a swallow's nest to the rocky eaves
of a great Sierran canyon, give way to a straggling, many-galleried
hotel; and a dozen blackened chimneys rise above the barren tableland
where once had stood the lonely forge. To that conservative orb of
light and heat there must have been a peculiar satisfaction in looking
down a few hours earlier upon the battlements and gables of
Oldenhurst, whose base was deeply embedded in the matured foundations and settled traditions of an English county. For the rising sun
had for the last ten centuries found Oldenhurst in its place, from the
heavy stone terrace that covered the dead-and-forgotten wall where a
Roman sentinel had once paced, to the little grating in the cloistered
quadrangle, where it had seen a Cistercian brother place the morning
dole. It had daily welcomed the growth of this vast and picturesque
excrescence of the times; it had smiled every morning upon this formidable yet quaint incrustation of power and custom, ignoring, as
Oldenhurst itself had ignored, the generations who possessed it, the
men who built it, the men who carried it with fire and sword, the men
who had lied and cringed for it, the king who had given it to a

favourite, the few brave hearts who had died for it in exile, and the one or two who had bought and paid for it. For Oldenhurst had absorbed all these and more until it had become a story of the past, incarnate in stone, greenwood, and flower; it had even drained the life-blood from adjacent hamlets, repaying them with tumuli growths like its own, in the shape of purposeless lodges, quaintly incompetent hospitals and schools, and churches where the inestimable blessing and knowledge of *its* gospel were taught and fostered. Nor had it dealt more kindly with the gentry within its walls, sending some to the scaffold, pillorying others in infamous office, reducing a few to poverty, and halting its later guests with gout and paralysis. It had given them in exchange the dubious immortality of a portrait gallery, from which they stared with stony and equal resignation; it had preserved their useless armour and accoutrements; it had set up their marble effigies in churches or laid them in cross-legged attitudes to trip up the unwary, until in death, as in life, they got between the congregation and the truth that was taught there. It had allowed an Oldenhurst crusader, with a broken nose like a pugilist, on the strength of his having been twice to the Holy Land, to hide the beautifully-illuminated Word from the lowlier worshipper on the humbler benches; it had sent an iconoclastic bishop of the Reformation to a nearer minster to ostentatiously occupy the place of the consecrated image he had overthrown. Small wonder that crowding the Oldenhurst retainers gradually into smaller space, with occasional Sabbath glimpses of the living rulers of Oldenhurst already in railed-off exaltation, it had forced them to accept Oldenhurst as a synonym of eternity, and left the knowledge of a higher Power to what time they should be turned out to their longer sleep under the tender grass of the beautiful outer churchyard.

And even thus, while every stone of the pile of Oldenhurst and every tree in its leafy park might have been eloquent with the story of vanity, selfishness, and unequal justice, it had been left to the infinite mercy of Nature to seal their lips with a spell of beauty that left mankind equally dumb; earth, air, and moisture had entered into a gentle conspiracy to soften, mellow, and clothe its external blemishes of breach and accident, its irregular design, its additions, accretions, ruins, and lapses with a harmonious charm of outline and colour; poets, romancers, and historians had equally conspired to illuminate the dark passages and uglier inconsistencies of its interior life with the glamour of their own fancy. The fragment of menacing keep, with its choked oubliettes, became a bower of tender ivy; the grim story of its crimes, properly edited by a contemporary bard of the family, passed into a charming ballad. Even the superstitious darkness of its religious house had escaped through fallen roof and shattered wall, leaving only the foliated and sun-pierced screen of front, with its rose-window and pinnacle of cross behind. Pilgrims from all lands had come to see it; fierce Republicans had crossed the seas to gaze at its mediæval outlines, and copy them in wood and stucco on their younger soil. Politicians had equally pointed to it as a convincing evidence of their own principles and in refutation of each other; and it had survived both. For it was this belief in its own perpetuity that was its strength and weakness. And that belief was never stronger than on this bright August morning, when it was on the verge of dissolution. A telegram brought to Sir Robert Mainwaring had even then as completely shattered and disintegrated Oldenhurst, in all it was and all it meant, as if the brown-paper envelope had been itself charged with the electric fluid.

Sir Robert Mainwaring, whose family had for three centuries possessed Oldenhurst, had received the news of his financial ruin; and the vast pile which had survived the repeated invasion of superstition, force, intrigue, and even progress, had succumbed to a foe its founders and proprietors had loftily ignored and left to Jews and traders. The acquisition of money, except by despoilment, gift, Royal favour, or inheritance, had been unknown at Oldenhurst. The present degenerate custodian of its fortunes, staggering under the weight of its sentimental mortmain already alluded to, had speculated in order to keep up its material strength, which was gradually shrinking through impoverished land and the ruined trade it had despised. He had invested largely in California mines, and was the chief shareholder in a San Francisco Bank. But the mines had proved worthless, the Bank had that morning suspended payment, owing to the failure of a large land and timber company on the Sierras, which it had imprudently "carried." The spark which had demolished Oldenhurst had been fired from the new telegraph-station in the hotel above the great Sierran canyon.

There was a large house-party at Oldenhurst that morning. But it had been a part of the history of the Mainwarings to accept defeat gallantly and as became their blood. Sir Percival—the second gentleman on the left as you entered the library—unhorsed, dying on a distant moor, with a handful of followers, abandoned by a charming Prince and a miserable cause, was scarcely a greater hero than this ruined but undaunted gentleman of eighty, entering the breakfast-room a few hours later as jauntily as his gout would permit, and conscientiously dispensing the hospitalities of his crumbling house. When he had arranged a few pleasure parties for the day, and himself thoughtfully anticipated the different tastes of his guests, he turned to Lady Mainwaring.

"Don't forget that somebody ought to go to the station to meet the Bradleys. Frank writes from St. Moritz that they are due here to-day."

Lady Mainwaring glanced quickly at her husband, and said *sotto voce,* "Do you think they'll care to come *now?* They probably have heard all about it."

"Not how it affects me," returned Sir Robert, in the same tone; "and as they might think that because Frank was with them on that California mountain we would believe it had something to do with Richardson involving the Bank in that wretched company, we must really *insist* upon their coming."

"Bradley!" echoed the Hon. Captain FitzHarry, overhearing the name during a late forage on the sideboard. "Bradley!—there was an awfully pretty American at Biarritz, travelling with a cousin, I think—a Miss Mason or Macy. Those sort of people, you know, who have a companion as pretty as themselves: bring you down with the other barrel if one misses—eh? Very clever, both of them, and hardly any accent."

"Mr. Bradley was a very dear friend of Frank's, and most kind to him," said Lady Mainwaring gravely.

"Didn't know there *was* a Mr. Bradley, really. He didn't come to the fore then," said the unabashed Captain. "Deuced hard to follow up those American husbands!"

"And their wives wouldn't thank you, if you did," said Lady Griselda Armiger, with a sweet smile.

"If it is the Mrs. Bradley I mean," said Lady Canterbridge from the lower end of the table, looking up from her letter, "who looks a little like Mrs. Summertree, and has a pretty cousin with her who wears very good frocks, I'm afraid you won't be able to get her down here. She's booked with engagements for the next six weeks. She and her cousin made all the running at Grigsby Royal, and she has quite deposed that other American beauty in Northforeland's good graces. She regularly *affiché'd* him, and it is piteous to see him follow her about. No, my dear; I don't believe they'll come to any one of less rank than a marquis. If they did, I'm sure Canterbridge would have had them at Buckenthorpe already."

"I wonder if there was ever anything in Frank's admiration of this Miss Macy?" said Lady Mainwaring a few moments later, lingering beside her husband in his study.

"I really don't know," said Sir Robert abstractedly; "his letters were filled with her praises, and Richardson thought"——

"Pray don't mention that man's name again," said Lady Mainwaring, with the first indication of feeling she had shown. "I shouldn't trust him."

"But why do you ask?" returned her husband.

Lady Mainwaring was silent for a moment. "She is very rich, I believe," she said slowly. "At least, Frank writes that some neighbours of theirs whom he met in the Engadine told him they had sold the site of that absurd cottage where he was ill for some extravagant sum."

"My dear Geraldine," said the old man affectionately, taking his wife's hand in his own, that now for the first time trembled, "if you have any hope based upon what you are thinking of now, let it be the last and least. You forget that Paget told us that with the best care he could scarcely ensure Frank's return to perfect health. Even if God in His mercy spared him long enough to take my place, what girl would be willing to tie herself to a man doomed to sickness and poverty? Hardly the one you speak of, my dear."

Lady Canterbridge proved a true prophet. Mrs. Bradley and Miss Macy did not come, regretfully alleging a previous engagement made on the Continent with the Duke of Northforeland and the Marquis of Dungeness; but the unexpected and apocryphal husband *did* arrive. "I have not seen my family," he said, "since I returned from visiting your son in Switzerland. I am glad they were able to amuse themselves without waiting for me at a London hotel, though I should prefer to have found them here." Sir Robert and Lady Mainwaring were courteous but slightly embarrassed. Lady Canterbridge, who had come to the station in bored curiosity, raised her clear blue eyes to his. He did not look like a fool, a complaisant or fashionably cynical husband— this well-dressed, well-mannered, but quietly and sympathetically observant man. Did he really care for his selfish wife? was it perfect trust or some absurd Transatlantic custom? She did not understand him. It wearied her, and she turned her eyes indifferently away. Bradley, a little irritated, he knew not why, at the scrutiny of this tall, handsome, gentlemanly-looking woman, who, however, in spite of her broad shoulders and narrow hips possessed a refined muliebrity superior to mere liberality of contour, turned slightly towards Sir Robert. "Lady Canterbridge, Frank's cousin," explained Sir Robert hesitatingly, as if conscious of some vague awkwardness. Bradley and Lady Canterbridge both bowed—possibly the latter's salutation was the most masculine—and Bradley, eventually forgetting her presence, plunged into an earnest, sympathetic, and intelligent account of the condition in which he had found the invalid at St. Moritz. The old man at first listened with an almost perfunctory courtesy and a hesitating reserve; but as Bradley was lapsing into equal reserve, and they drove up to the gates of the quadrangle, he unexpectedly warmed with a word or two of serious welcome. Looking up with a half-unconscious smile, Bradley met Lady Canterbridge's examining eyes.

The next morning, finding an opportunity to be alone with him, Bradley, with a tactful mingling of sympathy and directness, informed his host that he was cognisant of the disaster that had overtaken the Bank, and delicately begged him to accept of any service he could render him. "Pardon me," he said, "if I speak as plainly to you as I would to your son; my friendship for him justifies an equal frankness to any one he loves; but I should not intrude upon your confidence if I did not believe that my knowledge and assistance might be of benefit to you. Although *I* did not sell my lands to Richardson or approve of his methods," he continued, "I fear it was some suggestion of mine that eventually induced him to form the larger and more disastrous scheme that ruined the Bank. So you see," he added lightly, "I claim a right to offer you my services." Touched by Bradley's sincerity and discreet intelligence, Sir Robert was equally frank. During the recital of his Californian investments—a chronicle of almost fatuous speculation and imbecile enterprise—Bradley was profoundly moved at the naïve ignorance of business and hopeless ingenuousness of this old habitué of a cynical world and an insincere society, to whom no financial scheme had been too wild for acceptance. As Bradley listened with a half-saddened smile to the grave visions of this aged enthusiast, he remembered the son's unsophisticated simplicity; what he had considered as the "boyishness" of immaturity was the taint of the utterly unpractical Mainwaring blood. It was upon this blood, and others like it, that Oldenhurst had for centuries waxed and fattened.

Bradley was true to his promise of assistance, and with the aid of two or three of his brother millionaires, whose knowledge of the resources of the locality was no less powerful and convincing than the security of their actual wealth, managed to stay the immediate action of the catastrophe until the affairs of the Sierran Land and Timber Company could be examined and some plan of reconstruction arranged. During this interval of five months, in which the credit of Sir Robert Mainwaring was preserved with the secret of his disaster, Bradley was a frequent and welcome visitor to Oldenhurst. Apart from his strange and chivalrous friendship for the Mainwarings—which was as incomprehensible to Sir Robert as Sir Robert's equally eccentric and Quixotic speculations had been to Bradley—he began to feel a singular and weird fascination for the place. A patient martyr in the vast London house he had taken for his wife and cousin's amusement, he loved to escape the loneliness of its autumn solitude or the occasional greater loneliness of his wife's social triumphs. The handsome, thoughtful man who sometimes appeared at the foot of his wife's table or melted away like a well-bred ghost in the hollow emptiness of her brilliant receptions, piqued the languid curiosity of a few.

A distinguished personage, known for his tactful observance of *convenances* that others forgot, had made a point of challenging this gentlemanly apparition, and had followed it up with courteous civilities, which led to exchange of much respect but no increase of acquaintance. He had even spent a week at Buckenthorpe, with Canterbridge in the coverts and Lady Canterbridge in the music-room and library. He had returned more thoughtful, and for some time after was more frequent in his appearances at home, and more earnest in his renewed efforts to induce his wife to return to America with him.

"You'll never be happy anywhere but in California, among those common people," she replied; "and while I was willing to share your poverty *there,*" she added drily, "I prefer to share your wealth among civilised ladies and gentlemen. Besides," she continued, "we must consider Louise. She is as good as engaged to Lord Dunshunner, and I do not intend that you shall make a mess of her affairs here as you did in California."

It was the first time he had heard of Lord Dunshunner's proposals; it was the first allusion she had ever made to Louise and Mainwaring.

Meantime, the autumn leaves had fallen silently over the broad terraces of Oldenhurst, with little changes to the fortunes of the great house itself. The Christmas house-party included Lady Canterbridge, whose husband was still detained at Homburg in company with Dunshunner; and Bradley, whose wife and cousin lingered on the Continent. He was slightly embarrassed when Lady Canterbridge turned to him one afternoon as they were returning from the lake and congratulated him abruptly upon Louise's engagement.

"Perhaps you don't care to be congratulated," she said, as he did not immediately respond, "and you had as little to do with it as with that other? It is a woman's function."

"What other?" echoed Bradley.

Lady Canterbridge slightly turned her handsome head towards him as she walked unbendingly at his side. "Tell me how you manage to keep your absolute simplicity so fresh. Do you suppose it wasn't known at Oldenhurst that Frank had quite compromised himself with Miss Macy over there?"

"It certainly was not known 'over there,' " said Bradley curtly.

"Don't be angry with me."

Such an appeal from the tall, indifferent woman at his side, so confidently superior to criticism, and uttered in a lower tone, made him smile, albeit uneasily.

"I only meant to congratulate you," she continued carelessly. "Dunshunner is not a bad sort of fellow, and will come into a good property some day. And then, society is so made up of caprice, just now, that it is well for your wife's cousin to make the most of her opportunities while they last. She is very popular now; but next season"——Seeing that Bradley remained silent, she did not finish her sentence, but said with her usual abruptness, "Do you know a Miss Araminta Eulalie Sharpe?"

Bradley started. Could any one recognise honest Minty in the hopeless vulgarity which this fine lady had managed to carelessly import into her name? His eye kindled.

"She is an old friend of mine, Lady Canterbridge."

"How fortunate! Then I can please you by giving you good news of her. She is the coming sensation. They say she is very rich, but quite one of the people, you know; in fact, she makes no scruples of telling you her father was a blacksmith, I think, and takes the dear old man with her everywhere. FitzHarry raves about her, and says her *naïveté* is something too delicious. She is regularly in with some of the best people already. Lady Dungeness has taken her up, and Northforeland is only waiting for your cousin's engagement to be able to go over decently. Shall I ask her to Buckenthorpe?—come, now, as an apology for my rudeness to your cousin?" She was very womanly now in spite of her high collar, her straight back, and her tightly-fitting jacket, as she stood there smiling. Suddenly her smile faded; she drew her breath in quickly.

She had caught a glimpse of his usually thoughtful face and eyes, now illuminated with some pleasant memory.

"Thank you," he said smilingly, yet with a certain hesitation, as he thought of The Lookout and Araminta Eulalie Sharpe, and tried to reconcile them with the lady before him. "I should like it very much."

"Then you have known Miss Sharpe a long time?" continued Lady Canterbridge as they walked on.

"While we were at The Lookout she was our nearest neighbour."

"And I suppose your wife will consider it quite proper for you to see her again at my house?" said Lady Canterbridge, with a return of conventional levity.

"Oh! quite," said Bradley.

They had reached the low Norman-arched side entrance to the quadrangle. As Bradley swung open the bolt-studded oaken door to let her pass, she said carelessly—

"Then you are not coming in now?"

"No; I shall walk a little longer."

"And I am quite forgiven?"

"I am thanking you very much," he said, smiling directly into her blue eyes. She lowered them, and vanished into the darkness of the passage.

The news of Minty's success was further corroborated by Sir Robert, who later that evening called Bradley into the study. "Frank has been writing from Nice that he has renewed his acquaintance with some old Californian friends of yours—a Mr. and Miss Sharpe. Lady Canterbridge says that they are well known in London to some of our friends, but I would like to ask you something about them. Lady Mainwaring was on the point of inviting them here when I received a letter from Mr. Sharpe asking for a *business* interview. Pray, who is this Sharpe?"

"You say he writes for a *business* interview?" asked Bradley.

"Yes."

Bradley hesitated for a moment and then said quietly, "Perhaps, then, I am justified in a breach of confidence to him, in order to answer your question. He is the man who has assumed all the liabilities of the Sierran Land and Timber Company to enable the Bank to resume payment. But he did it on the condition that you were never to know it. For the rest he was a blacksmith who made a fortune, as Lady Canterbridge will tell you."

"How very odd—how kind, I mean! I should like to have been civil to him on Frank's account alone."

"I should see him on business and be civil to him afterwards." Sir Robert received the American's levity with his usual seriousness.

"No, they must come here for Christmas. His daughter is"——

"Araminta Eulalie Sharpe," said Bradley, in defiant memory of Lady Canterbridge.

Sir Robert winced audibly. "I shall rely on you, my dear boy, to help me make it pleasant for them," he said.

Christmas came, but not Minty. It drew a large contingent from Oldenhurst to the quaint old church, who came to view the green-wreathed monuments, and walls spotted with crimson berries, as if with the blood of former Oldenhurst warriors, and to impress the wondering villagers with the ineffable goodness and bounty of the Creator towards the Lords of Oldenhurst and their friends. Sir Robert, a little gouty, kept the house, and Bradley, somewhat uneasy at the Sharpes' absence, but more distrait with other thoughts, wandered listlessly in the long library. At the lower angle it was embayed into the octagon space of a former tower, which was furnished as a quaint recess for writing or study, pierced through its enormous walls with a lance-shaped window, hidden by heavy curtains. He was gazing abstractedly at the melancholy eyes of Sir Percival, looking down from the dark panel opposite, when he heard the crisp rustle of a skirt. Lady Canterbridge, tightly and stiffly buttoned in black from her long narrow boots to her slim white-collared neck, stood beside him with a

prayer-book in her ungloved hand. Bradley coloured quickly; the penetrating incense of the Christmas boughs and branches that decked the
walls and ceilings, mingling with some indefinable intoxicating aura
from the woman at his side, confused his senses. He seemed to be
losing himself in some forgotten past coeval with the long, quaintly
lighted room, the rich hangings, and the painted ancestor of this handsome woman. He recovered himself with an effort, and said, "You are
going to church?"

"I may meet them coming home; it's all the same. You like *him?*"
she said abruptly, pointing to the portrait. "I thought you did not care
for that sort of man over there."

"A man like that must have felt the impotence of his sacrifice before
he died, and that condoned everything," said Bradley thoughtfully.

"Then you don't think him a fool? Bob says it was a fair bargain for
a title and an office, and that by dying he escaped trial and the confiscation of what he had."

Bradley did not reply.

"I am disturbing your illusions again. Yet I rather like them. I think
you are quite capable of a sacrifice—perhaps you know what it is
already."

He felt that she was looking at him; he felt equally that he could not
respond with a commonplace. He was silent.

"I have offended you again, Mr. Bradley," she said. "Please be
Christian, and pardon me. You know this is a season of peace and
goodwill." She raised her blue eyes at the same moment to the Christmas decorations on the ceiling. They were standing before the parted
drapery of the lance window. Midway between the arched curtains
hung a spray of mistletoe—the conceit of a mischievous housemaid.
Their eyes met it simultaneously.

Bradley had Lady Canterbridge's slim, white hand in his own. The
next moment voices were heard in the passage, and the door nearly
opposite to them opened deliberately. The idea of their apparent seclusion and half compromising attitude flashed through the minds of both
at the same time. Lady Canterbridge stepped quickly backward, drawing Bradley with her, into the embrasure of the window; the folds of
the curtain swung together and concealed them from view.

The door had been opened by the footman, ushering in a broad-
shouldered man, who was carrying a travelling-bag and an umbrella in
his hand. Dropping into an arm-chair before the curtain, he waved
away the footman, who, even now, mechanically repeated a previously
vain attempt to relieve the stranger of his luggage.

"You leave that 'ere grip sack where it is, young man, and tell Sir
Robert Mainwaring that Mr. Demander Sharpe, of Californy, wishes

to see him—on business—on *business,* do ye hear? You hang onter that sentence—*on business!* it's about ez much ez you kin carry, I reckon, and leave that grip sack alone."

From behind the curtain Bradley made a sudden movement to go forward; but Lady Canterbridge—now quite pale but collected—restrained him with a warning movement of her hand. Sir Robert's stick and halting step were next heard along the passage, and he entered the room. His simple and courteous greeting of the stranger was instantly followed by a renewed attack upon the "grip sack," and a renewed defence of it by the stranger.

"No, Sir Robert," said the voice argumentatively, "this yer's a *business* interview, and until it's over—if *you* please—we'll remain ez we air. I'm Demander Sharpe, of Californy, and I and my darter, Minty, oncet had the pleasure of knowing your boy over thar, and of meeting him agin the other day at Nice."

"I think," said Sir Robert's voice gently, "that these are not the only claims you have upon me. I have only a day or two ago heard from Mr. Bradley that I owe to your generous hands and your disinterested liberality the saving of my California fortune."

There was the momentary sound of a pushed-back chair, a stamping of feet, and then Mr. Sharpe's voice rose high with the blacksmith's old querulous aggrieved utterance—

"So it's that finikin', conceited Bradley agin—that's giv' me away! Ef that man's all-fired belief in his being the Angel Gabriel and Dan'l Webster rolled inter one don't beat anythin'! I suppose that high-flyin' jay-bird kalkilated to put you and me and my gal and yer boy inter harness for his four-hoss chariot and he sittin' kam on the box drivin' us! Why don't he 'tend to his own business, and look arter his own concerns—instead o' leaving Jinny Bradley and Loo Macy dependent on Kings and Queens and titled folks gen'rally, and he, Jim Bradley, philanderin' with another man's wife—while that thar man is hard at work tryin' to make a honest livin' fer his wife, buckin' agin' faro an' the tiger gen'rally at Monaco! Eh? And that man a-intermeddlin' with me! Ef," continued the voice dropped to a tone of hopeless moral conviction, "Ef there's a man I mor'lly despise—it's that finikin' Jim Bradley."

"You quite misunderstand me, my dear sir," said Sir Robert's hurried voice; "he told me you had pledged him to secrecy, and he only revealed it to explain why you wished to see me."

There was a grunt of half-placated wrath from Sharpe, and then the voice resumed, but more deliberately, "Well, to come back to business: you've got a boy, Francis, and I've got a darter, Araminty. They've sorter taken a shine to each other and they want to get married. Mind

yer—wait a moment!—it wasn't allus so. No, sir; when my gal
Araminty first seed your boy in Californy she was poor, and she didn't
kalkilate to get into anybody's family unbeknownst or on sufferance.
Then she got rich and you got poor; and then—hold on a minit!—she
allows, does my girl, that there ain't any nearer chance o' their making
a match than they were afore, for she isn't goin' to hev it said that
she married your son fur the chance of some day becomin' Lady
Mainwaring."

"One moment, Mr. Sharpe," said the voice of the Baronet gravely:
"I am both flattered and pained by what I believe to be the kindly
object of your visit. Indeed, I may say I have gathered a suspicion of
what might be the sequel of this most unhappy acquaintance of my
son and your daughter; but I cannot believe that he has kept you in
ignorance of his unfortunate prospects and his still more unfortunate
state of health."

"When I told ye to hold on a minit," continued the blacksmith's
voice, with a touch of querulousness in its accent, "that was jist wot I
was comin' to. I knowed part of it from my own pocket, she knowed
the rest of it from his lips and the doctors she interviewed. And then
she says to me—sez my girl Minty—'Pop,' she sez, 'he's got nothing to
live for now but his title, and that he never may live to get, so that I
think ye kin jist go, Pop, and fairly and squarely, as a honest man, ask
his father to let me hev him.' Them's my darter's own words, Sir
Robert; and when I tell yer that she's got a million o' dollars to back
them, ye'll know she means business every time."

"Did Francis know that you were coming here?"

"Bless ye, no! He didn't know that she would have him. Ef it kem to
that, he ain't even asked her! She wouldn't let him until she was sure
of *you.*"

"Then you mean to say there is no engagement?"

"In course not. I reckoned to do the square thing first with ye."

The halting step of the Baronet crossing the room was heard distinctly. He had stopped beside Sharpe. "My dear Mr. Sharpe," he said,
in a troubled voice, "I cannot permit this sacrifice. It is too—too
great!"

"Then," said Sharpe's voice querulously, "I'm afraid we must do
without your permission. I didn't reckon to find a sort o' British Jim
Bradley in you. If *you* can't permit my darter to sacrifice herself by
marryin' your son, I can't permit her to sacrifice her love and him by
not marryin' him. So I reckon this yer interview is over."

"I am afraid we are both old fools, Mr. Sharpe; but—we will talk
this over with Lady Mainwaring. Come." There was evidently a slight
struggle near the chair over some inanimate object. But the next

moment the Baronet's voice rose, persuasively, "Really, I must insist upon relieving you of your bag and umbrella."

"Well, if you'll let me telegraph 'yes' to Minty, I don't care if yer do."

When the room was quiet again, Lady Canterbridge and James Bradley silently slipped from the curtain, and, without a word, separated at the door.

There was a merry Christmas at Oldenhurst and at Nice. But whether Minty's loving sacrifice was accepted or not, or whether she ever reigned as Lady Mainwaring, or lived an untitled widow, I cannot say. But as Oldenhurst still exists in all its pride and power, it is presumed that the peril that threatened its fortunes was averted, and that if another heroine was not found worthy of a frame in its picture-gallery, at least it had been sustained as of old by devotion and renunciation.

A Drift from
Redwood Camp

THEY HAD ALL known him as a shiftless, worthless creature. From the
time he first entered Redwood Camp, carrying his entire effects in a
red handkerchief on the end of a long-handled shovel, until he lazily
drifted out of it on a plank in the terrible inundation of 1856, they
never expected anything better of him. In a community of strong men
with sullen virtues and dangerously fascinating vices, he was tolerated
as possessing neither—not even rising by any dominant human weakness or ludicrous quality to the importance of a butt. In the *dramatis
personae* of Redwood Camp he was a simple "super"—who had only
passive, speechless rôles in those fierce dramas that were sometimes
unrolled beneath its green-curtained pines. Nameless and penniless, he
was overlooked by the census and ignored by the tax-collector, while
in a hotly-contested election for sheriff, when even the head-boards of
the scant cemetery were consulted to fill the poll-lists, it was discovered that neither candidate had thought fit to avail himself of his
actual vote. He was debarred the rude heraldry of a nickname of
achievement, and in a camp made up of "Euchre Bills," "Poker
Dicks," "Profane Pete," and "Snapshot Harry," was known vaguely
as "him," "Skeesicks," or "that coot." It was remembered long after,

with a feeling of superstition, that he had never even met with the dignity of an accident, nor received the fleeting honour of a chance shot meant for somebody else in any of the liberal and broadly comprehensive encounters which distinguished the camp. And the inundation that finally carried him out of it was partly anticipated by his passive incompetency, for while the others escaped—or were drowned in escaping—he calmly floated off on his plank without an opposing effort.

For all that Elijah Martin—which was his real name—was far from being unamiable or repellent. That he was cowardly, untruthful, selfish, and lazy, was undoubtedly the fact; perhaps it was his peculiar misfortune that, just then, courage, frankness, generosity, and activity were the dominant factors in the life of Redwood Camp. His submissive gentleness, his unquestioned modesty, his half refinement, and his amiable exterior consequently availed him nothing against the fact that he was missed during a raid of the Digger Indians, and lied to account for it; or that he lost his right to a gold discovery by failing to make it good against a bully, and selfishly kept this discovery from the knowledge of the camp. Yet this weakness awakened no animosity in his companions, and it is probably that the indifference of the camp to his fate in this final catastrophe came purely from a simple forgetfulness of one who at that supreme moment was weakly incapable.

Such was the reputation and such the antecedents of the man who, on the 15th of March 1856, found himself adrift in a swollen tributary of the Minyo. A spring freshet of unusual volume had flooded the adjacent river until, bursting its bounds, it escaped through the narrow, wedge-shaped valley that held Redwood Camp. For a day and a night the surcharged river poured half its waters through the straggling camp. At the end of that time every vestige of the little settlement was swept away; all that was left was scattered far and wide in the country, caught in the hanging branches of water-side willows and alders, embayed in sluggish pools, dragged over submerged meadows, and one fragment—bearing up Elijah Martin—pursuing the devious courses of an unknown tributary fifty miles away. Had he been a rash, impatient man, he would have been speedily drowned in some earlier desperate attempt to reach the shore; had he been an ordinarily bold man, he would have succeeded in transferring himself to the branches of some obstructing tree; but he was neither, and he clung to his broken raft-like berth with an endurance that was half the paralysis of terror and half the patience of habitual misfortune. Eventually he was caught in a side current, swept to the bank, and cast ashore on an unexplored wilderness.

His first consciousness was one of hunger, that usurped any

sentiment of gratitude for his escape from drowning. As soon as his cramped limbs permitted, he crawled out of the bushes in search of food. He did not know where he was; there was no sign of habitation —or even occupation—anywhere. He had been too terrified to notice the direction in which he had drifted—even if he had possessed the ordinary knowledge of a backwoodsman, which he did not. He was helpless. In his bewildered state, seeing a squirrel cracking a nut on the branch of a hollow tree near him, he made a half-frenzied dart at the frightened animal, which ran away. But the same association of ideas in his torpid and confused brain impelled him to search for the squirrel's hoard in the hollow of the tree. He ate the few hazel-nuts he found there ravenously. The purely animal instinct satisfied, he seemed to have borrowed from it a certain animal strength and intu-ition. He limped through the thicket not unlike some awkward, shy quadrumane, stopping here and there to peer out through the openings over the marshes that lay beyond. His sight, hearing, and even the sense of smell had become preternaturally acute. It was the latter which suddenly arrested his steps with the odour of dried fish. It had a significance beyond the mere instincts of hunger—it indicated the con-tiguity of some Indian encampment. And as such—it meant danger, torture, and death.

He stopped, trembled violently, and tried to collect his scattered senses. Redwood Camp had embroiled itself needlessly and brutally with the surrounding Indians, and only held its own against them by reckless courage and unerring marksmanship. The frequent use of a casual wandering Indian as a target for the practising rifles of its mem-bers had kept up an undying hatred in the heart of the aborigines and stimulated them to terrible and isolated reprisals. The scalped and skinned dead body of Jack Trainer, tied on his horse and held hid-eously upright by a cross of wood behind his saddle, had passed, one night, a slow and ghastly apparition, into camp; the corpse of Dick Ryner had been found anchored on the river-bed, disembowelled and filled with stone and gravel. The solitary and unprotected member of Redwood Camp who fell into the enemy's hands was doomed.

Elijah Martin remembered this, but his fears gradually began to subside in a certain apathy of the imagination, which, perhaps, dulled his apprehensions and allowed the instinct of hunger to become again uppermost. He knew that the low bark tents, or wigwams, of the Indians were hung with strips of dried salmon, and his whole being was now centred upon an attempt to stealthily procure a delicious morsel. As yet he had distinguished no other sign of life or habitation; a few moments later, however, and grown bolder with an animal-like trustfulness in his momentary security, he crept out of the thicket and found himself near a long, low mound or burrow-like structure of mud and bark on the river-bank. A single narrow opening, not unlike the entrance of an Esquimaux hut, gave upon the river. Martin had no difficulty in recognising the character of the building. It was a "sweat-house," an institution common to nearly all the aboriginal tribes of California. Half a religious temple, it was also half a sanitary asylum, was used as a Russian bath or superheated vault, from which the braves, sweltering and stifling all night, by smothered fires, at early dawn plunged, perspiring, into the ice-cold river. The heat and smoke were further utilised to dry and cure the long strips of fish hanging from the roof, and it was through the narrow aperture that served as a chimney that the odour escaped which Martin had detected. He knew that, as the bathers only occupied the house from midnight to early morn, it was now probably empty. He advanced confidently toward it.

He was a little surprised to find that the small open space between it and the river was occupied by a rude scaffolding, like that on which certain tribes exposed their dead, but in this instance it only contained the feathered leggings, fringed blanket, and eagle-plumed head-dress of some brave. He did not, however, linger in this plainly visible area, but quickly dropped on all-fours and crept into the interior of the house. Here he completed his feast with the fish, and warmed his chilled limbs on the embers of the still smouldering fires. It was while drying his tattered clothes and shoeless feet that he thought of the dead brave's useless leggings and moccasins, and it occurred to him that he would be less likely to attract the Indians' attention from a distance and provoke a ready arrow, if he were disguised as one of them. Crawling out again, he quickly secured, not only the leggings, but the blanket and head-dress, and putting them on, cast his own clothes into the stream. A bolder, more energetic, or more provident man would have followed the act by quickly making his way back to the thicket to reconnoitre, taking with him a supply of fish for future needs. But Elijah Martin succumbed again to the recklessness of inertia; he yielded once more to the animal instinct of momentary security. He returned to the interior of the hut, curled himself again on the ashes, and weakly resolving to sleep until moonrise, and as weakly hesitating, ended by falling into uneasy but helpless stupor.

When he awoke, the rising sun, almost level with the low entrance to the sweat-house, was darting its direct rays into the interior, as if searching it with fiery spears. He had slept ten hours. He rose tremblingly to his knees. Everything was quiet without; he might yet escape. He crawled to the opening. The open space before it was empty, but the scaffolding was gone. The clear, keen air revived him. As he sprang out, erect, a shout that nearly stunned him seemed to rise from the earth on all sides. He glanced around him in a helpless agony of fear. A dozen concentric circles of squatting Indians, whose heads were visible above the reeds, encompassed the banks around the sunken base of the sweat-house with successive dusky rings. Every avenue of escape seemed closed. Perhaps for that reason the attitude of his surrounding captors was passive rather than aggressive, and the shrewd, half-Hebraic profiles nearest him expressed only stoical waiting. There was a strange similarity of expression in his own immovable apathy of despair. His only sense of averting his fate was a confused idea of explaining his intrusion. His desperate memory yielded a few common Indian words. He pointed automatically to himself and the stream. His white lips moved.

"I come—from—the river!"

A guttural cry, as if the whole assembly were clearing their throats, went round the different circles. The nearest rocked themselves to and fro and bent their feathered heads toward him. A hollow-cheeked, decrepit old man arose and said, simply—

"It is he! The great chief has come!"

He was saved. More than that, he was re-created. For, by signs and intimations he was quickly made aware that since the death of their late chief, their medicine-men had prophesied that his perfect successor should appear miraculously before them, borne noiselessly on the river *from the sea,* in the plumes and insignia of his predecessor. This mere coincidence of appearance and costume might not have been convincing to the braves had not Elijah Martin's actual deficiencies contributed to their unquestioned faith in him. Not only his inert possession of the sweat-house and his apathetic attitude in their presence, but his utter and complete unlikeness to the white frontiersmen of their knowledge and tradition—creatures of fire and sword and malevolent activity—as well as his manifest dissimilarity to themselves, settled their conviction of his supernatural origin. His gentle, submissive voice, his yielding will, his lazy helplessness, the absence of strange weapons, and fierce explosives in his possession, his unwonted sobriety—all proved him an exception to his apparent race that was in itself miraculous. For it must be confessed that, in spite of the cherished theories of most romances and all statesmen and commanders, that *fear* is the great civiliser of the savage barbarian, and that he is supposed to regard the prowess of the white man and his mysterious death-dealing weapons as evidence of his supernatural origin and superior creation, the facts have generally pointed to the reverse. Elijah Martin was not long in discovering that when the Minyo hunter, with his obsolete bow, dropped dead by a bullet from a viewless and apparently noiseless space, it was *not* considered the lightnings of an avenging Deity, but was traced directly to the ambushed rifle of Kansas Joe, swayed by a viciousness quite as human as their own; the spectacle of Blizzard Dick, verging on *delirium tremens,* and riding "amuck" into an Indian village with a revolver in each hand, did *not* impress them as a supernatural act, nor excite their respectful awe as much as the less harmful frenzy of one of their own medicine-men; they were *not* influenced by implacable white gods, who relaxed only to drive hard bargains and exchange mildewed flour and shoddy blankets for their fish and furs. I am afraid they regarded these raids of Christian civilisation as they looked upon grasshopper plagues, famines, inundations, and epidemics; while an utterly impassive God washed his hands of the means he had employed, and even encouraged the faithful to resist and overcome his emissaries—the white devils! Had Elijah Martin been a student of theology, he would have been struck with the singular resemblance of these theories—although the application thereof was reversed—to the Christian faith. But Elijah Martin had neither the imagination of a theologian nor the insight of a politician. He only saw that he, hitherto ignored and despised in a community of half-barbaric men, now translated to a community of men wholly savage, was respected and worshipped!

It might have turned a stronger head than Elijah's. He was at first frightened, fearful lest his reception concealed some hidden irony, or that, like the flower-crowned victim of ancient sacrifice, he was exalted and sustained to give importance and majesty to some impending martyrdom. Then he began to dread that his innocent deceit—if deceit it was—should be discovered; at last, partly from meekness and partly from the animal contentment of present security, he accepted the situation. Fortunately for him it was purely passive. The great chief of the Minyo tribe was simply an expressionless idol of flesh and blood. The previous incumbent of that office had been an old man, impotent and senseless of late years through age and disease. The chieftains and braves had consulted in council before him, and perfunctorily submitted their decisions, like offerings, to his unresponsive shrine. In the same way, all material events—expeditions, trophies, industries—were supposed to pass before the dull, impassive eyes of the great chief, for direct acceptance. On the second day of Elijah's accession, two of the braves brought a bleeding human scalp before him. Elijah turned pale, trembled, and averted his head, and then, remembering the danger of giving way to his weakness, grew still more ghastly. The warriors watched him with impassioned faces. A grunt—but whether of astonishment, dissent, or approval, he could not tell—went round the circle.

But the scalp was taken away and never again appeared in his presence.

An incident still more alarming quickly followed. Two captives, white men, securely bound, were one day brought before him on their way to the stake, followed by a crowd of old and young squaws and children. The unhappy Elijah recognised in the prisoners two packers from a distant settlement who sometimes passed through Redwood Camp. An agony of terror, shame, and remorse shook the pseudo-chief to his crest of high feathers, and blanched his face beneath its paint and yellow ochre. To interfere to save them from the torture they were evidently to receive at the hands of those squaws and children, according to custom, would be exposure and death to him as well as themselves; while to assist by his passive presence at the horrible sacrifice of his countrymen was too much for even his weak selfishness. Scarcely knowing what he did as the lugubrious procession passed before him, he hurriedly hid his face in his blanket and turned his back upon the scene. There was a dead silence. The warriors were evidently unprepared for this extraordinary conduct of their chief. What might have been their action it was impossible to conjecture, for at that moment a little squaw, perhaps impatient for the sport and partly emboldened by the fact that she had been selected, only a few days before, as the betrothed of the new chief, approached him slyly from the other side. The horrified eyes of Elijah, momentarily raised from his blanket, saw and recognised her. The feebleness of a weak nature, that dared not measure itself directly with the real cause, vented its rage on a secondary object. He darted a quick glance of indignation and hatred at the young girl. She ran back in startled terror to her companions, a hurried consultation followed, and in another moment the whole bevy of girls, old women, and children were on the wing, shrieking and crying, to their wigwams.

"You see," said one of the prisoners coolly to the other in English, "I was right. They never intended to do anything to us. It was only a bluff. These Minyos are a different sort from the other tribes. They never kill anybody if they can help it."

"You're wrong," said the other excitedly. "It was that big chief there, with his head in a blanket, that sent those dogs to the right-about. Hell! did you see them run at just a look from him? He's a high and mighty feller, you bet. Look at his dignity!"

"That's so—he ain't no slouch," said the other, gazing at Elijah's muffled head critically. "D——d if he ain't a born king."

The sudden conflict and utter revulsion of emotion that those simple words caused in Elijah's breast was almost incredible. He had been at first astounded by the revelation of the peaceful reputation of the unknown tribe he had been called upon to govern; but even this comforting assurance was as nothing compared to the greater revelations implied in the speaker's praise of himself. He, Elijah Martin! the despised, the rejected, the worthless outcast of Redwood Camp, recognised as a "born king," a leader; his power felt by the very men who had scorned him! And he had done nothing—stop! had he actually done *nothing?* Was it not possible that he was *really* what they thought him? His brain reeled under the strong, unaccustomed wine of praise; acting upon his weak selfishness, it exalted him for a moment to their measure of his strength, even as their former belief in his inefficiency had kept him down. Courage is too often only the memory of past success. This was his first effort; he forgot he had not earned it, even as he now ignored the danger of earning it. The few words of unconscious praise had fallen like the blade of knighthood on his cowering shoulders; he had risen ennobled from the contact. Though his face was still muffled in his blanket, he stood erect and seemed to have gained in stature.

The braves had remained standing irresolute, and yet watchful, a few paces from their captives. Suddenly Elijah, still keeping his back to the prisoners, turned upon the braves with blazing eyes, violently throwing out his hands with the gesture of breaking bonds. Like all sudden demonstrations of undemonstrative men, it was extravagant, weird, and theatrical. But it was more potent than speech—the speech that, even if effective, would still have betrayed him to his countrymen. The braves hurriedly cut the thongs of the prisoners; another impulsive gesture from Elijah, and they, too, fled. When he lifted his eyes cautiously from his blanket, captors and captives had dispersed in opposite directions, and he was alone—and triumphant!

From that moment Elijah Martin was another man. He went to bed that night in an intoxicating dream of power; he arose a man of will, of strength. He read it in the eyes of the braves, albeit at times averted in wonder. He understood now, that although peace had been their habit and custom, they had nevertheless sought to test his theories of administration with the offering of the scalps and the captives, and in this detection of their common weakness he forgot his own. Most heroes require the contrast of the unheroic to set them off; and Elijah actually found himself devising means for strengthening the defensive and offensive character of the tribe, and was himself strengthened by it. Meanwhile the escaped packers did not fail to heighten the importance of their adventure by elevating the character and achievements of their deliverer; and it was presently announced throughout the frontier settlements that the hitherto insignificant and peaceful tribe of Minyos, who inhabited a large territory bordering on the Pacific Ocean, had developed into a powerful nation, only kept from the war-path by a more powerful but mysterious chief. The Government sent an Indian agent to treat with them, in its usual half-paternal, half-aggressive, and wholly inconsistent policy. Elijah, who still retained the imitative sense and adaptability to surroundings which belong to most lazy, impressible natures, and in striped yellow and vermilion features looked the chief he personated, met the agent with silent and becoming gravity. The council was carried on by signs. Never before had an Indian treaty been entered into with such perfect knowledge of the intentions and designs of the whites by the Indians, and such profound ignorance of the qualities of the Indians by the whites. It need scarcely be said that the treaty was an unquestionable Indian success. They did not give up their arable lands; what they did sell to the agent they refused to exchange for extravagant-priced shoddy blankets, worthless guns, damp powder, and mouldy meal. They took pay in dollars, and were thus enabled to open more profitable commerce with the traders at the settlements for better goods and better bargains; they simply declined beads, whisky, and Bibles at any price. The result was that the traders found it profitable to protect them from their countrymen, and the chances of wantonly shooting down a possible valuable customer stopped the old indiscriminate rifle-practice. The Indians were allowed to cultivate their fields in peace. Elijah purchased for them a few agricultural implements. The catching, curing, and smoking of salmon became an important branch of trade. They waxed prosperous and rich; they lost their nomadic habits—a centralised settlement bearing the external signs of an Indian village took the place of their old temporary encampments, but the huts were internally an improvement on the old wigwams. The dried fish were banished from the tentpoles to long sheds especially constructed for that purpose. The sweat-house was no longer utilised for worldly purposes. The wise and mighty Elijah did not attempt to reform their religion, but to preserve it in its integrity.

That these improvements and changes were due to the influence of one man was undoubtedly true, but that he was necessarily a superior man did not follow. Elijah's success was due partly to the fact that he had been enabled to impress certain negative virtues, which were part of his own nature, upon a community equally constituted to receive them. Each was strengthened by the recognition in each other of the unexpected value of those qualities; each acquired a confidence begotten of their success. *"He-hides-his-face,"* as Elijah Martin was known to the tribe after the episode of the released captives, was really not so much of an autocrat as many constitutional rulers.

Two years of tranquil prosperity passed. Elijah Martin, foundling, outcast, without civilised ties or relationship of any kind, forgotten by his countrymen, and lifted into alien power, wealth, security, and respect, became—homesick!

It was near the close of a summer afternoon. He was sitting at the door of his lodge, which overlooked, on one side, the far-shining levels of the Pacific, and, on the other, the slow descent to the cultivated meadows and banks of the Minyo River, that debouched through a waste of salt-marsh, beach-grass, sand-dunes, and foamy estuary into the ocean. The headland, or promontory—the only eminence of the Minyo territory—had been reserved by him for his lodge, partly on account of its isolation from the village at its base, and partly for the view it commanded of his territory. Yet his wearying and discontented eyes were more often found on the ocean, as a possible highway of escape from his irksome position, than on the plain and the distant range of mountains, so closely connected with the nearer past and his former detractors. In his vague longing he had no desire to return to them, even in triumph; in his present security there still lingered a doubt of his ability to cope with the old conditions. It was more like his easy, indolent nature—which revived in his prosperity—to trust to this least practical and remote solution of his trouble. His home-sickness was as vague as his plan for escape from it; he did not know exactly what he regretted, but it was probably some life he had not enjoyed, some pleasure that had escaped his former incompetency and poverty.

He had sat thus a hundred times, as aimlessly blinking at the vast possibilities of the shining sea beyond, turning his back upon the near and more practicable mountains, lulled by the far-off beating of monotonous rollers, the lonely cry of the curlew and plover, the drowsy changes of alternate breaths of cool, fragrant reeds and warm, spicy sands that blew across his eyelids, and succumbed to sleep, as he had done a hundred times before. The narrow strips of coloured cloth, insignia of his dignity, flapped lazily from his tent-poles, and at last seemed to slumber with him; the shadows of the leaf-tracery thrown by the bay-tree on the ground at his feet scarcely changed its pattern. Nothing moved but the round, restless, berry-like eyes of Wachita, his child-wife, the former heroine of the incident with the captive packers, who sat near her lord, armed with a willow wand, watchful of intruding wasps, sand-flies, and even the more ostentatious advances of a rotund and clerical-looking humble-bee, with his monotonous homily. Content, dumb, submissive, vacant, at such times, Wachita, debarred her husband's confidences through the native customs and his own indifferent taciturnity, satisfied herself by gazing at him with the wondering but ineffectual sympathy of a faithful dog. Unfortunately for Elijah her purely mechanical ministration could not prevent a more dangerous intrusion upon his security.

He awoke with a light start, and eyes that gradually fixed upon the woman a look of returning consciousness. Wachita pointed timidly to the village below.

"The Messenger of the Great White Father has come to-day, with his waggons and horses; he would see the chief of the Minyos, but I would not disturb my lord."

Elijah's brow contracted. Relieved of its characteristic metaphor, he knew that this meant that the new Indian agent had made his usual official visit, and had exhibited the usual anxiety to see the famous chieftain.

"Good!" he said. "White Rabbit (his lieutenant) will see the messenger and exchange gifts. It is enough."

"The white messenger has brought his wangee (white) woman with him. They would look upon the face of him who hides it," continued Wachita dubiously. "They would that Wachita should bring them nearer to where my lord is, that they might see him when he knew it not."

Elijah glanced moodily at his wife, with the half suspicion with which he still regarded her alien character. "Then let Wachita go back to the squaws and old women, and let her hide herself with them until the wangee strangers are gone," he said curtly. "I have spoken. Go!"

Accustomed to these abrupt dismissals, which did not necessarily indicate displeasure, Wachita disappeared without a word. Elijah, who had risen, remained for a few moments leaning against the tent-poles, gazing abstractedly toward the sea. The bees droned uninterruptedly in his ears; the far-off roll of the breakers came to him distinctly; but suddenly, with greater distinctness, came the murmur of a woman's voice.

"He don't look savage a bit! Why, he's real handsome."

"Hush! you"——said a second voice, in a frightened whisper.

"But if he *did* hear he couldn't understand," returned the first voice. A suppressed giggle followed.

Luckily, Elijah's natural and acquired habits of repression suited the emergency. He did not move, although he felt the quick blood fly to his face, and the voice of the first speaker had suffused him with a strange and delicious anticipation. He restrained himself, though the words she had naïvely dropped were filling him with new and tremulous suggestion. He was motionless, even while he felt that the vague longing and yearning which had possessed him hitherto was now mysteriously taking some unknown form and action.

The murmuring ceased. The humble-bee's drone again became ascendant—a sudden fear seized him. She was *going;* he should never see her! While he had stood there a dolt and sluggard, she had satisfied her curiosity and stolen away. With a sudden yielding to impulse, he darted quickly in the direction where he had heard her voice. The thicket moved, parted, crackled, and rustled, and then undulated thirty feet before him in a long wave, as if from the passage of some lithe, invisible figure. But at the same moment a little cry, half of alarm, half of laughter, broke from his very feet, and a bent manzanito-bush, relaxed by frightened fingers, flew back against his breast. Thrusting it hurriedly aside, his stooping, eager face came almost in contact with the pink, flushed cheeks and tangled curls of a woman's head. He was so near, her moist and laughing eyes almost drowned his eager glance; her parted lips and white teeth were so close to his that her quick breath took away his own.

She had dropped on one knee, as her companion fled, expecting he would overlook her as he passed, but his direct onset had extracted the feminine outcry. Yet even then she did not seem greatly frightened.

"It's only a joke, sir," she said, ignoring her late belief that he knew no English, but coolly lifting herself to her feet, by grasping his arm. "I'm Mrs. Dall, the Indian agent's wife. They said you wouldn't let anybody see you—and *I* determined I would. That's all!" She stopped, threw back her tangled curls behind her ears, shook the briars and thorns from her skirt, and added: "Well, I reckon you aren't afraid of a woman, are you? So no harm's done. Good-bye!"

She drew slightly back as if to retreat, but the elasticity of the manzanito against which she was leaning threw her forward once more. He again inhaled the perfume of her hair; he saw even the tiny freckles that darkened her upper lip and brought out the moist, red curve below. A sudden recollection of a playmate of his vagabond childhood flashed across his mind; a wild inspiration of lawlessness, begotten of his past experience, his solitude, his dictatorial power, and the beauty of the woman before him, mounted to his brain. He threw his arms passionately around her, pressed his lips to hers, and with a half-hysterical laugh drew back and disappeared in the thicket.

Mrs. Dall remained for an instant dazed and stupefied. Then she lifted her arm mechanically, and with her sleeve wiped her bruised mouth and the ochre stain that his paint had left, like blood, upon her cheek. Her laughing face had become instantly grave, but not from fear; her dark eyes had clouded, but not entirely with indignation. She suddenly brought down her hand sharply against her side with a gesture of discovery. "That's no Injun!" she said, with prompt decision. The next minute she plunged back into the trail again, and the dense foliage once more closed around her. But as she did so the broad, vacant face and the mutely wondering eyes of Wachita rose, like a placid moon, between the branches of a tree where she had been hidden, and shone serenely and impassively after her.

A month elapsed. But it was a month filled with more experience to Elijah than his past two years of exaltation. In the first few days following his meeting with Mrs. Dall, he was possessed by terror, mingled with flashes of desperation, at the remembrance of his rash imprudence. His recollection of extravagant frontier chivalry to womankind, and the swift retribution of the insulted husband or guardian, alternately filled him with abject fear or extravagant recklessness. At times prepared for flight, even to the desperate abandonment of himself in a canoe to the waters of the Pacific; at times he was on the point of inciting his braves to attack the Indian agency and precipitate the war that he felt would be inevitable. As the days passed, and there seemed to be no interruption to his friendly relations with the agency, with that relief a new, subtle joy crept into Elijah's heart. The image of the agent's wife framed in the leafy screen behind his lodge, the perfume of her hair and breath mingled with the spicing of the bay, the brief thrill and tantalisation of the stolen kiss still haunted him. Through his long, shy abstention from society, and his two years of solitary exile, the fresh beauty of this young Western wife, in whom the frank artlessness of girlhood still lingered, appeared to him like a superior creation. He forgot his vague longings in the inception of a more tangible but equally unpractical passion. He remembered her unconscious and spontaneous admiration of him; he dared to connect it with her forgiving silence. If she had withheld her confidences from her husband, he could hope—he knew not exactly what!

One afternoon Wachita put into his hand a folded note. With an instinctive presentiment of its contents, Elijah turned red and embarrassed in receiving it from the woman who was recognised as his wife. But the impassive, submissive manner of this household drudge, instead of touching his conscience, seemed to him a vulgar and brutal acceptance of the situation that dulled whatever compunction he might have had. He opened the note and read hurriedly as follows:—

You took a great freedom with me the other day, and I am justified in taking one with you now. I believe you understand English as well as I do. If you want to explain that, and your conduct to me, I will be at the same place this afternoon. My friend will accompany me, but she need not hear what you have to say.

Elijah read the letter, which might have been written by an ordinary school-girl, as if it had conveyed the veiled rendezvous of a princess. The reserve, caution, and shyness which had been the safeguard of his weak nature were swamped in a flow of immature passion. He flew to the interview with the eagerness and inexperience of first love. He was completely at her mercy. So utterly was he subjugated by her presence that she did not even run the risk of his passion. Whatever sentiment might have mingled with her curiosity, she was never conscious of a necessity to guard herself against it. At this second meeting she was in full possession of his secret. He had told her everything; she had promised nothing in return—she had not even accepted anything. Even her actual after-relations to the *dénouement* of his passion are still shrouded in mystery.

Nevertheless, Elijah lived two weeks on the unsubstantial memory of this meeting. What might have followed could not be known, for at the end of that time an outrage—so atrocious that even the peaceful Minyos were thrilled with savage indignation—was committed on the outskirts of the village. An old chief, who had been specially selected to deal with the Indian agent, and who kept a small trading outpost, had been killed and his goods despoiled by a reckless Redwood packer. The murderer had coolly said that he was only "serving out" the tool of a fraudulent imposture on the Government, and that he dared the arch-impostor himself, the so-called Minyo chief, to help himself. A wave of ungovernable fury surged up to the very tent-poles of Elijah's lodge and demanded vengeance. Elijah trembled and hesitated. In the thraldom of his selfish passion for Mrs. Dall he dared not contemplate a collision with her countrymen. He would have again sought refuge in his passive, non-committal attitude, but he knew the impersonal character of Indian retribution and compensation—a sacrifice of equal value, without reference to the culpability of the victim—and he dreaded some spontaneous outbreak. To prevent the enforced expiation of the crime by some innocent brother packer, he was obliged to give orders for the pursuit and arrest of the criminal, secretly hoping for his escape or the interposition of some circumstance to avert his punishment. A day of sullen expectancy to the old men and squaws in camp, of gloomy anxiety to Elijah alone in his lodge, followed the departure of the braves on the war-path. It was midnight when they returned. Elijah, who from his habitual reserve and the accepted etiquette of his exalted station had remained impassive in his tent, only knew from the guttural rejoicings of the squaws that the expedition had been successful and the captive was in their hands. At any other time he might have thought it an evidence of some growing scepticism of his infallibility of judgment and a diminution of respect that they did not confront him with their prisoner. But he was too glad to escape from the danger of exposure and possible arraignment of his past life by the desperate captive, even though it might not have been understood by the spectators. He reflected that the omission might have arisen from their recollection of his previous aversion to a retaliation on other prisoners. Enough that they would wait his signal for the torture and execution at sunrise the next day.

The night passed slowly. It is more than probable that the selfish and ignoble torments of the sleepless and vacillating judge were greater than those of the prisoner who dozed at the stake between his curses. Yet it was part of Elijah's fatal weakness that his kinder and more human instincts were dominated even at that moment by his lawless passion for the Indian agent's wife, and his indecision as to the fate of his captive was equally due to his preoccupation and a selfish consideration of her possible relations to the result. He hated the prisoner for his infelicitous and untimely crime, yet he could not make up his mind to his death. He paced the ground before his lodge in dishonourable incertitude. The small eyes of the submissive Wachita watched him with vague solicitude.

Towards morning he was struck by a shameful inspiration. He would creep unperceived to the victim's side, unloose his bonds, and bid him fly to the Indian agency! There he was to inform Mrs. Dall that her husband's safety depended upon his absenting himself for a few days, but that she was to remain and communicate with Elijah. She would understand everything, perhaps; at least she would know that the prisoner's release was to please her, and even if she did not, no harm would be done, a white man's life would be saved, and his real motive would not be suspected. He turned with feverish eagerness to the lodge. Wachita had disappeared—probably to join the other women. It was well; she would not suspect him.

The tree to which the doomed man was bound was, by custom, selected nearest the chief's lodge, within its sacred enclosure, with no other protection than that offered by its reserved seclusion and the outer semicircle of warriors' tents before it. To escape, the captive would therefore have to pass beside the chief's lodge to the rear and descend the hill towards the shore. Elijah would show him the way, and make it appear as if he had escaped unaided. As he glided into the shadow of a group of pines, he could dimly discern the outline of the destined victim, secured against one of the larger trees in a sitting posture, with his head fallen forward on his breast as if in sleep. But at the same moment another figure glided out from the shadow and approached the fatal tree. It was Wachita!

He stopped in amazement. But in another instant a flash of

intelligence made it clear to him. He remembered her vague uneasiness and solicitude at his agitation and her sudden disappearance; she had fathomed his perplexity, as she had once before! Of her own accord she was going to release the prisoner! The knife to cut his cords glittered in her hand. Brave and faithful animal!

He held his breath as he drew nearer. But, to his horror, the knife suddenly flashed in the air and darted down, again and again, upon the body of the helpless man. There was a convulsive struggle, but no outcry, and the next moment the body hung limp and inert in its cords. Elijah would himself have fallen, half fainting, against a tree, but by a revulsion of feeling, came the quick revelation that the desperate girl had rightly solved the problem! She had done what *he* ought to have done—and his loyalty and manhood were preserved. That conviction and the courage to act upon it—to have called the sleeping braves to witness his sacrifice—would have saved him, but—it was ordered otherwise!

As the girl rapidly passed him he threw out his hand and seized her wrist. "What did you do this for?" he demanded.

"For you," she said stupidly.

"And why?"

"Because you no kill him—you love his squaw."

"*His* squaw!" He staggered back. A terrible suspicion flashed upon him. He dashed Wachita aside and ran to the tree. It was the body of the Indian agent!

Aboriginal justice had been satisfied. The warriors had not caught the *murderer,* but, true to their idea of vicarious retribution, they had determined upon the expiatory sacrifice of a life as valuable and innocent as the one they had lost, and had carried off the unfortunate representative of the Government.

"So the Gov'rment hev at last woke up and wiped out them cussed Digger Minyos," said Snapshot Harry, three months later, as he laid down the newspaper, in the brand-new saloon of the brand-new town of Redwood. "I see they've stampeded both banks of the Minyo River, and sent off a lot to the reservation. I reckon the soldiers at Fort Cass got sick o' sentiment after those hounds killed the Injun agent, and are beginning to agree with us that the only 'good Injun' is a dead one."

"And it turns out that that wonderful chief, that them two packers used to rave about, woz about as big a devil ez any, and tried to run off with the agent's wife, only the warriors killed her. I'd like to know what become of him. Some says he was killed, others allow that he got away. I've heerd tell that he was originally some kind of Methodist preacher!—a kind o' saint that got a sort o' spiritooal holt on the old squaws and children."

"Why don't you ask old Skeesicks? I see he's back here ag'in—and grubbin' along at a dollar a day on tailin's He's been somewhere up north, they say."

"What, Skeesicks? That shiftless, o'n'ry cuss! You bet he wusn't anywhere where there was danger or fighting. Why, you might as well hev suspected *him* of being the big chief himself! There he comes—ask him."

And the laughter was so general that Elijah Martin—*alias* Skeesicks —lounging shyly into the bar-room, joined in it weakly.

A Ward of the Golden Gate

PROLOGUE

IN SAN FRANCISCO the "rainy season" had been making itself a reality to the wondering Eastern immigrant. There were short days of drifting clouds and flying sunshine, and long succeeding nights of incessant downpour, when the rain rattled on the thin shingles or drummed on the resounding zinc of pioneer roofs. The shifting sand-dunes on the outskirts were beaten motionless and sodden by the onslaught of consecutive storms; the south-east trades brought the saline breath of the outlying Pacific even to the busy haunts of Commercial and Kearney Streets; the low-lying Mission Road was a quagmire; along the City Front, despite of piles and pier and wharf, the Pacific tides still asserted themselves in mud and ooze as far as Sansome Street; the wooden side-walks of Clay and Montgomery Streets were mere floating bridges or buoyant pontoons superposed on elastic bogs; Battery Street was the Silurian beach of that early period on which tin cans, packing-boxes, freight, household furniture, and even the runaway crews of deserted ships had been cast away. There were dangerous and unknown depths in Montgomery Street and on the Plaza, and the wheels of a passing carriage hopelessly mired had to be lifted by the volunteer hands of a half-dozen high-booted wayfarers, whose wearers were sufficiently content to believe that a woman, a child, or an invalid was behind its closed windows, without troubling themselves or the occupant by looking through the glass.

It was a carriage that, thus released, eventually drew up before the superior public edifice known as the City Hall. From it a woman, closely veiled, alighted, and quickly entered the building. A few passers-by turned to look at her, partly from the rarity of the female figure at that period, and partly from the greater rarity of its being well-formed and even lady-like.

As she kept her way along the corridor and ascended an iron stair-case, she was passed by others more pre-occupied in business at the various public offices. One of these visitors, however, stopped as if struck by some fancied resemblance in her appearance, turned, and followed her. But when she halted before a door marked "Mayor's Office," he paused also, and, with a look of half-humorous bewilder-ment, and a slight glance around him as if seeking for some one to whom to impart his arch fancy, he turned away. The woman then entered a large ante-room with a certain quick feminine gesture of relief, and, finding it empty of other callers, summoned the porter, and asked him some question in a voice so suppressed by the official sever-ity of the apartment as to be hardly audible. The attendant replied by entering another room marked "Mayor's Secretary," and reappeared with a stripling of seventeen or eighteen, whose singularly bright eyes were all that was youthful in his composed features. After a slight scrutiny of the woman—half boyish, half official—he desired her, to be seated, with a certain exaggerated gravity as if he was over-acting a grown-up part, and, taking a card from her, re-entered his office. Here, however, he did *not* stand on his head or call out a confederate youth from a closet, as the woman might have expected. To the left was a green-baize door, outlined with brass-studded rivets like a cheerful coffin-lid, and bearing the mortuary inscription "Private." This he pushed open, and entered the Mayor's private office.

The municipal dignitary of San Francisco, although an erect, soldier-like man of strong middle age, was seated with his official chair tilted back against the wall and kept in position by his feet on the rungs of another, which in turn acted as a support for a second man, who was seated a few feet from him in an easy-chair. Both were lazily smoking.

The Mayor took the card from his secretary, glanced at it, said "Hullo!" and handed it to his companion, who read aloud "Kate Howard," and gave a prolonged whistle.

"Where is she?" asked the Mayor.

"In the ante-room, sir."

"Any one else there?"

"No, sir."

"Did you say I was engaged?"

"Yes, sir; but it appears she asked Sam who was with you, and when he told her she said, All right, she wanted to see Colonel Pendleton too."

The men glanced interrogatively at each other, but Colonel Pendleton, abruptly anticipating the Mayor's functions, said, "Have her in," and settled himself back in his chair.

A moment later the door opened, and the stranger appeared. As she closed the door behind her she removed her heavy veil, and displayed the face of a very handsome woman of past thirty. It is only necessary to add that it was a face known to the two men, and all San Francisco.

"Well, Kate," said the Mayor, motioning to a chair, but without rising or changing his attitude. "Here I am, and here is Colonel Pendleton, and these are office hours. What can we do for you?"

If he had received her with magisterial formality, or even politely, she would have been embarrassed, in spite of a certain boldness of her dark eyes and an ever-present consciousness of her power. It is possible that his own ease and that of his companion was part of their instinctive good-nature and perception. She accepted it as such, took the chair familiarly, and seated herself sideways upon it, her right arm half-encircling its back and hanging over it; altogether an easy and not ungraceful pose.

"Thank you, Jack—I mean, Mr. Mayor—and you too, Harry. I came on business. I want you two men to act as guardians for my little daughter."

"Your what?" asked the two men simultaneously.

"My daughter," she repeated, with a short laugh, which, however, ended with a note of defiance. "Of course, you don't know. Well," she added half-aggressively, and yet with the air of hurrying over a compromising and inexplicable weakness, "the long and short of it is I've got a little girl down at the Convent of Santa Clara, and have had—there! I've been taking care of her—*good* care, too, boys—for some time. And now I want to put things square for her for the future. See? I want to make over to her all my property—it's nigh on to seventy-five thousand dollars, for Bob Snelling put me up to getting those water lots a year ago—and, you see, I'll have to have regular guardians, trustees, or whatever you call 'em, to take care of the money for her."

"Who's her father?" asked the Mayor.

"What's that to do with it?" she said impetuously.

"Everything—because he's her natural guardian."

"Suppose he isn't known? Say dead, for instance."

"Dead will do," said the Mayor gravely. "Yes, dead will do," repeated Colonel Pendleton. After a pause, in which the two men seemed to have buried this vague relative, the Mayor looked keenly at the woman.

"Kate, have you and Bob Ridley had a quarrel?"

"Bob Ridley knows too much to quarrel with me," she said briefly.

"Then you are doing this for no motive other than that which you tell me?"

"Certainly. That's motive enough—ain't it?"

"Yes." The Mayor took his feet off his companion's chair and sat upright. Colonel Pendleton did the same, also removing his cigar from his lips. "I suppose you'll think this thing over?" he added.

"No—I want it done *now*—right here—in this office."

"But you know it will be irrevocable."

"That's what I want it to be—something might happen afterwards."

"But you are leaving nothing for yourself, and if you are going to devote everything to this daughter, and lead a different life, you'll——"

"Who said I was?"

The two men paused, and looked at her.

"Look here, boys, you don't understand. From the day that paper is signed, I've nothing to do with the child. She passes out of my hands into yours, to be schooled, educated, and made a rich girl out of—and never to know who or what or where *I* am. She doesn't know now. I haven't given her and myself away in that style—you bet! She thinks I'm only a friend. She hasn't seen me more than once or twice, and not to know me again. Why, I was down there the other day, and passed her walking out with the Sisters and the other scholars, and she didn't know me—though one of the Sisters did. But they're mum, *they* are, and don't let on. Why, now I think of it, *you* were down there, Jack, presiding in big style as Mr. Mayor at the exercises. You must have noticed her. Little thing, about nine—lot of hair, the same colour as mine, and brown eyes. White and yellow sash. Had a necklace on of real pearls I gave her. *I bought them,* you understand, myself at Tucker's—gave two hundred and fifty dollars for them—and a big bouquet of white rosebuds and lilacs I sent her."

"I remember her now on the platform," said the Mayor gravely. "So that is your child?"

"You bet—no slouch either. But that's neither here nor there. What I want now is you and Harry to look after her and her property the same as if I didn't live. More than that, as if I had *never lived.* I've come to you two boys, because I reckon you're square men and won't give me away. But I want to fix it even firmer than that. I want you to take hold of this trust not as Jack Hammersley, but as the *Mayor of San Francisco!* And when you make way for a new Mayor, *he* takes up the trust by virtue of his office, you see, so there's a trustee all along. I reckon there'll always be a San Francisco and always a Mayor—at least till the child's of age; and it gives her from the start a father, and a pretty big one too. Of course the new man isn't to know the why and wherefore of this. It's enough for him to take on that duty with his others, without asking questions. And he's only got to invest that money and pay it out as it's wanted, and consult Harry at times."

The two men looked at each other with approving intelligence. "But have you thought of a successor for *me,* in case somebody shoots me on sight any time in the next ten years?" asked Pendleton, with a gravity equal to her own.

"I reckon, as you're President of the El Dorado Bank, you'll make that a part of every President's duty too. You'll get the directors to agree to it, just as Jack here will get the Common Council to make it the Mayor's business."

The two men had risen to their feet, and, after exchanging glances, gazed at her silently. Presently the Mayor said—

"It can be done, Kate, and we'll do it for you—eh, Harry?"

"Count me in," said Pendleton, nodding.

"But you'll want a third man."

"What's that for?"

"The casting vote in case of any difficulty."

The woman's face fell. "I reckoned to keep it a secret with only you two," she said half-bitterly.

"No matter. We'll find some one to act, or you'll think of somebody and let us know."

"But I wanted to finish this thing right here," she said impatiently. She was silent for a moment, with her arched black brows knitted. Then she said abruptly, "Who's that smart little chap that let me in? He looks as if he might be trusted."

"That's Paul Hathaway, my secretary. He's sensible, but too young. Stop! I don't know about that. There's no legal age necessary, and he's got an awfully old head on him," said the Mayor thoughtfully.

"And *I* say his youth's in his favour," said Colonel Pendleton promptly. "He's been brought up in San Francisco, and he's got no d——d old-fashioned Eastern notions to get rid of, and will drop into this as a matter of business, without prying about or wondering. *I'll* serve with him."

"Call him in!" said the woman.

He came. Very luminous of eye, and composed of lip and brow, yet with the same suggestion of "making believe" very much, as if to offset the possible munching of forbidden cakes and apples in his own room, or the hidden presence of some still in his pocket.

The Mayor explained the case briefly, but with businesslike precision. "Your duty, Mr. Hathaway," he concluded, "at present will be merely nominal and, above all, confidential. Colonel Pendleton and myself will set the thing going." As the youth—who had apparently taken in and "illuminated" the whole subject with a single bright-eyed glance—bowed and was about to retire, as if to relieve himself of his real feelings behind the door, the woman stopped him with a gesture.

"Let's have this thing over now," she said to the Mayor. "You draw up something that we can all sign at once." She fixed her eyes on Paul, partly to satisfy her curiosity and justify her predilection for him, and partly to detect him in any overt act of boyishness. But the youth simply returned her glance with a cheerful, easy prescience, as if her past lay clearly open before him. For some minutes there was only the rapid scratching of the Mayor's pen over the paper. Suddenly he stopped and looked up.

"What's her name?"

"She mustn't have mine," said the woman quickly. "That's a part of my idea. I give that up with the rest. She must take a new name that gives no hint of me. Think of one, can't you, you two men? Something that would kind of show that she was the daughter of the city, you know."

"You couldn't call her 'Santa Francisca,' eh?" said Colonel Pendleton doubtingly.

"Not much," said the woman, with a seriousness that defied any ulterior insinuation.

"Nor Chrysopolinia?" said the Mayor musingly.

"But that's only a *first* name. She must have a family name," said the woman impatiently.

"Can *you* think of something, Paul?" said the Mayor, appealing to Hathaway. "You're a great reader, and later from your classics than I am." The Mayor, albeit practical and Western, liked to be ostentatiously forgetful of his old Alma Mater, Harvard, on occasions.

"How would *Yerba Buena* do, sir?" responded the youth gravely. "It's the old Spanish title of the first settlement here. It comes from the name that Father Junipero Serra gave to the pretty little vine that grows wild over the sandhills, and means 'Good herb.' He called it 'A balm for the wounded and sore.' "

"For the wounded and sore?" repeated the woman slowly.

"That's what they say," responded Hathaway.

"You ain't playing us, eh?" she said, with a half-laugh that, however, scarcely curved the open mouth with which she had been regarding the young secretary.

"No," said the Mayor hurriedly. "It's true. I've often heard it. And a capital name it would be for her too. *Yerba* the first name, *Buena* the second. She could be called Miss Buena when she grows up."

"Yerba Buena it is," she said suddenly. Then, indicating the youth with a slight toss of her handsome head, "His head's level—you can see that."

There was a silence again, and the scratching of the Mayor's pen continued. Colonel Pendleton buttoned up his coat, pulled his long moustache into shape, slightly arranged his collar, and walked to the window without looking at the woman. Presently the Mayor arose from his seat, and, with a certain formal courtesy that had been wanting in his previous manner, handed her his pen and arranged his chair for her at the desk. She took the pen, and rapidly appended her signature to the paper. The others followed, and, obedient to a sign from him, the porter was summoned from the outer office to witness the signatures. When this was over, the Mayor turned to his secretary. "That's all just now, Paul."

Accepting this implied dismissal with undisturbed gravity, the newly-made youthful guardian bowed and retired. When the green-baize door had closed upon him, the Mayor turned abruptly to the woman with the paper in his hand.

"Look here, Kate; there is still time for you to reconsider your action, and tear up this solitary record of it. If you choose to do so, say so, and I promise you that this interview, and all you have told us, shall never pass beyond these walls. No one will be the wiser for it, and we will give you full credit for having attempted something that was too much for you to perform."

She had half risen from her chair when he began, but fell back again in her former position and looked impatiently from him to his companion, who was also regarding her earnestly.

"What are you talking about?" she said sharply.

"*You,* Kate," said the Mayor. "You have given everything you possess to this child. What provision have you made for yourself?"

"Do I look played out?" she said, facing them.

She certainly did not look like anything but a strong, handsome, resolute woman; but the men did not reply.

"That is not all, Kate," continued the Mayor, folding his arms and looking down upon her. "Have you thought what this means? It is the complete renunciation not only of any claim but any interest in your child. That is what you have just signed, and what it will be our duty now to keep you to. From this moment we stand between you and her, as we stand between her and the world. Are you ready to see her grow up away from you, losing even the little recollection she has had of your kindness—passing you in the street without knowing you, perhaps even having you pointed out to her as a person she should avoid? Are you prepared to shut your eyes and ears henceforth to all that you may hear of her new life, when she is happy, rich, respectable, a courted heiress—perhaps the wife of some great man? Are you ready to accept that she will never know—that no one will ever know—that *you* had any share in making her so, and that if you should ever breathe it abroad we shall hold it our duty to deny it, and brand the man who takes it up for you as a liar and the slanderer of an honest girl?"

"That's what I came here for," she said curtly; then, regarding them curiously, and running her ringed hand up and down the railed back of her chair, she added, with a half-laugh, "What are you playin' me for, boys?"

"But," said Colonel Pendleton, without heeding her, "are you ready to know that in sickness or affliction you will be powerless to help her; that a stranger will take your place at her bedside, that as she has lived without knowing you she will die without that knowledge, or that if through any weakness of yours it came to her then, it would embitter her last thoughts of earth, and, dying, she would curse you?"

The smile upon her half-open mouth still fluttered around it, and her curved fingers still ran up and down the rails of the chair-back as if they were the chords of some mute instrument, to which she was trying to give voice. Her rings once or twice grated upon them as if she had at times gripped them closely. But she rose quickly when he paused, said "Yes" sharply, and put the chair back against the wall.

"Then I will send you copies of this to-morrow, and take an assignment of the property."

"I've got the cheque here for it now," she said, drawing it from her pocket and laying it upon the desk. "There; I reckon that's finished. Good-bye!"

The Mayor took up his hat, Colonel Pendleton did the same; both men preceded her to the door, and held it open with grave politeness for her to pass.

"Where are you boys going?" she asked, glancing from the one to the other.

"To see you to your carriage, Mrs. Howard," said the Mayor, in a voice that had become somewhat deeper.

"Through the whole building? Past all the people in the hall and on the stairs? Why, I passed Dan Stewart as I came in."

"If you will allow us?" he said, turning half-appealingly to Colonel Pendleton, who without speaking made a low bow of assent.

A slight flush rose to her face—the first and only change in the even healthy colour she had shown during the interview.

"I reckon I won't trouble you, boys, if it's all the same to you," she said, with her half-strident laugh. *"You* mightn't mind being seen—but *I* would. Good-bye."

She held out a hand to each of the men, who remained for an instant silently holding them. Then she passed out of the door, slipping on her close black veil as she did so with a half-funereal suggestion, and they saw her tall handsome figure fade into the shadows of the long corridor.

"Paul," said the Mayor, re-entering the office and turning to his secretary, "do you know who that woman is?"

"Yes, sir."

"She's one in a million! And now forget that you have ever seen her."

Chapter I

The principal parlour of the New Golden Gate Hotel in San Francisco, fairly reported by the local press as being "truly palatial" in its appointments and unrivalled in its upholstery, was nevertheless, on August 5, 1860, of that startling newness that checked any familiarity, and evidently had produced some embarrassment in the limbs of four visitors who had just been ushered into its glories. After hesitating before one or two gorgeous fawn-coloured brocaded easy-chairs of appalling and spotless virginity, one of them seated himself despairingly on a *tête-à-tête* sofa in marked and painful isolation, while another sat uncomfortably upright on a sofa. The two others remained standing, vaguely gazing at the ceiling, and exchanging ostentatiously admiring but hollow remarks about the furniture in unnecessary whispers. Yet they were apparently men of a certain habit of importance and small authority, with more or less critical attitude in their speech.

To them presently entered a young man of about five-and-twenty, with remarkably bright and singularly sympathetic eyes. Having swept the group in a smiling glance, he singled out the lonely occupier of the *tête-à-tête,* and moved pleasantly towards him. The man rose instantly with an eager, gratified look.

"Well, Paul, I didn't allow you'd remember me. It's a matter of four

years since we met at Marysville. And now you're bein' a great man,
you've——"

No one could have known from the young man's smiling face that
he really had not recognised his visitor at first, and that his greeting
was only an exhibition of one of those happy instincts for which he
was remarkable. But, following the clue suggested by his visitor, he
was able to say promptly and gaily—

"I don't know why I should forget Tony Shear or the Marysville
boys," turning with a half-confiding smile to the other visitors, who,
after the human fashion, were beginning to be resentfully impatient of
this special attention.

"Well, no—for I've allus said that you took your first start from
Marysville. But I've brought a few friends of our party—that I reckoned to introduce to you. Cap'en Stidger, Chairman of our Central
Committee; Mr. Henry J. Hoskins, of the firm of Hoskins & Bloomer;
and Joe Slate, of the *Union Press,* one of our most promising journal-
ists. Gentlemen," he continued, suddenly and without warning lifting
his voice to an oratorical plane in startling contrast to his previous
unaffected utterance, "I needn't say that this is the Honourable Paul
Hathaway—the youngest State Senator in the Legislature. You know
his record!" Then recovering the ordinary accents of humanity, he
added, "We read of your departure last night from Sacramento, and I
thought we'd come early, afore the crowd."

"Proud to know you, sir," said Captain Stidger, suddenly lifting the
conversation to the platform again. "I have followed your career, sir.
I've read your speech, Mr. Hathaway, and, as I was telling our mutual
friend, Mr. Shear, as we came along, I don't know any man that could
state the real Party issues as squarely. Your castigating exposition of
so-called Jeffersonian principles, and your relentless indictment of the
resolutions of '98 were—were"—coughed the Captain, dropping into
conversation again—"were the biggest thing out. You have only to
signify the day, sir, that you will address us, and I can promise you the
largest audience in San Francisco."

"I'm instructed by the proprietor of the *Union Press,* " said Mr.
Slate, feeling for his notebook and pencil, "to offer you its columns for
any explanations you may desire to make in the form of a personal
letter or an editorial in reply to the *Advertiser's* strictures on your
speech, or to take any information you may have for the benefit of our
readers and the Party."

"If you are ever down my way, Mr. Hathaway," said Mr. Hoskins,
placing a large business card in Hathaway's hand, "and will drop in as
a friend, I can show you about the largest business in the way of
canned provisions and domestic groceries in the State, and give you a

look around Battery Street generally. Or if you'll name your day, I've
got a pair of 2˙35 Blue Grass horses that'll spin you out to the Cliff
House to dinner and back. I've had Governor Fiske, and Senator Doo-
lan, and that big English capitalist who was here last year, and they—
well, sir—they were *pleased!* Or if you'd like to see the town—if this is
your first visit—I'm on hand to show you."

Nothing could exceed Mr. Hathaway's sympathetic acceptance of
their courtesies, nor was there the least affectation in it. Thoroughly
enjoying his fellow-men, even in their foibles, they found him irresistibly attractive. "I lived here seven years ago," he said smilingly to the
speaker.

"When the water came up to Montgomery Street," interposed Mr.
Shear, in a hoarse but admiring aside.

"When Mr. Hammersley was Mayor," continued Hathaway.

"Had an official position—private secretary—afore he was twenty,"
explained Shear, in perfectly audible confidence.

"Since then the city has made great strides, leaping full-grown, sir,
in a single night," said Captain Stidger, hastily ascending the rostrum
again with a mixed metaphor, to the apparent concern of a party of
handsomely dressed young ladies who had recently entered the parlour. "Stretching from South Park to Black Point, and running back
to the Mission Dolores and the Presidio, we are building up a metropolis, sir, worthy to be placed beside the Golden Gate that opens to the
broad Pacific and the shores of far Cathay! When the Pacific Railroad
is built we shall be the natural terminus of the Pathway of Nations!"

Mr. Hathaway's face betrayed no consciousness that he had heard
something like this eight years before, and that much of it had come
true, as he again sympathetically responded. Neither was his attention
attracted by a singular similarity which the attitude of the group of
ladies on the other side of the parlour bore to that of his own party.
They were clustered around one of their own number—a striking-
looking girl—who was apparently receiving their mingled flatteries
and caresses with a youthful yet critical sympathy which, singularly
enough, was not unlike his own. It was evident also that an odd sort of
rivalry seemed to spring up between the two parties, and that, in pro-
portion as Hathaway's admirers became more marked and ostentatious in their attentions, the supporters of the young girl were equally
effusive and enthusiastic in their devotion. As usual in such cases, the
real contest was between the partisans themselves; each successive
demonstration on either side was provocative or retaliatory, and when
they were apparently rendering homage to their idols they were really
distracted by and listening to each other. At last, Hathaway's party

being reinforced by fresh visitors, a tall brunette of the opposition remarked in a professedly confidential but perfectly audible tone—

"Well, my dear, as I don't suppose you want to take part in a political caucus, perhaps we'd better return to the Ladies' Boudoir, unless there's a committee sitting there too."

"I know how valuable your time must be, as you are all business men," said Hathaway, turning to his party, in an equally audible tone; "but before you go, gentlemen, you must let me offer you a little refreshment in a private room," and he moved naturally towards the door. The rival fair, who had already risen at their commander's suggestion, here paused awkwardly over an embarrassing victory. Should they go or stay? The object of their devotion, however, turned curiously towards Hathaway. For an instant their eyes met. The young girl turned carelessly to her companions and said, "No; stay here—it's the public parlour," and her followers, evidently accustomed to her authority, sat down again.

"A galaxy of young ladies from the Convent of Santa Clara, Mr. Hathaway," explained Captain Stidger, naïvely oblivious of any discourtesy on their part, as he followed Hathaway's glance and took his arm as they moved away. "Not the least of our treasures, sir. Most of them daughters of pioneers—and all Californian bred and educated. Connoisseurs have awarded them the palm, and declare that for Grace, Intelligence, and Woman's Highest Charms the East cannot furnish their equal." Having delivered this Parthian compliment in an oratorical passage through the doorway, the Captain descended, outside, into familiar speech. "But I suppose you will find that out for yourself if you stay here long. San Francisco might furnish a fitting bride to California's youngest Senator."

"I am afraid that my stay here must be brief, and limited to business," said Hathaway, who had merely noticed that the principal girl was handsome and original-looking. "In fact, I am here partly to see an old acquaintance—Colonel Pendleton."

The three men looked at each other curiously. "Oh! Harry Pendleton," said Mr. Hoskins incredulously. "You don't know *him?*"

"An old pioneer—of course," interposed Shear, explanatorily and apologetically. "Why, in Paul's time the Colonel was a big man here."

"I understand the Colonel has been unfortunate," said Hathaway gravely; "but in *my* time he was President of the El Dorado Bank."

"And the bank hasn't got through its settlement yet," said Hoskins. "I hope *you* ain't expecting to get anything out of it?"

"No," said Hathaway, smiling; "I was a boy at that time, and lived up to my salary. I know nothing of his bank difficulties, but it always struck me that Colonel Pendleton was himself an honourable man."

"It ain't that," said Captain Stidger energetically; "but the trouble with Harry Pendleton is that he hasn't grown with the State, and never adjusted himself to it. And he won't. He thinks the Millennium was between the fall of '49 and the spring of '50, and after that everything dropped. He belongs to the old days, when a man's simple *word* was good for any amount if you knew him; and they say that the old bank hadn't a scrap of paper for half that was owing to it. That was all very well, sir, in '49 and '50, and—Luck; but it won't do for '59 and '60, and—Business! And the old man can't see it."

"But he is ready to fight for it now, as in the old time," said Mr. Slate; "and that's another trouble with his chronology. He's done more to keep up duelling than any other man in the State, and don't know the whole spirit of progress and civilisation is against it."

It was impossible to tell from Paul Hathaway's face whether his sympathy with Colonel Pendleton's foibles or his assent to the criticisms of his visitors was the truer. Both were no doubt equally sincere. But the party was presently engaged in the absorption of refreshment, which, being of a purely spirituous and exhilarating quality, tended to increase their good humour with the host till they parted. Even then a gratuitous advertisement of his virtues and their own intentions in calling upon him was oratorically voiced from available platforms and landings, in the halls and stairways, until it was pretty well known throughout the Golden Gate Hotel that the Hon. Mr. Paul Hathaway had arrived from Sacramento, and had received a "spontaneous ovation."

Meantime the object of it had dropped into an easy-chair by the window of his room, and was endeavouring to recall a less profitable memory. The process of human forgetfulness is not a difficult one between the ages of eighteen and twenty-six, and Paul Hathaway had not only fulfilled the Mayor's request by forgetting the particulars of a certain transfer that he had witnessed in the Mayor's office, but in the year succeeding that request, being about to try his fortunes in the mountains, he had formally constituted Colonel Pendleton to act as his proxy in the administration of Mrs. Howard's singular Trust, in which, however, he had never participated except yearly to sign his name. He was, consequently, somewhat astonished to have received a letter a few days before from Colonel Pendleton, asking him to call and see him regarding it.

He vaguely remembered that it was eight years ago, and eight years had worked considerable change in the original trustees, greatest of all in his superior officer, the Mayor, who had died the year following, leaving his trusteeship to his successor in office, whom Paul Hathaway had never seen. The Bank of El Dorado, despite Mrs. Howard's

sanguine belief, had long been in bankruptcy, and, although Colonel
Pendleton still survived it, it was certain that no other president would
succeed to his office as trustee, and that the function would lapse with
him. Paul himself, a soldier of fortune, although habitually lucky, had
only lately succeeded to a profession—if his political functions could
be so described. Even with his luck, energy, and ambition, while everything was possible, nothing was secure. It seemed, therefore, as if
the soulless official must eventually assume the duties of the two
sympathising friends who had originated them, and had stood *in loco
parentis* to the constructive orphan. The mother, Mrs. Howard, had
disappeared a year after the Trust had been made—it was charitably
presumed in order to prevent any complications that might arise from
her presence in the country. With these facts before him, Paul Hathaway was more concerned in wondering what Pendleton could want
with him than, I fear, any direct sympathy with the situation. On the
contrary, it appeared to him more favourable for keeping the secret of
Mrs. Howard's relationship, which would now die with Colonel Pendleton and himself; and there was no danger of any emotional betrayal
of it in the cold official administration of a man who had received the
Trust through the formal hands of successive predecessors. He had
forgotten the time limited for the guardianship, but the girl must soon
be of age and off their hands. If there had ever been any romantic or
chivalrous impression left upon his memory by the scene in the May-
or's office, I fear he had put it away with various other foolish illusions
of his youth, to which he now believed he was superior.

Nevertheless, he would see the Colonel, and at once, and settle the
question. He looked at the address, "St. Charles Hotel." He remembered an old hostelry of that name, near the Plaza. Could it be possible
that it had survived the alterations and improvements of the city? It
was an easy walk through remembered streets, yet with changed shops
and houses and faces. When he reached the Plaza, scarce recognisable
in its later frontages of brick and stone, he found the old wooden
building still intact, with its villa-like galleries and verandahs incongruously and ostentatiously overlooked by two new and aspiring erec-
tions on either side. For an instant he tried to recall the glamour of old
days. He remembered when his boyish eyes regarded it as the crowning work of opulence and distinction; he remembered a ball given
there on some public occasion, which was to him the acme of social
brilliancy and display. How tawdry and trivial it looked beside those
later and more solid structures! How inconsistent were those long
latticed verandahs and balconies, pathetic record of that first illusion
of the pioneers that their climate was a tropical one! A restaurant and
billiard-saloon had aggrandised all of the lower storey; but there was

still the fanlight, over which the remembered title of "St. Charles," in gilded letters, was now reinforced by the too demonstrative legend, "Apartments and Board, by the Day or Week." Was it possible that this narrow, creaking staircase had once seemed to him the broad steps of Fame and Fortune? On the first landing a pre occupied Irish servant-girl, with a mop, directed him to a door at the end of the passage, at which he knocked. The door was opened by a grizzled negro servant, who was still holding a piece of oily chamois-leather in his hand; and the contents of a duelling-case, scattered upon a table in the centre of the room, showed what had been his occupation. Admitting Hathaway with great courtesy, he said—

"Marse Harry bin havin' his ole trubble, sah, and bin engaged just dis momen' on his toylet; ef yo'll accommodate yo'self on de sofa, I inform him yo' is heah."

As the negro passed into the next room, Paul cast a hasty glance around the apartment. The furniture, originally rich and elegant, was now worn threadbare and lustreless. A bookcase, containing, among other volumes, a few law books—there being a vague tradition, as Paul remembered, that Colonel Pendleton had once been connected with the law—a few French chairs of tarnished gilt, a rifle in the corner, a presentation sword in a mahogany case, a few classical prints on the walls, and one or two iron deed-boxes marked "El Dorado Bank," were the principal objects. A mild flavour of dry decay and methylated spirits pervaded the apartment. Yet it was scrupulously clean and well kept, and a few clothes neatly brushed and folded on a chair bore witness to the servant's care. As Paul, however, glanced behind the sofa, he was concerned to see a coat, which had evidently been thrust hurriedly in a corner, with the sleeve lining inside out, and a needle and thread still sticking in the seam. It struck him instantly that this had been the negro's occupation, and that the pistol-cleaning was a polite fiction.

"Yo'll have to skuse Marse Harry seein' yo' in bed, but his laig's pow'ful bad to-day, and he can't stand," said the servant, re-entering the room. "Skuse me, sah," he added in a dignified confidential whisper, half closing the door with his hand, "but if yo' wouldn't mind avoidin' 'xcitin' or controversical topics in yo' conversation it would be de better fo' him."

Paul smilingly assented, and the black retainer, with even more than the usual solemn ceremonious exaggeration of his race, ushered him into the bedroom. It was furnished in the same faded glory as the sitting-room, with the exception of a low iron camp-bedstead, in which the tall soldierly figure of Colonel Pendleton, clad in threadbare silk dressing-gown, was stretched. He had changed in eight years; his hair had become grey, and was thinned over the sunken temples, but his iron-grey moustache was still particularly long and well pointed. His face bore marks of illness and care; there were deep lines down the angle of the nostril that spoke of alternate savage outbreak and repression, and gave his smile a sardonic rigidity. His dark eyes, that shone with the exaltation of fever, fixed Paul's on entering, and with the tyranny of an invalid never left them.

"Well, Hathaway?"

With the sound of that voice Paul felt the years slip away, and he was again a boy, looking up admiringly to the strong man, who now lay helpless before him. He had entered the room with a faint sense of sympathising superiority and a consciousness of having had experience in controlling men. But all this fled before Colonel Pendleton's authoritative voice; even its broken tones carried the old dominant spirit of the man, and Paul found himself admiring a quality in his old acquaintance that he missed in his newer friends.

"I haven't seen you for eight years, Hathaway. Come here and let me look at you."

Paul approached the bedside with boyish obedience. Pendleton took his hand and gazed at him critically.

"I should have recognised you, sir, for all your moustache and your inches. The last time I saw you was in Jack Hammersley's office. Well, Jack's dead, and here *I* am, little better, I reckon. You remember Hammersley's house?"

"Yes," said Paul, albeit wondering at the question.

"Something like this, Swiss villa style. I remember when Jack put it up. Well, the last time I was out, I passed there. And what do you think they've done to it?"

Paul could not imagine.

"Well, sir," said the Colonel gravely, "they've changed it into a Church Missionary shop and Young Men's Christian Reading-room! But, that's 'progress' and 'improvement'!" He paused, and, slowly withdrawing his hand from Paul's, added with grim apology, "You're young, and belong to the new school, perhaps. Well, sir, I've read your speech; I don't belong to your Party—mine died ten years ago—but I congratulate you. George! Confound it! where's that boy gone?"

The negro indicated by this youthful title, although he must have been ten years older than his master, after a hurried shuffling in the sitting-room, eventually appeared at the door.

"George, champagne and materials for cocktails for the gentleman. The *best,* you understand. No new-fangled notions from that new barkeeper."

Paul, who thought he observed a troubled blinking in George's eyelid, and referred it to a fear of possible excitement for his patient, here begged his host not to trouble himself—that he seldom took anything in the morning.

"Possibly not, sir; possibly not," returned the Colonel hastily. "I know the new ideas are prohibitive and some other blank thing, but you're safe here from your constituents, and by gad, sir, I shan't force you to take it! It's *my* custom, Hathaway—an old one—played out, perhaps, like all the others, but a custom nevertheless, and I'm only surprised that George, who knows it, should have forgotten it."

"Fack is, Marse Harry," said George, with feverish apology, "it bin gone 'scaped my mind dis mo'nin' in de prerogation ob business, but I'm goin' now shuah!" and he disappeared.

"A good boy, sir, but beginning to be contaminated. Brought him here from Nashville over ten years ago. Eight years ago they proved to him that he was no longer a slave, and made him d——d unhappy until I promised him it should make no difference to him, and he could stay. I had to send for his wife and child—of course, a dead loss of eighteen hundred dollars when they set foot in the State—but I'm blanked if he isn't just as miserable with them here, for he has to take two hours in the morning and three in the afternoon every day to be with 'em. I tried to get him to take his family to the mines and make his fortune, like those fellows they call bankers and operators and stockbrokers nowadays; or to go to Oregon, where they'll make him some kind of a mayor or sheriff—but he won't. He collects my rents on some little property I have left, and pays my bills, sir, and, if this blank civilisation would only leave him alone, he'd be a good enough boy."

Paul couldn't help thinking that the rents George collected were somewhat inconsistent with those he was evidently mending when he arrived, but at that moment the jingle of glasses was heard in the sitting-room, and the old negro reappeared at the door. Drawing himself up with ceremonious courtesy, he addressed Paul. "Wo'd yo' mind, sah, taking a glance at de wine for yo' choice?" Paul rose, and followed him into the sitting-room, when George carefully closed the door. To his surprise Hathaway beheld a tray with two glasses of whisky and bitters, but no wine. "Skuse me, sah," said the old man with dignified apology, "but de Kernel won't have any but de best champagne for hono'ble gemmen like yo'self, and I'se despaired to say it can't be got in de house or de subburbs. De best champagne dat we gives visitors is the Widder Glencoe. Wo'd yo' mind, sah, for de sake o' not 'xcitin' de Kernel wid triflin' culinary matter, to say dat yo' don' take but de one brand?"

"Certainly," said Paul, smiling, "I really don't care for anything so early;" then, returning to the bedroom, he said carelessly, "You'll excuse me taking the liberty, Colonel, of sending away the champagne and contenting myself with whisky. Even the best brand—the Widow Cliquot"—with a glance at the gratified George—"I find rather trying so early in the morning."

"As you please, Hathaway," said the Colonel, somewhat stiffly. "I dare say there's a new fashion in drinks now, and a gentleman's stomach is a thing of the past. Then, I suppose, we can spare the boy, as this is his time for going home. Put that tin box with the Trust papers on the bed, George, and Mr. Hathaway will excuse your waiting." As the old servant made an exaggerated obeisance to each, Paul remarked, as the door closed upon him, "George certainly keeps his style, Colonel, in the face of the progress you deplore."

"He was always a 'dandy nigger,'" returned Pendleton, his face slightly relaxing as he glanced after his grizzled henchman, "but his exaggeration of courtesy is a blank sight more natural and manly than the exaggeration of discourtesy which your superior civilised 'helps' think is self-respect. The excuse of servitude of any kind is its spontaneity and affection. When you know a man hates you and serves you from interest, you know he's a cur and you're a tyrant. It's your blank progress that's made menial service degrading by teaching men to avoid it. Why, sir, when I first arrived here, Jack Hammersley and myself took turns as cook to the party. I didn't consider myself any the worse master for it. But enough of this." He paused, and, raising himself on his elbow, gazed for some seconds half-cautiously, half-doubtfully, upon his companion. "I've got something to tell you, Hathaway," he said slowly. "You've had an easy time with this Trust; your share of the work hasn't worried you, kept you awake nights, or interfered with your career. I understand perfectly," he continued, in reply to Hathaway's deprecating gesture. "I accepted to act as your proxy, and I *have*. I'm not complaining. But it is time that you should know what I've done, and what you may still have to do. Here is the record. On the day after that interview in the Mayor's office, the El Dorado Bank, of which I was and still am president, received seventy-five thousand dollars in trust from Mrs. Howard. Two years afterwards, on that same day, the bank had, by lucky speculations, increased that sum to the credit of the Trust one hundred and fifty thousand dollars, or double the original capital. In the following year the bank suspended payment."

Chapter II

In an instant the whole situation and his relations to it flashed upon Paul with a terrible but almost grotesque completeness. Here he was, at the outset of his career, responsible for the wasted fortune of the daughter of a social outcast, and saddled with her support! He now knew why Colonel Pendleton had wished to see him; for one shameful moment he believed he also knew why he had been content to take his proxy! The questionable character of the whole transaction, his own carelessness, which sprang from that very confidence and trust that Pendleton had lately extolled—what *would,* what *could* not be made of it! He already heard himself abused by his opponents—perhaps, more terrible still, faintly excused by his friends. All this was visible in his pale face and flashing eyes as he turned them on the helpless invalid.

Colonel Pendleton received his look with the same critical half-curious scrutiny that had accompanied his speech. At last his face changed slightly, a faint look of disappointment crossed his eyes, and a sardonic smile deepened the lines of his mouth.

"There, sir," he said hurriedly, as if dismissing an unpleasant revelation; "don't alarm yourself! Take a drink of that whisky. You look pale. Well; turn your eyes on those walls. You don't see any of that money laid out here—do you? Look at me. I don't look like a man enriched with other people's money—do I? Well, let that content you. Every dollar of that Trust fund, Hathaway, with all the interests and profits that have accrued to it, is *safe!* Every cent of it is locked up in Government Bonds with Rothschild's agent. There are the receipts, dated a week before the bank suspended. But enough of *that—that* isn't what I asked you to come and see me for."

The blood had rushed back to Paul's cheeks uncomfortably. He saw now, as impulsively as he had previously suspected his co-trustee, that the man had probably ruined himself to save the Trust. He stammered that he had not questioned the management of the fund nor asked to withdraw his proxy.

"No matter, sir," said the Colonel impatiently; "you had the right, and, I suppose," he added with half-concealed scorn, "it was your duty. But let that pass. The money is safe enough; but, Mr. Hathaway —and this is the point I want to discuss with you—it begins to look as if the *secret* was safe no longer!" He had raised himself with some pain and difficulty to draw nearer to Paul, and had again fixed his eyes eagerly upon him. But Paul's responsive glance was so vague that he added quickly, "You understand, sir; I believe that there are hounds— I say hounds!—who would be able to blurt out at any moment that that girl at Santa Clara is Kate Howard's daughter."

At any other moment Paul might have questioned the gravity of any

247

such contingency, but the terrible earnestness of the speaker, his dominant tone, and a certain respect which had lately sprung up in his breast for him, checked him, and he only asked, with as much concern as he could master for the moment—

"What makes you think so?"

"That's what I want to tell you, Hathaway, and how I, and I alone, am responsible for it. When the bank was in difficulty, and I made up my mind to guard the Trust with my own personal and private capital, I knew that there might be some comment on my action. It was a delicate matter to show any preference or exclusion at such a moment, and I took two or three of my brother directors whom I thought I could trust into my confidence. I told them the whole story, and how the Trust was sacred. I made a mistake, sir," continued Pendleton sardonically, "a grave mistake. I did not take into account that even in three years civilisation and religion had gained ground here. There was a hound there—a blank Judas in the Trust. Well; he didn't see it. I think he talked Scripture and morality. He said something about the wages of sin being infamous and only worthy of confiscation. He talked about the sins of the father being visited upon the children, and justly. I stopped him. Well! Do you know what's the matter with my ankle? Look!" He stopped, and with some difficulty and invincible gravity throwing aside his dressing-gown, turned down his stocking, and exposed to Paul's gaze the healed cicatrix of an old bullet-wound. "Troubled me damnably near a year. Where I hit *him*— hasn't troubled him at all since!

"I think," continued the Colonel, falling back upon the pillow with an air of relief, "that he told others—of his own kidney, sir—though it was a secret among gentlemen. But they have preferred to be silent now—than *afterwards.* They know that I'm ready. But I can't keep this up long; some time, you know, they're bound to improve in practice and hit higher up! As far as I'm concerned," he added, with a grim glance around the faded walls and threadbare furniture, "it don't mind; but *mine* isn't the mouth to be stopped." He paused, and then abruptly, yet with a sudden and pathetic dropping of his dominant note, said, "Hathaway, you're young, and Hammersley liked you— what's to be done? I thought of passing over my tools to you. You can shoot, and I hear you *have.* But the h—l of it is that if you dropped a man or two people would ask *why,* and want to know what it was about; while, when I do, nobody here thinks it anything but *my way!* I don't mean that it would hurt you with the crowd to wipe out one or two of these hounds during the canvass, but the trouble is that they belong to *your Party,* and," he added grimly, "that wouldn't help your career."

"But," said Paul, ignoring the sarcasm, "are you not magnifying the effect of a disclosure? The girl is an heiress, excellently brought up. Who will bother about the antecedents of the mother, who has disappeared, whom she never knew, and who is legally dead to her?"

"In my day, sir, no one who knew the circumstances," returned the Colonel quickly. "But we are living in a blessed era of Christian retribution and civilised propriety, and I believe there are a lot of men and women about who have no other way of showing their own virtue than by showing up another's vice. We're in a reaction of reform. It's the old drunkards who are always more clamorous for total abstinence than the moderately temperate. I tell you, Hathaway, there couldn't be an unluckier moment for our secret coming out."

"But she will be of age soon."

"In two months."

"And sure to marry."

"Marry!" repeated Pendleton, with grim irony. "Would *you* marry her?"

"That's another question," said the young man promptly, "and one of individual taste; but it does not affect my general belief that she could easily find a husband as good and better."

"Suppose she found one *before* the secret came out. Ought he to be told?"

"Certainly."

"And that would imply telling *her?*"

"Yes," said Paul, but not so promptly.

"And you consider *that* fulfilling the promise of the Trust—the pledges exchanged with that woman?" continued Pendleton, with glittering eyes and a return to his old dominant tone.

"My dear Colonel," said Paul, somewhat less positively, but still smiling, "you have made a romantic, almost impossible compact with Mrs. Howard, that, you yourself are now obliged to admit, circumstances may prevent your carrying out substantially. You forget, also, that you have just told me that you have already broken your pledge—under circumstances, it is true, that do you honour—and that now your desperate attempts to retrieve it have failed. Now I really see nothing wrong in your telling to a presumptive well-wisher of a girl what you have told to her enemy."

There was a dead silence. The prostrate man uttered a slight groan, as if in pain, and drew up his leg to change his position. After a pause he said, in a restrained voice, "I differ from you, Mr. Hathaway; but enough of this for the present. I have something else to say. It will be necessary for one of us to go at once to Santa Clara and see Miss Yerba Buena."

"Good heavens!" said Paul quickly. "Do you call her *that?*"

"Certainly, sir, *You* gave her the name. Have you forgotten?"

"I only suggested it," returned Paul hopelessly; "but no matter—go on."

"*I* cannot go there, as you see," continued Pendleton, with a weary gesture towards his crippled ankle; "and I should particularly like you to see her before we make the joint disposition of her affairs with the Mayor two months hence. I have some papers you can show her, and I have already written a letter introducing you to the Lady Superior at the convent and to her. You have never seen her?"

"No," said Paul. "But, of course, you have?"

"Not for three years."

Paul's eyes evidently expressed some wonder, for a moment after the Colonel added, "I believe, Hathaway, I am looked upon as a queer survival of a rather lawless and improper past. At least, I have thought it better not socially to compromise her by my presence. The Mayor goes there—at the examinations and exercises, I believe, sir; they make a sort of reception for him—with a—a—banquet—lemonade and speeches."

"I had intended to leave for Sacramento to-morrow night," said Paul, glancing curiously at the helpless man; "but I will go there if you wish."

"Thank you. It will be better."

There were a few words of further explanation of the papers, and Pendleton placed the packet in his visitor's hand. Paul rose. Somehow it appeared to him that the room looked more faded and forgotten than when he entered it, and the figure of the man before him more lonely, helpless, and abandoned. With one of his sympathetic impulses he said—

"I don't like to leave you here alone. Are you sure you can help yourself without George? Can I do anything before I go?"

"I am quite accustomed to it," said Pendleton quietly. "It happens once or twice a year, and when I go out—well—I miss more than I do here."

He took Paul's proffered hand mechanically, with a slight return of the critical doubting look he had cast upon him when he entered. His voice, too, had quite recovered its old dominance as he said, with half-patronising conventionality, "You'll have to find your way out alone. Let me know how you have sped at Santa Clara, will you? Good-bye."

The staircase and passage seemed to have grown shabbier and meaner as Paul slowly and hesitatingly descended to the street. At the foot of the stairs he paused irresolutely, and loitered with a vague idea of turning back on some pretence, only that he might relieve himself of the sense of desertion. He had already determined upon making that inquiry into the Colonel's personal and pecuniary affairs which he had not dared to offer personally, and had a half-formed plan of testing his own power and popularity in a certain line of relief that at once satisfied his sympathies and ambitions. Nevertheless, after reaching the street, he lingered a moment, when an odd idea of temporising with his inclinations struck him. At the farther end of the hotel—one of the parasites living on its decayed fortunes—was a small barber's shop. By having his hair trimmed and his clothes brushed, he could linger a little longer beneath the same roof with the helpless solitary, and perhaps come to some conclusion. He entered the clean but scantily-furnished shop, and threw himself into one of the nearest chairs, hardly noting that there were no other customers, and that a single assistant, stropping a razor behind a glass door, was the only occupant. But there was a familiar note of exaggerated politeness about the voice of this man as he opened the door and came towards the back of the chair with the formula—

"Mo'nin', sah! Shall we hab de pleshure of shavin' or hah-cuttin' dis mo'nin'?" Paul raised his eyes quickly to the mirror before him. It reflected the black face and grizzled hair of George.

More relieved at finding the old servant still near his master than caring to comprehend the reason, Hathaway said pleasantly, "Well, George, is this the way you look after your family?"

The old man started; for an instant his full red lips seemed to become dry and ashen, the whites of his eyes were suffused and staring, as he met Paul's smiling face in the glass. But almost as quickly he recovered himself, and, with a polite but deprecating bow, said, "For God sake, sah! I admit de sarkumstances is agin me, but de simple fack is dat I'm temper'ly occupyin' de place of an ole frien', sah, who is called round de cornah."

"And I'm devilish glad of any fact, George, that gives me a chance of having my hair cut by Colonel Pendleton's right-hand man. So fire away!"

The gratified smile which now suddenly overspread the whole of the old man's face, and seemed to quickly stiffen the rugged and wrinkled fingers that had at first trembled in drawing a pair of shears from a ragged pocket, appeared to satisfy Paul's curiosity for the present. But after a few moments' silent snipping, during which he could detect in the mirror some traces of agitation still twitching the negro's face, he said with an air of conviction—

"Look here, George—why don't you regularly use your leisure moments in this trade? You'd make your fortune by your taste and skill at it."

For the next half-minute the old man's frame shook with silent childlike laughter behind Paul's chair. "Well, Marse Hathaway, yo's an ole frien' o' my massa, and a gemman yo'self, sah, and a Senetah, and I doan' mind tellen' yo'—dat's jess what I bin gone done! It makes a little ready money for de ole woman and de chillern. But de Kernel don' know. Ah, sah, de Kernel kill me or hisself if he so much as spicioned me. De Kernel is high-toned, sah!—being a gemman yo'self, yo' understand. He wouldn't heah of his niggah worken' for two massas—for all he's agree'ble to lemme go and help myse'f. But, Lord bless yo,' sah, dat ain't in de category! De Kernel couldn't get along widout me."

"You collect his rents, don't you?" said Paul quietly.

"Yes, sah."

"Much?"

"Well, no, sah; not so much as fom'ly, sah! Yo' see, de Kernel's prop'ty lies in de ole parts of de town, where de po' white folks lib, and dey ain't reglar. De Kernel dat sof' in his heart, he doant press 'em; some of 'em is ole fo'ty-niners like hisself, sah; and some is Spanish, sah, and dey is sof' too, and ain't no more gumption dan chillern, and tink it's ole time come agin, and dey's in de ole places like afo' de Mexican Wah! and dey don' bin' payin' noffin'. But we gets along, sah —we gets along, not in de *prima facie* style, sah! mebbe not in de modden way dat de Kernel don't like; but we keeps ourse'f, sah, and has wine fo' our friends. When yo' come again, sah, yo'll find de Widder Glencoe on de sideboard."

"Has the Colonel many friends here?"

"Mos' de ole ones bin done gone, sah, and de Kernel don' cotton to de new. He don' mix much in sassiety till de bank settlements bin gone done. Skuse me, sah!—but yo' don' happen to know when dat is? It would be a pow'ful heap off de Kernel's mind if it was done. Bein' a high and mighty man in Committees up dah in Sacramento, sah, I didn't know but what yo' might know as it might come befo' yo'."

"I'll see about it," said Paul, with an odd abstracted smile.

"Shampoo dis mornen', sah?"

"Nothing more in this line," said Paul, rising from his chair, "but something more, perhaps, in the line of your other duties. You're a good barber for the public, George, and I don't take back what I said about your future; but *just now* I think the Colonel wants all your service. He's not at all well. Take this," he said, putting a twenty dollar gold piece in the astonished servant's hand, "and for the next three or four days drop the shop, and under some pretext or another arrange to be with him. That money will cover what you lose here, and as soon as the Colonel's all right again you can come back to work. But are you not afraid of being recognised by some one?"

"No, sah, dat's just it. On'y strangers dat don' know no better come yere."

"But suppose your master should drop in? It's quite convenient to his rooms."

"Marse Harry in a barber-shop!" said the old man, with a silent laugh. "Skuse me, sah," he added, with an apologetic mixture of respect and dignity, "but fo' twenty years no man hez touched de Kernel's chin but myself. When Marse Harry hez to go to a barber's shop, it won't make no matter who's dar."

"Let's hope he will not," said Paul gaily; then, anxious to evade the gratitude which since his munificence he had seen beaming in the old negro's eye and evidently trying to find polysyllabic and elevated expression on his lips, he said hurriedly, "I shall expect to find you with the Colonel when I call again in a day or two," and smilingly departed.

At the end of two hours George's barber-employer returned to relieve his assistant, and, on receiving from him an account and a certain percentage of the afternoon's fees (minus the gift from Paul), was informed by George that he should pretermit his attendance for a few days. "Udder private and personal affairs," explained the old negro, who made no social distinction in his vocabulary, "peroccupyin' dis niggah's time." The head barber, unwilling to lose a really good assistant, endeavoured to dissuade him by the offer of increased emolument, but George was firm.

As he entered the sitting-room the Colonel detected his step, and called him in.

"Another time, George, never allow a guest of mine to send away wine. If he don't care for it, put it on the sideboard."

"Yes, sah; but as yo' didn't like it yo'self, Marse Harry, and de wine was de most 'xpensive quality ob Glencoe——"

"D—n the expense!" He paused, and gazed searchingly at his old retainer.

"George," he said suddenly, yet in a gentle voice, "don't lie to me, or"—in a still kinder voice—"I'll flog the black skin off you! Listen to me. *Have* you got any money left?"

" 'Deed, sah, dere *is,* " said the negro earnestly. "I'll jist fetch it wid de accounts."

"Hold on! I've been thinking, lying here, that if the Widow Molloy can't pay because she sold out, and that tobacconist is ruined, and we've had to pay the water-tax for old Bill Soames, the rent last week don't amount to much, while there's the month's bill for the restaurant and that blank druggist's account for lotions and medicines to come out of it. It strikes me we're pretty near touching bottom. I've everything I want here, but, by God, sir, if I find *you* skimping yourself or lying to me, or borrowing money——"

"Yes, Marse Harry, but the Widow Molloy done gone and paid up dis afernoon. I'll bring de books and money to prove it," and he hurriedly re-entered the sitting-room.

Then with trembling hands he emptied his pockets on the table, including Paul's gift and the fees he had just received, and opening a desk-drawer, took from it a striped cotton handkerchief, such as negro women wear on their heads, containing a small quantity of silver tied up in a hard knot, and a boy's purse. This he emptied on the table with his own money.

They were the only rents of Colonel Henry Pendleton! They were contributed by "George Washington Thomson;" his wife, otherwise known as "Aunt Dinah," washerwoman; and "Scipio Thomson," their son, aged fourteen, bootblack. It did not amount to much. But in that happy moisture that dimmed the old man's eyes, God knows it looked large enough.

Chapter III

Although the rays of an unclouded sun were hot in the Santa Clara roads and byways, and the dry bleached dust had become an impalpable powder, the perspiring and parched pedestrian who rashly sought relief in the shade of the wayside oak was speedily chilled to the bone by the north-west trade-winds that on those August afternoons swept through the defiles of the coast range, and even penetrated the pastoral valley of San José. The anomaly of straw hats and overcoats with the occupants of buggies and station waggons was thus accounted for, and even in the sheltered garden of "El Rosario" two young girls in light summer dresses had thrown wraps over their shoulders as they lounged down a broad rose-alley at right angles with the deep long verandah of the *casa*. Yet, in spite of the chill, the old Spanish house and gardens presented a luxurious, almost tropical, picture from the roadside. Banks, beds, and bowers of roses lent their name and colour to the grounds; tree-like clusters of hanging-fuchsias, mound-like masses of variegated verbena, and tangled thickets of ceanothus and spreading heliotrope were set in boundaries of venerable olive, fig, and pear-trees. The old house itself, a picturesque relief to the glaring newness of the painted villas along the road, had been tastefully modified to suit the needs and habits of a later civilisation; the galleries of the inner courtyard, or *patio,* had been transferred to the outside walls in the form of deep verandahs, while the old adobe walls themselves were hidden beneath flowing Cape jessamine or bestarred passion vines, and topped by roofs of cylindrical red tiles.

"Miss Yerba!" said a dry masculine voice from the verandah.

The taller young girl started, and drew herself suddenly behind a large Castilian rose-tree, dragging her companion with her, and putting her finger imperatively upon a pretty but somewhat passionate mouth. The other girl checked a laugh, and remained watching her friend's wickedly levelled brows in amused surprise.

The call was repeated from the verandah. After a moment's pause there was the sound of retreating foot-steps, and all was quiet again.

"Why, for goodness' sake, didn't you answer, Yerba?" asked the shorter girl.

"Oh, I hate him!" responded Yerba. "He only wanted to bore me with his stupid, formal, sham-parental talk. Because he's my official guardian he thinks it necessary to assume this manner towards me when we meet, and treats me as if I were something between his stepdaughter and an almshouse orphan or a police board. It's perfectly ridiculous, for it's only put on while he is in office; and he knows it, and I know it, and I'm tired of making believe. Why, my dear, they change every election; I've had seven of them, all more or less of this kind, since I can remember."

"But I thought there were two others, dear, that were not official?" said her companion coaxingly.

Yerba sighed. "No; there was another, who was president of a bank, but that was also to be official if he died. I used to like him, he seemed to be the only gentleman among them; but it appears that he is dreadfully improper; shoots people now and then for nothing at all, and burst up his bank—and, of course, he's impossible, and, as there's no more bank, when he dies there'll be no more trustee."

"And there's the third, you know—a stranger, who never appears?" suggested the younger girl.

"And who do you suppose *he* turns out to be? Do you remember that conceited little wretch—that 'Baby Senator,' I think they called him—who was in the parlour of the Golden Gate the other morning surrounded by his idiotic worshippers and toadies and ballot-box stuffers? Well, if you please, *that's* Mr. Paul Hathaway—the Honourable Paul Hathaway, who washed his hands of me, my dear, at the beginning!"

"But really, Yerba, I thought that he looked and acted——"

"You thought of nothing at all, Milly," returned Yerba with authority. "I tell you he's a mass of conceit. What else could you expect of a

Man—toadied and fawned upon to that extent? It made me sick! I could have just shaken them!"

As if to emphasise her statement, she grasped one of the long willowy branches of the enormous rose-bush where she stood, and shook it lightly. The action detached a few of the maturer blossoms, and sent down a shower of faded pink petals on her dark hair and yellow dress. "I can't bear conceit," she added.

"Oh, Yerba, just stand as you are! I do wish the girls could see you. You make the *loveliest* picture!"

She certainly did look very pretty as she stood there—a few leaves lodged in her hair, clinging to her dress, and suggesting by reflection the colour that her delicate satin skin would have resented in its own texture. But she turned impatiently away—perhaps not before she had allowed this passing vision to impress the mind of her devoted adherent—and said, "Come along, or that dreadful man will be out on the verandah again."

"But, if you dislike him so, why did you accept the invitation to meet him here at luncheon?" said the curious Milly.

"*I* didn't accept; the Mother Superior did for me, because he's the Mayor of San Francisco visiting your uncle, and she's always anxious to please the powers that be. And I thought he might have some information that I could get out of him. And it was better than being in the convent all day. And I thought I could stand *him* if you were here."

Milly gratefully accepted this doubtful proof of affection by squeezing her companion's arm. "And you didn't get any information, dear?"

"Of course not! The idiot knows only the old tradition of his office— that I was a mysterious Trust left in Mayor Hammersley's hands. He actually informed me that 'Buena' meant 'Good'; that it was likely the name of the captain of some whaler that put into San Francisco in the early days, whose child I was, and that, if I chose to call myself 'Miss Good,' he would allow it, and get a Bill passed in the Legislature to legalise it. Think of it, my dear!—'Miss Good,' like one of Mrs. Barbauld's stories, or a moral governess in the 'Primary Reader.'"

" 'Miss Good,' " repeated Milly innocently. "Yes, you might put an *e* at the end—G-double-o-d-e. There are Goodes in Philadelphia. And then you won't have to sacrifice that sweet pretty 'Yerba,' that's so stylish and musical, for you'd still be 'Yerba Good.' But," she added, as Yerba made an impatient gesture, "why do you worry yourself about *that?* You wouldn't keep your own name long, whatever it was. An heiress like you, dear—lovely and accomplished—would have the best names as well as the best men in America to choose from."

"Now, please, don't repeat that idiot's words. That's what *he* says; that's what they *all* say!" returned Yerba pettishly. "One would really think it was necessary for me to get married to become anybody at all, or have any standing whatever. And, whatever you do, don't go talking of me as if I were named after a vegetable. 'Yerba Buena' is the name of an island in the bay just off San Francisco. I'm named after that."

"But I don't see the difference, dear. The island was named after the vine that grows on it."

"*You* don't see the difference?" said Yerba darkly. "Well, *I* do. But what are you looking at?"

Her companion had caught her arm, and was gazing intently at the house.

"Yerba," she said quickly, "there's the Mayor, and uncle, and a strange gentleman coming down the walk. They're looking for us. And, as I live, Yerb! the strange gentleman is that young Senator, Mr. Hathaway!"

"Mr. Hathaway? Nonsense!"

"Look for yourself."

Yerba glanced at the three gentlemen, who, a hundred yards distant, were slowly advancing in the direction of the ceanothus hedge, behind which the girls had instinctively strayed during their conversation.

"What are you going to do?" said Milly eagerly. "They're coming straight this way. Shall we stay here and let them pass, or make a run for the house?"

"No," said Yerba, to Milly's great surprise. "That would look as if we cared. Besides, I don't know that Mr. Hathaway has come to see *me*. We'll stroll out and meet them accidentally."

Milly was still more astonished. However, she said, "Wait a moment, dear!" and, with the instinctive deftness of her sex, in three small tugs and a gentle hitch, shook Yerba's gown into perfect folds, passed her fingers across her forehead and over her ears, securing, however, with a hairpin on their passage three of the rose petals where they had fallen. Then, discharging their faces of any previous expression, these two charming hypocrites sallied out innocently into the walk. Nothing could be more natural than their manner: if a criticism might be ventured upon, it was that their elbows were slightly drawn inwards and before them, leaving their hands gracefully advanced in the line of their figures, an attitude accepted throughout the civilised world of deportment as indicating fastidious refinement not unmingled with permissible hauteur.

The three gentlemen lifted their hats at this ravishing apparition, and halted. The Mayor advanced with great politeness.

"I feared you didn't hear me call you, Miss Yerba, so we ventured to seek you." As the two girls exchanged almost infantile glances of surprise, he continued, "Mr. Paul Hathaway has done us the honour of seeking you here, as he did not find you at the convent. You may have forgotten that Mr. Hathaway is the third one of your trustees."

"And so inefficient and worthless that I fear he doesn't count," said Paul; "but," raising his eyes to Yerba's, "I fancy that I have already had the pleasure of seeing you, and, I fear, the mortification of having disturbed you and your friends in the parlour of the Golden Gate Hotel yesterday."

The two girls looked at each other with the same child-like surprise. Yerba broke the silence by suddenly turning to Milly. "Certainly, you remember how greatly interested we were in the conversation of a party of gentlemen who were there when we came in. I am afraid our foolish prattle must have disturbed *you*. I know that we were struck with the intelligent and eloquent devotion of your friends."

"Oh, perfectly," chimed in the loyal but somewhat infelix Milly; "and it was so kind and thoughtful of Mr. Hathaway to take them away as he did."

"I felt the more embarrassed," continued Hathaway, smiling, but still critically examining Yerba for an indication of something characteristic beyond this palpable conventionality, "as I unfortunately must present my credentials from a gentleman as much of a stranger as myself—Colonel Pendleton."

The trade-wind was evidently making itself felt even in this pastoral retreat, for the two gentlemen appeared to shrink slightly within themselves, and a chill seemed to have passed over the group. The Mayor coughed. The avuncular Woods gazed abstractedly at a large cactus. Even Paul, prepared by previous experience, stopped short.

"Colonel Pendleton! Oh, do tell me all about him!" flashed out Yerba suddenly, with clasped hands and eager girlish breath.

Paul cast a quick, grateful glance at the girl. Whether assumed or not, her enthusiastic outburst was effective. The Mayor looked uneasily at Woods, and turned to Paul.

"Ah yes! You and he were original co-trustees. I believe Pendleton is in reduced circumstances. Never quite got over that bank trouble."

"That is only a question of legislative investigation and relief," said Paul lightly, yet with purposely vague official mystery of manner. Then, turning quickly to Yerba, as if replying to the only real question at issue, he continued pointedly, "I am sorry to say the Colonel's health is so poor that it keeps him quite a recluse. I have a letter from him and a message for you." His bright eyes added plainly, "as soon as we can get rid of those people."

"Then you think that a bill——" began the Mayor eagerly.

"I think, my dear sir," said Paul plaintively, "that I and my friends have already tried the patience of these two young ladies quite enough yesterday with politics and law-making. I have to catch the six-o'clock train to San Francisco this evening, and have already lost the time I hoped to spend with Miss Yerba by missing her at the convent. Let me stroll on here, if you like, and if I venture to monopolise the attention of this young lady for half an hour, you, my dear Mr. Mayor, who have more frequent access to her, I know will not begrudge it to me."

He placed himself beside Yerba and Milly, and began an entertaining, although, I fear, slightly exaggerated account of his reception by the Lady Superior, and her evident doubts of his identity with the trustee mentioned in Pendleton's letter of introduction. "I confess she frightened me," he continued, "when she remarked that, according to my statement, I could have been only eighteen years old when I became your guardian, and as much in want of one as you were. I think that only her belief that Mr. Woods and the Mayor would detect me as an impostor provoked her at last to tell me your whereabouts."

"But why *did* they ever make you a trustee, for goodness' sake?" said Milly naïvely. "Was there no one grown up at that time that they could have called upon?"

"Those were the *early* days of California," responded Paul, with great gravity, although he was conscious that Yerba was regarding him narrowly, "and I probably looked older and more intelligent than I really was. For, candidly," with the consciousness of Yerba's eyes still upon him, "I remember very little about it. I dare say I was selected, as you kindly suggest, 'for goodness' sake.' "

"After all," said the volatile Milly, who seemed inclined, as chaperon, to direct the conversation, "there was something pretty and romantic about it. You two poor young things taking care of each other, for, of course, there were no women here in those days."

"Of course there *were* women here," interrupted Yerba quickly, with a half-meaning, half-interrogative glance at Paul that made him instinctively uneasy. "You later comers"—to Milly—"always seem to think that there was nothing here before you!" She paused, and then added, with a naïve mixture of reproach and coquetry that was as charming as it was unexpected, "As to taking care of each other, Mr. Hathaway very quickly got rid of me, I believe."

"But I left you in better hands, Miss Yerba; and let me thank you now," he added in a lower tone, "for recognising it as you did a moment ago. I'm glad that you instinctively liked Colonel Pendleton. Had you known him better, you would have seen how truthful that instinct was. His chief fault in the eyes of our worthy friends is that he reminds them of a great deal they can't perpetuate and much they would like to forget." He checked himself abruptly. "But here is your letter," he resumed, drawing Colonel Pendleton's missive from his pocket; "perhaps you would like to read it now, in case you have any message to return by me. Miss Woods and I will excuse you."

They had reached the end of the rose-alley, where a summer-house that was in itself a rose-bower partly disclosed itself. The other gentlemen had lagged behind. "I will amuse *myself,* and console your other guardian, dear," said the vivacious Milly, with a rapid exchange of glances with Yerba, "until this horrid business is over. Besides," she added with cheerful vagueness, "after so long a separation you must have a great deal to say to each other."

Paul smiled as she rustled away, and Yerba, entering the summer-house, sat down and opened the letter. The young man remained leaning against the rustic archway, occasionally glancing at her and at the moving figures in the gardens. He was conscious of an odd excitement which he could trace to no particular cause. It was true that he had been annoyed at not finding the young girl at the convent, and at having to justify himself to the Lady Superior for what he conceived to be an act of gratuitous kindness; nor was he blind to the fact that his persistence in following her was more an act of aggression against the enemies of Pendleton than of concern for Yerba. She was certainly pretty; but he could not remember her mother sufficiently to trace any likeness, and he had never admired the mother's pronounced beauty. She had flashed out for an instant into what seemed originality and feeling. But it had passed, and she had asked no further questions in regard to the Colonel.

She had hurriedly skimmed through the letter, which seemed to be composed of certain figures and accounts. "I suppose it's all right," she said: "at least, you can say so if he asks you. It's only an explanation why he has transferred my money from the bank to Rothschild's agent years ago. I don't see why it should interest me *now."*

Paul made no doubt that it was the same transfer that had shipwrecked the Colonel's fortune and alienated his friends, and could not help replying somewhat pointedly, "But I think it should, Miss Yerba. I don't know what the Colonel explained to you—doubtless not the whole truth, for he is not a man to praise himself; but the fact is, the bank was in difficulties at the time of that transfer, and to make it he sacrificed his personal fortune, and, I think, awakened some of that ill-feeling you have just noticed." He checked himself too late: he had again lost not only his tact and self-control, but had nearly betrayed himself. He was surprised that the girl's justifiable ignorance should have irritated him. Yet she had evidently not noticed, or misunderstood it, for she said, with a certain precision that was almost studied—

"Yes, I suppose it would have been a terrible thing to him to have been suspected of misappropriating a Trust confided to him by parties who had already paid him the high compliment of confiding to his care a secret and a fortune."

Paul glanced at her quickly with astonishment. Was this ignorance, or suspicion? Her manner, however, suddenly changed, with the charming capriciousness of youth and conscious beauty. "He speaks of you in this letter," she said, letting her dark eyes rest on him provokingly.

"That accounts for your lack of interest, then," said Paul gaily, relieved to turn a conversation fraught with so much danger.

"But he speaks very flatteringly," she went on. "He seems to be another one of your admirers. I'm sure, Mr. Hathaway, after that scene in the hotel parlour yesterday, *you* at least cannot complain of having been misrepresented before *me*. To tell you the truth, I think I hated you a little for it."

"You were quite right," returned Paul. "I must have been insufferable! And I admit that I was slightly piqued against *you* for the idolatries showered upon you at the same moment by your friends."

Usually, when two young people have reached the point of confidingly exchanging their first impressions of each other, some progress has been made in first acquaintance. But it did not strike Paul in that way, and Yerba's next remark was discouraging.

"But I'm rather disappointed, for all that Colonel Pendleton tells me you know nothing of my family or of the secret."

Paul was this time quite prepared, and withstood the girl's scrutiny calmly. "Do you think," he asked lightly, "that even *he* knows?"

"Of course he does," she returned quickly. "Do you suppose he would have taken all that trouble you have just talked about if he didn't know it? And feared the consequences, perhaps?" she added, with a slight return of her previous expressive manner.

Again Paul was puzzled and irritated, he knew not why. But he only said pleasantly, "I differ from you there. I am afraid that such a thing as fear never entered into Colonel Pendleton's calculations on any subject. I think he would act the same towards the highest and the lowest, the powerful or the most weak." As she glanced at him quickly and mischievously, he added, "I am quite willing to believe that his knowledge of you made his duty pleasanter."

He was again quite sincere, and his slight sympathy had that irresistible quality of tone and look which made him so dangerous. For he was struck with the pretty soothed self-complacency that had shone in her face since he had spoken of Pendleton's equal disinterestedness. It seemed, too, as if what he had taken for passion or petulance in her manner had been only a resistance to some continual aggression of condition. With that remainder held in check, a certain latent nobility was apparent, as of her true self. In this moment of pleased abstraction she had drawn through the lattice-work of one of the windows a spray of roses still clinging to the vine, and, with her graceful head a little on one side, was softly caressing her cheek with it. She certainly was very pretty. From the crown of her dark little head to the narrow rosetted slipper that had been idly tapping the ground, but now seemed to tread it more proudly, with arched instep and small ankle, she was pleasant to look upon.

"But you surely have something else to think about, Miss Yerba?" said the young man with conviction. "In a few months you will be of age, and rid of those dreadfully stupid guardians; with your——"

The loosened rose-spray flew from her hand out of the window as she made a gesture, half real, half assumed, of imploring supplication. "Oh, please, Mr. Hathaway, for Heaven's sake don't *you* begin too! You are going to say that, with my wealth, my accomplishments, my beauty, my friends, what more can I want? What do I care about a secret that can neither add to them nor take them away? Yes, you were! It's the regular thing to say—everybody says it. Why, I should have thought 'the youngest Senator' could afford to have been more original."

"I plead guilty to *all* the weaknesses of humanity," said Paul warmly, again beginning to believe that he had been most unjust to her independence.

"Well, I forgive you, because you have forgotten to say that, if I don't like the name of Yerba Buena, I could *so* easily change that too."

"But you *do* like it," said Paul, touched with this first hearing of her name in her own musical accents, "or would like it if you heard yourself pronounce it." It suddenly recurred to him, with a strange thrill of pleasure, that he himself had given it to her. It was as if he had created some musical instrument to which she had just given voice. In his enthusiasm he had thrown himself on the bench beside her in an attitude that, I fear, was not as dignified as became his elderly office.

"But you don't think that is my *name,* " said the girl quickly.

"I beg your pardon?" said Paul hesitatingly.

"You don't think that anybody would have been so utterly idiotic as to call me after a ground-vine—a vegetable?" she continued petulantly.

"Eh?" stammered Paul.

"A name that could be so easily translated," she went on half-scornfully, "and, when translated, was no possible title for anybody? Think of it—Miss Good Herb! It is too ridiculous for anything."

Paul was not usually wanting in self-possession in an emergency, or in skill to meet attack. But he was so convinced of the truth of the girl's accusation, and now recalled so vividly his own consternation on hearing the result of his youthful and romantic sponsorship for the first time from Pendleton, that he was struck with confusion.

"But what do you suppose it was intended for?" he said at last vaguely. "It was certainly 'Yerba Buena' in the Trust. At least, I suppose so," he corrected himself hurriedly.

"It is only a supposition," she said quietly, "for you know it cannot be proved. The Trust was never recorded, and the only copy could not be found among Mr. Hammersley's papers. It is only part of the name, of which the first is lost."

"Part of the name?" repeated Paul uneasily.

"Part of it. It is a corruption of *de la Yerba Buena*—of the Yerba Buena—and refers to the island of Yerba Buena in the bay, and not to the plant. That island was part of the property of my family—the Arguellos—you will find it so recorded in the Spanish grants. My name is Arguello de la Yerba Buena."

It is impossible to describe the timid yet triumphant, the half-appealing yet complacent, conviction of the girl's utterance. A moment before Paul would have believed it impossible for him to have kept his gravity and his respect for his companion under this egregious illusion. But he kept both. For a sudden conviction that she suspected the truth, and had taken this audacious and original plan of crushing it, overpowered all other sense. The Arguellos, it flashed upon him, were an old Spanish family, former owners of Yerba Buena Island, who had in the last years become extinct. There had been a story that one of them had eloped with an American ship captain's wife at Monterey. The legendary history of early Spanish California was filled with more remarkable incidents, corroborated with little difficulty from Spanish authorities, who, it was alleged, lent themselves readily to any fabrication or forgery. There was no racial pride; on the contrary, they had shown an eager alacrity to ally themselves with their conquerors. The friends of the Arguellos would be proud to recognise and remember in the American heiress the descendant of their countrymen. All this passed rapidly through his mind after the first moment of surprise; all this must have been the deliberate reasoning of this girl of seventeen, whose dark eyes were bent upon him. Whether she was seeking corroboration or complicity he could not tell.

"Have you found this out yourself?" he asked, after a pause.

"Yes. One of my friends at the convent was Josita Castro; she knew all the history of the Arguellos. She is perfectly satisfied."

For an instant Paul wondered if it was a joint conception of the two schoolgirls. But, on reflection, he was persuaded that Yerba would commit herself to no accomplice—of her own sex. She might have dominated the girl, and would make her a firm partisan, while the girl would be convinced of it herself, and believe herself a free agent. He had had such experience with men himself.

"But why have you not spoken of it before—and to Colonel Pendleton?"

"He did not choose to tell *me*," said Yerba, with feminine dexterity. "I have preferred to keep it myself a secret till I am of age."

When Colonel Pendleton and some of the other trustees have no right to say anything, thought Paul quickly. She had evidently trusted *him*. Yet, fascinated as he had been by her audacity, he did not know whether to be pleased, or the reverse. He would have preferred to be placed on an equal footing with Josita Castro. She anticipated his thoughts by saying, with half-raised eyelids—

"What do *you* think of it?"

"It seems to be so natural and obvious an explanation of the mystery that I only wonder it was not thought of before," said Paul, with that perfect sincerity that made his sympathy so effective.

"You see"—still under her pretty eyelids, and the tender promise of a smile parting her little mouth—"I'm believing that you tell the truth when you say you don't know anything about it."

It was a desperate moment with Paul, but his sympathetic instincts, and possibly his luck, triumphed. His momentary hesitation easily simulated the caution of a conscientious man; his knit eyebrows and bright eyes, lowered in an effort of memory, did the rest. "I remember it all so indistinctly," he said, with literal truthfulness; "there was a veiled lady present, tall and dark, to whom Mayor Hammersley and the Colonel showed a singular, and it struck me as an almost superstitious, respect. I remember now, distinctly, I was impressed with the reverential way they both accompanied her to the door at the end of the interview." He raised his eyes slightly; the young girl's red lips were parted; that illumination of the skin, which was her nearest approach to colour, had quite transfigured her face. He felt suddenly that she believed it, yet he had no sense of remorse. He half believed it himself; at least, he remembered the nobility of the mother's self-renunciation and its effect upon the two men. Why should not the daughter preserve this truthful picture of the mother's momentary exaltation? Which was the most truthful—that, or the degrading facts? "You speak of a secret," he added. "I can remember little more than that the Mayor asked me to forget, from that moment, the whole occurrence. I did not know at the time how completely I should fulfill his request. You must remember, Miss Yerba, as your Lady Superior has, that I was absurdly young at the time. I don't know but that I may have thought, in my youthful inexperience, that this sort of thing was of common occurrence. And then, I had my own future to make —and youth is brutally selfish. I was quite friendless and unknown when I left San Francisco for the mines, at the time you entered the convent as Yerba Buena."

She smiled, and made a slight impulsive gesture, as if she would have drawn nearer to him, but checked herself, still smiling, and without embarrassment. It may have been a movement of youthful *camaraderie,* and that occasional maternal rather than sisterly instinct which sometimes influences a young girl's masculine friendship, and elevates the favoured friend to the plane of the doll she has outgrown. As he turned towards her, however, she rose, shook out her yellow dress, and said with pretty petulance—

"Then you must go so soon—and this your first and last visit as my guardian?"

"No one could regret that more than I," looking at her with undefined meaning.

"Yes," she said, with a tantalising coquetry that might have suggested an underlying seriousness, "I think you *have* lost a good deal. Perhaps so have I. We might have been good friends in all these years. But that is past."

"Why? Surely, I hope, my shortcomings with Miss Yerba Buena will not be remembered by Miss Arguello?" said Paul earnestly.

"Ah! *She* may be a very different person."

"I hope not," said the young man warmly. "But *how* different?"

"Well, she may not put herself in the way of receiving such point-blank compliments as that," said the young girl demurely.

"Not from her guardian?"

"She will have no guardian then." She said this gravely, but almost at the same moment turned and sat down again, throwing her linked hands over her knee, and looked at him mischievously. "You see what you have lost, sir."

"I see," said Paul, but with all the gravity that she had dropped.

"No; but you don't see all. I had no brother—no friend. You might have been both. You might have made me what you liked. You might have educated me far better than these teachers, or, at least, given me some pride in my studies. There were so many things I wanted to know that they couldn't teach me; so many times I wanted advice from some one that I could trust. Colonel Pendleton was very good to me when he came; he always treated me like a princess even when I wore short frocks. It was his manner that first made me think he knew my family; but I never felt as if I could tell him anything, and I don't think, with all his chivalrous respect, he ever understood me. As to the others—the Mayors—well, you may judge from Mr. Henderson. It is a wonder that I did not run away or do something desperate. Now, are you not a *little* sorry?"

Her voice, which had as many capricious changes as her manner, had been alternately coquettish, petulant, and serious, had now become playful again. But, like the rest of her sex, she was evidently more alert to her surroundings at such a moment than her companion, for before he could make any reply she said, without apparently looking, "But there is a deputation coming for you, Mr. Hathaway. You see, the case is hopeless. You never would be able to give to one what is claimed by the many."

Paul glanced down the rose-alley, and saw that the deputation in question was composed of the Mayor, Mr. Woods, a thin, delicate-looking woman—evidently Mrs. Woods—and Milly. The latter managed to reach the summer-house first, with apparently youthful alacrity, but really to exchange, in a single glance, some mysterious feminine signal with Yerba. Then she said with breathless infelicity—

"Before you two get bored with each other now, I must tell you there's a chance of you having more time. Aunty has promised to send off a note excusing you to the Reverend Mother, if she can persuade Mr. Hathaway to stay over to-night. But here they are. [To Yerba] Aunty is most anxious, and won't hear of his going."

Indeed, it seemed as if Mrs. Woods was, after a refined fashion, most concerned that a distinguished visitor like Mr. Hathaway should have to use her house as a mere accidental meeting-place with his ward, without deigning to accept her hospitality. She was reinforced by Mr. Woods, who enunciated the same idea with more masculine vigour; and by the Mayor, who expressed his conviction that a slight of this kind to Rosario would be felt in the Santa Clara valley. "After dinner, my dear Hathaway," concluded Mr. Woods, "a few of our neighbours may drop in, who would be glad to shake you by the hand—no formal meeting, my boy—but, hang it! *they* expect it."

Paul looked around for Yerba. There was really no reason why he shouldn't accept, although an hour ago the idea had never entered his mind. Yet, if he did, he would like the girl to know that it was for *her* sake. Unfortunately, far from exhibiting any concern in the matter, she seemed to be preoccupied with Milly, and only the charming back of her head was visible behind Mrs. Woods. He accepted, however, with a hesitation that took some of the graciousness from his yielding, and a sense that he was giving a strange importance to a trivial circumstance.

The necessity of attaching himself to his hostess, and making a more extended tour of the grounds, for a while diverted him from an uneasy consideration of his past interview. Mrs. Woods had known Yerba through the school friendship of Milly, and, as far as the religious rules of the convent would allow, had always been delighted to show her any hospitality. She was a beautiful girl—did not Mr. Hathaway think so?—and a girl of great character. It was a pity, of course, that she had never known a mother's care, and that the present routine of a boarding-school had usurped the tender influences of home. She believed, too, that the singular rotation of guardianship had left the girl practically without a counselling friend to rely upon, except perhaps Colonel Pendleton; and while she, Mrs. Woods, did not for a moment doubt that the Colonel might be a good friend and a pleasant companion of *men,* really he, Mr. Hathaway, must admit that, with his reputation and habits, he was hardly a fit associate for a young lady. Indeed, Mr. Woods would never have allowed Milly to invite Yerba here if Colonel Pendleton was to have been her escort. Of course, the poor girl could not choose her own guardian, but Mr. Woods said *he* had a right to choose who should be his niece's company. Perhaps Mr. Woods was prejudiced—most men were—yet surely Mr. Hathaway, although a loyal friend of Colonel Pendleton's, must admit that when it was an open scandal that the Colonel had fought a duel about a notoriously common woman, and even blasphemously defended her before a party of gentlemen, it was high time, as Mr. Woods said, that he should be remanded to their company exclusively. No; Mrs. Woods could not admit that this was owing to the injustice of her own sex! Men are really the ones who make the fuss over those things, just as they, as Mr. Hathaway well knew, made the laws! No; it was a great pity, as she and her husband had just agreed, that Mr. Hathaway, of all the guardians, could not have been always the help and counsellor —in fact, the elder brother—of poor Yerba! Paul was conscious that he winced slightly, consistently and conscientiously, at the recollection of certain passages of his youth; inconsistently and meanly, at this suggestion of a joint relationship with Yerba's mother.

"I think, too," continued Mrs. Woods, "she has worried foolishly about this ridiculous mystery of her parentage—as if it could make the slightest difference to a girl with a quarter of a million, or as if that didn't show quite conclusively that she *was* somebody!"

"Certainly," said Paul quickly, with a relief that he nevertheless felt was ridiculous.

"And, of course, I dare say it will all come out when she is of age. I suppose you know if any of the family are still living?"

"I really do not."

"I beg your pardon," said Mrs. Woods, with a smile, "I forgot it's a profound secret until then. But here we are at the house; I see the girls have walked over to our neighbours'. Perhaps you would like to have a few moments to yourself before you dress for dinner, and your portmanteau, which has been sent for, comes from your hotel. You must be tired of seeing so many people."

Paul was glad to accept any excuse for being alone, and, thanking his hostess, followed a servant to his room—a low-ceilinged but luxuriously furnished apartment on the first floor. Here he threw himself on a cushioned lounge that filled the angle of the deep embrasure—the thickness of the old adobe walls—that formed a part of the wooden-latticed window. A Cape jessamine climbing beside it filled the room with its subtle, intoxicating perfume. It was so strong, and he felt himself so irresistibly overpowered and impelled towards a merely idle reverie, that, in order to think more clearly and shut out some strange and unreasoning enthralment of his senses, he rose and sharply closed the window. Then he sat down and reflected.

What was he doing here? and what was the meaning of all this? He had come simply to fulfil a duty to his past, and please a helpless and misunderstood old acquaintance. He had performed that duty. But he had incidentally learned a certain fact that might be important to this friend, and clearly his duty was simply to go back and report it. He would gain nothing more in the way of corroboration of it by staying now, if further corroboration were required. Colonel Pendleton had already been uselessly and absurdly perplexed about the possible discovery of the girl's parentage, and its effect upon her fortunes and herself. She had just settled that of her own accord, and, without committing herself or others, had suggested a really sensible plan by which all trouble would be avoided in future. That was the common-sense way of looking at it. He would lay the plan before the Colonel, have him judge of its expediency and its ethics—and even the question whether she already knew the real truth, or was self-deceived. That done, he would return to his own affairs in Sacramento. There was nothing difficult in this, or that need worry him, only he could have done it just as well an hour ago.

He opened the window again. The scent of the jessamine came in as before, but mingled with the cooler breath of the roses. There was nothing intoxicating or unreal in it now; rather it seemed a gentle aromatic stimulant—of thought. Long shadows of unseen poplars beyond barred the garden lanes and alleys with bands of black and yellow. A slanting pencil of sunshine through the trees was for a moment focussed on a bed of waxen callas before a hedge of ceanothus, and struck into dazzling relief the cold white chalices of the flowers and the vivid shining green of their background. Presently it slid beyond to a tiny fountain, before invisible, and wrought a blinding miracle out of its flashing and leaping spray. Yet even as he gazed the fountain seemed to vanish slowly, the sunbeam slipped on, and beyond it moved the shimmer of white and yellow dresses. It was Yerba and Milly returning to the house. Well, he would not interrupt his reflections by idly watching them; he would probably see a great deal of Yerba that evening, and by that time he would have come to some conclusion in regard to her.

But he had not taken into consideration her voice, which, always musical in its Southern intonation and quite audible in the quiet garden, struck him now as being full of joyous sweetness. Well, she was certainly very happy—or very thoughtless. She was actually romping with Milly, and was now evidently being chased down the rose-alley by that volatile young woman. Then these swift Camillas apparently neared the house, there was the rapid rustle of skirts, the skurrying of little feet on the verandah, a stumble, a mouse-like shriek from Milly, and *her* voice, exhausted, dying, happy, broken with half-hushed laughter, rose to him on the breath of the jessamine and rose.

Surely she *was* a child, and, if a child, how he had misjudged her! What if all that he had believed was mature deliberation was only the innocent imaginings of a romantic girl, all that he had taken seriously only a schoolgirl's foolish dream! Instead of combating it, instead of reasoning with her, instead of trying to interest her in other things, he had even helped on her illusions. He had treated her as if the taint of her mother's worldliness and knowledge of evil was in her pure young flesh. He had recognised her as the daughter of an adventuress, and not as his ward, appealing to his chivalry through her very ignorance —it might be her very childish vanity. He had brought to a question of tender and pathetic interest only his selfish opinion of the world and the weaknesses of mankind. The blood came to his cheeks—with all his experienced self-control, he had not lost the youthful trick of blushing—and he turned away from the window as if it had breathed a reproach.

But ought he have even contented himself with destroying her illusions—ought he not have gone further and told her the whole truth? Ought he not first have won her confidence—he remembered bitterly, now, how she had intimated that she had no one to confide in—and, after revealing her mother's history, have still pledged himself to keep the secret from all others, and assisted her in her plan? It would not have altered the state of affairs, except so far as she was concerned: they could have combined together, his ready wit would have helped him, and his sympathy would have sustained her; but——

How and in what way could he have told her? Leaving out the delicate and difficult periphrase by which her mother's shame would have to be explained to an innocent schoolgirl—what right could he have assumed to tell it? As the guardian who had never counselled or protected her? As an acquaintance of hardly an hour ago? Who would have such a right? A lover—on whose lips it would only seem a tacit appeal to her gratitude or her fears, and whom no sensitive girl could accept thereafter? No. A husband? Yes! He remembered with a sudden start what Pendleton had said to him. Good heavens! Had Pendleton that idea in his mind? And yet—it seemed the only solution.

A knock at his door was followed by the appearance of Mr. Woods. Mr. Hathaway's portmanteau had come, and Mrs. Woods had sent a message, saying that in view of the limited time that Mr. Hathaway would have with his ward, Mrs. Woods would forego her right to keep him at her side at dinner, and yield her place to Yerba. Paul thanked him with a grave inward smile. What if he made his dramatic disclosure to her confidentially over the soup and fish? Yet, in his constantly recurring conviction of the girl's independence, he made no doubt she would have met his brutality with unflinching pride and self-possession. He began to dress slowly, at times almost forgetting himself in a new kind of pleasant apathy, which he attributed to the odour of the flowers, and the softer hush of twilight that had come on with the dying away of the trade winds, and the restful spice of the bay-trees near his window. He presently found himself not so much thinking of Yerba as *seeing* her. A picture of her in the summer-house caressing her cheek with the roses seemed to stand out from the shadows of the blank wall opposite him. When he passed into the dressing-room beyond, it was not his own face he saw in the glass, but hers. It was with a start, as if he had heard *her* voice, that he found upon his dressing-table a small vase containing a flower for his coat, with the pencilled words on a card in a schoolgirl's hand "From Yerba, with thanks for staying." It must have been placed there by a servant while he was musing at the window.

Half a dozen people were already in the drawing-room when Paul descended. It appeared that Mr. Woods had invited certain of his neighbours—among them a Judge Baker and his wife, and Don Caesar Briones, of the adjacent Rancho of Los Pajaros, and his sister, the Doña Anna. Milly and Yerba had not yet appeared. Don Caesar, a young man of a toreador build, roundly bland in face and murky in eye, seemed to notice their absence, and kept his glances towards the door, while Paul engaged in conversation with Doña Anna—if that word could convey an impression of a conventionality which that good-humoured young lady converted into an animated flirtation at the second sentence with a single glance and two shakes of her fan. And then Milly fluttered in—a vision of schoolgirl freshness and white tulle, and a moment later—with a pause of expectation—a tall, graceful figure, that at first Paul scarcely recognised.

It is a popular conceit of our sex that we are superior to any effect of feminine adornment, and that a pretty girl is equally pretty in the simplest frock. Yet there was not a man in the room who did not believe that Yerba in her present attire was not only far prettier than before, but that she indicated a new and more delicate form of beauty. It was not the mere revelation of contour and colour of an ordinary *décolleté* dress, it was a perfect presentment of pure symmetry and carriage. In this black grenadine dress, trimmed with jet, not only was the delicate satin sheen of her skin made clearer by contrast, but she looked every inch her full height, with an ideal exaltation of breeding and culture. She wore no jewellery except a small necklace of pearls— so small it might have been a child's—that fitted her slender throat so tightly that it could scarcely be told from the flesh that it clasped. Paul did not know that it was the gift of the mother to the child that she had forsworn only a few weeks before she parted from her for ever; but he had a vague feeling that, in that sable dress that seemed like mourning, she walked at the funeral of her mother's past. A few white flowers in her corsage, the companions of the solitary one in his buttonhole, were the only relief.

Their eyes met for a single moment, the look of admiration in Paul's being answered by the naïve consciousness in Yerba's of a woman looking her best; but the next moment she appeared preoccupied with the others, and the eager advances of Don Caesar.

"Your brother seems to admire Miss Yerba," said Paul.

"Ah, ye—es," returned Doña Anna. "And you?"

"Oh!" said Paul gaily. "*I? I* am her guardian—with me it is simple egotism, you know."

"Ah!" returned the arch Doña Anna, "you are then already *so* certain of her? Good! I shall warn him."

A precaution that did seem necessary; as later, when Paul, at a signal from his hostess, offered his arm to Yerba, the young Spaniard regarded him with a look of startled curiosity.

"I thank you for selecting me to wear your colours," said Paul, with a glance at the flowers in her corsage, as they sat at table, "and I think I deserve them, since, but for you, I should be on my way to San

Francisco at this moment. Shall I have an opportunity of talking to you a few moments later in the evening?" he added, in a lower tone.

"Why not now?" returned Yerba mischievously. "We are set here expressly for that purpose?"

"Surely not to talk of our own business—I should say, of our *family* affairs," said Paul, looking at her with equal playfulness; "though I believe your friend Don Caesar, opposite, would be more pleased if he were sure that was all we did."

"And you think his sister would share in that pleasure," retorted Yerba. "I warn you, Mr. Hathaway, that you have been quite justifying the Reverend Mother's doubts about your venerable pretensions. Everybody is staring at you now."

Paul looked up mechanically. It was true. Whether from some occult sympathy, from a human tendency to admire obvious fitness and symmetry, or the innocent love with which the world regards youthful lovers, they were all observing Yerba and himself with undisguised attention. A good talker, he quickly led the conversation to other topics. It was then that he discovered that Yerba was not only accomplished, but that this convent-bred girl had acquired a singular breadth of knowledge apart from the ordinary routine of the school curriculum. She spoke and thought with independent perceptions and clearness, yet without the tactlessness and masculine abruptness that is apt to detract from feminine originality of reflection. By some tacit understanding that had the charm of mutual confidence they both exerted themselves to please the company rather than each other, and Paul, in the interchange of sallies with Doña Anna, had a certain pleasure in hearing Yerba converse in Spanish with Don Caesar. But in a few moments he observed, with some uneasiness, that they were talking of the old Spanish occupation, and presently of the old Spanish families. Would she prematurely expose an ignorance that might be hereafter remembered against her, or invite some dreadful genealogical reminiscence that would destroy her hopes and raze her Spanish castles? Or was she simply collecting information? He admired the dexterity with which, without committing herself, she made Don Caesar openly and even confidentially communicative. And yet he was on thorns: at times it seemed as if he himself were playing a part in this imposture of Yerba's. He was aware that his wandering attention was noticed by the quick-witted Doña Anna, when he regained his self-possession by what appeared to be a happy diversion. It was the voice of Mrs. Judge Baker calling across the table to Yerba. By one of the peculiar accidents of general conversation, it was the one apparently trivial remark that in a pause challenged the ears of all.

"We were admiring your necklace, Miss Yerba."

Every eye was turned upon the slender throat of the handsome girl. The excuse was so natural.

Yerba put her hand to her neck with a smile. "You are joking, Mrs. Baker. I know it is ridiculously small; but it is a child's necklace, and I wear it because it was a gift from my mother."

Paul's heart sank again with consternation. It was the first time that he had heard the girl distinctly connect herself with her actual mother, and for an instant he felt as startled as if the forgotten Outcast herself had returned and taken a seat at the board.

"I told you it couldn't be so?" said Mrs. Baker, turning to her husband.

Everybody naturally looked inquiringly upon the couple, and Mrs. Baker explained with a smile: "Bob thinks he's seen it before; men are so obstinate."

"Pardon me, Miss Yerba," said the Judge blandly; "would you mind showing it to me, if it is not too much trouble?"

"Not at all," said Yerba, smiling, and detaching the circlet from her neck. "I'm afraid you'll find it rather old-fashioned."

"That's just what I hope to find it," said Judge Baker, with a triumphant glance at his wife. "It was eight years ago when I saw it in Tucker's jewellery shop. I wanted to buy it for my little Minnie, but as the price was steep I hesitated, and when I did make up my mind he had disposed of it to another customer. Yes," he added, examining the necklace that Yerba had handed to him, "I am certain it is the same; it was unique, like this. Odd, isn't it?"

Everybody said it *was* odd, and looked upon the occurrence with that unreasoning satisfaction with which average humanity receives the most trivial and unmeaning coincidences. It was left to Don Caesar to give it a gallant application.

"I have not-a the pleasure of knowing-a the Miss Minnie, but the jewellery, when she arrives to the throat-a of Miss Yerba, she has not lost the value—the beauty—the charm."

"No," said Woods cheerily. "The fact is, Baker, you were too slow. Miss Yerba's folks gobbled up the necklace while you were thinking. You were a new-comer. Old 'forty-niners' did not hesitate over a thing they wanted."

"You never knew who was your successful rival, eh?" said Doña Anna, turning to Judge Baker, with a curious glance at Paul's pale face in passing.

"No," said Baker, "but——" he stopped with a hesitating laugh and some little confusion. "No, I've mixed it up with something else. It's so long ago. I never knew, or if I did I've forgotten. But the necklace I remember." He handed it back to Yerba with a bow, and the incident ended.

Paul had not looked at Yerba during this conversation, an unreasoning instinct that he might confuse her, an equally unreasoning dread that he might see her confused by others, possessing him. And when he did glance at her calm, untroubled face, that seemed only a little surprised at his own singular coldness, he was by no means relieved. He was only convinced of one thing. In the last five minutes he had settled upon the irrevocable determination that his present relations with the girl could exist no longer. He must either tell her everything, or see her no more. There was no middle course. She was on the brink of an exposure at any moment, either through her ignorance or her unhappy pretension. In his intolerable position he was equally unable to contemplate her peril, accept her defence, or himself defend her.

As if, with some feminine instinct, she had attributed his silence to some jealousy of Don Caesar's attentions, she more than once turned from the Spaniard to Paul with an assuring smile. In his anxiety he half accepted the rather humiliating suggestion, and managed to say to her in a lower tone—

"On this last visit of your American guardian, one would think, you need not already anticipate your Spanish relations."

He was thrilled with the mischievous yet faintly tender pleasure that sparkled in her eyes as she said—

"You forget it is my American guardian's *first* visit, as well as his last."

"And as your guardian," he went on, with half-veiled seriousness, "I protest against your allowing your treasures, the property of the Trust," he gazed directly into her beautiful eyes, "being handled and commented upon by everybody."

When the ladies had left the table, he was, for a moment, relieved. But only for a moment. Judge Baker drew his chair beside Paul's, and taking his cigar from his lips, said with a perfunctory laugh—

"I say, Hathaway, I pulled up just in time to save myself from making an awful speech just now to your ward."

Paul looked at him with cold curiosity.

"Yes. Gad! Do you know *who* was my rival in that necklace transaction?"

"No," said Paul, with frigid carelessness.

"Why, Kate Howard! Fact, sir. She bought it right under my nose—and overbid me, too."

Paul did not lose his self-possession. Thanks to the fact that Yerba was not present, and that Don Caesar, who had overheard the speech, moved forward with a suggestive and unpleasant smile, his agitation congealed into a coldly placid fury.

"And I suppose," he returned, with perfect calmness, "that, after the usual habit of this class of women, the necklace very soon found its way back, through the pawn-broker, to the jeweller again. It's a common fate."

"Yes, of course," said Judge Baker cheerfully. "You're quite right. That's undoubtedly the solution of it. But," with a laugh, "I had a narrow escape from saying something—eh?"

"A very narrow escape from an apparently gratuitous insult," said Paul gravely, but fixing his eyes, now more luminous than ever with anger, not on the speaker, but on the face of Don Caesar, who was standing at his side. "You were about to say——"

"Eh—oh—ah! this Kate Howard? So! I have heard of her—yees! And Miss Yerba—ah—she is of my country—I think. Yes—we shall claim her—of a truth—yes."

"Your countrymen, I believe, are in the habit of making claims that are more often founded on profit than verity," said Paul, with smileless and insulting deliberation. He knew perfectly what he was saying, and the result he expected. Only twenty-four hours before he had smiled at Pendleton's idea of averting scandal and discovery by fighting, yet he was endeavouring to pick a quarrel with a man, merely on suspicion, for the same purpose, and he saw nothing strange in it. A vague idea, too, that this would irrevocably confirm him in opposition to Yerba's illusions probably determined him.

But Don Caesar, albeit smiling lividly, did not seem inclined to pick up the gauntlet, and Woods interfered hastily. "Don Caesar means that your ward has some idea herself that she is of Spanish origin—at least, Milly says so. But of course, as one of the oldest trustees, *you* know the facts."

In another moment Paul would have committed himself. "I think we'll leave Miss Yerba out of the question," he said coldly. "My remark was a general one, though, of course, I am responsible for any personal application of it."

"Spoken like a politician, Hathaway," said Judge Baker, with an effusive enthusiasm which he hoped would atone for the alarming results of his infelicitous speech. "That's right, gentlemen! You can't get the facts from him before he is ready to give them. Keep your secret, Mr. Hathaway; the Court is with you."

Nevertheless, as they passed out of the room to join the ladies, the Mayor lingered a little behind with Woods. "It's easy to see the influence of that Pendleton on our young friend," he said significantly.

"Somebody ought to tell him that it's played out down here—as Pendleton is. It's quite enough to ruin his career."

Paul was too observant not to notice this, but it brought him no sense of remorse; and his youthful belief in himself and his power kept him from concern. He felt as if he had done something, if only to show Don Caesar that the girl's weakness or ignorance could not be traded upon with impunity. But he was still undecided as to the course he should pursue. But he should determine that to-night. At present there seemed no chance of talking to her alone—she was unconcernedly conversing with Milly and Mrs. Woods, and already the visitors who had been invited to this hurried *levée* in his honour were arriving. In view of his late indiscretion, he nervously exerted his fullest powers, and in a very few minutes was surrounded by a breathless and admiring group of worshippers. A ludicrous resemblance to the scene in the Golden Gate Hotel passed through his mind; he involuntarily turned his eyes to seek Yerba in the half fear, half expectation of meeting her mischievous smile. Their glances met; to his surprise hers was smileless, and instantly withdrawn, but not until he had been thrilled by an unconscious prepossession in its luminous depths that he scarcely dared to dwell upon. What mattered now his passage with Don Caesar or the plaudits of his friends? *She* was proud of him!

Yet after that glance she was shy, preoccupying herself with Milly, or even listening sweetly to Judge Baker's somewhat practical and unromantic reminiscences of the deprivations and the hardships of Californian early days, as if to condone his past infelicity. She was pleasantly unaffected with Don Caesar, although she managed to draw Doña Anna into the conversation; she was unconventional, Paul fancied, to all but himself. Once or twice, when he had artfully drawn her towards the open French windows that led to the moonlit garden and shadowed verandah, she had managed to link Milly's arm in her own, and he was confident that a suggestion to stroll with him in the open air would be followed by her invitation to Milly to accompany them. Disappointed and mortified as he was, he found some solace in her manner, which he still believed suggested the hope that she might be made accessible to his persuasions. Persuasions to what? He did not know.

The last guest had departed; he lingered on the verandah with a cigar, begging his host and hostess not to trouble themselves to keep him company. Milly and Yerba had retired to the former's boudoir, but, as they had not yet formally bade him good-night, there was a chance of their returning. He still stayed on in this hope for half-an-hour, and then, accepting Yerba's continued absence as a tacit refusal of his request, he turned abruptly away. But as he glanced around the

garden before re-entering the house, he was struck by a singular circumstance—a white patch, like a forgotten shawl, which he had observed on the distant ceanothus hedge, and which had at first thrilled
him with expectation, had certainly *changed its position.* Before, it
seemed to be near the summer-house; now it was, undoubtedly, farther
away. Could they, or *she* alone, have slipped from the house and be
awaiting him there? With a muttered exclamation at his stupidity, he
stepped hastily from the verandah and walked towards it. But he had
scarcely proceeded a dozen yards before it disappeared. He reached
the summer-house—it was empty; he followed the line of hedge—no
one was there. It could not have been her, or she would have waited—
unless he were the victim of a practical joke. He turned impatiently
back to the house, re-entered the drawing-room by the French window, and was crossing the half-lit apartment, when he heard a slight
rustle in the shadow of the window. He looked around quickly, and
saw that it was Yerba, in a white loose gown, for which she had
already exchanged her black evening dress, leaning back composedly
on the sofa, her hands clasped behind her shapely head.

"I am waiting for Milly," she said, with a faint smile on her lips. He
fancied, in the moonlight that streamed upon her, that her beautiful
face was pale. "She has gone to the other wing to see one of the
servants who is ill. We thought you were on the verandah smoking and
I should have company, until I saw you start off, and rush up and
down the hedge like mad."

Paul felt that he was losing his self-possession, and becoming nervous in her presence.

"I thought it was *you,*" he stammered.

"Me! Out in the garden at this hour alone, and in the broad moonlight? What are you thinking of, Mr. Hathaway? Do you know anything of convent rules, or is that your idea of your ward's education?"

He fancied that, though she smiled faintly, her voice was as tremulous as his own.

"I want to speak with you," he said, with awkward directness. "I
even thought of asking you to stroll with me in the garden."

"Why not talk here?" she returned, changing her position, pointing
to the other end of the sofa, and drawing the whole overflow of her
skirt to one side. "It is not so very late, and Milly will return in a few
moments."

Her face was in shadow now, but there was a glow-worm light in
her beautiful eyes that seemed faintly to illuminate her whole face. He
sank down on the sofa at her side, no longer the brilliant and ambitious politician, but, it seemed to him, as hopelessly a dreaming,

inexperienced boy as when he had given her the name that now was all
he could think of, and the only word that rose to his feverish lips.
"Yerba!"

"I like to hear you say it," she said quickly, as if to gloss over his
first omission of her formal prefix, and leaning a little forward, with
her eyes on his. "One would think you had created it. You almost
make me regret to lose it."

He stopped! He felt that the last sentence had saved him. "It is of
that I want to speak," he broke out suddenly and almost rudely. "Are
you satisfied that it means nothing, and can mean nothing, to you?
Does it awaken no memory in your mind—recall nothing you care to
know? Think! I beg you, I implore you to be frank with me!"

She looked at him with surprise.

"I have told you already that my present name must be some absurd
blunder, or some intentional concealment. But why do you want to
know *now?*" she continued, adding her faint smile to the emphasis.

"To help you!" he said eagerly. "For that alone! To do all I can to
assist you, if you really believe, and want to believe, that you have
another. To ask you to confide in me; to tell me all you have been told,
all that you know, think you know, or *want* to know about your
relationship to the Arguellos—or to any one! And then to devote myself entirely to proving what you shall say is your desire. You see I am
frank with you Yerba! I only ask you to be as frank with me: to let me
know your doubts, that I may counsel you; your fears, that I may give
you courage."

"Is that all that you came here to tell me?" she asked quietly.

"No, Yerba," he said eagerly, taking her unresisting but indifferent
hand, "not all; but all that I must say, all that I have the right to say,
all that you, Yerba, would permit me to tell you *now.* But let me hope
that the day is not far distant when I can tell you *all,* when you will
understand that this silence has been the hardest sacrifice of the man
who now speaks to you."

"And yet not unworthy of a rising politician," she added, quickly
withdrawing her hand. "I agree," she went on, looking towards the
door, yet without appearing to avoid his eager eyes; "and when I have
settled upon 'a local habitation and a name' we shall renew this interesting conversation. Until then, as my fourth official guardian used to
say—he was a lawyer, Mr. Hathaway, like yourself—when he was
winding up his conjectures on the subject—all that has passed is to be
considered 'without prejudice'!"

"But, Yerba——" began Paul bitterly.

She slightly raised her hand as if to check him with a warning
gesture. "Yes, dear," she said suddenly, lifting her musical voice, with

a mischievous side-glance at Paul, as if to indicate her conception of the irony of a possible application, "this way! Here we are waiting for you!" Her listening ear had detected Milly's step in the passage, and in another moment that cheerful young woman discreetly stopped on the threshold of the room, with every expression of apologetic indiscretion in her face.

"We have finished our talk, and Mr. Hathaway has been so concerned about my having no real name that he has been promising me everything, but his own, for a suitable one. Haven't you, Mr. Hathaway?" She rose slowly, and, going over to Milly, put her arm around her waist and stood for one instant gazing at him between the curtains of the doorway. "Good-night. My very proper chaperon is dreadfully shocked at this midnight interview, and is taking me away. Only think of it, Milly: he actually proposed to me to walk in the garden with him! Good-night, or, as my ancestors—don't forget, *my ancestors* — used to say, *'Buena noche—hasta mañana!'* " She lingered over the Spanish syllables with an imitation of Doña Anna's lisp, and with another smile, but more faint and more ghost-like than before, vanished with her companion.

At eight o'clock the next morning Paul was standing beside his portmanteau on the verandah.

"But this is a sudden resolution of yours, Hathaway," said Mr. Woods. "Can you not possibly wait for the next train? The girls will be down then, and you can breakfast comfortably."

"I have much to do—more than I imagined—in San Francisco before I return," said Paul quickly. "You must make my excuses to them and to your wife."

"I hope," said Woods, with an uneasy laugh, "you have had no more words with Don Caesar, or he with you?"

"No," said Paul, with a reassuring smile; "nothing more, I assure you."

"For you know you're a devilish quick fellow, Hathaway," continued Woods; "quite as quick as your friend Pendleton. And, by the way, Baker is awfully cut up about that absurd speech of his, you know. Came to me last night and wondered if anybody could think it was intentional. I told him it was d—d stupid, that was all. I guess his wife had been at him. Ha! ha! You see, he remembers the old times, when everybody talked of these things, and that woman Howard was quite a character. I'm told she went off to the States years ago."

"Possibly," said Paul carelessly. After a pause, as the carriage drove up to the door, he turned to his host. "By the way, Woods, have you a ghost here?"

"The house is old enough for one. But no. Why?"

"I'll swear I saw a figure moving yonder in the shrubbery late last evening; and when I came up to it, it most unaccountably disappeared."

"One of Don Caesar's servants, I dare say. There is one of them, an Indian, prowling about here, I've been told, at all hours. I'll put a stop to it. Well, you must go, then? Dreadfully sorry you couldn't stop longer! Good-bye!"

Chapter IV

It was two months later that Mr. Tony Shear, of Marysville, but lately confidential clerk to the Hon. Paul Hathaway, entered his employer's chambers in Sacramento and handed the latter a letter.

"I only got back from San Francisco this morning; but Mr. Slate said I was to give you that, and if it satisfied you, and was what you wanted, you would send it back to him."

Paul took the envelope and opened it. It contained a printer's proof-slip, which he hurriedly glanced over. It read as follows:—

Those of our readers who are familiar with the early history of San Francisco will be interested to know that an eccentric and irregular trusteeship, vested for the last eight years in the Mayor of San Francisco and two of our oldest citizens, was terminated yesterday by the majority of a beautiful and accomplished young lady, a pupil of the Convent of Santa Clara. Very few, except the original trustees, were cognisant of the fact that the administration of the trustees has been a recognised function of the successive Mayors of San Francisco during this period; and the mystery surrounding it has been only lately divulged. It offers a touching and romantic instance of a survival of the old patriarchal duties of the former *Alcaldes* and the simplicity of pioneer days. It seems that, in the unsettled conditions of the Mexican land-titles that followed the American occupation, the consumptive widow of a scion of one of the oldest Californian families entrusted her property and the custody of her infant daughter virtually to the city of San Francisco, as represented by the trustees specified, until the girl should become of age. Within a year the invalid mother died. With what loyalty, sagacity, and prudence these gentlemen fulfilled their trust may be gathered from the fact that the property left in their charge has not only been secured and protected, but increased a hundredfold in value; and that the young lady who yesterday attained her majority is not only one of the richest landed heiresses on the Pacific Slope, but one of the most accomplished and thoroughly educated of her sex. It is now no secret that this

favoured child of Chrysopolis is the Doña Maria Concepcion de Arguello de la Yerba Buena, so called from her ancestral property on the
island, now owned by the Federal Government. But it is an affecting
and poetic tribute to the parent of her adoption that she has preferred to
pass under the old, quaintly typical name of the city, and has been
known to her friends simply as 'Miss Yerba Buena.' It is a no less
pleasant and suggestive circumstance that our 'youngest Senator,' the
Honourable Paul Hathaway, formerly private secretary to Mayor Hammersley, is one of the original unofficial trustees; while the chivalry of
the older days is perpetuated in the person of Colonel Harry Pendleton,
the remaining trustee.

As soon as he had finished, Paul took a pencil and crossed out the
last six lines; but instead of laying the proof aside, or returning it to
the waiting secretary, he remained with it in his hand, his silent, set
face turned towards the window. Whether the merely human secretary
was tired of waiting, or the devoted partisan saw something on his
young chief's face that disturbed him, he turned to Paul with that
exaggerated respect which his functions as secretary had grafted upon
his affection for his old associate and said—"I hope nothing's wrong,
sir. Not another of those scurrilous attacks on you for putting that bill
through to relieve Colonel Pendleton? Yet it was a risky thing for you,
sir."

Paul started, recovered himself as if from some remote abstraction,
and with a smile said, "No—nothing. Quite the reverse. Write to Mr.
Slate, thank him, and say that it will do very well—with the exception
of the lines I have marked out. Then bring me the letter, and I will add
this enclosure. Did you call on Colonel Pendleton?"

"Yes, sir. He was at Santa Clara, and had not yet returned—at least,
that's what that dandy nigger of his told me. The airs and graces that
that creature puts on since the Colonel's affairs have been straightened
out is a little too much for a white man to stand. Why, sir! d—d if he
didn't want to patronise *you,* and allowed to me that 'de Kernel' had a
'fah ideah' of you, 'and thought you a promisin' young man.' The fact
is, sir, the Party is making a big mistake trying to give votes to that
kind of cattle—it would only be giving two votes to the other side, for,
slave or free, they're the chattels of their old masters. And as to the
masters' gratitude for what you've done affecting a single vote of their
Party—you're mistaken."

"Colonel Pendleton belongs to no Party," said Paul curtly; "but if
his old constituents ever try to get into power again, they've lost their
only independent martyr."

He presently became abstracted again, and Shear produced from his overcoat pocket a series of official-looking documents.

"I've brought the reports, sir."

"Eh?" said Paul absently.

The secretary stared. "The reports of the San Francisco Chief of Police that you asked me to get." His employer was certainly very forgetful to-day.

"Oh yes; thank you. You can lay them on my desk. I'll look them over in Committee. You can go now, and if any one calls to see me, say I am busy."

The secretary disappeared in the adjoining room, and Paul leaned back in his chair, thinking. He had at last effected the work he had resolved upon when he left Rosario two months ago; the article he had just read, and which would appear as an editorial in the San Francisco paper the day after to-morrow, was the culmination of quietly persistent labour, inquiry, and deduction, and would be accepted hereafter as authentic history, which, if not thoroughly established, at least could not be gainsaid. Immediately on arriving at San Francisco, he had hastened to Pendleton's bedside and laid the facts and his plan before him. To his mingled astonishment and chagrin, the Colonel had objected vehemently to this "saddling of anybody's offspring on a gentleman who couldn't defend himself," and even Paul's explanation that the putative father was a myth scarcely appeased him. But Paul's timely demonstration, by relating the scene he had witnessed of Judge Baker's infelicitous memory, that the secret was likely to be revealed at any moment, and that if the girl continued to cling to her theory, as he feared she would, even to the parting with her fortune, they would be forced to accept it, or be placed in the hideous position of publishing her disgrace, at last convinced him. On the other hand, there was less danger of her *positive* imposition being discovered than of the *vague and impositive* truth. The real danger lay in the present uncertainty and mystery, which courted surmise and invited discovery. Paul himself was willing to take all the responsibility, and at last extracted from the Colonel a promise of passive assent. The only revelation he feared was from the interference of the mother, but Pendleton was strong in the belief that she had not only utterly abandoned the girl to the care of her guardians, but that she would never rescind her resolution to disclaim her relationship; that she had gone into self-exile for that purpose; and that if she *had* changed her mind he would be the first to know of it. On this they had parted. Meantime, Paul had not forgotten another resolution he had formed on his first visit to the Colonel, and had actually succeeded in getting Legislative relief for the

Golden Gate Bank, and restoring to the Colonel some of his private property that had been in the hands of a receiver.

This had been the background of Paul's meditation, which only threw into stronger relief the face and figure that moved before him as persistently as it had once before in the twilight of his room at Rosario. There were times when her moonlit face, with its faint strange smile, stood out before him as it had stood out of the shadows of the half-darkened drawing-room that night; as he had seen it—he believed for the last time—framed for an instant in the parted curtains of the doorway, when she bade him "Good-night." For he had never visited her since, and on the attainment of her majority had delegated his passing functions to Pendleton, whom he had induced to accompany the Mayor to Santa Clara for the final and formal ceremony. For the present she need not know how much she had been indebted to him for the accomplishment of her wishes.

With a sigh he at last recalled himself to his duty, and drawing the pile of reports which Shear had handed him, he began to examine them. These, again, bore reference to his silent, unobtrusive inquiries. In his function as chairman of committee he had taken advantage of a kind of advanced moral legislation then in vogue, and particularly in reference to a certain social reform, to examine statistics, authorities, and witnesses, and in this indirect but exhaustive manner had satisfied himself that the woman "Kate Howard," alias "Beverley," alias "Durfree," had long passed beyond the ken of local police supervision, and that in the record there was no trace or indication of her child. He was going over those infelix records of early transgressions with the eye of trained experience, making notes from time to time for his official use, and yet always watchful of his secret quest, when suddenly he stopped with a quickened pulse. In the record of an affray at a gambling-house, one of the parties had sought refuge in the room of "Kate Howard," who was represented before the magistrate by *her protector, Juan de Arguello.* The date given was contemporary with the beginning of the Trust, but that proved nothing. But the name—had it any significance, or was it a grim coincidence, that spoke even more terribly and hopelessly of the woman's promiscuous frailty? He again attacked the entire report, but there was no other record of her name. Even that would have passed any eye less eager and watchful than his own.

He laid the reports aside, and took up the proof-slip again. Was there any man living but himself and Pendleton who would connect these two statements? That her relations with this Arguello were brief and not generally known was evident from Pendleton's ignorance of the fact. But he must see him again, and at once. Perhaps he might have acquired some information from Yerba; the young girl might have given to his age that confidence she had withheld from the younger man; indeed, he remembered with a flush it was partly in that hope that he had induced the Colonel to go to Santa Clara. He put the proof-slip in his pocket and stepped to the door of the next room.

"You need not write that letter to Slate, Tony. I will see him myself. I am going to San Francisco to-night."

"And do you want anything copied from the reports, sir?"

Paul quickly swept them from the table into his drawer, and locked it. "Not now, thank you. I'll finish my notes later."

The next morning Paul was in San Francisco, and had again crossed the portals of the Golden Gate Hotel. He had been already told that the doom of that palatial edifice was sealed by the laying of the corner-stone of a new erection in the next square that should utterly eclipse it; he even fancied that it had already lost its freshness, and its meretricious glitter had been tarnished. But when he had ordered his breakfast he made his way to the public parlour, happily deserted at that early hour. It was here that he had first seen her. She was standing there, by that mirror, when their eyes first met in a sudden instinctive sympathy. She herself had remembered and confessed it. He recalled the pleased yet conscious girlish superiority with which she had received the adulation of her friends; his memory of her was broad enough now even to identify Milly, as it re-peopled the vacant and silent room.

An hour later he was making his way to Colonel Pendleton's lodgings, and half expecting to find the St. Charles Hotel itself transformed by the eager spirit of improvement. But it was still there in all its barbaric and provincial incongruity. Public opinion had evidently recognised that nothing save the absolute razing of its warped and flimsy walls could effect a change, and waited for it to collapse suddenly like the house of cards it resembled. Paul wondered for a moment if it were not ominous of its lodgers' hopeless inability to accept changed conditions, and it was with a feeling of doubt that he even now ascended the creaking staircase. But it was instantly dissipated on the threshold of the Colonel's sitting-room by the appearance of George and his reception of his master's guest.

The grizzled negro was arrayed in a surprisingly new suit of blue cloth with a portentous white waistcoat and an enormous crumpled white cravat, that gave him the appearance of suffering from a glandular swelling. His manner had, it seemed to Paul, advanced in exaggeration with his clothes. Dusting a chair and offering it to the visitor, he remained gracefully posed with his hand on the back of another.

"Yo' finds us heah yet, Marse Hathaway," he began, elegantly toying with an enormous silver watch-chain, "fo' de Kernel he don' bin find contagious apartments dat at all approximate, and he don' build, for his mind's not dat settled dat he ain't goin' to trabbel. De place is low down, sah, and de folks is low down, and dah's a heap o' white trash dat has congested under de roof ob de hotel since we came. But we uses it temper'ly, sah, fo' de present, and in a dissolutory fashion."

It struck Paul that the contiguity of a certain barber's shop and its dangerous reminiscences had something to do with George's lofty depreciation of his surroundings, and he could not help saying—

"Then you don't find it necessary to have it convenient to the barber's shop any more? I am glad of that, George."

The shot told. The unfortunate George, after an endeavor to collect himself by altering his pose two or three times in rapid succession, finally collapsed, and with an air of mingled pain and dignity, but without losing his ceremonious politeness or unique vocabulary, said—

"Yo' got me dah, sah! Yo' got me dah! De infirmities o' human natcheh, sah, is de common p'operty ob man, and a gemplum like yo'self, sah, a legislato' and a pow'ful speakah, is de las' one to hol' it agin de individal pusson. I confess, sah, de circumstances was propiskuous, de fees fahly good, and de risks inferior. De gemplum who kept de shop was an artess hisself, and had been niggah to Kernel Henderson of Tennessee, and de gemplum I relieved was a Mr. Johnson. But de Kernel, he wouldn't see it in that light, sah, and if you don' mind, sah——"

"I haven't the slightest idea of telling the Colonel or anybody, George," said Paul, smiling; "and I am glad to find on your own account that you are able to put aside any work beyond your duty here."

"Thank you, sah. If yo'll let me introduce yo' to de refreshment, yo'll find it all right now. De Glencoe is dah. De Kernel will be here soon, but he would be pow'ful mo'tified, sah, if yo' didn't hab something afo' he come." He opened a well-filled sideboard as he spoke. It was the first evidence Paul had seen of the Colonel's restored fortunes. He would willingly have contented himself with this mere outward manifestation, but in his desire to soothe the ruffled dignity of the old man he consented to partake of a small glass of spirits. George at once became radiant and communicative. "De Kernel bin gone to Santa Clara to see de young lady dat's finished her edercation dah—de Kernel's only ward, sah. She's one o' dose million-heiresses and highly connected, sah, wid de old Mexican Gobbermen, I understand. And I reckon dey's been big goin's on doun dar, fo' de Mayer kem hisself fo' de Kernel. Looks like dey might bin a proceshon, sah. Yo' don't know if de young lady bin hab a title, sah? I won't be shuah his honah de Mayer or de Kernel didn't say something about a 'Donna.' "

"Very likely," said Paul, turning away with a faint smile. So it was already in the air! Setting aside the old negro's characteristic exaggeration, there had already been some conversation between the Colonel and the Mayor, which George had vaguely overheard. He might be too late, the alternative might be no longer in his hands. But his discomposure was heightened a moment later by the actual apparition of the returning Pendleton.

He was dressed in a tightly-buttoned blue frock-coat, which fairly accented his tall, thin, military figure, although the top lappel was thrown far enough back to show a fine ruffled cambric shirt and checked gingham necktie, and was itself adorned with a white rosebud in the button-hole. Fawn-coloured trousers strapped over narrow patent-leather boots, and a tall white hat, whose broad mourning-band was a perpetual memory of his mother, who had died in his boyhood, completed his festal transformation. Yet his erect carriage, high aquiline nose, and long grey drooping moustache lent a distinguishing grace to this survival of a bygone fashion, and overrode any irreverent comment. Even his slight limp seemed to give a peculiar character to his massive gold-headed stick, and made it a part of his formal elegance.

Handing George his stick and a military cape he carried easily over his left arm, he greeted Paul warmly, yet with a return of his old dominant manner.

"Glad to see you, Hathaway, and glad to see the boy has served you better than the last time. If I had known you were coming, I would have tried to get back in time to have breakfast with you. But your friends at 'Rosario'—I think they call it; in my time it was owned by Colonel Briones, and *he* called it 'The Devil's Little Cañon'—detained me with some d—d civilities. Let's see—his name is Woods, isn't it? Used to sell rum to runaway sailors on Long Wharf, and take stores in exchange? Or was it Baker?—Judge Baker? I forget which. Well, sir, they wished to be remembered."

It struck Paul, perhaps unreasonably, that the Colonel's indifference and digression were both a little assumed, and he asked abruptly—

"And you fulfilled your mission?"

"I made the formal transfer, with the Mayor, of the property to Miss Arguello."

"To Miss Arguello?"

"To the Doña Maria Concepcion de Arguello de la Yerba Buena—to speak precisely," said the Colonel slowly. "George, you can take that hat to that blank hatter—what's his blanked name?—I read it only yesterday in a list of the prominent citizens here—and tell him, with my compliments, that I want a *gentleman's* mourning-band around my hat, and not a child's shoe-lace. It may be *his* idea of the value of his own parents—if he ever had any—but I don't care for him to appraise mine. Go!"

As the door closed upon George, Paul turned to the Colonel—

"Then am I to understand that you have agreed to her story?"

The Colonel rose, picked up the decanter, poured out a glass of whisky, and, holding it in his hand, said—

"My dear Hathaway, let us understand each other. As a gentleman, I have made a point through life never to question the age, name, or family of any lady of my acquaintance. Miss Yerba Buena came of age yesterday, and, as she is no longer my ward, she is certainly entitled to the consideration I have just mentioned. If she, therefore, chooses to tack to her name the whole Spanish directory, I don't see why I shouldn't accept it."

Characteristic as this speech appeared to be of the Colonel's ordinary manner, it struck Paul as being only an imitation of his usual frank independence, and made him uneasily conscious of some vague desertion on Pendleton's part. He fixed his bright eyes on his host, who was ostentatiously sipping his liquor, and said—

"Am I to understand that you have heard nothing more from Miss Yerba, either for or against her story? That you still do not know whether she has deceived herself, has been deceived by others, or is deceiving us?"

"After what I have just told you, Mr. Hathaway," said the Colonel, with an increased exaggeration of manner which Paul thought must be apparent even to himself, "I should have but one way of dealing with questions of that kind from anybody but yourself."

This culminating extravagance—taken in connection with Pendleton's passing doubts—actually forced a laugh from Paul in spite of his bitterness.

Colonel Pendleton's face flushed quickly. Like most positive one-idea'd men, he was restricted from any possible humorous combination, and only felt a mysterious sense of being detected in some weakness. He put down his glass.

"Mr. Hathaway," he began, with a slight vibration in his usual dominant accents, "you have lately put me under a sense of personal obligation for a favour which I felt I could accept without derogation from a younger man, because it seemed to be one not only of youthful generosity but of justice, and was not unworthy the exalted ambition of a young man like yourself or the simple deserts of an old man such as I am. I accepted it, sir, the more readily, because it was entirely unsolicited by me, and seemed to be the spontaneous offering of your own heart. If I have presumed upon it to express myself freely on other matters in a way that only excites your ridicule, I can but offer you an apology, sir. If I have accepted a favour I can neither renounce nor return, I must take the consequences to myself, and even beg *you,* sir, to put up with them."

Remorseful as Paul felt, there was a singular resemblance between the previous reproachful pose of George and this present attitude of his master, as if the mere propinquity of personal sacrifice had made them alike, that struck him with a mingled pathos and ludicrousness. But he said warmly "It is I who must apologise, my dear Colonel. I am not laughing at your conclusions, but at this singular coincidence with a discovery I have made."

"As how, sir?"

"I find in the report of the Chief of the Police for the year 1850 that Kate Howard was under the protection of a man named Arguello."

The Colonel's exaggeration instantly left him. He stared blankly at Paul. "And you call this a laughing matter, sir?" he said sternly, but in his more natural manner.

"Perhaps not; but I don't think, if you will allow me to say so, my dear Colonel, that *you* have been treating the whole affair very seriously. I left you two months ago utterly opposed to views which you are now treating as of no importance. And yet you wish me to believe that nothing has happened, and that you have no further information than you had then. That this is so, and that you are really no nearer the *facts,* I am willing to believe from your ignorance of what I have just told you, and your concern at it. But that you have not been influenced in your *judgment* of what you do know, I cannot believe." He drew nearer Pendleton, and laid his hand upon his arm. "I beg you to be frank with me, for the sake of the person whose interests I see you have at heart. In what way will the discovery I have just made affect them? You are not so far prejudiced as to be blind to the fact that it may be dangerous because it seems corroborative."

Pendleton coughed, rose, took his stick, and limped up and down the room, finally dropping into an arm-chair by the window, with his cane between his knees, and the drooping grey silken threads of his long moustache curled nervously between his fingers.

"Mr. Hathaway, I *will* be frank with you. I know nothing of this blank affair—blank it all!—but what I've told you. Your discovery may be a coincidence, nothing more. But I *have* been influenced, sir— influenced by one of the most perfect, goddess-like—yes, sir; one of the most simple girlish creatures that God ever sent upon earth. A woman that I should be proud to claim as my daughter, a woman that would always be the superior of any man who dare aspire to be her husband! A young lady as peerless in her beauty as she is in her accomplishments, and whose equal don't walk this planet! I know, sir, *you* don't follow me; I know, Mr. Hathaway, your Puritan prejudices; your Church proclivities; your worldly sense of propriety; and, above all, sir, the blanked hypocritical, Pharisaic doctrines of your Party—I mean no offence to *you,* sir, personally—blind you to that girl's perfections. She, poor child, herself has seen it and felt it; but never, in her blameless innocence and purity, suspecting the cause. 'There is,' she said to me last night confidentially, 'something strangely antagonistic and repellent in our natures, some undefined and nameless barrier between our ever understanding each other.' You comprehend, Mr. Hathaway, she does full justice to your intentions and your unquestioned abilities. 'I am not blind,' she said, 'to Mr. Hathaway's gifts, and it is very possible the fault lies with me.' Her very words, sir."

"Then you believe she is perfectly ignorant of her real mother?" asked Paul, with a steady voice, but a whitening face.

"As an unborn child," said the Colonel emphatically. "The snow on the Sierras is not more spotlessly pure of any trace or contamination of the mud of the mining ditches, than she of her mother and her past. The knowledge of it, the mere breath of suspicion of it, in her presence would be a profanation, sir! Look at her eye—open as the sky and as clear; look at her face and figure—as clean, sir, as a Blue-Grass thoroughbred! Look at the way she carries herself, whether in those white frillings of her simple school-gown, or that black evening-dress that makes her look like a princess! And, blank me, if she isn't one! There's no poor stock there—no white trash—no mixed blood, sir. Blank it all, sir, if it comes to *that*—the Arguellos—if there's a hound of them living—might go down on their knees to have their name borne by such a creature! By the Eternal, sir, if one of them dared to cross her path with a word that wasn't abject—yes, sir, *abject,* I'd wipe his dust off the earth and send it back to his ancestors before he knew where he was, or my name isn't Harry Pendleton!"

Hopeless and inconsistent as all this was, it was a wonderful sight to see the Colonel, his dark, stern face illuminated with a zealot's enthusiasm, his eyes on fire, the ends of his grey moustache curling around his set jaw, his head thrown back, his legs astride, and his gold-headed stick held in the hollow of his elbow, like a lance at rest! Paul saw it, and knew that this Quixotic transformation was part of *her* triumph, and yet had a miserable consciousness that the charms of this Dulcinea del Toboso had scarcely been exaggerated. He turned his eyes away and said quietly—

"Then you don't think this coincidence will ever awaken any suspicion in regard to her real mother?"

"Not in the least, sir—not in the least," said the Colonel, yet perhaps with more doggedness than conviction of accent. "Nobody but yourself would ever notice that police report, and the connection of that woman's name with his was not notorious, or I should have known it."

"And you believe," continued Paul hopelessly, "that Miss Yerba's selection of the name was purely accidental?"

"Purely—a schoolgirl's fancy. Fancy, did I say? No, sir; by Jove, an inspiration!"

"And," continued Paul, almost mechanically, "you do not think it may be some insidious suggestion of an enemy who knew of this transient relation that no one suspected?"

To his final amazement Pendleton's brow cleared! "An enemy? Gad! you may be right. I'll look into it; and, if that is the case, which I can scarcely dare hope for, Mr. Hathaway, you can safely leave him to *me.*"

He looked so supremely confident in his fatuous heroism that Paul could say no more. He rose, and with a faint smile upon his pale face held out his hand. "I think that is all I have to say. When you see Miss Yerba again—as you will, no doubt—you may tell her that I am conscious of no misunderstanding on my part, except perhaps as to the best way I could serve her, and that, but for what she has told *you,* I should certainly have carried away no remembrance of any misunderstanding of *hers.*"

"Certainly," said the Colonel, with cheerful philosophy; "I will carry your message with pleasure. You understand how it is, Mr. Hathaway. There is no accounting for these instincts—we can only accept them as they are. But I believe that your intentions, sir, were strictly according to what you conceived to be your duty. You won't take something before you go? Well, then—good-bye."

Two weeks later Paul found among his morning letters an envelope addressed in Colonel Pendleton's boyish scrawling hand. He opened it with an eagerness that no studied self-control nor rigid preoccupation of his duties had yet been able to subdue, and glanced hurriedly at its contents:—

DEAR SIR,—As I am on the point of sailing for Europe to-morrow to escort Miss Arguello and Miss Woods on an extended visit to England and the Continent, I am desirous of informing you that I have thus far been unable to find any foundation for the suggestions thrown out by you in our last interview. Miss Arguello's Spanish acquaintances have

been very select, and limited to a few school friends and Don Caesar
and Doña Anna Briones, tried friends, who are also fellow-passengers
with us to Europe. Miss Arguello suggests that some political difference
between you and Don Caesar, which occurred during your visit to Rosario three months ago, may have perhaps given rise to your supposition. She joins me in best wishes for your public career, which even in
the distractions of foreign travel and the obligations of her position she
will follow from time to time with the greatest interest.—Very respectfully yours,

HARRY PENDLETON

Chapter V

It was on an August day of 1863 that Paul Hathaway resigned himself
and his luggage to the care of the gold-laced, ostensible porter of the
Strudle Bad Hof, not without some uncertainty, in a land of uniforms,
whether he would eventually be conducted to the barracks, the police
office, or the Conservatoire. He was relieved when the omnibus drove
into the courtyard of the Bad Hof, and the gold-chained chamberlain,
flanked by two green tubs of oleanders, received him with a gravity
calculated to check any preconceived idea he might have that travelling was a trifling affair, or that an arrival at the Bad Hof was not of
serious moment. His letters had not yet arrived, for he had, in a fit of
restlessness, shortened his route, and he strolled listlessly into the
reading-room. Two or three English guests were evidently occupied in
eminently respectable reading and writing; two were sitting by the
window engaged in subdued but profitable conversation; and two
Americans from Boston were contentedly imitating them on the other
side of the room. A decent restraint, as of people who were not for a
moment to be led into any foreign idea of social gaiety at a watering-
place, was visible everywhere. A spectacled Prussian officer in full
uniform passed along the hall, halted for a moment at the doorway as
if contemplating an armed invasion, thought better of it, and took his
uniform away into the sunlight of the open square, where it was joined
by other uniforms, and became by contrast a miracle of unbraced
levity. Paul stood the Polar silence for a few moments, until one of the
readers arose and, taking his book—a Murray—in his hand, walked
slowly across the room to a companion, mutely pointed to a passage in
the book, remained silent until the other had dumbly perused it, and
then walked back again to his seat, having achieved the incident without a word. At which Paul, convinced of his own incongruity, softly

withdrew with his hat in his hand, and his eyes fixed devotionally upon it.

It was good after that to get into the slanting sunlight and chequered linden shadows of the *Allee;* to see even a tightly-jacketed cavalry-man naturally walking with Clärchen and her two round-faced and drab-haired young charges; to watch the returning invalid procession, very real and very human, each individual intensely involved in the atmosphere of his own symptoms; and very good after that to turn into the Thiergarten, where the animals were, however, chiefly of his own species, and shamelessly and openly amusing themselves. It was pleasant to contrast it with his first visit to the place three months before, and correct his crude impressions. And it was still more pleasant suddenly to recognise, under the round flat cap of a general officer, a former traveller who was fond of talking with him about America with an intelligence and understanding of it that Paul had often missed among his own travelled countrymen. It was pleasant to hear his unaffected and simple greeting, to renew their old acquaintance, and to saunter back to the hotel together through the long twilight.

They were only a few squares from the hotel, when Paul's attention was attracted by the curiosity and delight of two or three children before him, who seemed to be following a quaint-looking figure that was evidently not unfamiliar to them. It appeared to be a servant in a striking livery of green with yellow facings and crested silver buttons, but still more remarkable for the indescribable mingling of jaunty ease and conscious dignity with which he carried off his finery. There was something so singular and yet so vaguely reminiscent in his peculiar walk and the exaggerated swing of his light bamboo cane that Paul could not only understand the childish wonder of the passers-by, who turned to look after him, but was stirred with a deeper curiosity. He quickened his pace, but was unable to distinguish anything of the face or features of the stranger, except that his hair under his cocked hat appeared to be tightly curled and powdered. Paul's companion, who was amused at what seemed to be the American's national curiosity, had seen the figure before. "A servant in the suite of some Eastern *Altesse* visiting the baths. You will see stranger things, my friend, in the Strudle Bad. *Par exemple,* your own countrymen, too; the one who has enriched himself by that pork of Chicago, or that soap, or this candle, in a carriage with the crest of the title he has bought in Italy, with his dollars, and his beautiful daughters, who are seeking more titles with possible matrimonial contingencies."

After an early dinner, Paul found his way to the little theatre. He had already been struck by a highly coloured poster near the *Bahnhof,* purporting that a distinguished German company would give a representation of "Uncle Tom's Cabin," and certain peculiarities in the pictorial advertisement of the tableaux gave promise of some entertainment. He found the theatre fairly full: there was the usual contingent of *abonnirte* officers, a fair sprinkling of English and German travellers, but apparently none of his own countrymen. He had no time to examine the house more closely, for the play, commencing with simple punctuality, not only far exceeded the promise of the posters, but of any previous performance of the play he had witnessed. Transported at once to a gorgeous tropical region—the Slave States of America—resplendent with the fruits and palms of Mauritius, and peopled exclusively with Paul and Virginia's companions in striped cotton, Hathaway managed to keep a composed face, until the arrival of the good Southern planter St. Clair as one of the earlier portraits of Goethe, in top boots, light kerseymere breeches, redingote and loose Byron collar, compelled him to shrink into the upper corner of the box with his handkerchief to his face. Luckily, the action passed as the natural effect upon a highly sympathetic nature of religious interviews between a round-faced, flaxen-haired "Kleine Eva" and "Onkeel Tome," occasionally assisted by a Dissenting clergyman in Geneva bands; of excessive brutality with a cattle-whip by a Zamiel-like Legree; of the sufferings of a runaway negro *Zimmermädchen* with a child three shades lighter than herself; and of a painted canvas "man-hunt," where apparently four well-known German composers, on horseback, with flowing hair, top-boots, and a *cor de chasse,* were pursuing, with the aid of a pack of foxhounds, "the much too deeply abused and yet spiritually elevated Onkeel Tome." Paul did not wait for the final apotheosis of "der Kleine Eva," but, in the silence of a hushed audience, made his way into the corridor and down the staircase. He was passing an open door marked "Direction," when his attention was sharply attracted by a small gathering around it, and the sounds of indignant declamation. It was the voice of a countryman—more than that, it was a familiar voice, that he had not heard for three years—the voice of Colonel Harry Pendleton!

"Tell him," said Pendleton, in scathing tones, to some invisible interpreter—"tell him, sir, that a more infamous caricature of the blankest caricature that ever maligned a free people, sir, I never before had the honour of witnessing. Tell him that *I,* sir—I, Harry Pendleton, of Kentucky, a Southerner, sir—an old slaveholder, sir, declare it to be a tissue of falsehoods unworthy the credence of a Christian civilisation like this—unworthy the attention of the distinguished ladies and gentlemen that are gathered here to-night. Tell him, sir, he has been imposed upon. Tell him I am responsible—give him my card and address

—personally responsible for what I say. If he wants proofs—blank it all!—tell him you yourself have been a slave—*my* slave, sir! Take off your hat, sir! Ask him to look at you—ask him if he thinks you ever looked or could look like that lop-eared, psalm-singing, white-headed hypocrite on the stage! Ask him, sir, if he thinks that blank ringmaster they call St. Clair looks like *me!*"

At this astounding exordium Paul eagerly pressed forward and entered the bureau. There certainly was Colonel Pendleton, in spotless evening dress; erect, flashing, and indignant; his aquiline nose lifted like a hawk's beak over his quarry, his iron-grey moustache, now white and waxed, parted like a swallow's tail over his handsome mouth, and between him and the astounded "Direction" stood the apparition of the *Allee*—George! There was no mistaking him now. What Paul had thought was a curled wig or powder was the old negro's own white knotted wool, and the astounding livery he wore was carried off as no one but George could carry it.

But he was still more amazed when the old servant, in a German as exaggerated, as incoherent, but still as fluent and persuasive as his own native speech, began an extravagant but perfectly dignified and diplomatic translation of his master's protests. Where and when, and by what instinct, he had assimilated and made his own the grotesque inversions and ponderous sentimentalities of Teutonic phrasing, Paul could not guess; but it was with breathless wonder that he presently became aware that, so perfect and convincing was the old man's style and deportment, not only the simple officials but even the bystanders were profoundly impressed by this farrago of absurdity. A happy word here and there, the full title and rank given, even with a slight exaggeration, to each individual, brought a deep and guttural "So!" from lips that would have found it difficult to repeat a line of his ceremonious idiocy.

In their preoccupation neither the Colonel nor George had perceived Paul's entrance, but, as the old servant turned with magnificent courtesy towards the bystanders, his eyes fell upon Paul. A flash of surprise, triumph, and satisfaction lit up his rolling eyes. Paul instantly knew that he not only recognised him, but that he had already heard of and thoroughly appreciated a certain distinguished position that Paul had lately held, and was quick to apply it. Intensifying for a moment the grandiloquence of his manner, he called upon his master's most distinguished and happily arrived old friend, the Lord Lieutenant Governor of the Golden Californias, to corroborate his statement. Colonel Pendleton started, and grasped Paul's hand warmly. Paul turned to the already half-mollified Director with the diplomatic suggestion that the vivid and realistic acting of the admirable company which he himself had witnessed had perhaps unduly excited his old friend, even as it had undoubtedly thrown into greater relief the usual exaggerations of dramatic representation, and the incident terminated with a profusion of apologies, and the most cordial expressions of international good feeling on both sides.

Yet, as they turned away from the theatre together, Paul could not help noticing that, although the Colonel's first greeting had been spontaneous and unaffected, it was succeeded by an uneasy reserve. Paul made no attempt to break it, and confined himself to a few general inquiries, ending by inviting the Colonel to sup with him at the hotel. Pendleton hesitated. "At any other time, Mr. Hathaway, I should have insisted upon you, as the stranger, supping with me; but since the absence of—of—the rest of my party—I have given up my suite of rooms at the Bad Hof, and have taken smaller lodgings for myself and the boy at the Schwartze Adler. Miss Woods and Miss Arguello have accepted an invitation to spend a few days at the villa of the Baron and Baroness von Schilprecht—an hour or two from here." He lingered over the title with an odd mingling of impressiveness and inquiry, and glanced at Paul. But Hathaway exhibiting neither emotion nor surprise at the mention of Yerba's name or the title of her host, he continued, "Miss Arguello, I suppose you know, is immensely admired; she has been, sir, the acknowledged belle of Strudle Bad."

"I can readily believe it," said Paul simply.

"And has taken the position—the position, sir, to which she is entitled."

Without appearing to notice the slight challenge in Pendleton's tone, Paul returned, "I am glad to hear it. The more particularly as, I believe, the Germans are great sticklers for position and pedigree."

"You are right, sir—quite right: they are," said the Colonel proudly —"although"—with a certain premeditated deliberation—"I have been credibly informed that the King can, in certain cases, if he chooses, supply—yes, sir—*supply* a favoured person with ancestors— yes, sir, with *ancestors!*"

Paul cast a quick glance at his companion.

"Yes, sir—that is, we will say, in the case of a lady of inferior rank— or even birth, the King of these parts can, on her marriage with a nobleman—blank it all!—ennoble her father and mother, and their fathers and mothers, though they've been dead, or as good as dead, for years."

"I am afraid that's a slight exaggeration of the rare custom of granting 'noble lands,' or estates that carry hereditary titles with them," said Paul, more emphatically perhaps than the occasion demanded.

"Fact, sir—George there knows it all," said Pendleton. "He gets it from the other servants. I don't speak the language, sir, but *he* does. Picked it up in a year."

"I must compliment him on his fluency, certainly," said Paul, looking at George.

The old servant smiled, yet not without a certain condescension. "Yes, sah; I don' say to a scholar like yo'self, sah, dat I'se got de grandmatical presichion; but as fah, sah—as fah as de *idiotisms* ob de language goes, sah—it's gen'lly allowed I'm dar! As to what Marse Harry says ob de ignobling ob predecessors, I've had it, sah, from de best autority, sah—de furst, I may say, sah—de real *primâ facie* men —de gemplum ob his Serene Highness, in de korse ob ordinary conversashun, sah."

"That'll do, George," said Pendleton, with paternal brusqueness. "Run on ahead and tell that blank chamberlain that Mr. Hathaway is one of my friends—and have supper accordingly." As the negro hastened away he turned to Paul: "What he says is true: he's the most popular man or boy in all Strudle Bad—a devilish sight more than his master—and goes anywhere where *I* can't go. Princes and princesses stop and talk to him in the street; the Grand Duke asked permission to have him up in his carriage at the races the other day; and, by the Eternal, sir, he gives the style to all the flunkeys in town!"

"And, I see, he dresses the character," observed Paul.

"His own idea—entirely. And, by Jove! He proves to be right. You can't do anything here without a uniform. And they tell me he's got everything correct, down to the crest on the buttons."

They walked on in silence for a few moments, Pendleton retaining a certain rigidity of step and bearing which Paul had come to recognise as indicating some uneasiness or mental disturbance on his part. Hathaway had no intention of precipitating the confidence of his companion. Perhaps experience had told him it would come soon enough. So he spoke carelessly of himself. How the need of a year's relaxation and change had brought him abroad, his journeyings, and finally, how he had been advised by his German physician to spend a few weeks at Strudle Bad preparatory to the voyage home. Yet he was perfectly aware that the Colonel from time to time cast a furtive glance at his face. "And *you*," he said in conclusion, "when do you intend to return to California?"

The Colonel hesitated slightly. "I shall remain in Europe until Miss Arguello is—settled—I mean," he added hurriedly, "until she has— ahem!—completed her education in foreign ways and customs. You see, Hathaway, I have constituted myself, after a certain fashion, I may say—still her guardian. I am an old man, with neither kith nor kin myself, sir—I'm a little too old-fashioned for the boys over there"

—with a vague gesture towards the West, which, however, told Paul how near it still was to him. "But then, among the old fogeys here— blank it all!—it isn't noticed. So I look after her, you see, or rather make myself responsible for her generally—although, of course, she has other friends and associates, you understand, more of her own age and tastes."

"And I've no doubt she's perfectly satisfied," said Paul, in a tone of conviction.

"Well, yes, sir, I presume so," said the Colonel slowly; "but I've sometimes thought, Mr. Hathaway, that it would have been better if she'd have had a woman's care—the protection, you understand, of an elderly woman of society. That seems to be the style here, you know— a chaperon, they call it. Now, Milly Woods, you see, is about the same age, and the Doña Anna, of course, is older, but, blank it! she's as big a flirt as the rest—I mean," he added, correcting himself sharply, "she lacks balance, sir, and—what shall I call it?—self-abnegation."

"Then Doña Anna is still of your party?" asked Paul.

"She is, sir, and her brother, Don Caesar. I have thought it advis- able, on Yerba's account, to keep up as much as possible the sugges- tion of her Spanish relationship—although, by reason of their absurd ignorance of geography and political divisions out here, there is a prevailing impression that she is a South American. A fact, sir. I have myself been mistaken for the Dictator of one of those infernal Repub- lics, and I have been pointed out as ruling over a million or two of niggers like George!"

There was no trace of any conception of humour in the Colonel's face, although he uttered a short laugh, as if in polite acceptance of the possibility that Paul might have one. Far from that, his companion, looking at the striking profile and erect figure at his side—at the long white moustache which drooped from his dark cheeks, and remember- ing his own sensations at first seeing George—thought the popular belief not so wonderful. He was even forced to admit that the perfect unconsciousness on the part of master and man of any incongruity or peculiarity in themselves assisted the public misconception. And it was, I fear, with a feeling of wicked delight that, on entering the hotel, he hailed the evident consternation of those correct fellow-countrymen from whom he had lately fled, at what they apparently regarded as a national scandal. He overheard their hurried assurance to their Eng- lish friends that his companions were *not* from Boston, and enjoyed their mortification that this explanation did not seem to detract from the interest and relief with which the Britons surveyed them, or the open admiration of the Germans.

Although Pendleton somewhat unbent during supper, he did not allude to the secret of Yerba's parentage, nor of any tardy confidence of hers. To all appearance the situation remained as it was three years ago. He spoke of her great popularity as an heiress and a beautiful woman, and the marked attentions she received. He doubted not that she had rejected very distinguished offers, but she kept that to herself. She was perfectly competent to do so. She was no giddy girl, to be flattered or deceived; on the contrary, he had never known a cooler or more sensible woman. She knew her own worth. When she met the man who satisfied her ambition and understanding, she would marry, and not before. He did not know what that ambition was; it was something exalted, of course. He could only say, of his own knowledge, that last year, when they were on the Italian lakes, there was a certain Prince—Mr. Hathaway would understand why he did not mention names—who was not only attentive to her, but attentive to *him*, sir, by Jove! and most significant in his inquiries. It was the only occasion when he, the Colonel, had ever spoken to her on such subjects; and, knowing that she was not indifferent to the fellow, who was not bad of his kind, he had asked her why she had not encouraged his suit. She had said, with a laugh, that he couldn't marry her unless he gave up his claim of succession to a certain reigning house; and she wouldn't accept him *without it.* Those were her words, sir, and he could only say that the Prince left a few days afterwards, and they had never seen him since. As to the princelings and counts and barons, she knew to a day the date of their patents of nobility, and what privileges they were entitled to: she could tell to a dot the value of their estates, the amount of their debts, and, by Jove! sir, the amount of mortgages she was expected to pay off before she married them. She knew the amount of income she had to bring to the Prussian army, from the general to the lieutenant. She understood her own value and her rights. There was a young English lordling she met on the Rhine, whose boyish ways and simplicity seemed to please her. They were great friends; but he wanted him—the Colonel—to induce her to accept an invitation for both to visit his mother's home in England, that his people might see her. But she declined, sir! She declined to pass in review before his mother. She said it was for *him* to pass in review before *her* mother.

"Did she say that?" interrupted Paul, fixing his bright eyes upon the Colonel.

"If she had one, sir, if she had one," corrected the Colonel hastily. "Of course it was only an illustration. That she is an orphan is generally known, sir."

There was a dead silence for a few moments. The Colonel leant back in his chair and pulled his moustache. Paul turned away his eyes, and seemed absorbed in reflection. After a moment the Colonel coughed, pushed aside his glass, and leaning across the table, said, "I have a favour to ask of you, Mr. Hathaway."

There was such a singular change in the tone of his voice, an unexpected relaxation of some artificial tension—a relaxation which struck Paul so pathetically as being as much physical as mental, as if he had suddenly been overtaken in some exertion by the weakness of age— that he looked up quickly. Certainly, although still erect and lightly grasping his moustache, the Colonel looked older.

"By all means, my dear Colonel," said Paul warmly.

"During the time you remain here you can hardly help meeting Miss Arguello, perhaps frequently. It would be strange if you did not: it would appear to everybody still stranger. Give me your word as a gentleman that you will not make the least allusion to her of the past —nor reopen the subject."

Paul looked fixedly at the Colonel. "I certainly had no intention of doing so," he said after a pause, "for I thought it was already settled by you beyond disturbance or discussion. But do I understand you, that *she* has shown any uneasiness regarding it? From what you have just told me of her plans and ambition, I can scarcely imagine that she has any suspicion of the real facts."

"Certainly not," said the Colonel hurriedly. "But I have your promise."

"I promise you," said Paul, after a pause, "that I shall neither introduce nor refer to the subject myself, and that if *she* should question me again regarding it, which is hardly possible, I will reveal nothing without your consent."

"Thank you," said Pendleton, without, however, exhibiting much relief in his face. "She will return here to-morrow."

"I thought you said she was absent for some days," said Paul.

"Yes; but she is coming back to say good-bye to Doña Anna, who arrives here with her brother the same day, on their way to Paris."

It flashed through Paul's mind that the last time he had seen her was in the company of the Briones. It was not a pleasant coincidence. Yet he was not aware that it had affected him, until he saw the Colonel watching him.

"I believe you don't fancy the brother," said Pendleton.

For an instant Paul was strongly tempted to avow his old vague suspicions of Don Caesar, but the utter hopelessness of reopening the whole subject again, and his recollection of the passage in Pendleton's letter that purported to be Yerba's own theory of his dislike, checked him in time. He only said, "I don't remember whether I had any cause for disliking Don Caesar; I can tell better when I see him again," and changed the subject. A few moments later the Colonel summoned George from some lower region of the hotel, and rose to take his leave. "Miss Arguello, with her maid and courier, will occupy her old suite of rooms here," he remarked, with a return of his old imperiousness. "George has given the orders for her. *I* shall not change my present lodgings, but, of course, will call every day. Good-night!"

Chapter VI

The next morning Paul could not help noticing an increased and even exaggerated respect paid him by the hotel attendants. He was asked if his *Excellency* would be served with breakfast in a private room, and his condescension in selecting the public coffee-room struck the obsequious chamberlain, but did not prevent him from preceding Paul backwards to the table, and summoning a waiter to attend specially upon "milor." Surmising that George and the Colonel might be in some way connected with this extravagance, he postponed an investigation till he should have seen them again. And, although he hardly dared to confess it to himself, the unexpected prospect of meeting Yerba again fully preoccupied his thoughts. He had believed that he would eventually see her in Europe, in some vague and indefinite way and hour: it had been in his mind when he started from California. That it would be so soon, and in such a simple and natural manner, he had never conceived.

He had returned from his morning walk to the *Brunnen,* and was sitting idly in his room, when there was a knock at the door. It opened to a servant bearing a salver with a card. Paul lifted it with a slight tremor, not at the engraved name of "Maria Concepcion de Arguello de la Yerba Buena," but at the remembered school-girl hand that had pencilled underneath the words "wishes the favour of an audience with his Excellency the Lord Lieutenant Governor of the Californias."

Paul looked inquiringly at the servant. "The *gnädige Fräulein* was in her own salon. Would *Excellency* walk that way? It was but a step; in effect, the next apartment."

Paul followed him into the hall with wondering steps. The door of the next room was open, and disclosed a handsomely furnished salon. A tall graceful figure rose quickly from behind a writing-table, and advanced with outstretched hands and a frank yet mischievous smile. It was Yerba.

Standing there in a greyish hat, mantle, and travelling dress, all of one subdued yet alluring tone, she looked as beautiful as when he had last seen her—and yet—unlike. For a brief bitter moment his instincts revolted at this familiar yielding up in his fair countrywomen of all that was distinctively original in them to alien tastes and habits, and he resented the plastic yet characterless mobility which made Yerba's Parisian dress and European manner fit her so charmingly and yet express so little. For a brief critical moment he remembered the placid, unchanging simplicity of German and the inflexible and ingrained reserve of English girlhood, in opposition to this indistinctive cosmopolitan grace. But only for a moment. As soon as she spoke a certain flavour of individuality seemed to return to her speech.

"Confess," she said, "it was a courageous thing for me to do. You might have been somebody else—a real Excellency—or Heaven knows what! Or, what is worse, in your new magnificence you might have forgotten one of your oldest, most humble, but faithful subjects." She drew back and made him a mock ceremonious curtsey, that even in its charming exaggeration suggested to Paul, however, that she had already made it somewhere seriously.

"But what does it all mean?" he asked, smiling, feeling not only his doubts and uneasiness vanish, but even the years of separation melt away in her presence. "I know I went to bed last night a very humble individual, and yet I seem to awaken this morning a very exalted personage. Am I really Commander of the Faithful, or am I dreaming? Might I trouble you, as my predecessor Abou Hassan did Sweetlips, to bite my little finger?"

"Do you mean to say you have not seen the *Anzeiger?*" she returned, taking a small German printed sheet from the table and pointing to a paragraph. Paul took the paper. Certainly there was the plain announcement among the arrivals of "His Excellency Paul Hathaway, Lord Lieutenant Governor of the Californias." A light flashed upon him.

"This is George's work. He and Colonel Pendleton were here with me last night."

"Then you have seen the Colonel already?" she said, with a scarcely perceptible alteration of expression, which, however, struck Paul.

"Yes. I met him at the theatre last evening." He was about to plunge into an animated description of the Colonel's indignation, but checked himself, he knew not why. But he was thankful the next moment that he had.

"That accounts for everything," she said, lifting her pretty shoulders with a slight shrug of weariness. "I had to put a stop to George's talking about *me* three months ago—his extravagance is something *too* awful. And the Colonel, who is completely in his hands—trusting him for everything, even the language—doesn't see it."

"But he is extravagant in the praise of his friends only, and you certainly justify all he can say."

She was taking off her hat, and stopped for a moment to look at him thoughtfully, with the soft tendrils of her hair clinging to her forehead. "Did the Colonel talk much about me?"

"A great deal. In fact, I think we talked of nothing else. He has told me of your triumphs and your victims; of your various campaigns and your conquests. And yet I dare say he has not told me all—and I am dying to hear more."

She had laid down her hat and unloosed a large bow of her mantle, but stopped suddenly in the midst of it and sat down again. "I wish you'd do something for me."

"You have only to name it."

"Well, drop all this kind of talk! Try to think of me as if I had just come from California—or, better, as if you had never known anything of me at all—and we met for the first time. You could, I dare say, make yourself very agreeable to such a young lady who was willing to be pleased—why not to me? I venture to say you have not ever troubled yourself about me since we last met. No—hear me through—why then should you wish to talk over what didn't concern you at the time? Promise me you will stop this reminiscent gossip, and I promise you *I* will not only not bore you with it, but take care that it is not intruded upon you by others. Make yourself pleasant to me by talking about yourself and your prospects—anything but *me*—and I will throw over those princes and barons that the Colonel has raved about and devote myself to you while you are here. Does that suit your Excellency?" She had crossed her knees, and, with her hands clasped over them, and the toe of her small boot advanced behind her skirt, leaned forward in the attitude he remembered to have seen her take in the summer-house at Rosario.

"Perfectly," he said.

"How long will you be here?"

"About three weeks: that, I believe, is the time allotted for my cure."

"Are you really ill," she said quietly, "or imagine yourself so?"

"It amounts to about the same thing. But my cure may not take so long," he added, fixing his bright eyes upon her.

She returned his gaze thoughtfully, and they remained looking at each other silently.

"Then you are stronger than you give yourself credit for. That is very often the case," she said quietly. "There," she added in another tone, "it is settled. You will come and go as you like, using this salon as your own. Stay, we can do something to-day. What do you say to a ride in the forest this afternoon? Milly isn't here yet, but it will be quite proper for you to accompany me on horseback, though, of course, we couldn't walk a hundred yards down the *Allee* together unless we were *verlobt*."

"But," said Paul, "you are expecting company this afternoon. Don Caesar—I mean, Miss Briones and her brother are coming here to say good-bye."

She regarded him curiously, but without emotion.

"Colonel Pendleton should have added that they were to remain here overnight as my guests," she said composedly. "And of course we shall be back in time for dinner. But that is nothing to you. You have only to be ready at three o'clock. I will see that the horses are ordered. I often ride here, and the people know my tastes and habits. We will have a pleasant ride and a good long talk together, and I'll show you a ruin and a distant view of the villa where I have been staying." She held out her hand with a frank girlish smile, and even a girlish antici- pation of pleasure in her brown eyes. He bent over her slim fingers for a moment, and withdrew.

When he was in his own room again, he was conscious only of a strong desire to avoid the Colonel until after his ride with Yerba. He would keep his word so far as to abstain from allusion to her family or her past; indeed, he had his own opinion of its futility. But it would be strange if, with his past experience, he could not find some other way to determine her convictions or win her confidence during those two hours of companionship. He would accept her terms fairly; if she had any ulterior design in her advances, he would detect it; if she had the least concern for him, she could not continue long an artificial friend- ship. But he must not think of that!

By absenting himself from the hotel he managed to keep clear of Pendleton until the hour arrived. He was gratified to find Yerba in the simplest and most sensible of habits, as if she had already divined his tastes and had wished to avoid attracting undue attention. Neverthe- less, it very prettily accentuated her tall graceful figure, and Paul, albeit like most artistic admirers of the sex, not recognising a woman on a horse as a particularly harmonious spectacle, was forced to ad- mire her. Both rode well and naturally—having been brought up in the same Western school—the horses recognised it, and instinctively obeyed them, and their conversation had the easy deliberation and inflection of a *tête-à-tête*. Paul, in view of her previous hint, talked to her of himself and his fortunes—of which she appeared, however, to have some knowledge. His health had obliged him lately to abandon politics and office; he had been successful in some ventures, and had become a junior partner in a bank with foreign correspondence. She listened to him for some time with interest and attention, but at last her face became abstracted and thoughtful. "I wish I were a man!" she said suddenly.

Paul looked at her quickly. For the first time he detected in the ring of her voice something of the passionate quality he fancied he had always seen in her face.

"Except that it might give you better control of your horse, I don't see why," said Paul. "And I don't entirely believe you."

"Why?"

"Because no woman really wishes to be a man unless she is conscious of her failure as a woman."

"And how do you know I'm not?" she said, checking her horse and looking in his face. A quick conviction that she was on the point of some confession sprang into his mind, but unfortunately showed in his face. She beat back his eager look with a short laugh. "There, don't speak, and don't look like that. That remark was worthy the usual artless maiden's invitation to a compliment, wasn't it? Let us keep to the subject of yourself. Why, with your political influence, don't you get yourself appointed to some diplomatic position over here?"

"There are none in our service. You wouldn't want me to sink myself in some absurd social functions, which are called by that name, merely to become the envy and hatred of a few rich Republicans, like your friends who haunt foreign courts?"

"That's not a pretty speech—but I suppose I invited *that* too. Don't apologise. I'd rather see you flare out like that than pay compliments. Yet I fancy you're a diplomatist, for all that."

"You did me the honour to believe I was one once, when I was simply the most palpable ass and bungler living," said Paul bitterly.

She was still sweetly silent, apparently preoccupied in smoothing out the mane of her walking horse. "Did I?" she said softly. He drew close beside her.

"How different the vegetation is here from what it is with us!" she said with nervous quickness, directing his attention to the grass road beneath them, without lifting her eyes. "I don't mean what is cultivated—for I suppose it takes centuries to make the lawns they have in England—but even here the blades of grass seem to press closer together, as if they were crowded or overpopulated, like the country; and this forest, which has been always wild and was a hunting park, has a *blasé* look, as if it was already tired of the unchanging traditions and monotony around it. I think over there Nature affects and influences us; here, I fancy, it is itself affected by the people."

"I think a good deal of Nature comes over from America for that purpose," he said drily.

"And I think you are breaking your promise—besides being a goose!" she retorted smartly. Nevertheless, for some occult reason they both seemed relieved by this exquisite witticism, and trotted on amicably together. When Paul lifted his eyes to hers he could see that they were suffused with a tender mischief, as of a reproving yet secretly admiring sister, and her strangely delicate complexion had taken on itself that faint Alpine glow that was more of an illumination than a colour. "There," she said gaily, pointing with her whip as the wood opened upon a glade through which the parted trees showed a long blue curvature of distant hills; "you see that white thing lying like a snowdrift on the hills?"

"Or the family washing on a hedge."

"As you please. Well, that is the villa."

"And you were very happy there?" said Paul, watching her girlishly animated face.

"Yes; and as you don't ask questions, I'll tell you why. There is one of the sweetest old ladies there that I ever met—the perfection of old-time courtliness with all the motherishness of a German woman. She was very kind to me, and, as she had no daughter of her own, I think she treated me as if I was one. At least, I can imagine how one would feel to her, and what a woman like that could make of any girl. You laugh, Mr. Hathaway, you don't understand—but you don't know what an advantage it would be to a girl to have a mother like that, and know that she could fall back on her and hold her own against anybody. She's equipped from the start, instead of being handicapped. It's all very well to talk about the value of money. It can give you everything but one thing—the power to do without it."

"I think its purchasing value would include even the *gnädige Frau,*" said Paul, who had laughed only to hide the uneasiness that Yerba's approach to the tabooed subject had revived in him.

She shook her head; then, recovering her tone of gentle banter, said: "There—I've made a confession. If the Colonel talks to you again about my conquests, you will know that at present my affections are centred on the Baron's mother. I admit it's a strong point in his—in *anybody's*—favour, who can show an unblemished maternal pedigree. What a pity it is you are an orphan, like myself, Mr. Hathaway! For I fancy your mother must have been a very perfect woman. A great deal of her tact and propriety has descended to you. Only it would have been nicer if she had given it to you, like pocket-money, as occasion required—which you might have shared with me—than leaving it to you in one thumping legacy."

It was impossible to tell how far the playfulness of her brown eyes suggested any ulterior meaning, for, as Paul again drew eagerly towards her, she sent her horse into a rapid canter before him. When he was at her side again she said, "There is still the ruin to see on our way home. It is just off here to the right. But if you wish to go over it we shall have to dismount at the foot of the slope and walk up. It hasn't any story or legend that I know of; I looked over the guide-book to cram for it before you came—but there was nothing. So you can invent what you like."

They dismounted at the beginning of a gentle acclivity, where an ancient waggon-road, now grass-grown, rose smooth as a glacis. Tying their horses to two moplike bushes, they climbed the slope hand in hand like children. There were a few winding broken steps, part of a fallen archway, a few feet of vaulted corridor, a sudden breach—the sky beyond—and that was all! Not all—for before them, overlooked at first, lay a chasm covering half an acre, in which the whole of the original edifice—tower, turrets, walls, and battlements—had been apparently cast, inextricably mixed and mingled at different depths and angles, with here and there, like mushrooms from a dustheap, a score of trees upspringing.

"This is not Time—but gunpowder," said Paul, leaning over a parapet of the wall and gazing at the abyss, with a slight grimace.

"It don't look very romantic, certainly," said Yerba. "I only saw it from the road before. I'm dreadfully sorry," she added, with mock penitence. "I suppose, however, *something* must have happened here."

"There may have been nobody in the house at the time," said Paul gravely. "The family may have been at the baths."

They stood close together, their elbows resting upon the broken wall, and almost touching. Beyond the abyss and darker forest they could see the more vivid green and regular lines of the plane-trees of Strudle Bad, the glitter of a spire, or the flash of a dome. From the abyss itself arose a cool odour of moist green leaves, the scent of some unseen blossoms, and around the baking vines on the hot wall the hum of apparently taskless and disappointed bees. There was nobody in sight in the forest road, no one working in the bordering fields, and no suggestion of the present. There might have been three or four centuries between them and Strudle Bad.

"The legend of this place," said Paul, glancing at the long brown lashes and oval outline of the cheek so near his own, "is simple, yet affecting. A cruel, remorseless, but fascinating Hexie was once loved by a simple shepherd. He had never dared to syllable his hopeless affection, or claim from her a syllabled—perhaps I should say a one-syllabled—reply. He had followed her from remote lands, dumbly worshipping her, building in his foolish brain an air-castle of happiness, which by reason of her magic power she could always see plainly in his eyes. And one day, beguiling him in the depths of the forest, she led him to a fair-seeming castle, and, bidding him enter its portals, offered to show him a realisation of his dream. But, lo! even as he entered the stately corridor it seemed to crumble away before him, and disclosed a hideous abyss beyond, in which the whole of that goodly palace lay in heaped and tangled ruins—the fitting symbol of his wrecked and shattered hopes."

She drew back a little way from him, but still holding on to the top of the broken wall with one slim gauntleted hand, and swung herself to one side, while she surveyed him with smiling parted lips and conscious eyelids. He promptly covered her hand with his own, but she did not seem to notice it.

"That is not the story," she said, in a faint voice that even her struggling sauciness could not make steadier. "The true story is called 'The Legend of the Goose-Girl of Strudle Bad and the enterprising Gosling.' There was once a goose-girl of the plain who tried honestly to drive her geese to market, but one eccentric and wilful gosling—— Mr. Hathaway! Stop—please—I beg you let me go!"

He had caught her in his arms—the one encircling her waist, the other hand still grasping hers. She struggled, half laughing; yielding for a breathless moment as his lips brushed her cheek, and—threw him off. "There!" she said; "that will do: the story was not illustrated."

"But, Yerba," he said, with passionate eagerness, "hear me—it is all God's truth—I love you!"

She drew back farther, shaking the dust of the wall from the folds of her habit. Then, with a lower voice and a paler cheek, as if his lips had sent her blood and utterance back to her heart, she said, "Come, let us go."

"But not until you've heard me, Yerba."

"Well, then—I believe you—there!" she said, looking at him.

"You believe me?" he repeated eagerly, attempting to take her hand again.

She drew back still farther. "Yes," she said, "or I shouldn't be here now. There! that must suffice you. And if you wish me still to believe you, you will not speak of this again while we are out together. Come, let us go back to the horses."

He looked at her with all his soul. She was pale, but composed, and —he could see—determined. He followed her without a word. She accepted his hand to support her again down the slope without embarrassment or reminiscent emotion. The whole scene through which he had just passed might have been buried in the abyss and ruins behind her. As she placed her foot in his hand to remount, and for a moment rested her weight upon his shoulder, her brown eyes met his frankly and without a tremor.

Nor was she content with this. As Paul at first rode on silently, his heart filled with unsatisfied yearning, she rallied him mischievously. Was it kind in him on this, their first day together, to sulk in this fashion? Was it a promise for their future excursions? Did he intend to carry his lugubrious visage through the *Allee* and up to the courtyard of the hotel, to proclaim his sentimental condition to the world? At least she trusted he would not show it to Milly, who might remember that this was only the *second time* they had met each other. There was something so sweetly reasonable in this, and withal not without a certain hopefulness for the future, to say nothing of the half-mischievous, half-reproachful smile that accompanied it, that Paul exerted himself, and eventually recovered his lost gaiety. When they at last drew up in the courtyard, with the flush of youth and exercise in their faces, Paul felt he was the object of envy to the loungers, and of fresh gossip to Strudle Bad. It struck him less pleasantly that two dark faces, which had been previously regarding him in the gloom of the corridor and vanished as he approached, reappeared some moments later in Yerba's salon as Don Caesar and Doña Anna, with a benignly different expression. Doña Anna especially greeted him with so much of the ostentatious archness of a confident and forgiving woman to a momentarily recreant lover that he felt absurdly embarrassed in Yerba's presence. He was thinking how he could excuse himself, when he noticed a beautiful basket of flowers on the table and a tiny note bearing a baron's crest. Yerba had put it aside with—as it seemed to him at the moment—an almost too pronounced indifference—and an indifference that was strongly contrasted to Doña Anna's eagerly expressed enthusiasm over the offering, and her ultimate supplications to Paul and her brother to admire its beauties and the wonderful taste of the donor.

All this seemed so incongruous with Paul's feelings, and above all with the recollection of his scene with Yerba, that he excused himself from dining with the party, alleging an engagement with his old fellow-traveller the German officer, whose acquaintance he had renewed. Yerba did not press him; he even fancied she looked relieved. Colonel Pendleton was coming; Paul was not loth, in his present frame of mind, to dispense with his company. A conviction that the Colonel's counsel was not the best guide for Yerba, and that in some vague way their interests were antagonistic, had begun to force itself upon him. He had no intention of being disloyal to her old guardian, but he felt that Pendleton had not been frank with him since his return from

Rosario. Had he ever been so with *her?* He sometimes doubted his disclaimer.

He was lucky in finding the General disengaged, and together they dined at a restaurant and spent the evening at the *Kursaal.* Later, at the Residenz Club, the General leaned over his beer-glass and smilingly addressed his companion.

"So I hear you, too, are a conquest of the beautiful South American."

For an instant Paul, recognising only Doña Anna under that epithet, looked puzzled.

"Come, my friend," said the General, regarding him with some amusement, "I am an older man than you, yet I hardly think I could have ridden out with such a goddess without becoming her slave."

Paul felt his face flush in spite of himself. "Ah! you mean Miss Arguello," he said hurriedly, his colour increasing at his own mention of that name as if he were imposing it upon his honest companion. "She is an old acquaintance of mine—from my own state—California."

"Ah, so," said the General, lifting his eyebrows in profound apology. "A thousand pardons."

"Surely," said Paul, with a desperate attempt to recover his equanimity, *"you* ought to know our geography better."

"So, I am wrong. But still the name—Arguello—surely that is not American? Still, they say she has no accent, and does not look like a Mexican."

For an instant Paul was superstitiously struck with the fatal infelicity of Yerba's selection of a foreign name, that now seemed only to invite that comment and criticism which she should have avoided. Nor could he explain it at length to the General without assisting and accentuating the deception, which he was always hoping in some vague way to bring to an end. He was sorry he had corrected the General; he was furious that he had allowed himself to be confused.

Happily his companion had misinterpreted his annoyance, and with impulsive German friendship threw himself into what he believed to be Paul's feelings. *"Donnerwetter!* Your beautiful countrywoman is made the subject of curiosity just because that stupid Baron is persistent in his serious attentions. That is quite enough, my good friend, to make *Klatschen* here among those animals who do not understand the freedom of an American girl, or that an heiress may have something else to do with her money than to expend it on the Baron's mortgages. But"—he stopped, and his simple, honest face assumed an air of profound and sagacious cunning—"I am glad to talk about it with you, who, of course, are perfectly familiar with the affair. I shall now be able to know what to say. My word, my friend, has some weight here, and I shall use it. And now you shall tell me *who* is our lovely friend, and *who* were her parents and her kindred in her own home. Her associates here, you possibly know, are an impossible Colonel and his never-before-approached valet, with some South American Indian planters, and, I believe, a pork-butcher's daughter. But of *them*—it makes nothing. Tell me of *her* people."

With his kindly serious face within a few inches of Paul's, and sympathising curiosity beaming from his pince-nez, he obliged the wretched and conscience-stricken Hathaway to respond with a detailed account of Yerba's parentage as projected by herself and indorsed by Colonel Pendleton. He dwelt somewhat particularly on the romantic character of the Trust, hoping to draw the General's attention away from the question of relationship, but he was chagrined to find that the honest warrior evidently confounded the Trust with some eleemosynary institution, and sympathetically glossed it over. "Of course," he said, "the Mexican Minister at Berlin would know all about the Arguello family; so there would be no question there."

Paul was not sorry when the time came to take leave of his friend; but, once again in the clear moonlight and fresh, balmy air of the *Allee,* he forgot the unpleasantness of the interview. He found himself thinking only of his ride with Yerba. Well! he had told her that he loved her. She knew it now, and, although she had forbidden him to speak further, she had not wholly rejected it. It must be her morbid consciousness of the mystery of her birth that withheld a return of her affections—some half-knowledge, perhaps, that she would not divulge, yet that kept her unduly sensitive of accepting his love. He was satisfied there was no entanglement; her heart was virgin. He even dared to hope that she had *always* cared for him. It was for *him* to remove all obstacles—to prevail upon her to leave this place and return to America with him as her husband, the guardian of her good name, and the custodian of her secret. At times the strains of a dreamy German waltz, played in the distance, brought back to him the brief moment that his arm had encircled her waist by the crumbling wall, and his pulses grew languid, only to leap firmer the next moment with more desperate resolve. He would win her, come what may! He could never have been in earnest before; he loathed and hated himself for his previous passive acquiescence to her fate. He had been a weak tool of the Colonel's from the first; he was even now handicapped by a preposterous promise he had given him! Yes, she was right to hesitate—to question his ability to make her happy! He had found her here, surrounded by stupidity and cupidity—to give it no other name—so patent that she was the common gossip, and had offered nothing but a boyish declaration! As he strode into the hotel that night, it was well that he did not meet the unfortunate Colonel on the staircase!

It was very late, although there was still visible a light in Yerba's salon, shining on her balcony, which extended before and included his own window. From time to time he could hear the murmur of voices. It was too late to avail himself of the invitation to join them, even if his frame of mind had permitted it. He was too nervous and excited to go to bed, and, without lighting his candle, he opened the French window that gave upon the balcony, drew a chair in the recess behind the curtain, and gazed upon the night. It was very quiet; the moon was high, the square was sleeping in a trance of chequered shadows, like a gigantic chessboard, with black foreshortened trees for pawns. The click of a cavalry sabre, the sound of a footfall on the pavement of the distant Königsstrasse were distinctly audible; a far-off railway whistle was startling in its abruptness. In the midst of this calm the opening of the door of the salon, with the sudden uplifting of voices in the hall, told Paul that Yerba's guests were leaving. He heard Doña Anna's arch accents—arch even to Colonel Pendleton's monotonous baritone! —Milly's high, rapid utterances, the suave falsetto of Don Caesar, and *her* voice, he thought a trifle wearied—the sound of retiring footsteps, and all was still again.

So still that the rhythmic beat of the distant waltz returned to him with a distinctiveness that he could idly follow. He thought of Rosario and the rose-breath of the open windows with a strange longing, and remembered the half-stifled sweetness of her happy voice rising with it from the verandah. Why had he ever let it pass from him then, and waft its fragrance elsewhere? Why——What was that?

The slight turning of a latch! The creaking of the French window of the salon, and somebody had slipped softly half out on the balcony. His heart stopped beating. From his position in the recess of his own window, with his back to the partition of the salon, he could see nothing. Yet he did not dare to move. For with the quickened senses of a lover he felt the diffused and perfumed aura of *her* presence, of *her* garments, of *her* flesh flow in upon him through the open window, and possess his whole breathless being! It was *she!* Like him, perhaps, longing to enjoy the perfect night—like him, perhaps, thinking of——

"So you ar-range to get rid of me—ha! like thees? To tur-rn me off from your heels like a dog who have follow you—but without a word —without a—a—thanks—without a 'ope! Ah!—we have ser-rved you —me and my sister; we are the or-range dry—now we can go! Like the old shoe, we are to be flung away! Good! But I am here again—you see. I shall speak, and you shall hear."

Don Caesar's voice—alone with her! Paul gripped his chair and sat upright.

"Stop! Stay where you are! How dared you return here?" It was Yerba's voice, on the balcony, low and distinct.

"Shut the window! I shall speak with you what you will not the world to hear."

"I prefer to keep where I am, since you have crept into this room like a thief."

"A thief! Good!" He broke out in Spanish, and, as if no longer fearful of being overheard, had evidently drawn nearer the window. "A thief. Ha! *muy bueno*—but it is not *I*, you understand—I, Caesar Briones, who am the thief! No! It is that swaggering *espadachin*—that *fanfarron* of a Colonel Pendleton—that pattern of an official, Mr. Hathaway—that most beautiful heiress of the Californias, Miss Arguello—that are thieves! Yes—of a *name*—Miss Arguello—of a *name!* The name of Arguello!"

Paul rose to his feet.

"Ah, so! You start—you turn pale—you flash your eyes, Señora, but you think you have deceived me all these years. You think I did not see your game at Rosario—yes, even when that foolish Castro *muchacha* first put that idea in your head. Who furnished you the facts you wanted? I—Mother of God!—*such facts!*—I, who knew the Arguello pedigree—I, who know it was as impossible for you to be a daughter of them as—what? let me think—as—as it is impossible for you to be the wife of that Baron whom you would deceive with the rest! Ah, yes; it was a high flight for you, Mees—Mees—Doña Fulana—a noble game for you to bring down!"

Why did she not speak? What was she doing? If she had but uttered a single word of protest, of angry dismissal, Paul would have flown to her side. It could not be the paralysis of personal fear: the balcony was wide; she could easily pass to the end; she could even see his open window.

"Why did I do this? Because I loved you, Señora—and you knew it! Ah! you can turn your face away now; you can pretend to misunderstand me, as you did a moment ago; you can part from me now like a mere acquaintance—but it was not always so! No; it was *you* who brought me here, your eyes that smiled into mine—and drove home the Colonel's request that I and my sister should accompany you. God! I was weak then! You smile, Señora; you think you have succeeded—you and your pompous Colonel and your clever Governor! You think you have compromised me, and perjured *me*, because of this. You are wrong! You think I dare not speak to this puppet of a Baron, and that I have no proofs. You are wrong!"

"And even if you can produce them, what care I?" said Yerba unexpectedly, yet in a voice so free from excitement and passion that the weariness which Paul had at first noticed seemed to be the only dominant tone. "Suppose you prove that I am not an Arguello. Good! You have yet to show that a connection with any of your race would be anything but a disgrace."

"Ah! you defy me, little one! *Caramba!* Listen, then! You do not know all! When you thought I was only helping you to fabricate your claim to the Arguellos' name, I was finding out *who you really were!* Ah! It was not so difficult as you fondly hope, Señora. We were not all brutes and fools in the early days, though we stood aside to let your people run their vulgar course. It was your hired bully—your respected guardian—this dog of an *espadachin,* who let out a hint of the secret—with a prick of his blade—and a scandal. One of my *peon* women was a servant at the convent when you were a child, and recognised the woman who put you there and came to see you as a friend. She overheard the Mother Superior say it was your mother, and saw a necklace that was left for you to wear. Ah! you begin to believe! When I had put this and that together I found that Pepita could not identify you with the child that she had seen. But you, Señora, you *yourself* supplied the missing proof. Yes! you supplied it with the *necklace* that you wore that evening at Rosario, when you wished to do honour to this young Hathaway—the guardian who had always thrown you off! Ah! you now suspect why, perhaps! It was your mother's necklace that you wore, and you said so! That night I sent the good Pepita to identify it; to watch through the window from the garden when you were wearing it; to make it sure as the Creed. I sent her to your room late that night when you had changed your dress, that she might examine it among your jewels. And she did—and will swear—look you!—*swear* that it is the one given you as a child by the woman at the convent, who was your mother! And who was that woman—eh? Who was the mother of the Arguello de la Yerba Buena? —who this noble ancestress?"

"Excuse me—but perhaps you are not aware that you are raising your voice in a lady's drawing-room, and that, although you are speaking a language no one here understands, you are disturbing the hotel."

It was Paul, quiet, pale in the moonlight, erect on the balcony before the window. As Yerba, with a start, retreated quickly into the room, Don Caesar stepped forward angrily and suspiciously towards the window. He had his hand reached forward towards the handle as if to close the swinging sash against the intruder, when in an instant he was seized by Paul, tightly locked in a desperate grip, and whirled out on the balcony. Before he could gain breath to utter a cry, Hathaway had passed his right arm around the Mexican's throat, effectively stopping his utterance, and, with a supreme effort of strength, dragged him along the wall, falling with him into the open window of his own room. As he did so, to his inexpressible relief he heard the sash closed and the bolt drawn of the salon window, and regained his feet, collected, quiet, and triumphant.

"I am sorry," he said, coolly dusting his clothes, "to have been obliged to change the scene of this discussion so roughly, but you will observe that you can speak more freely *here,* and that any altercation *we* may have in this room will be less likely to attract comment."

"Assassin!" said Don Caesar chokingly, as he struggled to his feet.

"Thank you. Relieve your feelings as much as you like here; in fact, if you would speak a little louder you would oblige me. The guests are beginning to be awake," continued Paul, with a wicked smile, indicating the noise of an opening door and footsteps in the passage, "and are now able to locate without difficulty the scene of the disturbance."

Briones apparently understood his meaning, and the success of his stratagem. "You think you have saved *her* from disgrace," he said, with a livid smile, in a lower tone and a desperate attempt to imitate Paul's coolness. "For the present—ah—yees! perhaps in this hotel and this evening. But you have not stop my mouth for—a—tomorrow—and the whole world, Mr. Hathaway."

"Well," said Paul, looking at him critically, "I don't know about that. Of course, there's the equal chance that you may kill me—but that's a question for to-morrow, too."

The Mexican cast a quick glance at the door and window. Paul, as if carelessly, changed the key of the former from one pocket to the other, and stepped before the window.

"So this is a plot to murder me. Have a care! You are not in your own brigand California!"

"If you think so, alarm the house. They will find us quarrelling, and you will only precipitate matters by receiving the insult that will make you fight—before them."

"I am r-ready, sir, when and where you will," said Briones, with a swaggering air but a shifting, furtive eye. "Open—a—the door."

"Pardon me. We will leave this room *together* in an hour for the station. We will board the night express that will take us in three hours beyond the frontier, where we can each find a friend."

"But my affairs here—my sister—I must see her."

"You shall write a note to her at that table, saying that important business—a despatch—has called you away, and we will leave it with the porter to be delivered *in the morning.* Or—I do not restrict you—

you can say what you like, provided she don't get it until we have left."

"And you make of me a prisoner, sir?"

"No; a visitor, Don Caesar—a visitor whose conversation is so interesting that I am forced to detain him to hear more. You can pass the time pleasantly by finishing the story I was obliged to interrupt a moment ago. Do you know this mother of Miss Yerba, of whom you spoke?"

"That's m—my affair."

"That means you don't know her. If you did, you'd have had her within call. And, as she is the only person who is able to say that Miss Yerba is *not* an Arguello, you have been very remiss."

"Ah, bah! I am not one of your—a—lawyers."

"No; or you would know that, with no better evidence than you have, you might be sued for slander."

"Ah! Why does not Miss Yerba sue, then?"

"Because she probably expects that somebody will shoot you."

"As *you,* for instance?"

"Perhaps."

"And if you do *not*—eh? you have not stop my mouth, but your own. And if you *do,* you help her to marry the Baron, your rival. You are not wise, friend Hathaway."

"May I remind you that you have not yet written to your sister, and you may prefer to do it carefully and deliberately!"

Don Caesar arose, with a vindictive glance at Paul, and pulled a chair before the table, as the latter placed pen, ink, and paper before him. "Take your time," he added, folding his arms and walking towards the window. "Say what you like, and don't let my presence restrain you."

The Mexican began to write furiously, then spasmodically, then slowly and reluctantly. "I war-r-n you, I shall expose all," he said suddenly.

"As you please."

"And shall say that if I disappear, you are my murderer—you understand—my *murderer?*"

"Don't consult me on a question of epithets, but go on."

Don Caesar recommenced his writing with a malign smile. There was a sudden sharp rap at the door.

Don Caesar leaped to his feet, grasped his papers, and rushed to the door; but Paul was before him. "Who is there?" he demanded.

"Pendleton."

At the sound of the Colonel's voice Don Caesar fell back. Paul opened the door, admitted the tall figure of the Colonel, and was about to turn the key again. But Pendleton lifted his hand in grim deprecation.

"That will do, Mr. Hathaway. I know all. But I wish to speak with Briones elsewhere, alone."

"Excuse me, Colonel Pendleton," said Paul firmly, "but I have the prior claim. Words have passed between this gentleman and myself which we are now on our way to the station and the frontier to settle. If you are willing to accompany us, I shall give you every opportunity to converse with him alone, and arrange whatever business you may have with him, provided it does not interfere with mine."

"My business," said Pendleton, "is of a personal nature, that will not interfere with any claim of yours that Mr. Briones may choose to admit, but is of a private quality that must be transacted between us now." His face was pale, and his voice, although steady and self-controlled, had that same strange suggestion of sudden age in it which Paul had before noticed. Whether Don Caesar detected it, or whether he had some other instinctive appreciation of greater security, Paul could not tell. He seemed to recover his swagger again as he said—

"I shall hear what Colonel Pendleton has to say first. But I shall hold myself in readiness to meet you afterwards—you shall not fear, sir!"

Paul remained looking from the one to the other without speaking. It was Don Caesar who returned his glance boldly and defiantly, Colonel Pendleton who, with thin white fingers pulling his moustache, evaded it. Then Paul unlocked the door, and said slowly, "In five minutes I leave this house for the station. I shall wait there until the train arrives. If this gentleman does not join me, I shall be better able to understand all this and take measures accordingly."

"And I tell to you, Meester Hathaway, sir," said Don Caesar, striking an attitude in the doorway, "you shall do as *I* please—*Caramba!* —and shall beg——"

"Hold your tongue, sir—or, by the Eternal——" burst out Pendleton suddenly, bringing down his thin hand on the Mexican's shoulder. He stopped as suddenly. "Gentlemen, this is childish. Go, sir!" to Don Caesar, pointing with a gaunt white finger into the darkened hall. "I will follow you. Mr. Hathaway, as an older man, and one who has seen a good deal of foolish altercation, I regret, sir, deeply regret, to be a witness to this belligerent quality in a law-maker and a public man; and I must deprecate, sir—deprecate your demand on that gentleman for what, in the folly of youth, you are pleased to call personal satisfaction."

As he moved with dignity out of the room, Paul remained blankly staring after him. Was it all a dream?—or was this Colonel Pendleton, the duellist? Had the old man gone crazy, or was he merely acting to veil some wild purpose? His sudden arrival showed that Yerba must have sent for him and told him of Don Caesar's threats: would he be wild enough to attempt to strangle the man in some remote room or in the darkness of the passage? He stepped softly into the hall: he could still hear the double tread of the two men; they had reached the staircase—they were *descending!* He heard the drowsy accents of the night porter and the swinging of the door—they were in the street!

Wherever they were going, or for what purpose, *he* must be at the station, as he had warned them he would be. He hastily threw a few things into his valise, and prepared to follow them. When he went downstairs he informed the porter that owing to an urgent call of business he should try to catch the through express at three o'clock, but they must retain his room and luggage until they heard from him. He remembered Don Caesar's letter. Had either of the gentlemen, his friends who had just gone out, left a letter or message? No, Excellency; the gentlemen were talking earnestly—he believed, in the South American language—and had not spoken to him.

Perhaps it was this that reminded Paul, as he crossed the square again, that he had made no preparation for any possible fatal issue to himself in this adventure. *She* would know it, however, and why he had undertaken it. He tried to think that perhaps some interest in himself had prompted her to send the Colonel to him. Yet mingled with this was an odd sense of a certain ridiculousness in his position; there was the absurdity of his prospective antagonist being even now in confidential consultation with his own friend and ally, whose functions he had usurped, and in whose interests he was about to risk his life. And as he walked away through the silent streets the conviction more than once was forced upon him that he was going to an appointment that would not be kept.

He reached the station some ten minutes before the train was due. Two or three half-drowsy, wrapped-up passengers were already on the platform; but neither Don Caesar nor Colonel Pendleton was among them. He explored the waiting-rooms and even the half-lit buffet, but with no better success. Telling the *Bahnhof Inspector* that his passage was only contingent upon the arrival of one or two companions, and describing them minutely to prevent mistakes, he began gloomily to pace before the ticket-office. Five minutes passed—the number of passengers did not increase; ten minutes; a distant shriek—the hoarse inquiry of the inspector—had the Herr's companions yet *gekommt?* the sudden glare of a Cyclopean eye in the darkness, the ongliding of the long-jointed and gleaming-spotted serpent, the train—a hurried glance around the platform, one or two guttural orders, the slamming of doors, the remounting of black-uniformed figures like caryatides along the *marchepieds,* a puff of vapour, and the train had come and gone without them.

Yet he would give his adversary fifteen minutes more to allow for accident or delay, or the possible arrival of the Colonel with an explanation, and recommenced his gloomy pacing, as the *Bahnhof* sank back into half-lit repose. At the end of five minutes there was another shriek. Paul turned quickly to the inspector. Ah, then, there was another train? No; it was only the *up express* for Basle, going the other way, and stopping at the *Nord Station,* half a mile away. It would not stop here, but the Herr would see it pass in a few moments at full speed.

It came presently, with a prolonged despairing shriek, out of the darkness; a flash, a rush and roar at his side, a plunge into the darkness again with the same despairing cry; a flutter of something white from one of the windows, like a loosened curtain, that at last seemed to detach itself, and, after a wild attempt to follow, suddenly soared aloft, whirled over and over, dropped, and drifted slowly, slantwise, to the ground.

The inspector had seen it, ran down the line, and picked it up. Then he returned with it to Paul with a look of sympathising concern. It was a lady's handkerchief, evidently some signal waved to the well-born Herr, who was the only passenger on the platform. So, possibly, it might be from his friends, who by some stupid mischance had gone to the wrong station, and—*Gott im Himmel!*—it was hideously stupid, yet possible, got on the wrong train!

The Herr, a little pale, but composed, thought it *was* possible. No; he would not telegraph to the next station—not yet—he would inquire.

He walked quickly away, reaching the hotel breathlessly, yet in a space that seemed all too brief for his disconnected thought. There were signs of animation in the hall, and an empty carriage was just re-entering the courtyard. The hallporter met him with demonstrative concern and apology. Ah! if he had only understood his Excellency better, he could have saved him all this trouble. Evidently his Excellency was going with the Arguello party, who had ordered a carriage, doubtless for the same important journey, an hour before, yet had left only a few moments after his Excellency. And his Excellency, it would appear, had gone to the wrong station.

Paul pushed hurriedly past the man and ascended to his room. Both windows were open, and in the faint moonlight he could see that something white was pinned to his pillow. With nervous fingers he relit his candles, and found it was a note in Yerba's handwriting. As he opened it, a tiny spray of the vine that had grown on the crumbling wall fell at his feet. He picked it up, pressed it to his lips, and read, with dim eyes, as follows:

You know now why I spoke to you as I did to-day, and why the other half of this precious spray is the only memory I care to carry with me out of this crumbling ruin of all my hopes. You were right, Paul: my taking you there *was an omen*—not to you, who can never be anything but proud, beloved, and true—but to *me* of all this shame and misery. Thank you for all you have done—for all you would do, my friend, and don't think me ungrateful, only because I am unworthy of it. Try to forgive me, but don't forget me—you might still love a little the poor girl to whom you have already given the only name she can ever take from you—YERBA BUENA!

Chapter VII

It was already autumn, and in the city of New York an early Sunday morning breeze was sweeping up the leaves that had fallen from the regularly planted ailanthus trees before the brown-stone frontage of a row of monotonously alike five-storeyed houses on one of the principal avenues. The Pastor of the Third Presbyterian Church, that uplifted its double towers on the corner, stopped before one of these dwellings, ran up the dozen broad steps, and rang the bell. He was presently admitted to the sombre richness of a hall and drawing-room with high-backed furniture of dark carved wood, like cathedral stalls, and, hat in hand, somewhat impatiently awaited the arrival of his hostess and parishioner. The door opened to a tall, white-haired woman in lustreless black silk. She was regular and resolute in features, of fine but unbending presence, and, though somewhat past middle age, showed no signs of either the weakness or mellowness of years.

"I am sorry to disturb your Sabbath morning meditations, Sister Argalls, nor would I if it were not in the line of Christian duty; but Sister Robbins is unable to-day to make her usual Sabbath hospital visit, and I thought if you were excused from the Foreign Missionary class and Bible instruction at three you might undertake her functions. I know, my dear old friend," he continued, with bland deprecation of her hard-set eyes, "how distasteful this promiscuous mingling with the rough and ungodly has always been to you, and how reluctant you are to be placed in the position of being liable to hear coarse, vulgar, or irreverent speech. I think, too, in our long and pleasant pastoral relations, you have always found me mindful of it. I admit I have sometimes regretted that your late husband had not more generally familiarised you with the ways of the world. But so it is—we all have our weaknesses. If not one thing, another. And as envy and uncharitableness sometimes find their way in even Christian hearts, I should like you to undertake this office for the sake of example. There are some, dear Sister Argalls, who think that the rich widow who is most liberal in the endowment of the goods that Providence has entrusted to her hands claims therefore to be exempt from labour in the Christian vineyard. Let us teach them how unjust they are."

"I am willing," said the lady, with a dry, determined air. "I suppose these patients are not professedly bad characters?"

"By no means. A few, perhaps; but the majority are unfortunates—dependent either upon public charity or some small provision made by their friends."

"Very well."

"And you understand that, though they have the privilege of rejecting your Christian ministrations, dear Sister Argalls, you are free to judge when you may be patient or importunate with them."

"I understand."

The Pastor was not an unkindly man, and, as he glanced at the uncompromising look in Mrs. Argalls' eyes, felt for a moment some inconsistency between his humane instincts and his Christian duty. "Some of them may require, and be benefited by, a stern monitress, and Sister Robbins, I fear, was weak," he said consolingly to himself, as he descended the steps again.

At three o'clock Mrs. Argalls, with a reticule and a few tracts, was at the door of St. John's Hospital. As she displayed her testimonials and announced that she had taken Mrs. Robbins' place, the officials received her respectfully, and gave some instructions to the attendants, which, however, did not stop some individual comments.

"I say, Jim, it doesn't seem the square thing to let that grim old girl loose among them poor convalescents."

"Well, I don't know: they say she's rich and gives a lot o' money away, but if she tackles that swearing old Kentuckian in No. 3, she'll have her hands full."

However, the criticism was scarcely fair, for Mrs. Argalls, although moving rigidly along from bed to bed of the ward, equipped with a certain formula of phrases, nevertheless dropped from time to time some practical common-sense questions that showed an almost masculine intuition of the patients' needs and requirements. Nor did she betray any of that over-sensitive shrinking from coarseness which the good Pastor had feared, albeit she was quick to correct its exhibition.

The languid men listened to her with half-aggressive, half-amused interest, and some of the satisfaction of taking a bitter but wholesome tonic. It was not until she reached the bed at the farther end of the ward that she seemed to meet with any check.

It was occupied by a haggard man, with a long white moustache and features that seemed wasted by inward struggle and fever. At the first sound of her voice he turned quickly towards her, lifted himself on his elbow, and gazed fixedly in her face.

"Kate Howard—by the Eternal!" he said, in a low voice.

Despite her rigid self-possession the woman started, glanced hurriedly around, and drew nearer to him.

"Pendleton!" she said, in an equally suppressed voice. "What, in God's name, are you doing here?"

"Dying, I reckon—sooner or later," he said grimly; "that's what they do here."

"But—what," she went on hurriedly, still glancing over her shoulder as if she suspected some trick—"what has brought you to this?"

"*You!*" said the Colonel, dropping back exhaustedly on his pillow. "You and your daughter."

"I don't understand you," she said quickly, yet regarding him with stern rigidity. "You know perfectly well I have *no* daughter. You know perfectly well that I've kept the word I gave you ten years ago, and that I have been dead to her as she has been to me."

"I know," said the Colonel, "that within the last three months I have paid away my last cent to keep the mouth of an infernal scoundrel shut who *knows* that you are her mother, and threatens to expose her to her friends. I know that I'm dying here of an old wound that I got when I shut the mouth of another hound who was ready to bark at her two years after you disappeared. I know that between you and her I've let my old nigger die of a broken heart, because I couldn't keep him to suffer with me, and I know that I'm here a pauper on the State. I know that, Kate, and when I say it I don't regret it. I've kept my word to *you,* and, by the Eternal, your daughter's worth it! For if there ever was a fair and peerless creature—it's your child!"

"And she—a rich woman—unless she squandered the fortune I gave her—lets you lie here!" said the woman grimly.

"She don't know it."

"She *should* know it! Have you quarrelled?" She was looking at him keenly.

"She distrusts me, because she half suspects the secret, and I hadn't the heart to tell her all."

"All? What does she know? What does this man know? What has been told her?" she said rapidly.

"She only knows that the name she has taken she has no right to."

"Right to? Why, it was written on the Trust—Yerba Buena."

"No, not that. She thought it was a mistake. She took the name of Arguello."

"What?" said Mrs. Argalls, suddenly grasping the invalid's wrist with both hands. "What name?" Her eyes were startled from their rigid coldness, her lips were colourless.

"Arguello! It was some foolish schoolgirl fancy which that hound helped to foster in her. Why—what's the matter, Kate?"

The woman dropped the helpless man's wrist, then, with an effort, recovered herself sufficiently to rise, and with an air of increased decorum, as if the spiritual character of their interview excluded worldly intrusion, adjusted the screen around his bed, so as partly to hide her own face and Pendleton's. Then, dropping into the chair beside him, she said in her old voice, from which the burden of ten long years seemed to have been lifted.

"Harry, what's that you're playing on me?"

"I don't understand you," said Pendleton amazedly.

"Do you mean to say you don't know it, and didn't tell her yourself?" she said curtly.

"What? Tell her what?" he repeated impatiently.

"That Arguello *was* her father!"

"Her father?" He tried to struggle to his elbow again, but she laid her hand masterfully upon his shoulder and forced him back. "Her father!" he repeated hurriedly. "José Arguello! Great God!—are you sure?"

Quietly and yet mechanically gathering the scattered tracts from the coverlet, and putting them back one by one in her reticule, she closed it and her lips with a snap as she uttered "Yes."

Pendleton remained staring at her silently. "Yes," he muttered; "it may have been some instinct of the child's, or some diabolical fancy of Briones'. But," he said bitterly, "true or not, she has no right to his name."

"And I say she *has.*"

She had risen to her feet, with her arms folded across her breast, in an attitude of such Puritan composure that the distant spectators might have thought she was delivering an exordium to the prostrate man.

"I met José Arguello, for the second time, in New Orleans," she said slowly, "eight years ago. He was still rich, but ruined in health by dissipation. I was tired of my way of life. He proposed that I should marry him to take care of him and legitimatise our child. I was forced to tell him what I had done with her, and that the Trust could not be disturbed until she was of age and her own mistress. He assented. We married, but he died within a year. He died, leaving with me his acknowledgment of her as his child, and the right to claim her if I chose."

"And?" interrupted the Colonel with sparkling eyes.

"I don't choose."

"Hear me!" she continued firmly. "With his name and my own mistress, and the girl, as I believed, properly provided for and ignorant of my existence, I saw no necessity for reopening the past. I resolved to lead a new life as his widow. I came North. In the little New England town where I first stopped the country people contracted my name to Mrs. Argalls. I let it stand so. I came to New York and entered the service of the Lord and the bonds of the Church, Henry Pendleton, as Mrs. Argalls, and have remained so ever since."

"But you would not object to Yerba knowing that you lived, and rightly bore her father's name?" said Pendleton eagerly.

The woman looked at him with compressed lips. "I should. I have buried all my past and all its consequences. Let me not seek to reopen it or recall them."

"But if you knew that she was as proud as yourself, and that this very uncertainty as to her name and parentage, although she has never known the whole truth, kept her from taking the name and becoming the wife of a man whom she loves?"

"Whom she loves!"

"Yes; one of her guardians—Hathaway—to whom you entrusted her when she was a child."

"Paul Hathaway—but *he* knew it."

"Yes. But *she* does not know he does. He has kept the secret faithfully even when she refused him."

She was silent for a moment, and then said—

"So be it. I consent."

"And you'll write to her?" said the Colonel eagerly.

"No. But *you* may, and if you want them I will furnish you with such proofs as you may require."

"Thank you." He held out his hand with such a happy, yet childish gratitude upon his worn face, that her own trembled slightly as she took it. "Good-bye!"

"I shall see you soon," she said.

"I shall be here," he said grimly.

"I think not," she returned, with the first relaxation of her smileless face, and moved away.

As she passed out she asked to see the house surgeon. How soon did he think the patient she had been conversing with could be removed

from the hospital with safety? Did Mrs. Argalls mean "far"? Mrs.
Argalls meant as far as *that*—tendering her card and eminently respectable address. Ah!—perhaps in a week. Not before? Perhaps before, unless complications ensued; the patient had been much run
down physically, though, as Mrs. Argalls had probably noticed, he
was singularly strong in nervous will force. Mrs. Argalls *had* noticed
it, and considered it an extraordinary case of conviction—worthy of
the closest watching and care. When he was able to be moved she
would send her own carriage and her own physician to superintend his
transfer. In the meantime he was to want for nothing. Certainly, he
had given very little trouble, and, in fact, wanted very little. Just now
he had only asked for paper, pens, and ink.

Chapter VIII

As Mrs. Argalls' carriage rolled into Fifth Avenue, it for a moment
narrowly grazed another carriage, loaded with luggage, driving up to
an hotel. The abstracted traveller within it was Paul Hathaway, who
had returned from Europe that morning.

Paul entered the hotel, and, going to the register mechanically,
turned its leaves for the previous arrivals, with the same hopeless
patience that had for the last six weeks accompanied this habitual
preliminary performance on his arrival at the principal European hotels. For he had lost all trace of Yerba, Pendleton, Milly, and the
Briones from the day of their departure. The entire party seemed to
have separated at Basle; and, in that eight-hours start they had of him,
to have disappeared to the four cardinal points. He had lingered a few
days in London to transact some business; he would linger a few days
longer in New York before returning to San Francisco.

The daily papers already contained his name in the list of the
steamer passengers who arrived that morning. It might meet *her* eye,
although he had been haunted during the voyage by a terrible fancy
that she was still in Europe, and had either hidden herself in some
obscure provincial town with the half-crazy Pendleton, or had entered
a convent, or even, in reckless despair, had accepted the name and title
of some penniless nobleman. It was this miserable doubt that had
made his homeward journey at times seem like a cruel desertion of
her, while at other moments the conviction that Milly's Californian
relatives might give him some clue to her whereabouts made him
feverishly fearful of delaying an hour on his way to San Francisco. He
did not believe that she had tolerated the company of Briones a single
moment after the scene at the Bad Hof, and yet he had no confidence

in the Colonel's attitude towards the Mexican. Hopeless of the future as her letter seemed, still its naïve and tacit confession of her feelings at the moment was all that sustained him.

Two days passed, and he still lingered aimlessly in New York. In two days more the Panama steamer would sail—yet in his hesitation he had put off securing his passage. He visited the offices of the different European steamer lines, and examined the recent passenger lists, but there was no record of any of the party. What made his quest seem the more hopeless was his belief that, after Briones' revelation, she had cast off the name of Arguello and taken some other. She might even be in New York under that new name now.

On the morning of the third day, among his letters was one that bore the postmark of a noted suburban settlement of wealthy villa-owners on the Hudson River. It was from Milly Woods, stating that her father had read of his arrival in the papers, and begged he would dine and stay the next night with them at "Under Cliff," if he "still had any interest in the fortunes of old friends. Of course," added the perennially incoherent Milly, "if it bores you we shan't expect you." The quick colour came to Paul's careworn cheek. He telegraphed assent, and at sunset that afternoon stepped off the train at a little private woodland station—so abnormally rustic and picturesque, in its brown-bark walls covered with scarlet Virginia creepers, that it looked like a theatrical erection.

Mr. Woods's station waggon was in waiting, but Paul, handing the driver his valise, and ascertaining the general direction of the house, and that it was not far distant, told him to go on and he would follow afoot. The tremor of vague anticipation had already come upon him; something that he knew not whether he feared or longed for, only that it was inevitable, had begun to possess him. He would soon recover himself in the flaring glory of this woodland, and the invigoration of this hale October air.

It was a beautiful and brilliant sunset, yet not so beautiful and brilliant but that the whole opulent forest around him seemed to challenge and repeat its richest as well as its most delicate dyes. The reddening west, seen through an opening of scarlet maples, was no longer red; the golden glory of the sun, sinking over a promontory of gleaming yellow sumach that jutted out into the noble river, was shorn of its intense radiance; at times in the thickest woods he seemed surrounded by a yellow nimbus; at times so luminous was the glow of these translucent leaves that the position of the sun itself seemed changed, or the shadows cast in defiance of its glory. As he walked on, long reaches of the lordly placid stream at his side were visible, as far as the terraces of the opposite shore, lifted on basaltic columns, themselves streaked and veined with gold and fire. Paul had seen nothing like this since his boyhood; for an instant the great heroics of the Sierran landscape were forgotten in this magnificent harlequinade.

A dim footpath crossed the road in the direction of the house, which for the last few moments had been slowly etching itself as a soft vignette in a tinted aureole of walnut and maple upon the steel blue of the river. He was hesitating whether to take this short cut or continue on by the road, when he heard the rustling of quick footsteps among the fallen leaves of the variegated thicket through which it stole. He stopped short, the leafy screen shivered and parted, and a tall graceful figure, like a draped and hidden Columbine, burst through its painted foliage. It was Yerba!

She ran quickly towards him, with parted lips, shining eyes, and a few scarlet leaves clinging to the stuff of her worsted dress in a way that recalled the pink petals of Rosario.

"When I saw you were not in the waggon and knew you were walking, I slipped out to intercept you, as I had something to tell you before you saw the others. I thought you wouldn't mind." She stopped, and suddenly hesitated.

What was this new strange shyness that seemed to droop her eyelids, her proud head, and even the slim hand that had been so impulsively and frankly outstretched towards him? And he—Paul—what was he doing? Where was this passionate outburst that had filled his heart for nights and days? Where this eager, tumultuous questioning that his feverish lips had rehearsed hour by hour? Where this desperate courage that would sweep the whole world away if it stood between them? Where, indeed? He was standing only a few feet from her —cold, silent, and tremulous!

She drew back a step, lifted her head with a quick toss that seemed to condense the moisture in her shining eyes, and sent what might have been a glittering dewdrop flying into the loosed tendrils of her hair. Calm and erect again, she put her little hand to her jacket pocket.

"I only wanted you to read a letter I got yesterday," she said, taking out an envelope.

The spell was broken. Paul caught eagerly at the hand that held the letter, and would have drawn her to him; but she put him aside gravely but sweetly.

"Read that letter!"

"Tell me of *yourself* first!" he broke out passionately. "Why you fled from me, and why I now find you here, by the merest chance, without a word of summons from yourself, Yerba? Tell me who is with you? Are you free and your own mistress—free to act for yourself and me? Speak, darling—don't be cruel! Since that night I have longed for you, sought for you, and suffered for you every day and hour. Tell me if I find you the same Yerba who wrote——"

"Read that letter!"

"I care for none but the one you left me. I have read and re-read it, Yerba—carried it always with me. See! I have it here!" He was in the act of withdrawing it from his breast-pocket, when she put up her hand piteously.

"Please, Paul, please—read this letter first!"

There was something in her new supplicating grace, still retaining the faintest suggestion of her old girlish archness, that struck him. He took the letter and opened it. It was from Colonel Pendleton.

Plainly, concisely, and formally, without giving the name of his authority or suggesting his interview with Mrs. Argalls, he had informed Yerba that he had documentary testimony that she was the daughter of the late José de Arguello, and legally entitled to bear his name. A copy of the instructions given to his wife, recognising Yerba Buena, the ward of the San Francisco Trust, as his child and hers, and leaving to the mother the choice of making it known to her and others, was enclosed.

Paul turned an unchanged face upon Yerba, who was watching him eagerly, uneasily, almost breathlessly.

"And you think this concerns *me!*" he said bitterly. "You think only of this, when I speak of the precious letter that bade me hope, and brought me to you?"

"Paul," said the girl, with wondering eyes and hesitating lips; "do you mean to say that—that—this is—nothing to you?"

"Yes—but forgive me, darling!" he broke out again, with a sudden vague remorsefulness, as he once more sought her elusive hand. "I am a brute—an egotist! I forgot that it might be something to *you.*"

"Paul," continued the girl, her voice quivering with a strange joy, "do you say that you—*you* yourself, care nothing for this?"

"Nothing," he answered, gazing at her transfigured face with admiring wonder.

"And"—more timidly, as a faint aurora kindled in her cheeks— "that you don't care—that—that—I am coming to you *with a name* to give you in—exchange?"

He started.

"Yerba, you are not mocking me? You will be my wife?"

She smiled, yet moving softly backwards with the grave stateliness of a vanishing yet beckoning goddess, until she reached the sumach-bush from which she had emerged. He followed. Another backward step, and it yielded to let her through; but even as it did so she caught him in her arms and for a single moment it closed upon them both,

and hid them in its glory. A still lingering song-bird, possibly convinced that he had mistaken the season, and that spring had really
come, flew out with a little cry to carry the message south; but even
then Paul and Yerba emerged with such innocent, childlike gravity,
and side by side walked so composedly towards the house, that he
thought better of it.

Chapter IX

It was only the *third* time they had ever met—did Paul consider that
when he thought her cold? Did he know now why she had not understood him at Rosario? Did he understand now how calculating and
selfish he had seemed to her that night? Could he look her in the face
now—no, he must be quiet—they were so near the house, and everybody could see them!—and say that he had ever believed her capable
of making up that story of the Arguellos? Could he not have guessed
that she had some memory of that name in her childish recollections,
how or where she knew not? Was it strange that a daughter should
have an instinct of her father? Was it kind to her to know all this
himself and yet reveal nothing? Because her mother and father had
quarrelled, and her mother had run away with somebody and left her
a ward to strangers—was that to be concealed from her, and she left
without a name? This, and much more, tenderly reproachful, bewildering and sweetly illogical, yet inexpressibly dear to Paul as they
walked on in the gloaming.

More to the purpose, however, the fact that Briones, as far as she
knew, did not know her mother, and never before the night at Strudle
Bad had ever spoken of her. Still more to the purpose, that he had
disappeared after an interview with the Colonel that night, and that
she believed always that the Colonel had bought him off. It was not
with *her* money. She had sometimes thought that the Colonel and he
were in confidence, and that was why she had lately distrusted Pendleton. But she had refused to take the name of Arguello again after that
scene, and had called herself only by the name he had given her—
would he forgive her for ever speaking of it as she had?—Yerba Buena.
But on shipboard, at Milly's suggestion, and to keep away from
Briones, her name had appeared on the passenger list as Miss Good,
and they had come, not to New York, but Boston.

It was possible that the Colonel had extracted the information he
sent her *from* Briones. They had parted from Pendleton in London, as
he was grumpy and queer, and, as Milly thought, becoming very mi-
serly and avaricious as he grew older, for he was always quarrelling

over the hotel bills. But he had Mrs. Woods's New York address at Under Cliff, and, of course, guessed where she was. There was no address on his letter; he had said he would write again.

Thus much until they reached the steps of the verandah, and Milly, flying down, was ostentatiously overwhelmed with the unexpected appearance of Mr. Paul Hathaway and Yerba, whom she had been watching from the window for the last ten minutes. Then the appearance of Mr. Woods, Californian and reminiscent, and Mrs. Woods, metropolitan, languid, and forgetful, and the sudden and formal retirement of the girls. An arch and indefinable mystery in the air whenever Paul and Yerba appeared together—of which even the servants were discreetly conscious.

At dinner Mr. Woods again became retrospective and Californian, and dwelt upon the changes he had noticed. It appeared the old pioneers had in few cases attained a comfortable fortune for their old age. "I know," he added, "that your friend Colonel Pendleton has dropped a good deal of money over in Europe. Somebody told me that he actually was reduced to take a steerage passage home. It looks as if he might gamble—it's an old Californian complaint." As Paul, who had become suddenly grave again, did not speak, Mrs. Woods reminded them that she had always doubted the Colonel's moral principles. Old as he was, he had never got over that freedom of life and social opinion which he had imbibed in early days. For her part, she was very glad that he had not returned from Europe with the girls, though, of course, the presence of Don Caesar and his sister during their European sojourn was a corrective. As Paul's face grew darker during this languid criticism, Yerba, who had been watching it with a new and absorbing sympathy, seized the first moment when they left the table to interrogate him with heart-breaking eyes.

"You don't think, Paul, that the Colonel is really poor?"

"God only knows," said Paul. "I tremble to think how that scoundrel may have bled him."

"And all for me! Paul, dear, you know you were saying in the woods that you would never, never touch my money. What"—exultingly—"if we gave it to him?"

What answer Paul made did not transpire, for it seemed to have been indicated by an interval of profound silence.

But the next morning, as he and Mr. Woods were closeted in the library, Yerba broke in upon them with a pathetic face and a telegram in her hand. "Oh, Paul—Mr. Hathaway—*it's true!*"

Paul seized the telegram quickly; it had no signature, only the line: "Colonel Pendleton is dangerously ill at St. John's Hospital."

"I must go at once," said Paul, rising.

"Oh, Paul"—imploringly—"let me go with you! I should never forgive myself if—*and it's addressed to me;* and what would he think if I didn't come?"

Paul hesitated. "Mrs. Woods will let Milly go with us—and she can stay at the hotel. Say yes," she continued, seeking his eyes eagerly.

He consented, and in half an hour they were in the train for New York. Leaving Milly at the hotel, ostensibly in deference to the Woods's prejudices, but really to save the presence of a third party at this meeting, Paul drove with Yerba rapidly to the hospital. They were admitted to an anteroom. The house surgeon received them respectfully, but doubtingly. The patient was a little better this morning, but very weak. There was a lady now with him—a member of a religious and charitable guild, who had taken the greatest interest in him—indeed, she had wished to take him to her own home—but he had declined at first, and now he was too weak to be removed.

"But I received this telegram; it must have been sent at his request," protested Yerba.

The house surgeon looked at the beautiful face. He was mortal. He would see if the patient was able to stand another interview; possibly the regular visitor might withdraw.

When he had gone, an attendant volunteered the information that the old gentleman was perhaps a little excited at times. He was a wonderful man; he had seen a great deal; he talked much of California and the early days; he was very interesting. Ah, it would be all right now if the doctor found him well enough, for the lady was already going—that was she coming through the hall.

She came slowly towards them—erect, grey, grim—a still handsome apparition. Paul started. To his horror, Yerba ran impulsively forward and said eagerly, "Is he better? Can he see us now?"

The woman halted an instant, seemed to gather the prayer-book and reticule she was carrying closer to her breast, but was otherwise unchanged. Replying to Paul rather than the young girl, she said rigidly, "The patient is able to see Mr. Hathaway and Miss Yerba Buena," and passed slowly on. But as she reached the door she unloosed her black mourning veil from her bonnet, and seemed to drop it across her face with a gesture that Paul remembered she had used twelve years ago.

"She frightens me!" said Yerba, turning a suddenly startled face on Paul. "Oh, Paul, I hope it isn't an omen, but she looked like some one from the grave!"

"Hush!" said Paul, turning away a face that was whiter than her own. "They are coming now."

The house surgeon had returned a trifle graver. They might see him now, but they must be warned that he wandered at times a little; and, if he might suggest, if it was anything of family importance, they had better make the most of their time and his lucid intervals. Perhaps, if they were old friends—*very* old friends—he would recognise them. He was wandering much in the past—always in the past.

They found him in the end of the ward, but so carefully protected and partitioned off by screens that the space around his cot had all the privacy and security of an apartment. He was very much changed; they would scarcely have known him but for the delicately curved aquiline profile and the long white moustache—now so faint and etherealised as to seem a mere spirit wing that rested on his pillow. To their surprise he opened his eyes with a smile of perfect recognition, and with thin fingers beyond the coverlid beckoned to them to approach. Yet there was still a shadow of his old reserve in his reception of Paul, and, although one hand interlocked the fingers of Yerba—who had at first rushed impulsively forward and fallen on her knees beside the bed—and the other softly placed itself upon her head, his eyes were fixed upon the young man's with the ceremoniousness due to a stranger.

"I am glad to see, sir," he began in a slow, broken, but perfectly audible voice, "that now you are—satisfied with the right—of this young lady—to bear the name of—Arguello—and her relationship— sir—to one of the oldest——"

"But, my dear old friend," broke out Paul earnestly, "I *never* cared for that—I beg you to believe——"

"He never—never—cared for it—dear, dear Colonel," sobbed Yerba passionately; "it was all my fault—he thought only of me—you wrong him!"

"*I* think otherwise," said the Colonel, with grim and relentless deliberation. "I have a vivid—impression—sir—of an—interview I had with you—at the St. Charles—where you said——" He was silent for a moment, and then in a quite different voice called faintly—

"George!"

Paul and Yerba glanced quickly at each other.

"George, set out some refreshment for the Honourable Paul Hathaway. The best, sir—you understand. . . . A good nigger, sir—a good boy; and he never leaves me, sir. Only, by gad! sir, he will starve himself and his family to be with me. I brought him with me to California away back in the fall of forty-nine. Those were the early days, sir—the early days."

His head had fallen back quite easily on the pillow now; but a slight film seemed to be closing over his dark eyes, like the inner lid of an eagle when it gazes upon the sun.

"They were the old days, sir—the days of Men—when a man's *word* was enough for anything, and his trigger-finger settled any doubt. When the Trust that he took from Man, Woman, or Child was never broken. When the tide, sir, that swept through the Golden Gate came up as far as Montgomery Street."

He did not speak again. But they who stood beside him knew that the tide had once more come up to Montgomery Street, and was carrying Harry Pendleton away with it.

The Châtelaine of
Burnt Ridge

Chapter I

IT HAD GROWN dark on Burnt Ridge. Seen from below, the whole
serrated crest that had glittered in the sunset as if its interstices were
eaten by consuming fires, now closed up its ranks of blackened shafts
and became again harsh and sombre *chevaux de frise* against the sky.
A faint glow still lingered over the red valley road as if it were its own
reflection, rather than any light from beyond the darkened ridge.
Night was already creeping up out of remote cañons and along the
furrowed flanks of the mountain, or settling on the nearer woods with
the sound of home-coming and innumerable wings. At a point where
the road began to encroach upon the mountain-side in its slow winding ascent the darkness had become so real that a young girl cantering
along the rising terrace found difficulty in guiding her horse, with eyes
still dazzled by the sunset fires.

In spite of her precautions, the animal suddenly shied at some object
in the obscured roadway, and nearly unseated her. The accident disclosed not only the fact that she was riding in a man's saddle, but also
a foot and ankle that her ordinary walking-dress was too short to hide.

It was evident that her equestrian exercise was extempore, and that at that hour and on that road she had not expected to meet company. But she was apparently a good horsewoman, for the mischance that might have thrown a less practical or more timid rider seemed of little moment to her. With a strong hand and determined gesture she wheeled her frightened horse back into the track, and rode him directly at the object. But here she herself slightly recoiled—for it was the body of a man lying in the road.

As she leaned forward over her horse's shoulder she could see by the dim light that he was a miner, and that, though motionless, he was breathing stertorously. Drunk, no doubt!—an accident of the locality alarming only to her horse. But although she cantered impatiently forward, she had not proceeded a hundred yards before she stopped reflectively and trotted back again. He had not moved. She could now see that his head and shoulders were covered with broken clods of earth and gravel, and smaller fragments lay at his side. A dozen feet above him on the hillside there was a foot trail which ran parallel with the bridle-road, and occasionally overhung it. It seemed possible that he might have fallen from the trail and been stunned.

Dismounting, she succeeded in dragging him to a safer position by the bank. The act discovered his face, which was young, and unknown to her. Wiping it with the silk handkerchief which was loosely slung around his neck after the fashion of his class, she gave a quick feminine glance around her, and then approached her own and rather handsome face near his lips. There was no odour of alcohol in the thick and heavy respiration. Mounting again, she rode forward at an accelerated pace, and in twenty minutes had reached a higher table-land of the mountain, a cleared opening in the forest that showed signs of careful cultivation, and a large, rambling, yet picturesque-looking dwelling, whose unpainted red-wood walls were hidden in roses and creepers. Pushing open a swinging gate, she entered the enclosure as a brown-faced man, dressed as a vaquero, came towards her as if to assist her to alight. But she had already leaped to the ground and thrown him the reins.

"Miguel," she said, with a mistress's quiet authority in her boyish contralto voice, "put Glory in the covered waggon, and drive down the road as far as the valley turning. There's a man lying near the right bank, drunk, or sick maybe, or perhaps crippled by a fall. Bring him up here, unless somebody has found him already, or you happen to know who he is and where to take him."

The vaquero raised his shoulders, half in deprecation, half in disappointed expectation of some other command. "And your brother, señora, he has not himself arrived?"

A light shadow of impatience crossed her face. "No," she said bluntly. "Come, be quick."

She turned towards the house as the man moved away. Already a gaunt-looking old man had appeared in the porch, and was awaiting her with his hand shadowing his angry, suspicious eyes, and his lips moving querulously.

"Of course, you've got to stand out there and give orders and 'tend to your own business afore you think o' speaking to your own flesh and blood," he said aggrievedly. "That's all *you* care!"

"There was a sick man lying in the road, and I've sent Miguel to look after him," returned the girl, with a certain contemptuous resignation.

"Oh yes!" struck in another voice, which seemed to belong to the female of the first speaker's species, and to be its equal in age and temper, "and I reckon you saw a jay-bird on a tree, or a squirrel on the fence, and either of 'em was more important to you than your own brother."

"Steve didn't come by the stage, and didn't send any message," continued the young girl, with the same coldly resigned manner. "No one had any news of him, and, as I told you before, I didn't expect any."

"Why don't you say right out you didn't *want* any?" said the old man sneeringly. "Much you inquired! No; I orter hev gone myself, and I would if I was master here, instead of me and your mother bein' the dust of the yearth beneath your feet."

The young girl entered the house, followed by the old man, passing an old woman seated by the window, who seemed to be nursing her resentment and a large Bible which she held clasped against her shawled bosom at the same moment. Going to the wall, she hung up her large hat and slightly shook the red dust from her skirts as she continued her explanation, in the same deep voice, with a certain monotony of logic and possibly of purpose and practice also.

"You and mother know as well as I do, father, that Stephen is no more to be depended upon than the wind that blows. It's three years since he set foot here; it's three years since he has been promising to come, and even getting money to come, and yet he has never showed his face, though he has been a dozen times within five miles of this house. He doesn't come, because he doesn't want to come. As to *your* going over to the stage-office, I went there myself at the last moment to save you the mortification of asking questions of strangers that they know have been a dozen times answered already."

There was such a ring of absolute truthfulness, albeit worn by repetition, in the young girl's deep honest voice, that for one instant her two more emotional relatives quailed before it; but only for a moment.

"That's right!" shrilled the old woman. "Go on and abuse your own brother. It's only the fear you have that he'll make his fortune yet and shame you before the father and mother you despise."

The young girl remained standing by the window motionless and apparently passive, as if receiving an accepted and usual punishment. But here the elder woman gave way to sobs and some incoherent snuffling, at which the younger went away. Whether she recognised in her mother's tears the ordinary deliquescence of emotion, or whether, as a woman herself, she knew that this mere feminine conventionality could not possibly be directed at her, and that the actual conflict between them had ceased, she passed slowly on to an inner hall, leaving the male victim, her unfortunate father, to succumb, as he always did sooner or later, to their influence. Crossing the hall, which was decorated with a few elk horns, Indian trophies, and mountain pelts, she entered another room, and closed the door behind her with a gesture of relief.

The room, which looked upon a porch, presented a singular combination of masculine business occupations and feminine taste and adornment. A desk covered with papers, a shelf displaying a ledger and account-books, another containing works of reference, a table with a vase of flowers and a lady's riding-whip upon it, a map of California flanked on either side by an embroidered silken workbag and an oval mirror decked with grasses, a calendar and interest-table hanging below two schoolgirl crayons of classic heads, with the legend, "Josephine Forsyth *fecit*"—were part of its incongruous accessories. The young girl went to her desk, but presently moved and turned towards the window thoughtfully. The last gleam had died from the steel-blue sky; a few lights like star points began to prick out the lower valley. The expression of monotonous restraint and endurance had not yet faded from her face.

Yet she had been accustomed to scenes like the one she had just passed through since her girlhood. Five years ago Alexander Forsyth, her uncle, had brought her to this spot—then a mere log cabin on the hillside—as a refuge from the impoverished and shiftless home of his elder brother Thomas and his ill-tempered wife. Here Alexander Forsyth, by reason of his more dominant character and business capacity, had prospered until he became a rich and influential ranche owner. Notwithstanding her father's jealousy of Alexander's fortune, and the open rupture that followed between the brothers, Josephine retained her position in the heart and home of her uncle without espousing the cause of either; and her father was too prudent not to recognise the

near and prospective advantages of such a mediator. Accustomed to
her parents' extravagant denunciations, and her uncle's more repressed but practical contempt of them, the unfortunate girl early
developed a cynical disbelief in the virtues of kinship in the abstract,
and a philosophical resignation to its effects upon her personally. Believing that her father and uncle fairly represented the fraternal principle, she was quite prepared for the early defection and distrust of her
vagabond and dissipated brother Stephen, and accepted it calmly.
True to an odd standard of justice, which she had erected from the
crumbling ruins of her own domestic life, she was tolerant of everything but human perfection. This quality, however fatal to her higher
growth, had given her a peculiar capacity for business which endeared
her to her uncle. Familiar with the strong passions and prejudices of
men, she had none of those feminine meannesses, a wholesome distrust
of which had kept her uncle a bachelor. It was not strange, therefore,
that when he died two years ago it was found that he had left her his
entire property, real and personal, limited only by a single condition.
She was to undertake the vocation of a "sole trader," and carry on the
business under the name of "J. Forsyth." If she married, the estate and
property was to be held distinct from her husband's, inalienable under
the "Married Woman's Property Act," and subject during her life only
to her own control and personal responsibilities as a trader.

The intense disgust and discomfiture of her parents, who had expected to more actively participate in their brother's fortune, may be
imagined. But it was not equal to their fury when Josephine, instead of
providing for them a separate maintenance out of her abundance, simply offered to transfer them and her brother to her own house on a
domestic but not a business equality. There being no alternative but
their former precarious shiftless life in their "played out" claim in the
valley, they wisely consented, reserving the sacred right of daily protest and objurgation. In the economy of Burnt Ridge Ranche they
alone took it upon themselves to represent the shattered domestic altar
and its outraged Lares and Penates. So conscientiously did they perform their task as to even occasionally impede the business visitor to
the ranche, and to cause some of the more practical neighbours to
seriously doubt the young girl's commercial wisdom. But she was firm.
Whether she thought her parents a necessity of respectable domestic-
ity, or whether she regarded their presence in the light of a penitential
atonement for some previous disregard of them, no one knew. Public
opinion inclined to the latter.

The black line of ridge faded out with her abstraction, and she
turned from the window and lit the lamp on her desk. The yellow light
illuminated her face and figure. In their womanly graces there was no

trace of what some people believed to be a masculine character, except a singularly frank look of critical inquiry and patient attention in her dark eyes. Her long brown hair was somewhat rigidly twisted into a knot on the top of her head, as if more for security than ornament. Brown was also the prevailing tint of her eyebrows, thickly-set eyelashes, and eyes, and was even suggested in the slight sallowness of her complexion. But her lips were well-cut and fresh-coloured, and her hands and feet small and finely formed. She would have passed for a pretty girl had she not suggested something more.

She sat down, and began to examine a pile of papers before her with that concentration and attention to detail which was characteristic of her eyes, pausing at times with prettily knit brows, and her penholder between her lips, in the semblance of a pout that was pleasant enough to see. Suddenly the rattle of hoofs and wheels struck her with a sense of something forgotten, and she put down her work quickly and stood up listening. The sound of rough voices and her father's querulous accents was broken upon by a cultivated and more familiar utterance: "All right; I'll speak to her at once. Wait there," and the door opened to the well-known physician of Burnt Ridge, Dr. Duchesne.

"Look here," he said, with an abruptness that was only saved from being brusque by a softer intonation and a reassuring smile, "I met Miguel helping an accident into your buggy. Your orders, eh?"

"Oh yes," said Josephine quietly. "A man I saw on the road."

"Well, it's a bad case, and wants prompt attention. And as your house is the nearest, I came with him here."

"Certainly," she said gravely. "Take him to the second room beyond—Steve's room—it's ready," she explained to two dusky shadows in the hall behind the doctor.

"And look here," said the doctor, partly closing the door behind him and regarding her with critical eyes—"you always said you'd like to see some of my queer cases. Well, this is one—a serious one, too; in fact, it's just touch and go with him. There's a piece of the bone pressing on the brain no bigger than that, but as much as if all Burnt Ridge was atop of him! I'm going to lift it. I want somebody here to stand by, some one who can lend a hand with a sponge, eh?—some one who isn't going to faint or scream, or even shake a hair's breadth, eh?"

The colour rose quickly to the girl's cheek, and her eyes kindled. "I'll come," she said thoughtfully. "Who is he?"

The doctor stared slightly at the unessential query. "Don't know; one of the river miners, I reckon. It's an urgent case. I'll go and get everything ready. You'd better," he added, with an ominous glance at her grey frock, "put something over your dress." The suggestion made her grave, but did not alter her colour.

A moment later she entered the room. It was the one that had always been set apart for her brother; the very bed on which the unconscious man lay had been arranged that morning with her own hands. Something of this passed through her mind as she saw that the doctor had wheeled it beneath the strong light in the centre of the room, stripped its outer coverings with professional thoughtfulness, and rearranged the mattresses. But it did not seem like the same room. There was a pungent odour in the air from some freshly-opened phial; an almost feminine neatness and luxury in an open morocco case like a jewel-box on the table, shining with spotless steel. At the head of the bed one of her own servants, the powerful mill foreman, was assisting with the mingled curiosity and *blasé* experience of one accustomed to smashed and lacerated digits. At first she did not look at the central unconscious figure on the bed, whose sufferings seemed to her to have been vicariously transferred to the concerned, eager, and drawn faces that looked down upon its immunity. Then she femininely recoiled before the bared white neck and shoulders displayed above the quilt, until, forcing herself to look upon the face half concealed by bandages, and the head from which the dark tangles of hair had been ruthlessly sheared, she began to share the doctor's unconcern in his personality. What mattered who or what *he* was? It was—a case!

The operation began. With the same earnest intelligence she had previously shown, she quickly and noiselessly obeyed the doctor's whispered orders, and even half anticipated them. She was conscious of a singular curiosity that, far from being mean or ignoble, seemed to lift her not only above the ordinary weaknesses of her own sex, but made her superior to the men around her. Almost before she knew it, the operation was over, and she regarded with equal curiosity the ostentatious solicitude with which the doctor seemed to be wiping his fateful instrument, that bore an odd resemblance to a silver-handled centre-bit. The stertorous breathing below the bandages had given way to a fainter but more natural respiration. There was a moment of suspense. The doctor's hand left the pulse and lifted the closed eyelid of the sufferer. A slight movement passed over the figure. The sluggish face had cleared, life seemed to struggle back into it before even the dull eyes participated in the glow. Dr. Duchesne with a sudden gesture waved aside his companions, but not before Josephine had bent her head eagerly forward.

"He is coming to," she said.

At the sound of that deep clear voice—the first to break the hush of the room—the dull eyes leaped up and the head turned in its direction. The lips moved and uttered a single rapid sentence. The girl recoiled.

"You're all right now," said the doctor cheerfully, intent only upon the form before him.

The lips moved again, but this time feebly and vacantly; the eyes were staring vaguely around.

"What's matter? What's all about?" said the man thickly.

"You've had a fall. Think a moment. Where do you live?"

Again the lips moved, but this time only to emit a confused, incoherent murmur. Dr. Duchesne looked grave, but recovered himself quickly.

"That will do. Leave him alone now," he said brusquely to the others.

But Josephine lingered.

"He spoke well enough just now," she said eagerly. "Did you hear what he said?"

"Not exactly," said the doctor abstractedly, gazing at the man.

"He said, 'You'll have to kill me first,' " said Josephine slowly.

"Humph," said the doctor abstractedly, passing his hand backwards and forwards before the man's eyes to note any change in the staring pupils.

"Yes," continued Josephine gravely. "I suppose," she added cautiously, "he was thinking of the operation—of what you had just done to him?"

"What *I* had done to him? Oh yes!"

Chapter II

Before noon the next day it was known throughout Burnt Ridge Valley that Dr. Duchesne had performed a difficult operation upon an unknown man, who had been picked up unconscious from a fall, and carried to Burnt Ridge Ranche. But although the unfortunate man's life was saved by the operation, he had only momentarily recovered consciousness—relapsing into a semi-idiotic state, which effectively stopped the discovery of any clue to his friends or his identity. As it was evidently an *accident,* which, in that rude community—and even in some more civilised ones—conveyed a vague impression of some contributory incapacity on the part of the victim, or some Providential interference of a retributive character, Burnt Ridge gave itself little trouble about it. It is unnecessary to say that Mr. and Mrs. Forsyth gave themselves and Josephine much more. They had a theory and a grievance. Satisfied from the first that the alleged victim was a drunken tramp, who submitted to have a hole bored in his head in order to foist himself upon the ranche, they were loud in their protests, even hinting at a conspiracy between Josephine and the stranger to supplant her brother in the property, as he had already in the spare bedroom. "Didn't all that yer happen *the very night* she pretended to go for Stephen—eh?" said Mrs. Forsyth. "Tell me that! And didn't she have it all arranged with the buggy to bring him here, as that sneaking doctor himself let out—eh? Looks mighty curious, don't it?" she muttered darkly to the old man. But although that gentleman, even from his own selfish view, would scarcely have submitted to a surgical operation and later idiocy as the price of insuring comfortable dependency, he had no doubt others were base enough to do it, and lent a willing ear to his wife's suspicions.

Josephine's personal knowledge of the stranger went little further. Doctor Duchesne had confessed to her his professional disappointment at the incomplete results of the operation. He had saved the man's life, but as yet not his reason. There was still hope, however, for the diagnosis revealed nothing that might prejudice a favourable progress. It was a most interesting case. He would watch it carefully, and as soon as the patient could be removed would take him to the county hospital, where, under his own eyes, the poor fellow would have the benefit of the latest science and the highest specialists. Physically he was doing remarkably well; indeed, he must have been a fine young chap, free from blood taint or vicious complication, whose flesh had healed like an infant's. It should be recorded that it was at this juncture that Mrs. Forsyth first learnt that a *silver plate* let into the artful stranger's skull was an adjunct of the healing process! Convinced that this infamous extravagance was part and parcel of the conspiracy, and was only the beginning of other assimilations of the Forsyths' metallic substance; that the plate was probably polished and burnished with a fulsome inscription to the doctor's skill, and would pass into the possession and adornment of a perfect stranger, her rage knew no bounds. He or his friends ought to be made to pay for it or work it out! In vain it was declared that a few dollars were all that was found in the man's pocket, and that no memoranda gave any indication of his name, friends, or history beyond the suggestion that he came from a distance. This was clearly a part of the conspiracy! Even Josephine's practical good sense was obliged to take note of this singular absence of all record regarding him, and the apparent obliteration of everything that might be responsible for his ultimate fate.

Homeless, friendless, helpless, and even nameless, the unfortunate man of twenty-five was thus left to the tender mercies of the mistress of Burnt Ridge Ranche as if he had been a new-born foundling laid at

her door. But this mere claim of weakness was not all; it was supple-
mented by a singular personal appeal to Josephine's nature. From the
time that he turned his head towards her voice on that fateful night his
eyes had always followed her around the room with a wondering,
yearning, canine half-intelligence. Without being able to convince herself that he understood her better than his regular attendant furnished
by the doctor, she could not fail to see that he obeyed her implicitly,
and that whenever any difficulty arose between him and his nurse she
was always appealed to. Her pride in this proof of her practical sover-
eignty was flattered; and when Doctor Duchesne finally admitted that
although the patient was now physically able to be removed to the
hospital, yet he would lose in the change that very strong factor which
Josephine had become in his mental recovery, the young girl as frankly
suggested that he should stay as long as there was any hope of restoring his reason. Doctor Duchesne was delighted. With all his enthusiasm for science, he had a professional distrust of some of its disciples,
and perhaps was not sorry to keep this most interesting case in his own
hands. To him her suggestion was only a womanly kindness, tempered
with womanly curiosity. But the astonishment and stupefaction of her
parents at this evident corroboration of suspicions they had as yet only
half believed, was tinged with superstitious dread. Had she fallen in
love with this helpless stranger? or, more awful to contemplate, was he
really no stranger, but a surreptitious lover thus strategically brought
under her roof? For once they refrained from open criticism. The very
magnitude of their suspicion left them dumb.

It was thus that the virgin Châtelaine of Burnt Ridge Ranche was
left to gaze untrammelled upon her pale and handsome guest, whose
silken-bearded lips and sad childlike eyes might have suggested a more
exalted Sufferer in their absence of any suggestion of a grosser material
manhood. But even this imaginative appeal did not enter into her
feelings. She felt for her good-looking, helpless patient a profound and
honest pity. I do not know whether she had ever heard that "pity was
akin to love." She would probably have resented that utterly untenable
and atrocious commonplace. There was no suggestion, real or illusive,
of any previous masterful quality in the man which might have made
his present dependent condition picturesque by contrast. He had come
to her handicapped by an unromantic accident and a practical want of
energy and intellect. He would have to touch her interest anew if,
indeed, he would ever succeed in dispelling the old impression. His
beauty, in a community of picturesquely handsome men, had little
weight with her, except to accent the contrast with their fuller
manhood.

Her life had given her no illusions in regard to the other sex. She had found them, however, more congenial and safer companions than women, and more accessible to her own sense of justice and honour. In return they had respected and admired rather than loved her, in spite of her womanly graces. If she had at times contemplated eventual marriage, it was only as a possible practical partnership in her business; but as she lived in a country where men thought it dishonourable and a proof of incompetency to rise by their wives' superior fortune, she had been free from that kind of mercenary persecution, even from men who might have worshipped her in hopeless and silent honour.

For this reason there was nothing in the situation that suggested a single compromising speculation in the minds of the neighbours, or disturbed her own tranquillity. There seemed to be nothing in the future except a possible relief to her curiosity. Some day the unfortunate man's reason would be restored, and he would tell his simple history. Perhaps he might explain what was in his mind when he turned to her the first evening with that singular sentence which had often recurred strangely to her, she knew not why. It did not strike her until later that it was because it had been the solitary indication of an energy and capacity that seemed unlike him. Nevertheless, after that explanation she would have been quite willing to have shaken hands with him and parted.

And yet—for there was an unexpressed remainder in her thought— she was never entirely free or uninfluenced in his presence. The flickering vacancy of his sad eyes sometimes became fixed with a resolute immobility under the gentle questioning with which she had sought to draw out his faculties, that both piqued and exasperated her. He could say "yes" and "no," as she thought, intelligently, but he could not utter a coherent sentence nor write a word, except like a child in imitation of his copy. She taught him to repeat after her the names of the inanimate objects in the room, then the names of the doctor, his attendant, the servant, and finally her own under her Christian prenomen, with frontier familiarity; but when she pointed to himself he waited for *her* to name him! In vain she tried him with all the masculine names she knew; his was not one of them, or he would not or could not speak it. For at times she rejected the professional dictum of the doctor that the faculty of memory was wholly paralysed or held in abeyance, even to the half-automatic recollection of his letters, yet she inconsistently began to teach him the alphabet with the same method, and—in her sublime unconsciousness of his manhood—with the same discipline as if he were a very child. When he had recovered sufficiently to leave his room, she would lead him to the porch before her window, and make him contented and happy by allowing him to watch her at work at her desk, occasionally answering his wondering eyes with a word, or stirring his faculties with a question. I grieve to say that her parents had taken advantage of this publicity and his supposed helpless condition to show their disgust of his assumption, to the extreme of making faces at him—an act which he resented with such a furious glare that they retreated hurriedly to their own verandah. A fresh though somewhat inconsistent grievance was added to their previous indictment of him: "If we ain't found dead in our bed with our throats cut by that woman's crazy husband" (they had settled by this time that there had been a clandestine marriage), "we'll be lucky," groaned Mrs. Forsyth.

Meantime the mountain summer waxed to its fulness of fire and fruition. There were days when the crowded forest seemed choked and impeded with its own foliage, and pungent and stifling with its own rank maturity; when the long hillside ranks of wild oats, thick-set and impassable, filled the air with the heated dust of germination. In this quickening irritation of life it would be strange if the unfortunate man's torpid intellect was not helped in its awakening, and he was allowed to ramble at will over the ranche; but with the instinct of a domestic animal he always returned to the house and sat in the porch, where Josephine usually found him awaiting her when she herself returned from a visit to the mill. Coming thence one day, she espied him on the mountain-side leaning against a projecting ledge in an attitude so rapt and immovable that she felt compelled to approach him. He appeared to be dumbly absorbed in the prospect, which might have intoxicated a saner mind.

Half veiled by the heat that rose quiveringly from the fiery cañon below, the domain of Burnt Ridge stretched away before him, until, lifted in successive terraces hearsed and plumed with pines, it was at last lost in the ghostly snow-peaks. But the practical Josephine seized the opportunity to try once more to awaken the slumbering memory of her pupil. Following his gaze, with signs and questions she sought to draw from him some indication of familiar recollection of certain points of the map thus unrolled behind him. But in vain. She even pointed out the fateful shadow of the overhanging ledge on the road where she had picked him up—there was no response in his abstracted eyes. She bit her lips; she was becoming irritated again. Then it occurred to her that, instead of appealing to his hopeless memory, she had better trust to some unreflective automatic instinct independent of it, and she put the question a little forward: "When you leave us, where will you go from here?" He stirred slightly, and turned towards her. She repeated her query slowly and patiently, with signs and gestures recognised between them. A faint glow of intelligence struggled into his eyes; he lifted his arm slowly and pointed.

"Ah! those white peaks—the Sierras?" she asked eagerly. No reply.
"Beyond them?"

"Yes."

"The States?" No reply. "Farther still?"

He remained so patiently quiet and still pointing, that she leaned
forward, and, following with her eyes the direction of his hand, saw
that he was pointing to the sky!

Then a great quiet fell upon them. The whole mountainside seemed
to her to be hushed as if to allow her to grasp and realise for the first
time the pathos of the ruined life at her side, which *it* had known so
long, but which she had never felt till now. The tears came to her eyes;
in her swift revulsion of feeling she caught the thin uplifted hand
between her own. It seemed to her that he was about to raise them to
his lips, but she withdrew them hastily, and moved away. She had a
strange fear that if he had kissed them it might seem as if some dumb
animal had touched them—or—*it might not.* The next day she felt a
consciousness of this in his presence, and a wish that he was well cured
and away. She determined to consult Dr. Duchesne on the subject
when he next called.

But the doctor, secure in the welfare of his patient, had not visited
him lately, and she found herself presently absorbed in the business of
the ranche, which at this season was particularly trying. There had
also been a quarrel between Dick Shipley, her mill foreman, and Miguel, her ablest and most trusted vaquero, and in her strict sense of
impartial justice she was obliged to side on the merits of the case with
Shipley against her oldest retainer. This troubled her, as she knew that
with the Mexican nature, fidelity and loyalty were not unmixed with
quick and unreasoning jealousy. For this reason she was somewhat
watchful of the two men when work was over and there was a chance
of their being thrown together. Once or twice she had remained up late
to meet Miguel returning from the Posada at San Ramon, filled with
aguardiente and a recollection of his wrongs, and to see him safely
bestowed before she herself retired. It was on one of those occasions,
however, that she learned that Dick Shipley, hearing that Miguel had
disparaged him freely at the Posada, had broken the discipline of the
ranche and absented himself the same night that Miguel "had leave"
with a view of facing his antagonist on his own ground. To prevent this
the fearless girl at once secretly set out alone to overtake and bring
back the delinquent.

For two or three hours the house was thus left to the sole occupancy
of Mr. and Mrs. Forsyth and the invalid—a fact only dimly suspected
by the latter, who had become vaguely conscious of Josephine's anxiety, and had noticed the absence of light and movement in her room.

It was therefore that, having risen again and mechanically taken his seat in the porch to await her return, he was startled by hearing *her* voice in the shadow of the lower porch, accompanied by a hurried tapping against the door of the old couple. The half-reasoning man arose and would have moved towards it, but suddenly he stopped rigidly, with white and parted lips and vacantly distended eyeballs.

Meantime the voice and muffled tapping had brought the tremulous fingers of old Forsyth to the door-latch. He opened the door partly; a slight figure that had been lurking in the shadow of the porch pushed rapidly through the opening. There was a faint outcry quickly hushed, and the door closed again. The rays of a single candle showed the two old people hysterically clasping in their arms the figure that had entered—a slight but vicious-looking young fellow of five-and-twenty.

"There, d—n it!" he said impatiently, in a voice whose rich depth was like Josephine's, but whose querulous action was that of the two old people before him, "let me go, and quit that. I didn't come here to be strangled. I want some money—money, you hear! Devilish quick, too, for I've got to be off again before daylight. So look sharp, will you?"

"But, Stevy dear, when you didn't come that time three months ago, but wrote from Los Angelos, you said you'd made a strike at last, and——"

"What are you talking about?" he interrupted violently. "That was just my lyin' to keep you from worryin' me. Three months ago—three months ago! Why, you must have been crazy to have swallowed it; I hadn't a cent."

"Nor have we," said the old woman shrilly. "That hellish sister of yours still keeps us like beggars. Our only hope was you, our own boy. And now you only come to—to go again."

"But *she* has money; *she's* doing well, and *she* shall give it to me," he went on angrily. "She can't bully me with her business airs and morality. Who else has got a right to share, if it is not her own brother?"

Alas for the fatuousness of human malevolence! Had the unhappy couple related only the simple facts they knew about the new guest of Burnt Ridge Ranche, and the manner of his introduction, they might have spared what followed.

But the old woman broke into a vindictive cry, "Who else, Steve—who else? Why, the slut has brought a *man* here—a sneaking, deceitful, underhanded, crazy lover!"

"Oh, has she?" said the young man fiercely, yet secretly pleased at this promising evidence of his sister's human weakness. "Where is she? I'll go to her. She's in her room, I suppose," and before they could restrain him, he had thrown off their impeding embraces and darted across the hall.

The two old people stared doubtfully at each other. For even this powerful ally, whose strength, however, they were by no means sure of, might succumb before the determined Josephine! Prudence demanded a middle course. "Ain't they brother and sister?" said the old man, with an air of virtuous toleration. "Let 'em fight it out."

The young man impatiently entered the room he remembered to have been his sister's. By the light of the moon that streamed upon the window he could see she was not there. He passed hurriedly to the door of her bedroom; it was open; the room was empty, the bed unturned. She was not in the house—she had gone to the mill. Ah! What was that they had said! An infamous thought passed through the scoundrel's mind. Then, in what he half believed was an access of virtuous fury, he began by the dim light to rummage in the drawers of the desk for such loose coin or valuables as, in the perfect security of the ranche, were often left unguarded. Suddenly he heard a heavy footstep on the threshold, and turned.

An awful vision—a recollection, so unexpected, so ghost-like in that weird light that he thought he was losing his senses—stood before him. It moved forwards with staring eyeballs and white and open lips from which a horrible inarticulate sound issued that was the speech of no living man! With a single desperate, almost superhuman effort Stephen Forsyth bounded aside, leaped from the window, and ran like a madman from the house. Then the apparition trembled, collapsed, and sank in an undistinguishable heap to the ground.

When Josephine Forsyth returned an hour later with her mill foreman, she was startled to find her helpless patient in a fit on the floor of her room. With the assistance of her now converted and penitent employé, she had the unfortunate man conveyed to his room—but not until she had thoughtfully rearranged the disorder of her desk and closed the open drawers without attracting Dick Shipley's attention. In the morning, hearing that the patient was still in the semi-conscious exhaustion of his late attack, but without seeing him, she sent for Dr. Duchesne. The doctor arrived while she was absent at the mill, where, after a careful examination of his patient, he sought her with some little excitement.

"Well?" she said with eager gravity.

"Well, it looks as if your wish would be gratified. Your friend has had an epileptic fit, but the physical shock has started his mental machinery again. He has recovered his faculties: his memory is returning; he thinks and speaks coherently; he is as sane as you and I."

"And—" said Josephine questioning the doctor's knitted eyebrows.

"I am not yet sure whether it was the result of some shock he doesn't remember, or an irritation of the brain, which would indicate that the operation had not been successful, and that there was still some physical pressure or obstruction there—in which case he would be subject to these attacks all his life."

"Do you think his reason came before the fit or after?" asked the girl anxiously.

"I couldn't say. Had anything happened?"

"I was away, and found him on the floor on my return," she answered half uneasily. After a pause she said, "Then he has told you his name, and all about himself?"

"Yes; it's nothing at all! He was a stranger just arrived from the States, going to the mines—the old story; had no near relations, of course; wasn't missed or asked after; remembers walking along the ridge and falling over; name, John Baxter of Maine." He paused, and relaxing into a slight smile, added, "I haven't spoiled your romance, have I?"

"No," she said, with an answering smile. Then as the doctor walked briskly away she slightly knitted her pretty brows, hung her head, patted the ground with her little foot beyond the hem of her gown, and said to herself, "The man was lying to him."

Chapter III

On her return to the house, Josephine apparently contented herself with receiving the bulletin of the stranger's condition from the servant, for she did not enter his room. She had obtained no theory of last night's incident from her parents, who, beyond a querulous agitation that was quickened by the news of his return to reason, refrained from even that insidious comment which she half feared would follow. When another day passed without her seeing him, she nevertheless was conscious of a little embarrassment when his attendant brought her the request that she would give him a moment's speech in the porch, whither he had been removed.

She found him physically weaker; indeed, so much so that she was fain, even in her embarrassment, to assist him back to the bench from which he had ceremoniously risen. But she was so struck with the change in his face and manner, a change so virile and masterful, in spite of its gentle sadness of manner, that she recoiled with a slight timidity as if he had been a stranger, although she was also conscious that he seemed to be more at his ease than she was. He began in a low exhausted voice, but before he had finished his first sentence she felt herself in the presence of a superior.

"My thanks come very late, Miss Forsyth," he said, with a faint smile; "but no one knows better than yourself the reason why, or can better understand that they mean that the burden you have so generously taken on yourself is about to be lifted. I know all, Miss Forsyth. Since yesterday I have learned how much I owe you—even my life, I believe, though I am afraid I must tell you in the same breath that *that* is of little worth to any one. You have kindly helped and interested yourself in a poor stranger who turns out to be a nobody, without friends, without romance, and without even mystery. You found me lying in the road down yonder, after a stupid accident that might have happened to any other careless tramp, and which scarcely gave me a claim to a bed in the county hospital, much less under this kindly roof. It was not my fault, as you know, that all this did not come out sooner; but while it doesn't lessen your generosity, it doesn't lessen my debt, and although I cannot hope to ever repay you, I can at least keep the score from running on. Pardon my speaking so bluntly, but my excuse for speaking at all was to say 'Good-bye' and 'God bless you.' Dr. Duchesne has promised to give me a lift on my way in his buggy when he goes."

There was a slight touch of consciousness in his voice in spite of its sadness, which struck the young girl as a weak and even ungentlemanly note in his otherwise self-abnegating and undemonstrative attitude. If he was a common tramp, he wouldn't talk in that way, and if he wasn't, why did he lie? Her practical good sense here asserted itself.

"But you are far from strong yet; in fact, the doctor says you might have a relapse at any moment, and you have—that is, you *seem* to have, no money," she said gravely.

"That's true," he said quickly. "I remember I was quite played out when I entered the settlement, and I think I had parted from even some little trifles I carried with me. I am afraid I was a poor find to those who picked me up, and you ought to have taken warning. But the doctor has offered to lend me enough to take me to San Francisco, if only to give a fair trial to the machine he has set once more a-going."

"Then you have friends in San Francisco?" said the young girl quickly. "Those who know you? Why not write to them first, and tell them you are here?"

"I don't think your postmaster here would be preoccupied with letters for John Baxter if I did," he said quietly. "But here is the doctor waiting. Good-bye."

He stood looking at her in a peculiar, yet half-resigned way, and held out his hand. For a moment she hesitated. Had he been less independent and strong she would have refused to let him go—have offered him some slight employment at the ranche; for oddly enough, in spite of the suspicion that he was concealing something, she felt that she would have trusted him, and he would have been a help to her. But he was not only determined, but *she* was all the time conscious that he was a totally different man from the one she had taken care of, and merely ordinary prudence demanded that she should know something more of him first. She gave him her hand constrainedly; he pressed it warmly.

Dr. Duchesne drove up, helped him into the buggy, smiled a good-natured but half-perfunctory assurance that he would look after "her patient," and drove away.

The whole thing was over, but so unexpectedly, so suddenly, so unromantically, so unsatisfactorily, that, although her common-sense told her that it was perfectly natural, proper, business-like, and reasonable, and, above all, final and complete, she did not know whether to laugh or be angry. Yet this was her parting from the man who had but a few days ago moved her to tears with a single hopeless gesture. Well, this would teach her what to expect. Well, what had she expected? Nothing!

Yet for the rest of the day she was unreasonably irritable, and if the conjointure be not paradoxical, severely practical and inhumanly just. Falling foul of some presumption of Miguel's, based upon his prescriptive rights through long service on the estate, with the recollection of her severity towards his antagonist in her mind, she rated that trusted retainer with such pitiless equity and unfeminine logic that his hot Latin blood chilled in his veins, and he stood livid on the road. Then, informing Dick Shipley with equally relentless calm that she might feel it necessary to change *all* her foremen unless they could agree in harmony, she sought the dignified seclusion of her castle. But her respected parents, whose triumphant relief at the stranger's departure had emboldened them to await her return in the porch with bended bows of invective and lifted javelins of aggression, recoiled before the resistless helm of this cold-browed Minerva, who galloped contemptuously past them.

Nevertheless, she sat late that night at her desk. The cold moon looked down upon her window and lit up the empty porch where her silent guest had mutely watched her. For a moment she regretted that he had recovered his reason, excusing herself on the practical ground that he would never have known his dependence, and he would have been better cared for by her. She felt restless and uneasy. This slight divergence from the practical groove in which her life had been set had disturbed her in many other things, and given her the first views of the narrowness of it.

Suddenly she heard a step in the porch. The lateness of the hour, perhaps some other reason, seemed to startle her, and she half rose. The next moment the figure of Miguel appeared at the doorway, and with a quick hurried look around him and at the open window he approached her. He was evidently under great excitement. His hollow shaven cheek looked like a waxen effigy in the mission church, his yellow tobacco-stained eye glittered like phosphorescent amber, his lank grey hair was damp and perspiring; but more striking than this was the evident restraint he had put upon himself, pressing his broad-brimmed *sombrero* with both of his trembling yellow hands against his breast. The young girl cast a hurried glance at the open window and at the gun which stood in the corner, and then confronted him with clear and steady eyes, but a paler cheek.

Ah, he began in Spanish, which he himself had taught her as a child. It was a strange thing, his coming there tonight; but then, Mother of God! it was a strange, a terrible thing that she had done to him—old Miguel, her uncle's servant: he that had known her as a *muchacha;* he that had lived all his life at the ranche—ay, and whose fathers before him had lived there all *their* lives and driven the cattle over the very spot where she now stood, before the thieving Americans came here! But he would be calm; yes, the señora should find him calm, even as she was when she told him to go. He would not speak. No, he—Miguel—would contain himself; yes, he *had* mastered himself, but could he restrain others? Ah yes, *others*—that was it. Could he keep Manuel and Pepe and Dominguez from talking to the millman —that leaking sieve, that gabbling brute of a Shipley, for whose sake she had cast off her old servant that very day.

She looked at him with cold astonishment, but without fear. Was he drunk with *aguardiente,* or had his jealousy turned his brain? He continued gasping, but still pressing his hat against his breast.

Ah, he saw it all! Yes, it was to-day, the day he left. Yes, she had thought it safe to cast Miguel off now—now that *he* was gone.

Without in the least understanding him, the colour had leaped to her cheek, and the consciousness of it made her furious.

"How dare you?" she said passionately. "What has that stranger to do with my affairs or your insolence?"

He stopped and gazed at her with a certain admiring loyalty. "Ah! so," he said, with a deep breath, "the señora is the niece of her uncle. She does well not to fear *him*—a dog"—with a slight shrug—"who is more than repaid by the señora's condescension. *He* dare not speak!"

"Who dare not speak? Are you mad?" She stopped with a sudden terrible instinct of apprehension. "Miguel," she said in her deepest voice, "answer me, I command you! Do you know anything of this man?"

It was Miguel's turn to recoil from his mistress. "Ah! my God, is it possible the señora has not suspect?"

"Suspect!" said Josephine haughtily, albeit her proud heart was beating quickly. "I *suspect* nothing. I command you to tell me what you *know.*"

Miguel turned with a rapid gesture and closed the door. Then, drawing her away from the window, he said in a hurried whisper—

"I know that that man has not the name of Baxter! I know that he has the name of Randolph, a young gambler, who have won a large sum at Sacramento, and, fearing to be robbed by those he won of, have walk to himself through the road in disguise of a miner. I know that your brother Esteban have decoyed him here, and have fallen on him."

"Stop!" said the young girl, her eyes, which had been fixed with the agony of conviction, suddenly flashing with the energy of despair. "And you call yourself the servant of my uncle, and dare say this of his nephew?"

"Yes, señora," broke out the old man passionately. "It is because I am the servant of your uncle that I, and *I alone,* dare say it to you! It is because I perjured my soul, and have perjured my soul to deny it elsewhere, that I now dare to say it! It is because I, your servant, knew it from one of my countrymen who was of the gang—because I, Miguel, knew that your brother was not far away that night, and because I, whom you would dismiss, have picked up this pocket-book of Randolph's and your brother's ring which he have dropped and I have found beneath the body of the man you sent me to fetch."

He drew a packet from his bosom, and tossed it on the desk before her.

"And why have you not told me this before?" said Josephine passionately.

Miguel shrugged his shoulders.

"What good? Possibly this dog Randolph would die. Possibly he would live—as a lunatic. Possibly would happen what has happened. The señora is beautiful. The American has eyes. If the Doña Josephine's beauty shall finish what the silly Don Esteban's arm have begun—what matter?"

"Stop!" cried Josephine, pressing her hands across her shuddering eyelids. Then uncovering her white and set face, she said rapidly, "Saddle my horse and your own at once. Then take your choice! Come with me and repeat all that you have said in the presence of that man, or leave this ranche for ever. For if I live I shall go to him to-night, and tell the whole story."

The old man cast a single glance at his mistress, shrugged his shoulders, and, without a word, left the room. But in ten minutes they were on their way to the county town.

Day was breaking over the distant Burnt Ridge—a faint sombre level, like a funeral pall, in the dim horizon—as they drew up before the gaunt white-painted pile of the hospital building. Josephine uttered a cry; Dr. Duchesne's buggy was before the door. On its very threshold they met the doctor, dark and irritated. "Then you heard the news?" he said quickly.

Josephine turned her white face to the doctor's. "What news?" she asked, in a voice that seemed strangely deep and resonant.

"The poor fellow had another attack last night, and died of exhaustion about an hour ago. I was too late to save him."

"Did he say anything? Was he conscious?" asked the girl hoarsely.

"No; incoherent! Now I think of it, he harped on the same string as he did the night of the operation. What was it he said? you remember."

" 'You'll have to kill me first,' " repeated Josephine in a choking voice.

"Yes; something about his dying before he'd tell. Well, he came back to it before he went off—they often do. You seem a little hoarse with your morning ride. You should take care of that voice of yours. By the way, it's a good deal like your brother's."

The Châtelaine of Burnt Ridge never married.

Through the Santa Clara Wheat

Chapter I

IT WAS AN enormous wheat-field in the Santa Clara valley, stretching to the horizon line unbroken. The meridian sun shone upon it without glint or shadow; but at times, when a stronger gust of the trade winds passed over it, there was a quick slanting impression of the whole surface that was, however, as unlike a billow as itself was unlike a sea. Even when a lighter zephyr played down its long level the agitation was superficial, and seemed only to momentarily lift a veil of greenish mist that hung above its immovable depths. Occasional puffs of dust alternately rose and fell along an imaginary line across the field, as if a current of air were passing through it, but were otherwise inexplicable.

Suddenly a faint shout, apparently somewhere in the vicinity of the line, brought out a perfectly clear response, followed by the audible murmur of voices which it was impossible to localise. Yet the whole field was so devoid of any suggestion of human life or motion that it seemed rather as if the vast expanse itself had become suddenly articulate and intelligible.

"Wot say?"

354

"Wheel off."

"Whar?"

"In the road."

One of the voices here indicated itself in the direction of the line of dust, and said, "Comin'," and a man stepped out from the wheat into a broad and dusty avenue.

With his presence three things became apparent.

First, that the puffs of dust indicated the existence of the invisible avenue through the unlimited and unfenced field of grain; secondly, that the stalks of wheat on either side of it were so tall as to actually hide a passing vehicle; and thirdly, that a vehicle had just passed, had lost a wheel, and been dragged partly into the grain by its frightened horse, which a dusty man was trying to restrain and pacify.

The horse, given up to equine hysterics, and evidently convinced that the ordinary buggy behind him had been changed into some dangerous and appalling creation, still plunged and kicked violently to rid himself of it. The man who had stepped out of the depths of the wheat quickly crossed the road, unhitched the traces, drew back the vehicle, and, glancing at the traveller's dusty and disordered clothes, said, with curt sympathy—

"Spilt, too; but not hurt, eh?"

"No, neither of us. I went over with the buggy when the wheel cramped, but *she* jumped clear."

He made a gesture indicating the presence of another. The man turned quickly. There was a second figure, a young girl standing beside the grain from which he had emerged, embracing a few stalks of wheat with one arm and a hand in which she still held her parasol, while she grasped her gathered skirts with the other, and trying to find a secure foothold for her two neat narrow slippers on a crumbling cake of adobe above the fathomless dust of the roadway. Her face, although annoyed and discontented, was pretty, and her light dress and slim figure were suggestive of a certain superior condition.

The man's manner at once softened with Western courtesy. He swung his broad-brimmed hat from his head, and bent his body with the ceremoniousness of the country ball-room. "I reckon the lady had better come up to the shanty out o' the dust and sun till we kin help you get these things fixed," he said to the driver. "I'll send round by the road for your hoss, and have one of mine fetch up your waggon."

"Is it far?" asked the girl, slightly acknowledging his salutation, without waiting for her companion to reply.

"Only a step this way," he answered, motioning to the field of wheat beside her.

"What! In *there?* I never could go in there," she said decidedly.

"It's a heap shorter than by the road, and not so dusty. I'll go with
you and pilot you."

The young girl cast a vexed look at her companion as the probable
cause of all this trouble, and shook her head. But at the same moment
one little foot slipped from the adobe into the dust again. She instantly
clambered back with a little feminine shriek, and ejaculated, "Well, of
all things!" and then, fixing her blue annoyed eyes on the stranger,
asked impatiently, "Why couldn't I go there by the road in the waggon? I could manage to hold on and keep in."

"Because I reckon you'd find it too pow'ful hot waitin' here till we
got round to ye."

There was no doubt it was very hot, the radiation from the baking
roadway beating up under her parasol and pricking her cheek-bones
and eyeballs like needles. She gave a fastidious little shudder, furled
her parasol, gathered her skirts still tighter, faced about, and said, "Go
on, then." The man slipped backwards into the ranks of stalks, parting
them with one hand and holding out the other as if to lead her. But
she evaded the invitation by holding her tightly-drawn skirt with both
hands and bending her head forward as if she had not noticed it. The
next moment the road, and even the whole outer world disappeared
behind them, and they seemed floating in a choking green translucent
mist.

But the effect was only momentary; a few steps farther she found
that she could walk with little difficulty between the ranks of stalks,
which were regularly spaced, and the resemblance now changed to
that of a long pillared conservatory of greenish glass, that touched all
objects with its pervading hue. She also found that the close air above
her head was continually freshened by the interchange of currents of
lower temperature from below—as if the whole vast field had a circu-
lation of its own—and that the adobe beneath her feet was gratefully
cool to her tread. There was no dust, as he had said; what had at first
half suffocated her seemed to be some stimulating aroma of creation
that filled the narrow green aisles, and now imparted a strange vigour
and excitement to her as she walked along. Meantime her guide was
not conversationally idle. Now, no doubt, she had never seen anything
like this before? It was ordinary wheat, only it was grown on adobe
soil—the richest in the valley. These stalks, she could see herself, were
ten and twelve feet high. That was the trouble, they all ran too much
to stalk, although the grain yield was "suthen' pow'ful." She could tell
that to her friends, for he reckoned she was the only young lady that
had ever walked under such a growth. Perhaps she was new to
Californy? He thought so from the start. Well, this was Californy, and
this was not the least of the ways it could "lay over" every other

country on God's yearth. Many folks thought it was the gold and the climate, but she could see for herself what it could do with wheat. He wondered if her brother had ever told her of it? No, the stranger wasn't her brother. Nor cousin, nor company? No; only the hired driver from a San José hotel, who was takin' her over to Major Randolph's. Yes, he knew the old Major; the ranche was a pretty place, nigh unto three miles farther on. Now that he knew the driver was no relation of hers he didn't mind telling her that the buggy was a "rather old consarn," and the driver didn't know his business. Yes, it might be fixed up so as to take her over to the Major's; there was one of their own men—a young fellow—who could do anything that *could* be done with wood and iron—a reg'lar genius!—and *he'd* tackle it. It might take an hour, but she'd find it quite cool waiting in the shanty. It was a rough place, for they only camped out there during the season to look after the crop, and lived at their own homes the rest of the time. Was she going to stay long at the Major's? He noticed she had not brought her trunk with her. Had she known the Major's wife long? Perhaps she thought of settling in the neighbourhood?

All this naïve, good-humoured questioning—so often cruelly misunderstood as mere vulgar curiosity, but as often the courteous instinct of simple unaffected people to entertain the stranger by inviting him to talk of what concerns himself rather than their ownselves—was nevertheless, I fear, met only by monosyllables from the young lady or an impatient question in return. She scarcely raised her eyes to the broad jean-shirted back that preceded her through the grain until the man abruptly ceased talking, and his manner, without losing its half-paternal courtesy, became graver. She was beginning to be conscious of her incivility, and was trying to think of something to say, when he exclaimed, with a slight air of relief, "Here we are!" and the shanty suddenly appeared before them.

It certainly was very rough—a mere shell of unpainted boards that scarcely rose above the level of the surrounding grain, and a few yards distant was invisible. Its slightly sloping roof, already warped and shrunken into long fissures that permitted glimpses of the steel-blue sky above, was evidently intended only as a shelter from the cloudless sun in those two months of rainless days and dewless nights when it was inhabited. Through the open doors and windows she could see a row of "bunks" or rude sleeping berths against the walls, furnished with coarse mattresses and blankets. As the young girl halted, the man with an instinct of delicacy hurried forward, entered the shanty, and dragging a rude bench to the doorway, placed it so that she could sit beneath the shade of the roof yet with her back to these domestic revelations. Two or three men, who had been apparently lounging

there, rose quietly and unobtrusively withdrew. Her guide brought her
a tin cup of deliciously cool water, exchanged a few hurried words
with his companions, and then disappeared with them, leaving her
alone.

Her first sense of relief from their company was, I fear, stronger
than any other feeling. After a hurried glance around the deserted
apartment she arose, shook out her dress and mantle, and then going
into the darkest corner supported herself with one hand against the
wall while with the other she drew off, one by one, her slippers from
her slim, striped-stockinged feet, shook and blew out the dust that had
penetrated within, and put them on again. Then, perceiving a triangular fragment of looking-glass nailed against the wall, she settled the
strings of her bonnet by the aid of its reflection, patted the fringe of
brown hair on her forehead with her separated five fingers as if playing
an imaginary tune on her brow, and came back with maidenly abstraction to the doorway.

Everything was quiet, and her seclusion seemed unbroken. A smile
played for an instant in the soft shadows of her eyes and mouth as she
recalled the abrupt withdrawal of the men. Then her mouth straightened and her brows slightly bent. It was certainly very unmannerly in
them to go off in that way. "Good heavens! couldn't they have stayed
around without talking? Surely it didn't require four men to go and
bring up that waggon?" She picked up her parasol from the bench
with an impatient little jerk. Then she held out her ungloved hand into
the hot sunshine beyond the door with the gesture she would have
used had it been raining, and withdrew it as quickly—her hand quite
scorched in the burning rays. Nevertheless, after another impatient
pause she desperately put up her parasol and stepped from the shanty.

Presently she was conscious of a faint sound of hammering not far
away. Perhaps there was another shed, but hidden like everything else
in this monotonous ridiculous grain. Some stalks, however, were trodden down and broken around the shanty; she could move more easily
and see where she was going. To her delight, a few steps farther
brought her into a current of the trade-wind and a cooler atmosphere.
And a short distance beyond them, certainly, was the shed from which
the hammering proceeded. She approached it boldly.

It was simply a roof upheld by rude uprights and crossbeams, and
open to the breeze that swept through it. At one end was a small
blacksmith's forge, some machinery, and what appeared to be part of a
small steam-engine. Midway of the shed was a closet or cupboard
fastened with a large padlock. Occupying its whole length on the other
side was a work-bench, and at the farther end stood the workman she
had heard.

He was apparently only a year or two older than herself, and clad in blue jean overalls, blackened and smeared with oil and coal-dust. Even his youthful face, which he turned towards her, had a black smudge running across it and almost obliterating a small auburn moustache. The look of surprise that he gave her, however, quickly passed; he remained patiently and in a half-preoccupied way, holding his hammer in his hand as she advanced. This was evidently the young fellow who could "do anything that could be done with wood and iron."

She was very sorry to disturb him, but could he tell her how long it would be before the waggon could be brought up and mended? He could not say that until he himself saw what was to be done; if it was only a matter of the wheel he could fix it up in a few moments; if, as he had been told, it was a case of twisted or bent axle it would take longer, but it would be here very soon. Ah, then, would he let her wait here, as she was very anxious to know at once, and it was much cooler than in the other shed? Certainly; he would go over and bring her a bench. But here she begged he wouldn't trouble himself; she could sit anywhere comfortably.

The lower end of the work-bench was covered with clean and odorous shavings; she lightly brushed them aside and, with a youthful movement, swung herself to a seat upon it, supporting herself on one hand as she leaned towards him. She could thus see that his eyes were of a light yellowish-brown, like clarified honey, with a singular look of clear concentration in them, which, however, was the same whether turned upon his work, the surrounding grain, or upon her. This, and his sublime unconsciousness of the smudge across his face and his blackened hands, made her wonder if the man who could do everything with wood and iron was above doing anything with water. She had half a mind to tell him of it, particularly as she noticed also that his throat below the line of sunburn disclosed by his open collar was quite white, and his grimy hands well-made. She was wondering whether he would be affronted if she said in her politest way, "I beg your pardon, but do you know you have quite accidentally got something on your face," and offer her handkerchief, which, of course, he would decline, when her eye fell on the steam-engine.

"How odd! Do you use that on the farm?"

"No"—he smiled here, the smudge accenting it and setting off his white teeth in a Christy Minstrel fashion that exasperated her—no, although it *could* be used, and had been. But it was his first effort, made two years ago, when he was younger and more inexperienced. It was a rather rough thing, she could see—but he had to make it at odd times with what iron he could pick up or pay for, and at different forges where he worked.

She begged his pardon—where—
Where he worked.
Ah, then he was the machinist or engineer here?
No, he worked here just like the others, only he was allowed to put up a forge while the grain was green, and have his bench in consideration of the odd jobs he could do in the way of mending tools, &c. There was a heap of mending and welding to do—she had no idea how quickly agricultural machines got out of order! He had done much of his work on the steam-engine on moonlit nights. Yes; she had no idea how perfectly clear and light it was here in the valley on such nights; although of course the shadows were very dark, and when he dropped a screw or a nut it was difficult to find. He had worked there because it saved time and because it didn't cost anything, and he had nobody to look on or interfere with him. No, it was not lonely; the coyotes and wild cats sometimes came very near, but were always more surprised and frightened than he was; and once a horseman who had strayed off the distant road yonder mistook him for an animal and shot at him twice.

He told all this with such freedom from embarrassment, and with such apparent unconsciousness of the blue eyes that were following him, and the light, graceful figure—which was so near his own that in some of his gestures his grimy hands almost touched its delicate garments—that, accustomed as she was to a certain masculine aberration in her presence, she was greatly amused by his naïve acceptance of her as an equal. Suddenly, looking frankly in her face, he said—

"I'll show you a secret, if you care to see it."

Nothing would please her more.

He glanced hurriedly around, took a key from his pocket, and unlocked the padlock that secured the closet she had noticed. Then, reaching within, with infinite care he brought out a small mechanical model.

"There's an invention of my own. A reaper and thresher combined. I'm going to have it patented and have a big one made from this model. This will work, as you see."

He then explained to her with great precision how as it moved over the field the double operation was performed by the same motive-power. That it would be a saving of a certain amount of labour and time which she could not remember. She did not understand a word of his explanations; she saw only a clean and pretty but complicated toy, that under the manipulation of his grimy fingers rattled a number of frail-like staves and worked a number of wheels and drums, yet there was no indication of her ignorance in her sparkling eyes and smiling, breathless attitude. Perhaps she was interested in his own absorption;

the revelation of his pre-occupation with this model struck her as if he had made her a *confidante* of some boyish passion for one of her own sex, and she regarded him with the same sympathising superiority.

"You will make a fortune out of it," she said pleasantly.

Well, he might make enough to be able to go on with some other inventions he had in his mind. They cost money and time, no matter how careful one was.

This was another interesting revelation to the young girl. He not only did not seem to care for the profit his devotion brought him, but even his one beloved ideal might be displaced by another. So like a man after all!

Her reflections were broken upon by the sound of voices. The young man carefully replaced the model in its closet with a parting glance as if he was closing a shrine, and said, "There comes the waggon." The young girl turned to face the men who were dragging it from the road, with the half-complacent air of having been victorious over their late rude abandonment, but they did not seem to notice it or to be surprised at her companion, who quickly stepped forward and examined the broken vehicle with workmanlike deliberation.

"I hope you will be able to do something with it," she said sweetly, appealing directly to him. "I should thank you *so much.*"

He did not reply. Presently he looked up to the man who had brought her to the shanty, and said, "The axle's strained, but it's safe for five or six miles more of this road. I'll put the wheel on easily." He paused, and without glancing at her continued, "You might send her on by the cart."

"Pray don't trouble yourselves," interrupted the young girl, with a pink uprising in her cheeks; "I shall be quite satisfied with the buggy as it stands." Send her on in the cart, indeed! Really they were a rude set—*all* of them.

Without taking the slightest notice of her remark, the man replied gravely to the young mechanic, "Yes, but we'll be wanting the cart before it can get back from taking her."

"Her" again. "I assure you the buggy will serve perfectly well—if this—gentleman—will only be kind enough to put on the wheel again," she returned hotly.

The young mechanic at once set to work. The young girl walked apart silently until the wheel was restored to its axle. But to her surprise a different horse was led forward to be harnessed.

"We thought your horse wasn't safe in case of another accident," said the first man, with the same smileless consideration. "This one wouldn't cut up if he was harnessed to an earthquake or a worse driver than you've got."

It occurred to her instantly that the more obvious remedy of sending another driver had been already discussed and rejected by them.
Yet, when her own driver appeared a moment afterwards, she ascended to her seat with some dignity and a slight increase of colour.

"I am very much obliged to you all," she said, without glancing at
the young inventor.

"Don't mention it, miss."

"Good afternoon."

"Good afternoon." They all took off their hats with the same formal
gravity as the horse moved forward, but turned back to their work
again before she was out of the field.

Chapter II

The ranche of Major Randolph lay on a rich *falda* of the Coast Range,
and overlooked the great wheat plains that the young girl had just left.
The house of wood and adobe, buried to its first storey in rose-trees
and passion vines, was large and commodious. Yet it contained only
the Major, his wife, her son and daughter, and the few occasional
visitors from San Francisco whom he entertained and she tolerated.

For the Major's household was not entirely harmonious. While a
young infantry subaltern at a Gulf station, he had been attracted by
the piquant foreign accent and dramatic gestures of a French Creole
widow, and—believing them, in the first flush of his youthful passion,
more than an offset to the encumbrance of her two children who, with
the memory of various marital infidelities, were all her late husband
had left her—had proposed, been accepted, and promptly married to
her. Before he obtained his captaincy she had partly lost her accent,
and those dramatic gestures, which had accented the passion of their
brief courtship, began to intensify domestic altercation and the bursts
of idle jealousy to which she was subject. Whether she was revenging
herself on her second husband for the faults of her first is not known,
but it was certain that she brought an unhallowed knowledge of the
weaknesses, cheap cynicism, and vanity of a foreign predecessor to sit
in judgment upon the simple-minded and chivalrous American soldier
who had succeeded him, and who was, in fact, the most loyal of husbands. The natural result of her scepticism was an espionage and criticism of the wives of the Major's brother officers that compelled a
frequent change of quarters. When to this was finally added a racial
divergence and antipathy, the public disparagement of the customs
and education of her female colleagues, and the sudden insistence of a
foreign and French dominance in her household beyond any ordinary

Creole justification, Randolph, presumably to avoid later international complications, resigned while he was as yet a major. Luckily his latest banishment to an extreme Western outpost had placed him in California during the flood of a speculation epoch. He purchased a valuable Spanish grant to three leagues of land for little over a three months' pay. Following that yearning which compels retired ship-captains and rovers of all degrees to buy a farm in their old days, the Major, professionally and socially inured to border strife, sought surcease and Arcadian repose in ranching.

It was here that Mrs. Randolph, late relict of the late Scipion l'Hommadieu, devoted herself to bringing up her children after the extremest of French methods, and in resurrecting a "de" from her own family to give a distinct and aristocratic character to their name. The "de Fontanges l'Hommadieu" were, however, only known to their neighbours—after the Western fashion—by their stepfather's name, when they were known at all, which was seldom. For the boy was unpleasantly conceited as a precocious worldling, and the girl as unpleasantly complacent in her *rôle of ingénue*. The household was completely dominated by Mrs. Randolph. A punctilious Catholic, she attended all the functions of the adjacent Mission, and the shadow of a black *soutane* at twilight gliding through the wild oat-fields behind the ranche had often been mistaken for a coyote. The peace-loving Major did not object to a piety which, while it left his own conscience free, imparted a respectable religious air to his household, and kept him from the equally distasteful approaches of the Puritanism of his neighbours, and was blissfully unconscious that he was strengthening the antagonistic foreign element in his family with an alien Church.

Meantime, as the repaired buggy was slowly making its way towards his house, Major Randolph entered his wife's boudoir with a letter which the San Francisco post had just brought him. A look of embarrassment on his good-humoured face strengthened the hard lines of hers; she felt some momentary weakness of her natural enemy, and prepared to give battle.

"I'm afraid here's something of a muddle, Josephine," he began, with a deprecating smile. "Mallory, who was coming down here with his daughter, you know——"

"This is the first intimation *I* have had that anything has been settled upon," interrupted the lady, with appalling deliberation.

"However, my dear, you know I told you last week that he thought of bringing her here while he went South on business. You know, being a widower, he has no one to leave her with."

"And I suppose it is the American fashion to entrust one's daughters to any old boon companions?"

"Mallory is an old friend," interrupted the Major impatiently. "He knows I'm married, and although he has never seen *you*, he is quite willing to leave his daughter here."

"Thank you!"

"Come, you know what I mean. The man naturally believes that my wife will be a proper chaperon for his daughter. But that is not the present question. He intended to call here; I expected to take you over to San José to see her and all that, you know; but the fact of it is—that is—it seems from this letter that—he's been called away sooner than he expected, and that—well—hang it! the girl is actually on her way here now."

"Alone?"

"I suppose so. You know one thinks nothing of that here."

"Or any other propriety, for that matter."

"For heaven's sake, Josephine, don't be ridiculous! Of course it's stupid her coming in this way, and Mallory ought to have brought her —but she's coming, and we must receive her. By Jove! Here she is now!" he added, starting up after a hurried glance through the window. "But what kind of a d——d turn-out is that, anyhow?"

It certainly was an odd-looking conveyance that had entered the gates, and was now slowly coming up the drive towards the house. A large draught horse harnessed to a dust-covered buggy, whose strained fore-axle, bent by the last mile of heavy road, had slanted the tops of the forewheels towards each other at an alarming angle. The light, graceful dress and elegant parasol of the young girl, who occupied half of its single seat, looked ludicrously pronounced by the side of the slouching figure and grimy duster of the driver, who occupied the other half.

Mrs. Randolph gave a gritty laugh. "I thought you said she was alone. Is that an escort she has picked up, American fashion, on the road?"

"That's her hired driver, no doubt. Hang it! she can't drive here by herself," retorted the Major impatiently, hurrying to the door and down the staircase. But he was instantly followed by his wife. She had no idea of permitting a possible understanding to be exchanged in their first greeting. The late M. l'Hommadieu had been able to impart a whole plan of intrigue in a single word and glance.

Happily, Rose Mallory, already in the hall, in a few words detailed the accident that had befallen her, to the honest sympathy of the Major and the coldly polite concern of Mrs. Randolph, who in deliberately chosen sentences managed to convey to the young girl the conviction that accidents of any kind to young ladies were to be regarded as only a shade removed from indiscretions. Rose was impressed, and even flattered, by the fastidiousness of this foreign-appearing woman, and after the fashion of youthful natures, accorded to her the respect due to recognised authority. When to this authority, which was evident, she added a depreciation of the Major, I fear that some common instinct of feminine tyranny responded in Rose's breast, and that on the very threshold of the honest soldier's home she tacitly agreed with the wife to look down upon him. Mrs. Randolph departed to inform her son and daughter of their guest's arrival. As a matter of fact, however, they had already observed her approach to the house through the slits of their drawn window-blinds, and those even narrower prejudices and limited comprehensions which their education had fostered. The girl, Adele, had only grasped the fact that Rose had come to their house in fine clothes, alone with a man, in a broken-down vehicle, and was moved to easy mirth and righteous wonder. The young man, Emile, had agreed with her, with the mental reservation that the guest was pretty, and must eventually fall in love with him. They both, however, welcomed her with a trained politeness and a superficial attention that, while the indifference of her own countrymen in the wheat-field was still fresh in her recollection, struck her with grateful contrast; the Major's quiet and unobtrusive kindliness naturally made less impression, or was accepted as a matter of course.

"Well," said the Major, cheerfully but tentatively, to his wife when they were alone again, "she seems a nice girl after all; and a good deal of pluck and character, by Jove! to push on in that broken buggy rather than linger or come in a farm cart, eh?"

"She was alone in that wheat-field," said Mrs. Randolph, with grim deliberation, "for half an hour, she confesses it herself—*talking with a young man!*"

"Yes, but the others had gone for the buggy. And, in the name of Heaven, what would you have her do—hide herself in the grain?" said the Major desperately. "Besides," he added, with a recklessness he afterwards regretted, "that mechanical chap they've got there is really intelligent and worth talking to."

"I have no doubt *she* thought so," said Mrs. Randolph, with a mirthless smile. "In fact, I have observed that the American freedom generally means doing what you *want* to do. Indeed, I wonder she didn't bring him with her! Only I beg, Major, that you will not again, in the presence of my daughter—and, I may even say, of my son—talk lightly of the solitary meetings of young ladies with mechanics, even though their faces were smutty and their clothes covered with oil."

The Major here muttered something about there being less danger in a young lady listening to the intelligence of a coarsely-dressed labourer than to the compliments of a rose-scented fop, but Mrs. Randolph walked out of the room before he finished the evident platitude.

That night Rose Mallory retired to her room in a state of self-satisfaction that she even felt was to a certain extent a virtue. She was delighted with her reception, and with her hostess and family. It was strange her father had not spoken more of *Mrs.* Randolph, who was clearly the superior of his old friend. What fine manners they all had, so different from other people she had known! There was quite an old-world civilisation about them; really it was like going abroad! She would make the most of her opportunity, and profit by her visit. She would begin by improving her French; they spoke it perfectly, and with such a pure accent. She would correct certain errors she was conscious of in her own manners, and copy Mrs. Randolph as much as possible. Certainly there was a great deal to be said of Mrs. Randolph's way of looking at things. Now she thought of it calmly, there *was* too much informality and freedom in American ways! There was not enough respect due to position and circumstances. Take those men in the wheat-field, for example. Yet here she found it difficult to formulate an indictment against them for "freedom." She would like to go there some day with the Randolphs and let them see what company manners were! She was thoroughly convinced now that her father had done wrong in sending her alone; it certainly was most disrespectful to them and careless of him (she had quite forgotten that she had herself proposed to her father to go alone rather than wait at the hotel), and she must have looked very ridiculous in her fine clothes and the broken-down buggy. When her trunk came by express to-morrow she would look out something more sober. She must remember that she was in a Catholic and religious household now. Ah yes! how very fine it was to see that priest at dinner in his *soutane,* sitting down like one of the family, and making them all seem like a picture of some historical and aristocratic romance! And then they were actually "de Fontanges l'Hommadieu." How different he was from that shabby Methodist minister who used to come to see her father in a black cravat with a hideous bow! Really there was something to say for a religion that contained so much picturesque refinement; and for her part—— But that will do. I beg to say that I am not writing of any particular snob nor feminine monstrosity, but of a very charming creature, who was quite able to say her prayers afterwards like a good girl, and lay her pretty cheek upon her pillow without a blush.

She opened her window and looked out. The moon, a great silver dome, was uplifting itself from a bluish-grey level, which she knew was the distant plain of wheat. Somewhere in its midst appeared a dull star, at times brightening as if blown upon or drawn upwards in a comet-like trail. By some odd instinct she felt that it was the solitary forge of the young inventor, and pictured him standing before it with his abstracted hazel eyes and a face more begrimed in the moonlight than ever. When *did* he wash himself? Perhaps not until Sunday. How lonely it must be out there! She slightly shivered and turned from the window. As she did so, it seemed to her that something knocked against her door from without. Opening it quickly, she was almost certain that the sound of a rustling skirt retreated along the passage. It was very late; perhaps she had disturbed the house by shutting her window. No doubt it was the motherly interest of Mrs. Randolph that impelled her to softly come and look after her; and for once her simple surmises were correct. For not only the inspecting eyes of her hostess, but the amatory glances of the youthful Emile, had been fastened upon her window until the light disappeared, and even the Holy Mission Church of San José had assured itself of the dear child's safety with a large and supple ear at her keyhole.

The next morning Major Randolph took her with Adele in a light carriole over the ranche. Although his domain was nearly as large as the adjoining wheat-plain, it was not, like that, monopolised by one enormous characteristic yield, but embraced a more diversified product. There were acres and acres of potatoes in rows of endless and varying succession; there were miles of wild oats and barley, which overtopped them as they drove in narrow lanes of dry and dusty monotony; there were orchards of pears, apricots, peaches, and nectarines, and vineyards of grapes, so comparatively dwarfed in height that they scarcely reached to the level of their eyes, yet laden and breaking beneath the weight of their ludicrously disproportionate fruit. What seemed to be a vast green plateau covered with tiny patches, that bounded the northern edge of the prospect, was an enormous bed of strawberry plants. But everywhere, crossing the track, bounding the fields, orchards, and vineyards, intersecting the paths of the whole domain, were narrow irrigating ducts and channels of running water.

"Those," said the Major poetically, "are the veins and arteries of the ranche. Come with me now, and I'll show you its pulsating heart." Descending from the waggon into pedestrian prose again, he led Rose a hundred yards farther to a shed that covered a wonderful artesian well. In the centre of a basin a column of water rose regularly with the even flow and volume of a brook. "It is one of the largest in the State," said the Major, "and is the life of all that grows here during six months of the year."

Pleased as the young girl was with those evidences of the prosperity and position of her host, she was struck, however, with the fact that the farm-labourers, vine-growers, nurserymen, and all field hands scattered on the vast estate were apparently of the same independent, unpastoral, and unprofessional character as the men of the wheat-field. There were no cottages or farm buildings that she could see, nor any apparent connection between the household and the estate; far from suggesting tenantry or retainers, the men who were working in the fields glanced at them as they passed with the indifference of strangers, or replied to the Major's greetings or questionings with perfect equality of manner, or even business-like reserve and caution. Her host explained that the ranche was worked by a company "on shares," that those labourers were, in fact, the bulk of the company, and that he, the Major, only furnished the land, the seed, and the implements. "That man who was driving the long roller, and with whom you were indignant because he wouldn't get out of our way, is the president of the company."

"That needn't make him so uncivil," said Rose poutingly, "for if it comes to that, you're the *landlord,*" she added triumphantly.

"No," said the Major good-humouredly. "I am simply the man driving the lighter and more easily-managed team for pleasure, and he's the man driving the heavier and more difficult machine for work. It's for me to get out of his way; and looked at in the light of my being *the landlord,* it is still worse, for as we're working 'on shares' I'm interrupting *his* work and reducing *his* profits merely because I choose to sacrifice my own."

I need not say that those atrociously levelling sentiments were received by the young ladies with that feminine scorn which is only qualified by misconception. Rose, who, under the influence of her hostess, had a vague impression that they sounded something like the French Revolution, and that Adele must feel like the Princess Elizabeth, rushed to her relief like a good girl. "But, Major, now, *you're* a gentleman, and if *you* had been driving that roller you know you would have turned out for us."

"I don't know about that," said the Major mischievously; "but if I had, I should have known that the other fellow who accepted it wasn't a gentleman."

But Rose, having sufficiently shown her partisanship in the discussion, after the feminine fashion, did not care particularly for the logical result. After a moment's silence she resumed. "And the wheat ranche below—is that carried on in the same way?"

"Yes. But their landlord is a bank, who advances not only the land but the money to work it, and doesn't ride around in a buggy with a couple of charmingly distracting young ladies."

"And do they all share alike?" continued Rose, ignoring the pleasantry, "big and little—that young inventor with the rest?"

She stopped. She felt the *ingénue's* usually complacent eyes suddenly fixed upon her with an unhallowed precocity, and as quickly withdrawn. Without knowing why, she felt embarrassed, and changed the subject.

The next day they drove to the Convent of Santa Clara and the Mission College of San José. Their welcome at both places seemed to Rose to be a mingling of caste greeting and spiritual zeal, and the austere seclusion and reserve of those cloisters repeated that suggestion of an old-world civilisation that had already fascinated the young Western girl. They made other excursions in the vicinity, but did not extend it to a visit to their few neighbours. With their reserved and exclusive ideas this fact did not strike Rose as peculiar, but on a later shopping expedition to the town of San José, a certain reticence and aggressive sensitiveness on the part of the shopkeepers and tradespeople towards the Randolphs produced an unpleasant impression on her mind. She could not help noticing, too, that after the first stare of astonishment which greeted her appearance with her hostess, she herself was included in the antagonism. With her youthful prepossession for her friends, this distinction she regarded as flattering and aristocratic, and I fear she accented it still more by discussing with Mrs. Randolph the merits of the shopkeepers' wares in schoolgirl French before them. She was unfortunate enough, however, to do this in the shop of a polyglot German.

"Oxcoos me, mees," he said gravely, "but dot lady speeks Engeleesh so goot mit yourselluf, and ven you dells to her dot silk is hallf gotton in English, she onderstand you mooch better and it don't make nodings to me." The laugh which would have followed from her own countrywoman did not, however, break upon the trained faces of the "de Fontanges l'Hommadieus," yet while Rose would have joined in it, albeit a little ruefully, she felt for the first time mortified at their civil insincerity.

At the end of two weeks Major Randolph received a letter from Mr. Mallory. When he had read it, he turned to his wife: "He thanks you," he said, "for your kindness to his daughter, and explains that his sudden departure was owing to the necessity of his taking advantage of a great opportunity for speculation that had offered." As Mrs. Randolph turned away with a slight shrug of the shoulders, the Major continued: "But you haven't heard all! That opportunity was the securing of a half interest in a Cinnabar lode in Sonora, which has already gone up a hundred thousand dollars in his hands! By Jove! a man can afford to drop a little social ceremony on those terms—eh, Josephine?" he concluded, with a triumphant chuckle.

"He's as likely to lose his hundred thousand tomorrow, while his manners will remain," said Mrs. Randolph. "I've no faith in these sudden California fortunes."

"You're wrong as regards Mallory, for he's as careful as he is lucky. He don't throw money away for appearance's sake, or he'd have a rich home for that daughter. He could afford it."

Mrs. Randolph was silent. "She is his only daughter, I believe?" she continued presently.

"Yes—he has no other kith or kin," returned the Major.

"She seems to be very much impressed by Emile," said Mrs. Randolph.

Major Randolph faced his wife quickly. "In the name of all that's ridiculous, my dear, you are not already thinking of——" he gasped.

"I should be very loth to give *my* sanction to anything of the kind, knowing the difference of her birth, education, and religion—although the latter I believe she would readily change," said Mrs. Randolph severely. "But when you speak of *my* already thinking of 'such things,' do you suppose that your friend, Mr. Mallory, didn't consider all that when he sent that girl here?"

"Never," said the Major vehemently; "and if it entered his head now, by Jove, he'd take her away to-morrow—always supposing I didn't anticipate him by sending her off myself."

Mrs. Randolph uttered her mirthless laugh. "And you suppose the girl would go? Really, Major, you don't seem to understand this boasted liberty of your own countrywoman. What does she care for her father's control? Why, she'd make him do just what *she* wanted. But," she added, with an expression of dignity, "perhaps we had better not discuss this until we know something of Emile's feelings in the matter. That is the only question that concerns us." With this she swept out of the room, leaving the Major at first speechless with honest indignation, and then, after the fashion of all guileless natures, a little uneasy and suspicious of his own guilelessness. For a day or two after he found himself, not without a sensation of meanness, watching Rose when in Emile's presence, but he could distinguish nothing more than the frank satisfaction she showed equally to the others. Yet he found himself regretting even that, so subtle was the contagion of his wife's suspicions.

Chapter III

It had been a warm morning; an unusual mist, which the sun had not dissipated, had crept on from the great grainfields beyond, and hung around the house charged with a dry, dusty closeness that seemed to be quite independent of the sun's rays, and more like a heated exhalation or emanation of the soil itself. In its acrid irritation Rose thought she could detect the breath of the wheat as on the day she had plunged into its pale green shadows. By the afternoon this mist had disappeared, apparently in the same mysterious manner, but not scattered by the usual trade wind, which—another unusual circumstance—that day was not forthcoming. There was a breathlessness in the air like the hush of listening expectancy, which filled the young girl with a vague restlessness, and seemed to even affect a scattered company of crows in the field beyond the house, who rose suddenly with startled but aimless wings, and then dropped vacantly among the grain again.

Major Randolph was inspecting a distant part of the ranche, Mrs. Randolph was presumably engaged in her boudoir, and Rose was sitting between Adele and Emile before the piano in the drawing-room, listlessly turning over the leaves of some music. There had been an odd mingling of eagerness and abstraction in the usual attentions of the young man that morning, and a certain nervous affectation in his manner of twisting the ends of a small black moustache, which resembled his mother's eyebrows, that had affected Rose with a half-amused, half-uneasy consciousness, but which she had, however, referred to the restlessness produced by the weather. It occurred to her also that the vacuously amiable Adele had once or twice regarded her with the same precocious childlike curiosity and infantine cunning she had once before exhibited. All this did not, however, abate her admiration for both—perhaps particularly for this picturesquely gentlemanly young fellow, with his gentle audacities of compliment, his caressing attentions, and his unfailing and equal address. And when, discovering that she had mislaid her fan for the fifth time that morning, he started up with equal and undiminished fire to go again and fetch it, the look of grateful pleasure and pleading perplexity in her pretty eyes might have turned a less conceited brain than his.

"But you don't know where it is?"

"I shall find it by instinct."

"You are spoiling me—you two." The parenthesis was a hesitating addition, but she continued, with fresh sincerity, "I shall be quite helpless when I leave here—if I am ever able to go by myself."

"Don't ever go, then."

"But just now I want my fan; it is so close everywhere to-day."

"I fly, mademoiselle."

He started to the door.

She called after him.

"Let me help your instinct, then; I had it last in the Major's study."

"That was where I was going."

He disappeared. Rose got up and moved uneasily towards the window. "How queer and quiet it looks outside. It's really too bad that he should be sent after that fan again. He'll never find it." She resumed her place at the piano, Adele following her with round, expectant eyes. After a pause she started up again. "I'll go and fetch it myself," she said, with a half-embarrassed laugh, and ran to the door.

Scarcely understanding her own nervousness, but finding relief in rapid movement, Rose flew lightly up the staircase. The Major's study, where she had been writing letters during his absence that morning, was at the farther end of a long passage, and near her own bedroom, the door of which, as she passed, she noticed, half-abstractedly, was open, but she continued on and hurriedly entered the study. At the same moment Emile, with a smile on his face, turned towards her with the fan in his hand.

"Oh, you've found it," she said, with nervous eagerness. "I was so afraid you'd have all your trouble for nothing."

She extended her hand, with a half-breathless smile, for the fan, but he caught her outstretched little palm in his own, and held it.

"Ah! but you are not going to leave us, are you?"

In a flash of consciousness she understood him, and as it seemed to her, her own nervousness, and all, and everything. And with it came a swift appreciation of all it meant to her and her future. To be always with him and like him, a part of this refined and restful seclusion—akin to all that had so attracted her in this house; not to be obliged to educate herself up to it, but to be in it on equal terms at once; to know that it was no wild, foolish, youthful fancy, but a wise, thoughtful, and prudent resolve, that her father would understand and her friends respect: these were the thoughts that crowded quickly upon her, more like an explanation of her feelings than a revelation, in the brief second that he held her hand. It was not, perhaps, love as she had dreamed it, and even *believed* it, before. She was not ashamed or embarrassed; she even felt, with a slight pride, that she was not blushing. She raised her eyes frankly. What she *would* have said she did not know, for the door, which he had closed behind her, began to shake violently.

It was not the fear of some angry intrusion or interference surely that made him drop her hand instantly. It was not—her second thought—the idea that some one had fallen in a fit against it that blanched his face with abject and unreasoning terror! It must have been something else that caused him to utter an inarticulate cry and dash out of the room and down the stairs like a madman? What had happened?

In her own self-possession she knew that all this was passing rapidly, that it was not the door now that was still shaking, for it had swung almost shut again—but it was the windows, the book-shelves, the floor beneath her feet, that were all shaking. She heard a hurried scrambling, the trampling of feet below, and the quick rustling of a skirt in the passage, as if some one had precipitately fled from her room. Yet no one had called to her—even *he* had said nothing—whatever had happened they clearly had not cared for her to know.

The jarring and rattling ceased as suddenly, but the house seemed silent and empty. She moved to the door, which had now swung open a few inches, but to her astonishment it was fixed in that position, and she could not pass. As yet she had been free from any personal fear, and even now it was with a half smile at her imprisonment in the Major's study that she rang the bell and turned to the window. A man, whom she recognised as one of the ranche labourers, was standing a hundred feet away in the garden, looking curiously at the house. He saw her face as she tried to raise the sash, uttered an exclamation, and ran forward. But before she could understand what he said, the sash began to rattle in her hand, the jarring recommenced, the floor shook beneath her feet, a hideous sound of grinding seemed to come from the walls, a thin seam of dust-like smoke broke from the ceiling, and with the noise of falling plaster a dozen books followed each other from the shelves, in what, in the frantic hurry of that moment, seemed a grimly deliberate succession; a picture hanging against the wall, to her dazed wonder, swung forward, and appeared to stand at right angles from it; she felt herself reeling against the furniture, a deadly nausea overtook her, and she glanced despairingly towards the window; the outlying fields beyond the garden seemed to be undulating like a sea. For the first time she raised her voice, not in fear, but in a pathetic little cry of apology for her awkwardness in tumbling about, and not being able to grapple this new experience, and then she found herself near the door, which had once more swung free. She grasped it eagerly, and darted out of the study into the deserted passage. Here some instinct made her follow the line of the wall, rather than the shaking balusters of the corridor and staircase, but before she reached the bottom she heard a shout, and the farm labourer she had seen coming towards her seized her by the arm, dragged her to the open doorway of the drawing-room, and halted beneath its arch in the wall. Another thrill, but lighter than before, passed through the building, then all was still again.

"It's over; I reckon that's all just now," said the man coolly. "It's quite safe to cut and run for the garden now, through this window." He half led, half lifted her through the French window to the verandah and the ground, and locking her arm in his, ran quickly forward a hundred feet from the house, stopping at last beneath a large post oak where there was a rustic seat, into which she sank. "You're safe now, I reckon," he said grimly.

She looked towards the house; the sun was shining brightly, a cool breeze seemed to have sprung up as they ran. She could see a quantity of rubbish lying on the roof, from which a dozen yards of zinc gutter were perilously hanging; the broken shafts of the farther cluster of chimneys, a pile of bricks scattered upon the ground and among the battered down beams of the end of the verandah—but that was all. She lifted her now whitened face to the man, and with the apologetic smile still lingering on her lips, asked—

"What does it all mean? What has happened?"

The man stared at her. "D'ye mean to say ye don't know?"

"How could I? They must have all left the house as soon as it began. I was talking to—to M. l'Hommadieu, and he suddenly left."

The man brought his face angrily down within an inch of her own. "D'ye mean to say that them d——d French half-breeds stampeded and left yer there alone?"

She was still too much stupefied by the reaction to fully comprehend his meaning, and repeated feebly, with her smile still faintly lingering, "But you don't tell me *what* it was?"

"An earthquake," said the man roughly, "and if it had lasted ten seconds longer it would have shook the whole shanty down and left you under it. Yer kin tell *that* to them, if they don't know it; but from the way they made tracks to the fields, I reckon they did. They're coming now."

Without another word he turned away half surlily, half defiantly, passing scarce fifty yards away Mrs. Randolph and her daughter, who were hastening towards their guest.

"Oh, here you are!" said Mrs. Randolph, with the nearest approach to effusion that Rose had yet seen in her manner. "We were wondering where you had run to, and were getting quite concerned. Emile was looking for you everywhere."

The recollection of his blank and abject face, his vague outcry and blind fright, came back to Rose with a shock that sent a flash of sympathetic shame to her face. The ingenuous Adele noticed it, and dutifully pinched her mother's arm.

"Emile?" echoed Rose faintly—"looking for *me?*"

Mother and daughter exchanged glances.

"Yes," said Mrs. Randolph cheerfully; "he says he started to run with you, but you got ahead and slipped out of the garden door—or something of the kind," she added, with the air of making light of Rose's girlish fears. "You know one scarcely knows what one does at such times, and it must have been all frightfully strange to *you*—and he's been quite distracted—lest you should have wandered away. Adele, run and tell him Miss Mallory has been here under the oak all the time."

Rose started—and then fell hopelessly back in her seat. Perhaps it *was* true! Perhaps he had not rushed off with that awful face and without a word. Perhaps she herself had been half frightened out of her reason. In the simple weak kindness of her nature it seemed less dreadful to believe that the fault was partly her own.

"And you went back into the house to look for us when all was over," said Mrs. Randolph, fixing her black beady magnetic eyes on Rose, "and that stupid yokel Jake brought you out again. He needn't have clutched your arm so closely, my dear—I must speak to the Major about his excessive familiarity—but I suppose I shall be told that that is American freedom. I call it 'a liberty.' "

It struck Rose that she had not even thanked the man—in the same flash that she remembered something dreadful that he had said. She covered her face with her hands and tried to recall herself.

Mrs. Randolph gently tapped her shoulder with a mixture of maternal philosophy and discipline, and continued: "Of course it's an upset —and you're confused still. That's nothing. They say, dear, it's perfectly well known that no two people's recollections of these things ever are the same. It's really ridiculous, the contradictory stories one hears. Isn't it, Emile?"

Rose felt that the young man had joined them, and was looking at her. In the fear that she should still see some trace of the startled selfish animal in his face, she did not dare to raise her eyes to his, but looked at his mother. Mrs. Randolph was standing then, collected but impatient.

"It's all over now," said Emile in his usual voice, "and except the chimneys and some fallen plaster there's really no damage done. But I'm afraid they have caught it pretty badly at the Mission and at San Francisco, in those tall, flashy, rattle-trap buildings they're putting up. I've just sent off one of the men for news."

Her father was in San Francisco by that time; and she had never thought of *him!* In her quick remorse she now forgot all else and rose to her feet.

"I must telegraph to my father at once," she said hurriedly; "he is there."

"You had better wait until the messenger returns and hear his news," said Emile. "If the shock was only a slight one in San Francisco, your father might not understand you, and would be alarmed."

She could see his face now—there was no record of the past expression upon it, but he was watching her eagerly. Mrs. Randolph and Adele had moved away to speak to the servants. Emile drew nearer.

"You surely will not desert us now?" he said in a low voice.

"Please don't," she said vaguely. "I'm so worried," and, pushing quickly past him, she hurriedly rejoined the two women.

They were superintending the erection of a long tent or marquee in the garden, hastily extemporised from the awnings of the verandah and other cloth. Mrs. Randolph explained that, although all danger was over, there was the possibility of the recurrence of lighter shocks during the day and night, and that they would all feel much more secure and comfortable to camp out for the next twenty-four hours in the open air.

"Only imagine you're picnicking, and you'll enjoy it as most people usually enjoy those horrid *al fresco* entertainments. I don't believe there's the slightest real necessity for it, but," she added in a lower voice, "the Irish and Chinese servants are so demoralised now, they wouldn't stay indoors with us. It's a common practice here, I believe, for a day or two after the shock, and it gives time to put things right again and clear up. The old, one-storied, Spanish houses, with walls three feet thick, and built round a courtyard or *patio,* were much safer. It's only when the Americans try to improve upon the old order of things with their pinchbeck shams and stucco that Providence interferes like this to punish them."

It was the fact, however, that Rose was more impressed by what seemed to her the absolute indifference of Providence in the matter, and the cool resumption by Nature of her ordinary conditions. The sky above their heads was as rigidly blue as ever, and as smilingly monotonous; the distant prospect, with its clear, well-known silhouettes, had not changed; the crows swung on lazy, deliberate wings over the grain as before; and the trade wind was again blowing in its quiet persistency. And yet she knew that something had happened that would never again make her enjoyment of the prospect the same; that nothing would ever be as it was yesterday. I think at first she referred only to the material and larger phenomena, and did not confound this revelation of the insecurity of the universe with her experience of man. Yet the fact also remained that to the conservative, correct, and, as she believed, secure condition to which she had been approximating, all her relations were rudely shaken and upset. It really seemed to this simple-minded young woman that the revolutionary disturbance of settled conditions might have as Providential an origin as the "Divine Right" of which she had heard so much.

Chapter IV

In her desire to be alone and to evade the now significant attentions of Emile, she took advantage of the bustle that followed the hurried transfer of furniture and articles from the house to escape through the garden to the outlying fields. Striking into one of the dusty lanes that she remembered, she wandered on for half an hour, until her progress and meditation were suddenly arrested. She had come upon a long chasm or crack in the soil, fully twenty feet wide and as many in depth, crossing her path at right angles. She did not remember having seen it before; the track of wheels went up to its precipitous edge; she could see the track on the other side, but the hiatus remained unbridged and uncovered. It was not there yesterday. She glanced right and left; the fissure seemed to extend like a moat or ditch, from the distant road to the upland between her and the great wheat valley below, from which she was shut off. An odd sense of being in some way a prisoner confronted her. She drew back with an impatient start, and perhaps her first real sense of indignation. A voice behind her, which she at once recognised, scarcely restored her calmness.

"You can't get across there, miss."

She turned. It was the young inventor from the wheat ranche, on horseback and with a clean face. He had just ridden out of the grain on the same side of the chasm as herself.

"But you seem to have got over," she said bluntly.

"Yes, but it was farther up the field. I reckoned that the split might be deeper but not so broad in the rock out-crop over there than in the adobe here. I found it so, and jumped it."

He looked as if he might—alert, intelligent, and self-contained. He lingered a moment, and then continued—

"I'm afraid you must have been badly shaken and a little frightened up there before the chimneys came down?"

"No," she was glad to say, briefly and she believed truthfully, "I wasn't frightened. I didn't even know it was an earthquake."

"Ah!" he reflected, "that was because you were a stranger. It's odd —they're all like that. I suppose it's because nobody really expects or believes in the unlooked-for thing, and yet that's the thing that always happens. And then, of course, that other affair, which really is serious, startled you the more."

She felt herself ridiculously and angrily blushing. "I don't know what you mean," she said icily. "What other affair?"

"Why, the well."

"The well?" she repeated vacantly.

"Yes; the artesian well has stopped. Didn't the Major tell you?"

"No," said the girl. "He was away; I haven't seen him yet."

"Well, the flow of water has ceased completely. That's what I'm here for. The Major sent for me, and I've been to examine it."

"And is that stoppage so very important?" she said dubiously.

It was his turn to look at her wonderingly.

"If it's *lost* entirely it means ruin for the ranche," he said sharply. He wheeled his horse, nodded gravely, and trotted off.

Major Randolph's figure of the "life-blood of the ranche" flashed across her suddenly. She knew nothing of irrigation, or the costly appliances by which the Californian agriculturist opposed the long summer droughts. She only vaguely guessed that the dreadful earthquake had struck at the prosperity of those people whom only a few hours ago she had been proud to call her friends. The underlying goodness of her nature was touched. Should she let a momentary fault —if it were not really, after all, only a misunderstanding—rise between her and them at such a moment? She turned and hurried quickly towards the house.

Hastening onward, she found time, however, to wonder also why these common men—she now included even the young inventor in that category—were all so rude and uncivil to *her!* She had never before been treated in this way; she had always been rather embarrassed by the admiring attentions of young men, clerks and collegians, in her Atlantic home, and of professional men—merchants and stockbrokers—in San Francisco. It was true they were not as continually devoted to her and to the nice art and etiquette of pleasing as Emile— they had other things to think about, being in business and not being *gentlemen*—but then they were greatly superior to these clowns, who took no notice of her, and rode off without lingering or formal leave-taking when their selfish affairs were concluded. It must be the contact of the vulgar earth—this wretched, cracking, material, and yet ungovernable and lawless earth—that so depraved them. She felt she would like to say this to some one—not her father, for he wouldn't listen to her, nor to the Major, who would laughingly argue with her, but to Mrs. Randolph, who would understand her, and perhaps say it some day in her own sharp, sneering way to those very clowns. With these gentle sentiments irradiating her blue eyes and putting a pink flush upon her fair cheeks, Rose reached the garden with the intention of rushing sympathetically into Mrs. Randolph's arms. But it suddenly occurred to her that she would be obliged to state how she became aware of this misfortune, and with it came an instinctive aversion to speak of her meeting with the inventor. She would wait until Mrs. Randolph told her. But although that lady was engaged in a low-voiced discussion in French with Emile and Adele, which instantly ceased at her approach, there was no allusion made to the new calamity. "You need not telegraph to your father," she said as Rose approached; "he has already telegraphed to you for news. As you were out and the messenger was waiting an answer, we opened the despatch, and sent one telling him that you were all right, and that he need not hurry here on your account. So you are satisfied, I hope." A few hours ago this would have been true, and Rose would have probably seen in the action of her hostess only a flattering motherly supervision; there was, in fact, still a lingering trace of trust in her mind; yet she was conscious that she would have preferred to answer the despatch herself, and to have let her father come. To a girl brought up with a belief in the right of individual independence of thought and action there was something in Mrs. Randolph's practical ignoring of that right which startled her in spite of her new conservatism, while, as the daughter of a business man, her instincts revolted against Mrs. Randolph's unbusiness-like action with the telegram, however vulgar and unrefined she may have begun to consider a life of business. The result was a certain constraint and embarrassment in her manner, which, however, had the laudable effect of limiting Emile's attention to significant glances, and was no doubt variously interpreted by the others. But she satisfied her conscience by determining to make a confidence of her sympathy to the Major on the first opportunity.

This she presently found when the others were preoccupied; the Major greeting her with a somewhat careworn face, but a voice whose habitual kindness was unchanged. When he had condoled with her on the terrifying phenomenon that had marred her visit to the ranche—and she could not help impatiently noticing that he too seemed to have accepted his wife's theory that she had been half deliriously frightened —he regretted that her father had not concluded to come down to the ranche, as his practical advice would have been invaluable in this emergency. She was about to eagerly explain why, when it occurred to her that Mrs. Randolph had only given him a suppressed version of the telegram, and that she would be betraying her or again taking sides in this partisan-divided home. With some hesitation she had at last alluded to the accident to the artesian well. The Major did not ask her how she had heard of it; it was a bad business, he thought, but it might not be a total loss. The water may have been only diverted by the shock, and might be found again at the lower level, or in some lateral fissure. He had sent hurriedly for Tom Bent—that clever young engineer at the wheat ranche, who was always studying up these things with his inventions—and that was his opinion. No, Tom was not a well-digger, but it was generally known that he had "located" one or two, and had long ago advised the tapping of that flow by a second boring, in case of just such an emergency. He was coming again to-morrow. By the way, he had asked how the young lady visitor was, and hoped she had not been alarmed by the earthquake!

Rose felt herself again blushing, and, what was more singular, with an unexpected and it seemed to her ridiculous pleasure, although outwardly she appeared to ignore the civility completely. And she had no intention of being so easily placated. If this young man thought by mere perfunctory civilities to her *host* to make up for his clownishness to *her,* he was mistaken. She would let him see it when he called tomorrow. She quickly turned the subject by assuring the Major of her sympathy and her intention of sending for her father. For the rest of the afternoon and during their *al fresco* dinner she solved the difficulty of her strained relations with Mrs. Randolph and Emile by conversing chiefly with the Major, tacitly avoiding, however, any allusion to this Mr. Bent. But Mrs. Randolph was less careful.

"You don't really mean to say, Major," she began in her driest, grittiest manner, "that instead of sending to San Francisco for some skilled master-mechanic, you are going to listen to the vagaries of a conceited, half-educated farm-labourer, and employ him? You might as well call in some of those wizards or water-witches at once." But the Major, like many other well-managed husbands who are good-humouredly content to suffer in the sunshine of prosperity, had no idea of doing so in adversity, and the prospect of being obliged to go back to youthful struggles had recalled some of the independence of that period. He looked up quietly and said—

"If his conclusions are as clear and satisfactory tomorrow as they were to-day, I shall certainly try to secure his services."

"Then I can only say *I* would prefer the water-witch. He at least would not represent a class of neighbours who have made themselves systematically uncivil and disagreeable to us."

"I am afraid, Josephine, we have not tried to make ourselves particularly agreeable to *them,*" said the Major.

"If that can only be done by admitting their equality, I prefer they should remain uncivil. Only let it be understood, Major, that if you choose to take this Tom-the-ploughboy to mend your well, you will at least keep him there while he is on the property."

With what retort the Major would have kept up this conjugal discussion already beginning to be awkward to the discreet visitor is not known, as it was suddenly stopped by a bullet from the rosebud lips of the ingenuous Adele.

"Why, he's very handsome when his face is clean, and his hands are small and not at all hard. And he doesn't talk the least bit queer or common."

There was a dead silence. "And pray, where did *you* see him, and what do you know about his hands?" asked Mrs. Randolph, in her most desiccated voice. "Or has the Major already presented you to him? I shouldn't be surprised."

"No, but"—hesitated the young girl, with a certain mouse-like audacity—"when you sent me to look after Miss Mallory, I came up to him just after he had spoken to her, and he stopped to ask me how we all were, and if Miss Mallory was really frightened by the earthquake, and he shook hands for good afternoon—that's all."

"And who taught you to converse with common strangers and shake hands with them?" continued Mrs. Randolph, with narrowing lips.

"Nobody, mamma; but I thought if Miss Mallory, who is a young lady, could speak to him, so could I, who am not out yet."

"We won't discuss this any further at present," said Mrs. Randolph stiffly, as the Major smiled grimly at Rose. "The earthquake seems to have shaken down in this house more than the chimneys."

It certainly had shaken all power of sleep from the eyes of Rose when the household at last dispersed to lie down in their clothes on the mattresses which had been arranged under the awnings. She was continually starting up from confused dreams of the ground shaking under her, or she seemed to be standing on the brink of some dreadful abyss like the great chasm on the grain-field, when it began to tremble and crumble beneath her feet. It was near morning when, unable to endure it any longer, she managed without disturbing the sleeping Adele, who occupied the same curtained recess with her, to slip out from the awning. Wrapped in a thick shawl, she made her way through the encompassing trees and bushes of the garden that had seemed to imprison and suffocate her to the edge of the grain-field, where she could breathe the fresh air beneath an open, starlit sky. There was no moon, and the darkness favoured her; she had no fears that weighed against the horror of seclusion with her own fancies. Besides, they were camping *out* of the house, and if she chose to sit up or walk about no one could think it strange. She wished her father were here, that she might have some one of her own kin to talk to, yet she knew not what to say to him if he had come. She wanted somebody to sympathise with her feelings—or rather, perhaps, some one to combat and even ridicule the uneasiness that had lately come over her. She knew what her father would say: "Do you want to go, or do you want to stay here? Do you like these people, or do you not?" She remembered the one or two glowing and enthusiastic accounts she had written him of her visit here, and felt herself blushing again. What would he think of Mrs. Randolph's opening and answering the telegram? Wouldn't he find out from the Major if she had garbled the sense of his despatch?

Away to the right, in the midst of the distant and invisible wheat-field, there was the same intermittent star, which like a living, breath-ing thing seemed to dilate in glowing respiration, as she had seen it the first night of her visit. Mr. Bent's forge! It must be nearly daylight now; the poor fellow had been up all night, or else was stealing this early march on the day. She recalled Adele's sudden eulogium of him. The first natural smile that had come to her lips since the earthquake broke up her nervous restraint, and sent her back more like her old self to her couch.

But she had not proceeded far towards the tent, when she heard the sound of low voices approaching her. It was the Major and his wife, who, like herself, had evidently been unable to sleep, and were up betimes. A new instinct of secretiveness which she felt was partly the effect of her artificial surroundings checked her first natural instinct to call to them, and she drew back deeper in the shadow to let them pass. But to her great discomfiture, the Major in a conversational emphasis stopped directly in front of her.

"You are wrong, I tell you, a thousand times wrong. The girl is simply upset by this earthquake. It's a great pity her father didn't come instead of telegraphing. And, by Jove, rather than hear any more of this, I'll send for him myself," said the Major, in an energetic but suppressed voice.

"And the girl won't thank you, and you'll be a fool for your pains," returned Mrs. Randolph, with dry persistency.

"But, according to your own ideas of propriety, Mallory ought to be the first one to be consulted—and by me, too."

"Not in this case. Of course, before any actual engagement is on, you can speak of Emile's attentions."

"But suppose Mallory has other views? Suppose he declines the honour? The man is no fool."

"Thank you. But for that very reason he must. Listen to me, Major: if he doesn't care to please his daughter for her own sake, he will have to do so for the sake of decency. Yes, I tell you, she has thoroughly compromised herself—quite enough, if it is ever known, to spoil any other engagement her father may make. Why, ask Adele! The day of the earthquake she *absolutely* had the audacity to send him out of the room upstairs into your study for her fan, and then follow him up there alone. The servants knew it. I knew it, for I was in her room at the time with Father Antonio. The earthquake made it plain to everybody. Decline it!—No. Mr. Mallory will think twice about it before he does that.—What's that? Who's there?"

There was a sudden rustle in the bushes like the passage of some frightened animal—and then all was still again.

Chapter V

The sun, an hour high, but only just topping the greenish crests of the wheat, was streaming like the morning breeze through the open length of Tom Bent's workshed. An exaggerated and prolonged shadow of the young inventor himself at work beside his bench was stretching itself far into the broken-down ranks of stalks towards the invisible road, and falling at the very feet of Rose Mallory as she emerged from them.

She was very pale, very quiet, and very determined. The travelling mantle thrown over her shoulders was dusty, the ribbons that tied her hat under her round chin had become unloosed. She advanced, walking down the line of shadow directly towards him.

"I am afraid I will have to trouble you once more," she said, with a faint smile, which did not, however, reach her perplexed eyes. "Could you give me any kind of a conveyance that would take me to San José at once?"

The young man had started at the rustling of her dress in the shavings and turned eagerly. The faintest indication of a loss of interest was visible for an instant in his face, but it quickly passed into a smile of recognition. Yet she felt that he had neither noticed any change in her appearance, nor experienced any wonder at seeing her there at that hour.

"I did not take a buggy from the house," she went on quickly, "for I left early, and did not want to disturb them. In fact, they don't know that I am gone. I was worried at not hearing news from my father in San Francisco since the earthquake, and I thought I would run down to San José to inquire without putting them to any trouble. Anything will do that you have ready, if I can take it at once."

Still without exhibiting the least surprise, Bent nodded affirmatively, put down his tools, begged her to wait a moment, and ran off in the direction of the cabin. As he disappeared behind the wheat she lapsed quite suddenly against the work-bench, but recovered herself a moment later, leaning with her back against it, her hands grasping it on either side, and her knit brows and determined little face turned towards the road. Then she stood erect again, shook the dust out of her skirts, lifted her veil, wiped her cheeks and brow with the corner of a small handkerchief, and began walking up and down the length of the shed as Bent reappeared.

He was accompanied by the man who had first led her through the wheat. He gazed upon her with apparently all the curiosity and concern that the other had lacked.

"You want to get to San José as quick as you can?" he said interrogatively.

"Yes," she said quickly, "if you can help me."

"You walked all the way from the Major's here?" he continued, without taking his eyes from her face.

"Yes," she answered, with an affectation of carelessness she had not shown to Bent. "But I started very early, it was cool and pleasant, and didn't seem far."

"I'll put you down in San José inside the hour. You shall have my horse and trotting sulky, and I'll drive you myself. Will that do?"

She looked at him wonderingly. She had not forgotten his previous restraint and gravity, but now his face seemed to have relaxed with some humorous satisfaction. She felt herself colouring slightly, but whether with shame or relief she could not tell.

"I shall be *so* much obliged to you," she replied hesitatingly; "and so will my father, I know."

"I reckon," said the man, with the same look of amused conjecture; then, with a quick, assuring nod, he turned away and dived into the wheat again.

"You're all right now, Miss Mallory," said Bent complacently. "Dawson will fix it. He's got a good horse, and he's a good driver too." He paused, and then added pleasantly, "I suppose they're all well up at the house?"

It was so evident that his remark carried no personal meaning to herself that she was obliged to answer carelessly, "Oh yes."

"I suppose you see a good deal of Miss Randolph—Miss Adele, I think you call her?" he remarked tentatively, and with a certain boyish enthusiasm which she had never conceived possible to his nature.

"Yes," she replied a little dryly; "she is the only young lady there." She stopped, remembering Adele's naïve description of the man before her, and said abruptly, "You know her, then?"

"A little," replied the young man modestly. "I see her pretty often when I am passing the upper end of the ranche. She's very well brought up, and her manners are very refined—don't you think so?— and yet she's just as simple and natural as a country girl. There's a great deal in education after all, isn't there?" he went on confidentially, "and although," he lowered his voice and looked cautiously around him, "I believe that some of us here don't fancy her mother much, there's no doubt that Mrs. Randolph knows how to bring up her children. Some people think that kind of education is all artificial, and don't believe in it, but *I* do!"

With the consciousness that she was running away from these people, and the shameful disclosure she had heard last night—with the recollection of Adele's scandalous interpretation of her most innocent actions, and her sudden and complete revulsion against all that she had previously admired in that household—to hear this man, who had seemed to her a living protest against their ideas and principles, now expressing them and holding them up for emulation, almost took her breath away.

"I suppose that means you intend to fix Major Randolph's well for him?" she said dryly.

"Yes," he returned, without noticing her manner; "and I think I can find that water again. I've been studying it up all night, and do you know what I'm going to do? I am going to make the earthquake that lost it help me to find it again." He paused, and looked at her with a smile and a return of his former enthusiasm. "Do you remember the crack in the adobe field that stopped you yesterday?"

"Yes," said the girl, with a slight shiver.

"I told you then that the same crack was a split in the rock outcrop farther up the plain, and was deeper. I am satisfied now, from what I have seen, that it is really a rupture of the whole strata all the way down. That's the one weak point that the imprisoned water is sure to find, and that's where the borer will tap it—in the new well that the earthquake itself has sunk."

It seemed to her now that she understood his explanation perfectly, and she wondered the more he had been so mistaken in his estimate of Adele. She turned away a little impatiently and looked anxiously towards the point where Dawson had disappeared. Bent followed her eyes.

"He'll be here in a moment, Miss Mallory. He has to drive slowly through the grain, but I hear the wheels." He stopped, and his voice took up its previous note of boyish hesitation. "By the way—I'll—I'll be going up to the Rancho this afternoon to see the Major. Have you any message for Mrs. Randolph—or for—for Miss Adele?"

"No—," said Rose hesitatingly, "and—and——"

"I see," interrupted Bent carelessly. "You don't want anything said about your coming here. I won't."

It struck her that he seemed to have no ulterior meaning in the suggestion. But before she could make any reply, Dawson reappeared, driving a handsome mare harnessed to a light spider-like vehicle. He had also assumed, evidently in great haste, a black frock-coat buttoned over his waistcoatless and cravatless shirt, and a tall black hat, that already seemed to be cracking in the sunlight. He drove up, at once assisted her to the narrow perch beside him, and with a nod to Bent drove off. His breathless expedition relieved the leave-taking of these young people of any ceremony.

"I suppose," said Mr. Dawson, giving a half glance over his shoulder as they struck into the dusty highway, "I suppose you don't care to see anybody before you get to San José?"

"No—o—o," said Rose timidly.

"And I reckon you wouldn't mind my racin' a bit if anybody kem up?"

"No."

"The mare's sort o' fastidious about takin' anybody's dust."

"Is she?" said Rose, with a faint smile.

"Awful," responded her companion; "and the queerest thing of all is, she can't bear to have any one behind her either."

He leaned forward, with his expression of humorous enjoyment of some latent joke, and did something with the reins—Rose never could clearly understand what, though it seemed to her that he simply lifted them with ostentatious lightness—but the mare suddenly appeared to *lengthen* herself and lose her height, and the stalks of wheat on either side of the dusty track began to melt into each other, and then slipped like a flash into one long continuous shimmering green hedge. So perfect was the mare's action that the girl was scarcely conscious of any increased effort; so harmonious the whole movement that the light skeleton waggon seemed only a prolonged process of that long slim body and free collarless neck, both straight as the thin shafts on each side and straighter than the delicate ribbon-like traces which, in what seemed a mere affectation of conscious power hung at times almost limp between the whiffle-tree and the narrow breast-band which was all that confined the animal's powerful fore-quarters. So superb was the reach of its long easy stride that Rose could scarcely see any undulations in the brown shining back, on which she could have placed her foot, nor feel the soft beat of the delicate hoofs that took the dust so firmly and yet so lightly.

The rapidity of motion, which kept them both with heads bent forward and seemed to force back any utterance that rose to their lips, spared Rose the obligation of conversation, and her companion was equally reticent. But it was evident to her that he half suspected she was running away from the Randolphs, and that she wished to avoid the embarrassment of being overtaken even in persuasive pursuit. It was not possible that he knew the cause of her flight, and yet she could not account for his evident desire to befriend her, nor, above all, for his apparently humorous enjoyment of the situation. Had he taken it gravely she might have been tempted to partly confide in him and ask his advice. Was she doing right, after all? Ought she not to have stayed long enough to speak her mind to Mrs. Randolph and demand to be sent home. No! She had not only shrunk from repeating the infamous slander she had overheard, but she had a terrible fear that if she had done so Mrs. Randolph was capable of denying it or even charging her with being still under the influence of the earthquake shock and of walking in her sleep. No! She could not trust her—she could trust no one there. Had not even the Major listened to those infamous lies? Had she not seen that he was helpless in the hands of this cabal in his own household—a cabal that she herself had thoughtlessly joined against him.

They had reached the first slight ascent. Her companion drew out his watch, looked at it with satisfaction, and changed the position of his hands on the reins. Without being able to detect the difference, she felt they were slackening speed. She turned inquiringly towards him; he nodded his head, with a half smile and a gesture to her to look ahead. The spires of San José were already faintly uplifting from the distant fringe of oaks.

So soon! In fifteen minutes she would be there—and *then!* She remembered suddenly she had not yet determined what to do. Should she go on at once to San Francisco, or telegraph to her father and await him at San José? In either case a new fear of the precipitancy of her action and the inadequacy of her reasons had sprung up in her mind. Would her father understand her? Would he underrate the cause and be mortified at the insult she had given the family of his old friend, or, more dreadful still, would he exaggerate her wrongs, and seek a personal quarrel with the Major? He was a man of quick temper, and had the Western ideas of redress. Perhaps even now she was precipitating a duel between them. Her cheeks grew wan again, her breath came quickly, tears gathered in her eyes. Oh, she was a dreadful girl, she knew it; she was an utterly miserable one, and she knew that too!

The reins were tightened. The pace lessened, and at last fell to a walk. Conscious of her tell-tale eyes and troubled face, she dared not turn to her companion to ask him why, but glanced across the fields.

"When you first came I didn't get to know your name, Miss Mallory, but I reckon I know your father."

Her father! What made him say that? She wanted to speak, but she felt she could not. In another moment, if he went on, she must do *something*—she would cry!

"I reckon you'll be wanting to go to the hotel first, anyway?"

There!—she knew it! He *would* keep on! And now she had burst into tears.

The mare was still walking slowly; the man was lazily bending forward over the shafts as if nothing had occurred. Then suddenly, illogically, and without a moment's warning, the pride that had sustained her crumbled and became as the dust of the road.

She burst out and told him—this stranger!—this man she had disliked!—all and *everything.* How she had felt, how she had been deceived, and what she had overheard!

"I thought as much," said her companion quietly, "and that's why I sent for your father."

"You sent for my father!—when?—where?" echoed Rose, in astonishment.

"Yesterday. He was to come to-day, and if we don't find him at the hotel it will be because he has already started to come here by the upper and longer road. But you leave it to *me,* and don't you say anything to him of this now. If he's at the hotel I'll say I drove you down there to show off the mare. *Sabe?* If he isn't, I'll leave you there and come back here to find him. I've got something to tell him that will set *you* all right." He smiled grimly, lifted the reins, the mare started forward again, and the vehicle and its occupants disappeared in a vanishing dust cloud.

Chapter VI

It was nearly noon when Mr. Dawson finished rubbing down his sweating mare in the little stable shed among the wheat. He had left Rose at the hotel, for they found Mr. Mallory had previously started by a circuitous route for the wheat ranche. He had resumed not only his working clothes but his working expression. He was now superintending the unloading of a wain of stores and implements when the light carry-all of the Randolphs rolled into the field. It contained only Mrs. Randolph and the driver. A slight look of intelligence passed between the latter and the nearest one of Dawson's companions, succeeded, however, by a dull look of stupid vacancy on the faces of all the others, including Dawson. Mrs. Randolph noticed it, and was forewarned. She reflected that no human beings ever looked *naturally* as stupid as that and were able to work. She smiled sarcastically, and then began with dry distinctness and narrowing lips.

"Miss Mallory, a young lady visiting us, went out for an early walk this morning, and has not returned. It is possible she may have lost her way among your wheat. Have you seen anything of her?"

Dawson raised his eyes from his work and glanced slowly around at his companions, as if taking the heavy sense of the assembly. One or two shook their heads mechanically, and returned to their suspended labour. He said coolly—

"Nobody here seems to."

She felt that they were lying. She was only a woman against five men. She was only a petty domestic tyrant; she might have been a larger one. But she had all the courage of that possibility.

"Major Randolph and my son are away," she went on, drawing herself erect. "But I know that the Major will pay liberally if these men will search the field, besides making it all right with your—*employers*—for the loss of time."

Dawson uttered a single word in a low voice to the man nearest him, who apparently communicated it to the others, for the four men stopped unloading and moved away one after the other—even the driver joining in the exodus. Mrs. Randolph smiled sarcastically; it was plain that these people, with all their boasted independence, were quite amenable to pecuniary considerations. Nevertheless, as Dawson remained looking quietly at her, she said—

"Then I suppose they've concluded to go and see?"

"No; I've sent them away so that they couldn't *hear.*"

"Hear what?"

"What I've got to say to you."

She looked at him suddenly. Then she said, with a disdainful glance around her, "I see I am helpless here, and—thanks to your trickery—alone. Have a care, sir; I warn you that you will have to answer to Major Randolph for any insolence."

"I reckon you won't tell Major Randolph what I have to say to you," he returned coolly.

Her lips were nearly a greyish hue, but she said scornfully, "And why not? Do you know who you are talking to?"

The man came lazily forward to the carry-all, carelessly brushed aside the slack reins, and resting his elbows on the horse's back, laid his chin on his hands, as he looked up in the woman's face.

"Yes; *I* know who I'm talking to," he said coolly. "But as the Major don't, I reckon you won't tell him."

"Stand away from that horse," she said, her whole face taking the greyish colour of her lips, but her black eyes growing smaller and brighter. "Hand me those reins and let me pass. What *canaille* are you to stop me?"

"I thought so," returned the man, without altering his position, "you don't know *me.* You never saw *me* before. Well, I'm Jim Dawson, the nephew of L'Hommadieu, *your old master!*"

She gripped the iron rail of the seat as if to leap from it, but checked herself suddenly and leaned back, with a set smile on her mouth that seemed stamped there. It was remarkable that with that smile she flung away her old affectation of superciliousness for an older and ruder audacity, and that not only the expression but the type of her face appeared to have changed.

"I don't say," continued the man quietly, "that he didn't *marry* you before he died. But you know as well as I do that the laws of his State didn't recognise the marriage of a master with his Octoroon slave! And you know as well as I do that even if he had freed you he couldn't change your blood. Why, if I'd been willing to stay at Avoyelles to be a nigger-driver like him, the plantation of 'de Fontanges'—whose name you have taken—would have been left to me. If *you* had stayed there you might have been my property instead of *your* owning a square man like Randolph. You didn't think of that when you came here, did you?" he added composedly.

"Oh, mon Dieu!" she said, dropping rapidly into a different accent, with her white teeth and fixed mirthless smile, "so it is a claim for *property,* eh? You're wanting money—you? *Très bien,* you forget we are in California, where one does not own a slave. And you have a fine story there, my poor friend. Very pretty, but very hard to prove, *m'sieu.* And these peasants are in it, eh, working it on shares like the farm, eh?"

"Well," said Dawson, slightly changing his position, and passing his hand over the horse's neck with a half-wearied contempt, "one of these men is from Plaquemine and the other from Coupée. They know all the L'Hommadieus' history. And they know a streak of the tarbrush when they see it. They took your measure when they came here last year, and sized you up fairly. So had I, for the matter of that, when I *first* saw you. And we compared notes. But the Major is a square man, for all he is your husband, and we reckoned he had a big enough contract on his hands to take care of you and L'Hommadieu's half-breeds, and so"—he tossed the reins contemptuously aside—"we kept this to ourselves."

"And now you want—what—eh?"

"We want an end to this foolery," he broke out roughly, stepping back from the vehicle and facing her suddenly, with his first angry gesture. "We want an end to these airs and grimaces, and all this dandy nigger business; we want an end to this 'cake-walking' through the wheat, and flouting of the honest labour of your betters. We want you and your 'de Fontanges' to climb down. And we want an end to this ropin'-in of white folks to suit your little game; we want an end to your trying to mix your nigger blood with any one here, and we intend to stop it. We draw the line at the Major."

Lashed as she had been by those words apparently out of all semblance of her former social arrogance, a lower and more stubborn resistance seemed to have sprung up in her, as she sat sideways, watching him with her set smile and contracting eyes.

"Ah," she said dryly, "so *she is here*. I thought so. Which of you is it, eh? It's a good spec—Mallory's a rich man. She's not particular."

The man had stopped as if listening, his head turned towards the road. Then he turned carelessly, and facing her again, waved his hand with a gesture of tired dismissal, and said, "Go! You'll find your driver over there by the tool-shed. He has heard nothing yet—but I've given you fair warning. Go!"

He walked slowly back towards the shed as the woman, snatching up the reins, drove violently off in the direction where the men had disappeared. But she turned aside, ignoring her waiting driver in her wild and reckless abandonment of all her old conventional attitudes, and lashing her horse forward with the same set smile on her face, the same odd relaxation of figure, and the same squaring of her elbows.

Avoiding the main road, she pushed into a narrow track that intersected another nearer the scene of the accident to Rose's buggy three weeks before. She had nearly passed it when she was hailed by a strange voice, and looking up, perceived a horseman floundering in the mazes of the wheat to one side of the track. Whatever mean thought of her past life she was flying from, whatever mean purpose she was flying to, she pulled up suddenly, and as suddenly resumed her erect aggressive stiffness. The stranger was a middle-aged man, in dress and appearance a dweller of cities. He lifted his hat as he perceived the occupant of the waggon to be a lady.

"I beg your pardon, but I fear I've lost my way in trying to make a short cut to the Excelsior Company's Ranche."

"You are in it now," said Mrs. Randolph quickly.

"Thank you, but where can I find the farmhouse?"

"There is none," she returned, with her old superciliousness, "unless you choose to give that name to the shanties and sheds where the labourers and servants live near the road."

The stranger looked puzzled. "I'm looking for a Mr. Dawson," he said reflectively, "but I may have made some mistake. Do you know Major Randolph's house hereabouts?"

"I do. I am Mrs. Randolph," she said stiffly.

The stranger's brow cleared, and he smiled pleasantly. "Then this is a fortunate meeting," he said, raising his hat again as he reined in his horse beside the waggon, "for I am Mr. Mallory, and I was looking forward to the pleasure of presenting myself to you an hour or two later. The fact is, an old acquaintance, Mr. Dawson, telegraphed me yesterday to meet him here on urgent business, and I felt obliged to go there first."

Mrs. Randolph's eyes sparkled with a sudden gratified intelligence, but her manner seemed rather to increase than abate its grim precision.

"Our meeting this morning, Mr. Mallory, is both fortunate and unfortunate, for I regret to say that your daughter, who has not been quite herself since the earthquake, was missing early this morning and has not yet been found, though we have searched everywhere. Understand me," she said, as the stranger started, "I have no fear for her *personal* safety; I am only concerned for any *indiscretion* that she may commit in the presence of these strangers whose company she would seem to prefer to ours."

"But I don't understand you, madam," said Mallory sternly; "you are speaking of my daughter, and——"

"Excuse me, Mr. Mallory," said Mrs. Randolph, lifting her hand with her driest deprecation and her most desiccating smile, "I'm not passing judgment or criticism. I am of a foreign race, and consequently do not understand the freedom of American young ladies, and their familiarity with the opposite sex. I make no charges; I only wish to assure you that she will no doubt be found in the company and under the protection of her own countrymen. There is," she added with ironical distinctness, "a young mechanic, or field hand, or 'quack well-doctor,' whom she seems to admire, and with whom she appears to be on equal terms."

Mallory regarded her for a moment fixedly, and then his sternness relaxed to a mischievously complacent smile. "That must be young Bent, of whom I've heard," he said, with unabated cheerfulness. "And I don't know but what she may be with him, after all. For now I think of it, a chuckle-headed fellow, of whom a moment ago I inquired the way to your house, told me I'd better ask the young man and young woman who were 'philandering through the wheat' yonder. Suppose we look for them. From what I've heard of Bent, he's too much wrapped up in his inventions for flirtation, but it would be a good joke to stumble upon them."

Mrs. Randolph's eyes sparkled with a mingling of gratified malice and undisguised contempt for the fatuous father beside her. But before she could accept or decline the challenge, it had become useless. A murmur of youthful voices struck her ear, and she suddenly stood upright and transfixed in the carriage. For lounging down slowly towards them out of the dim green aisles of the arboured wheat, lost in themselves and the shimmering veil of their seclusion, came the engineer, Thomas Bent, and on his arm, gazing ingenuously into his face, the figure of Adele—her own perfect daughter.

"I don't think, my dear," said Mr. Mallory, as the anxious Rose flew into his arms on his return to San José a few hours later, "that it will be necessary for you to go back again to Major Randolph's before we leave. I have said 'Good-bye' for you and thanked them, and your trunks are packed and will be sent here. The fact is, my dear, you see this affair of the earthquake and the disaster to the artesian well have upset all their arrangements, and I am afraid that my little girl would be only in their way just now."

"And you have seen Mr. Dawson—and you know why he sent for you?" asked the young girl, with nervous eagerness.

"Ah, yes," said Mr. Mallory thoughtfully, *"that* was really important. You see, my child," he continued, taking her hand in one of his own and patting the back of it gently with the other, "we think, Dawson and I, of taking over the Major's ranche and incorporating it with the Excelsior in one, to be worked on shares like the Excelsior; and as Mrs. Randolph is very anxious to return to the Atlantic States with her children, it is quite possible. Mrs. Randolph, as you have possibly noticed," Mr. Mallory went on, still patting his daughter's hand, "does not feel entirely at home here, and will consequently leave the Major free to rearrange by himself the ranche on the new basis. In fact, as the change must be made before the crops come in, she talks of going next week. But if you like the place, Rose, I've no doubt the Major and Dawson will always find room for you and me when we run down there for a little fresh air."

"And did you have all that in your mind, papa, when you came down here, and was that what you and Mr. Dawson wanted to talk about?" said the astonished Rose.

"Mainly, my dear, mainly. You see I'm a capitalist now, and the real value of capital is to know how and when to apply it to certain conditions."

"And this Mr.—Mr. Bent—do you think—he will go on and find the water, papa?" said Rose hesitatingly.

"Ah! Bent—Tom Bent—oh yes," said Mallory with great heartiness. "Capital fellow, Bent! and mighty ingenious! Glad you met him! Well," thoughtfully but still heartily, "he may not find it exactly where he expected, but he'll find it or something better. We can't part with him, and he has promised Dawson to stay. We'll utilise *him,* you may be sure."

It would seem that they did, and from certain interviews and conversations that took place between Mr. Bent and Miss Mallory on a later visit, it would also appear that her father had exercised a discreet reticence in regard to a certain experiment of the young inventor, of which he had been an accidental witness.

A Night at "Hays"

Chapter I

IT WAS DIFFICULT to say if Hays' farmhouse or "Hays," as it was familiarly called, looked any more bleak and cheerless that winter afternoon than it usually did in the strong summer sunshine. Painted a cold merciless white, with scant projections for shadows, a roof of white-pine shingles, bleached lighter through sun and wind, and covered with low, white-capped chimneys, it looked even more stark and chilly than the drifts which had climbed its low roadside fence, and yet seemed hopeless of gaining a foothold on the glancing walls, or slippery, wind-swept roof. The storm, which had already heaped the hollows of the road with snow, hurled its finely-granulated flakes against the building, but they were whirled along the gutters and ridges, and disappeared in smoke-like puffs across the icy roof. The granite outcrop in the hilly field beyond had long ago whitened and vanished; the dwarf-firs and larches, which had at first taken uncouth shapes in the drift, blended vaguely together, and then merged into an unbroken formless wave. But the gaunt angles and rigid outlines of the building remained sharp and unchanged. It would seem as if the rigours of winter had only accented their hardness, as the fierceness of summer had previously made them intolerable.

It was believed that some of this unyielding grimness attached to Hays himself. Certain it is that neither hardship nor prosperity had touched his character. Years ago his emigrant team had broken down in this wild but wooded defile of the Sierras, and he had been forced to a winter encampment, with only a rude log-cabin for shelter, on the very verge of the promised land. Unable to enter it himself, he was nevertheless able to assist the better-equipped teams that followed him with wood and water and a coarse forage gathered from a sheltered slope of wild oats. This was the beginning of a rude "supply station," which afterwards became so profitable that when spring came, and Hays' team were sufficiently recruited to follow the flood of immigrating gold-seekers to the placers and valleys, there seemed no occasion for it. His fortune had been already found in the belt of arable slope behind the wooded defile, and in the miraculously located coign of vantage on what was now the great highway of travel and the only oasis and first relief of the weary journey; the breaking down of his own team at that spot had not only been the salvation of those who found at "Hays" the means of prosecuting the last part of their pilgrimage, but later provided the equipment of returning teams.

The first two years of this experience had not been without hardship and danger. He had been raided by Indians and besieged for three days in his stockaded cabin; he had been invested by wintry drifts of twenty feet of snow, cut off equally from incoming teams from the pass and the valley below. During the second year his wife had joined him with four children, but whether the enforced separation had dulled her conjugal affection, or whether she was tempted by a natural feminine longing for the land of promise beyond, she sought it one morning with a fascinating teamster, leaving her two sons and two daughters behind her; two years later the elder of the daughters followed the mother's example, with such maidenly discretion, however, as to forbear compromising herself by any previous matrimonial formality whatever. From that day Hays had no further personal intercourse with the valley below. He put up an hotel a mile away from the farmhouse, that he might not have to dispense hospitality to his customers, nor accept their near companionship. Always a severe Presbyterian, and an uncompromising deacon of a far-scattered and scanty community who occasionally held their service in one of his barns, he grew more rigid, sectarian, and narrow day by day. He was feared, and although neither respected nor loved, his domination and endurance were accepted. A grim landlord, hard creditor, close-fisted patron, and a smileless neighbour who neither gambled nor drank, "Old Hays," as he was called while yet scarce fifty, had few acquaintances and fewer friends. There were those who believed that his domestic infelicities were the result of his unsympathetic nature; it never occurred to any one (but himself probably) that they might have been the cause. In those Sierran altitudes, as elsewhere, the belief in original sin—popularly known as "pure cussedness"—dominated and overbore any consideration of passive, impelling circumstances or temptation, unless they had been actively demonstrated with a revolver. The passive expression of harshness, suspicion, distrust, and moroseness was looked upon as inherent wickedness.

The storm raged violently as Hays emerged from the last of a long range of outbuildings and sheds, and crossed the open space between him and the farmhouse. Before he had reached the porch, with its scant shelter, he had floundered through a snow-drift and faced the full fury of the storm. But the snow seemed to have glanced from his hard angular figure as it had from his roof-ridge, for when he entered the narrow hall-way his pilot jacket was unmarked, except where a narrow line of powdered flakes outlined the seams as if worn. To the right was an apartment, half office, half sitting-room, furnished with a dark and chilly iron safe, a sofa and chairs covered with black and coldly shining horsehair. Here Hays not only removed his upper coat but his under one also, and drawing a chair before the fire, sat down in his shirt-sleeves. It was his usual rustic pioneer habit, and might have been some lingering reminiscence of certain remote ancestors to whom clothes were an impediment. He was warming his hands and placidly ignoring his gaunt arms in their thinly-clad "hickory" sleeves, when a young girl of eighteen sauntered, half-perfunctorily, half-inquisitively, into the room. It was his only remaining daughter. Already elected by circumstances to a dry household virginity, her somewhat large features, sallow complexion, and tasteless, unattractive dress did not obviously suggest a sacrifice. Since her sister's departure she had taken sole charge of her father's domestic affairs and the few rude servants he employed, with a certain inherited following of his own moods and methods. To the neighbours she was known as "Miss Hays"—a dubious respect that in a community of familiar "Sallys," "Mamies," "Pussies," was grimly prophetic. Yet she rejoiced in the Oriental appellation of "Zuleika." To this it is needless to add that it was impossible to conceive any one who looked more decidedly Western.

"Ye kin put some things in my carpet bag agin the time the sled comes round," said her father meditatively, without looking up.

"Then you're not coming back to-night?" asked the girl curiously. "What's goin' on at the summit, father?"

"*I* am," he said grimly. "You don't reckon I kalkilate to stop thar! I'm going on as far as Horseley's to close up that contract afore the weather changes."

"I kinder allowed it was funny you'd go to the hotel to-night. There's a dance there; those two Wetherbee girls and Mamie Harris passed up the road an hour ago on a wood sled, nigh blown to pieces and sittin' up in the snow like skeert white rabbits."

Hays' brow darkened heavily.

"Let 'em go," he said, in a hard voice that the fire did not seem to have softened. "Let 'em go for all the good their fool-parents will ever get outer them, or the herd of way-side cattle they've let them loose among."

"I reckon they haven't much to do at home, or are hard put for company, to travel six miles in the snow to show off their prinkin' to a lot of idle louts, shiny with bear's grease and scented up with doctor's stuff," added the girl, shrugging her shoulders, with a touch of her father's mood and manner.

Perhaps it struck Hays at that moment that her attitude was somewhat monstrous and unnatural for one still young and presumably like other girls, for, after glancing at her under his heavy brows, he said in a gentler tone—

"Never *you* mind, Zuly. When your brother Jack comes home he'll know what's what, and have all the proper New York ways and style. It's nigh on three years now that he's had the best training Dr. Dawson's Academy could give—sayin' nothing of the pow'ful Christian example of one of the best preachers in the States. They mayn't have worldly, ungodly fandangoes where he is, and riotous livin', and scarlet abominations, but I've been told that they've 'tea circles,' and 'assemblies,' and 'harmony concerts' of young folks—and dancin'—yes, fine square dancin' under control. No, I ain't stinted him in anythin'. You kin remember that, Zuleika, when you hear any more gossip and backbitin' about your father's meanness. I ain't spared no money for him."

"I reckon not," said the girl a little sharply. "Why, there's that draft fur two hundred and fifty dollars that kem only last week from the Doctor's fur extras."

"Yes," replied Hays, with a slight knitting of the brows; "the Doctor mout hev writ more particklers, but parsons ain't allus business men. I reckon these here extrys were to push Jack along in the term, as the Doctor knew I wanted him back here in the spring, now that his brother has got to be too stiff-necked and self-opinionated to do his father's work." It seemed from this that there had been a quarrel between Hays and his eldest son, who conducted his branch business at Sacramento, and who had in a passion threatened to set up a rival establishment to his father's. And it was also evident from the manner of the girl that she was by no means a strong partisan of her father in the quarrel.

"You'd better find out first how all the schoolin' and trainin' of Jack's is going to jibe with the Ranch, and if he ain't been eddicated out of all knowledge of station business or keer for it. New York ain't Hays' Ranch, and these yer 'assemblies' and 'harmony' doin's and their airs and graces may put him out of conceit with our plain ways. I reckon ye didn't take that to mind when you've been hustlin' round payin' two hundred and fifty dollar drafts for Jack and quo'llin with Bijah! I ain't sayin' nothin', father; only mebbe if Bijah had had drafts and extrys flourished around him a little more, mebbe he'd have been more polite and not so rough spoken. Mebbe," she continued, with a little laugh, "even *I'd* be a little more in the style to suit Master Jack when he comes ef I had three hundred dollars worth of convent schoolin' like Mamie Harris."

"Yes, and you'd have only made yourself fair game for ev'ry schemin', lazy sport or counter-jumper along the road from this to Sacramento!" responded Hays savagely.

Zuleika laughed again constrainedly, but in a way that might have suggested that this dreadful contingency was still one that it was possible to contemplate without entire consternation. As she moved slowly towards the door she stopped with her hand on the lock and said tentatively, "I reckon you won't be wantin' any supper before you go? You're almost sure to be offered somethin' up at Horseley's, while if I have to cook you up suthin' now and still have the men's regular supper to get at seven, it makes all the expense of an extra meal."

Hays hesitated. He would have preferred his supper now, and had his daughter pressed him would have accepted it. But economy, which was one of Zuleika's inherited instincts, vaguely appearing to him to be a virtue, interchangeable with chastity and abstemiousness, was certainly to be encouraged in a young girl. It hardly seems possible that with an eye single to the integrity of the larder she could ever look kindly on the blandishments of his sex, or indeed be exposed to them. He said simply, "Don't cook for me," and resumed his attitude before the fire as the girl left the room.

As he sat there, grim and immovable as one of the battered fire-dogs before him, the wind in the chimney seemed to carry on a deep-throated, dejected, and confidential conversation with him, but really had very little to reveal. There were no haunting reminiscences of his married life in this room, which he had always occupied in preference to the company or sitting-room beyond. There were no familiar shadows of the past lurking in its corners to pervade his reverie. When he did reflect, which was seldom, there was always in his mind a vague idea of a central injustice to which he had been subjected, that was to be avoided by a circuitous movement, to be hidden by work, but never to be surmounted. And to-night he was going out in the storm, which he could understand and fight, as he had often done before, and he was going to drive a bargain with a man like himself, and get the better of him if he could, as he had done before, and another day would be gone, and that central injustice which he could not understand would be circumvented, and he would still be holding his own in the world. And the God of Israel whom he believed in, and who was a hard but conscientious Providence, something like himself, would assist him perhaps some day to the understanding of this same vague injustice which He was, for some strange reason, permitting. But never more unrelenting and unsparing of others than when under conviction of sin himself, and never more harsh and unforgiving than when fresh from the contemplation of the Divine mercy, he still sat there grimly holding his hands to a warmth that never seemed to get nearer his heart than that, when his daughter re-entered the room with his carpet bag.

To rise, put on his coat and overcoat, secure a fur cap on his head by a woollen comforter, covering his ears and twined round his throat, and to rigidly offer a square and weather-beaten cheek to his daughter's dusty kiss, did not apparently suggest any lingering or hesitation. The sled was at the door, which for a tumultuous moment opened on the storm and the white vision of a horse knee-deep in a drift, and then closed behind him. Zuleika shot the bolt, brushed some flakes of the invading snow from the mat, and, after frugally raking down the fire on the hearth her father had just quitted, retired through the long passage to the kitchen and her domestic supervision.

It was a few hours later; supper had long past, the "hands" had one by one returned to their quarters under the roof or in the adjacent lofts, and Zuleika and the two maids had at last abandoned the kitchen for their bedroom beyond. Zuleika herself, by the light of a solitary candle, had entered the office and had dropped meditatively into a chair, as she slowly raked the warm ashes over the still smouldering fire. The barking of dogs had momentarily attracted her attention, but it had suddenly ceased. It was followed, however, by a more startling incident—a slight movement outside, and an attempt to raise the window!

She was not frightened; perhaps there was little for her to fear: it was known that Hays kept no money in the house; the safe was only used for securities and contracts, and there were half a dozen men within call. It was, therefore, only her usual active, burning curiosity for novel incident that made her run to the window and peer out; but it was with a spontaneous cry of astonishment she turned and darted to the front door, and opened it to the muffled figure of a young man.

"Jack! Saints alive! Why, of all things!" she gasped incoherently.

He stopped her with an impatient gesture, and a hand that prevented her from closing the door again.

"Dad ain't here?" he asked quickly.

"No."

"When'll he be back?"

"Not to-night."

"Good," he said, turning to the door again. She could see a motionless horse and sleigh in the road, with a woman holding the reins.

He beckoned to the woman, who drove to the door and jumped out. Tall, handsome, and audacious, she looked at Zuleika with a quick laugh of confidence, as at some recognised absurdity.

"Go in there," said the young man, opening the door of the office; "I'll come back in a minute."

As she entered, still smiling, as if taking part in some humorous but risky situation, he turned quickly to Zuleika and said in a low voice, "Where can we talk?"

The girl held out her hand and glided hurriedly through the passage until she reached a door, which she opened. By the light of a dying fire he could see it was her bedroom. Lighting a candle on the mantel, she looked eagerly in his face as he threw aside his muffler and opened his coat. It disclosed a spare, youthful figure, and a thin, weak face that a budding moustache only seemed to make still more immature. For an instant brother and sister gazed at each other. Astonishment on her part, nervous impatience on his, apparently repressed any demonstration of family affection. Yet when she was about to speak he stopped her roughly.

"There now; don't talk. I know what you're goin' to say—could say it myself if I wanted to—and it's no use. Well then, here I am. You saw *her*. Well, she's *my wife*—we've been married three months. Yes, my *wife;* married three months ago. I'm here because I ran away from school—that is, I *haven't been there* for the last three months. I came out with her last steamer; we went up to the Summit Hotel last night —where they didn't know me—until we could see how the land lay before popping down on dad. I happened to learn that he was out to-night, and I brought her down here to have a talk. We can go back again before he comes, you know, unless——"

"But," interrupted the girl, with sudden practicality, "you say you ain't been at Doctor Dawson's for three months! Why, only last week he drew on dad for two hundred and fifty dollars for your extras!"

He glanced around him, and then arranged his necktie in the glass above the mantel with a nervous laugh.

"*Oh, that!* I fixed that up, and got the money for it in New York to pay our passage with. It's all right, you know."

Chapter II

The girl stood looking at the ingenious forger with an odd, breathless smile. It was difficult to determine, however, if gratified curiosity were not its most dominant expression.

"And you've got a wife—and *that's* her?" she resumed.

"Yes."

"Where did you first meet her? Who is she?"

"She's an actress—mighty popular in 'Frisco—I mean New York. Lot o' chaps tried to get her—I cut 'em out. For all dad's trying to keep me at Dawson's—I ain't such a fool, eh?"

Nevertheless, as he stood there stroking his fair moustache, his astuteness did not seem to impress his sister to enthusiastic assent. Yet she did not relax her breathless, inquisitive smile as she went on—

"And what are you going to do about dad?"

He turned upon her querulously.

"Well, that's what I want to talk about."

"You'll catch it!" she said impressively.

But here her brother's nervousness broke out into a weak, impotent fury. It was evident, too, that in spite of its apparent spontaneous irritation its intent was studied. Catch it! Would he? Oh yes! Well, she'd see *who'd* catch it! Not him. No, he'd had enough of this meanness, and wanted it ended! He wasn't a woman, to be treated like his sister—like their mother—like their brother, if it came to that, for he knew how he was to be brought back to take Bijah's place in the spring; he'd heard the whole story. No, he was going to stand up for his rights—he was going to be treated as the son of a man who was worth half a million ought to be treated! He wasn't going to be skimped, while his father was wallowing in money that he didn't know what to do with—money that by rights ought to have been given to their mother and their sister. Why, even the law wouldn't permit such meanness—if he was dead. No, he'd come back with Lottie, his wife, to show his father that there was one of the family that couldn't be fooled and bullied, and wouldn't put up with it any longer. There was going to be a fair division of the property, and his sister Annie's property, and hers—Zuleika's—too, if she'd have the pluck to speak up for herself. All this and much more he said. Yet even while his small fury was genuine and characteristic, there was such an evident incongruity between himself and his speech that it seemed to fit him loosely, and in a measure flapped in his gestures like another's garment. Zuleika, who had exhibited neither disgust nor sympathy with his rebellion, but had rather appeared to enjoy it as a novel domestic performance, the morality of which devolved solely upon the performer, retained her curious smile. And then a knock at the door startled them.

It was the stranger—slightly apologetic and still humorous, but firm and self-confident withal. She was sorry to interrupt their family council, but the fire was going out where she sat, and she would like a cup of tea or some refreshment. She did not look at Jack, but, completely ignoring him, addressed herself to Zuleika with what seemed to be a direct challenge; in that feminine eye-grapple there was a quick, instinctive, and final struggle between the two women. The stranger triumphed. Zuleika's vacant smile changed to one of submission, and then equally ignoring her brother in this double defeat, she hastened to the kitchen to do the visitor's bidding. The woman closed the door behind her, and took Zuleika's place before the fire.

"Well?" she said, in a half-contemptuous toleration.

"Well?" said Jack, in an equally ill-disguised discontent, but an evident desire to placate the woman before him. "It's all right, you know. I've had my say. It'll come right, Lottie, you'll see."

The woman smiled again, and glanced around the bare walls of the room.

"And I suppose," she said dryly, "when it comes right I'm to take the place of your sister in the charge of this workhouse, and succeed to the keys of that safe in the other room?"

"It'll come all right, I tell you; you can fix things up here any way you'll like when we get the old man straight," said Jack, with the iteration of feebleness. "And as to that safe, I've seen it chock full of securities."

"It'll hold one less to-night," she said, looking at the fire.

"What are you talking about?" he asked, in querulous suspicion.

She drew a paper from her pocket.

"It's that draft of yours that you were crazy enough to sign Dawson's name to. It was lying out there on the desk. I reckon it isn't a thing you care to have kept as evidence, even by your father."

She held it in the flames until it was consumed.

"By Jove, your head is level, Lottie!" he said, with an admiration that was not, however, without a weak reserve of suspicion.

"No, it isn't, or I wouldn't be here," she said curtly. Then she added, as if dismissing the subject, "Well, what did you tell her?"

"Oh, I said I met you in New York. You see I thought she might think it queer if she knew I only met you in San Francisco three weeks ago. Of course I said we were married."

She looked at him with weary astonishment.

"And of course, whether things go right or not, she'll find out that I've got a husband living, that I never met you in New York, but on the steamer, and that you've lied. I don't see the *use* of it. You said you were going to tell the whole thing squarely and say the truth, and that's why I came to help you."

"Yes; but don't you see, hang it all!" he stammered, in the irritation of weak confusion, "I had to tell her *something*. Father won't dare to tell her the truth, no more than he will the neighbours. He'll hush it up, you bet; and when we get this thing fixed you'll go and get your divorce, you know, and we'll be married privately on the square."

He looked so vague, so immature, yet so fatuously self-confident, that the woman extended her hand with a laugh and tapped him on the back as she might have patted a dog. Then she disappeared to follow Zuleika in the kitchen.

When the two women returned together they were evidently on the best of terms. So much so that the man, with the easy reaction of a shallow nature, became sanguine and exalted, even to an ostentatious exhibition of those New York graces on which the paternal Hays had set such store. He complacently explained the methods by which he had deceived Doctor Dawson; how he had himself written a letter from his father commanding him to return to take his brother's place, and how he had shown it to the Doctor and been three months in San Francisco looking for work and assisting Lottie at the theatre, until a conviction of the righteousness of his cause, perhaps combined with the fact that they were also short of money and she had no engagement, impelled him to his present heroic step. All of which Zuleika listened to with childish interest, but superior appreciation of his companion. The fact that this woman was an actress, an abomination vaguely alluded to by her father as being even more mysteriously wicked than her sister and mother, and correspondingly exciting, as offering a possible permanent relief to the monotony of her home life, seemed to excuse her brother's weakness. She was almost ready to become his partisan—*after* she had seen her father.

They had talked largely of their plans; they had settled small details of the future and the arrangement of the property; they had agreed that Zuleika should be relieved of her household drudgery, and sent to a fashionable school in San Francisco with a music teacher and a dressmaker. They had discussed everything but the precise manner in which the revelation should be conveyed to Hays. There was still plenty of time for that, for he would not return until to-morrow at

noon, and it was already tacitly understood that the vehicle of trans-
mission should be a letter from the Summit Hotel. The possible contingency of a sudden outburst of human passion not entirely controlled by religious feeling was to be guarded against.

They were sitting comfortably before the replenished fire; the wind
was still moaning in the chimney, when suddenly in a lull of the storm
the sound of sleigh bells seemed to fill the room. It was followed by a
voice from without, and with a hysterical cry Zuleika started to her
feet. The same breathless smile with which she had greeted her brother
an hour ago was upon her lips as she gasped—

"Lord, save us!—but it's dad come back!"

I grieve to say that here the doughty redresser of domestic wrongs
and retriever of the family honour lapsed white-faced in his chair
idealess and tremulous. It was his frailer companion who rose to the
occasion and even partly dragged him with her. "Go back to the
hotel," she said quickly, "and take the sled with you—you are not fit
to face him now! But he does not know *me,* and I will stay!" To the
staring Zuleika, "I am a stranger stopped by a broken sleigh on my
way to the hotel. Leave the rest to me. Now clear out, both of you. I'll
let him in."

She looked so confident, self-contained, and superior, that the
thought of opposition never entered their minds, and as an impatient
rapping rose from the door they let her, with a half-impatient, half-
laughing gesture, drive them before her from the room. When they
had disappeared in the distance, she turned to the front door, unbolted
and opened it. Hays blundered in out of the snow with a muttered
exclamation, and then, as the light from the open office door revealed
a stranger, started and fell back.

"Miss Hays is busy," said the woman quietly, "I am afraid on my
account. But my sleigh broke down on the way to the hotel, and I was
forced to get out here. I suppose this is Mr. Hays?"

A strange woman—by her dress and appearance a very worldling—
and even braver in looks and apparel than many he had seen in the
cities—seemed, in spite of all his precautions, to have fallen short of
the hotel and been precipitated upon him! Yet under the influence of
some odd abstraction he was affected by it less than he could have
believed. He even achieved a rude bow as he bolted the door and
ushered her into the office. More than that, he found himself explaining to the fair trespasser the reasons of his return to his own home.
For, like a direct man, he had a consciousness of some inconsistency in
his return—or in the circumstances that induced a change of plans
which might conscientiously require an explanation.

"You see, ma'am, a rather singular thing happened to me after I passed the summit. Three times I lost the track, got off it somehow, and found myself travelling in a circle. The third time, when I struck my own tracks again, I concluded I'd just follow them back here. I suppose I might have got the road again by tryin' and fightin' the snow —but there's some things not worth the fightin'. This was a matter of business—and, after all, ma'am, business ain't everythin'—is it?"

He was evidently in some unusual mood, the mood that with certain reticent natures often compels them to make their brief confidences to utter strangers rather than impart them to those intimate friends who might remind them of their weakness. She agreed with him pleasantly, but not so obviously as to excite suspicion. "And you preferred to let your business go, and come back to the comfort of your own home and family."

"The comfort of my home and family?" he repeated in a dry, deliberate voice. "Well, I reckon I ain't been tempted much by *that*. That isn't what I meant." But he went back to the phrase, repeating it grimly as if it were some mandatory text. "The comfort of my *own home and family*! Well, Satan hasn't set *that* trap for my feet yet, ma'am. No; ye saw my daughter? well, that's all my family; ye see this room? that's all my home. My wife ran away from me; my daughter cleared out too; my eldest son as was with me here has quo'lled with me, and reckons to set up a rival business agin me. No," he said, still more meditatively and deliberately; "it wasn't to come back to the comforts of my own home and family that I faced round on Heavy Tree Hill, I reckon."

As the woman, for certain reasons, had no desire to check this auspicious and unlooked-for confidence, she waited patiently. Hays remained silent for an instant warming his hands before the fire, and then looked up interrogatively.

"A professor of religion, ma'am, or under conviction?"

"Not exactly," said the lady, smiling.

"Excuse me, but in spite of your fine clothes I reckoned you had a serious look just now. A reader of Scripture, maybe?"

"I know the Bible."

"You remember when the angel with the flamin' sword appeared unto Saul on the road to Damascus?"

"Yes."

"It mout hev been suthin' in that style that stopped me," he said slowly and tentatively. "Though nat'rally *I* didn't *see* anything, and only had the queer feelin'. It might hev been *that* shied my mare off the track."

"But Saul was up to some wickedness, wasn't he?" said the lady smilingly, "while *you* were simply going somewhere on business?"

"Yes," said Hays thoughtfully; "but my *business* might hev seemed like persecution. I don't mind tellin' you what it was if you'd care to listen. But mebbe you're tired. Mebbe you want to retire. You know," he went on with a sudden hospitable outburst, "you needn't be in any hurry to go; we kin take care of you here to-night, and it'll cost you nothin'. And I'll send you on with my sleigh in the mornin'. Per'aps you'd like suthin' to eat—a cup of tea—or—I'll call Zuleika," and he rose, with an expression of awkward courtesy.

But the lady, albeit with a self-satisfied sparkle in her dark eyes, here carelessly assured him that Zuleika had already given her refreshment, and indeed was at that moment preparing her own room for her. She begged he would not interrupt this interesting story.

Hays looked relieved.

"Well, I reckon I won't call her, for what I was goin' to say ain't exakly the sort o' thin' for an innocent, simple sort o' thing like her to hear—I mean," he interrupted himself hastily—"that folks of more experience of the world like you and me don't mind speakin' of—I'm sorter takin' it for granted that you're a married woman, ma'am."

The lady, who had regarded him with a sudden rigidity, here relaxed her expression and nodded.

"Well," continued Hays, resuming his place by the fire, "you see this yer man I was goin' to see lives about four miles beyond the summit on a ranch that furnishes most of the hay for the stock that side of the Divide. He's bin holdin' off his next year's contracts with me, hopin' to make better terms from the prospects of a late spring and higher prices. He held his head mighty high, and talked big of waitin' his own time. I happened to know he couldn't do it."

He put his hands on his knees and stared at the fire, and then went on—

"Ye see this man had had crosses and family trials. He had a wife that left him to jine a lot of bally dancers and painted women in the 'Frisco playhouses when he was livin' in the southern country. You'll say that was like *my* own case—and mebbe that was why it came to him to tell me about it—but the difference betwixt *him* and *me* was that instead of restin' unto the Lord and findin' Him, and pluckin' out the eye that offended him 'cordin' to Scripter, as I did, *he* followed after *her* tryin' to get her back, until, findin' that wasn't no use, he took a big disgust and came up here to hide hisself, where there wasn't no playhouse nor play-actors, and no wimmen but Injin squaws. He preempted the land, and nat'rally, there bein' no one ez cared to live there but himself, he had it all his own way, made it pay, and, as I was sayin' before, held his head high for prices. Well—you ain't gettin' tired, ma'am?"

"No," said the lady, resting her cheek on her hand and gazing at the fire; "it's all very interesting, and so odd that you two men, with nearly the same experiences, should be neighbours."

"Say buyer and seller, ma'am, not neighbours—at least Scriptoorily —nor friends. Well—now this is where the Speshal Providence comes in—only this afternoon Jim Briggs, hearin' me speak of Horseley's offishness——"

"*Whose* offishness?" asked the lady.

"Horseley's offishness—Horseley's the name of the man I'm talkin' about. Well, hearin' that, he says, 'You hold on, Hays, and he'll climb down. That wife of his has left the stage—got sick of it—and is driftin' round in 'Frisco with some fellow. When Horseley gets to hear that, you can't keep him here—he'll settle up, sell out, and realise on everything he's got to go after her agin—you bet.' That's what Briggs said. Well, that's what sent me up to Horseley's to-night—to get there, drop the news, and then pin him down to that contract."

"It looked like a good stroke of business and a fair one," said the lady in an odd voice. It was so odd that Hays looked up. But she had somewhat altered her position, and was gazing at the ceiling, and with her hand to her face seemed to have just recovered from a slight yawn, at which he hesitated with a new and timid sense of politeness.

"You're gettin' tired, ma'am?"

"Oh dear, no!" she said in the same voice, but clearing her throat with a little cough. "And why didn't you see this Mr. Horseley after all? Oh, I forgot!—you said you changed your mind from something you'd heard."

He had turned his eyes to the fire again, but without noticing as he did so that she slowly moved her face, still half hidden by her hand, towards him, and was watching him intently.

"No," he said; slowly "nothin' I heard, somethin' I felt. It mout hev been that that set off on the track. It kem to me all of a sudden that he might be sittin' thar calm and peaceful like ez I might be here, hevin' forgot all about her and his trouble, and here was me goin' to drop down upon him and start it all fresh agin. It looked a little like persecution—yes, like persecution. I got rid of it, sayin' to myself it was business. But I'd got off the road meantime, and had to find it again, and whenever I got back to the track and was pointed for his house, it all seemed to come back on me and set me off again. When that had happened three times, I turned round and started for home."

"And do you mean to say," said the lady, with a discordant laugh, "that you believe, because *you* didn't go there and break the news, that nobody else will? That he won't hear of it from the first man he meets?"

"He don't meet any one up where he lives, and only Briggs and myself know it, and I'll see that Briggs don't tell. But it was mighty queer this whole thing comin' upon me suddenly—wasn't it?"

"Very queer," replied the lady, "for," with the same metallic laugh, "you don't seem to be given to this kind of weakness with your own family."

If there was any doubt as to the sarcastic suggestion of her voice, there certainly could be none in the wicked glitter of her eyes fixed upon his face under her shading hand. But haply he seemed unconscious of both, and even accepted her statement without an ulterior significance.

"Yes," he said communingly, to the glaring embers of the hearth, "it must have been a special revelation."

There was something so fatuous and one-idead in his attitude and expression, so monstrously inconsistent and inadequate to what was going on around him, and so hopelessly stupid—if a mere simulation —that the angry suspicion that he was acting a part slowly faded from her eyes, and a hysterical smile began to twitch her set lips. She still gazed at him. The wind howled drearily in the chimney; all that was economic, grim, and cheerless in the room seemed to gather as flitting shadows around that central figure. Suddenly she arose with such a quick rustling of her skirts that he lifted his eyes with a start; for she was standing immediately before him, her hands behind her, her handsome, audacious face bent smilingly forward, and her bold brilliant eyes within a foot of his own.

"Now, Mr. Hays, do you want to know what this warning or special revelation of yours *really* meant? Well, it had nothing whatever to do with that man on the summit. No. The whole interest, gist, and meaning of it was simply this, that you should turn round and come straight back here and"—she drew back and made him an exaggerated theatrical curtsey—"have the supreme pleasure of making *my* acquaintance! That was all. And now, as you've *had it,* in five minutes I must be off. You've offered me already your horse and sleigh to go to the summit. I accept it and go! Good-bye!"

He knew nothing of a woman's coquettish humour; he knew still less of that mimic stage from which her present voice, gesture, and expression were borrowed; he had no knowledge of the burlesque emotions which that voice, gesture, and expression were supposed to portray, and finally and fatally he was unable to detect the feminine hysteric jar and discord that underlay it all. He thought it was strong, characteristic, and real, and accepted it literally. He rose.

"Ef you allow you can't stay, why, I'll go and get the horse. I reckon he ain't bin put up yet."

"Do, please."

He grimly resumed his coat and hat and disappeared through the passage into the kitchen, whence, a moment later, Zuleika came flying.

"Well, what has happened?" she said eagerly.

"It's all right," said the woman quickly, "though he knows nothing yet. But I've got things fixed generally, so that he'll be quite ready to have it broken to him by this time to-morrow. But don't you say anything till I've seen Jack and you hear from *him*. Remember."

She spoke rapidly; her cheeks were quite glowing from some sudden energy; so were Zuleika's with the excitement of curiosity. Presently the sound of sleigh bells again filled the room. It was Hays leading the horse and sleigh to the door, beneath a sky now starlit and crisp under a north-east wind. The fair stranger cast a significant glance at Zuleika, and whispered hurriedly, "You know he must not come with me. You must keep him here."

She ran to the door muffled and hooded, leaped into the sleigh, and gathered up the reins.

"But you cannot go alone," said Hays, with awkward courtesy. "I was kalkilatin'——"

"You're too tired to go out again, dad," broke in Zuleika's voice quickly. "You ain't fit; you're all grey and krinkly now, like as when you had one of your last spells. She'll send the sleigh back to-morrow."

"I can find my way," said the lady briskly; "there's only one turn off, I believe, and that——"

"Leads to the stage station three miles west. You needn't be afraid of gettin' off on that, for you'll likely see the down stage crossin' your road as soon ez you get clear of the Ranch."

"Good-night," said the lady. An arc of white spray sprang before the forward runner, and the sleigh vanished in the road.

Father and daughter returned to the office.

"You didn't get to know her, dad, did ye?" queried Zuleika.

"No," responded Hays gravely; "except to see she wasn't no backwoods or mountaineering sort. Now, there's the kind of woman, Zuly, as knows her own mind and yours too; that a man like your brother Jack oughter pick out when he marries."

Zuleika's face beamed behind her father. "You ain't goin' to sit up any longer, dad?" she said, as she noticed him resume his seat by the fire. "It's gettin' late, and you look mighty tuckered out with your night's work."

"Do you know what she said, Zuly?" returned her father, after a pause, which turned out to have been a long silent laugh.

"No."

"She said," he repeated slowly, "that she reckoned I came back here to-night to have the pleasure of her acquaintance!" He brought his two hands heavily down upon his knees, rubbing them down deliberately towards his ankles, and leaning forward with his face to the fire and a long-sustained smile of complete though tardy appreciation.

He was still in this attitude when Zuleika left him. The wind crooned over him confidentially, but he still sat there, given up apparently to some posthumous enjoyment of his visitor's departing witticism.

It was scarcely daylight when Zuleika, while dressing, heard a quick tapping upon her shutter. She opened it to the scared and bewildered face of her brother.

"What happened with her and father last night?" he said hoarsely.

"Nothing—why?"

"Read that. It was brought to me half an hour ago by a man in dad's sleigh, from the stage station."

He handed her a crumpled note with trembling fingers. She took it and read—

"The game's up, and I'm out of it! Take my advice and clear out of it too, until you can come back in better shape. Don't be such a fool as to try and follow me. Your father isn't one, and that's where you've slipped up."

"He shall pay for it, whatever he's done," said her brother, with an access of wild passion. "Where is he?"

"Why, Jack, you wouldn't dare to see him now?"

"Wouldn't I?" He turned and ran, convulsed with passion, before the windows towards the front of the house. Zuleika slipped out of her bedroom and ran to her father's room. He was not there. Already she could hear her brother hammering frantically against the locked front door.

The door of the office was partly open. Her father was still there. Asleep? Yes, for he had apparently sank forward before the cold hearth. But the hands that he had always been trying to warm were colder than the hearth or ashes, and he himself never again spoke nor stirred.

It was deemed providential by the neighbours that his youngest and favourite son, alarmed by news of his father's failing health, had arrived from the Atlantic States just at the last moment. But it was thought singular that after the division of the property he entirely abandoned the Ranch, and that even pending the division his beautiful but fastidious Eastern bride declined to visit it with her husband.

Johnson's
"Old Woman"

IT WAS GROWING dark, and the Sonora trail was becoming more indistinct before me at every step. The difficulty had increased over the grassy slope, where the overflow from some smaller watercourse above had worn a number of diverging gullies so like the trail as to be undistinguishable from it. Unable to determine which was the right one, I threw the reins over the mule's neck and resolved to trust to that superior animal's sagacity, of which I had heard so much. But I had not taken into account the equally well-known weaknesses of sex and species, and Chu Chu had already shown uncontrollable signs of wanting her own way. Without a moment's hesitation, feeling the relaxed bridle, she laid down and rolled over.

In this perplexity the sound of horse's hoofs ringing out of the rocky cañon beyond was a relief, even if momentarily embarrassing. An instant afterwards a horse and rider appeared cantering round the hill on what was evidently the lost trail, and pulled up as I succeeded in forcing Chu Chu to her legs again.

"Is that the trail from Sonora?" I asked.

"Yes;" but with a critical glance at the mule, "I reckon you ain't going thar to-night."

"Why not?"

"It's a matter of eighteen miles, and most of it a blind trail through the woods after you take the valley."

"Is it worse than this?"

"What's the matter with this trail? Ye ain't expecting a racecourse or a shell road over the foot hills—are ye?"

"No. Is there any hotel where I can stop?"

"Nary."

"Nor any house?"

"No."

"Thank you. Good-night."

He had already passed on, when he halted again and turned in his saddle. "Look yer. Just a spell over yon cañon ye'll find a patch o' buckeyes; turn to the right and ye'll see a trail. That'll take ye to a shanty. You ask if it's Johnson's."

"Who's Johnson?"

"I am. You ain't lookin' for Vanderbilt or God Almighty up here, are you? Well then, you hark to me, will you? You say to my old woman to give you supper and a shake-down somewhar to-night. Say *I* sent you. So long."

He was gone before I could accept or decline. An extraordinary noise proceeded from Chu Chu, not unlike a suppressed chuckle. I looked sharply at her; she coughed affectedly, and, with her head and neck stretched to their greatest length, appeared to contemplate her neat little off fore shoe with admiring abstraction. But as soon as I had mounted she set off abruptly, crossed the rocky cañon, apparently sighted the patch of buckeyes of her own volition, and without the slightest hesitation found the trail to the right, and in half an hour stood before the shanty.

It was a log cabin, with an additional "lean-to" of the same material, roofed with bark, and on the other side a larger and more ambitious "extension" built of rough, unplaned, and unpainted redwood boards, lightly shingled. The "lean-to" was evidently used as a kitchen, and the central cabin as a living-room. The barking of a dog as I approached called four children of different sizes to the open door, where already an enterprising baby was feebly essaying to crawl over a bar of wood laid across the threshold to restrain it.

"Is this Johnson's house?"

My remark was really addressed to the eldest, a boy of apparently nine or ten, but I felt that my attention was unduly fascinated by the baby, who at that moment had toppled over the bar, and was calmly eyeing me upside down, while silently and heroically suffocating in its petticoats. The boy disappeared without replying, but presently

returned with a taller girl of fourteen or fifteen. I was struck with the
way that, as she reached the door, she passed her hands rapidly over
the heads of the others as if counting them, picked up the baby, reversed it, shook out its clothes, and returned it to the inside without
even looking at it. The act was evidently automatic and habitual.

I repeated my question timidly.

Yes, it *was* Johnson's, but he had just gone to King's Mills. I replied
hurriedly that I knew it—that I had met him beyond the cañon. As I
had lost my way and couldn't get to Sonora to-night, he had been good
enough to say that I might stay until morning. My voice was slightly
raised for the benefit of Mr. Johnson's "old woman," who, I had no
doubt, was inspecting me furtively from some corner.

The girl drew the children away, except the boy. To him she said
simply, "Show the stranger whar to stake out his mule, 'Dolphus,"
and disappeared in the "extension" without another word. I followed
my little guide, who was perhaps more actively curious, but equally
unresponsive. To my various questions he simply returned a smile of
exasperating vacuity. But he never took his eager eyes from me, and I
was satisfied that not a detail of my appearance escaped him. Leading
the way behind the house to a little wood, whose only "clearing" had
been effected by decay or storm, he stood silently apart while I pick-
eted Chu Chu, neither offering to assist me nor opposing any interruption to my survey of the locality. There was no trace of human cultivation in the surroundings of the cabin; the wilderness still trod sharply
on the heels of the pioneer's fresh footprints, and even seemed to
obliterate them. For a few yards around the actual dwelling there was
an unsavoury fringe of civilisation in the shape of cast off clothes,
empty bottles, and tin cans, and the adjacent thorn and elder bushes
blossomed unwholesomely with bits of torn white paper and bleaching
dish-cloths. This hideous circle never widened; Nature always appeared to roll back the intruding *débris;* no bird nor beast carried it
away; no animal ever forced the uncleanly barrier; civilisation remained grimly trenched in its own exuvia. The old terrifying girdle of
fire around the hunters' camp was not more deterring to curious night
prowlers than this coarse and accidental outwork.

When I regained the cabin I found it empty, the doors of the lean-to
and extension closed, but there was a stool set before a rude table,
upon which smoked a tin cup of coffee, a tin dish of hot saleratus
biscuit, and a plate of fried beef. There was something odd and depressing in this silent exclusion of my presence. Had Johnson's "old
woman" from some dark post of observation taken a dislike to my
appearance, or was this churlish withdrawal a peculiarity of Sierran
hospitality? Or was Mrs. Johnson young and pretty, and hidden under

the restricting ban of Johnson's jealousy, or was she a deformed crip-
ple, or even a bed-ridden crone? From the extension at times came a
murmur of voices, but never the accents of adult womanhood. The
gathering darkness, relieved only by a dull glow from the smouldering
logs in the adobe chimney, added to my loneliness. In the circumstances I knew I ought to have put aside the repast and given myself
up to gloomy and pessimistic reflection; but Nature is often inconsistent, and in that keen mountain air, I grieve to say, my physical and
moral condition was not in that perfect accord always indicated by
romancers. I had an appetite, and I gratified it; dyspepsia and ethical
reflections might come later. I ate the saleratus biscuit cheerfully, and
was meditatively finishing my coffee when a gurgling sound from the
rafters above attracted my attention. I looked up; under the overhang
of the bark roof three pairs of round eyes were fixed upon me. They
belonged to the children I had previously seen, who, in the attitude of
Raphael's cherubs, had evidently been deeply interested spectators of
my repast. As our eyes met an inarticulate giggle escaped the lips of
the youngest.

I never could understand why the shy amusement of children over
their elders is not accepted as philosophically by its object as when it
proceeds from an equal. We fondly believe that when Jones or Brown
laughs at us it is from malice, ignorance, or a desire to show his
superiority, but there is always a haunting suspicion in our minds that
these little critics *really* see something in us to laugh at. I, however,
smiled affably in return, ignoring any possible grotesqueness in my
manner of eating in private.

"Come here, Johnny," I said blandly.

The two elder ones, a girl and a boy, disappeared instantly, as if the
crowning joke of this remark was too much for them. From a scraping
and kicking against the log wall I judged that they had quickly
dropped to the ground outside. The younger one, the giggler, remained fascinated, but ready to fly at a moment's warning.

"Come here, Johnny, boy," I repeated gently. "I want you to go to
your mother, please, and tell her——"

But here the child, who had been working its face convulsively,
suddenly uttered a lugubrious howl and disappeared also. I ran to the
front door and looked out in time to see the tallest girl, who had
received me, walking away with it under her arm, pushing the boy
ahead of her and looking back over her shoulder, not unlike a youthful
she-bear conducting her cubs from danger. She disappeared at the end
of the extension, where there was evidently another door.

It was very extraordinary. It was not strange that I turned back to
the cabin with a chagrin and mortification which for a moment made

me entertain the wild idea of saddling Chu Chu and shaking the dust of that taciturn house from my feet. But the ridiculousness of such an act, to say nothing of its ingratitude, as quickly presented itself to me. Johnson had offered me only food and shelter; I could have claimed no more from the inn I had asked him to direct me to. I did not re-enter the house, but, lighting my last cigar, began to walk gloomily up and down the trail. With the outcoming of the stars it had grown lighter; through a wind opening in the trees I could see the heavy bulk of the opposite mountain, and beyond it a superior crest defined by a red line of forest fire, which, however, cast no reflection on the surrounding earth or sky. Faint woodland currents of air, still warm from the afternoon sun, stirred the leaves around me with long-drawn aromatic breaths. But these in time gave way to the steady Sierran night wind sweeping down from the higher summits, and rocking the tops of the tallest pines, yet leaving the tranquillity of the dark lower aisles unshaken. It was very quiet; there was no cry nor call of beast or bird in the darkness; the long rustle of the tree-tops sounded as faint as the far-off wash of distant seas. Nor did the resemblance cease there; the close-set files of the pines and cedars, stretching in illimitable ranks to the horizon, were filled with the immeasureable loneliness of an ocean shore. In this vast silence I began to think I understood the taciturnity of the dwellers in the solitary cabin.

When I returned, however, I was surprised to find the tallest girl standing by the door. As I approached she retreated before me, and, pointing to the corner where a common cot bed had been evidently just put up, said, "Ye can turn in thar, only ye'll have to rouse out early when 'Dolphus does the chores," and was turning towards the extension again, when I stopped her almost appealingly.

"One moment, please. Can I see your mother?"

She stopped and looked at me with a singular expression. Then she said sharply—

"You know, fust rate, she's dead."

She was turning away again, but I think she must have seen my concern in my face, for she hesitated. "But," I said quickly, "I certainly understood your father, that is, Mr. Johnson," I added interrogatively, "to say that—that I was to speak to"—I didn't like to repeat the exact phrase—"his *wife.*"

"I don't know what he was playin' ye for," she said shortly. "Mar has been dead mor'n a year."

"But," I persisted, "is there no grown-up woman here?"

"No."

"Then who takes care of you and the children?"

"I do."

"Yourself and your father—eh?"

"Dad ain't here two days running, and then on'y to sleep."

"And you take the entire charge of the house?"

"Yes, and the log tallies."

"The log tallies?"

"Yes; keep count and measure the logs that go by the slide."

It flashed upon me that I had passed the slide or declivity on the hill side, where logs were slipped down into the valley, and I inferred that Johnson's business was cutting timber for the mill.

"But you're rather young for all this work," I suggested.

"I'm goin' on sixteen," she said gravely.

Indeed, for the matter of that, she might have been any age. Her face, on which sunburn took the place of complexion, was already hard and set. But on a nearer view I was struck with the fact that her eyes, which were not large, were almost indistinguishable from the presence of the most singular eyelashes I had ever seen. Intensely black, intensely thick, and even tangled in their profusion, they bristled rather than fringed her eyelids, obliterating everything but the shining black pupils beneath, which were like certain lustrous hairy mountain berries. It was this woodland suggestion that seemed to uncannily connect her with the locality. I went on playfully—

"That's not *very* old; but tell me—does your father, or *did* your father, ever speak of you as 'his old woman?'"

She nodded. "Then you thought I was mar?" she said, smiling.

It was such a relief to see her worn face relax its expression of pathetic gravity—although this operation quite buried her eyes in their black thickset hedge again—that I continued cheerfully, "It wasn't much of a mistake, considering all you do for the house and family."

"Then you didn't tell Billy 'to go and be dead in the ground with mar,' as he 'lows you did?" she said half suspiciously, yet trembling on the edge of a smile.

No, I had not; but I admitted that my asking him to go to his mother might have been open to this dismal construction by a sensitive infant mind. She seemed mollified, and again turned to go.

"Good-night, miss—; you know your father didn't tell me your real name," I said.

"Karline!"

"Good-night, Miss Karline."

I held out my hand.

She looked at it and then at me through her intricate eyelashes. Then she struck it aside briskly, but not unkindly, said "Quit foolin', now," as she might have said to one of the children, and disappeared through the inner door. Not knowing whether to be amused or indignant, I remained silent a moment. Then I took a turn outside in the increasing darkness, listened to the now hurrying wind over the tree-tops, re-entered the cabin, closed the door, and went to bed.

But not to sleep. Perhaps the responsibility towards these solitary children, which Johnson had so lightly shaken off, devolved upon me as I lay there, for I found myself imagining a dozen emergencies of their unprotected state which the elder girl could scarcely grapple. There was little to fear from depredatory man or beast—desperadoes of the mountain trail never stooped to ignoble burglary, bear or panther seldom approached a cabin—but there was the chance of sudden illness, fire, the accidents that beset childhood, to say nothing of the narrowing moral and mental effect of their isolation at that tender age. It was scandalous in Johnson to leave them alone.

In the silence I found I could hear quite distinctly the sound of their voices in the extension, and it was evident that Caroline was putting them to bed. Suddenly a voice was uplifted—her own! She began to sing and the others to join her. It was the repetition of a single verse of a well-known lugubrious negro melody. "All the world am sad and dreary," wailed Caroline, in a high head-note, "everywhere I roam." "O, darkieth," lisped the younger girl in response, "how my heart growth weary, far from the old folkth at h-o-o-me." This was repeated two or three times before the others seemed to get the full swing of it, and then the lines rose and fell sadly and monotonously in the darkness. I don't know why, but I at once got the impression that those motherless little creatures were under a vague belief that their performance was devotional, and was really filling the place of an evening hymn. A brief and indistinct kind of recitation, followed by a dead silence, broken only by the slow creaking of new timber, as if the house were stretching itself to sleep too, confirmed my impression. Then all became quiet again.

But I was more wide awake than before. Finally I rose, dressed myself, and dragging my stool to the fire, took a book from my knapsack, and by the light of a guttering candle, which I discovered in a bottle in the corner of the hearth, began to read. Presently I fell into a doze. How long I slept I could not tell, for it seemed to me that a dreamy consciousness of a dog barking at last forced itself upon me so strongly that I awoke. The barking appeared to come from behind the cabin, in the direction of the clearing where I had tethered Chu Chu. I opened the door hurriedly, ran round the cabin towards the hollow, and was almost at once met by the bulk of the frightened Chu Chu, plunging out of the darkness towards me, kept only in check by her riata in the hand of a blanketed shape slowly advancing with a gun over its shoulder out of the hollow. Before I had time to recover from my astonishment I was thrown into greater confusion by recognising the shape as none other than Caroline!

Without the least embarrassment or even self-consciousness of her appearance, she tossed the end of the riata to me with the curtest explanation as she passed by. Some prowling bear or catamount had frightened the mule. I had better tether it before the cabin away from the wind.

"But I thought wild beasts never came so near," I said quickly.

"Mule meat's mighty temptin'," said the girl sententiously and passed on. I wanted to thank her; I wanted to say how sorry I was that she had been disturbed; I wanted to compliment her on her quiet midnight courage, and yet warn her against recklessness; I wanted to know whether she had been accustomed to such alarms; and if the gun she carried was really a necessity. But I could only respect her reticence, and I was turning away when I was struck by a more inexplicable spectacle. As she neared the end of the extension I distinctly saw the tall figure of a man, moving with a certain diffidence and hesitation that did not, however, suggest any intention of concealment, among the trees; the girl apparently saw him at the same moment, and slightly slackened her pace. Not more than a dozen feet separated them. He said something that was inaudible to my ears—but whether from his hesitation or the distance, I could not determine. There was no such uncertainty in her reply, however, which was given in her usual curt fashion—"All right. You kin trapse along home now and turn in."

She turned the corner of the extension and disappeared. The tall figure of the man wavered hesitatingly for a moment, and then vanished also. But I was too much excited by curiosity to accept this unsatisfactory conclusion, and, hastily picketing Chu Chu a few rods from the front door, I ran after him, with an instinctive feeling that he had not gone far. I was right. A few paces distant he had halted in the same dubious, lingering way. "Hallo!" I said.

He turned towards me in the like awkward fashion, but with neither astonishment nor concern.

"Come up and take a drink with me before you go," I said, "if you're not in a hurry. I'm alone here, and since I *have* turned out I don't see why we mightn't have a smoke and a talk together."

"I dursn't."

I looked up at the six feet of strength before me and repeated wonderingly, "Dare not?"

"*She* wouldn't like it." He made a movement with his right shoulder towards the extension.

"Who?"

"Miss Karline."

"Nonsense!" I said. "She isn't in the cabin—you won't see *her*. Come along." He hesitated, although from what I could discern of his bearded face it was weakly smiling.

"Come."

He obeyed, following me not unlike Chu Chu, I fancied, with the same sense of superior size and strength and a slight whitening of the eye, as if ready to shy at any moment. At the door he "backed." Then he entered sideways. I noticed that he cleared the doorway at the top and the sides only by a hair's-breadth.

By the light of the fire I could see that, in spite of his full first growth of beard, he was young—even younger than myself, and that he was by no means bad-looking. As he still showed signs of retreating at any moment, I took my flask and tobacco from my saddle-bags, handed them to him, pointed to the stool, and sat down myself upon the bed.

"You live near here?"

"Yes," he said a little abstractedly, as if listening for some interruption, "at Ten Mile Crossing."

"Why, that's two miles away."

"I reckon."

"Then you don't live here—on the clearing?"

"No. I b'long to the mill at 'Ten Mile.' "

"You were on your way home?"

"No," he hesitated, looking at his pipe; "I kinder meander round here at this time, when Johnson's away, to see if everything's goin' straight."

"I see—you're a friend of the family."

" 'Deed no!" He stopped, laughed, looked confused, and added, apparently to his pipe, "That is, a sorter friend. Not much. *She*"—he lowered his voice, as if that potential personality filled the whole cabin —"wouldn't like it."

"Then at night, when Johnson's away, you do sentry duty round the house?"

"Yes, 'sentry dooty,' that's it"—he seemed impressed with the suggestion—"that's it! Sentry dooty. You've struck it, pardner."

"And how often is Johnson away?"

" 'Bout two or three times a week on an average."

"But Miss Caroline appears to be able to take care of herself. She has no fear."

"Fear! Fear wasn't hangin' round when *she* was born!" He paused. "No, sir. Did ye ever look into them eyes?"

I hadn't, on account of the lashes. But I didn't care to say this, and only nodded.

"There ain't the created thing livin' or dead that she can't stand straight up to and look at."

I wondered if he had fancied she experienced any difficulty in standing up before that innocently good-humoured face, but I could not resist saying—

"Then I don't see the use of your walking four miles to look after her."

I was sorry for it the next minute, for he seemed to have awkwardly broken his pipe, and had to bend down for a long time afterwards to laboriously pick up the smallest fragments of it. At last he said cautiously—

"Ye noticed them bits o' flannin' round the chillern's throats?"

I remembered that I had, but was uncertain whether it was intended as a preventive of cold or a child's idea of decoration. I nodded.

"That's their trouble. One night, when old Johnson had been off for three days to Coulterville, I was prowling round here and I didn't git to see no one, though there was a light burnin' in the shanty all night. The next night I was here again—the same light twinklin', but no one about. I reckoned that was mighty queer, and I jess crep' up to the house an' listened. I heard suthin' like a little cough onest in a while, and times suthin' like a little moan. I didn't durst to sing out, for I knew *she* wouldn't like it, but I whistled keerless like, to let the chillern know I was there. But it didn't seem to take. I was jess goin' off, when—darn my skin!—if I didn't come across the bucket of water I'd fetched up from the spring *that mornin',* standin' there full, and *never taken in!* When I saw that I reckoned I'd jess wade in, anyhow, and I knocked. Pooty soon the door was half opened, and I saw her eyes blazin' at me like them coals. Then *she* 'lowed I'd better 'git up and get,' and shet the door too! Then I 'lowed she might tell me what was up—through the door. Then she said—through the door—as how the chillern lay all sick with that hoss-distemper, diphthery. Then she 'lowed she'd use a doctor ef I'd fetch him. Then she 'lowed again I'd better take the baby, that hadn't ketched it yet, along with me, and leave it where it was safe. Then she passed out the baby through the door all wrapped up in a blankit like a papoose, and you bet I made tracks with it. I knowed thar wasn't no good going to the mill, so I let out for White's, four miles beyond, whar there was White's old mother. I told her how things were pointin', and she lent me a hoss, and I jess rounded on Doctor Green at Mountain Jim's, and had him back here afore sun up! And then I heard she wilted—regularly played out, you see—for she had it all along wuss than the lot, and never let on or whimpered!"

"It was well you persisted in seeing her that night," I said, watching the rapt expression of his face. He looked up quickly, became conscious of my scrutiny, and dropped his eyes again, smiled feebly, and drawing a circle in the ashes with the broken pipe-stem, said—

"But *she* didn't like it, though."

I suggested, a little warmly, that if she allowed her father to leave her alone at night with delicate children, she had no right to choose *who* should assist her in an emergency. It struck me afterwards that this was not very complimentary to him, and I added hastily that I wondered if she expected some young lady to be passing along the trail at midnight! But this reminded me of Johnson's style of argument, and I stopped.

"Yes," he said meekly; "and ef she didn't keer enough for herself and her brothers and sisters, she orter remember them Beazeley chillern."

"Beazeley children?" I repeated wonderingly.

"Yes; them two little ones, the size of Mirandy; they're Beazeley's."

"Who is Beazeley, and what are his children doing here?"

"Beazeley up and died at the mill, and she bedeviled her father to let her take his two young 'uns here."

"You don't mean to say that with her other work she's taking care of other people's children too?"

"Yes, and eddicatin' them."

"Educating them?"

"Yes; teachin' them to read and write and do sums. One of our loggers ketched her at it when she was keepin' tally."

We were both silent for some moments.

"I suppose you know Johnson?" I said finally.

"Not much."

"But you call here at other times than when you're helping her?"

"Never been in the house before."

He looked slowly around him as he spoke, raising his eyes to the bare rafters above, and drawing a few long breaths, as if he were inhaling the aura of some unseen presence. He appeared so perfectly gratified and contented, and I was so impressed with this humble and silent absorption of the sacred interior, that I felt vaguely conscious that any interruption of it was a profanation, and I sat still, gazing at the dying fire. Presently he arose, stretched out his hand, shook mine warmly, said, "I reckon I'll meander along," took another long breath, this time secretly, as if conscious of my eyes, and then slouched sideways out of the house into the darkness again, where he seemed suddenly to attain his full height, and so looming, disappeared. I shut the door, went to bed, and slept soundly.

So soundly that when I awoke the sun was streaming on my bed from the open door. On the table before me my breakfast was already laid. When I had dressed and eaten it, struck by the silence, I went to the door and looked out. 'Dolphus was holding Chu Chu by the riata a few paces from the cabin.

"Where's Caroline?" I asked.

He pointed to the woods and said, "Over yon; keeping tally."

"Did she leave any message?"

"Said I was to git your mule for you."

"Anything else?"

"Yes; said you was to go."

I went, but not until I had scrawled a few words of thanks on a leaf of my note-book, which I wrapped about my last Spanish dollar, addressed it to "Miss Johnson," and laid it upon the table.

It was more than a year later that in the bar-room of the Mariposas Hotel a hand was laid upon my sleeve. I looked up. It was Johnson.

He drew from his pocket a Spanish dollar. "I reckoned," he said cheerfully, "I'd run again ye somewhar some time. My old woman told me to give ye that when I did, and say that she 'didn't keep no hotel.' But she allowed she'd keep the letter, and has spelled it out to the chillern."

Here was the opportunity I had longed for to touch Johnson's pride and affection in the brave but unprotected girl. "I want to talk to you about Miss Johnson," I said eagerly.

"I reckon so," he said, with an exasperating smile. "Most fellers do. But she ain't *Miss* Johnson no more. She's married."

"Not to that big chap over from Ten Mile Mills?" I said breathlessly.

"What's the matter with *him,*" said Johnson. "Ye didn't expect her to marry a nobleman, did ye?"

I said I didn't see why she shouldn't—and believed that she *had.*

Out of a
Pioneer's Trunk

IT WAS A slightly cynical, but fairly good-humoured crowd that had gathered before a warehouse on Long Wharf in San Francisco one afternoon in the summer of '51. Although the occasion was an auction, the bidders' chances more than usually hazardous, and the season and locality famous for reckless speculation, there was scarcely any excitement among the bystanders, and a lazy, half-humorous curiosity seemed to have taken the place of any zeal for gain.

It was an auction of unclaimed trunks and boxes—the personal luggage of early emigrants—which had been left on storage in hulk or warehouse at San Francisco, while the owner was seeking his fortune in the mines. The difficulty and expense of transport, often obliging the gold-seeker to make part of his journey on foot, restricted him to the smallest *impedimenta,* and that of a kind not often found in the luggage of ordinary civilisation. As a consequence, during the emigration of '49, he was apt on landing to avail himself of the invitation usually displayed on some of the doors of the rude hostelries on the shore: "Rest for the Weary and Storage for Trunks." In a majority of cases he never returned to claim his stored property. Enforced absence, protracted equally by good or evil fortune, accumulated the high storage charges until they usually far exceeded the actual value of the goods; sickness, further emigration, or death also reduced the number of possible claimants, and that more wonderful human frailty—absolute forgetfulness of deposited possessions—combined together to leave the bulk of the property in the custodian's hands. Under an understood agreement they were always sold at public auction after a given time. Although the contents of some of the trunks were exposed, it was found more in keeping with the public sentiment to sell the trunks *locked* and *unopened*. The element of curiosity was kept up from time to time by the incautious disclosures of the lucky or unlucky purchaser, and general bidding thus encouraged—except when the speculator, with the true gambling instinct, gave no indication in his face of what was drawn in this lottery. Generally, however, some suggestion in the exterior of the trunk, a label or initials; some conjectural knowledge of its former owner, or the idea that he might be secretly present in the hope of getting his property back for less than the accumulated dues, kept up the bidding and interest.

A modest-looking, well-worn portmanteau had been just put up at a small opening bid, when Harry Flint joined the crowd. The young man had arrived a week before at San Francisco friendless and penniless, and had been forced to part with his own effects to procure necessary food and lodging while looking for an employment. In the irony of fate that morning the proprietors of a dry-goods store, struck with his good looks and manners, had offered him a situation, if he could make himself more presentable to their fair clients. Harry Flint was gazing half abstractedly, half hopelessly, at the portmanteau, without noticing the auctioneer's persuasive challenge. In his abstraction he was not aware that the auctioneer's assistant was also looking at him curiously, and that possibly his dejected and half-clad appearance had excited the attention of one of the cynical bystanders, who was exchanging a few words with the assistant. He was, however, recalled to himself a moment later when the portmanteau was knocked down at fifteen dollars, and considerably startled when the assistant placed it at his feet with a grim smile. "That's your property, Fowler, and I reckon you look as if you wanted it back bad."

"But—there's some mistake," stammered Flint. "I didn't bid."

"No, but Tom Flynn did for you. You see, I spotted you from the first, and told Flynn I reckoned you were one of those chaps who came back from the mines dead broke. And he up and bought your things for you—like a square man. That's Flynn's style, if he is a gambler."

"But," persisted Flint, "this never was my property. My name isn't Fowler, and I never left anything here."

The assistant looked at him with a grim, half-credulous, half-scornful smile. "Have it your own way," he said, "but I oughter tell yer, old man, that I'm the warehouse clerk, and I remember *you*. I'm here for that purpose. But as that thar valise is bought and paid for by somebody else and given to you, it's nothing more to me. Take or leave it."

The ridiculousness of quarrelling over the mere form of his good fortune here struck Flint, and, as his abrupt benefactor had as abruptly disappeared, he hurried off with his prize. Reaching his cheap lodging-house, he examined its contents. As he had surmised, it contained a full suit of clothing of the better sort, and suitable to his urban needs. There were a few articles of jewellery, which he put religiously aside. There were some letters, which seemed to be of a purely business character. There were a few daguerreotypes of pretty faces, one of which was singularly fascinating to him. But there was another, of a young man, which startled him with its marvellous resemblance *to himself!* In a flash of intelligence he understood it all now. It was the likeness of the former owner of the trunk, for whom the assistant had actually mistaken him! He glanced hurriedly at the envelopes of the letters. They were addressed to Shelby Fowler, the name by which the assistant had just called him. The mystery was plain now. And for the present he could fairly accept his good luck, and trust to later fortune to justify himself.

Transformed in his new garb, he left his lodgings to present himself once more to his possible employer. His way led past one of the large gambling saloons. It was yet too early to find the dry-goods trader disengaged; perhaps the consciousness of more decent, civilised garb emboldened him to mingle more freely with strangers, and he entered the saloon. He was scarcely abreast of one of the faro tables when a man suddenly leaped up with an oath and discharged a revolver full in his face. The shot missed. Before his unknown assailant could fire again the astonished Flint had closed with him, and instinctively clutched the weapon. A brief but violent struggle ensued. Flint felt his strength failing him, when suddenly a look of astonishment came into the furious eyes of his adversary, and the man's grasp mechanically relaxed. The half-freed pistol, thrown upwards by this movement, was accidentally discharged point blank into his temples, and he fell dead. No one in the crowd had stirred or interfered.

"You've done for Australian Pete this time, Mr. Fowler," said a voice at his elbow. He turned gaspingly, and recognised his strange benefactor, Flynn. "I call you all to witness, gentlemen," continued the gambler, turning dictatorially to the crowd, "that this man was *first* attacked and was *unarmed.*" He lifted Flint's limp and empty hands and then pointed to the dead man, who was still grasping the weapon. "Come!" He caught the half-paralysed arm of Flint and dragged him into the street.

"But," stammered the horrified Flint, as he was borne along, "what does it all mean? What made that man attack me?"

"I reckon it was a case of shooting on sight, Mr. Fowler; but he missed it by not waiting to see if you were armed. It wasn't the square thing, and you're all right with the crowd now, whatever he might have had agin' you."

"But," protested the unhappy Flint, "I never laid eyes on the man before, and my name isn't Fowler."

Flynn halted, and dragged him in a doorway. "Who the devil are you?" he asked roughly.

Briefly, passionately, almost hysterically, Flint told him his scant story. An odd expression came over the gambler's face.

"Look here," he said abruptly; "I have passed my word to the crowd yonder that you are a dead-broke miner called Fowler. I allowed that you might have had some row with that Sydney Dick, Australian Pete, in the mines. That satisfied them. If I go back now, and say it's a lie, that your name ain't Fowler, and you never knew who Pete was, they'll jest pass you over to the police to deal with you, and wash their hands of it altogether. You may prove to the police who you are, and how that d——d clerk mistook you, but it will give you trouble. And who is there here who knows who you really are?"

"No one," said Flint, with sudden hopelessness.

"And you say you're an orphan, and ain't got any relations livin' that you're beholden to?"

"No one."

"Then take my advice, and *be* Fowler, and stick to it! Be Fowler until Fowler turns up, and thanks you for it; for you've saved Fowler's life, as Pete would never have funked and lost his grit over Fowler as he did with you; and you've a right to his name."

He stopped, and the same odd superstitious look came into his dark eyes.

"Don't you see what all that means? Well, I'll tell you. You're in the biggest streak of luck a man ever had. You've got the cards in your own hands! They spell 'Fowler'! Play Fowler first, last, and all the time. Good-night, and good luck, *Mr. Fowler.*"

The next morning's journal contained an account of the justifiable killing of the notorious desperado and ex-convict, Australian Pete, by a courageous young miner by the name of Fowler. "An act of firmness and daring," said the *Pioneer*, "which will go far to counteract the terrorism produced by those lawless ruffians."

In his new suit of clothes, and with this paper in his hand, Flint sought the dry-goods proprietor—the latter was satisfied and convinced. That morning Harry Flint began his career as salesman and as "Shelby Fowler."

From that day Shelby Fowler's career was one of uninterrupted prosperity. Within the year he became a partner. The same miraculous fortune followed other ventures later. He was mill owner, mine owner, bank director—a millionaire! He was popular, the reputation of his brief achievement over the desperado kept him secure from the attack of envy and rivalry. He never was confronted by the real Fowler. There was no danger of exposure by others—the one custodian of his secret, Tom Flynn, died in Nevada the year following. He had quite forgotten his youthful past, and even the more recent lucky portmanteau; remembered nothing, perhaps, but the pretty face of the daguerreotype that had fascinated him. There seemed to be no reason why he should not live and die as Shelby Fowler.

His business a year later took him to Europe. He was entering a train at one of the great railway stations of London, when the porter, who had just deposited his portmanteau in a compartment, reappeared at the window followed by a young lady in mourning.

"Beg pardon, sir, but I handed you the wrong portmanteau. That belongs to this young lady. This is yours."

Flint glanced at the portmanteau on the seat before him. It certainly was not his, although it bore the initials "S.F." He was mechanically handing it back to the porter, when his eyes fell on the young lady's face. For an instant he stood petrified. It was the face of the daguerreotype. "I beg pardon," he stammered, "but are these your initials?" She hesitated; perhaps it was the abruptness of the question, but he saw she looked confused.

"No. A friend's."

She disappeared into another carriage, but from that moment Harry Flint knew that he had no other aim in life but to follow this clue and the beautiful girl who had dropped it. He bribed the guard at the next station, and discovered that she was going to York. On their arrival, he was ready on the platform to respectfully assist her. A few words disclosed the fact that she was a fellow-countrywoman, although residing in England, and at present on her way to join some friends at Harrogate. Her name was West. At the mention of his, he again fancied she looked disturbed.

They met again and again; the informality of his introduction was overlooked by her friends, as his assumed name was already respectably and responsibly known beyond California. He thought no more of his future. He was in love. He even dared to think it might be returned; but he felt he had no right to seek that knowledge until he had told her his real name and how he came to assume another's. He did so alone—scarcely a month after their first meeting. To his alarm, she burst into a flood of tears, and showed an agitation that seemed far beyond any apparent cause. When she had partly recovered, she said, in a low frightened voice—

"You are bearing *my brother's* name. But it was a name that the unhappy boy had so shamefully disgraced in Australia that he abandoned it, and, as he lay upon his death-bed, the last act of his wasted life was to write an imploring letter begging me to change mine too. For the infamous companion of his crime who had first tempted, then betrayed him, had possession of all his papers and letters, many of them from *me,* and was threatening to bring them to our Virginia home and expose him to our neighbours. Maddened by desperation, the miserable boy twice attempted the life of the scoundrel, and might have added that blood-guiltiness to his other sins had he lived. I *did* change my name to my mother's maiden one, left the country, and have lived here to escape the revelations of that desperado, should he fulfil his threat."

In a flash of recollection Flint remembered the startled look that had come into his assailant's eye after they had clinched. It was the same man who had too late realised that his antagonist was not Fowler. "Thank God! you are for ever safe from any exposure from that man," he said gravely, "and the name of Fowler has never been known in San Francisco save in all respect and honour. It is for you to take back—fearlessly and alone!"

She did—but not alone, for she shared it with her husband.

The Great
Deadwood Mystery

PART I

IT WAS GROWING quite dark in the telegraph office at Cottonwood,
Tuolumne Co., California. The office, a box-like enclosure, was separated from the public room of the Miners' Hotel by a thin partition,
and the operator, who was also news and express agent at Cottonwood, had closed his window, and was lounging by his news-stand
preparatory to going home. Accustomed as he was to long intervals of
idleness, he was fast becoming bored.

The tread of mud-muffled boots on the verandah, and the entrance
of two men, offered a momentary excitement. He recognised in the
strangers two prominent citizens of Cottonwood, and their manner
bespoke business. One of them proceeded to the desk, wrote a despatch, and handed it to the other interrogatively.

"That's about the way the thing p'ints," responded his companion.
"I reckoned it only squar to use his dientikal words?"
"That's so."
The first speaker turned to the operator with the despatch.
"How soon can you shove her through?"

The operator glanced professionally over the address and the length of the despatch.

"Now," he answered promptly.

"And she gets there——?"

"To-night; but there's no delivery until to-morrow."

"Shove her through to-night, and say there's an extra twenty left here for delivery"

The operator, accustomed to all kinds of extravagant outlay for expedition, replied that he would lay this proposition, with the despatch, before the San Francisco office. He then took it and read it—and re-read it. He preserved the usual professional apathy—had doubtless sent many more enigmatical and mysterious messages—but, nevertheless, when he finished he raised his eyes inquiringly to his customer. That gentleman, who enjoyed a reputation for equal spontaneity of temper and revolver, met his gaze a little impatiently. The operator had recourse to a trick. Under the pretence of misunderstanding the message, he obliged the sender to repeat it aloud for the sake of accuracy, and even suggested a few verbal alterations, ostensibly to insure correctness, but really to extract further information. Nevertheless, the man doggedly persisted in a literal transcript of his message. The operator went to his instrument hesitatingly.

"I suppose," he added half questioningly, "there ain't no chance of a mistake? This address is Rightbody, that rich old Bostonian that everybody knows. There ain't but one?"

"That's the address," responded the first speaker coolly.

"Didn't know the old chap had investments out here," suggested the operator, lingering at his instrument.

"No more did I," was the insufficient reply.

For some few moments nothing was heard but the click of the instrument, as the operator worked the key with the usual appearance of imparting confidence to a somewhat reluctant hearer who preferred to talk himself. The two men stood by, watching his motions with the usual awe of the unprofessional. When he had finished, they laid before him two gold pieces. As the operator took them up, he could not help saying—

"The old man went off kinder sudden, didn't he? Had no time to write?"

"Not sudden for that kind o' man," was the exasperating reply.

But the speaker was not to be disconcerted. "If there is an answer——"

"There ain't any," replied the first speaker quietly.

"Why?"

"Because the man ez sent the message is dead."

"But it's signed by you two."

"On'y ez witnesses—eh?" appealed the first speaker to his comrade.

"On'y ez witnesses," responded the other.

The operator shrugged his shoulders. The business concluded, the first speaker slightly relaxed. He nodded to the operator, and turned to the bar-room with a pleasing social impulse. When their glasses were set down empty, the first speaker, with a cheerful condemnation of the hard times and the weather, apparently dismissed all previous proceedings from his mind, and lounged out with his companion. At the corner of the street they stopped.

"Well, that job's done," said the first speaker, by way of relieving the slight social embarrassment of parting.

"That's so," responded his companion, and shook his hand.

They parted. A gust of wind swept through the pines, and struck a faint Aeolian cry from the wires above their heads, and the rain and the darkness again slowly settled upon Cottonwood.

The message lagged a little at San Francisco, laid over half-an-hour at Chicago, and fought longitude the whole way, so that it was past midnight when the "all night" operator took it from the wires at Boston. But it was freighted with a mandate from the San Francisco office, and a messenger was procured, who sped with it through dark snow-bound streets, between the high walls of close-shuttered rayless houses to a certain formal square, ghostly with snow-covered statues. Here he ascended the broad steps of a reserved and solid-looking mansion, and pulled a bronze bell knob that, somewhere within those chaste recesses, after an apparent reflective pause, coldly communicated the fact that a stranger was waiting without—as he ought. Despite the lateness of the hour, there was a slight glow from the windows, clearly not enough to warm the messenger with indications of a festivity within, but yet bespeaking, as it were, some prolonged though subdued excitement. The sober servant, who took the despatch and receipted for it as gravely as if witnessing a last will and testament, respectfully paused before the entrance of the drawing-room. The sound of measured and rhetorical speech, through which the occasional catarrhal cough of the New England coast struggled, as the only effort of nature not wholly repressed, came from its heavily-curtained recesses, for the occasion of the evening had been the reception and entertainment of various distinguished persons, and, as had been epigrammatically expressed by one of the guests, "the history of the country" was taking its leave in phrases more or less memorable and characteristic. Some of these valedictory axioms were clever, some witty, a few profound, but always left as a genteel contribution to the entertainer. Some had been already prepared, and, like a card, had served and identified the guest at other mansions.

The last guest departed, the last carriage rolled away, when the servant ventured to indicate the existence of the despatch to his master, who was standing on the hearthrug in an attitude of wearied self-righteousness. He took it, opened it, read it, re-read it, and said—

"There must be some mistake! It is not for me; call the boy, Waters."

Waters, who was perfectly aware that the boy had left, nevertheless obediently walked towards the hall door, but was recalled by his master.

"No matter—at present!"

"It's nothing serious, William?" asked Mrs. Rightbody, with languid wifely concern.

"No, nothing. Is there a light in my study?"

"Yes. But before you go—can you give me a moment or two?"

Mr. Rightbody turned a little impatiently towards his wife. She had thrown herself languidly on the sofa, her hair was slightly disarranged, and part of a slippered foot was visible. She might have been a finely-formed woman, but even her careless *déshabille* left the general impression that she was severely flannelled throughout, and that any ostentation of womanly charm was under vigorous sanitary surveillance.

"Mrs. Marvin told me to-night that her son made no secret of his serious attachment for our Alice, and that if I was satisfied, Mr. Marvin would be glad to confer with you at once."

The information did not seem to absorb Mr. Rightbody's wandering attention, but rather increased his impatience. He said hastily that he would speak of that to-morrow; and, partly by way of reprisal, and partly to dismiss the subject, added—

"Positively James must pay some attention to the register and thermometer. It was over 70° to-night, and the ventilating draught was closed in the drawing-room."

"That was because Professor Ammon sat near it, and the old gentleman's tonsils are so sensitive."

"He ought to know from Dr. Dyer Doit that systematic and regular exposure to draughts stimulates the mucous membrane, while fixed air over 60° invariably——"

"I am afraid, William," interrupted Mrs. Rightbody, with feminine adroitness, adopting her husband's topic with a view of thereby directing him from it, "I'm afraid that people do not yet appreciate the substitution of *bouillon* for punch and ices. I observed that Mr.

Spondee declined it, and I fancied looked disappointed. The fibrine and wheat in liqueur-glasses passed quite unnoticed too."

"And yet each half-drachm contained the half-digested substance of a pound of beef. I'm surprised at Spondee," continued Mr. Rightbody aggrievedly. "Exhausting his brain and nerve force by the highest creative efforts of the Muse, he prefers perfumed and diluted alchohol flavoured with carbonic acid gas. Even Mrs. Faringway admitted to me that the sudden lowering of the temperature of the stomach by the introduction of ice——"

"Yes, but she took a lemon ice at the last Dorothea Reception, and asked me if I had observed that the lower animals refused their food at a temperature over 60°."

Mr. Rightbody again moved impatiently towards the door. Mrs. Rightbody eyed him curiously.

"You will not write, I hope? Dr. Kepler told me to-night that your cerebral symptoms interdicted any prolonged mental strain."

"I must consult a few papers," responded Mr. Rightbody curtly, as he entered his library.

It was a richly furnished apartment, morbidly severe in its decorations, which were symptomatic of a gloomy dyspepsia of art, then quite prevalent. A few curios, very ugly, but providentially equally rare, were scattered about; there were various bronzes, marbles, and casts, all requiring explanation, and so fulfilling their purpose of promoting conversation and exhibiting the erudition of their owner. There were souvenirs of travel with a history, old *bric-a-brac* with a pedigree, but little or nothing that challenged attention for itself alone. In all cases the superiority of the owner to his possessions was admitted. As a natural result, nobody ever lingered there, the servants avoided the room, and no child was ever known to play in it.

Mr. Rightbody turned up the gas, and from a cabinet of drawers, precisely labelled, drew a package of letters. These he carefully examined. All were discoloured, and made dignified by age; but some, in their original freshness, must have appeared trifling and inconsistent with any correspondent of Mr. Rightbody. Nevertheless, that gentleman spent some moments in carefully perusing them, occasionally referring to the telegram in his hand. Suddenly there was a knock at the door. Mr. Rightbody started, made a half-unconscious movement to return the letters to the drawer, turned the telegram face downwards, and then somewhat harshly stammered—

"Eh? Who's there? Come in!"

"I beg your pardon, papa," said a very pretty girl, entering, without, however, the slightest trace of apology or awe in her manner, and taking a chair with the self-possession and familiarity of an *habitué* of the room; "but I knew it was not your habit to write late, so I supposed you were not busy. I am on my way to bed."

She was so very pretty, and withal so utterly unconscious of it, or perhaps so consciously superior to it, that one was provoked into a more critical examination of her face. But this only resulted in a reiteration of her beauty, and, perhaps, the added facts that her dark eyes were very womanly, her rich complexion eloquent, and her chiselled lips full enough to be passionate or capricious, notwithstanding that their general effect suggested neither caprice, womanly weakness, nor passion.

With the instinct of an embarrassed man, Mr. Rightbody touched the topic he would have preferred to avoid.

"I suppose we must talk over to-morrow," he hesitated, "this matter of yours and Mr. Marvin's? Mrs. Marvin has formally spoken to your mother."

Miss Alice lifted her bright eyes intelligently, but not joyfully, and the colour of action rather than embarrassment rose to her round checks.

"Yes, *he* said she would," she answered simply.

"At present," continued Mr. Rightbody, still awkwardly, "I see no objection to the proposed arrangement."

Miss Alice opened her round eyes at this. "Why, papa, I thought it had been all settled long ago. Mamma knew it, you knew it. Last July mamma and you talked it over."

"Yes, yes," returned her father, fumbling his papers; "that is—well, we will talk of it to-morrow." In fact, Mr. Rightbody *had* intended to give the affair a proper attitude of seriousness and solemnity by due precision of speech and some apposite reflections when he should impart the news to his daughter, but felt himself unable to do it now. "I am glad, Alice," he said at last, "that you have quite forgotten your previous whims and fancies. You see *we* are right."

"Oh, I dare say, papa, if I'm to be married at all, that Mr. Marvin is in every way suitable."

Mr. Rightbody looked at his daughter narrowly. There was not the slightest impatience nor bitterness in her manner; it was as well regulated as the sentiment she expressed.

"Mr. Marvin is——" he began.

"I know what Mr. Marvin *is,*" interrupted Miss Alice, "and he has promised me that I shall be allowed to go on with my studies the same as before. I shall graduate with my class, and if I prefer to practise my profession, I can do so in two years after our marriage."

"In two years?" queried Mr. Rightbody curiously.

"Yes. You see, in case we should have a child, that would give me time enough to wean it."

Mr. Rightbody looked at this flesh of his flesh, pretty and palpable flesh as it was; but being confronted as equally with the brain of his brain, all he could do was to say meekly—

"Yes, certainly. We will see about all that to-morrow."

Miss Alice rose. Something in the free, unfettered swing of her arms, as she rested them, lightly, after a half yawn, on her lithe hips, suggested his next speech, although still *distrait* and impatient.

"You continue your exercise with the Health Lift yet, I see."

"Yes, papa, but I had to give up the flannels. I don't see how mamma could wear them. But my dresses are high-necked, and by bathing I toughen my skin. See," she added, as with a childlike unconsciousness she unfastened two or three buttons of her gown, and exposed the white surface of her throat and neck to her father; "I can defy a chill."

Mr. Rightbody, with something akin to a genuine playful, paternal laugh, leaned forward and kissed her forehead.

"It's getting late, Ally," he said parentally, but not dictatorially. "Go to bed."

"I took a nap of three hours this afternoon," said Miss Alice, with a dazzling smile, "to anticipate this dissipation. Good-night, papa. To-morrow, then."

"To-morrow," repeated Mr. Rightbody, with his eyes still fixed upon the girl vaguely. "Good-night."

Miss Alice tripped from the room, possibly a trifle the more light-heartedly that she had parted from her father in one of his rare moments of illogical human weakness. And perhaps it was well for the poor girl that she kept this single remembrance of him, when, I fear, in after years, his methods, his reasoning, and indeed all he had tried to impress upon her childhood, had faded from her memory.

For, when she had left, Mr. Rightbody fell again to the examination of his old letters. This was quite absorbing; so much so that he did not notice the footsteps of Mrs. Rightbody on the staircase as she passed to her chamber, nor that she had paused on the landing to look through the glass half-door on her husband, as he sat there with the letters beside him and the telegram opened before him. Had she waited a moment later, she would have seen him rise and walk to the sofa with a disturbed air and a slight confusion, so that on reaching it he seemed to hesitate to lie down, although pale and evidently faint. Had she still waited, she would have seen him rise again with an agonised effort, stagger to the table, fumblingly refold and replace the papers in the cabinet, and lock it; and although now but half-conscious, hold the telegram over the gas-flame till it was consumed. For had she waited until this moment, she would have flown unhesitatingly to his aid, as, this act completed, he staggered again, reached his hand toward the bell, but vainly, and then fell prone upon the sofa.

But alas, no providential nor accidental hand was raised to save him, or anticipate the progress of this story. And when, half-an-hour later, Mrs. Rightbody, a little alarmed and more indignant at his violation of the doctor's rules, appeared upon the threshold, Mr. Rightbody lay upon the sofa, dead!

With bustle, with thronging feet, with the irruption of strangers, and a hurrying to and fro, but, more than all, with an impulse and emotion unknown to the mansion when its owner was in life, Mrs. Rightbody strove to call back the vanished life; but in vain. The highest medical intelligence, called from its bed at this strange hour, saw only the demonstration of its theories, made a year before. Mr. Rightbody was dead—without doubt—without mystery—even as a correct man should die; logically, and endorsed by the highest medical authority.

But even in the confusion Mrs. Rightbody managed to speed a messenger to the telegraph office for a copy of the despatch received by Mr. Rightbody, but now missing.

In the solitude of her own room, and without a confidant, she read these words—

Copy.

To Mr. Adams Rightbody, Boston, Mass.

Joshua Silsbee died suddenly this morning. His last request was that you should remember your sacred compact with him of thirty years ago.

(Signed)   SEVENTY-FOUR.
                  SEVENTY-FIVE.

In the darkened home, and amid the formal condolements of their friends, who had called to gaze upon the scarcely cold features of their late associate, Mrs. Rightbody managed to send another despatch. It was addressed to "Seventy-Four and Seventy-Five," Cottonwood. In a few hours she received the following enigmatical response:—

A horse thief, named Josh Silsbee, was lynched yesterday morning by the Vigilantes at Deadwood.

PART II

The spring of 1874 was retarded in the Californian Sierras. So much so, that certain Eastern tourists who had early ventured into the Yo Semite Valley, found themselves, one May morning, snow-bound against the tempestuous shoulders of *El Capitan.* So furious was the onset of the wind at the Upper Merced Cañon, that even so respectable a lady as Mrs. Rightbody was fain to cling to the neck of her guide to keep her seat in the saddle; while Miss Alice, scorning all masculine assistance, was hurled, a lovely chaos, against the snowy wall of the chasm. Mrs. Rightbody screamed; Miss Alice raged under her breath, but scrambled to her feet again in silence.

"I told you so," said Mrs. Rightbody, in an indignant whisper, as her daughter again ranged beside her—"I warned you especially, Alice —that—that—"

"What?" interrupted Miss Alice curtly.

"That you would need your chemiloons and high boots," said Mrs. Rightbody, in a regretful undertone, slightly increasing her distance from the guides.

Miss Alice shrugged her pretty shoulders scornfully, but ignored her mother's implication.

"You were particularly warned against going into the Valley at this season," she only replied grimly.

Mrs. Rightbody raised her eyes impatiently.

"You know how anxious I was to discover your poor father's strange correspondent, Alice; you have no consideration."

"But when you *have* discovered him—what then?" queried Miss Alice.

"What then?"

"Yes. My belief is that you will find the telegram only a mere business cypher. And all this quest mere nonsense."

"Alice! why, *you* yourself thought your father's conduct that night very strange. Have you forgotten?"

The young lady had *not,* but for some far-reaching feminine reason, chose to ignore it at that moment, when her late tumble in the snow was still fresh in her mind.

"And this woman—whoever she may be——" continued Mrs. Rightbody.

"How do you know there's a woman in the case?" interrupted Miss Alice, wickedly, I fear.

"How do—I—know—there's a woman?" slowly ejaculated Mrs. Rightbody, floundering in the snow and the unexpected possibility of such a ridiculous question. But here her guide flew to her assistance, and estopped further speech. And indeed a grave problem was before them.

The road that led to their single place of refuge—a cabin, half hotel, half trading-post, scarce a mile away—skirted the base of the rocky dome, and passed perilously near the precipitous wall of the valley. There was a rapid descent of a hundred yards or more to this terrace-like passage, and the guides paused for a moment of consultation, coolly oblivious alike to the terrified questioning of Mrs. Rightbody or the half-insolent independence of the daughter. The elder guide was russet-bearded, stout, and humorous; the younger was dark-bearded, slight, and serious.

"Ef you kin get young Bunker Hill to let you tote her on your shoulders, I'll git the madam to hang on to me," came to Mrs. Rightbody's horrified ears as the expression of her particular companion.

"Freeze to the old gal, and don't reckon on me if the daughter starts in to play it alone," was the enigmatical response of the younger guide.

Miss Alice overheard both propositions; and before the two men returned to their side, that high-spirited young lady had urged her horse down the declivity.

Alas, at this moment a gust of whirling snow swept down upon her. There was a flounder, a mis-step, a fatal strain on the wrong rein, a fall, a few plucky but unavailing struggles, and both horse and rider slid ignominiously down toward the rocky shelf. Mrs. Rightbody screamed. Miss Alice, from a confused *débris* of snow and ice, uplifted a vexed and colouring face to the younger guide—a little the more angrily, perhaps, that she saw a shade of impatience on his face.

"Don't move, but tie one end of the 'lass' under your arms, and throw me the other," he said quietly.

"What do you mean by 'lass'—the lasso?" asked Miss Alice disgustedly.

"Yes, ma'am."

"Then why don't you say so?"

"Oh, Alice!" reproachfully interpolated Mrs. Rightbody, encircled by the elder guide's stalwart arm.

Miss Alice deigned no reply, but drew the loop of the lasso over her shoulders, and let it drop to her round waist. Then she essayed to throw the other end to her guide. Dismal failure! The first fling nearly knocked her off the ledge, the second went all wild against the rocky wall, the third caught in a thorn bush, twenty feet below her companion's feet. Miss Alice's arm sunk helplessly to her side, at which signal of unqualified surrender the younger guide threw himself half-way down the slope, worked his way to the thorn bush, hung for a moment

perilously over the parapet, secured the lasso, and then began to pull
away at his lovely burden. Miss Alice was no dead weight, however,
but steadily half-scrambled on her hands and knees to within a foot or
two of her rescuer. At this too familiar proximity, she stood up and
leaned a little stiffly against the line, causing the guide to give an extra
pull, which had the lamentable effect of landing her almost in his
arms. As it was, her intelligent forehead struck his nose sharply, and, I
regret to add, treating of a romantic situation, caused that somewhat
prominent sign and token of a hero to bleed freely. Miss Alice instantly clapped a handful of snow over his nostrils.

"Now elevate your right arm," she said commandingly.

He did as he was bidden—but sulkily.

"That compresses the artery."

No man, with a pretty woman's hand and a handful of snow over
his mouth and nose, could effectively utter a heroic sentence, nor
with his arm elevated stiffly over his head assume a heroic attitude.
But when his mouth was free again he said half-sulkily, half-
apologetically—

"I might have known a girl couldn't throw worth a cent."

"Why?" demanded Alice sharply.

"Because—why—because—you see—they haven't got the experience," he stammered feebly.

"Nonsense; they haven't the *clavicle*—that's all! It's because I'm a
woman, and smaller in the collar-bone, that I haven't the play of the
fore-arm which you have. See!" She squared her shoulders slightly,
and turned the blaze of her dark eyes full on his. "Experience, indeed!
A girl can learn anything a boy can."

Apprehension took the place of ill-humour in her hearer. He turned
his eyes hastily away, and glanced above him. The elder guide had
gone forward to catch Miss Alice's horse, which, relieved of his rider,
was floundering towards the trail. Mrs. Rightbody was nowhere to be
seen. And these two were still twenty feet below the trail!

There was an awkward pause.

"Shall I pull you up the same way?" he queried. Miss Alice looked
at his nose, and hesitated. "Or will you take my hand?" he added, in
surly impatience. To his surprise, Miss Alice took his hand, and they
began the ascent together.

But the way was difficult and dangerous. Once or twice her feet
slipped on the smoothly-worn rock beneath, and she confessed to an
inward thankfulness when her uncertain feminine hand-grip was exchanged for his strong arm around her waist. Not that he was ungen-
tle, but Miss Alice angrily felt that he had once or twice exercised his
superior masculine functions in a rough way; and yet the next moment

she would have probably rejected the idea that she had even noticed it. There was no doubt, however, that he *was* a little surly.

A fierce scramble finally brought them back in safety to the trail; but in the action Miss Alice's shoulder, striking a projecting boulder, wrung from her a feminine cry of pain, her first sign of womanly weakness. The guide stopped instantly.

"I am afraid I hurt you?"

She raised her brown lashes, a trifle moist from suffering, looked in his eyes, and dropped her own. Why, she could not tell. And yet he had certainly a kind face, despite its seriousness; and a fine face, albeit unshorn and weather-beaten. Her own eyes had never been so near to any man's before, save her lover's; and yet she had never seen so much in even his. She slipped her hand away, not with any reference to him, but rather to ponder over this singular experience, and somehow felt uncomfortable thereat.

Nor was he less so. It was but a few days ago that he had accepted the charge of this young woman from the elder guide, who was the recognised escort of the Rightbody party, having been a former correspondent of her father's. He had been hired like any other guide, but had undertaken the task with that chivalrous enthusiasm which the average Californian always extends to the sex so rare to him. But the illusion had passed, and he had dropped into a sulky practical sense of his situation, perhaps fraught with less danger to himself. Only when appealed to by his manhood or her weakness, he had forgotten his wounded vanity.

He strode moodily ahead, dutifully breaking the path for her in the direction of the distant cañon, where Mrs. Rightbody and her friend awaited them. Miss Alice was first to speak. In this trackless, uncharted *terra incognita* of the passions, it is always the woman who steps out to lead the way.

"You know this place very well. I suppose you have lived here long?"

"Yes."

"You were not born here—no?"

A long pause.

"I observe they call you 'Stanislaus Joe.' Of course that is not your real name?" *(Mem.* Miss Alice had never called him *anything,* usually prefacing any request with a languid, "O-er-er, please, mister-er-a!" explicit enough for his station.)

"No."

Miss Alice (trotting after him, and bawling in his ear), *"What* name did you say?"

The man (doggedly), "I don't know."

Nevertheless, when they reached the cabin, after a half-hour's buffeting with the storm, Miss Alice applied herself to her mother's escort, Mr. Ryder.

"What's the name of the man who takes care of my horse?"

"Stanislaus Joe," responded Mr. Ryder.

"Is that all?"

"No; sometimes he's called Joe Stanislaus."

Miss Alice (satirically), "I suppose it's the custom here to send young ladies out with gentlemen who hide their names under an *alias?*"

Mr. Ryder (greatly perplexed), "Why, dear me, Miss Alice, you allers 'peared to me as a gal as was able to take keer——"

Miss Alice (interrupting with a wounded dove-like timidity), "Oh, never mind, please!"

The cabin offered but scanty accommodation to the tourists, which fact, when indignantly presented by Mrs. Rightbody, was explained by the good-humoured Ryder from the circumstance that the usual hotel was only a slight affair of boards, cloth, and paper, put up during the season and partly dismantled in the fall. "You couldn't be kept warm enough there," he added. Nevertheless Miss Alice noticed that both Mr. Ryder and Stanislaus Joe retired there with their pipes, after having prepared the ladies' supper with the assistance of an Indian woman, who apparently emerged from the earth at the coming of the party, and disappeared as mysteriously.

The stars came out brightly before they slept, and the next morning a clear unwinking sun beamed with almost summer power through the shutterless window of their cabin, and ironically disclosed the details of its rude interior. Two or three mangy, half-eaten buffalo robes, a bear-skin, some suspicious-looking blankets, rifles and saddles, deal tables and barrels made up its scant inventory. A strip of faded calico hung before a recess near the chimney, but so blackened by smoke and age that even feminine curiosity respected its secret. Mrs. Rightbody was in high spirits, and informed her daughter that she was at last on the track of her husband's unknown correspondent. " 'Seventy-Four and Seventy-Five' represent two members of the Vigilance Committee, my dear, and Mr. Ryder will assist me to find them."

"Mr. Ryder!" ejaculated Miss Alice, in scornful astonishment.

"Alice," said Mrs. Rightbody, with a suspicious assumption of sudden defence, "you injure yourself—you injure me by this exclusive attitude. Mr. Ryder is a friend of your father's, an exceedingly well-informed gentleman. I have not, of course, imparted to him the extent of my suspicions. But he can help me to what I must and will know. You might treat him a little more civilly—or, at least, a little better than you do his servant, your guide. Mr. Ryder is a gentleman, and not a paid courier."

Miss Alice was suddenly attentive. When she spoke again she asked, "Why do you not find something about this Silsbee—who died—or was hung—or something of that kind?"

"Child," said Mrs. Rightbody, "don't you see, there was no Silsbee, or if there was, he was simply the confidant of that—woman!"

A knock at the door, announcing the presence of Mr. Ryder and Stanislaus Joe with the horses, checked Mrs. Rightbody's speech. As the animals were being packed, Mrs. Rightbody for a moment withdrew in confidential conversation with Mr. Ryder, and, to the young lady's still greater annoyance, left her alone with Stanislaus Joe. Miss Alice was not in a good temper, but she felt it necessary to say something.

"I hope the hotel offers better quarters for travellers than this in summer," she began.

"It does."

"Then this does not belong to it?"

"No, ma'am."

"Who lives here, then?"

"I do."

"I beg your pardon," stammered Miss Alice; "I thought you lived where we hired—where we met you—in—in—you must excuse me."

"I'm not a regular guide, but as times were hard, and I was out of grub, I took the job."

"Out of grub!" "job!" And *she* was the "job." What would Henry Marvin say? It would nearly kill him. She began herself to feel a little frightened, and walked towards the door.

"One moment, miss!"

The young girl hesitated. The man's tone was surly, and yet indicated a certain kind of half-pathetic grievance. Her curiosity got the better of her prudence, and she turned back.

"That morning," he began hastily, "when we were coming down the valley, you picked me up twice."

"I picked *you* up?" repeated the astonished Alice.

"Yes—*contradicted* me, that's what I mean. Once when you said those rocks were volcanic; once when you said the flower you picked was a poppy. I didn't let on at the time, for it wasn't my say; but all the while you were talking I might have laid for you——"

"I don't understand you," said Alice haughtily.

"I might have entrapped you before folks. But I only want you to know that *I'm* right, and here are the books to show it."

He drew aside the dingy calico curtain, revealed a small shelf of bulky books, took down two large volumes, one of botany, one of geology, nervously sought his text, and put them in Alice's outstretched hands.

"I had no intention——" she began, half-proudly, half-embarrassed.

"Am I right, miss?" he interrupted.

"I presume you are, if you say so."

"That's all, ma'am! Thank you."

Before the girl had time to reply, he was gone. When he again returned, it was with her horse, and Mrs. Rightbody and Ryder were awaiting her. But Miss Alice noticed that his own horse was missing.

"Are you not going with us?" she asked.

"No, ma'am."

"Oh, indeed!"

Miss Alice felt her speech was a feeble conventionalism, but it was all she could say. She, however, *did* something. Hitherto it had been her habit to systematically reject his assistance in mounting to her seat. Now she awaited him. As he approached, she smiled and put out her little foot. He instantly stooped; she placed it in his hand, rose with a spring, and for one supreme moment Stanislaus Joe held her unresistingly in his arms. The next moment she was in the saddle, but in that brief interval of sixty seconds she had uttered a volume in a single sentence—

"I hope you will forgive me!"

He muttered a reply, and turned his face aside quickly, as if to hide it.

Miss Alice cantered forward with a smile, but pulled her hat down over her eyes as she joined her mother. She was blushing.

PART III

Mr. Ryder was as good as his word. A day or two later he entered Mrs. Rightbody's parlour at the Chrysopolis Hotel in Stockton, with the information that he had seen the mysterious senders of the despatch, and that they were now in the office of the hotel waiting her pleasure. Mr. Ryder further informed her that these gentlemen had only stipulated that they should not reveal their real names, and that they should be introduced to her simply as the respective "Seventy-Four" and "Seventy-Five" who had signed the despatch sent to the late Mr. Rightbody.

Mrs. Rightbody at first demurred to this; but on the assurance from

Mr. Ryder that this was the only condition on which an interview would be granted, finally consented.

"You will find them square men, even if they are a little rough, ma'am; but if you'd like me to be present, I'll stop; though I reckon if ye'd calkilated on that, you'd have had me take care o' your business by proxy, and not come yourself three thousand miles to do it."

Mrs. Rightbody believed it better to see them alone.

"All right, ma'am. I'll hang round out here, and ef ye should happen to hev a ticklin' in your throat and a bad spell o' coughin', I'll drop in, careless like, to see if you don't want them drops. *Sabe?*"

And with an exceedingly arch wink, and a slight familiar tap on Mrs. Rightbody's shoulder, which might have caused the late Mr. Rightbody to burst his sepulchre, he withdrew.

A very timid, hesitating tap on the door was followed by the entrance of two men, both of whom in general size, strength, and uncouthness, were ludicrously inconsistent with their diffident announcement. They proceeded in Indian file to the centre of the room, faced Mrs. Rightbody, acknowledged her deep courtesy by a strong shake of the hand, and drawing two chairs opposite to her, sat down side by side.

"I presume I have the pleasure of addressing——" began Mrs. Rightbody.

The man directly opposite Mrs. Rightbody turned to the other inquiringly.

The other man nodded his head, and replied—

"Seventy-Four."

"Seventy-Five," promptly followed the other.

Mrs. Rightbody paused, a little confused.

"I have sent for you," she began again, "to learn something more of the circumstances under which you gentlemen sent a despatch to my late husband."

"The circumstances," replied Seventy-Four quietly, with a side glance at his companion, "panned out about in this yer style. We hung a man named Josh Silsbee down at Deadwood for hoss-stealin'. When I say *we,* I speak for Seventy-Five yer, as is present, as well as representin', so to speak, seventy-two other gents as is scattered. We hung Josh Silsbee on squar, pretty squar evidence. Afore he was strung up, Seventy-Five yer axed him, accordin' to custom, ef there was ennything he had to say, or enny request that he allowed to make of us. He turns to Seventy-Five yer, and——"

Here he paused suddenly, looking at his companion.

"He sez, sez he," began Seventy-Five, taking up the narrative; "he sez, 'Kin I write a letter?' sez he. Sez I, 'Not much, ole man; ye've got no time.' Sez he, 'Kin I send a despatch by telegraph?' I sez, 'Heave ahead.' He sez—these is his dientikal words—'Send to Adams Rightbody, Boston. Tell him to remember his sacred compack with me thirty years ago.' "

" 'His sacred compack with me thirty years ago,' " echoed Seventy-Four. "His dientikal words."

"What was the compact?" asked Mrs. Rightbody anxiously.

Seventy-Four looked at Seventy-Five, and then both arose and retired to the corner of the parlour, where they engaged in a slow but whispered deliberation. Presently they returned, and sat down again.

"We allow," said Seventy-Four quietly but decidedly, "that *you* know what that sacred compact was."

Mrs. Rightbody lost her temper and her truthfulness together. "Of course," she said hurriedly, "I know; but do you mean to say that you gave this poor man no further chance to explain before you murdered him?"

Seventy-Four and Seventy-Five both rose again slowly and retired. When they returned again and sat down, Seventy-Five, who by this time, through some subtle magnetism, Mrs. Rightbody began to recognise as the superior power, said gravely—

"We wish to say, regarding this yer murder, that Seventy-Four and me is equally responsible. That we reckon also to represent, so to speak, seventy-two other gentlemen as is scattered. That we are ready, Seventy-Four and me, to take and holt that responsibility now and at any time, afore every man or men as kin be fetched agin us. We wish to say that this yer say of ours holds good yer in Californy or in any part of these United States."

"Or in Canady," suggested Seventy-Four.

"Or in Canady. We wouldn't agree to cross the water or go to furrin parts, unless absolutely necessary. We leaves the chise of weppings to your principal, ma'am, or being a lady, ma'am, and interested, to any one you may fetch to act for him. An advertisement in any of the Sacramento papers, or a playcard or handbill stuck into a tree near Deadwood saying that Seventy-Four or Seventy-Five will communicate with this yer principal or agent of yours, will fetch us—allers."

Mrs. Rightbody, a little alarmed and desperate, saw her blunder. "I mean nothing of the kind," she said hastily. "I only expected that you might have some further details of this interview with Silsbee—that perhaps you could tell me—" a bold bright thought crossed Mrs. Rightbody's mind, "something more about *her.*"

The two men looked at each other.

"I suppose your society have no objection to giving me information about *her?*" said Mrs. Rightbody eagerly.

Another quiet conversation in the corner, and the return of both men.

"We want to say that we've no objection."

Mrs. Rightbody's heart beat high. Her boldness had made her penetration good. Yet she felt she must not alarm the men heedlessly.

"Will you inform me to what extent Mr. Rightbody, my late husband, was interested in her?"

This time it seemed an age to Mrs. Rightbody before the men returned from their solemn consultation in the corner. She could both hear and feel that their discussion was more animated than their previous conferences. She was a little mortified, however, when they sat down, to hear Seventy-Four say slowly—

"We wish to say that we don't allow to say *how* much."

"Do you not think that the 'sacred compact' between Mr. Rightbody and Mr. Silsbee referred to her."

"We reckon it do."

Mrs. Rightbody, flushed and animated, would have given worlds had her daughter been present to hear this undoubted confirmation of her theory. Yet she felt a little nervous and uncomfortable, even on this threshold of discovery.

"Is she here now?"

"She's in Tuolumne," said Seventy-Four.

"A little better looked arter than formerly," added Seventy-Five.

"I see. Then Mr. Silsbee *enticed* her away?"

"Well, ma'am, it *was* allowed as she runned away. But it wasn't proved, and it generally wasn't her style."

Mrs. Rightbody trifled with her next question. "She was pretty, of course?"

The eyes of both men brightened.

"She was *that!*" said Seventy-Four emphatically.

"It would have done you good to see her," added Seventy-Five.

Mrs. Rightbody inwardly doubted it; but before she could ask another question, the two men again retired to the corner for consultation. When they came back there was a shade more of kindliness and confidence in their manner, and Seventy-Four opened his mind more freely.

"We wish to say, ma'am, looking at the thing, by and large, in a far-minded way—that ez *you* seem interested, and ez Mr. Rightbody was interested, and was according to all accounts deceived and led away by Silsbee, that we don't mind listening to any proposition *you* might make, as a lady—allowin' you was ekally interested."

"I understand," said Mrs. Rightbody quickly. "And you will furnish me with any papers."

The two men again consulted.

"We wish to say, ma'am, that we think she's got papers, but——"

"I *must* have them, you understand," interrupted Mrs. Rightbody, "at any price!"

"We was about to say, ma'am," said Seventy-Five slowly, "that, considerin' all things—and you being a lady—you kin have *her,* papers, pedigree, and guarantee, for twelve hundred dollars!"

It has been alleged that Mrs. Rightbody asked only one question more, and then fainted. It is known, however, that by the next day it was understood in Deadwood that Mrs. Rightbody had confessed to the Vigilance Committee that her husband, a celebrated Boston millionaire, anxious to gain possession of Abner Springer's well-known sorrel mare, had incited the unfortunate Josh Silsbee to steal it; and that finally, failing in this, the widow of the deceased Boston millionaire was now in personal negotiation with the owners.

Howbeit, Miss Alice, returning home that afternoon, found her mother with a violent headache.

"We will leave here by the next steamer," said Mrs. Rightbody languidly. "Mr. Ryder has promised to accompany us."

"But, mother——"

"The climate, Alice, is over-rated. My nerves are already suffering from it. The associations are unfit for you, and Mr. Marvin is naturally impatient."

Miss Alice coloured slightly.

"But your quest, mother?"

"I've abandoned it."

"But *I* have not," said Alice quietly. "Do you remember my guide at the Yo Semite, Stanislaus Joe? Well, Stanislaus Joe is—who do you think?"

Mrs. Rightbody was languidly indifferent.

"Well, Stanislaus Joe is the son of Joshua Silsbee."

Mrs. Rightbody sat upright in astonishment.

"Yes; but, mother, he knows nothing of what we know. His father treated him shamefully, and set him cruelly adrift years ago; and when he was hung, the poor fellow, in sheer disgrace, changed his name."

"But if he knows nothing of his father's compact, of what interest is this?"

"Oh, nothing! Only I thought it might lead to something."

Mrs. Rightbody suspected that "something," and asked sharply, "And pray how did *you* find it out? You did not speak of it in the Valley."

"Oh, I didn't find it out till to-day," said Miss Alice, walking to the window. "He happened to be here, and—told me."

PART IV

If Mrs. Rightbody's friends had been astounded by her singular and unexpected pilgrimage to California so soon after her husband's decease, they were still more astounded by the information a year later that she was engaged to be married to a Mr. Ryder, of whom only the scant history was known that he was a Californian, and former correspondent of her husband. It was undeniable that the man was wealthy, and evidently no mere adventurer; it was rumoured that he was courageous and manly; but even those who delighted in his odd humour were shocked at his grammar and slang. It was said that Mr. Marvin had but one interview with his father-in-law elect, and returned so supremely disgusted that the match was broken off. The horse-stealing story, more or less garbled, found its way through lips that pretended to decry it, yet eagerly repeated it. Only one member of the Rightbody family—and a new one—saved them from utter ostracism. It was young Mr. Ryder, the adopted son of the prospective head of the household, whose culture, manners, and general elegance fascinated and thrilled Boston with a new sensation. It seemed to many that Miss Alice should in the vicinity of this rare exotic forget her former enthusiasm for a professional life, but the young man was pitied by society, and various plans for diverting him from any *mésalliance* with the Rightbody family were concocted.

It was a wintry night, and the second anniversary of Mr. Rightbody's death, that a light was burning in his library. But the dead man's chair was occupied by young Mr. Ryder, adopted son of the new proprietor of the mansion, and before him stood Alice, with her dark eyes fixed on the table.

"There must have been something in it, Joe, believe me. Did you never hear your father speak of mine?"

"Never."

"But you say he was college bred, and born a gentleman, and in his youth he must have had many friends."

"Alice," said the young man gravely, "when I have done something to redeem my name, and wear it again before these people, before *you,* it would be well to revive the past. But till then——"

But Alice was not to be put down. "I remember," she went on, scarcely heeding him, "that when I came in that night, papa was reading a letter, and seemed to be disconcerted."

"A letter?"

"Yes; but," added Alice, with a sigh, "when we found him here insensible, there was no letter on his person. He must have destroyed it."

"Did you ever look among his papers? If found, it might be a clue."

449

The young man glanced toward the cabinet. Alice read his eyes, and answered—

"Oh dear, no. The cabinet contained only his papers, all perfectly arranged—you know how methodical were his habits—and some old business and private letters, all carefully put away."

"Let us see them," said the young man, rising.

They opened drawer after drawer; files upon files of letters and business papers, accurately folded and filed. Suddenly Alice uttered a little cry, and picked up a quaint ivory paper-knife lying at the bottom of a drawer.

"It was missing the next day, and never could be found. He must have mislaid it here. This is the drawer," said Alice eagerly.

Here was a clue. But the lower part of the drawer was filled with old letters, not labelled, yet neatly arranged in files. Suddenly he stopped, and said, "Put them back, Alice, at once."

"Why?"

"Some of these letters are in my father's handwriting."

"The more reason why *I* should see them," said the girl imperatively. "Here, you take part and I'll take part, and we'll get through quicker."

There was a certain decision and independence in her manner which he had learned to respect. He took the letters, and in silence read them with her. They were old college letters, so filled with boyish dreams, ambitions, aspirations, and Utopian theories, that I fear neither of these young people even recognised their parents in the dead ashes of the past. They were both grave, until Alice uttered a little hysterical cry, and dropped her face in her hands. Joe was instantly beside her.

"It's nothing, Joe, nothing. Don't read it, please; please, don't. It's so funny—it's so very queer."

But Joe had, after a slight, half-playful struggle, taken the letter from the girl. Then he read aloud the words written by his father thirty years ago.

"I thank you, dear friend, for all you say about my wife and boy. I thank you for reminding me of our boyish compact. He will be ready to fulfil it, I know, if he loves those his father loves, even if you should marry years later. I am glad for your sake, for both our sakes, that it is a boy. Heaven send you a good wife, dear Adams, and a daughter, to make my son equally happy."

Joe Silsbee looked down, took the half-laughing, half-tearful face in his hands, kissed her forehead, and with tears in his grave eyes, said "Amen!"

I am inclined to think that this sentiment was echoed heartily by Mrs. Rightbody's former acquaintances, when, a year later, Miss Alice was united to a professional gentleman of honour and renown, yet who was known to be the son of a convicted horse-thief. A few remembered the previous Californian story, and found corroboration therefor; but a majority believed it a just reward to Miss Alice for her conduct to Mr. Marvin, and as Miss Alice cheerfully accepted it in that light, I do not see why I may not end my story with happiness to all concerned.

How Santa Claus
Came to Simpson's Bar

IT HAD BEEN raining in the valley of the Sacramento. The North Fork had overflowed its banks, and Rattlesnake Creek was impassable. The few boulders that had marked the summer ford at Simpson's Crossing were obliterated by a vast sheet of water stretching to the foothills. The up-stage was stopped at Granger's; the last mail had been abandoned in the *tules,* the rider swimming for his life. "An area," remarked the "Sierra Avalanche," with pensive local pride, "as large as the State of Massachusetts is now under water."

Nor was the weather any better in the foothills. The mud lay deep on the mountain road; waggons that neither physical force nor moral objurgation could move from the evil ways into which they had fallen encumbered the track, and the way to Simpson's Bar was indicated by brokendown teams and hard swearing. And farther on, cut off and inaccessible, rained upon and bedraggled, smitten by high winds and threatened by high water, Simpson's Bar, on the eve of Christmas Day, 1862, clung like a swallow's nest to the rocky entablature and splintered capitals of Table Mountain, and shook in the blast.

As night shut down on the settlement, a few lights gleamed through the mist from the windows of cabins on either side of the highway now, crossed and gullied by lawless streams and swept by marauding winds. Happily most of the population were gathered at Thompson's store, clustered around a redhot stove, at which they silently spat in some accepted sense of social communion that perhaps rendered conversation unnecessary. Indeed, most methods of diversion had long since been exhausted on Simpson's Bar; high water had suspended the regular occupations on gulch and on river, and a consequent lack of money and whisky had taken the zest from most illegitimate recreation. Even Mr. Hamlin was fain to leave the Bar with fifty dollars in his pocket—the only amount actually realised of the large sums won by him in the successful exercise of his arduous profession. "Ef I was asked," he remarked somewhat later,—"ef I was asked to pint out a purty little village where a retired sport as didn't care for money could exercise hisself, frequent and lively, I'd say Simpson's Bar; but for a young man with a large family depending on his exertions it don't pay." As Mr. Hamlin's family consisted mainly of female adults, this remark is quoted rather to show the breadth of his humour than the exact extent of his responsibilities.

Howbeit, the unconscious objects of this satire sat that evening in the listless apathy begotten of idleness and lack of excitement. Even the sudden splashing of hoofs before the door did not arouse them. Dick Bullen alone paused in the act of scraping out his pipe, and lifted his head, but no other one of the group indicated any interest in, or recognition of, the man who entered.

It was a figure familiar enough to the company, and known in Simpson's Bar as "The Old Man." A man of perhaps fifty years; grizzled and scant of hair, but still fresh and youthful of complexion. A face full of ready but not very powerful sympathy, with a chameleon-like aptitude for taking on the shade and colour of contiguous moods and feelings. He had evidently just left some hilarious companions, and did not at first notice the gravity of the group, but clapped the shoulder of the nearest man jocularly, and threw himself into a vacant chair.

"Jest heard the best thing out, boys! Ye know Smiley, over yar—Jim Smiley—funniest man in the Bar? Well, Jim was jest telling the richest yarn about"——

"Smiley's a——fool," interrupted a gloomy voice.

"A particular——skunk," added another in sepulchral accents.

A silence followed these positive statements. The Old Man glanced quickly around the group. Then his face slowly changed. "That's so," he said reflectively, after a pause, "certinly a sort of a skunk and suthin' of a fool. In course." He was silent for a moment as in painful contemplation of the unsavouriness and folly of the unpopular Smiley. "Dismal weather, ain't it?" he added, now fully embarked on the current of prevailing sentiment. "Mighty rough papers on the boys, and no show for money this season. And to-morrow's Christmas."

There was a movement among the men at this announcement, but whether of satisfaction or disgust was not plain. "Yes," continued the Old Man in the lugubrious tone he had, within the last few moments, unconsciously adopted,—"yes, Christmas, and to-night's Christmas Eve. Ye see, boys, I kinder thought—that is, I sorter had an idee, just passin' like, you know—that maybe ye'd all like to come over to my house to-night and have a sort of tear round. But I suppose, now, you wouldn't? Don't feel like it, maybe?" he added with anxious sympathy, peering into the faces of his companions.

"Well, I don't know," responded Tom Flynn with some cheerfulness. "P'r'aps we may. But how about your wife, Old Man? What does *she* say to it?"

The Old Man hesitated. His conjugal experience had not been a happy one, and the fact was known to Simpson's Bar. His first wife, a delicate, pretty little woman, had suffered keenly and secretly from the jealous suspicions of her husband, until one day he invited the whole Bar to his house to expose her infidelity. On arriving, the party found the shy, *petite* creature quietly engaged in her household duties, and retired abashed and discomfited. But the sensitive woman did not easily recover from the shock of this extraordinary outrage. It was with difficulty she regained her equanimity sufficiently to release her lover from the closet in which he was concealed, and escape with him. She left a boy of three years to comfort her bereaved husband. The Old Man's present wife had been his cook. She was large, loyal, and aggressive.

Before he could reply, Joe Dimmick suggested with great directness that it was the "Old Man's house," and that, invoking the Divine Power, if the case were his own, he would invite whom he pleased, even if in so doing he imperilled his salvation. The Powers of Evil, he further remarked, should contend against him vainly. All this delivered with a terseness and vigour lost in this necessary translation.

"In course. Certainly. Thet's it," said the Old Man with a sympathetic frown. "Thar's no trouble about *thet.* It's my own house, built every stick on it myself. Don't you be afeard o' her, boys. She *may* cut up a trifle rough—ez wimmin do—but she'll come round." Secretly the Old Man trusted to the exaltation of liquor and the power of courageous example to sustain him in such an emergency.

As yet, Dick Bullen, the oracle and leader of Simpson's Bar, had not spoken. He now took his pipe from his lips. "Old Man, how's that yer Johnny gettin' on? Seems to me he didn't look so peart last time I seed him on the bluff heavin' rocks at Chinamen. Didn't seem to take much interest in it. Thar was a gang of 'em by yar yesterday—drownded out up the river—and I kinder thought o' Johnny, and how he'd miss 'em! Maybe now, we'd be in the way ef he wus sick?"

The father, evidently touched not only by this pathetic picture of Johnny's deprivation, but by the considerate delicacy of the speaker, hastened to assure him that Johnny was better and that a "little fun might 'liven him up.' Whereupon Dick arose, shook himself, and saying, "I'm ready. Lead the way, Old Man: here goes," himself led the way with a leap, a characteristic howl, and darted out into the night. As he passed through the outer room he caught up a blazing brand from the hearth. The action was repeated by the rest of the party, closely following and elbowing each other, and before the astonished proprietor of Thompson's grocery was aware of the intention of his guests, the room was deserted.

The night was pitchy dark. In the first gust of wind their temporary torches were extinguished, and only the red brands dancing and flitting in the gloom like drunken will-o'-the-wisps indicated their whereabouts. Their way led up Pine-Tree Cañon, at the head of which a broad, low, bark-thatched cabin burrowed in the mountain-side. It was the home of the Old Man, and the entrance to the tunnel in which he worked when he worked at all. Here the crowd paused for a moment, out of delicate deference to their host, who came up panting in the rear.

"P'r'aps ye'd better hold on a second out yer, whilst I go in and see that things is all right," said the Old Man, with an indifference he was far from feeling. The suggestion was graciously accepted, the door opened and closed on the host, and the crowd, leaning their backs against the wall and cowering under the eaves, waited and listened.

For a few moments there was no sound but the dripping of water from the eaves, and the stir and rustle of wrestling boughs above them. Then the men became uneasy, and whispered suggestion and suspicion passed from the one to the other. "Reckon she's caved in his head the first lick!" "Decoyed him inter the tunnel and barred him up, likely." "Got him down and sittin' on him." "Prob'ly biling suthin' to heave on us: stand clear the door, boys!" For just then the latch clicked, the door slowly opened, and a voice said, "Come in out o' the wet."

The voice was neither that of the Old Man nor of his wife. It was the voice of a small boy, its weak treble broken by that preternatural hoarseness which only vagabondage and the habit of premature self-assertion can give. It was the face of a small boy that looked up at theirs,—a face that might have been pretty, and even refined, but that it was darkened by evil knowledge from within, and dirt and hard experience from without. He had a blanket around his shoulders, and had evidently just risen from his bed. "Come in," he repeated, "and don't make no noise. The Old Man's in there talking to mar," he continued, pointing to an adjacent room which seemed to be a kitchen, from which the Old Man's voice came in deprecating accents. "Let me be," he added querulously, to Dick Bullen, who had caught him up, blanket and all, and was affecting to toss him into the fire, "let go o' me, you d—d old fool, d'ye hear?"

Thus adjured, Dick Bullen lowered Johnny to the ground with a smothered laugh, while the men, entering quietly, ranged themselves around a long table of rough boards which occupied the centre of the room. Johnny then gravely proceeded to a cupboard and brought out several articles, which he deposited on the table. "Thar's whisky. And crackers. And red herons. And cheese." He took a bite of the latter on his way to the table. "And sugar." He scooped up a mouthful *en route* with a small and very dirty hand. "And terbacker. Thar's dried appils too on the shelf, but I don't admire 'em. Appils is swellin'. Thar," he concluded, "now wade in, and don't be afeard. *I* don't mind the old woman. She don't b'long to *me*. S'long."

He had stepped to the threshold of a small room, scarcely larger than a closet, partitioned off from the main apartment, and holding in its dim recess a small bed. He stood there a moment looking at the company, his bare feet peeping from the blanket, and nodded.

"Hello, Johnny! You ain't goin' to turn in agin, are ye?" said Dick.

"Yes, I are," responded Johnny decidedly.

"Why, wot's up, old fellow?"

"I'm sick."

"How sick?"

"I've got a fevier. And childblains. And roomatiz," returned Johnny, and vanished within. After a moment's pause, he added in the dark, apparently from under the bedclothes,—"And biles!"

There was an embarrassing silence. The men looked at each other and at the fire. Even with the appetising banquet before them, it seemed as if they might again fall into the despondency of Thompson's grocery, when the voice of the Old Man, incautiously lifted, came deprecatingly from the kitchen.

"Certainly! Thet's so. In course they is. A gang o' lazy, drunken loafers, and that ar Dick Bullen's the orneriest of all. Didn't hev no more *sabe* than to come round yar with sickness in the house and no provision. Thet's what I said: 'Bullen,' sez I, 'it's crazy drunk you are, or a fool,' sez I, 'to think o' such a thing.' 'Staples,' I sez, 'be you a man, Staples, and 'spect to raise h—ll under my roof and invalids lyin' round?' But they would come,—they would. Thet's wot you must 'spect o' such trash as lays round the Bar."

A burst of laughter from the men followed this unfortunate exposure. Whether it was overheard in the kitchen, or whether the Old Man's irate companion had just then exhausted all other modes of expressing her contemptuous indignation, I cannot say, but a back door was suddenly slammed with great violence. A moment later and the Old Man reappeared, haply unconscious of the cause of the late hilarious outburst, and smiled blandly.

"The old woman thought she'd jest run over to Mrs. MacFadden's for a sociable call," he explained with jaunty indifference as he took a seat at the board.

Oddly enough it needed this untoward incident to relieve the embarrassment that was beginning to be felt by the party, and their natural audacity returned with their host. I do not propose to record the convivialities of that evening. The inquisitive reader will accept the statement that the conversation was characterised by the same intellectual exaltation, the same cautious reverence, the same fastidious delicacy, the same rhetorical precision, and the same logical and coherent discourse somewhat later in the evening, which distinguish similar gatherings of the masculine sex in more civilised localities and under more favourable auspices. No glasses were broken in the absence of any; no liquor was uselessly spilt on the floor or table in the scarcity of that article.

It was nearly midnight when the festivities were interrupted. "Hush," said Dick Bullen, holding up his hand. It was the querulous voice of Johnny from his adjacent closet: "O dad!"

The Old Man arose hurriedly and disappeared in the closet. Presently he reappeared. "His rheumatiz is coming on agin bad," he explained, "and he wants rubbin'." He lifted the demijohn of whisky from the table and shook it. It was empty. Dick Bullen put down his tin cup with an embarrassed laugh. So did the others. The Old Man examined their contents and said hopefully, "I reckon that's enough; he don't need much. You hold on all o' you for a spell, and I'll be back;" and vanished in the closet with an old flannel shirt and the whisky. The door closed but imperfectly, and the following dialogue was distinctly audible:

"Now, sonny, whar does she ache worst?"

"Sometimes over yar and sometimes under yer; but it's most powerful from yer to yer. Rub yer, dad."

A silence seemed to indicate a brisk rubbing. Then Johnny:

"Hevin' a good time out yer, dad?"

"Yes, sonny."

"To-morrer's Chrismiss,—ain't it?"

"Yes, sonny. How does she feel now?"

"Better. Rub a little furder down. Wot's Chrismiss, anyway? Wot's it all about?"

"Oh, it's a day."

This exhaustive definition was apparently satisfactory, for there was a silent interval of rubbing. Presently Johnny again:

"Mar sez that everywhere else but yer everybody gives things to everybody Chrismiss, and then she jist waded inter you. She sez thar's a man they call Sandy Claws, not a white man, you know, but a kind o' Chinemin, comes down the chimbley night afore Chrismiss and gives things to chillern,—boys like me. Puts 'em in their butes! Thet's what she tried to play upon me. Easy now, pop, whar are you rubbin' to,—thet's a mile from the place. She jest made that up, didn't she, jest to aggrewate me and you? Don't rub thar. . . . Why, dad!"

In the great quiet that seemed to have fallen upon the house the sigh of the near pines and the drip of leaves without was very distinct. Johnny's voice, too, was lowered as he went on, "Don't you take on now, for I'm gettin' all right fast. Wot's the boys doin' out thar?"

The Old Man partly opened the door and peered through. His guests were sitting there sociably enough, and there were a few silver coins and a lean buckskin purse on the table. "Bettin' on suthin'— some little game or 'nother. They're all right," he replied to Johnny, and recommenced his rubbing.

"I'd like to take a hand and win some money," said Johnny reflectively after a pause.

The Old Man glibly repeated what was evidently a familiar formula, that if Johnny would wait until he struck it rich in the tunnel he'd have lots of money, &c., &c.

"Yes," said Johnny, "but you don't. And whether you strike it or I win it, it's about the same. It's all luck. But it's mighty cur'o's about Chrismiss—ain't it? Why do they call it Chrismiss?"

Perhaps from some instinctive deference to the overhearing of his guests, or from some vague sense of incongruity, the Old Man's reply was so low as to be inaudible beyond the room.

"Yes," said Johnny, with some slight abatement of interest, "I've heerd o' *him* before. Thar, that'll do, dad. I don't ache near so bad as I did. Now wrap me tight in this yer blanket. So. Now," he added in a muffled whisper, "sit down yer by me till I go asleep." To assure himself of obedience, he disengaged one hand from the blanket and, grasping his father's sleeve, again composed himself to rest.

For some moments the Old Man waited patiently. Then the un- wonted stillness of the house excited his curiosity, and without moving from the bed he cautiously opened the door with his disengaged hand, and looked into the main room. To his infinite surprise it was dark and deserted. But even then a smouldering log on the hearth broke, and by the upspringing blaze he saw the figure of Dick Bullen sitting by the dying embers.

"Hello!"

Dick started, rose, and came somewhat unsteadily toward him.

"Whar's the boys?" said the Old Man.

"Gone up the cañon on a little *pasear*. They're coming back for me in a minit. I'm waitin' round for 'em. What are you starin' at, Old Man?" he added with a forced laugh; "do you think I'm drunk?"

The Old Man might have been pardoned the supposition, for Dick's eyes were humid and his face flushed. He loitered and lounged back to the chimney, yawned, shook himself, buttoned up his coat and laughed. "Liquor ain't so plenty as that, Old Man. Now don't you git up," he continued, as the Old Man made a movement to release his sleeve from Johnny's hand. "Don't you mind manners. Sit jest whar you be; I'm goin' in a jiffy. Thar, that's them now."

There was a low tap at the door. Dick Bullen opened it quickly, nodded "Good night" to his host, and disappeared. The Old Man would have followed him but for the hand that still unconsciously grasped his sleeve. He could have easily disengaged it: it was small, weak, and emaciated. But perhaps because it *was* small, weak, and emaciated he changed his mind, and, drawing his chair closer to the bed, rested his head upon it. In this defenceless attitude the potency of his earlier potations surprised him. The room flickered and faded before his eyes, reappeared, faded again, went out, and left him—asleep.

Meantime Dick Bullen, closing the door, confronted his companions. "Are you ready?" said Staples. "Ready," said Dick; "what's the time?" "Past twelve," was the reply; "can you make it?—it's nigh on fifty miles, the round trip hither and yon." "I reckon," returned Dick shortly. "Whar's the mare?" "Bill and Jack's holdin' her at the crossin'." "Let 'em hold on a minit longer," said Dick.

He turned and re-entered the house softly. By the light of the guttering candle and dying fire he saw that the door of the little room was open. He stepped toward it on tiptoe and looked in. The Old Man had fallen back in his chair, snoring, his helpless feet thrust out in a line with his collapsed shoulders, and his hat pulled over his eyes. Beside him, on a narrow wooden bedstead, lay Johnny, muffled tightly in a blanket that hid all save a strip of forehead and a few curls damp with perspiration. Dick Bullen made a step forward, hesitated, and glanced over his shoulder into the deserted room. Everything was quiet. With a sudden resolution he parted his huge moustaches with both hands and stooped over the sleeping boy. But even as he did so a mischievous blast, lying in wait, swooped down the chimney, rekindled the hearth, and lit up the room with a shameless glow from which Dick fled in bashful terror.

His companions were already waiting for him at the crossing. Two of them were struggling in the darkness with some strange misshapen bulk, which as Dick came nearer took the semblance of a great yellow horse.

It was the mare. She was not a pretty picture. From her Roman nose to her rising haunches, from her arched spine hidden by the stiff *machillas* of a Mexican saddle, to her thick, straight, bony legs, there was not a line of equine grace. In her half-blind but wholly vicious white eyes, in her protruding under-lip, in her monstrous colour, there was nothing but ugliness and vice.

"Now then," said Staples, "stand cl'ar of her heels, boys, and up with you. Don't miss your first holt of her mane, and mind ye get your off stirrup *quick*. Ready!"

There was a leap, a scrambling struggle, a bound, a wild retreat of the crowd, a circle of flying hoofs, two springless leaps that jarred the earth, a rapid play and jingle of spurs, a plunge, and then the voice of Dick somewhere in the darkness. "All right!"

"Don't take the lower road back onless you're hard pushed for time! Don't hold her in down hill. We'll be at the ford at five. G'lang! Hoopa! Mula! GO!"

A splash, a spark struck from the ledge in the road, a clatter in the rocky cut beyond, and Dick was gone.

Sing, O Muse, the ride of Richard Bullen! Sing, O Muse, of chivalrous men! the sacred quest, the doughty deeds, the battery of low churls, the fearsome ride and gruesome perils of the Flower of Simpson's Bar! Alack! she is dainty, this Muse! She will have none of this bucking brute and swaggering, ragged rider, and I must fain follow him in prose, afoot!

It was one o'clock, and yet he had only gained Rattlesnake Hill. For in that time Jovita had rehearsed to him all her imperfections and practised all her vices. Thrice had she stumbled. Twice had she thrown up her Roman nose in a straight line with the reins, and, resisting bit and spur, struck out madly across country. Twice had she reared, and, rearing, fallen backward; and twice had the agile Dick, unharmed, regained his seat before she found her vicious legs again. And a mile beyond them, at the foot of a long hill, was Rattlesnake Creek. Dick knew that here was the crucial test of his ability to perform his enterprise, set his teeth grimly, put his knees well into her flanks, and changed his defensive tactics to brisk aggression. Bullied and maddened, Jovita began the descent of the hill. Here the artful

Richard pretended to hold her in with ostentatious objurgation and well-feigned cries of alarm. It is unnecessary to add that Jovita instantly ran away. Nor need I state the time made in the descent; it is written in the chronicles of Simpson's Bar. Enough that in another moment, as it seemed to Dick, she was splashing on the overflowed banks of Rattlesnake Creek. As Dick expected, the momentum she had acquired carried her beyond the point of balking, and, holding her well together for a mighty leap, they dashed into the middle of the swiftly flowing current. A few moments of kicking, wading, and swimming, and Dick drew a long breath on the opposite bank.

The road from Rattlesnake Creek to Red Mountain was tolerably level. Either the plunge in Rattlesnake Creek had dampened her baleful fire, or the art which led to it had shown her the superior wickedness of her rider, for Jovita no longer wasted her surplus energy in wanton conceits. Once she bucked, but it was from force of habit; once she shied, but it was from a new, freshly-painted meeting-house at the crossing of the country road. Hollows, ditches, gravelly deposits, patches of freshly-springing grasses, flew from beneath her rattling hoofs. She began to smell unpleasantly, once or twice she coughed slightly, but there was no abatement of her strength or speed. By two o'clock he had passed Red Mountain and begun the descent to the plain. Ten minutes later the driver of the fast Pioneer coach was overtaken and passed by a "man on a Pinto hoss,"—an event sufficiently notable for remark. At halfpast two Dick rose in his stirrups with a great shout. Stars were glittering through the rifted clouds, and beyond him, out of the plain, rose two spires, a flagstaff, and a straggling line of black objects. Dick jingled his spurs and swung his *riata,* Jovita bounded forward, and in another moment they swept into Tuttleville, and drew up before the wooden piazza of "The Hotel of All Nations."

What transpired that night at Tuttleville is not strictly a part of this record. Briefly I may state, however, that after Jovita had been handed over to a sleepy ostler, whom she at once kicked into unpleasant consciousness, Dick sallied out with the barkeeper for a tour of the sleeping town. Lights still gleamed from a few saloons and gambling-houses; but, avoiding these, they stopped before several closed shops, and by persistent tapping and judicious outcry roused the proprietors from their beds, and made them unbar the doors of their magazines and expose their wares. Sometimes they were met by curses, but oftener by interest and some concern in their needs, and the interview was invariably concluded by a drink. It was three o'clock before this pleasantry was given over, and with a small waterproof bag of indiarubber strapped on his shoulders Dick returned to the hotel. But here he was waylaid by Beauty,—Beauty opulent in charms, affluent in dress, persuasive in speech, and Spanish in accent! In vain she repeated the invitation in "Excelsior," happily scorned by all Alpine-climbing youth, and rejected by this child of the Sierras,—a rejection softened in this instance by a laugh and his last gold coin. And then he sprang to the saddle and dashed down the lonely street and out into the lonelier plain, where presently the lights, the black line of houses, the spires, and the flagstaff sank into the earth behind him again and were lost in the distance.

The storm had cleared away, the air was brisk and cold the outlines of adjacent landmarks were distinct, but it was half-past four before Dick reached the meeting-house and the crossing of the county road. To avoid the rising grade he had taken a longer and more circuitous road, in whose viscid mud Jovita sank fetlock deep at every bound. It was a poor preparation for a steady ascent of five miles more; but Jovita, gathering her legs under her, took it with her usual blind, unreasoning fury, and a half-hour later reached the long level that led to Rattlesnake Creek. Another half-hour would bring him to the creek. He threw the reins lightly upon the neck of the mare, chirruped to her, and began to sing.

Suddenly Jovita shied with a bound that would have unseated a less practised rider. Hanging to her rein was a figure that had leaped from the bank, and at the same time from the road before her arose a shadowy horse and rider. "Throw up your hands," commanded the second apparition, with an oath.

Dick felt the mare tremble, quiver, and apparently sink under him. He knew what it meant and was prepared.

"Stand aside, Jack Simpson. I know you, you d—d thief! Let me pass, or"——

He did not finish the sentence. Jovita rose straight in the air with a terrific bound, throwing the figure from her bit with a single shake of her vicious head, and charged with deadly malevolence down on the impediment before her. An oath, a pistol-shot, horse and highwayman rolled over in the road, and the next moment Jovita was a hundred yards away. But the good right arm of her rider, shattered by a bullet, dropped helplessly at his side.

Without slacking his speed he shifted the reins to his left hand. But a few moments later he was obliged to halt and tighten the saddle-girths that had slipped in the onset. This in his crippled condition took some time. He had no fear of pursuit, but looking up he saw that the eastern stars were already paling, and that the distant peaks had lost their ghostly whiteness, and now stood out blackly against a lighter sky. Day was upon him. Then completely absorbed in a single idea, he forgot the pain of his wound, and mounting again dashed on toward

Rattlesnake Creek. But now Jovita's breath came broken by gasps, Dick reeled in his saddle, and brighter and brighter grew the sky.

Ride, Richard; run, Jovita; linger, O day!

For the last few rods there was a roaring in his ears. Was it exhaustion from loss of blood, or what? He was dazed and giddy as he swept down the hill, and did not recognise his surroundings. Had he taken the wrong road, or was this Rattlesnake Creek?

It was. But the brawling creek he had swam a few hours before had risen, more than doubled its volume, and now rolled a swift and resistless river between him and Rattlesnake Hill. For the first time that night Richard's heart sank within him. The river, the mountain, the quickening east, swam before his eyes. He shut them to recover his self-control. In that brief interval, by some fantastic mental process, the little room at Simpson's Bar and the figures of the sleeping father and son rose upon him. He opened his eyes wildly, cast off his coat, pistol, boots, and saddle, bound his precious pack tightly to his shoulders, grasped the bare flanks of Jovita with his bared knees, and with a shout dashed into the yellow water. A cry rose from the opposite bank as the head of a man and horse struggled for a few moments against the battling current, and then were swept away amidst uprooted trees and whirling driftwood.

The Old Man started and woke. The fire on the hearth was dead, the candle in the outer room flickering in its socket, and somebody was rapping at the door. He opened it, but fell back with a cry before the dripping, half-naked figure that reeled against the doorpost.

"Dick?"

"Hush! Is he awake yet?"

"No; but, Dick?"——

"Dry up, you old fool! Get me some whisky, *quick!*" The Old Man flew and returned with—an empty bottle! Dick would have sworn, but his strength was not equal to the occasion. He staggered, caught at the handle of the door, and motioned to the Old Man.

"Thar's suthin' in my pack yer for Johnny, Take it off. I can't."

The Old Man unstrapped the pack, and laid it before the exhausted man.

"Open it, quick."

He did so with trembling fingers. It contained only a few poor toys, —cheap and barbaric enough, goodness knows, but bright with paint and tinsel. One of them was broken; another, I fear, was irretrievably ruined by water, and on the third—ah me! there was a cruel spot.

"It don't look like much, that's a fact," said Dick ruefully. . . . "But it's the best we could do. . . . Take 'em, Old Man, and put 'em in his stocking, and tell him—tell him, you know—hold me, Old Man"——The Old Man caught at his sinking figure. "Tell him," said Dick, with a weak little laugh,—"tell him Sandy Claus has come."

And even so, bedraggled, ragged, unshaven and unshorn, with one arm hanging helplessly at his side, Santa Claus came to Simpson's Bar and fell fainting on the first threshold. The Christmas dawn came slowly after, touching the remoter peaks with the rosy warmth of ineffable love. And it looked so tenderly on Simpson's Bar that the whole mountain, as if caught in a generous action, blushed to the skies.

A Monte Flat Pastoral

HOW OLD MAN PLUNKETT WENT HOME

I THINK WE all loved him. Even after he mismanaged the affairs of the Amity Ditch Company, we commiserated him, although most of us were stockholders and lost heavily. I remember that the blacksmith went so far as to say that "them chaps as put that responsibility on the old man oughter be lynched." But the blacksmith was not a stockholder, and the expression was looked upon as the excusable extravagance of a large, sympathising nature, that, when combined with a powerful frame, was unworthy of notice. At least, that was the way they put it. Yet I think there was a general feeling of regret that this misfortune would interfere with the old man's long-cherished plan of "going home."

Indeed, for the last ten years he had been "going home." He was going home after a six months' sojourn at Monte Flat. He was going home after the first rains. He was going home when the rains were over. He was going home when he had cut the timber on Buckeye Hill, when there was pasture on Dow's Flat, when he struck pay-dirt on Eureka Hill, when the Amity Company paid its first dividend, when the election was over, when he had received an answer from his wife. And so the years rolled by, the spring rains came and went, the woods of Buckeye Hill were level with the ground, the pasture on Dow's Flat grew sere and dry, Eureka Hill yielded its pay-dirt and swamped its owner, the first dividends of the Amity Company were made from the assessments of stockholders, there were new county officers at Monte Flat, his wife's answer had changed into a persistent question, and still old man Plunkett remained.

It is only fair to say that he had made several distinct essays towards going. Five years before he had bidden good-bye to Monte Hill with much effusion and hand-shaking. But he never got any farther than the next town. Here he was induced to trade the sorrel colt he was riding for a bay mare—a transaction that at once opened to his lively fancy a vista of vast and successful future speculation. A few days after, Abner Dean of Angel's received a letter from him stating that he was going to Visalia to buy horses. "I am satisfied," wrote Plunkett, with that elevated rhetoric for which his correspondence was remarkable, "I am satisfied that we are at last developing the real resources of California. The world will yet look to Dow's Flat as the great stock-raising centre. In view of the interests involved I have deferred my departure for a month." It was two months before he again returned to us, penniless. Six months later he was again enabled to start for the Eastern States, and this time he got as far as San Francisco. I have before me a letter which I received a few days after his arrival, from which I venture to give an extract: "You know, my dear boy, that I have always believed that gambling, as it is absurdly called, is still in its infancy in California. I have always maintained that a perfect system might be invented, by which the game of poker may be made to yield a certain percentage to the intelligent player. I am not at liberty at present to disclose the system, but before leaving this city I intend to perfect it." He seems to have done so, and returned to Monte Flat with two dollars and thirty-seven cents, the absolute remainder of his capital after such perfection.

It was not until 1868 that he appeared to have finally succeeded in going home. He left us by the overland route—a route which he declared would give great opportunity for the discovery of undeveloped resources. His last letter was dated Virginia City. He was absent three years. At the close of a very hot day in midsummer he alighted from the Wingdam stage with hair and beard powdered with dust and age. There was a certain shyness about his greeting, quite different from his usual frank volubility, that did not, however, impress us as any accession of character. For some days he was reserved regarding his recent visit, contenting himself with asserting, with more or less aggressiveness, that he had "always said he was going home, and now he had been there." Later, he grew more communicative, and spoke freely and critically of the manners and customs of New York and Boston, commented on the social changes in the years of his absence, and, I remember, was very hard upon what he deemed the follies incidental to a high state of civilisation. Still later, he darkly alluded to the moral laxity of the higher planes of Eastern society, but it was not long before he completely tore away the veil and revealed the naked wickedness of New York social life in a way I even now shudder to recall. Vinous intoxication, it appeared, was a common habit of the first ladies of the city; immoralities which he scarcely dared name were daily practised by the refined of both sexes; niggardliness and greed were the common vices of the rich. "I have always asserted," he continued, "that corruption must exist where luxury and riches are rampant, and capital is not used to develop the natural resources of the country. Thank you—I will take mine without sugar." It is possible that some of these painful details crept into the local journals. I remember an editorial in the "Monte Flat Monitor," entitled "The Effete East," in which the fatal decadence of New York and New England was elaborately stated, and California offered as a means of natural salvation. "Perhaps," said the "Monitor," "we might add that Calaveras County offers superior inducements to the Eastern visitor with capital."

Later he spoke of his family. The daughter he had left a child had grown into beautiful womanhood; the son was already taller and larger than his father, and in a playful trial of strength, "the young rascal," added Plunkett, with a voice broken with paternal pride and humorous objurgation, had twice thrown his doting parent to the ground. But it was of his daughter he chiefly spoke. Perhaps emboldened by the evident interest which masculine Monte Flat held in feminine beauty, he expatiated at some length on her various charms and accomplishments, and finally produced her photograph—that of a very pretty girl—to their infinite peril. But his account of his first meeting with her was so peculiar that I must fain give it after his own methods, which were, perhaps, some shades less precise and elegant than his written style.

"You see, boys, it's always been my opinion that a man oughter be able to tell his own flesh and blood by instinct. It's ten years since I'd seen my Melindy, and she was then only seven, and about so high. So, when I went to New York, what did I do? Did I go straight to my house and ask for my wife and daughter, like other folks? No, sir! I rigged myself up as a pedlar, as a pedlar, sir, and I rung the bell. When the servant came to the door, I wanted—don't you see—to show the ladies some trinkets. Then there was a voice over the banister, says, 'Don't want anything—send him away.' 'Some nice laces, ma'am, smuggled,' I says, looking up. 'Get out, you wretch,' says she. I knew the voice, boys—it was my wife; sure as a gun—thar wasn't any instinct thar. 'Maybe the young ladies want somethin',' I said. 'Did you hear me!' says she, and with that she jumps forward and I left. It's ten years, boys, since I've seen the old woman, but somehow, when she fetched that leap, I naterally left."

He had been standing beside the bar—his usual attitude—when he made this speech, but at this point he half-faced his auditors with a look that was very effective. Indeed, a few, who had exhibited some signs of scepticism and lack of interest, at once assumed an appearance of intense gratification and curiosity as he went on.

"Well, by hangin' round there for a day or two, I found out at last it was to be Melindy's birthday next week, and that she was goin' to have a big party. I tell ye what, boys, it weren't no slouch of a reception. The whole house was bloomin' with flowers, and blazin' with lights, and there was no end of servants and plate and refreshments and fixin's"——

"Uncle Joe."

"Well?"

"Where did they get the money?"

Plunkett faced his interlocutor with a severe glance. "I always said," he replied slowly, "that when I went home, I'd send on ahead of me a draft for ten thousand dollars. I always said that, didn't I? Eh? And I said I was goin' home—and I've been home—haven't I? Well?"

Either there was something irresistibly conclusive in this logic, or else the desire to hear the remainder of Plunkett's story was stronger, but there was no more interruption. His ready good-humour quickly returned, and, with a slight chuckle, he went on.

"I went to the biggest jewellery shop in town, and I bought a pair of diamond earrings and put them in my pocket, and went to the house. 'What name?' says the chap who opened the door, and he looked like a cross 'twixt a restaurant waiter and a parson. 'Skeesicks,' said I. He takes me in, and pretty soon my wife comes sailin' into the parlour, and says, 'Excuse me, but I don't think I recognise the name.' She was mighty polite, for I had on a red wig and side-whiskers. 'A friend of your husband's from California, ma'am, with a present for your daughter, Miss'——, and I made as I had forgot the name. But all of a sudden a voice said, 'That's too thin,' and in walked Melindy. 'It's playin' it rather low down, father, to pretend you don't know your daughter's name—ain't it now? How are you, old man?' And with that she tears off my wig and whiskers, and throws her arms around my neck,—instinct, sir, pure instinct!"

Emboldened by the laughter which followed his description of the filial utterances of Melinda, he again repeated her speech, with more or less elaboration, joining in with, and indeed often leading, the hilarity that accompanied it, and returning to it with more or less incoherency, several times during the evening.

And so at various times, and at various places—but chiefly in barrooms—did this Ulysses of Monte Flat recount the story of his wanderings. There were several discrepancies in his statement, there was sometimes considerable prolixity of detail, there was occasional change of character and scenery, there was once or twice an absolute change in the denouement, but always the fact of his having visited his wife and children remained. Of course in a sceptical community like that of Monte Flat—a community accustomed to great expectation and small realisation—a community wherein, to use the local dialect, "they got the colour and struck hardpan," more frequently than any other mining camp—in such a community the fullest credence was not given to old man Plunkett's facts. There was only one exception to the general unbelief—Henry York of Sandy Bar. It was he who was always an attentive listener; it was his scant purse that had often furnished Plunkett with means to pursue his unprofitable speculations; it was to him that the charms of Melinda were more frequently rehearsed; it was he that had borrowed her photograph; and it was he that, sitting alone in his little cabin one night, kissed that photograph until his honest, handsome face glowed again in the firelight.

It was dusty in Monte Flat. The ruins of the long, dry season were crumbling everywhere; everywhere the dying summer had strewn its red ashes a foot deep or exhaled its last breath in a red cloud above the troubled highways. The alders and cotton-woods that marked the line of the watercourses were grimy with dust, and looked as if they might have taken root in the open air; the gleaming stones of the parched water-courses themselves were as dry bones in the valley of death. The dusty sunset at times painted the flanks of the distant hills a dull, coppery hue; on other days there was an odd, indefinable earthquake halo on the volcanic cones of the farther coast spurs; again, an acid, resinous smoke from the burning wood on Heavytree Hill smarted the eyes and choked the free breath of Monte Flat, or a fierce wind, driving everything—including the shrivelled summer like a curled leaf—before it, swept down the flanks of the Sierras and chased the inhabitants to the doors of their cabins, and shook its red fist in at their windows. And on such a night as this—the dust having, in some way, choked the wheels of material progress in Monte Flat—most of the inhabitants were gathered listlessly in the gilded bar-room of the Moquelumne Hotel, spitting silently at the redhot stove that tempered the mountain winds to the shorn lambs of Monte Flat, and waiting for the rain.

Every method known to the Flat of beguiling the time until the
advent of this long-looked-for phenomenon had been tried. It is true
the methods were not many, being limited chiefly to that form of
popular facetiae known as practical joking; and even this had assumed
the seriousness of a business pursuit. Tommy Roy, who had spent two
hours in digging a ditch in front of his own door—into which a few
friends casually dropped during the evening—looked *ennuyé* and dissatisfied; the four prominent citizens, who, disguised as footpads, had
stopped the County Treasurer on the Wingdam road, were jaded from
their playful efforts next morning; the principal physician and lawyer
of Monte Flat, who had entered into an unhallowed conspiracy to
compel the Sheriff of Calaveras and his *posse* to serve a writ of eject-
ment on a grizzly bear, feebly disguised under the name of "one Major
Ursus," who haunted the groves of Heavytree Hill, wore an expression
of resigned weariness. Even the editor of the "Monte Flat Monitor,"
who had that morning written a glowing account of a battle with the
Wipneck Indians for the benefit of Eastern readers—even *he* looked
grave and worn. When, at last, Abner Dean of Angel's, who had been
on a visit to San Francisco, walked into the room, he was, of course,
victimised in the usual way by one or two apparently honest questions
which ended in his answering them, and then falling into the trap of
asking another to his utter and complete shame and mortification—
but that was all. Nobody laughed, and Abner, although a victim, did
not lose his good-humour. He turned quietly on his tormentors and
said—

"I've got something better than that—you know old man
Plunkett?"

Everybody simultaneously spat at the stove and nodded his head.

"You know he went home three years ago?" Two or three changed
the position of their legs from the backs of different chairs, and one
man said "Yes."

"Had a good time home?"

Everybody looked cautiously at the man who had said "Yes," and
he, accepting the responsibility with a fainthearted smile, said "Yes"
again, and breathed hard.

"Saw his wife and child, purty gal?" said Abner cautiously.

"Yes," answered the man doggedly.

"Saw her photograph, perhaps?" continued Abner Dean quietly.

The man looked hopelessly around for support. Two or three who
had been sitting near him and evidently encouraging him with a look
of interest, now shamelessly abandoned him and looked another way.
Henry York flushed a little and veiled his brown eyes. The man hesitated, and then with a sickly smile that was intended to convey the fact

that he was perfectly aware of the object of this questioning, and was only humouring it from abstract good feeling, returned "Yes," again.

"Sent home—let's see—ten thousand dollars, wasn't it?" Abner Dean went on.

"Yes," reiterated the man, with the same smile.

"Well, I thought so," said Abner quietly; "but the fact is, you see, that he never went home at all—nary time."

Everybody stared at Abner in genuine surprise and interest, as with provoking calmness and a half-lazy manner he went on.

"You see, thar was a man down in 'Frisco as knowed him and saw him in Sonora during the whole of that three years. He was herding sheep or tending cattle, or spekilating all that time, and hadn't a red cent. Well, it 'mounts to this—that 'ar Plunkett ain't been east of the Rocky Mountains since '49."

The laugh which Abner Dean had the right to confidently expect came, but it was bitter and sardonic. I think indignation was apparent in the minds of his hearers. It was felt, for the first time, that there was a limit to practical joking. A deception carried on for a year, compromising the sagacity of Monte Flat, was deserving the severest reprobation. Of course nobody had believed Plunkett; but then the supposition that it might be believed in adjacent camps that they *had* believed him was gall and bitterness. The lawyer thought that an indictment for obtaining money under false pretences might be found, the physician had long suspected him of insanity, and was not certain but that he ought to be confined. The four prominent merchants thought that the business interests of Monte Flat demanded that something should be done. In the midst of an excited and angry discussion the door slowly opened, and old man Plunkett staggered into the room.

He had changed pitifully in the last six months. His hair was a dusty yellowish-gray, like the chimisal on the flanks of Heavytree Hill; his face was waxen-white and blue and puffy under the eyes; his clothes were soiled and shabby—streaked in front with the stains of hurried luncheons eaten standing, and fluffy behind with the wool and hair of hurriedly extemporised couches. In obedience to that odd law, that the more seedy and soiled a man's garments become the less does he seem inclined to part with them, even during that portion of the twenty-four hours when they are deemed least essential, Plunkett's clothes had gradually taken on the appearance of a kind of bark, or an out-growth from within, for which their possessor was not entirely responsible. Howbeit, as he entered the room he attempted to button his coat over a dirty shirt, and passed his fingers, after the manner of some animal, over his cracker-strewn beard—in recognition of a cleanly public sentiment. But even as he did so the weak smile faded from his lips, and his hand, after fumbling aimlessly around a button, dropped helplessly at his side. For, as he leaned his back against the bar and faced the group, he for the first time became aware that every eye but one was fixed upon him. His quick, nervous apprehension at once leaped to the truth. His miserable secret was out and abroad in the very air about him. As a last resort, he glanced despairingly at Henry York, but his flushed face was turned toward the windows.

No word was spoken. As the barkeeper silently swung a decanter and glass before him, he took a cracker from a dish and mumbled it with affected unconcern. He lingered over his liquor, until its potency stiffened his relaxed sinews and dulled the nervous edge of his apprehension, and then he suddenly faced around. "It don't look as if we were goin' to hev any rain much afore Christmas," he said with defiant ease.

No one made any reply.

"Just like this in '52 and again in '60. It's always been my opinion that these dry seasons come reg'lar. I've said it afore. I say it again. It's jist as I said about going home, you know," he added with desperate recklessness.

"Thar's a man," said Abner Dean lazily, "ez sez you never went home. Thar's a man ez sez you've been three years in Sonora. Thar's a man ez sez you haint seen your wife and daughter since '49. Thar's a man ez sez you've been playin' this camp for six months."

There was a dead silence. Then a voice said, quite as quietly—

"That man lies."

It was not the old man's voice. Everybody turned as Henry York slowly rose, stretching out his six feet of length, and, brushing away the ashes that had fallen from his pipe upon his breast, deliberately placed himself beside Plunkett, and faced the others.

"That man ain't here," continued Abner Dean with listless indifference of voice and a gentle preoccupation of manner, as he carelessly allowed his right hand to rest on his hip near his revolver. "That man ain't here, but if I'm called upon to make good what he says, why, I'm on hand."

All rose as the two men—perhaps the least externally agitated of them all—approached each other. The lawyer stepped in between them.

"Perhaps there's some mistake here. York, do you *know* that the old man has been home?"

"Yes."

"How do you know it?"

York turned his clear, honest, frank eyes on his questioner, and without a tremor told the only direct and unmitigated lie of his life. "Because I've seen him there."

The answer was conclusive. It was known that York had been visiting the East during the old man's absence. The colloquy had diverted attention from Plunkett, who, pale and breathless, was staring at his unexpected deliverer. As he turned again toward his tormentors, there was something in the expression of his eye that caused those that were nearest to him to fall back, and sent a strange, indefinable thrill through the boldest and most reckless. As he made a step forward the physician almost unconsciously raised his hand with a warning gesture, and old man Plunkett, with his eyes fixed upon the redhot stove, and an odd smile playing about his mouth, began—

"Yes—of course you did. Who says you didn't? It ain't no lie; I said I was goin' home, and I've been home. Haven't I? My God! I have. Who says I've been lyin'? Who says I'm dreamin'? Is it true—why don't you speak? It is true, after all. You say you saw me there, why don't you speak again? Say! Say!—is it true? It's going now, O my God—it's going again. It's going now. Save me!" and with a fierce cry he fell forward in a fit upon the floor.

When the old man regained his senses he found himself in York's cabin. A flickering fire of pine boughs lit up the rude rafters, and fell upon a photograph tastefully framed with fir-cones and hung above the brush whereon he lay. It was the portrait of a young girl. It was the first object to meet the old man's gaze, and it brought with it a flush of such painful consciousness that he started and glanced quickly around. But his eyes only encountered those of York—clear, brown, critical and patient, and they fell again.

"Tell me, old man," said York, not unkindly, but with the same cold, clear tone in his voice that his eye betrayed a moment ago, "tell me, is *that* a lie too?" and he pointed to the picture.

The old man closed his eyes and did not reply. Two hours before the question would have stung him into some evasion or bravado. But the revelation contained in the question, as well as the tone of York's voice, was to him now, in his pitiable condition, a relief. It was plain even to his confused brain that York had lied when he had endorsed his story in the bar-room—it was clear to him now that he had not been home—that he was not, as he had begun to fear, going mad. It was such a relief that, with characteristic weakness, his former recklessness and extravagance returned. He began to chuckle—finally, to laugh uproariously.

York, with his eyes still fixed on the old man, withdrew the hand with which he had taken his.

"Didn't we fool 'em nicely, eh, Yorky? He! he! The biggest thing yet ever played in this camp! I always said I'd play 'em all some day, and I have—played 'em for six months. Ain't it rich—ain't it the richest thing you ever seed? Did you see Abner's face when he spoke 'bout that man as seed me in Sonora?—warn't it good as the minstrels? Oh, it's too much!" and striking his leg with the palm of his hand, he almost threw himself from the bed in a paroxysm of laughter—a paroxysm that, nevertheless, appeared to be half real and half affected.

"Is that photograph hers?" said York in a low voice, after a slight pause.

"Hers? No! It's one of the San Francisco actresses, he! he! Don't you see—I bought it for two bits in one of the book-stores. I never thought they'd swaller *that* too! but they did! Oh, but the old man played 'em this time, didn't he—eh?" and he peered curiously in York's face.

"Yes, and he played *me* too," said York, looking steadily in the old man's eye.

"Yes, of course," interposed Plunkett hastily, "but you know, Yorky, you got out of it well! You've sold 'em too. We've both got 'em on a string now—you and me—got to stick together now. You did it well, Yorky, you did it well. Why, when you said you'd seen me in York city, I'm d—d if I didn't"——

"Didn't what?" said York gently, for the old man had stopped with a pale face and wandering eye.

"Eh?"

"You say when I said I had seen you in New York you thought"——

"You lie!" said the old man fiercely, "I didn't say I thought anything. What are you trying to go back on me for? Eh?" His hands were trembling as he rose, muttering, from the bed and made his way toward the hearth.

"Gimme some whisky," he said presently, "and dry up. You oughter treat, anyway. Them fellows oughter treated last night. By hookey, I'd made 'em—only I fell sick."

York placed the liquor and a tin cup on the table beside him, and going to the door turned his back upon his guest and looked out on the night. Although it was clear moonlight the familiar prospect never to him seemed so dreary. The dead waste of the broad Wingdam highway never seemed so monotonous—so like the days that he had passed and were to come to him—so like the old man in its suggestion of going somewhere and never getting there. He turned, and going up to Plunkett put his hand upon his shoulder and said—

"I want you to answer one question fairly and squarely."

The liquor seemed to have warmed the torpid blood in the old man's veins and softened his acerbity, for the face he turned up to

York was mellowed in its rugged outline and more thoughtful in expression as he said—

"Go on, my boy."

"Have you a wife and—daughter?"

"Before God, I have!"

The two men were silent for a moment, both gazing at the fire. Then Plunkett began rubbing his knees slowly.

"The wife, if it comes to that, ain't much," he began cautiously, "being a little on the shoulder, you know, and wantin', so to speak, a liberal California education—which makes, you know, a bad combination. It's always been my opinion that there ain't any worse. Why, she's as ready with her tongue as Abner Dean is with his revolver, only with the difference that she shoots from principle, as she calls it, and the consequence is she's always layin' for you. It's the effete East, my boy, that's ruinin' her; it's them ideas she gets in New York and Boston that's made her and me what we are. I don't mind her havin' 'em if she didn't shoot. But havin' that propensity, them principles oughtn't to be lying round loose no more'n firearms."

"But your daughter?" said York.

The old man's hands went up to his eyes here, and then both hands and head dropped forward on the table. "Don't say anything 'bout her, my boy, don't ask me now." With one hand concealing his eyes he fumbled about with the other in his pockets for his handkerchief—but vainly. Perhaps it was owing to this fact that he repressed his tears, for when he removed his hand from his eyes they were quite dry. Then he found his voice.

"She's a beautiful girl, beautiful, though I say it—and you shall see her, my boy, you shall see her, sure. I've got things about fixed now. I shall have my plan for reducin' ores perfected in a day or two, and I've got proposals from all the smeltin' works here"—here he hastily produced a bundle of papers that fell upon the floor—"and I'm goin' to send for 'em. I've got the papers here as will give me ten thousand dollars clear in the next month," he added, as he strove to collect the valuable documents again. "I'll have 'em here by Christmas, if I live, and you shall eat your Christmas dinner with me, York, my boy—you shall, sure."

With his tongue now fairly loosened by liquor and the suggestive vastness of his prospects, he rambled on more or less incoherently, elaborating and amplifying his plans—occasionally even speaking of them as already accomplished, until the moon rode high in the heavens, and York led him again to his couch. Here he lay for some time muttering to himself, until at last he sank into a heavy sleep. When York had satisfied himself of the fact, he gently took down the picture and frame, and, going to the hearth, tossed them on the dying embers, and sat down to see them burn.

The fir-cones leaped instantly into flame; then the features that had entranced San Francisco audiences nightly flashed up and passed away —as such things are apt to pass—and even the cynical smile on York's lips faded too. And then there came a supplemental and unexpected flash as the embers fell together, and by its light York saw a paper upon the floor. It was one that had fallen from the old man's pocket. As he picked it up listlessly a photograph slipped from its folds. It was the portrait of a young girl, and on its reverse was written, in a scrawling hand, "Melinda to Father."

It was at best a cheap picture, but, ah me! I fear even the deft graciousness of the highest art could not have softened the rigid angularities of that youthful figure, its self-complacent vulgarity, its cheap finery, its expressionless ill-favour. York did not look at it the second time. He turned to the letter for relief.

It was misspelled, it was unpunctuated, it was almost illegible, it was fretful in tone and selfish in sentiment. It was not, I fear, even original in the story of its woes. It was the harsh recital of poverty, of suspicion, of mean makeshifts and compromises, of low pains and lower longings, of sorrows that were degrading, of a grief that was pitiable. Yet it was sincere in a certain kind of vague yearning for the presence of the degraded man to whom it was written—an affection that was more like a confused instinct than a sentiment.

York folded it again carefully, and placed it beneath the old man's pillow. Then he returned to his seat by the fire. A smile that had been playing upon his face, deepening the curves behind his moustache and gradually overrunning his clear brown eyes, presently faded away. It was last to go from his eyes, and it left there—oddly enough to those who did not know him—a tear.

He sat there for a long time, leaning forward, his head upon his hands. The wind that had been striving with the canvas roof all at once lifted its edges and a moonbeam slipped suddenly in, and lay for a moment like a shining blade upon his shoulder. And knighted by its touch, straightway plain Henry York arose—sustained, high-purposed and self-reliant!

The rains had come at last. There was already a visible greenness on the slopes of Heavytree Hill, and the long white track of the Wingdam road was lost in outlying pools and ponds a hundred rods from Monte Flat. The spent water-courses, whose white bones had been sinuously trailed over the flat, like the vertebrae of some forgotten Saurian, were full again; the dry bones moved once more in the valley, and there was joy in the ditches, and a pardonable extravagance in the columns of the "Monte Flat Monitor." "Never before in the history of the county has the yield been so satisfactory. Our contemporary of the 'Hillside Beacon,' who yesterday facetiously alluded to the fact(?) that our best citizens were leaving town, in 'dug-outs,' on account of the flood, will be glad to hear that our distinguished fellow-townsman, Mr. Henry York, now on a visit to his relatives in the East, lately took with him, in his 'dug-out,' the modest sum of fifty thousand dollars, the result of one week's clean-up. We can imagine," continued that sprightly journal, "that no such misfortune is likely to overtake Hillside this season. And yet we believe the 'Beacon' man wants a railroad." A few journals broke out into poetry. The operator at Simpson's Crossing telegraphed to the Sacramento "Universe:" "All day the low clouds have shook their garnered fulness down." A San Francisco journal lapsed into noble verse, thinly disguised as editorial prose: "Rejoice, the gentle rain has come, the bright and pearly rain, which scatters blessings on the hills, and sifts them o'er the plain. Rejoice," etc. Indeed, there was only one to whom the rain had not brought blessing, and that was Plunkett. In some mysterious and darksome way, it had interfered with the perfection of his new method of reducing ores, and thrown the advent of that invention back another season. It had brought him down to an habitual seat in the bar-room, where, to heedless and inattentive ears, he sat and discoursed of the East and his family.

No one disturbed him. Indeed, it was rumoured that some funds had been lodged with the landlord, by a person or persons unknown, whereby his few wants were provided for. His mania—for that was the charitable construction which Monte Flat put upon his conduct—was indulged, even to the extent of Monte Flat's accepting his invitation to dine with his family on Christmas Day—an invitation extended frankly to every one with whom the old man drank or talked. But one day, to everybody's astonishment, he burst into the bar-room, holding an open letter in his hand. It read as follows:—

Be ready to meet your family at the new cottage on Heavytree Hill on Christmas Day. Invite what friends you choose.   HENRY YORK

The letter was handed round in silence. The old man, with a look alternating between hope and fear, gazed in the faces of the group. The Doctor looked up significantly, after a pause. "It's a forgery, evidently," he said in a low voice; "he's cunning enough to conceive it—they always are—but you'll find he'll fail in executing it. Watch his face! Old man," he said suddenly, in a loud, peremptory tone, "this is a trick—a forgery—and you know it. Answer me squarely, and look me in the eye. Isn't it so?"

The eyes of Plunkett stared a moment, and then dropped weakly. Then, with a feebler smile, he said, "You're too many for me, boys. The Doc's right. The little game's up. You can take the old man's hat," and so, tottering, trembling, and chuckling, he dropped into silence and his accustomed seat. But the next day he seemed to have forgotten this episode, and talked as glibly as ever of the approaching festivity.

And so the days and weeks passed until Christmas—a bright, clear day, warmed with south winds, and joyous with the resurrection of springing grasses—broke upon Monte Flat. And then there was a sudden commotion in the hotel bar-room and Abner Dean stood beside the old man's chair, and shook him out of a slumber to his feet. "Rouse up, old man! York is here, with your wife and daughter at the cottage on Heavytree. Come, old man. Here, boys, give him a lift," and in another moment a dozen strong and willing hands had raised the old man, and bore him in triumph to the street, up the steep grade of Heavytree Hill, and deposited him, struggling and confused, in the porch of a little cottage. At the same instant, two women rushed forward, but were restrained by a gesture from Henry York. The old man was struggling to his feet. With an effort, at last, he stood erect, trembling, his eye fixed, a gray pallor on his cheek, and a deep resonance in his voice.

"It's all a trick, and a lie! They ain't no flesh and blood or kin o' mine. It ain't my wife, nor child. My daughter's a beautiful girl—a beautiful girl—d'ye hear? She's in New York, with her mother, and I'm going to fetch her here. I said I'd go home, and I've been home— d'ye hear me?—I've been home! It's a mean trick you're playin' on the old man. Let me go, d'ye hear? Keep them women off me! Let me go! I'm going—I'm going home!"

His hands were thrown up convulsively in the air, and, half turning round, he fell sideways on the porch, and so to the ground. They picked him up hurriedly; but too late. He had gone home.

Baby Sylvester

IT WAS AT a little mining camp in the California Sierras that he first dawned upon me in all his grotesque sweetness.

I had arrived early in the morning, but not in time to intercept the friend who was the object of my visit. He had gone "prospecting"—so they told me on the river—and would not probably return until late in the afternoon. They could not say what direction he had taken; they could not suggest that I would be likely to find him if I followed. But it was the general opinion that I had better wait.

I looked around me. I was standing upon the bank of the river; and, apparently, the only other human beings in the world were my interlocutors, who were even then just disappearing from my horizon down the steep bank toward the river's dry bed. I approached the edge of the bank.

Where could I wait?

Oh, anywhere; down with them on the river-bar, where they were working, if I liked! Or I could make myself at home in any of those cabins that I found lying round loose. Or, perhaps it would be cooler and pleasanter for me in my friend's cabin on the hill. Did I see those three large sugarpines? And, a little to the right, a canvas roof and chimney over the bushes? Well, that was my friend's—that was Dick Sylvester's cabin. I could stake my horse in that little hollow, and just

479

hang round there till he came. I would find some books in the shanty;
I could amuse myself with them. Or I could play with the baby.

Do what?

But they had already gone. I leaned over the bank and called after
their vanishing figures—

"What did you say I could do?"

The answer floated slowly up on the hot, sluggish air—

"Pla-a-y with the ba-by."

The lazy echoes took it up and tossed it languidly from hill to hill,
until Bald Mountain opposite made some incoherent remark about the
baby, and then all was still.

I must have been mistaken. My friend was not a man of family;
there was not a woman within forty miles of the river camp; he never
was so passionately devoted to children as to import a luxury so expensive. I must have been mistaken.

I turned my horse's head toward the hill. As we slowly climbed the
narrow trail, the little settlement might have been some exhumed
Pompeian suburb, so deserted and silent were its habitations. The open
doors plainly disclosed each rudely-furnished interior—the rough pine
table, with the scant equipage of the morning meal still standing; the
wooden bunk, with its tumbled and dishevelled blankets. A golden
lizard—the very genius of desolate stillness—had stopped breathless
upon the threshold of one cabin; a squirrel peeped impudently into the
window of another; a woodpecker, with the general flavour of under-
taking which distinguishes that bird, withheld his sepulchral hammer
from the coffin-lid of the roof on which he was professionally engaged,
as we passed. For a moment, I half-regretted that I had not accepted
the invitation to the riverbed; but, the next moment, a breeze swept up
the long, dark cañon, and the waiting files of the pines beyond bent
toward me in salutation. I think my horse understood as well as myself
that it was the cabins that made the solitude human, and therefore
unbearable, for he quickened his pace, and with a gentle trot brought
me to the edge of the wood and the three pines that stood like videttes
before the Sylvester outpost.

Unsaddling my horse in the little hollow, I unslung the long *riata*
from the saddlebow, and tethering him to a young sapling, turned
toward the cabin. But I had gone only a few steps when I heard a
quick trot behind me, and poor Pomposo, with every fibre tingling
with fear, was at my heels. I looked hurriedly around. The breeze had
died away, and only an occasional breath from the deep-chested
woods, more like a long sigh than any articulate sound, or the dry
singing of a cicala in the heated cañon, were to be heard. I examined
the ground carefully for rattlesnakes, but in vain. Yet here was

Pomposo shivering from his arched neck to his sensitive haunches, his very flanks pulsating with terror. I soothed him as well as I could, and then walked to the edge of the wood and peered into its dark recesses. The bright flash of a bird's wing, or the quick dart of a squirrel, was all I saw. I confess it was with something of superstitious expectation that I again turned toward the cabin. A fairy child, attended by Titania and her train, lying in an expensive cradle, would not have surprised me; a Sleeping Beauty, whose awakening would have repeopled these solitudes with life and energy, I am afraid I began to confidently look for, and would have kissed without hesitation.

But I found none of these. Here was the evidence of my friend's taste and refinement in the hearth swept scrupulously clean, in the picturesque arrangement of the fur skins that covered the floor and furniture, and the *serápe* lying on the wooden couch. Here were the walls fancifully papered with illustrations from the "London News;" here was the wood-cut portrait of Mr. Emerson over the chimney, quaintly framed with blue jays' wings; here were his few favourite books on the swinging shelf; and here, lying upon the couch, the latest copy of "Punch." Dear Dick! The flour-sack was sometimes empty, but the gentle satirist seldom missed his weekly visit.

I threw myself on the couch and tried to read. But I soon exhausted my interest in my friend's library, and lay there staring through the open door on the green hillside beyond. The breeze again sprang up, and a delicious coolness, mixed with the rare incense of the woods, stole through the cabin. The slumbrous droning of bumble-bees outside the canvas roof, the faint cawing of rooks on the opposite mountain, and the fatigue of my morning ride, began to droop my eyelids. I pulled the *serápe* over me as a precaution against the freshening mountain breeze, and in a few moments was asleep.

I do not remember how long I slept. I must have been conscious, however, during my slumber, of my inability to keep myself covered by the *serápe*, for I awoke once or twice clutching it with a despairing hand as it was disappearing over the foot of the couch. Then I became suddenly aroused to the fact that my efforts to retain it were resisted by some equally persistent force, and letting it go, I was horrified at seeing it swiftly drawn under the couch. At this point I sat up completely awake; for immediately after, what seemed to be an exaggerated muff began to emerge from under the couch. Presently it appeared fully, dragging the *serápe* after it. There was no mistaking it now—it was a baby bear. A mere suckling, it was true—a helpless roll of fat and fur—but unmistakably, a grizzly cub!

I cannot recall anything more irresistibly ludicrous than its aspect as it slowly raised its small wondering eyes to mine. It was so much

taller in its haunches than its shoulders—its fore-legs were so dispro-
portionately small—that in walking its hind-feet invariably took prece-
dence. It was perpetually pitching forward over its pointed, inoffensive
nose, and recovering itself always, after these involuntary somersaults,
with the gravest astonishment. To add to its preposterous appearance,
one of its hind-feet was adorned by a shoe of Sylvester's, into which it
had accidentally and inextricably stepped. As this somewhat impeded
its first impulse to fly, it turned to me; and then, possibly recognising
in the stranger the same species as its master, it paused. Presently, it
slowly raised itself on its hind-legs, and vaguely and deprecatingly
waved a baby paw, fringed with little hooks of steel. I took the paw
and shook it gravely. From that moment we were friends. The little
affair of the *serápe* was forgotten.

Nevertheless, I was wise enough to cement our friendship by an act
of delicate courtesy. Following the direction of his eyes, I had no
difficulty in finding, on a shelf near the ridge-pole, the sugarbox and
the square lumps of white sugar that even the poorest miner is never
without. While he was eating them I had time to examine him more
closely. His body was a silky, dark, but exquisitely modulated grey,
deepening to black in his paws and muzzle. His fur was excessively
long, thick, and soft as eider down, the cushions of flesh beneath perfectly infantine in their texture and contour. He was so very young
that the palms of his half-human feet were still tender as a baby's.
Except for the bright blue, steely hooks, half-sheathed in his little toes,
there was not a single harsh outline or detail in his plump figure. He
was as free from angles as one of Leda's offspring. Your caressing hand
sank away in his fur with dreamy languor. To look at him long was an
intoxication of the senses; to pat him was a wild delirium; to embrace
him, an utter demoralisation of the intellectual faculties.

When he had finished the sugar he rolled out of the door with a
half-diffident, half-inviting look in his eye, as if he expected me to
follow. I did so, but the sniffing and snorting of the keen-scented
Pomposo in the hollow, not only revealed the cause of his former
terror, but decided me to take another direction. After a moment's
hesitation he concluded to go with me, although I am satisfied, from a
certain impish look in his eye, that he fully understood and rather
enjoyed the fright of Pomposo. As he rolled along at my side, with a
gait not unlike a drunken sailor, I discovered that his long hair concealed a leather collar around his neck, which bore for its legend the
single word, "Baby!" I recalled the mysterious suggestion of the two
miners. This, then, was the "baby" with whom I was to "play."

How we "played;" how Baby allowed me to roll him down hill,
crawling and puffing up again each time, with perfect good humour;

how he climbed a young sapling after my Panama hat, which I had "shied" into one of the topmost branches; how after getting it he refused to descend until it suited his pleasure; how when he did come down he persisted in walking about on three legs, carrying my hat, a crushed and shapeless mass, clasped to his breast with the remaining one; how I missed him at last, and finally discovered him seated on a table in one of the tenantless cabins, with a bottle of syrup between his paws, vainly endeavouring to extract its contents—these and other details of that eventful day I shall not weary the reader with now. Enough, that when Dick Sylvester returned, I was pretty well fagged out, and the baby was rolled up, an immense bolster at the foot of the couch, asleep, Sylvester's first words after our greeting were—

"Isn't he delicious?"

"Perfectly. Where did you get him?"

"Lying under his dead mother, five miles from here," said Dick, lighting his pipe. "Knocked her over at fifty yards; perfectly clean shot —never moved afterwards! Baby crawled out, scared but unhurt. She must have been carrying him in her mouth, and dropped him when she faced me, for he wasn't more than three days old, and not steady on his pins. He takes the only milk that comes to the settlement— brought up by Adams Express at seven o'clock every morning. They say he looks like me. Do you think so?" asked Dick, with perfect gravity, stroking his hay-coloured moustachios, and evidently assuming his best expression.

I took leave of the baby early the next morning in Sylvester's cabin, and, out of respect for Pomposo's feelings, rode by without any postscript of expression. But the night before I had made Sylvester solemnly swear that, in the event of any separation between himself and Baby, it should revert to me. "At the same time," he had added, "it's only fair to say that I don't think of dying just yet, old fellow, and I don't know of anything else that would part the cub and me."

Two months after this conversation, as I was turning over the morning's mail at my office in San Francisco, I noticed a letter bearing Sylvester's familiar hand. But it was post-marked "Stockton," and I opened it with some anxiety at once. Its contents were as follows:—

O Frank! Don't you remember what we agreed upon anent the baby? Well, consider me as dead for the next six months, or gone where cubs can't follow me—East. I know you love the baby; but do you think, dear boy—now, really, do you think you *could* be a father to it? Consider this well. You are young, thoughtless, well-meaning enough; but dare you take upon yourself the functions of guide, genius, or guardian to one so young and guileless? Could you be the mentor to this

Telemachus? Think of the temptations of a metropolis. Look at the question well, and let me know speedily, for I've got him as far as this place, and he's kicking up an awful row in the hotelyard and rattling his chain like a maniac. Let me know by telegraph at once.SYLVESTER

P.S. —Of course he's grown a little, and doesn't take things always as quietly as he did. He dropped rather heavily on two of Watson's 'purps' last week, and snatched old Watson himself, bald-headed, for interfering. You remember Watson: for an intelligent man, he knows very little of California fauna. How are you fixed for bears on Montgomery street —I mean in regard to corrals and things?   S.

P.P.S. —He's got some new tricks. The boys have been teaching him to put up his hands with them. He slings an ugly left.   S.

I am afraid that my desire to possess myself of Baby overcame all other considerations, and I telegraphed an affirmative at once to Sylvester. When I reached my lodgings late that afternoon, my landlady was awaiting me with a telegram. It was two lines from Sylvester—

All right. Baby goes down on night-boat. Be a father to him.   S.

It was due, then, at one o'clock that night. For a moment I was staggered at my own precipitation. I had as yet made no preparations —had said nothing to my landlady about her new guest. I expected to arrange everything in time; and now, through Sylvester's indecent haste, that time had been shortened twelve hours.

Something, however, must be done at once. I turned to Mrs. Brown. I had great reliance in her maternal instincts; I had that still greater reliance, common to our sex, in the general tender-heartedness of pretty women. But I confess I was alarmed. Yet, with a feeble smile, I tried to introduce the subject with classical ease and lightness. I even said, "If Shakespeare's Athenian clown, Mrs. Brown, believed that a lion among ladies was a dreadful thing, what must"——But here I broke down, for Mrs. Brown, with the awful intuition of her sex, I saw at once was more occupied with my manner than my speech. So I tried a business *brusquerie,* and, placing the telegram in her hand, said hurriedly, "We must do something about this at once. It's perfectly absurd, but he will be here at one to-night. Beg thousand pardons, but business prevented my speaking before"——and paused, out of breath and courage.

Mrs. Brown read the telegram gravely, lifted her pretty eyebrows, turned the paper over and looked on the other side, and then, in a remote and chilling voice, asked me if she understood me to say that the mother was coming also.

"Oh, dear no," I exclaimed, with considerable relief; "the mother is dead, you know. Sylvester—that is my friend, who sent this—shot her when the baby was only three days old"——But the expression of Mrs. Brown's face at this moment was so alarming that I saw that nothing but the fullest explanation would save me. Hastily, and I fear not very coherently, I told her all.

She relaxed sweetly. She said I had frightened her with my talk about lions. Indeed, I think my picture of poor Baby—albeit a trifle highly coloured—touched her motherly heart. She was even a little vexed at what she called Sylvester's "hard-heartedness." Still, I was not without some apprehension. It was two months since I had seen him, and Sylvester's vague allusion to his "slinging an ugly left" pained me. I looked at sympathetic little Mrs. Brown, and the thought of Watson's pups covered me with guilty confusion.

Mrs. Brown had agreed to sit up with me until he arrived. One o'clock came, but no Baby. Two o'clock—three o'clock passed. It was almost four when there was a wild clatter of horses' hoofs outside, and with a jerk a waggon stopped at the door. In an instant I had opened it and confronted a stranger. Almost at the same moment the horses attempted to run away with the waggon.

The stranger's appearance was, to say the least, disconcerting. His clothes were badly torn and frayed; his linen sack hung from his shoulders like a herald's apron; one of his hands was bandaged; his face scratched, and there was no hat on his disheveled head. To add to the general effect, he had evidently sought relief from his woes in drink, and he swayed from side to side as he clung to the door handle, and in a very thick voice stated that he had "suthin' " for me outside. When he had finished the horses made another plunge.

Mrs. Brown thought they must be frightened at something.

"Frightened!" laughed the stranger with bitter irony. "Oh no! Hossish ain't frightened! On'y ran away four timesh comin' here. Oh no! Nobody's frightened. Everythin's all ri'. Ain't it, Bill?" he said, addressing the driver. "On'y been overboard twish; knocked down a hatchway once. Thash nothin'! On'y two men unner doctor's han's at Stockton. Thash nothin'! Six hunner dollarsh cover all dammish."

I was too much disheartened to reply, but moved toward the waggon. The stranger eyed me with an astonishment that almost sobered him.

"Do you reckon to tackle that animile yourself?" he asked, as he surveyed me from head to foot.

I did not speak, but, with an appearance of boldness I was far from feeling, walked to the waggon and called "Baby!"

"All ri'. Cash loosh them straps, Bill, and stan' clear."

The straps were cut loose, and Baby—the remorseless, the terrible—quietly tumbled to the ground, and, rolling to my side, rubbed his foolish head against me.

I think the astonishment of the two men was beyond any vocal expression. Without a word the drunken stranger got into the waggon and drove away.

And Baby? He had grown, it is true, a trifle larger; but he was thin, and bore the marks of evident ill-usage. His beautiful coat was matted and unkempt, and his claws—those bright steel hooks—had been ruthlessly pared to the quick. His eyes were furtive and restless, and the old expression of stupid good-humour had changed to one of intelligent distrust. His intercourse with mankind had evidently quickened his intellect without broadening his moral nature.

I had great difficulty in keeping Mrs. Brown from smothering him in blankets and ruining his digestion with the delicacies of her larder; but I at last got him completely rolled up in the corner of my room and asleep. I lay awake some time later with plans for his future. I finally determined to take him to Oakland, where I had built a little cottage and always spent my Sundays, the very next day. And in the midst of a rosy picture of domestic felicity I fell asleep.

When I awoke it was broad day. My eyes at once sought the corner where Baby had been lying. But he was gone. I sprang from the bed, looked under it, searched the closet, but in vain. The door was still locked; but there were the marks of his blunted claws upon the sill of the window that I had forgotten to close. He had evidently escaped that way—but where? The window opened upon a balcony, to which the only other entrance was through the hall. He must be still in the house.

My hand was already upon the bell-rope, but I stayed it in time. If he had not made himself known, why should I disturb the house? I dressed myself hurriedly and slipped into the hall. The first object that met my eyes was a boot lying upon the stairs. It bore the marks of Baby's teeth, and as I looked along the hall I saw too plainly that the usual array of freshly-blackened boots and shoes before the lodgers' doors was not there. As I ascended the stairs I found another, but with the blacking carefully licked off. On the third floor were two or three more boots, slightly mouthed; but at this point Baby's taste for blacking had evidently palled. A little farther on was a ladder, leading to an open scuttle. I mounted the ladder, and reached the flat roof that formed a continuous level over the row of houses to the corner of the street. Behind the chimney on the very last roof something was lurking. It was the fugitive Baby. He was covered with dust and dirt and fragments of glass. But he was sitting on his hind-legs, and was eating an enormous slab of pea-nut candy with a look of mingled guilt and infinite satisfaction. He even, I fancied, slightly stroked his stomach with his disengaged fore-paw as I approached. He knew that I was looking for him, and the expression of his eye said plainly, "The past, at least, is secure."

I hurried him, with the evidences of his guilt, back to the scuttle, and descended on tip-toe to the floor beneath. Providence favoured us; I met no one on the stairs, and his own cushioned tread was inaudible. I think he was conscious of the dangers of detection, for he even forbore to breathe, or much less chew the last mouthful he had taken; and he skulked at my side, with the syrup dropping from his motionless jaws. I think he would have silently choked to death just then for my sake, and it was not until I had reached my room again, and threw myself panting on the sofa, that I saw how near strangulation he had been. He gulped once or twice, apologetically, and then walked to the corner of his own accord, and rolled himself up like an immense sugar-plum, sweating remorse and treacle at every pore.

I locked him in when I went to breakfast, when I found Mrs. Brown's lodgers in a state of intense excitement over certain mysterious events of the night before, and the dreadful revelations of the morning. It appeared that burglars had entered the block from the scuttles; that, being suddenly alarmed, they had quitted our house without committing any depredation, dropping even the boots they had collected in the halls; but that a desperate attempt had been made to force the till in the confectioner's shop on the corner, and that the glass show-cases had been ruthlessly smashed. A courageous servant in No. 4 had seen a masked burglar, on his hands and knees, attempting to enter their scuttle; but on her shouting, "Away wid yees," he instantly fled.

I sat through this recital with cheeks that burned uncomfortably; nor was I the less embarrassed on raising my eyes to meet Mrs. Brown's fixed curiously and mischievously on mine. As soon as I could make my escape from the table I did so, and, running rapidly upstairs, sought refuge from any possible inquiry in my own room. Baby was still asleep in the corner. It would not be safe to remove him until the lodgers had gone down town, and I was revolving in my mind the expediency of keeping him until night veiled his obtrusive eccentricity from the public eye, when there came a cautious tap at my door. I opened it. Mrs. Brown slipped in quietly, closed the door softly, stood with her back against it and her hand on the knob, and beckoned me mysteriously towards her. Then she asked, in a low voice—

"Is hair-dye poisonous?"

I was too confounded to speak.

"Oh do! you know what I mean," she said impatiently. "This stuff." She produced suddenly from behind her a bottle with a Greek label— so long as to run two or three times spirally around it from top to bottom. "He says it isn't a dye; it's a vegetable preparation, for invigo- rating"——

"Who says?" I asked despairingly.

"Why, Mr. Parker, of course," said Mrs. Brown severely, with the air of having repeated the name a great many times—"the old gen- tleman in the room above. The simple question I want to ask," she continued, with the calm manner of one who has just convicted an- other of gross ambiguity of language, "is only this: If some of this stuff were put in a saucer and left carelessly on the table, and a child, or a baby, or a cat, or any young animal, should come in at the window and drink it up—a whole saucer full—because it had a sweet taste, would it be likely to hurt them?"

I cast an anxious glance at Baby, sleeping peacefully in the corner, and a very grateful one at Mrs. Brown, and said I didn't think it would.

"Because," said Mrs. Brown loftily, as she opened the door, "I thought if it was poisonous, remedies might be used in time. Because," she added suddenly, abandoning her lofty manner and wildly rushing to the corner, with a frantic embrace of the unconscious Baby, "be- cause if any nasty stuff should turn its booful hair a horrid green or a naughty pink, it would break its own muzzer's heart, it would!"

But before I could assure Mrs. Brown of the inefficiency of hair-dye as an internal application, she had darted from the room.

That night, with the secrecy of defaulters, Baby and I decamped from Mrs. Brown's. Distrusting the too emotional nature of that noble animal, the horse, I had recourse to a hand-cart, drawn by a stout Irishman, to convey my charge to the ferry. Even then Baby refused to go unless I walked by the cart, and at times rode in it.

"I wish," said Mrs. Brown, as she stood by the door, wrapped in an immense shawl, and saw us depart, "I wish it looked less solemn—less like a pauper's funeral."

I must admit that, as I walked by the cart that night, I felt very much as if I were accompanying the remains of some humble friend to his last resting-place; and that, when I was obliged to ride in it, I never could entirely convince myself that I was not helplessly overcome by liquor, or the victim of an accident, *en route* to the hospital. But at last we reached the ferry. On the boat I think no one discovered Baby except a drunken man, who approached me to ask for a light for his cigar, but who suddenly dropped it and fled in dismay to the gentlemen's cabin, where his incoherent ravings were luckily taken for the earlier indications of *delirium tremens.*

It was nearly midnight when I reached my little cottage on the outskirts of Oakland; and it was with a feeling of relief and security that I entered, locked the door, and turned him loose in the hall, satisfied that henceforward his depredations would be limited to my own property. He was very quiet that night, and after he had tried to mount the hat-rack, under the mistaken impression that it was intended for his own gymnastic exercise, and knocked all the hats off, he went peaceably to sleep on the rug.

In a week, with the exercise afforded him by the run of a large, carefully-boarded enclosure, he recovered his health, strength, spirits, and much of his former beauty. His presence was unknown to my neighbours, although it was noticeable that horses invariably "shied" in passing to the windward of my house, and that the baker and milkman had great difficulty in the delivery of their wares in the morning, and indulged in unseemly and unnecessary profanity in so doing.

At the end of the week, I determined to invite a few friends to see the Baby, and to that purpose wrote a number of formal invitations. After descanting, at some length, on the great expense and danger attending his capture and training, I offered a programme of the performances of the "Infant Phenomenon of Sierran Solitudes," drawn up into the highest professional profusion of alliteration and capital letters. A few extracts will give the reader some idea of his educational progress—

1. He will, rolled up in a Round Ball, roll down the Wood Shed, Rapidly, illustrating His manner of Escaping from His Enemy in his Native Wilds.
2. He will Ascend the Well Pole, and remove from the Very Top a Hat, and as much of the Crown and Brim thereof as May be Permitted.
3. He will perform in a pantomime, descriptive of the Conduct of the Big Bear, The Middle-Sized Bear, and The Little Bear of the Popular Nursery Legend.
4. He will shake his chain Rapidly, showing his Manner of striking Dismay and Terror in the Breasts of Wanderers in Ursine Wildernesses.

The morning of the exhibition came, but an hour before the performance the wretched Baby was missing. The Chinese cook could not indicate his whereabouts. I searched the premises thoroughly, and then, in despair, took my hat and hurried out into the narrow lane that led toward the open fields and the woods beyond. But I found no trace nor track of Baby Sylvester. I returned, after an hour's fruitless search, to find my guests already assembled on the rear veranda. I briefly recounted my disappointment, my probable loss, and begged their assistance.

"Why," said a Spanish friend, who prided himself on his accurate knowledge of English, to Barker, who seemed to be trying vainly to rise from his reclining position on the veranda, "Why do you not disengage yourself from the veranda of our friend? and why, in the name of Heaven, do you attach to yourself so much of this thing, and make to yourself such unnecessary contortion? Ah," he continued, suddenly withdrawing one of his own feet from the veranda with an evident effort, "I am myself attached! Surely it is something here!"

It evidently was. My guests were all rising with difficulty,—the floor of the veranda was covered with some glutinous substance. It was— syrup!

I saw it all in a flash. I ran to the barn; the keg of "golden syrup," purchased only the day before, lay empty upon the floor. There were sticky tracks all over the enclosure, but still no Baby.

"There's something moving the ground over there by that pile of dirt," said Barker.

He was right; the earth was shaking in one corner of the enclosure like an earthquake. I approached cautiously. I saw, what I had not before noticed, that the ground was thrown up; and there, in the middle of an immense grave-like cavity, crouched Baby Sylvester, still digging, and slowly, but surely, sinking from sight in a mass of dust and clay.

What were his intentions? Whether he was stung by remorse, and wished to hide himself from my reproachful eyes, or whether he was simply trying to dry his syrup-besmeared coat, I never shall know, for that day, alas! was his last with me.

He was pumped upon for two hours, at the end of which time he still yielded a thin treacle. He was then taken and carefully enwrapped in blankets and locked up in the storeroom. The next morning he was gone! The lower portion of the window sash and pane were gone too. His successful experiments on the fragile texture of glass at the confectioner's, on the first day of his entrance to civilisation, had not been lost upon him. His first essay at combining cause and effect ended in his escape.

Where he went, where he hid, who captured him if he did not succeed in reaching the foot-hills beyond Oakland, even the offer of a large reward, backed by the efforts of an intelligent police, could not discover. I never saw him again from that day until——

Did I see him? I was in a horse-car on Sixth Avenue, a few days ago, when the horses suddenly became unmanageable and left the track for the sidewalk, amid the oaths and execrations of the driver. Immediately in front of the car a crowd had gathered around two performing bears and a showman. One of the animals—thin, emaciated, and the mere wreck of his native strength—attracted my attention. I endeavoured to attract his. He turned a pair of bleared, sightless eyes in my direction, but there was no sign of recognition. I leaned from the car-window and called softly, "Baby!" But he did not heed. I closed the window. The car was just moving on, when he suddenly turned, and, either by accident or design, thrust a callous paw through the glass.

"It's worth a dollar-and-a-half to put in a new pane," said the conductor, "if folks will play with bears!"——

The Man on the Beach

I

HE LIVED BESIDE a river that emptied into a great ocean. The narrow strip of land that lay between him and the estuary was covered at high tide by a shining film of water, at low tide with the cast-up offerings of sea and shore. Logs yet green, and saplings washed away from inland banks, battered fragments of wrecks and orange crates of bamboo, broken into tiny rafts yet odorous with their lost freight, lay in long successive curves—the fringes and over-lappings of the sea. At high noon the shadow of a seagull's wing, or a sudden flurry and gray squall of sandpipers, themselves but shadows, was all that broke the monotonous glare of the level sands.

He had lived there alone for a twelvemonth. Although but a few miles from a thriving settlement, during that time his retirement had never been intruded upon, his seclusion remained unbroken. In any other community he might have been the subject of rumour or criticism, but the miners at Camp Rogue and the traders at Trinidad Head, themselves individual and eccentric, were profoundly indifferent to all other forms of eccentricity or heterodoxy that did not come in contact with their own. And certainly there was no form of eccentricity less aggressive than that of a hermit, had they chosen to give him that

492

appellation. But they did not even do that, probably from lack of interest or perception. To the various traders who supplied his small wants he was known as "Kernel," "Judge," and "Boss." To the general public "The Man on the Beach" was considered a sufficiently distinguishing title. His name, his occupation, rank, or antecedents, nobody cared to inquire. Whether this arose from a fear of reciprocal inquiry and interest, or from the profound indifference before referred to, I cannot say.

He did not look like a hermit. A man yet young, erect, well-dressed, clean-shaven, with a low voice, and a smile half-melancholy, half-cynical, was scarcely the conventional idea of a solitary. His dwelling, a rude improvement on a fisherman's cabin, had all the severe exterior simplicity of frontier architecture, but within it was comfortable and wholesome. Three rooms—a kitchen, a living-room, and a bedroom—were all it contained.

He had lived there long enough to see the dull monotony of one season lapse into the dull monotony of the other. The bleak north-west trade-winds had brought him mornings of staring sunlight and nights of fog and silence. The warmer south-west trades had brought him clouds, rain, and the transient glories of quick grasses and ordorous beach blossoms. But summer or winter, wet or dry season, on one side rose always the sharply-defined hills with their changeless background of evergreens; on the other side stretched always the illimitable ocean as sharply defined against the horizon, and as unchanging in its hue. The onset of spring and autumn tides, some changes among his feathered neighbours, the footprints of certain wild animals along the river's bank, and the hanging out of parti-coloured signals from the wooded hillside far inland, helped him to record the slow months. On summer afternoons, when the sun sank behind a bank of fog that, moving solemnly shoreward, at last encompassed him and blotted out sea and sky, his isolation was complete. The damp gray sea that flowed above and around and about him always seemed to shut out an intangible world beyond, and to be the only real presence. The booming of breakers scarce a dozen rods from his dwelling was but a vague and unintelligible sound, or the echo of something past for ever. Every morning when the sun tore away the misty curtain he awoke, dazed and bewildered, as upon a new world. The first sense of oppression over, he came to love at last this subtle spirit of oblivion; and at night, when its cloudy wings were folded over his cabin, he would sit alone with a sense of security he had never felt before. On such occasions he was apt to leave his door open, and listen as for footsteps; for what might not come to him out of this vague, nebulous world beyond? Perhaps even *she;* for this strange solitary was not insane nor visionary. He was never in spirit alone. For night and day, sleeping or waking, pacing the beach or crouching over his driftwood fire, a woman's face was always before him—the face for whose sake and for cause of whom he sat there alone. He saw it in the morning sunlight; it was her white hands that were lifted from the crested breakers; it was the rustling of her skirt when the sea wind swept through the beach grasses; it was the loving whisper of her low voice when the long waves sank and died among the sedge and rushes. She was as omnipresent as sea and sky and level sand. Hence, when the fog wiped them away, she seemed to draw closer to him in the darkness. On one or two more gracious nights in midsummer, when the influence of the fervid noonday sun was still felt on the heated sands, the warm breath of the fog touched his cheek as if he had been hers, and the tears started to his eyes.

Before the fogs came—for he arrived there in winter—he had found surcease and rest in the steady glow of a lighthouse upon the little promontory a league below his habitation. Even on the darkest nights, and in the tumults of storm, it spoke to him of a patience that was enduring and a steadfastness that was immutable. Later on he found a certain dumb companionship in an uprooted tree, which, floating down the river, had stranded hopelessly upon his beach, but in the evening had again drifted away. Rowing across the estuary a day or two afterward, he recognised the tree again from a "blaze" of the settler's axe still upon its trunk. He was not surprised a week later to find the same tree in the sands before his dwelling, or that the next morning it should be again launched on its purposeless wanderings. And so, impelled by wind or tide, but always haunting his seclusion, he would meet it voyaging up the river at the flood, or see it tossing among the breakers on the bar, but always with the confidence of its returning sooner or later to an anchorage beside him. After the third month of his self-imposed exile, he was forced into a more human companionship, that was brief but regular. He was obliged to have menial assistance. While he might have eaten his bread "in sorrow" carelessly and mechanically, if it had been prepared for him, the occupation of cooking his own food brought the vulgarity and materialness of existence so near to his morbid sensitiveness that he could not eat the meal he had himself prepared. He did not yet wish to die, and when starvation or society seemed to be the only alternative, he chose the latter. An Indian woman, so hideous as to scarcely suggest humanity, at stated times performed for him these offices. When she did not come, which was not infrequent, he did not eat.

Such was the mental and physical condition of the Man on the Beach on January 1, 1869.

It was a still, bright day, following a week of rain and wind. Low down the horizon still lingered a few white flecks—the flying squadrons of the storm—as vague as distant sails. Southward the harbour bar whitened occasionally but lazily; even the turbulent Pacific swell stretched its length wearily upon the shore. And toiling from the settlement over the low sand dunes, a carriage at last halted half a mile from the solitary's dwelling.

"I reckon ye'll hev to git out here," said the driver, pulling up to breathe his panting horses. "Ye can't git any nigher."

There was a groan of execration from the interior of the vehicle, a hysterical little shriek, and one or two shrill expressions of feminine disapprobation, but the driver moved not. At last a masculine head expostulated from the window: "Look here; you agreed to take us to the house. Why, it's a mile away at least!"

"Thar, or tharabouts, I reckon," said the driver, coolly crossing his legs on the box.

"It's no use talking; *I* can never walk through this sand and horrid glare," said a female voice quickly and imperatively. Then, apprehensively, "Well of all the places!"

"Well, I never!"

"This *does* exceed everything."

"It's really *too* idiotic for anything."

It was noticeable that while the voices betrayed the difference of age and sex, they bore a singular resemblance to each other, and a certain querulousness of pitch that was dominant.

"I reckon I've gone about as fur as I allow to go with them hosses," continued the driver suggestively, "and as time's vallyble, ye'd better onload."

"The wretch does not mean to leave us here alone?" said a female voice in shrill indignation. "You'll wait for us, driver?" said a masculine voice confidently.

"How long?" asked the driver.

There was a hurried consultation within. The words "Might send us packing," "May take all night to get him to listen to reason," "Bother! whole thing over in ten minutes," came from the window. The driver meanwhile had settled himself back in his seat, and whistled in patient contempt of a fashionable fare that didn't know its own mind nor destination. Finally, the masculine head was thrust out, and, with a certain potential air of judicially ending a difficulty, said—

"You're to follow us slowly, and put up your horses in the stable or barn until we want you."

An ironical laugh burst from the driver. "Oh yes—in the stable or

barn—in course. But, my eyes sorter failin' me, mebbee, now, some ev
you younger folks will kindly pint out the stable or barn of the Kernel's. Woa!—will ye?—woa! Give me a chance to pick out that there
barn or stable to put ye in!" This in arch confidence to the horses, who
had not moved.

Here the previous speaker, rotund, dignified, and elderly, alighted
indignantly, closely followed by the rest of the party, two ladies and a
gentleman. One of the ladies was past the age, but not the fashion, of
youth, and her Parisian dress clung over her wasted figure and well-
bred bones artistically if not gracefully; the younger lady, evidently
her daughter, was crisp and pretty, and carried off the aquiline nose
and aristocratic emaciation of her mother with a certain piquancy and
a dash that was charming. The gentleman was young, thin, with the
family characteristics, but otherwise indistinctive.

With one accord they all faced directly toward the spot indicated by
the driver's whip. Nothing but the bare, bleak, rectangular outlines of
the cabin of the Man on the Beach met their eyes. All else was a
desolate expanse, unrelieved by any structure higher than the tussocks
of scant beach grass that clothed it. They were so utterly helpless that
the driver's derisive laughter gave way at last to good humour and
suggestion. "Look yer," he said finally, "I don't know ez it's your fault
you don't know this kentry ez well ez you do Yurup; so I'll drag this
yer team over to Robinson's on the river, give the horses a bite, and
then meander down this yer ridge, and wait for ye. Ye'll see me from
the Kernel's." And without waiting for a reply, he swung his horses'
heads toward the river, and rolled away.

The same querulous protest that had come from the windows arose
from the group, but vainly. Then followed accusations and recrimina-
tion. "It's *your* fault; you might have written, and had him meet us at
the settlement." "You wanted to take him by surprise!" "I didn't."
"You know if I'd written that we were coming, he'd have taken good
care to run away from us." "Yes, to some more inaccessible place."
"There can be none worse than this," &c., &c. But it was so clearly
evident that nothing was to be done but to go forward, that even in the
midst of their wrangling they straggled on in Indian file toward the
distant cabin, sinking ankle-deep in the yielding sand, punctuating
their verbal altercation with sighs, and only abating it at a scream
from the elder lady.

"Where's Maria?"

"Gone on ahead!" grunted the younger gentleman, in a bass voice,
so incongruously large for him that it seemed to have been a ventrilo-
quistic contribution by somebody else.

It was too true. Maria, after adding her pungency to the general conversation, had darted on ahead. But alas! that swift Camilla, after scouring the plain some two hundred feet with her demitrain, came to grief on an unbending tussock and sat down, panting but savage. As they plodded wearily toward her, she bit her red lips, smacked them on her cruel little white teeth like a festive and sprightly ghoul, and lisped:—

"You *do* look so like guys! For all the world like those English shopkeepers we met on the Righi, doing the three-guinea excursion in their Sunday clothes!"

Certainly the spectacle of these exotically plumed bipeds, whose fine feathers were already bedrabbled by sand and growing limp in the sea breeze, was somewhat dissonant with the rudeness of sea and sky and shore. A few gulls screamed at them; a loon, startled from the lagoon, arose shrieking and protesting, with painfully extended legs, in obvious burlesque of the younger gentleman. The elder lady felt the justice of her gentle daughter's criticism, and retaliated with simple directness—

"Your skirt is ruined, your hair is coming down, your hat is half off your head, and your shoes—in Heaven's name, Maria! what *have* you done with your shoes?"

Maria had exhibited a slim stockinged foot from under her skirt. It was scarcely three fingers broad, with an arch as patrician as her nose. "Somewhere between here and the carriage," she answered; "Dick can run back and find it, while he is looking for your brooch, mamma. Dick's so obliging."

The robust voice of Dick thundered, but the wasted figure of Dick feebly ploughed its way back, and returned with the missing buskin.

"I may as well carry them in my hand like the market girls at Saumur, for we have got to wade soon," said Miss Maria, sinking her own terrors in the delightful contemplation of the horror in her parent's face, as she pointed to a shining film of water slowly deepening in a narrow swale in the sands between them and the cabin.

"It's the tide," said the elder gentleman. "If we intend to go on we must hasten; permit me, my dear madam," and before she could reply he had lifted the astounded matron in his arms and made gallantly for the ford. The gentle Maria cast an ominous eye on her brother, who, with manifest reluctance, performed for her the same office. But that acute young lady kept her eyes upon the preceding figure of the elder gentleman, and seeing him suddenly and mysteriously disappear to his armpits, unhesitatingly threw herself from her brother's protecting arms—an action which instantly precipitated him into the water—and paddled hastily to the opposite bank, where she eventually assisted in pulling the elderly gentleman out of the hollow into which he had fallen, and in rescuing her mother, who floated helplessly on the surface, upheld by her skirts, like a gigantic and variegated water-lily. Dick followed with a single gaiter. In another minute they were safe on the opposite bank.

The elder lady gave way to tears; Maria laughed hysterically; Dick mingled a bass oath with the now audible surf; the elder gentleman, whose florid face the salt water had bleached, and whose dignity seemed to have been washed away, accounted for both by saying he thought it was a quicksand.

"It might have been," said a quiet voice behind them; "you should have followed the sand-dunes half a mile farther to the estuary."

They turned instantly at the voice. It was that of the Man on the Beach. They all rose to their feet and uttered together, save one, the single exclamation, "James!" The elder gentleman said, "Mr. North," and, with a slight resumption of his former dignity, buttoned his coat over his damp shirt front.

There was a silence, in which the Man on the Beach looked gravely down upon them. If they had intended to impress him by any suggestion of a gay, brilliant, and sensuous world beyond in their own persons, they had failed, and they knew it. Keenly alive as they had always been to external prepossession, they felt that they looked forlorn and ludicrous, and that the situation lay in his hands. The elderly lady again burst into tears of genuine distress, Maria coloured over her cheek-bones, and Dick stared at the ground in sullen disquiet.

"You had better get up," said the Man on the Beach, after a moment's thought, "and come up to the cabin. I cannot offer you a change of garments, but you can dry them by the fire."

They all rose together, and again said in chorus, "James!" but this time with an evident effort to recall some speech or action previously resolved upon and committed to memory. The elder lady got so far as to clasp her hands and add, "You have not forgotten us, James, O James!" the younger gentleman to attempt a brusque "Why, Jim, old boy," that ended in querulous incoherence; the young lady to cast a half-searching, half-coquettish look at him; and the old gentleman to begin, "Our desire, Mr. North"—but the effort was futile. Mr. James North, standing before them with folded arms, looked from the one to the other.

"I have not thought much of you for a twelvemonth," he said quietly, "but I have not forgotten you. Come!"

He led the way a few steps in advance, they following silently. In this brief interview they felt he had resumed the old dominance and independence, against which they had rebelled; more than that, in this half failure of their first concerted action they had changed their querulous bickerings to a sullen distrust of each other, and walked moodily apart as they followed James North into his house. A fire blazed brightly on the hearth; a few extra seats were quickly extemporised from boxes and chests, and the elder lady, with the skirt of her dress folded over her knees—looking not unlike an exceedingly overdressed jointed doll—dried her flounces and her tears together. Miss Maria took in the scant appointments of the house in one single glance, and then fixed her eyes upon James North, who, the least concerned of the party, stood before them, grave and patiently expectant.

"Well," began the elder lady in a high key, "after all this worry and trouble you have given us, James, haven't you anything to say? Do you know—have you the least idea what you are doing? what egregious folly you are committing? what everybody is saying? Eh? Heavens and earth! do you know who I am?"

"You are my father's brother's widow, Aunt Mary," returned James quietly. "If I am committing any folly it only concerns myself; if I cared for what people said I should not be here; if I loved society enough to appreciate its good report I should stay with it."

"But they say you have run away from society to pine alone for a worthless creature—a woman who has used you, as she has used and thrown away others—a"——

"A woman," chimed in Dick, who had thrown himself on James's bed while his patent leathers were drying—"a woman that all the fellers know never intended"——here, however, he met James North's eye, and muttering something about "whole thing being too idiotic to talk about," relapsed into silence.

"You know," continued Mrs. North, "that while we and all our set shut our eyes to your very obvious relations with that woman, and while I myself often spoke of it to others as a simple flirtation, and averted a scandal for your sake, and when the climax was reached, and she herself gave you an opportunity to sever your relations, and nobody need have been wiser—and she'd have had all the blame—and it's only what she's accustomed to—you—you! you, James North!—you must nonsensically go, and, by this extravagant piece of idiocy and sentimental tomfoolery, let everybody see how serious the whole affair was, and how deep it hurt you! and here in this awful place, alone—where you're half drowned to get to it, and are willing to be wholly drowned to get away! Oh, don't talk to me! I won't hear it—it's just too idiotic for anything!"

The subject of this outburst neither spoke nor moved a single muscle.

"Your aunt, Mr. North, speaks excitedly," said the elder gentleman;

"yet I think she does not over-estimate the unfortunate position in which your odd fancy places you. I know nothing of the reasons that have impelled you to this step; I only know that the popular opinion is that the cause is utterly inadequate. You are still young, with a future before you. I need not say how your present conduct may imperil that. If you expected to achieve any good—even to your own satisfaction— by this conduct"——

"Yes—if there was anything to be gained by it!" broke in Mrs. North.

"If you ever thought she'd come back!—but that kind of woman don't. They must have change. Why"——began Dick suddenly, and as suddenly lying down again.

"Is this all you have come to say?" asked James North, after a moment's patient silence, looking from one to the other.

"All!" screamed Mrs. North; "is it not enough?"

"Not to change my mind nor my residence at present," replied North coolly.

"Do you mean to continue this folly all your life?"

"And have a coroner's inquest, and advertisements and all the facts in the papers?"

"And have *her* read the melancholy details, and know that you were faithful and she was not?"

This last shot was from the gentle Maria, who bit her lips as it glanced from the immovable man.

"I believe there is nothing more to say," continued North quietly. "I am willing to believe your intentions are as worthy as your zeal. Let us say no more," he added with grave weariness; "the tide is rising, and your coachman is signalling you from the bank."

There was no mistaking the unshaken positiveness of the man, which was all the more noticeable from its gentle but utter indifference to the wishes of the party. He turned his back upon them as they gathered hurriedly around the elder gentleman, while the words, "He cannot be in his right mind," "It's your duty to do it," "It's sheer insanity," "Look at his eye!" all fell unconsciously upon his ear.

"One word more, Mr. North," said the elder gentleman a little portentously, to conceal an evident embarrassment. "It may be that your conduct might suggest to minds more practical than your own the existence of some aberration of the intellect—some temporary mania—that might force your best friends into a quasi-legal attitude of"——

"Declaring me insane," interrupted James North, with the slight impatience of a man more anxious to end a prolix interview than to combat an argument. "I think differently. As my aunt's lawyer, you know that within the last year I have deeded most of my property to her and her family. I cannot believe that so shrewd an adviser as Mr. Edmund Carter would ever permit proceedings that would invalidate that conveyance."

Maria burst into a laugh of such wicked gratification that James North, for the first time, raised his eyes with something of interest to her face. She coloured under them, but returned his glance with another like a bayonet flash. The party slowly moved toward the door, James North following.

"Then this is your final answer?" asked Mrs. North, stopping imperiously on the threshold.

"I beg your pardon?" queried North, half abstractedly.

"Your final answer?"

"Oh, certainly."

Mrs. North flounced away a dozen rods in rage. This was unfortunate for North. It gave them the final attack in detail. Dick began: "Come along! You know you can advertise for her with a personal down there, and the old woman wouldn't object as long as you were careful and put in an appearance now and then!"

As Dick limped away, Mr. Carter thought, in confidence, that the whole matter—even to suit Mr. North's sensitive nature—might be settled there. "*She* evidently expects you to return. My opinion is that she never left San Francisco. You can't tell anything about these women."

With this last sentence on his indifferent ear, James North seemed to be left free. Maria had rejoined her mother; but as they crossed the ford, and an intervening sand-hill hid the others from sight, that piquant young lady suddenly appeared on the hill and stood before him.

"And you're not coming back?" she said directly.

"No."

"Never?"

"I cannot say."

"Tell me! what is there about some women to make men love them so?"

"Love," replied North quietly.

"No, it cannot be—it is not *that!*"

North looked over the hill and round the hill, and looked bored.

"Oh, I'm going now. But one moment, Jim! I didn't want to come. They dragged me here. Good-bye." She raised a burning face and eyes to his. He leaned forward and imprinted the perfunctory, cousinly kiss of the period upon her cheek.

"Not that way," she said angrily, clutching his wrists with her long, thin fingers; "you shan't kiss me in that way, James North."

With the faintest, ghost-like passing of a twinkle in the corners of his sad eyes, he touched his lips to hers. With the contact, she caught him round the neck, pressed her burning lips and face to his forehead, his cheeks, the very curves of his chin and throat, and—with a laugh was gone.

II

Had the kinsfolk of James North any hope that their visit might revive some lingering desire he still combated to enter once more the world they represented, that hope would have soon died. Whatever effect this episode had upon the solitary—and he had become so self-indulgent of his sorrow, and so careless of all that came between him and it, as to meet opposition with profound indifference—the only appreciable result was a greater attraction for the solitude that protected him, and he grew even to love the bleak shore and barren sands that had proved so inhospitable to others. There was a new meaning to the roar of the surges, an honest, loyal sturdiness in the unchanging persistency of the uncouth and blustering trade-winds, and a mute fidelity in the shining sands, treacherous to all but him. With such bandogs to lie in wait for trespassers, should he not be grateful?

If no bitterness was awakened by the repeated avowal of the unfaithfulness of the woman he loved, it was because he had always made the observation and experience of others give way to the dominance of his own insight. No array of contradictory facts ever shook his belief or unbelief; like all egotists, he accepted them as truths controlled by a larger truth of which he alone was cognisant. His simplicity, which was but another form of his egotism, was so complete as to baffle ordinary malicious cunning, and so he was spared the experience and knowledge that come to a lower nature, and help to debase it.

Exercise and the stimulus of the few wants that sent him hunting or fishing kept up his physical health. Never a lover of rude freedom or outdoor life, his sedentary predilections and nice tastes kept him from lapsing into barbarian excess; never a sportsman, he followed the chase with no feverish exultation. Even dumb creatures found out his secret, and at times, stalking moodily over the upland, the brown deer and elk would cross his path without fear or molestation, or, idly lounging in his canoe within the river bar, flocks of wild fowl would settle within stroke of his listless oar. And so the second winter of his hermitage drew near its close, and with it came a storm that passed into local history, and is still remembered. It uprooted giant trees along the river, and with them the tiny rootlets of the life he was idly fostering.

The morning had been fitfully turbulent, the wind veering several points south and west, with suspicious lulls, unlike the steady onset of the regular south-west trades. High overhead the long manes of racing *cirro stratus* streamed with flying gulls and hurrying water-fowl; plover piped incessantly, and a flock of timorous sandpipers sought the low ridge of his cabin, while a wrecking crew of curlew hastily manned the uprooted tree that tossed wearily beyond the bar. By noon the flying clouds huddled together in masses, and then were suddenly exploded in one vast opaque sheet over the heavens. The sea became gray, and suddenly wrinkled and old. There was a dumb, half-articulate cry in the air—rather a confusion of many sounds, as of the booming of distant guns, the clangour of a bell, the trampling of many waves, the creaking of timbers and soughing of leaves, that sank and fell ere you could yet distinguish them. And then it came on to blow. For two hours it blew strongly. At the time the sun should have set the wind had increased; in fifteen minutes darkness shut down, even the white sands lost their outlines, and sea and shore and sky lay in the grip of a relentless and aggressive power.

Within his cabin, by the leaping light of his gusty fire, North sat alone. His first curiosity passed, the turmoil without no longer carried his thought beyond its one converging centre. *She* had come to him on the wings of the storm, even as she had been borne to him on the summer fog-cloud. Now and then the wind shook the cabin, but he heeded it not. He had no fears for its safety; it presented its low gable to the full fury of the wind that year by year had piled, and was even now piling, protecting buttresses of sand against it. With each succeeding gust it seemed to nestle more closely to its foundations, in the whirl of flying sand that rattled against its roof and windows. It was nearly midnight when a sudden thought brought him to his feet. What if *she* were exposed to the fury of such a night as this? What could he do to help her? Perhaps even now, as he sat there idle, she—— Hark! was not that a gun—No? Yes, surely!

He hurriedly unbolted the door, but the strength of the wind and the impact of drifted sand resisted his efforts. With a new and feverish strength possessing him he forced it open wide enough to permit his egress, when the wind caught him as a feather, rolled him over and over, and then, grappling him again, held him down hard and fast against the drift. Unharmed, but unable to move, he lay there, hearing the multitudinous roar of the storm, but unable to distinguish one familiar sound in the savage medley. At last he managed to crawl flat on his face to the cabin, and, refastening the door, threw himself upon his bed.

He was awakened from a fitful dream of his cousin Maria. She with a supernatural strength seemed to be holding the door against some unseen, unknown power that moaned and strove without, and threw itself in despairing force against the cabin. He could see the lithe undulations of her form as she alternately yielded to its power, and again drew the door against it, coiling herself around the loghewn doorpost with a hideous, snake-like suggestion. And then a struggle and a heavy blow, which shook the very foundations of the structure, awoke him. He leaped to his feet, and into an inch of water! By the flickering firelight he could see it oozing and dripping from the crevices of the logs and broadening into a pool by the chimney. A scrap of paper torn from an envelope was floating idly on its current. Was it the overflow of the backed-up waters of the river? He was not left long in doubt. Another blow upon the gable of the house, and a torrent of spray leaped down the chimney, scattered the embers far and wide, and left him in utter darkness. Some of the spray clung to his lips. It was salt. The great ocean had beaten down the river bar and was upon him!

Was there aught to fly to? No! The cabin stood upon the highest point of the sandspit, and the low swale on one side crossed by his late visitors was a seething mass of breakers, while the estuary behind him was now the ocean itself. There was nothing to do but to wait.

The very helplessness of his situation was, to a man of his peculiar temperament, an element of patient strength. The instinct of self-preservation was still strong in him, but he had no fear of death, nor, indeed, any presentiment of it; yet if it came, it was an easy solution of the problem that had been troubling him, and it wiped off the slate! He thought of the sarcastic prediction of his cousin, and death in the form that threatened him was the obliteration of his home and even the ground upon which it stood. There would be nothing to record, no stain could come upon the living. The instinct that kept him true to *her* would tell her how he died; if it did not, it was equally well. And with this simple fatalism his only belief, this strange man groped his way to his bed, lay down, and in a few moments was asleep. The storm still roared without. Once again the surges leaped against the cabin, but it was evident that the wind was abating with the tide.

When he awoke it was high noon, and the sun was shining brightly. For some time he lay in a delicious languor, doubting if he was alive or dead, but feeling through every nerve and fibre an exquisite sense of peace—a rest he had not known since his boyhood—a relief he scarcely knew from what. He felt that he was smiling, and yet his pillow was wet with the tears that glittered still on his lashes. The sand blocking up his doorway, he leaped lightly from his window. A few clouds were still sailing slowly in the heavens, the trailing plumes of a great benediction that lay on sea and shore. He scarcely recognised the familiar landscape; a new bar had been formed in the river, and a narrow causeway of sand that crossed the lagoon and marches to the river bank and the upland trail seemed to bring him nearer to humanity again. He was conscious of a fresh, childlike delight in all this, and when, a moment later, he saw the old uprooted tree, now apparently for ever moored and imbedded in the sand beside his cabin, he ran to it with a sense of joy.

Its trailing roots were festooned with clinging seaweed and the long, snaky, undulating stems of the sea-turnip; and fixed between two crossing roots was a bamboo orange crate, almost intact. As he walked toward it he heard a strange cry, unlike anything the barren sands had borne before. Thinking it might be some strange sea-bird caught in the meshes of the seaweed, he ran to the crate and looked within. It was half filled with sea-moss and feathery algae. The cry was repeated. He brushed aside the weeds with his hands. It was not a wounded sea-bird, but a living human child!

As he lifted it from its damp enwrappings he saw that it was an infant eight or nine months old. How and when it had been brought there, or what force had guided that elfish cradle to his very door, he could not determine; but it must have been left early, for it was quite warm, and its clothing almost dried by the blazing morning sun. To wrap his coat about it, to run to his cabin with it, to start out again with the appalling conviction that nothing could be done for it there, occupied some moments. His nearest neighbour was Trinidad Joe, a "logger," three miles up the river. He remembered to have heard vaguely that he was a man of family. To half strangle the child with a few drops from his whisky flask, to extricate his canoe from the marsh, and strike out into the river with his waif, was at least to do something. In half an hour he had reached the straggling cabin and sheds of Trinidad Joe, and from the few scanty flowers that mingled with the brushwood fence, and a surplus of linen fluttering on the line, he knew that his surmise as to Trinidad Joe's domestic establishment was correct.

The door at which he knocked opened upon a neat, plainly-furnished room, and the figure of a buxom woman of twenty-five. With an awkwardness new to him, North stammered out the circumstances of his finding the infant, and the object of his visit. Before he had finished, the woman, by some feminine trick, had taken the child from his hands ere he knew it; and when he paused, out of breath, burst into a fit of laughter. North tried to laugh too, but failed.

When the woman had wiped the tears from a pair of very frank blue eyes, and hidden two rows of very strong white teeth again, she said—

"Look yar! You're that looney sort o' chap that lives alone over on the spit yonder, ain't ye?"

North hastened to admit all that the statement might imply.

"And so ye've had a baby left ye to keep you company? Lordy!" Here she looked as if dangerously near a relapse, and then added, as if in explanation of her conduct—

"When I saw ye paddlin' down here—you thet ez shy as elk in summer—I sez, 'He's sick.' But a baby—O Lordy!"

For a moment North almost hated her. A woman who, in this pathetic, perhaps almost tragic, picture saw only a ludicrous image, and that image himself, was of another race than he had ever mingled with. Profoundly indifferent as he had always been to the criticism of his equals in station, the mischievous laughter of this illiterate woman jarred upon him worse than his cousin's sarcasm. It was with a little dignity that he pointed out the fact that at present the child needed nourishment. "It's very young," he added. "I'm afraid it wants its natural nourishment."

"Whar is it to get it?" asked the woman.

James North hesitated, and looked around. There should be a baby somewhere! there *must* be a baby somewhere! "I thought that you," he stammered, conscious of an awkward colouring,—"I—that is—I"

——He stopped short, for she was already cramming her apron into her mouth, too late, however, to stop the laugh that overflowed it. When she found her breath again, she said—

"Look yar! I don't wonder they said you was looney! I'm Trinidad Joe's onmarried darter, and the only woman in this house. Any fool could have told you that. Now, ef you can rig us up a baby out o' them facts, I'd like to see it done."

Inwardly furious but outwardly polite, James North begged her pardon, deplored his ignorance, and, with a courtly bow, made a movement to take the child. But the woman as quickly drew it away.

"Not much," she said hastily. "What! trust that poor critter to you? No, sir! Thar's more ways of feeding a baby, young man, than you knows on, with all your 'nat'ral nourishment.' But it looks kinder logy and stupid."

North freezingly admitted that he had given the infant whisky as a stimulant.

"You did? Come, now, that ain't so looney after all. Well, I'll take the baby, and when dad comes home we'll see what can be done."

North hesitated. His dislike of the woman was intense, and yet he knew no one else, and the baby needed instant care. Besides, he began

to see the ludicrousness of his making a first call on his neighbours
with a foundling to dispose of. She saw his hesitation, and said—

"Ye don't know me, in course. Well, I'm Bessy Robinson, Trinidad
Joe Robinson's daughter. I reckon dad will give me a character if you
want references, or any of the boys on the river."

"I'm only thinking of the trouble I'm giving you, Miss Robinson, I
assure you. Any expense you may incur"——

"Young man," said Bessy Robinson, turning sharply on her heel,
and facing him with her black brows a little contracted, "if it comes to
expenses, I reckon I'll pay you for that baby, or not take it at all. But I
don't know you well enough to quarrel with you on sight. So leave the
child to me, and if you choose, paddle down here tomorrow, after sun
up—the ride will do you good—and see it, and dad thrown in. Good-
bye!" and with one powerful but well-shaped arm thrown around the
child, and the other crooked at the dimpled elbow a little aggressively,
she swept by James North and entered a bedroom, closing the door
behind her.

When Mr. James North reached his cabin it was dark. As he rebuilt
his fire, and tried to rearrange the scattered and disordered furniture,
and remove the débris of last night's storm, he was conscious for the
first time of feeling lonely. He did not miss the child. Beyond the
instincts of humanity and duty he had really no interest in its welfare
or future. He was rather glad to get rid of it, he would have preferred
to some one else, and yet *she* looked as if she were competent. And
then came the reflection that since the morning he had not once
thought of the woman he loved. The like had never occurred in his
twelvemonth's solitude. So he set to work, thinking of her and of his
sorrows, until the word "looney," in connection with his suffering,
flashed across his memory. "Looney!" It was not a nice word. It suggested something less than insanity; something that might happen to a
common, unintellectual sort of person. He remembered the loon, an
ungainly feathered neighbour, that was popularly supposed to have
lent its name to the adjective. Could it be possible that people looked
upon him as one too hopelessly and uninterestingly afflicted for sympathy or companionship, too unimportant and common for even ridicule; or was this but the coarse interpretation of that vulgar girl?

Nevertheless, the next morning "after sun up" James North was at
Trinidad Joe's cabin. That worthy proprietor himself—a long, lank
man, with even more than the ordinary rural Western characteristics
of ill-health, ill-feeding, and melancholy—met him on the bank,
clothed in a manner and costume that was a singular combination of
the frontiersman and the sailor. When North had again related the
story of his finding the child, Trinidad Joe pondered.

"It mout hev been stowed away in one of them crates for safe-keeping," he said, musingly, "and washed off the deck o' one o' them Tahiti brigs goin' down fer oranges. Leastways, it never got thar from these parts."

"But it's a miracle its life was saved at all. It must have been some hours in the water."

"Them brigs lays their course well inshore, and it was just mebbee a toss up if the vessel clawed off the reef at all! And ez to the child keepin' up, why, dog my skin! that's just the contrariness o' things," continued Joe, in sententious cynicism. "Ef an able seaman had fallen from the yard-arm that night he'd been sunk in sight o' the ship, and thet baby ez can't swim a stroke sails ashore, sound asleep, with the waves for a baby-jumper."

North, who was half relieved, yet half-awkwardly disappointed at not seeing Bessy, ventured to ask how the child was doing.

"She'll do all right now," said a frank voice above, and, looking up, North discerned the round arms, blue eyes, and white teeth of the daughter at the window. "She's all hunky, and has an appetite—ef she hezn't got her 'nat'ral nourishment.' Come, dad! heave ahead, and tell the stranger what you and me allow we'll do, and don't stand there swappin' lies with him."

"Weel," said Trinidad Joe dejectedly, "Bess allows she can rar that baby and do justice to it. And I don't say—though I'm her father—that she can't. But when Bess wants anything she wants it all, clean down; no half-ways nor leavin's for her."

"That's me! go on, dad—you're chippin' in the same notch every time," said Miss Robinson with cheerful directness.

"Well, we agree to put the job up this way. We'll take the child and you'll give us a paper or writin' makin' over all your right and title. How's that?"

Without knowing exactly why he did, Mr. North objected decidedly.

"Do you think we won't take good care of it?" asked Miss Bessy sharply.

"That is not the question," said North a little hotly. "In the first place, the child is not mine to give. It has fallen into my hands as a trust—the first hands that received it from its parents. I do not think it right to allow any other hands to come between theirs and mine."

Miss Bessy left the window. In another moment she appeared from the house, and, walking directly toward North, held out a somewhat substantial hand. "Good!" she said, as she gave his fingers an honest squeeze. "You ain't so looney after all. Dad, he's right! He shan't gin it up, but we'll go halves in it, he and me. He'll be father and I'll be mother 'till death do us part, or the reg'lar family turns up. Well—what do you say?"

More pleased than he dared confess to himself with the praise of this common girl, Mr. James North assented. Then would he see the baby? He would, and Trinidad Joe, having already seen the baby, and talked of the baby, and felt the baby, and indeed had the baby offered to him in every way during the past night, concluded to give some of his valuable time to logging, and left them together.

Mr. North was obliged to admit that the baby was thriving. He, moreover, listened with polite interest to the statement that the baby's eyes were hazel, like his own; that it had five teeth; that she was, for a girl of that probable age, a robust child; and yet Mr. North lingered. Finally, with his hand on the door-lock, he turned to Bessy and said—

"May I ask you an odd question, Miss Robinson?"

"Go on."

"Why did you think I was—'looney'?"

The frank Miss Robinson bent her head over the baby.

"Why?"

"Yes, why?"

"Because you *were* looney."

"Oh!"

"But"——

"Yes"——

"You'll get over it."

And under the shallow pretext of getting the baby's food, she retired to the kitchen, where Mr. North had the supreme satisfaction of seeing her, as he passed the window, sitting on a chair with her apron over her head, shaking with laughter.

For the next two or three days he did not visit the Robinsons, but gave himself up to past memories. On the third day he had—it must be confessed not without some effort—brought himself into that condition of patient sorrow which had been his habit. The episode of the storm and the finding of the baby began to fade, as had faded the visit of his relatives. It had been a dull, wet day, and he was sitting by his fire, when there came a tap at his door. "Flora," by which juvenescent name his aged Indian handmaid was known, usually announced her presence with an imitation of a curlew's cry: it could not be her. He fancied he heard the trailing of a woman's dress against the boards, and started to his feet, deathly pale, with a name upon his lips. But the door was impatiently thrown open, and showed Bessy Robinson! And the baby!

With a feeling of relief he could not understand, he offered her a seat. She turned her frank eyes on him curiously.

"You look skeert!"

"I was startled. You know I see nobody here!"

"Thet's so. But look yar, do you ever use a doctor?"

Not clearly understanding her, he in turn asked, "Why?"

"Cause you must rise up and get one now—thet's why. This yer baby of ours is sick. We don't use a doctor at our house, we don't beleeve in 'em, hain't no call for 'em—but this yer baby's parents mebbee did. So rise up out o' that cheer, and get one."

James North looked at Miss Robinson and rose, albeit a little in doubt, and hesitating.

Miss Robinson saw it. "I shouldn't hev troubled ye, nor ridden three mile to do it, if ther hed been any one else to send. But dad's over at Eureka, buying logs, and I'm alone. Hello—wher' yer goin'?"

North had seized his hat and opened the door. "For a doctor," he replied amazedly.

"Did ye kalkilate to walk six miles and back?"

"Certainly—I have no horse."

"But *I* have, and you'll find her tethered outside. She ain't much to look at, but when you strike the trail she'll go."

"But *you*—how will *you* return?"

"Well," said Miss Robinson, drawing her chair to the fire, taking off her hat and shawl, and warming her knees by the blaze, "I didn't reckon to return. You'll find me here when you come back with the doctor. Go! Skedaddle quick."

She did not have to repeat the command. In another instant James North was in Miss Bessy's seat—a man's dragoon saddle—and pounding away through the sand. Two facts were in his mind: one was that he, the "looney," was about to open communication with the wisdom and contemporary criticism of the settlement, by going for a doctor to administer to a sick and anonymous infant in his possession; the other was that his solitary house was in the hands of a self-invited, large-limbed, illiterate, but rather comely young woman. These facts he could not gallop away from, but to his credit be it recorded that he fulfilled his mission zealously, if not coherently, to the doctor, who during the rapid ride gathered the idea that North had rescued a young married woman from drowning, who had since given birth to a child.

The few words that set the doctor right when he arrived at the cabin might in any other community have required further explanation, but Dr. Duchesne, an old army surgeon, was prepared for everything and indifferent to all. "The infant," he said, "was threatened with inflammation of the lungs; at present there was no danger, but the greatest care and caution must be exercised. Particularly exposure should be avoided." "That settles the whole matter then," said Bessy potentially. Both gentlemen looked their surprise. "It means," she condescended to further explain, "that *you* must ride that filly home, wait for the old man to come to-morrow, and then ride back here with some of my duds, for thar's no 'day-days' nor picnicing for that baby ontil she's better. And I reckon to stay with her ontil she is."

"She certainly is unable to bear any exposure at present," said the doctor, with an amused side glance at North's perplexed face. "Miss Robinson is right." I'll ride with you over the sands as far as the trail."

"I'm afraid," said North, feeling it incumbent upon him to say something, "that you'll hardly find it as comfortable here as"——

"I reckon not," she said simply, "but I didn't expect much."

North turned a little wearily away. "Good night," she said suddenly, extending her hand, with a gentler smile of lip and eye than he had ever before noticed, "good night—take good care of dad."

The doctor and North rode together some moments in silence. North had another fact presented to him, *i.e.,* that he was going a-visiting, and that he had virtually abandoned his former life; also that it would be profanation to think of his sacred woe in the house of a stranger.

"I daresay," said the doctor suddenly, "you are not familiar with the type of woman Miss Bessy presents so perfectly. Your life has been spent among the conventional class."

North froze instantly at what seemed to be a probing of his secret. Disregarding the last suggestion, he made answer simply and truthfully that he had never met any Western girl like Bessy.

"That's your bad luck," said the doctor. "You think her coarse and illiterate?"

Mr. North had been so much struck with her kindness that really he had not thought of it.

"That's not so," said the doctor curtly; "although even if you told her so she would not think any the less of you—nor of herself. If she spoke rustic Greek instead of bad English, and wore a *cestus* in place of an ill-fitting corset, you'd swear she was a goddess. There's your trail. Good night."

III

James North did not sleep well that night. He had taken Miss Bessy's bedroom, at her suggestion, there being but two, and "dad never using sheets and not bein' keerful in his habits." It was neat, but that was all. The scant ornamentation was atrocious; two or three highly-coloured prints, a shell work-box, a ghastly winter bouquet of skeleton leaves and mosses, a starfish, and two china vases hideous enough to have been worshipped as Buddhist idols, exhibited the gentle recreation of the fair occupant, and the possible future education of the child. In the morning he was met by Joe, who received the message of his daughter with his usual dejection, and suggested that North stay with him until the child was better. That event was still remote; North found, on his return to his cabin, that the child had been worse; but he did not know, until Miss Bessy dropped a casual remark, that she had not closed her own eyes that night. It was a week before he regained his own quarters, but an active week—indeed, on the whole, a rather pleasant week. For there was a delicate flattery in being domineered by a wholesome and handsome woman, and Mr. James North had by this time made up his mind that she was both. Once or twice he found himself contemplating her splendid figure with a recollection of the doctor's compliment, and later, emulating her own frankness, told her of it.

"And what did *you* say?" she asked.

"Oh, I laughed and said—nothing."

And so did she.

A month after this interchange of frankness, she asked him if he could spend the next evening at her house. "You see," she said, "there's to be a dance down at the hall at Eureka, and I haven't kicked a fut since last spring. Hank Fisher's comin' up to take me over, and I'm goin' to let the shanty slide for the night."

"But what's to become of the baby?" asked North, a little testily.

"Well," said Miss Robinson, facing him somewhat aggressively, "I reckon it won't hurt ye to take care of it for a night. Dad can't—and if he could, he don't know how. Liked to have pizened me after mar died. No, young man, I don't propose to ask Hank Fisher to tote thet child over to Eureka and back, and spile his fun."

"Then I suppose I must make way for Mr. Hank—Hank—Fisher?" said North, with the least tinge of sarcasm in his speech.

"Of course. You've got nothing else to do, you know."

North would have given worlds to have pleaded a previous engagement on business of importance, but he knew that Bessy spoke truly. He had nothing to do. "And Fisher has, I suppose?" he asked.

"Of course—to look after *me!*"

A more unpleasant evening James North had not spent since the first day of his solitude. He almost began to hate the unconscious cause of his absurd position, as he paced up and down the floor with it. "Was there ever such egregious folly?" he began, but remembering he was quoting Maria North's favourite *résumé* of his own conduct, he stopped. The child cried, missing, no doubt, the full rounded curves and plump arm of its nurse. North danced it violently, with an inward accompaniment that was not musical, and thought of the other dancers. "Doubtless," he mused, "she has told this beau of hers that she has left the baby with the 'looney' Man on the Beach. Perhaps I may be offered a permanent engagement as a harmless simpleton accustomed to the care of children. Mothers may cry for me. The doctor is at Eureka. Of course, he will be there to see his untranslated goddess, and condole with her over the imbecility of the Man on the Beach." Once he carelessly asked Joe who the company were.

"Well," said Joe mournfully, "thar's Widder Higsby and darter; the four Stubbs gals; in course Polly Doble will be on hand with that feller that's clerking over at the Head for Jones, and Jones's wife. Then thar's French Pete, and Whisky Ben, and that chap that shot Archer —I disremember his name—and the barber—what's that little mulatto's name—that 'ar Kanaka? I swow!" continued Joe drearily, "I'll be forgettin' my own next—and"——

"That will do," interrupted North, only half concealing his disgust as he rose and carried the baby to the other room, beyond the reach of names that might shock its ladylike ears. The next morning he met the from-dance-returning Bessy abstractedly, and soon took his leave, full of a disloyal plan, conceived in the sleeplessness of her own bedchamber. He was satisfied that he owed a duty to its unknown parents to remove the child from the degrading influences of the barber Kanaka, and Hank Fisher especially, and he resolved to write to his relatives, stating the case, asking a home for the waif and assistance to find its parents. He addressed this letter to his cousin Maria, partly in consideration of the dramatic farewell of that young lady, and its possible influence in turning her susceptible heart towards his *protégé*. He then quietly settled back to his old solitary habits, and for a week left the Robinsons unvisited. The result was a morning call by Trinidad Joe on the hermit. "It's a whim of my gal's, Mr. North," he said dejectedly, "and ez I told you before and warned ye, when that gal hez an idee, fower yoke or oxen and seving men can't drag it outer her. She's got a idee o' larnin'—never hevin' hed much schoolin', and we ony takin' the papers, permiskiss like—and she says *you* can teach her—not hevin' anythin' else to do. Do ye folly me?"

"Yes," said North, "certainly."

"Well, she allows ez mebbe you're proud, and didn't like her takin' care of the baby for nowt; and she reckons that ef you'll gin her some book larnin', and get her to sling some fancy talk in fash'n'ble style— why, she'll call it squar."

"You can tell her," said North, very honestly, "that I shall be only too glad to help her in any way, without ever hoping to cancel my debt of obligation to her."

"Then it's a go?" said the mystified Joe, with a desperate attempt to convey the foregoing statement to his own intellect in three Saxon words.

"It's a go," replied North cheerfully.

And he felt relieved. For he was not quite satisfied with his own want of frankness to her. But here was a way to pay off the debt he owed her, and yet retain his own dignity. And now he could tell her what he had done, and he trusted to the ambitious instinct that prompted her to seek a better education to explain his reasons for it.

He saw her that evening and confessed all to her frankly. She kept her head averted, but when she turned her blue eyes to him they were wet with honest tears. North had a man's horror of a ready feminine lachrymal gland; but it was not like Bessy to cry, and it meant something; and then she did it in a large, goddess-like way, without sniffling, or choking, or getting her nose red, but rather with a gentle deliquescence, a harmonious melting, so that he was fain to comfort her with nearer contact, gentleness in his own sad eyes, and a pressure of her large hand.

"It's all right, I s'pose," she said sadly; "but I didn't reckon on yer havin' any relations, but thought you was alone, like me."

James North, thinking of Hank Fisher and the "mullater," could not help intimating that his relations were very wealthy and fashionable people, and had visited him last summer. A recollection of the manner in which they had so visited him, and his own reception of them, prevented his saying more. But Miss Bessy could not forego a certain feminine curiosity, and asked—

"Did they come with Sam Baker's team?"

"Yes."

"Last July?"

"Yes."

"And Sam drove the horses here for a bite?"

"I believe so."

"And them's your relations?"

"They are."

Miss Robinson reached over the cradle and enfolded the sleeping infant in her powerful arms. Then she lifted her eyes, wrathful through her still glittering tears, and said, slowly, "They don't—have—this—child—then!"

"But why?"

"Oh, why? *I* saw them! That's why, and enough! You can't play any such gay and festive skeletons on this poor baby for flesh and blood parents. No, sir!"

"I think you judge them hastily, Miss Bessy," said North, secretly amused; "my aunt may not, at first, favourably impress strangers, yet she has many friends. But surely you do not object to my cousin Maria, the young lady?"

"What! that dried cuttle-fish, with nothing livin' about her but her eyes? James North, ye may be a fool like the old woman—perhaps it's in the family—but ye ain't a devil like that gal! That ends it."

And it did. North despatched a second letter to Maria saying that he had already made other arrangements for the baby. Pleased with her easy victory, Miss Bessy became more than usually gracious, and the next day bowed her shapely neck meekly to the yoke of her teacher, and became a docile pupil. James North could not have helped noticing her ready intelligence, even had he been less prejudiced in her favour than he was fast becoming now. If he had found it pleasant before to be admonished by her, there was still more delicious flattery in her perfect trust in his omniscient skill as a pilot over this unknown sea. There was a certain enjoyment in guiding her hand over the writingbook, that I fear he could not have obtained from an intellect less graciously sustained by its physical nature. The weeks flew quickly by on gossamer wings, and when she placed a bunch of larkspurs and poppies in his hand one morning, he remembered for the first time that it was spring.

I cannot say that there was more to record of Miss Bessy's education than this. Once North, half jestingly, remarked that he had never yet seen her admirer, Mr. Hank Fisher. Miss Bessy (colouring but cool)—"You never will!" North (white but hot)—"Why?" Miss Bessy (faintly)—"I'd rather not." (North resolutely)—"I insist." Bessy (yielding)—"As my teacher?" North (hesitatingly, at the limitation of the epithet)—"Y-e-e-s!" Bessy—"And you'll promise never to speak of it again?" North—"Never." Bessy (slowly)—"Well, he said I did an awful thing to go over to your cabin and stay." North (in the genuine simplicity of a refined nature)—"But how?" Miss Bessy (half piqued, but absolutely admiring that nature)—"Quit! and keep your promise!"

They were so happy in these new relations that it occurred to Miss Bessy one day to take James North to task for obliging her to ask to be his pupil. "You knew how ignorant I was," she added; and Mr. North retorted by relating to her the doctor's criticism on her independence. "To tell you the truth," he added, "I was afraid you would not take it as kindly as he thought."

"That is, you thought me as vain as yourself. It seems to me you and the doctor had a great deal to say to each other."

"On the contrary," laughed North, "that was all we said."

"And you didn't make fun of me?"

Perhaps it was not necessary for North to take her hand to emphasise his denial, but he did.

Miss Bessy, being still reminiscent, perhaps did not notice it. "If it hadn't been for that ar—I mean that thar—no, that baby—I wouldn't have known you!" she said dreamily.

"No," returned North mischievously, "but you still would have known Hank Fisher."

No woman is perfect. Miss Bessy looked at him with a sudden—her first and last—flash of coquetry. Then stooped and kissed—the baby.

James North was a simple gentleman, but not altogether a fool. He returned the kiss, but not vicariously.

There was a footstep on the porch. These two turned the hues of a dying dolphin, and then laughed. It was Joe. He held a newspaper in his hand. "I reckon ye woz right, Mr. North, about my takin' these yar papers reg'lar. For I allow here's suthin' that may clar up the mystery o' that baby's parents." With the hesitation of a slowly grappling intellect, Joe sat down on the table and read from the San Francisco "Herald" as follows:—" 'It is now ascertained beyond doubt that the wreck reported by the "Aeolus" was the American brig "Pompare," bound hence to Tahiti. The worst surmises are found correct. The body of the woman has been since identified as that of the beauti-ful daughter of—of—of—Terp—Terp—Terpish'—Well! I swow that name just tackles me."

"Gin it to me, dad," said Bessy pertly. "You never had any education, any way. Hear your accomplished daughter." With a mock bow to the new schoolmaster, and a capital burlesque of a confident schoolgirl, she strode to the middle of the room, the paper held and folded bookwise in her hands. "Ahem! Where did you leave off? Oh, 'the beautiful daughter of Terpsichore—whose name was prom-i-nently connected with a mysterious social scandal of last year—the gifted but unfortunate Grace Chatterton'—No—don't stop me—there's some more! 'The body of her child, a lovely infant of six months, has not been recovered, and it is supposed was washed overboard.' There! maybe that's the child, Mr. North. Why, dad! Look, O my God! He's falling. Catch him, dad! Quick!"

But her strong arm had anticipated her father's. She caught him, lifted him to the bed, on which he lay henceforth for many days unconscious. Then fever supervened, and delirium, and Dr. Duchesne telegraphed for his friends; but at the end of a week and the opening of a summer day the storm passed, as the other storm had passed, and he awoke, enfeebled, but at peace. Bessy was at his side—he was glad to see—alone. "Bessy, dear," he said hesitatingly, "when I am stronger I have something to tell you."

"I know it all, Jem," she said with a trembling lip; "I heard it all—no, not from *them,* but from your own lips in your delirium. I'm glad it came from *you*—even then."

"Do you forgive me, Bessy?"

She pressed her lips to his forehead and said hastily, and then falteringly, as if afraid of her impulse—

"Yes. Yes."

"And you will still be mother to the child?"

"Her child?"

"No, dear, not hers, but *mine!"*

She started, cried a little, and then putting her arms around him, said, "Yes."

And as there was but one way of fulfilling that sacred promise, they were married in the autumn.

Two Saints of the Foot-Hills

IT NEVER WAS clearly ascertained how long they had been there. The first settler of Rough-and-Ready—one Low, playfully known to his familiars as "The Poor Indian"—declared that the Saints were afore his time, and occupied a cabin in the brush when he "blazed" his way to the North Fork. It is certain that the two were present when the water was first turned on the Union Ditch, and then and there received the designation of Daddy Downey and Mammy Downey, which they kept to the last. As they tottered toward the refreshment tent, they were welcomed with the greatest enthusiasm by the boys; or, to borrow the more refined language of the "Union Recorder,"— "Their gray hairs and bent figures, recalling as they did the happy paternal eastern homes of the spectators, and the blessings that fell from venerable lips when they left those homes to journey in quest of the Golden Fleece on Occidental Slopes, caused many to burst into tears." The nearer facts, that many of these spectators were orphans, that a few were unable to establish any legal parentage whatever, that others had enjoyed a State's guardianship and discipline, and that a majority had left their parental roofs without any embarrassing preliminary formula, were mere passing clouds that did not dim the

518

golden imagery of the writer. From that day the Saints were adopted as historical lay figures, and entered at once into possession of uninterrupted gratuities and endowment.

It was not strange that, in a country largely made up of ambitious and reckless youth, these two—types of conservative and settled forms —should be thus celebrated. Apart from any sentiment or veneration, they were admirable foils to the community's youthful progress and energy. They were put forward at every social gathering, occupied prominent seats on the platform at every public meeting, walked first in every procession, were conspicuous at the frequent funeral and rarer wedding, and were godfather and godmother to the first baby born in Rough-and-Ready. At the first poll opened in that precinct, Daddy Downey cast the first vote, and, as was his custom on all momentous occasions, became volubly reminiscent. "The first vote I ever cast," said Daddy, "was for Andrew Jackson—the father o' some on you peart young chaps wasn't born then; he! he!—that was 'way long in '33, wasn't it? I disremember now, but if Mammy was here, she bein' a school-gal at the time, she could say. But my memory's failin' me. I'm an old man, boys; yet I likes to see the young ones go ahead. I recklect that thar vote from a suckumstance. Squire Adams was present, and seein' it was my first vote, he put a goold piece into my hand, and, sez he, sez Squire Adams, 'Let that always be a reminder of the exercise of a glorious freeman's privilege!' He did; he! he! Lord, boys! I feel so proud of ye, that I wish I had a hundred votes to cast for ye all."

It is hardly necessary to say that the memorial tribute of Squire Adams was increased tenfold by the judges, inspectors, and clerks, and that the old man tottered back to Mammy considerably heavier than he came. As both of the rival candidates were equally sure of his vote, and each had called upon him and offered a conveyance, it is but fair to presume they were equally beneficent. But Daddy insisted upon walking to the polls,—a distance of two miles,—as a moral-example, and a text for the Californian paragraphers, who hastened to record that such was the influence of the foothill climate, that "a citizen of Rough-and-Ready, aged eighty-four, rose at six o'clock, and, after milking two cows, walked a distance of twelve miles to the polls, and returned in time to chop a cord of wood before dinner." Slightly exaggerated as this statement may have been, the fact that Daddy was always found by the visitor to be engaged at his woodpile, which seemed neither to increase nor diminish under his axe, a fact, doubtless, owing to the activity of Mammy, who was always at the same time making pies, seemed to give some credence to the story. Indeed, the wood-pile of Daddy Downey was a standing reproof to the indolent and sluggish miner.

"Ole Daddy must use up a pow'ful sight of wood; every time I've passed by his shanty he's been makin' the chips fly. But what gets me is, that the pile don't seem to come down," said Whisky Dick to his neighbour.

"Well, you derned fool!" growled his neighbour, "spose some chap happens to pass by thar, and sees the ole man doin' at man's work at eighty, and slouches like you and me lying round drunk, and that chap, feelin' kinder humped, goes up some dark night and heaves a load of cut pine over his fence, who's got anything to say about it? say?"

Certainly not the speaker, who had done the act suggested, nor the penitent and remorseful hearer, who repeated it next day.

The pies and cakes made by the old woman were, I think, remarkable rather for their inducing the same loyal and generous spirit than for their intrinsic excellence, and, it may be said, appealed more strongly to the nobler aspirations of humanity than its vulgar appetite. Howbeit, everybody ate Mammy Downey's pies, and thought of his childhood. "Take 'em, dear boys," the old lady would say; "it does me good to see you eat 'em; reminds me kinder of my poor Sammy, that ef he'd lived, would hev been ez strong and big ez you be, but was taken down with lung fever at Sweetwater. I kin see him yet; that's forty year ago, dear! comin' out o' the lot to the bakehouse, and smilin' such a beautiful smile, like yours, dear boy, as I handed him a mince or a lemming turnover. Dear, dear, how I do run on! and those days is past! but I seems to live in you again!" The wife of the hotel-keeper, actuated by a low jealousy, had suggested that she "seemed to live *off* them;" but as that person tried to demonstrate the truth of her statement by reference to the cost of the raw material used by the old lady, it was considered by the camp as too practical and economical for consideration. "Besides," added Cy Perkins, "ef old Mammy wants to turn an honest penny in her old age, let her do it. How would you like your old mother to make pies on grub wages? eh?" A suggestion that so affected his hearer (who had no mother) that he bought three on the spot. The quality of these pies had never been discussed but once. It is related that a young lawyer from San Francisco, dining at the Palmetto restaurant, pushed away one of Mammy Downey's pies with every expression of disgust and dissatisfaction. At this juncture, Whisky Dick, considerably affected by his favourite stimulant, approached the stranger's table, and, drawing up a chair, sat uninvited before him.

"Mebbee, young man," he began gravely, "ye don't like Mammy Downey's pies?"

The stranger replied curtly, and in some astonishment, that he did not, as a rule, "eat pie."

"Young man," continued Dick with drunken gravity, "mebbee you're accustomed to Charlotte rusks and blue mange; mebbee ye can't eat unless your grub is got up by one o' them French cooks? Yet *we*— us boys yar in this camp—calls that pie—a good—a com-pe-tent pie!"

The stranger again disclaimed anything but a general dislike of that form of pastry.

"Young man," continued Dick, utterly unheeding the explanation, —"young man, mebbee you onst had an ole—a very ole mother, who, tottering down the vale o' years, made pies. Mebbee, and it's like your blank epicurean soul, ye turned up your nose on the ole woman, and went back on the pies, and on her! She that dandled ye when ye woz a baby,—a little baby! Mebbee ye went back on her, and shook her, and played off on her, and gave her away—dead away! And now, mebbee young man—I wouldn't hurt ye for the world, but mebbee, afore ye leave this yar table, YE'LL EAT THAT PIE! "

The stranger rose to his feet, but the muzzle of a dragoon revolver in the unsteady hands of Whisky Dick caused him to sit down again. He ate the pie, and lost his case likewise before a Rough-and-Ready jury.

Indeed, far from exhibiting the cynical doubts and distrusts of age, Daddy Downey received always with childlike delight the progress of modern improvement and energy. "In my day, long back in the twenties, it took us nigh a week—a week, boys—to get up a barn, and all the young ones—I was one then—for miles round at the raisin'; and yer's you boys—rascals ye are, too—runs up this yer shanty for Mammy and me 'twixt sun-up and dark! Eh, eh, you're teachin' the old folks new tricks, are ye? Ah, get along, you!" and in playful simulation of anger he would shake his white hair and his hickory staff at the "rascals." The only indication of the conservative tendencies of age was visible in his continual protest against the extravagance of the boys. "Why," he would say, "a family, a hull family,—leavin' alone me and the old woman,—might be supported on what you young rascals throw away in a single spree. Ah, you young dogs, didn't I hear about your scattering half-dollars on the stage the other night when that Eyetalian Papist was singin'. And that money goes out of Ameriky—ivry cent!"

There was little doubt that the old couple were saving, if not avaricious. But when it was known, through the indiscreet volubility of Mammy Downey, that Daddy Downey sent the bulk of their savings, gratuities, and gifts, to a dissipated and prodigal son in the East,—

whose photograph the old man always carried with him, it rather elevated him in their regard. "When ye write to that gay and festive son o' yourn, Daddy," said Joe Robinson, "send him this yer specimen. Give him my compliments, and tell him, ef he kin spend money faster than I can, I call him! Tell him, ef he wants a first-class jamboree, to kem out here, and me and the boys will show him what a square drunk is!" In vain would the old man continue to protest against the spirit of the gift; the miner generally returned with his pockets that much the lighter, and it is not improbable a little less intoxicated than he otherwise might have been. It may be premised that Daddy Downey was strictly temperate. The only way he managed to avoid hurting the feelings of the camp was by accepting the frequent donations of whisky to be used for the purposes of liniment.

"Next to snake-oil, my son," he would say, "and dilberry-juice,— and ye don't seem to pro-duce 'em hereabouts,—whisky is good for rubbin' onto old bones to make 'em limber. But pure cold water, 'sparklin' and bright in its liquid light,' and, so to speak, reflectin' of God's own linyments on its surfiss, is the best, onless, like poor ol' Mammy and me, ye gets the dumb-agur from over-use."

The fame of the Downey couple was not confined to the foot-hills. The Rev. Henry Gushington, D.D., of Boston, making a bronchial tour of California, wrote to the "Christian Pathfinder" an affecting account of his visit to them, placed Daddy Downey's age at 102, and attributed the recent conversions in Rough-and-Ready to their influence. That gifted literary Hessian, Bill Smith, travelling in the interests of various capitalists, and the trustworthy correspondent of four "only independent American journals," quoted him as an evidence of the longevity superinduced by the climate, offered him as an example of the security of helpless life and property in the mountains, used him as an advertisement of the Union Ditch, and it is said, in some vague way, cited him as proving the collateral facts of a timber and ore-producing region existing in the foot-hills worthy the attention of Eastern capitalists.

Praised thus by the lips of distinguished report, fostered by the care and sustained by the pecuniary offerings of their fellow-citizens, the Saints led for two years a peaceful life of gentle absorption. To relieve them from the embarrassing appearance of eleemosynary receipts,—an embarrassment felt more by the givers than the recipients,—the postmastership of Rough-and-Ready was procured for Daddy, and the duty of receiving and delivering the United States mails performed by him, with the advice and assistance of the boys. If a few letters went astray at this time, it was easily attributed to this undisciplined aid, and the boys themselves were always ready to make up the value of a missing money-letter and "keep the old man's accounts square." To these functions presently were added the treasurerships of the Masons' and Odd Fellows' charitable funds,—the old man being far advanced in their respective degrees,—and even the position of almoner of their bounties was superadded. Here, unfortunately, Daddy's habits of economy and avaricious propensity came near making him unpopular, and very often needy brothers were forced to object to the quantity and quality of the help extended. They always met with more generous relief from the private hands of the brothers themselves, and the remark, "that the ol' man was trying to set an example,—that he meant well,"—and that they would yet be thankful for his zealous care and economy. A few, I think, suffered in noble silence, rather than bring the old man's infirmity to the public notice.

And so with this honour of Daddy and Mammy, the days of the miners were long and profitable in the land of the foot-hills. The mines yielded their abundance, the winters were singularly open, and yet there was no drouth nor lack of water, and peace and plenty smiled on the Sierrean foot-hills, from their highest sunny upland to the trailing *falda* of wild oats and poppies. If a certain superstition got abroad among the other camps, connecting the fortunes of Rough-and-Ready with Daddy and Mammy, it was a gentle, harmless fancy, and was not, I think, altogether rejected by the old people. A certain large, patriarchal, bountiful manner, of late visible in Daddy, and the increase of much white hair and beard, kept up the poetic illusion, while Mammy, day by day, grew more and more like somebody's fairy godmother. An attempt was made by a rival camp to emulate these paying virtues of reverence, and an aged mariner was procured from the Sailor's Snug Harbour in San Francisco on trial. But the unfortunate seaman was more or less diseased, was not always presentable, through a weakness for ardent spirits, and finally, to use the powerful idiom of one of his disappointed foster-children, "up and died in a week, without slinging ary blessin'."

But vicissitude reaches young and old alike. Youthful Rough-and-Ready and the Saints had climbed to their meridian together, and it seemed fit that they should together decline. The first shadow fell with the immigration to Rough-and-Ready of a second aged pair. The landlady of the Independence Hotel had not abated her malevolence towards the Saints, and had imported at considerable expense her grand-aunt and grand-uncle, who had been enjoying for some years a sequestered retirement in the poorhouse at East Machias. They were indeed very old. By what miracle, even as anatomical specimens, they had been preserved during their long journey was a mystery to the camp. In some respects they had superior memories and reminiscences. The

old man—Abner Trix—had shouldered a musket in the war of 1812;
his wife, Abigail, had seen Lady Washington. She could sing hymns;
he knew every text between "the leds" of a Bible. There is little doubt
but that in many respects, to the superficial and giddy crowd of youthful spectators, they were the more interesting spectacle.

Whether it was jealousy, distrust, or timidity that overcame the
Saints, was never known, but they studiously declined to meet the
strangers. When directly approached upon the subject, Daddy Downey pleaded illness, kept himself in close seclusion, and the Sunday
that the Trixes attended church in the schoolhouse on the hill, the
triumph of the Trix party was mitigated by the fact that the Downeys
were not in their accustomed pew. "You bet that Daddy and Mammy
is lying low jest to ketch them old mummies yet," explained a Downeyite. For by this time schism and division had crept into the camp;
the younger and later members of the settlement adhering to the
Trixes, while the older pioneers stood not only loyal to their own
favourites, but even, in the true spirit of partisanship, began to seek for
a principle underlying their personal feelings. "I tell ye what, boys,"
observed Sweetwater Joe, "if this yer camp is goin' to be run by greenhorns, and old pioneers, like Daddy and the rest of us, must take back
seats, it's time we emigrated and shoved out, and tuk Daddy with us.
Why, they're talkin' of rotation in offiss, and of putting that skeleton
that Ma'am Decker sets up at the table to take her boarders' appetites
away, into the post-office in place o' Daddy." And, indeed, there were
some fears of such a conclusion; the newer men of Rough-and-Ready
were in the majority, and wielded a more than equal influence of
wealth and outside enterprise. "Frisco," as a Downeyite bitterly remarked, "already owned half the town." The old friends that rallied
around Daddy and Mammy were, like most loyal friends in adversity,
in bad case themselves, and were beginning to look and act, it was
observed, not unlike their old favourites.

At this juncture Mammy died.

The sudden blow for a few days seemed to reunite dissevered
Rough-and-Ready. Both factions hastened to the bereaved Daddy
with condolements, and offers of aid and assistance. But the old man
received them sternly. A change had come over the weak and yielding
octogenarian. Those who expected to find him maudlin, helpless, dis-
consolate, shrank from the cold, hard eyes and truculent voice that
bade them "begone," and "leave him with his dead." Even his own
friends failed to make him respond to their sympathy, and were fain to
content themselves with his cold intimation that both the wishes of his
dead wife and his own instincts were against any display, or the reception of any favour from the camp that might tend to keep up the

divisions they had innocently created. The refusal of Daddy to accept any service offered was so unlike him as to have but one dreadful meaning! The sudden shock had turned his brain! Yet so impressed were they with his resolution that they permitted him to perform the last sad offices himself, and only a select few of his nearer neighbours assisted him in carrying the plain deal coffin from his lonely cabin in the woods to the still lonelier cemetery on the hilltop. When the shallow grave was filled, he dismissed even these curtly, shut himself up in his cabin, and for days remained unseen. It was evident that he was no longer in his right mind.

His harmless aberration was accepted and treated with a degree of intelligent delicacy hardly to be believed of so rough a community. During his wife's sudden and severe illness, the safe containing the funds intrusted to his care by the various benevolent associations was broken into and robbed, and although the act was clearly attributable to his carelessness and preoccupation, all allusion to the fact was withheld from him in his severe affliction. When he appeared again before the camp, and the circumstances were considerately explained to him, with the remark that "the boys had made it all right," the vacant, hopeless, unintelligent eye that he turned upon the speaker showed too plainly that he had forgotten all about it. "Don't trouble the old man," said Whisky Dick, with a burst of honest poetry. "Don't ye see his memory's dead, and lying there in the coffin with Mammy?" Perhaps the speaker was nearer right than he imagined.

Failing in religious consolation, they took various means of diverting his mind with worldly amusements, and one was a visit to a travelling variety troupe, then performing in the town. The result of the visit was briefly told by Whisky Dick. "Well, sir, we went in, and I sot the old man down in a front seat, and kinder propped him up with some other of the fellers round him, and there he sot as silent and awful ez the grave. And then that fancy dancer, Miss Grace Somerset, comes in, and dern my skin, ef the old man didn't get to trembling and fidgeting all over, as she cut them pidgin wings. I tell ye what, boys, men is men, way down to their boots,—whether they're crazy or not! Well, he took on so, that I'm blamed if at last that gal *herself* didn't notice him! and she ups, suddenly, and blows him a kiss—so! with her fingers!"

Whether this narration were exaggerated or not, it is certain that the old man Downey every succeeding night of the performance was a spectator. That he may have aspired to more than that was suggested a day or two later in the following incident: A number of the boys were sitting around the stove in the Magnolia saloon, listening to the onset of a winter storm against the windows, when Whisky Dick, tremulous, excited, and bristling with rain-drops and information, broke in upon them.

"Well, boys, I've got just the biggest thing out. Ef I hadn't seed it myself, I wouldn't hev believed it!"

"It ain't thet ghost ag'in?" growled Robinson, from the depths of his arm-chair; "thet ghost's about played."

"Wot ghost?" asked a new-comer.

"Why, ole Mammy's ghost, that every feller about yer sees when he's half full and out late o' nights."

"Where?"

"Where? Why, where should a ghost be? Meanderin' round her grave on the hill, yander, in course."

"It's suthin bigger nor thet, pard," said Dick confidently; "no ghost kin rake down the pot ag'in the keerds I've got here. This ain't no bluff!"

"Well, go on!" said a dozen excited voices.

Dick paused a moment diffidently, with the hesitation of an artistic *raconteur.*

"Well," he said, with affected deliberation, "let's see! It's nigh onto an hour ago ez I was down thar at the variety show. When the curtain was down betwixt the ax, I looks round fer Daddy. No Daddy thar! I goes out and asks some o' the boys. 'Daddy *was* there a minnit ago,' they say; 'must hev gone home.' Bein' kinder responsible for the old man, I hangs around, and goes out in the hall and sees a passage leadin' behind the scenes. Now the queer thing about this, boys, ez that suthin in my bones tells me the old man is *thar.* I pushes in, and, sure as a gun, I hear his voice. Kinder pathetic, kinder pleadin', kinder"——

"Love-makin!" broke in the impatient Robinson.

"You've hit it, pard,—you've rung the bell every time! But she says, 'I wants thet money down, or I'll'—and here I couldn't get to hear the rest. And then he kinder coaxes; and she says, sorter sassy, but listenin' all the time,—woman like, ye know, Eve and the sarpint!—and she says, 'I'll see to-morrow.' And he says, 'You won't blow on me?' and I gets excited and peeps in, and may I be teetotally durned ef I didn't see"——

"What?" yelled the crowd.

"Why, *Daddy on his knees to that there fancy dancer,* Grace Somerset! Now, if Mammy's ghost is meanderin' round, why, et's about time she left the cemetery and put in an appearance in Jackson's Hall. Thet's all!"

"Look yar, boys," said Robinson, rising, "I don't know ez it's the square thing to spile Daddy's fun. I don't object to it, provided she ain't takin' in the old man, and givin' him dead away. But ez we're his guardeens, I propose that we go down thar and see the lady, and find out ef her intentions is honourable. If she means marry, and the old man persists, why, I reckon we kin give the young couple a send-off thet won't disgrace this yer camp! Hey, boys?"

It is unnecessary to say that the proposition was received with acclamation, and that the crowd at once departed on their discreet mission. But the result was never known, for the next morning brought a shock to Rough-and-Ready before which all other interest paled to nothingness.

The grave of Mammy Downey was found violated and despoiled; the coffin opened, and half filled with the papers and accounts of the robbed benevolent associations; but the body of Mammy was gone! Nor, on examination, did it appear that the sacred and ancient form of that female had ever reposed in its recesses!

Daddy Downey was not to be found, nor is it necessary to say that the ingenuous Grace Somerset was also missing.

For three days the reason of Rough-and-Ready trembled in the balance. No work was done in the ditches, in the flume, nor in the mills. Groups of men stood by the grave of the lamented relict of Daddy Downey, as open-mouthed and vacant as that sepulchre. Never since the great earthquake of '52 had Rough-and-Ready been so stirred to its deepest foundations.

On the third day the sheriff of Calaveras—a quiet, gentle, thoughtful man—arrived in town, and passed from one to the other of excited groups, dropping here and there detached but concise and practical information.

"Yes, gentlemen, you are right, Mrs. Downey is not dead, because there wasn't any Mrs. Downey! Her part was played by George F. Fenwick, of Sydney,—a 'ticket-of-leave-man,' who was, they say, a good actor. Downey? Oh yes! Downey was Jem Flanigan, who, in '52, used to run the variety troupe in Australia, where Miss Somerset made her *début*. Stand back a little, boys. Steady! The money? Oh yes, they've got away with that, sure! How are ye, Joe? Why, you're looking well and hearty! I rather expected ye court week. How's things your way?"

"Then they were only play-actors, Joe Hall?" broke in a dozen voices.

"I reckon!" returned the sheriff coolly.

"And for a matter o' five blank years," said Whisky Dick sadly, "they played this camp!"

"Who was my Quiet Friend?"

"STRANGER!"

The voice was not loud, but clear and penetrating. I looked vainly up and down the narrow, darkening trail. No one in the fringe of alder ahead; no one on the gullied slope behind.

"Oh! stranger!"

This time a little impatiently. The Californian classical vocative, "Oh," always meant business.

I looked up, and perceived for the first time on the ledge, thirty feet above me, another trail parallel with my own, and looking down upon me through the buckeye bushes a small man on a black horse.

Five things to be here noted by the circumspect mountaineer. *First*, the locality,—lonely and inaccessible, and away from the regular faring of teamsters and miners. *Secondly*, the stranger's superior knowledge of the road, from the fact that the other trail was unknown to the ordinary traveller. *Thirdly*, that he was well armed and equipped. *Fourthly*, that he was better mounted. *Fifthly*, that any distrust or timidity arising from the contemplation of these facts had better be kept to one's self.

All this passed rapidly through my mind as I returned his salutation.

"Got any tobacco?" he asked.

I had, and signified the fact, holding up the pouch inquiringly.

"All right, I'll come down. Ride on, and I'll jine ye on the slide."

"The slide!" Here was a new geographical discovery as odd as the second trail. I had ridden over the trail a dozen times, and seen no communication between the ledge and trail. Nevertheless, I went on a hundred yards or so, when there was a sharp crackling in the underbrush, a shower of stones on the trail, and my friend plunged through the bushes to my side, down a grade that I should scarcely have dared to lead my horse. There was no doubt he was an accomplished rider,—another fact to be noted.

As he ranged beside me, I found I was not mistaken as to his size; he was quite under the medium height, and but for a pair of cold, grey eyes, was rather commonplace in feature.

"You've got a good horse there," I suggested.

He was filling his pipe from my pouch, but looked up a little surprised, and said, "Of course." He then puffed away with the nervous eagerness of a man long deprived of that sedative. Finally, between the puffs, he asked me whence I came.

I replied, "From Lagrange."

He looked at me a few moments curiously, but on my adding that I had only halted there for a few hours, he said: "I thought I knew every man between Lagrange and Indian Spring, but somehow I sorter disremember your face and your name."

Not particularly caring that he should remember either, I replied half laughingly, that, as I lived the other side of Indian Spring, it was quite natural. He took the rebuff, if such it was, so quietly that as an act of mere perfunctory politeness I asked him where *he* came from.

"Lagrange."

"And are you going to——"

"Well! that depends pretty much on how things pan out, and whether I can make the riffle." He let his hand rest quite unconsciously on the leathern holster of his dragoon revolver, yet with a strong suggestion to me of his ability "to make the riffle" if he wanted to, and added: "But just now I was reck'nin' on taking a little *pasear* with you."

There was nothing offensive in his speech save its familiarity, and the reflection, perhaps, that whether I objected or not, he was quite able to do as he said. I only replied that if our *pasear* was prolonged beyond Heavy-tree Hill, I should have to borrow his beast. To my surprise he replied quietly, "That's so," adding that the horse was at my disposal when he wasn't using it, and *half* of it when he was. "Dick has carried double many a time before this," he continued, "and kin do it again; when your mustang gives out I'll give you a lift and room to spare."

I could not help smiling at the idea of appearing before the boys at Red Gulch *en croupe* with the stranger; but neither could I help being oddly affected by the suggestion that his horse had done double duty before. "On what occasion, and why?" was a question I kept to myself. We were ascending the long, rocky flank of the divide; the narrowness of the trail obliged us to proceed slowly, and in file, so that there was little chance for conversation, had he been disposed to satisfy my curiosity.

We toiled on in silence, the buckeye giving way to chimisal, the westering sun, reflected again from the blank walls beside us, blinding our eyes with its glare. The pines in the cañon below were olive gulfs of heat, over which a hawk here and there drifted lazily, or, rising to our level, cast a weird and gigantic shadow of slowly moving wings on the mountain side. The superiority of the stranger's horse led him often far in advance, and made me hope that he might forget me entirely, or push on, growing weary of waiting. But regularly he would halt by a boulder, or reappear from some chimisal, where he had patiently halted. I was beginning to hate him mildly, when at one of those reappearances he drew up to my side, and asked me how I liked Dickens!

Had he asked my opinion of Huxley or Darwin, I could not have been more astonished. Thinking it were possible that he referred to some local celebrity of Lagrange, I said, hesitatingly:—

"You mean"——

"Charles Dickens. Of course you've read him? Which of his books do you like best?"

I replied with considerable embarrassment that I liked them all,—as I certainly did.

He grasped my hand for a moment with a fervour quite unlike his usual phlegm, and said, "That's me, old man. Dickens ain't no slouch. You can count on him pretty much all the time."

With this rough preface, he launched into a criticism of the novelist, which for intelligent sympathy and hearty appreciation I had rarely heard equalled. Not only did he dwell upon the exuberance of his humour, but upon the power of his pathos and the all-pervading element of his poetry. I looked at the man in astonishment. I had considered myself a rather diligent student of the great master of fiction, but the stranger's felicity of quotation and illustration staggered me. It is true, that his thought was not always clothed in the best language, and

often appeared in the slouching, slangy undress of the place and period, yet it never was rustic nor homespun, and sometimes struck me
with its precision and fitness. Considerably softened toward him, I
tried him with other literature. But vainly. Beyond a few of the lyrical
and emotional poets, he knew nothing. Under the influence and enthusiasm of his own speech, he himself had softened considerably; offered
to change horses with me, readjusted my saddle with professional skill,
transferred my pack to his own horse, insisted upon my sharing the
contents of his whisky flask, and noticing that I was unarmed, pressed
upon me a silver-mounted Derringer, which he assured me he could
"warrant." These various offices of good will and the diversion of his
talk beguiled me from noticing the fact that the trail was beginning to
become obscure and unrecognisable. We were evidently pursuing a
route unknown before to me. I pointed out the fact to my companion,
a little impatiently. He instantly resumed his old manner and dialect.

"Well, I reckon one trail's as good as another, and what hev ye got
to say about it?"

I pointed out, with some dignity, that I preferred the old trail.

"Mebbe you did. But you're jiss now takin' a *pasear* with *me*. This
yer trail will bring you right into Indian Spring, and *onnoticed,* and no
questions asked. Don't you mind now, I'll see you through."

It was necessary here to make some stand against my strange companion. I said firmly, yet as politely as I could, that I had proposed
stopping over night with a friend.

"Whar?"

I hesitated. The friend was an eccentric Eastern man, well known in
the locality for his fastidiousness and his habits as a recluse. A misan-
thrope, of ample family and ample means, he had chosen a secluded
but picturesque valley in the Sierras where he could rail against the
world without opposition. "Lone Valley," or "Boston Ranch," as it
was familiarly called, was the one spot that the average miner both
respected and feared. Mr. Sylvester, its proprietor, had never affiliated
with "the boys," nor had he ever lost their respect by any active
opposition to their ideas. If seclusion had been his object, he certainly
was gratified. Nevertheless, in the darkening shadows of the night, and
on a lonely and unknown trail, I hesitated a little at repeating his name
to a stranger of whom I knew so little. But my mysterious companion
took the matter out of my hands.

"Look yar," he said, suddenly, "thar ain't but one place 'twixt yer
and Indian Spring whar ye can stop, and that is Sylvester's."

I assented, a little sullenly.

"Well," said the stranger, quietly, and with a slight suggestion of
conferring a favour on me, "ef yer pointed for Sylvester's—why—*I*

don't mind stopping thar with ye. It's a little off the road—I'll lose some time—but taking it by and large, I don't much mind."

I stated, as rapidly and as strongly as I could, that my acquaintance with Mr. Sylvester did not justify the introduction of a stranger to his hospitality; that he was unlike most of the people here,—in short, that he was a queer man, &c., &c.

To my surprise my companion answered quietly: "Oh, that's all right. I've heerd of him. Ef you don't feel like checking me through, or if you'd rather put 'C.O.D.' on my back, why it's all the same to me. I'll play it alone. Only you just count me in. Say 'Sylvester' all the time. That's me!"

What could I oppose to this man's quiet assurance? I felt myself growing red with anger and nervous with embarrassment. What would the correct Sylvester say to me? What would the girls,—I was a young man then, and had won an *entrée* to their domestic circle by my reserve, known by a less complimentary adjective among "the boys," —what would they say to my new acquaintance? Yet I certainly could not object to his assuming all risks on his own personal recognisances, nor could I resist a certain feeling of shame at my embarrassment.

We were beginning to descend. In the distance below us already twinkled the lights in the solitary rancho of Lone Valley. I turned to my companion. "But you have forgotten that I don't even know your name. What am I to call you?"

"That's so," he said, musingly. "Now, let's see. 'Kearney' would be a good name. It's short and easy like. Thar's a street in 'Frisco the same title; Kearney it is."

"But"——I began impatiently.

"Now you leave all that to me," he interrupted, with a superb self-confidence that I could not but admire. "The name ain't no account. It's the man that's responsible. Ef I was to lay for a man that I reckoned was named Jones, and after I fetched him I found out on the inquest that his real name was Smith, that wouldn't make no matter, as long as I got the man."

The illustration, forcible as it was, did not strike me as offering a prepossessing introduction, but we were already at the rancho. The barking of dogs brought Sylvester to the door of the pretty little cottage which his taste had adorned.

I briefly introduced Mr. Kearney. "Kearney will do—Kearney's good enough for me," commented the *soi-disant* Kearney half-aloud, to my own horror and Sylvester's evident mystification, and then he blandly excused himself for a moment that he might personally supervise the care of his own beast. When he was out of ear-shot I drew the puzzled Sylvester aside.

"I have picked up—I mean I have been picked up on the road by a gentle maniac, whose name is not Kearney. He is well armed and quotes Dickens. With care, acquiescence in his views on all subjects, and general submission to his commands, he may be placated. Doubtless the spectacle of your helpless family, the contemplation of your daughter's beauty and innocence, may touch his fine sense of humour and pathos. Meanwhile, Heaven help you, and forgive me."

I ran upstairs to the little den that my hospitable host had kept always reserved for me in my wanderings. I lingered some time over my ablutions, hearing the languid, gentlemanly drawl of Sylvester below, mingled with the equally cool, easy slang of my mysterious acquaintance. When I came down to the sitting-room I was surprised, however, to find the self-styled Kearney quietly seated on the sofa, the gentle May Sylvester, the "Lily of Lone Valley," sitting with maidenly awe and unaffected interest on one side of him, while on the other that arrant flirt, her cousin Kate, was practising the pitiless archery of her eyes, with an excitement that seemed almost real.

"Who is your deliciously cool friend?" she managed to whisper to me at supper, as I sat utterly dazed and bewildered between the enrapt May Sylvester, who seemed to hang upon his words, and this giddy girl of the period, who was emptying the battery of her charms in active rivalry upon him. "Of course we know his name isn't Kearney. But how romantic! And isn't he perfectly lovely? And who is he?"

I replied with severe irony that I was not aware what foreign potentate was then travelling *incognito* in the Sierras of California, but that when his royal highness was pleased to inform me, I should be glad to introduce him properly. "Until then," I added, "I fear the acquaintance must be Morganatic."

"You're only jealous of him," she said pertly. "Look at May—she is completely fascinated. And her father, too." And actually, the languid, world-sick, cynical Sylvester was regarding him with a boyish interest and enthusiasm almost incompatible with his nature. Yet I submit honestly to the clear-headed reason of my own sex, that I could see nothing more in the man than I have already delivered to the reader.

In the middle of an exciting story of adventure, of which he, to the already prejudiced mind of his fair auditors, was evidently the hero, he stopped suddenly.

"It's only some pack train passing the bridge on the lower trail," explained Sylvester; "go on."

"It may be my horse is a trifle oneasy in the stable," said the alleged Kearney; "he ain't used to boards and covering." Heaven only knows what wild and delicious revelation lay in the statement of this fact, but the girls looked at each other with cheeks pink with excitement as Kearney arose, and with quiet absence of ceremony quitted the table.

"Ain't he just lovely?" said Kate, gasping for breath, "and so witty."

"Witty!" said the gentle May, with just the slightest trace of defiance in her sweet voice; "witty, my dear? why, don't you see that his heart is just breaking with pathos? Witty, indeed; why, when he was speaking of that poor Mexican woman that was hung, I saw the tears gather in his eyes. Witty, indeed!"

"Tears," laughed the cynical Sylvester, "tears, idle tears. Why, you silly children, the man is a man of the world, a philosopher, quiet, observant, unassuming."

"Unassuming!" Was Sylvester intoxicated, or had the mysterious stranger mixed the "insane verb" with the family pottage? He returned before I could answer this self-asked inquiry, and resumed coolly his broken narrative. Finding myself forgotten in the man I had so long hesitated to introduce to my friends, I retired to rest early, only to hear, through the thin partitions, two hours later, enthusiastic praises of the new guest from the voluble lips of the girls, as they chatted in the next room before retiring.

At midnight I was startled by the sound of horses' hoofs and the jingling of spurs below. A conversation between my host and some mysterious personage in the darkness was carried on in such a low tone that I could not learn its import. As the cavalcade rode away I raised the window.

"What's the matter?"

"Nothing," said Sylvester, coolly, "only another one of those playful homicidal freaks peculiar to the country. A man was shot by Cherokee Jack over at Lagrange this morning, and that was the sheriff of Calaveras and his posse hunting him. I told him I'd seen nobody but you and your friend. By the way, I hope the cursed noise hasn't disturbed him. The poor fellow looked as if he wanted rest."

I thought so too. Nevertheless, I went softly to his room. It was empty. My impression was that he had distanced the sheriff of Calaveras about two hours.

The Fool of Five Forks

HE LIVED ALONE. I do not think this peculiarity arose from any wish
to withdraw his foolishness from the rest of the camp, nor was it
probable that the combined wisdom of Five Forks ever drove him into
exile. My impression is, that he lived alone from choice—a choice he
made long before the camp indulged in any criticism of his mental
capacity. He was much given to moody reticence, and although to
outward appearances a strong man, was always complaining of ill
health. Indeed, one theory of his isolation was that it afforded him
better opportunities for taking medicine, of which he habitually consumed large quantities.

His folly first dawned upon Five Forks through the Post Office
windows. He was for a long time the only man who wrote home by
every mail, his letters being always directed to the same person—a
woman. Now it so happened that the bulk of the Five Forks' correspondence was usually the other way; there were many letters received
—the majority being in the female hand—but very few answered.

The men received them indifferently, or as a matter of course; a few
opened and read them on the spot with a barely repressed smile of self-
conceit, or quite as frequently glanced over them with undisguised
impatience. Some of the letters began with "My dear husband," and
some were never called for. But the fact that the only regular

correspondent of Five Forks never received any reply became at last quite notorious. Consequently, when an envelope was received bearing the stamp of the "Dead Letter Office," addressed to the Fool under the more conventional title of "Cyrus Hawkins," there was quite a fever of excitement. I do not know how the secret leaked out, but it was eventually known to the camp that the envelope contained Hawkins' own letters returned. This was the first evidence of his weakness; any man who repeatedly wrote to a woman who did not reply must be a fool. I think Hawkins suspected that his folly was known to the camp, but he took refuge in symptoms of chills and fever, which he at once developed, and effected a diversion with three bottles of Indian chologogue and two boxes of pills. At all events, at the end of a week he resumed a pen, stiffened by tonics, with all his old epistolatory pertinacity. This time the letters had a new address.

In those days a popular belief obtained in the mines that Luck particularly favoured the foolish and unscientific. Consequently, when Hawkins struck a "pocket" in the hill-side near his solitary cabin, there was but little surprise. "He will sink it all in the next hole," was the prevailing belief, predicated upon the usual manner in which the possessor of "nigger luck" disposed of his fortune. To everybody's astonishment, Hawkins, after taking out about eight thousand dollars and exhausting the pocket, did not prospect for another. The camp then waited patiently to see what he would do with his money. I think, however, that it was with the greatest difficulty their indignation was kept from taking the form of a personal assault, when it became known that he had purchased a draft for eight thousand dollars in favour of "that woman." More than this, it was finally whispered that the draft was returned to him as his letters had been, and that he was ashamed to reclaim the money at the express office. "It wouldn't be a bad specilation to go East, get some smart gal for a hundred dollars to dress herself up and represent that hag, and jest freeze onto that eight thousand," suggested a far-seeing financier. I may state here that we always alluded to Hawkins' fair unknown as "The Hag," without having, I am confident, the least justification for that epithet.

That the Fool should gamble seemed eminently fit and proper. That he should occasionally win a large stake, according to that popular theory which I have recorded in the preceding paragraph, appeared also a not improbable or inconsistent fact. That he should, however, break the faro bank which Mr. John Hamlin had set up in Five Forks, and carry off a sum variously estimated at from ten to twenty thousand dollars, and not return the next day and lose the money at the same table, really appeared incredible. Yet such was the fact. A day or two passed without any known investment of Mr. Hawkins' recently-acquired capital. "Ef he allows to send it to that Hag," said one prominent citizen, "suthin' ought to be done! It's jest ruinin' the reputation of this yer camp—this sloshin' around o' capital on non-residents ez don't claim it!" "It's settin' an example o' extravagance," said another, "ez is little better nor a swindle. Thars mor'n five men in this camp thet, hearin' thet Hawkins had sent home eight thousand dollars, must jest rise up and send home their hard earnings, too! And then to think thet that eight thousand was only a bluff, after all, and thet it's lyin' there on call in Adams & Co.'s bank! Well! I say it's one o' them things a vigilance committee oughter look into!"

When there seemed no possibility of this repetition of Hawkins' folly, the anxiety to know what he had really done with his money became intense. At last a self-appointed committee of four citizens dropped artfully, but to outward appearances carelessly, upon him in his seclusion. When some polite formalities had been exchanged, and some easy vituperation of a backward season offered by each of the parties, Tom Wingate approached the subject—

"Sorter dropped heavy on Jack Hamlin the other night, didn't ye? He allows you didn't give him no show for revenge. I said you wasn't no such d—d fool—didn't I, Dick?" continued the artful Wingate, appealing to a confederate.

"Yes," said Dick promptly. "You said twenty thousand dollars wasn't goin' to be thrown around recklessly. You said Cyrus had suthin' better to do with his capital," superadded Dick, with gratuitous mendacity. "I disremember now what partickler investment you said he was goin' to make with it," he continued, appealing with easy indifference to his friend.

Of course Wingate did not reply, but looked at the Fool, who with a troubled face, was rubbing his legs softly. After a pause he turned deprecatingly toward his visitors.

"Ye didn't enny of ye ever hev a sort of tremblin' in your legs—a kind o' shakiness from the knee down? Suthin'," he continued, slightly brightening with his topic, "suthin' that begins like chills, and yet ain't chills. A kind o' sensation of goneness here, and a kind o' feelin' as if you might die suddent! When Wright's Pills don't somehow reach the spot, and Quinine don't fetch you?"

"No!" said Wingate, with a curt directness, and the air of authoritatively responding for his friends. "No, never had. You was speakin' of this yer investment."

"And your bowels all the time irregular!" continued Hawkins, blushing under Wingate's eye, and yet clinging despairingly to his theme like a shipwrecked mariner to his plank.

Wingate did not reply, but glanced significantly at the rest. Hawkins evidently saw this recognition of his mental deficiency, and said apologetically, "You was saying suthin' about my investment?"

"Yes," said Wingate, so rapidly as to almost take Hawkins' breath away—"the investment you made in"——

"Rafferty's Ditch," said the Fool, timidly.

For a moment the visitors could only stare blankly at each other. "Rafferty's Ditch," the one notorious failure of Five Forks! Rafferty's Ditch, the impracticable scheme of an utterly unpractical man; Rafferty's Ditch, a ridiculous plan for taking water that could not be got to a place where it wasn't wanted! Rafferty's Ditch, that had buried the fortunes of Rafferty and twenty wretched stockholders in its muddy depths!

"And thet's it—is it?" said Wingate, after a gloomy pause. "Thet's it! I see it all now, boys. That's how ragged Pat Rafferty went down to San Francisco yesterday in store clothes, and his wife and four children went off in a kerridge to Sacramento. Thet's why them ten workmen of his, ez hedn't a cent to bless themselves with, was playin' billiards last night and eatin' isters. Thet's whar that money kum frum —one hundred dollars—to pay for thet long advertisement of the new issue of Ditch stock in the *Times* yesterday. Thet's why them six strangers were booked at the Magnolia Hotel yesterday. Don't you see —it's thet money and thet Fool!"

The Fool sat silent. The visitors rose without a word.

"You never took any of them Indian Vegetable Pills?" asked Hawkins timidly, of Wingate.

"No," roared Wingate, as he opened the door.

"They tell me that took with the Panacea—they was out o' the Panacea when I went to the drug store last week—they say that, took with the Panacea, they always effect a certing cure."—But by this time Wingate and his disgusted friends had retreated, slamming the door on the Fool and his ailments.

Nevertheless in six months the whole affair was forgotten, the money had been spent—the "Ditch" had been purchased by a company of Boston capitalists, fired by the glowing description of an Eastern tourist, who had spent one drunken night at Five Forks—and I think even the mental condition of Hawkins might have remained undisturbed by criticism, but for a singular incident.

It was during an exciting political campaign, when party feeling ran high, that the irascible Captain McFadden, of Sacramento, visited Five Forks. During a heated discussion in the Prairie Rose Saloon words passed between the Captain and the Honourable Calhoun Bungstarter, ending in a challenge. The Captain bore the infelix reputation of being a notorious duellist and a dead shot: the Captain was unpopular; the

Captain was believed to have been sent by the opposition for a deadly purpose, and the Captain was, moreover, a stranger. I am sorry to say that with Five Forks this latter condition did not carry the quality of sanctity or reverence that usually obtains among other nomads. There was consequently some little hesitation when the Captain turned upon the crowd and asked for some one to act as his friend. To everybody's astonishment, and to the indignation of many, the Fool stepped forward and offered himself in that capacity. I do not know whether Captain McFadden would have chosen him voluntarily, but he was constrained, in the absence of a better man, to accept his services.

The duel never took place! The preliminaries were all arranged, the spot indicated, the men were present with their seconds, there was no interruption from without, there was no explanation or apology passed —but the duel did *not* take place. It may be readily imagined that these facts, which were all known to Five Forks, threw the whole community into a fever of curiosity. The principals, the surgeon, and one second left town the next day. Only the Fool remained. *He* resisted all questioning—declaring himself held in honour not to divulge—in short, conducted himself with consistent but exasperating folly. It was not until six months had passed that Colonel Starbottle, the second of Calhoun Bungstarter, in a moment of weakness superinduced by the social glass, condescended to explain. I should not do justice to the parties if I did not give that explanation in the Colonel's own words. I may remark, in passing, that the characteristic dignity of Colonel Starbottle always became intensified by stimulants, and that by the same process all sense of humour was utterly eliminated.

"With the understanding that I am addressing myself confidentially to men of honour," said the Colonel, elevating his chest above the barroom counter of the Prairie Rose Saloon, "I trust that it will not be necessary for me to protect myself from levity, as I was forced to do in Sacramento on the only other occasion when I entered into an explanation of this delicate affair by—er—er—calling the individual to a personal account—er! I do not believe," added the Colonel, slightly waving his glass of liquor in the air with a graceful gesture of courteous deprecation—"knowing what I do of the present company—that such a course of action is required here. Certainly not—Sir—in the home of Mr. Hawkins—er—the gentleman who represented Mr. Bungstarter, whose conduct, ged, Sir, is worthy of praise, blank me!"

Apparently satisfied with the gravity and respectful attention of his listeners, Colonel Starbottle smiled relentingly and sweetly, closed his eyes half dreamily, as if to recall his wandering thoughts, and began—

"As the spot selected was nearest the tenement of Mr. Hawkins, it was agreed that the parties should meet there. They did so promptly at

half past six. The morning being chilly, Mr. Hawkins extended the
hospitalities of his house with a bottle of Bourbon whisky—of which
all partook but myself. The reason for that exception is, I believe, well
known. It is my invariable custom to take brandy—a wine-glassful in a
cup of strong coffee, immediately on rising. It stimulates the functions,
sir, without producing any blank derangement of the nerves."

The barkeeper, to whom, as an expert, the Colonel had graciously
imparted this information, nodded approvingly, and the Colonel, amid
a breathless silence, went on—

"We were about twenty minutes in reaching the spot. The ground
was measured, the weapons were loaded, when Mr. Bungstarter confided to me the information that he was unwell and in great *pain!* On
consultation with Mr. Hawkins, it appeared that his principal in a
distant part of the field was also suffering and in great pain. The
symptoms were such as a medical man would pronounce 'choleraic.' I
say *would* have pronounced, for on examination the surgeon was also
found to be—er—in pain, and I regret to say, expressing himself in
language unbecoming the occasion. His impression was that some
powerful drug had been administered. On referring the question to
Mr. Hawkins, he remembered that the bottle of whisky partaken by
them contained a medicine which he had been in the habit of taking,
but which, having failed to act upon him, he had concluded to be
generally ineffective, and had forgotten. His perfect willingness to hold
himself personally responsible to each of the parties, his genuine concern at the disastrous effect of the mistake, mingled with his own
alarm at the state of his system, which—er—failed to—er—respond to
the peculiar qualities of the medicine, was most becoming to him as a
man of honour and a gentleman! After an hour's delay, both principals
being completely exhausted, and abandoned by the surgeon, who was
unreasonably alarmed at his own condition, Mr. Hawkins and I
agreed to remove our men to Markleville. There, after a further consultation with Mr. Hawkins, an amicable adjustment of all difficulties,
honourable to both parties, and governed by profound secrecy, was
arranged. I believe," added the Colonel, looking around and setting
down his glass, "no gentleman has yet expressed himself other than
satisfied with the result."

Perhaps it was the Colonel's manner, but whatever was the opinion
of Five Forks regarding the intellectual display of Mr. Hawkins in this
affair, there was very little outspoken criticism at the moment. In a
few weeks the whole thing was forgotten, except as part of the necessary record of Hawkins' blunders, which was already a pretty full one.
Again some later follies conspired to obliterate the past, until, a year
later, a valuable lead was discovered in the "Blazing Star" Tunnel, in

the hill where he lived, and a large sum was offered him for a portion of his land on the hill-top. Accustomed as Five Forks had become to the exhibition of his folly, it was with astonishment that they learned that he resolutely and decidedly refused the offer. The reason that he gave was still more astounding. He was about to build!

To build a house upon property available for mining purposes was preposterous; to build at all with a roof already covering him, was an act of extravagance; to build a house of the style he proposed was simply madness!

Yet here were facts. The plans were made and the lumber for the new building was already on the ground, while the shaft of the "Blazing Star" was being sunk below. The site was, in reality, a very picturesque one—the building itself of a style and quality hitherto unknown in Five Forks. The citizens, at first sceptical, during their moments of recreation and idleness gathered doubtingly about the locality. Day by day, in that climate of rapid growths, the building, pleasantly known in the slang of Five Forks as "the Idiot Asylum," rose beside the green oaks and clustering firs of Hawkins Hill, as if it were part of the natural phenomena. At last it was completed. Then Mr. Hawkins proceeded to furnish it with an expensiveness and extravagance of outlay quite in keeping with his former idiocy. Carpets, sofas, mirrors, and finally a piano—the only one known in the county, and brought at great expense from Sacramento—kept curiosity at a fever heat. More than that, there were articles and ornaments which a few married experts declared only fit for women. When the furnishing of the house was complete—it had occupied two months of the speculative and curious attention of the camp—Mr. Hawkins locked the front door, put the key in his pocket, and quietly retired to his more humble roof, lower on the hill side!

I have not deemed it necessary to indicate to the intelligent reader all of the theories which obtained in Five Forks during the erection of the building. Some of them may be readily imagined. That "the Hag" had by artful coyness and systematic reticence at last completely subjugated the Fool, and that the new house was intended for the nuptial bower of the (predestined) unhappy pair, was of course the prevailing opinion. But when, after a reasonable time had elapsed, and the house still remained untenanted, the more exasperating conviction forced itself upon the general mind that the Fool had been for the third time imposed upon. When two months had elapsed and there seemed no prospect of a mistress for the new house, I think public indignation became so strong that had "the Hag" arrived, the marriage would have been publicly prevented. But no one appeared that seemed to answer to this idea of an available tenant, and all inquiry of Mr.

Hawkins as to his intention in building a house and not renting it or occupying it, failed to elicit any further information. The reasons that he gave were felt to be vague, evasive, and unsatisfactory. He was in no hurry to move, he said; when he *was* ready, it surely was not strange that he should like to have his house all ready to receive him. He was often seen upon the veranda of a summer evening smoking a cigar. It is reported that one night the house was observed to be brilliantly lighted from garret to basement; that a neighbour, observing this, crept toward the open parlour window, and, looking in, espied the Fool accurately dressed in evening costume, lounging upon a sofa in the drawing-room, with the easy air of socially entertaining a large party. Notwithstanding this, the house was unmistakably vacant that evening, save for the presence of the owner, as the witnesses afterward testified. When this story was first related, a few practical men suggested the theory that Mr. Hawkins was simply drilling himself in the elaborate duties of hospitality against a probable event in his history. A few ventured the belief that the house was haunted. The imaginative editor of the Five Forks "Record" evolved from the depths of his professional consciousness a story that Hawkins' sweetheart had died, and that he regularly entertained her spirit in this beautifully-furnished mausoleum. The occasional spectacle of Hawkins' tall figure pacing the veranda on moonlight nights lent some credence to this theory, until an unlooked-for incident diverted all speculation into another channel.

It was about this time that a certain wild, rude valley, in the neighbourhood of Five Forks, had become famous as a picturesque resort. Travellers had visited it, and declared that there were more cubic yards of rough stone cliff and a waterfall of greater height, than any they had visited. Correspondents had written it up with extravagant rhetoric and inordinate poetical quotation. Men and women who had never enjoyed a sunset, a tree, or a flower—who had never appreciated the graciousness or meaning of the yellow sunlight that flecked their homely doorways, or the tenderness of a midsummer's night, to whose moon-light they bared their shirt-sleeves or their *tulle* dresses—came from thousands of miles away to calculate the height of this rock, to observe the depth of this chasm, to remark upon the enormous size of this unsightly tree, and to believe with ineffable self-complacency that they really admired nature. And so it came to pass that, in accordance with the tastes or weaknesses of the individual, the more prominent and salient points of the valley were christened, and there was a "Lace Handkerchief Fall," and the "Tears of Sympathy Cataract," and one distinguished orator's "Peak," and several "Mounts" of various noted people, living or dead; and an "Exclamation Point," and a "Valley of

Silent Adoration." And, in course of time, empty soda-water bottles were found at the base of the cataract, and greasy newspapers and fragments of ham sandwiches lay at the dusty roots of giant trees. With this, there were frequent irruptions of closely-shaven and tightly-cravated men and delicate-faced women in the one long street of Five Forks, and a scampering of mules, and an occasional procession of dusty brown-linen cavalry.

A year after "Hawkins' Idiot Asylum" was completed, one day there drifted into the valley a riotous cavalcade of "school-marms," teachers of the San Francisco public schools, out for a holiday. Not severely-spectacled Minervas and chastely armed and mailed Pallases, but, I fear for the security of Five Forks, very human, charming, and mischievous young women. At least, so the men thought, working in the ditches and tunnelling on the hill-side; and when, in the interests of Science and the mental advancement of Juvenile Posterity, it was finally settled that they should stay in Five Forks two or three days for the sake of visiting the various mines, and particularly the "Blazing Star" Tunnel, there was some flutter of masculine anxiety. There was a considerable inquiry for "store clothes," a hopeless overhauling of old and disused raiment, and a general demand for "boiled shirts" and the barber.

Meanwhile, with that supreme audacity and impudent hardihood of the sex when gregarious, the school-marms rode through the town, admiring openly the handsome faces and manly figures that looked up from the ditches or rose behind the cars of ore at the mouths of tunnels. Indeed, it is alleged that Jenny Forester, backed and supported by seven other equally shameless young women, had openly and publicly waved her handkerchief to the florid Hercules of Five Forks—one Tom Flynn, formerly of Virginia—leaving that good-natured but not over-bright giant pulling his blonde moustaches in bashful amazement.

It was a pleasant June afternoon that Miss Nelly Arnot, Principal of the primary department of one of the public schools of San Francisco, having evaded her companions, resolved to put into operation a plan which had lately sprung up in her courageous and mischief-loving fancy. With that wonderful and mysterious instinct of her sex, from whom no secrets of the affections are hid and to whom all hearts are laid open, she had heard the story of Hawkins' folly and the existence of the "Idiot Asylum." Alone, on Hawkins' Hill, she had determined to penetrate its seclusion. Skirting the underbrush at the foot of the hill, she managed to keep the heaviest timber between herself and the "Blazing Star" Tunnel at its base, as well as the cabin of Hawkins, half-way up the ascent, until, by a circuitous route, at last she reached, unobserved, the summit. Before her rose, silent, darkened, and motionless, the object of her search. Here her courage failed her, with all the characteristic inconsequence of her sex. A sudden fear of all the dangers she had safely passed—bears, tarantulas, drunken men, and lizards—came upon her. For a moment, as she afterwards expressed it, "She thought she should die." With this belief, probably, she gathered three large stones, which she could hardly lift, for the purpose of throwing a great distance; put two hairpins in her mouth, and carefully readjusted with both hands two stray braids of her lovely blue-black mane which had fallen in gathering the stones. Then she felt in the pockets of her linen duster for her card-case, handkerchief, pocket-book, and smelling-bottle, and finding them intact, suddenly assumed an air of easy, ladylike unconcern, went up the steps of the veranda, and demurely pulled the front door-bell, which she knew would not be answered. After a decent pause, she walked around the encompassing veranda, examining the closed shutters of the French windows until she found one that yielded to her touch. Here she paused again to adjust her coquettish hat by the mirror-like surface of the long sash window that reflected the full length of her pretty figure. And then she opened the window and entered the room.

Although long closed, the house had a smell of newness and of fresh paint that was quite unlike the mouldiness of the conventional haunted house. The bright carpets, the cheerful walls, the glistening oil-cloths were quite inconsistent with the idea of a ghost. With childish curiosity she began to explore the silent house, at first timidly—opening the doors with a violent push, and then stepping back from the threshold to make good a possible retreat; and then more boldly, as she became convinced of her security and absolute loneliness. In one of the chambers, the largest, there were fresh flowers in a vase—evidently gathered that morning; and what seemed still more remarkable, the pitchers and ewers were freshly filled with water. This obliged Miss Nelly to notice another singular fact, namely, that the house was free from dust—the one most obtrusive and penetrating visitor of Five Forks. The floors and carpets had been recently swept, the chairs and furniture carefully wiped and dusted. If the house *was* haunted, it was possessed by a spirit who had none of the usual indifference to decay and mould. And yet the beds had evidently never been slept in, the very springs of the chair in which she sat creaked stiffly at the novelty, the closet doors opened with the reluctance of fresh paint and varnish, and in spite of the warmth, cleanliness, and cheerfulness of furniture and decoration, there was none of the ease of tenancy and occupation. As Miss Nelly afterwards confessed, she longed to "tumble things around," and when she reached the parlour or drawing-room again, she could hardly resist the desire. Particularly was she tempted by a closed piano, that stood mutely against the wall. She thought she would open it just to see who was the maker. That done, it would be no harm to try its tone. She did so, with one little foot on the soft pedal. But Miss Nelly was too good a player, and too enthusiastic a musician, to stop at half measures. She tried it again— this time so sincerely that the whole house seemed to spring into voice. Then she stopped and listened. There was no response—the empty rooms seemed to have relapsed into their old stillness. She stepped out on the veranda—a woodpecker recommenced his tapping on an adjacent tree, the rattle of a cart in the rocky gulch below the hill came faintly up. No one was to be seen far or near. Miss Nelly, reassured, returned. She again ran her fingers over the keys—stopped, caught at a melody running in her mind, half played it, and then threw away all caution. Before five minutes had elapsed she had entirely forgotten herself, and with her linen duster thrown aside, her straw hat flung on the piano, her white hands bared, and a black loop of her braided hair hanging upon her shoulder, was fairly embarked upon a flowing sea of musical recollection.

She had played perhaps half-an-hour, when, having just finished an elaborate symphony and resting her hands on the keys, she heard very distinctly and unmistakably the sound of applause from without. In an instant the fires of shame and indignation leaped into her cheeks, and she rose from the instrument and ran to the window, only in time to catch sight of a dozen figures in blue and red flannel shirts vanishing hurriedly through the trees below.

Miss Nelly's mind was instantly made up. I think I have already intimated that under the stimulus of excitement she was not wanting in courage, and as she quietly resumed her gloves, hat, and duster, she was not perhaps exactly the young person that it would be entirely safe for the timid, embarrassed, or inexperienced of my sex to meet alone. She shut down the piano, and having carefully reclosed all the windows and doors, and restored the house to its former desolate condition, she stepped from the veranda, and proceeded directly to the cabin of the unintellectual Hawkins, that reared its adobe chimney above the umbrage a quarter of a mile below.

The door opened instantly to her impulsive knock, and the Fool of Five Forks stood before her. Miss Nelly had never before seen the man designated by this infelicitous title, and as he stepped backward in half courtesy and half astonishment she was for the moment disconcerted. He was tall, finely formed, and dark-bearded. Above cheeks a little hollowed by care and ill-health shone a pair of hazel eyes, very large, very gentle, but inexpressibly sad and mournful. This was certainly not the kind of man Miss Nelly had expected to see, yet after her first embarrassment had passed, the very circumstance, oddly enough, added to her indignation, and stung her wounded pride still more deeply. Nevertheless, the arch hypocrite instantly changed her tactics with the swift intuition of her sex.

"I have come," she said with a dazzling smile, infinitely more dangerous than her former dignified severity, "I have come to ask your pardon for a great liberty I have just taken. I believe the new house above us on the hill is yours. I was so much pleased with its exterior that I left my friends for a moment below here," she continued artfully, with a slight wave of the hand, as if indicating a band of fearless Amazons without, and waiting to avenge any possible insult offered to one of their number, "and ventured to enter it. Finding it unoccupied, as I had been told, I am afraid I had the audacity to sit down and amuse myself for a few moments at the piano—while waiting for my friends."

Hawkins raised his beautiful eyes to hers. He saw a very pretty girl, with frank gray eyes glistening with excitement, with two red, slightly freckled cheeks, glowing a little under his eyes, with a short scarlet upper lip turned back, like a rose leaf, over a little line of white teeth, as she breathed somewhat hurriedly in her nervous excitement. He saw all this calmly, quietly, and, save for the natural uneasiness of a shy, reticent man, I fear without a quickening of his pulse.

"I knowed it," he said simply. "I heerd ye as I kem up."

Miss Nelly was furious at his grammar, his dialect, his coolness, and still more at the suspicion that he was an active member of her invisible *claque.*

"Ah," she said, still smiling, "then I think I heard *you*"——

"I reckon not," he interrupted gravely. "I didn't stay long. I found the boys hanging round the house, and I allowed at first I'd go in and kinder warn you, but they promised to keep still, and you looked so comfortable and wrapped up in your music, that I hadn't the heart to disturb you, and kem away. I hope," he added earnestly, "they didn't let on ez they heerd you. They ain't a bad lot—them Blazin' Star boys —though they're a little hard at times. But they'd no more hurt ye then they would a—a—a cat!" continued Mr. Hawkins, blushing with a faint apprehension of the inelegance of his simile.

"No! no!" said Miss Nelly, feeling suddenly very angry with herself, the Fool, and the entire male population of Five Forks. "No! I have behaved foolishly, I suppose—and if they *had* it would have served me right. But I only wanted to apologise to you. You'll find everything as you left it. Good day!"

She turned to go. Mr. Hawkins began to feel embarrassed. "I'd have asked ye to sit down," he said, finally, "if it hed been a place fit for a lady. I oughter done so, enny way. I don't know what kept me from it. But I ain't well, Miss. Times I get a sort o' dumb ager—it's the ditches, I think, Miss—and I don't seem to hev my wits about me."

Instantly Miss Arnot was all sympathy—her quick woman's heart was touched.

"Can I—can anything be done?" she asked, more timidly than she had before spoken.

"No!—not onless ye remember suthin' about these pills." He exhibited a box containing about half-a-dozen. "I forget the direction—I don't seem to remember much, any way, these times—they're 'Jones' Vegetable Compound.' If ye've ever took 'em ye'll remember whether the reg'lar dose is eight. They ain't but six here. But perhaps ye never tuk any," he added deprecatingly.

"No," said Miss Nelly, curtly. She had usually a keen sense of the ludicrous, but somehow Mr. Hawkins' eccentricity only pained her.

"Will you let me see you to the foot of the hill?" he said again, after another embarrassing pause.

Miss Arnot felt instantly that such an act would condone her trespass in the eyes of the world. She might meet some of her invisible admirers—or even her companions—and, with all her erratic impulses, she was nevertheless a woman, and did not entirely despise the verdict of conventionality. She smiled sweetly and assented, and in another moment the two were lost in the shadows of the wood.

Like many other apparently trivial acts in an uneventful life, it was decisive. As she expected, she met two or three of her late applauders, whom, she fancied, looked sheepish and embarrassed; she met also her companions looking for her in some alarm, who really appeared astonished at her escort, and, she fancied, a trifle envious of her evident success. I fear that Miss Arnot, in response to their anxious inquiries, did not state entirely the truth, but, without actual assertion, led them to believe that she had at a very early stage of the proceeding completely subjugated this weak-minded giant, and had brought him triumphantly to her feet. From telling this story two or three times she got finally to believing that she had some foundation for it; then to a vague sort of desire that it would eventually prove to be true, and then to an equally vague yearning to hasten that consummation. That it would redound to any satisfaction of the Fool she did not stop to doubt. That it would cure him of his folly she was quite confident. Indeed, there are very few of us—men or women—who do not believe that even a hopeless love for ourselves is more conducive to the salvation of the lover than a requited affection for another.

The criticism of Five Forks was, as the reader may imagine, swift and conclusive. When it was found out that Miss Arnot was not "the Hag" masquerading as a young and pretty girl, to the ultimate deception of Five Forks in general and the Fool in particular, it was decided at once that nothing but the speedy union of the Fool and the "pretty school-marm" was consistent with ordinary common sense. The singular good fortune of Hawkins was quite in accordance with the theory of his luck as propounded by the camp. That after "the Hag" failed to make her appearance he should "strike a lead" in his own house, without the trouble of "prospectin'," seemed to these casuists as a wonderful but inevitable law. To add to these fateful probabilities, Miss Arnot fell and sprained her ankle in the ascent of Mount Lincoln, and was confined for some weeks to the hotel after her companions had departed. During this period Hawkins was civilly but grotesquely attentive. When, after a reasonable time had elapsed, there still appeared to be no immediate prospect of the occupancy of the new house, public opinion experienced a singular change in regard to its theories of Mr. Hawkins' conduct. "The Hag" was looked upon as a saint-like and long-suffering martyr to the weaknesses and inconsistency of the Fool. That, after erecting this new house at her request, he had suddenly "gone back" on her; that his celibacy was the result of a long habit of weak proposal and subsequent shameless rejection, and that he was now trying his hand on the helpless school-marm, was perfectly plain to Five Forks. That he should be frustrated in his attempts at any cost was equally plain. Miss Nelly suddenly found herself invested with a rude chivalry that would have been amusing had it not been at times embarrassing; that would have been impertinent but for the almost superstitious respect with which it was proffered. Every day somebody from Five Forks rode out to inquire the health of the fair patient. "Hez Hawkins bin over yer to-day?" queried Tom Flynn, with artful ease and indifference as he leaned over Miss Nelly's easychair on the veranda. Miss Nelly, with a faint pink flush on her cheek, was constrained to answer "No." "Well, he sorter sprained his foot agin a rock yesterday," continued Flynn, with shameless untruthfulness. "You mus'n't think anything o' that, Miss Arnot. He'll be over yer to-morrer, and meantime he told me to hand this yer bookay with his regards, and this yer specimen!" And Mr. Flynn laid down the flowers he had picked *en route* against such an emergency, and presented respectfully a piece of quartz and gold which he had taken that morning from his own sluice-box. "You mus'n't mind Hawkins' ways, Miss Nelly," said another sympathising miner. "There ain't a better man in camp than that theer Cy Hawkins!—but he don't understand the ways o' the world with wimen. He hasn't mixed as much with society as the rest of us," he added, with an elaborate Chesterfieldian

ease of manner, "but he means well." Meanwhile a few other sympathetic tunnel-men were impressing upon Mr. Hawkins the necessity of
the greatest attention to the invalid. "It won't do, Hawkins," they
explained, "to let that there gal go back to San Francisco and say that
when she was sick and alone, the only man in Five Forks under whose
roof she had rested, and at whose table she had sat"—this was considered a natural but pardonable exaggeration of rhetoric—"ever threw
off on her; and it shan't be done. It ain't the square thing to Five
Forks." And then the Fool would rush away to the valley, and be
received by Miss Nelly with a certain reserve of manner that finally
disappeared in a flush of colour, some increased vivacity, and a pardonable coquetry. And so the days passed; Miss Nelly grew better in
health and more troubled in mind, and Mr. Hawkins became more
and more embarrassed, and Five Forks smiled and rubbed its hands,
and waited for the approaching denouement. And then it came. But
not perhaps in the manner that Five Forks had imagined.

It was a lovely afternoon in July that a party of Eastern tourists
rode into Five Forks. They had just "done" the Valley of Big Things,
and there being one or two Eastern capitalists among the party, it was
deemed advisable that a proper knowledge of the practical mining
resources of California should be added to their experience of the
merely picturesque in Nature. Thus far everything had been satisfactory; the amount of water which passed over the Fall was large, owing
to a backward season; some snow still remained in the cañons near the
highest peaks; they had ridden round one of the biggest trees, and
through the prostrate trunk of another. To say that they were delighted is to express feebly the enthusiasm of these ladies and gentlemen, drunk with the champagny hospitality of their entertainers, the
utter novelty of scene, and the dry, exhilarating air of the valley. One
or two had already expressed themselves ready to live and die there;
another had written a glowing account to the Eastern press, depreciat-
ing all other scenery in Europe and America; and under these circumstances it was reasonably expected that Five Forks would do its duty,
and equally impress the stranger after its own fashion.

Letters to this effect were sent from San Francisco by prominent
capitalists there, and under the able superintendence of one of their
agents, the visitors were taken in hand, shown "what was to be seen,"
carefully restrained from observing what ought not to be visible, and
so kept in a blissful and enthusiastic condition. And so the graveyard
of Five Forks, in which but two of the occupants had died natural
deaths, the dreary, ragged cabins on the hill-sides, with their sad-eyed,
cynical, broken-spirited occupants, toiling on, day by day, for a miserable pittance and a fare that a self-respecting Eastern mechanic would

have scornfully rejected, were not a part of the Eastern visitors' recollection. But the hoisting works and machinery of the "Blazing Star
Tunnel Company" was—the Blazing Star Tunnel Company, whose
"gentlemanly Superintendent" had received private information from
San Francisco to do the "proper thing" for the party. Wherefore the
valuable heaps of ore in the company's works were shown, the oblong
bars of gold—ready for shipment—were playfully offered to the ladies
who could lift and carry them away unaided, and even the tunnel
itself, gloomy, fateful, and peculiar, was shown as part of the experience; and, in the noble language of one correspondent, "the wealth of
Five Forks and the peculiar inducements that it offered to Eastern
capitalists" were established beyond a doubt. And then occurred a
little incident which, as an unbiassed spectator, I am free to say offered
no inducements to anybody whatever, but which, for its bearing upon
the central figure of this veracious chronicle, I cannot pass over.

It had become apparent to one or two more practical and sober-
minded in the party that certain portions of the "Blazing Star" Tunnel
—(owing, perhaps, to the exigencies of a flattering annual dividend)—
were economically and imperfectly "shored" and supported, and were
consequently unsafe, insecure, and to be avoided. Nevertheless, at a
time when champagne corks were popping in dark corners, and enthusiastic voices and happy laughter rang through the half-lighted levels
and galleries, there came a sudden and mysterious silence. A few lights
dashed swiftly by in the direction of a distant part of the gallery, and
then there was a sudden sharp issuing of orders and a dull, ominous
rumble. Some of the visitors turned pale—one woman fainted!

Something had happened. What? "Nothing"—the speaker is fluent
but uneasy—"one of the gentlemen in trying to dislodge a 'specimen'
from the wall had knocked away a support. There had been a 'cave'—
the gentleman was caught and buried below his shoulders. It was all
right—they'd get him out in a moment—only it required great care to
keep from extending the 'cave.' Didn't know his name—it was that
little man—the husband of that lively lady with the black eyes. Eh!
Hullo there! Stop her. For God's sake!—not that way! She'll fall from
that shaft. She'll be killed!"

But the lively lady was already gone. With staring black eyes, imploringly trying to pierce the gloom, with hands and feet that sought
to batter and break down the thick darkness, with incoherent cries and
supplications, following the moving of *ignis fatuus* lights ahead, she
ran and ran swiftly! Ran over treacherous foundations, ran by yawning
gulfs, ran past branching galleries and arches, ran wildly, ran despairingly, ran blindly, and at last ran into the arms of the Fool of Five
Forks.

In an instant she caught at his hand. "Oh, save him!" she cried; "you belong here—you know this dreadful place; bring me to him. Tell me where to go and what to do, I implore you! Quick, he is dying. Come!"

He raised his eyes to hers, and then, with a sudden cry, dropped the rope and crowbar he was carrying, and reeled against the wall. "Annie!" he gasped, slowly, "is it you?"

She caught at both his hands, brought her face to his with staring eyes, murmured "Good God, Cyrus!" and sank upon her knees before him.

He tried to disengage the hand that she wrung with passionate entreaty.

"No, no! Cyrus, you will forgive me—you will forget the past! God has sent you here to-day. You will come with me. You will—you must —save him!"

"Save who?" cried Cyrus hoarsely.

"My husband!"

The blow was so direct—so strong and overwhelming—that even through her own stronger and more selfish absorption she saw it in the face of the man, and pitied him.

"I thought—you—knew—it!" she faltered. He did not speak, but looked at her with fixed, dumb eyes. And then the sound of distant voices and hurrying feet started her again into passionate life. She once more caught his hand.

"O Cyrus! hear me! If you have loved me through all these years, you will not fail me now. You must save him! You can! You are brave and strong—you always were, Cyrus! You will save him, Cyrus, for my sake—for the sake of your love for me! You will—I know it! God bless you!"

She rose as if to follow him, but at a gesture of command she stood still. He picked up the rope and crowbar slowly, and in a dazed, blinded way that, in her agony of impatience and alarm, seemed protracted to cruel infinity. Then he turned, and raising her hand to his lips, he kissed it slowly, looked at her again—and the next moment was gone.

He did not return. For at the end of the next half-hour, when they laid before her the half-conscious breathing body of her husband, safe and unharmed but for exhaustion and some slight bruises, she learned that the worst fears of the workmen had been realised. In releasing him a second "cave" had taken place. They had barely time to snatch away the helpless body of her husband before the strong frame of his rescuer, Cyrus Hawkins, was struck and smitten down in his place.

For two hours he lay there, crushed and broken-limbed, with a heavy beam lying across his breast, in sight of all, conscious and patient. For two hours they had laboured around him, wildly, despairingly, hopefully, with the wills of gods and the strength of giants, and at the end of that time they came to an upright timber, which rested its base upon the beam. There was a cry for axes, and one was already swinging in the air, when the dying man called to them, feebly—

"Don't cut that upright!"

"Why?"

"It will bring down the whole gallery with it."

"How?"

"It's one of the foundations of my house."

The axe fell from the workman's hand, and with a blanched face he turned to his fellows. It was too true. They were in the uppermost gallery, and the "cave" had taken place directly below the new house. After a pause the Fool spoke again more feebly.

"The lady!—quick."

They brought her—a wretched, fainting creature, with pallid face and streaming eyes—and fell back as she bent her face above him.

"It was built for you, Annie, darling," he said in a hurried whisper, "and has been waiting up there for you and me all these long days. It's deeded to you, Annie, and you must—live there—with *him!* He will not mind that I shall be always near you—for it stands above—my grave!"

And he was right. In a few minutes later, when he had passed away, they did not move him, but sat by his body all night with a torch at his feet and head. And the next day they walled up the gallery as a vault, but they put no mark or any sign thereon, trusting rather to the monument that, bright and cheerful, rose above him in the sunlight of the hill. For they said: "This is not an evidence of death and gloom and sorrow, as are other monuments, but is a sign of Life and Light and Hope, wherefore shall all men know that he who lies under it—is a Fool!"

The Man from Solano

HE CAME TOWARD me out of an opera lobby, between the acts—a figure as remarkable as anything in the performance. His clothes, no two articles of which were of the same colour, had the appearance of having been purchased and put on only an hour or two before—a fact more directly established by the clothes-dealer's ticket which still adhered to his coat-collar, giving the number, size, and general dimensions of that garment somewhat obtrusively to an uninterested public. His trousers had a straight line down each leg, as if he had been born flat but had since developed; and there was another crease down his back, like those figures children cut out of folded paper. I may add that there was no consciousness of this in his face, which was good-natured, and, but for a certain squareness in the angle of his lower jaw, utterly uninteresting and commonplace.

"You disremember me," he said briefly, as he extended his hand, "but I'm from Solano, in Californy. I met you there in the spring of '57. I was tendin' sheep, and you was burnin' charcoal."

There was not the slightest trace of any intentional rudeness in the reminder. It was simply a statement of fact, and as such to be accepted.

"What I hailed ye for was only this," he said, after I had shaken hands with him. "I saw you a minnit ago standin' over in yon box—

553

chirpin' with a lady—a young lady, peart and pretty. Might you be telling me her name?"

I gave him the name of a certain noted belle of a neighbouring city, who had lately stirred the hearts of the metropolis, and who was especially admired by the brilliant and fascinating young Dashboard, who stood beside me.

The Man from Solano mused for a moment, and then said, "Thet's so! thet's the name! It's the same gal!"

"You have met her, then?" I asked, in surprise.

"Ye-es," he responded slowly; "I met her about fower months ago. She'd bin makin' a tour of Californy with some friends, and I first saw her aboard the cars this side of Reno. She lost her baggage checks, and I found them on the floor and gave 'em back to her, and she thanked me. I reckon now it would be about the square thing to go over thar and sorter recognise her." He stopped a moment, and looked at us inquiringly.

"My dear sir," struck in the brilliant and fascinating young Dashboard, "if your hesitation proceeds from any doubt as to the propriety of your attire, I beg you to dismiss it from your mind at once. The tyranny of custom, it is true, compels your friend and myself to dress peculiarly, but I assure you nothing could be finer than the way that the olive green of your coat melts in the delicate yellow of your cravat, or the pearl gray of your trousers blends with the bright blue of your waistcoat, and lends additional brilliancy to that massive oroid watch-chain which you wear."

To my surprise, the Man from Solano did not strike him. He looked at the ironical Dashboard with grave earnestness, and then said quietly—

"Then I reckon you wouldn't mind showin' me in thar?"

Dashboard was, I admit, a little staggered at this. But he recovered himself, and, bowing ironically, led the way to the box. I followed him and the Man from Solano.

Now the belle in question happened to be a gentlewoman—descended from gentlewomen—and after Dashboard's ironical introduction, in which the Man from Solano was not spared, she comprehended the situation instantly. To Dashboard's surprise she drew a chair to her side, made the Man from Solano sit down, quietly turned her back on Dashboard, and in full view of the brilliant audience and the focus of a hundred lorgnettes, entered into conversation with him.

Here, for the sake of romance, I should like to say he became animated, and exhibited some trait of excellence—some rare wit or solid sense. But the fact is he was dull and stupid to the last degree. He persisted in keeping the conversation upon the subject of the lost baggage-checks, and every bright attempt of the lady to divert him failed signally. At last, to everybody's relief, he rose, and leaning over her chair, said—

"I calklate to stop over here some time, miss, and you and me bein' sorter strangers here, maybe when there's any show like this goin' on you'll let me"——

Miss X. said somewhat hastily that the multiplicity of her engagements and the brief limit of her stay in New York she feared would, &c., &c. The two other ladies had their handkerchiefs over their mouths, and were staring intently on the stage, when the Man from Solano continued—

"Then, maybe, miss, whenever there is a show goin' on that you'll attend, you'll just drop me word to Earle's Hotel, to this yer address," and he pulled from his pocket a dozen well-worn letters, and taking the buff envelope from one, handed it to her with something like a bow.

"Certainly," broke in the facetious Dashboard; "Miss X. goes to the Charity Ball to-morrow night. The tickets are but a trifle to an opulent Californian, and a man of your evident means, and the object a worthy one. You will, no doubt, easily secure an invitation."

Miss X. raised her handsome eyes for a moment to Dashboard. "By all means," she said, turning to the Man from Solano; "and as Mr. Dashboard is one of the managers, and you are a stranger, he will, of course, send you a complimentary ticket. I have known Mr. Dashboard long enough to know that he is invariably courteous to strangers and a gentleman." She settled herself in her chair again and fixed her eyes upon the stage.

The Man from Solano thanked the Man of New York, and then, after shaking hands with everybody in the box, turned to go. When he had reached the door he looked back to Miss X., and said—

"It *was* one of the queerest things in the world, miss, that my findin' them checks"——

But the curtain had just then risen on the garden scene in "Faust," and Miss X. was absorbed. The Man from Solano carefully shut the box door and retired. I followed him.

He was silent until he reached the lobby, and then he said, as if renewing a previous conversation, "She *is* a mighty peart gal—that's so. She's just my kind, and will make a stavin' good wife."

I thought I saw danger ahead for the Man from Solano, so I hastened to tell him that she was beset by attentions, that she could have her pick and choice of the best of society, and finally, that she was, most probably, engaged to Dashboard.

"That's so," he said quietly, without the slightest trace of feeling.

"It would be mighty queer if she wasn't. But I reckon I'll steer down to the ho-tel. I don't care much for this yellin'." (He was alluding to a cadenza of that famous cantatrice, Signora Batti Batti.) "What's the time?"

He pulled out his watch. It was such a glaring chain, so obviously bogus, that my eyes were fascinated by it. "You're looking at that watch," he said; "it's purty to look at, but she don't go worth a cent. And yet her price was $125, gold. I gobbled her up in Chatham Street day before yesterday, where they were selling 'em very cheap at auction."

"You have been outrageously swindled," I said indignantly. "Watch and chain are not worth twenty dollars."

"Are they worth fifteen?" he asked gravely.

"Possibly."

"Then I reckon it's a fair trade. Ye see, I told 'em I was a Californian from Solano, and hadn't anything about me of greenbacks. I had three slugs with me. Ye remember them slugs?" (I did; the "slug" was a "token" issued in the early days—a hexagonal piece of gold a little over twice the size of a twenty-dollar gold piece—worth and accepted for fifty dollars.)

"Well, I handed them that, and they handed me the watch. You see them slugs I had made myself outer brass filings and iron pyrites, and used to slap 'em down on the boys for a bluff in a game of draw poker. You see, not being reg'lar gov'ment money, it wasn't counterfeiting. I reckon they cost me, counting time and anxiety, about fifteen dollars. So, if this yer watch is worth that, it's about a square game, ain't it?"

I began to understand the Man from Solano, and said it was. He returned his watch to his pocket, toyed playfully with the chain, and remarked, "Kinder makes a man look fash'nable and wealthy, don't it?"

I agreed with him. "But what do you intend to do here?" I asked.

"Well, I've got a cash capital of nigh on seven hundred dollars. I guess until I get into reg'lar business I'll skirmish round Wall Street, and sorter lay low." I was about to give him a few words of warning, but I remembered his watch, and desisted. We shook hands and parted.

A few days after I met him on Broadway. He was attired in another new suit, but I think I saw a slight improvement in his general appearance. Only five distinct colours were visible in his attire. But this, I had reason to believe afterwards, was accidental.

I asked him if he had been to the ball. He said he had. "That gal, and a mighty peart gal she was too, was there, but she sorter fought shy of me. I got this new suit to go in, but those waiters sorter run me into a private box, and I didn't get much chance to continner our talk about them checks. But that young feller, Dashboard, was mighty perlite. He brought lots of fellers and young women round to the box to see me, and he made up a party that night to take me round Wall Street and in them Stock Boards. And the next day he called for me, and took me, and I invested about five hundred dollars in them stocks —maybe more. You see, we sorter swopped stocks. You know I had ten shares in the Peacock Copper Mine, that you was once secretary of."

"But those shares are not worth a cent. The whole thing exploded ten years ago."

"That's so, maybe; *you* say so. But then I didn't know anything more about Communipaw Central, or the Naphtha Gaslight Company, and so I thought it was a square game. Only I realised on the stocks I bought, and I kem up outer Wall Street about four hundred dollars better. You see it was a sorter risk, after all, for them Peacock stocks *might* come up!"

I looked into his face: it was immeasurably serene and commonplace. I began to be a little afraid of the man, or, rather, of my want of judgment of the man; and after a few words we shook hands and parted.

It was some months before I again saw the Man from Solano. When I did, I found that he had actually become a member of the Stock Board, and had a little office on Broad Street, where he transacted a fair business. My remembrance going back to the first night I met him, I inquired if he had renewed his acquaintance with Miss X.

"I heerd that she was in Newport this summer, and I ran down there fur a week."

"And you talked with her about the baggage-checks?"

"No," he said seriously; "she gave me a commission to buy some stocks for her. You see, I guess them fash'nable fellers sorter got to runnin' her about me, and so she put our acquaintance on a square business footing. I tell you, she's a right peart gal. Did ye hear of the accident that happened to her?"

I had not.

"Well, you see, she was out yachting, and I managed through one of those fellers to get an invite too. The whole thing was got up by a man that they say is going to marry her. Well, one afternoon the boom swings round in a little squall and knocks her overboard. There was an awful excitement,—you've heard about it, maybe?"

"No!" But I saw it all with a romancer's instinct in a flash of poetry! This poor fellow, debarred through uncouthness from expressing his affection for her, had at last found his fitting opportunity. He had——

"Thar was an awful row," he went on. "I ran out on the taffrail, and there a dozen yards away was that purty creature, that peart gal, and —I"——

"You jumped for her," I said hastily.

"No!" he said gravely. "I let the other man do the jumping. I sorter looked on."

I stared at him in astonishment.

"No," he went on seriously. "He was the man who jumped—that was just then his 'put'—his line of business. You see if I had waltzed over the side of that ship, and cavoorted in, and flummuxed round and finally flopped to the bottom, that other man would have jumped nateral-like and saved her; and ez he was going to marry her any way, I don't exactly see where *I'd* hev been represented in the transaction. But don't you see, ef, after he'd jumped and hadn't got her, he'd gone down himself, I'd hev had the next best chance, and the advantage of heving him outer the way. You see, you don't understand me—I don't think you did in Californy."

"Then he did save her?"

"Of course. Don't you see she was all right. If he'd missed her, I'd have chipped in. Thar warn't no sense in my doing his duty onless he failed."

Somehow the story got out. The Man from Solano as a butt became more popular than ever, and of course received invitations to burlesque receptions, and naturally met a great many people whom otherwise he would not have seen. It was observed also that his seven hundred dollars were steadily growing, and that he seemed to be getting on in his business. Certain Californian stocks which I had seen quietly interred in the old days in the tombs of their fathers were magically revived; and I remember, as one who has seen a ghost, to have been shocked as I looked over the quotations one morning to have seen the ghastly face of the "Dead Beach Mining Co.," rouged and plastered, looking out from the columns of the morning paper. At last a few people began to respect, or suspect, the Man from Solano. At last suspicion culminated with this incident:—

He had long expressed a wish to belong to a certain "fash'n'ble" club, and with a view of burlesque he was invited to visit the club, where a series of ridiculous entertainments were given him, winding up with a card party. As I passed the steps of the club-house early next morning, I overheard two or three members talking excitedly,—

"He cleaned everybody out." "Why, he must have raked in nigh on $40,000."

"Who?" I asked.

"The Man from Solano."

As I turned away, one of the gentlemen, a victim, noted for his sporting propensities, followed me, and laying his hand on my shoulder, asked—

"Tell me fairly now. What business did your friend follow in California?"

"He was a shepherd."

"A what?"

"A shepherd. Tended his flocks on the honey-scented hills of Solano."

"Well, all I can say is, d—n your Californian pastorals!"

A Ghost of the Sierras

IT WAS A vast silence of pines, redolent with balsamic breath, and muffled with the dry dust of dead bark and matted mosses. Lying on our backs, we looked upward through a hundred feet of clear, unbroken interval to the first lateral branches that formed the flat canopy above us. Here and there the fierce sun, from whose active persecution we had just escaped, searched for us through the woods, but its keen blade was dulled and turned aside by intercostal boughs, and its brightness dissipated in nebulous mists throughout the roofing of the dim, brown aisles around us. We were in another atmosphere, under another sky; indeed, in another world than the dazzling one we had just quitted. The grave silence seemed so much a part of the grateful coolness, that we hesitated to speak, and for some moments lay quietly outstretched on the pine tassels where we had first thrown ourselves. Finally, a voice broke the silence—

"Ask the old Major; he knows all about it!"

The person here alluded to under that military title was myself. I hardly need explain to any Californian that it by no means followed that I was a "Major," or that I was "old," or that I knew anything about "it," or indeed what "it" referred to. The whole remark was merely one of the usual conventional feelers to conversation,—a kind of social preamble, quite common to our slangy camp intercourse.

Nevertheless, as I was always known as the Major, perhaps for no better reason than that the speaker, an old journalist, was always called Doctor, I recognised the fact so far as to kick aside an intervening saddle, so that I could see the speaker's face on a level with my own, and said nothing.

"About ghosts!" said the Doctor, after a pause, which nobody broke or was expected to break. "Ghosts, sir! That's what we want to know. What are we doing here in this blank old mausoleum of Calaveras County, if it isn't to find out something about 'em, eh?"

Nobody replied.

"Thar's that haunted house at Cave City. Can't be more than a mile or two away, anyhow. Used to be just off the trail."

A dead silence.

The Doctor (addressing space generally): "Yes, sir; it *was* a mighty queer story."

Still the same reposeful indifference. We all knew the Doctor's skill as a *raconteur;* we all knew that a story was coming, and we all knew that any interruption would be fatal. Time and time again, in our prospecting experience, had a word of polite encouragement, a rash expression of interest, even a too eager attitude of silent expectancy, brought the Doctor to a sudden change of subject. Time and time again have we seen the unwary stranger stand amazed and bewildered between our own indifference and the sudden termination of a promising anecdote, through his own unlucky interference. So we said nothing. "The Judge"—another instance of arbitrary nomenclature—pretended to sleep. Jack began to twist a *cigarrito.* Thornton bit off the ends of pine needles reflectively.

"Yes, sir," continued the Doctor, coolly resting the back of his head on the palms of his hands, "it *was* rather curious. All except the murder. *That's* what gets me, for the murder had no new points, no fancy touches, no sentiment, no mystery. Was just one of the old style, "subhead" paragraphs. Old-fashioned miner scrubs along on hardtack and beans, and saves up a little money to go home and see relations. Old-fashioned assassin sharpens up knife, old style; loads old flint-lock, brass-mounted pistols; walks in on old-fashioned miner one dark night, sends him home to his relations away back to several generations, and walks off with the swag. No mystery *there;* nothing to clear up; subsequent revelations only impertinence. Nothing for any ghost to do—who meant business. More than that, over forty murders, same old kind, committed every year in Calaveras, and no spiritual post obits coming due every anniversary; no assessments made on the peace and quiet of the surviving community. I tell you what, boys, I've always been inclined to throw off on the Cave City ghost for that alone. It's a bad precedent, sir. If that kind o' thing is going to obtain in the foot-hills, we'll have the trails full of chaps formerly knocked over by Mexicans and road agents; every little camp and grocery will have stock enough on hand to go into business, and where's there any security for surviving life and property, eh? What's your opinion, Judge, as a fair-minded legislator?"

Of course there was no response. Yet it was part of the Doctor's system of aggravation to become discursive at these moments, in the hope of interruption, and he continued for some moments to dwell on the terrible possibility of a state of affairs in which a gentleman could no longer settle a dispute with an enemy without being subjected to succeeding spiritual embarrassment. But all this digression fell upon apparently inattentive ears.

"Well, sir, after the murder, the cabin stood for a long time deserted and tenantless. Popular opinion was against it. One day a ragged prospector, savage with hard labour and harder luck, came to the camp, looking for a place to live and a chance to prospect. After the boys had taken his measure, they concluded that he'd already tackled so much in the way of difficulties that a ghost more or less wouldn't be of much account. So they sent him to the haunted cabin. He had a big yellow dog with him, about as ugly and as savage as himself; and the boys sort o' congratulated themselves, from a practical view point, that while they were giving the old ruffian a shelter, they were helping in the cause of Christianity against ghosts and goblins. They had little faith in the old man, but went their whole pile on that dog. That's where they were mistaken.

"The house stood almost three hundred feet from the nearest cave, and on dark nights, being in a hollow, was as lonely as if it had been on the top of Shasta. If you ever saw the spot when there was just moon enough to bring out the little surrounding clumps of chaparral until they looked like crouching figures, and make the bits of broken quartz glisten like skulls, you'd begin to understand how bit a contract that man and that yellow dog undertook.

"They went into possession that afternoon, and old Hard Times set out to cook his supper. When it was over he sat down by the embers and lit his pipe, the yellow dog lying at his feet. Suddenly 'Rap! rap!' comes from the door. 'Come in,' says the man gruffly. 'Rap!' again. 'Come in and be d—d to you,' says the man, who had no idea of getting up to open the door. But no one responded, and the next moment smash goes the only sound pane in the only window. Seeing this, old Hard Times gets up, with the devil in his eye, and a revolver in his hand, followed by the yellow dog, with every teeth showing, and swings open the door. No one there! But as the man opened the door, that yellow dog, that had been so chipper before, suddenly begins to crouch and step backward, step by step, trembling and shivering, and at last crouches down in the chimney, without even so much as looking at his master. The man slams the door shut again, but there comes another smash. This time it seems to come from inside the cabin, and it isn't until the man looks around and sees everything quiet that he gets up, without speaking, and makes a dash for the door, and tears round outside the cabin like mad, but finds nothing but silence and darkness. Then he comes back swearing and calls the dog. But that great yellow dog that the boys would have staked all their money on is crouching under the bunk, and has to be dragged out like a coon from a hollow tree, and lies there, his eyes starting from their sockets; every limb and muscle quivering with fear, and his very hair drawn up in bristling ridges. The man calls him to the door. He drags himself a few steps, stops, sniffs, and refuses to go farther. The man calls him again, with an oath and a threat. Then, what does that yellow dog do? He crawls edgewise towards the door, crouching himself against the bunk, till he's flatter than a knife blade; then, half-way, he stops. Then that d —d yellow dog begins to walk gingerly—lifting each foot up in the air, one after the other, still trembling in every limb. Then he stops again. Then he crouches. Then he gives one little shuddering leap—not straight forward, but up,—clearing the floor about six inches, as if"——

"Over something," interrupted the Judge hastily, lifting himself on his elbow.

The Doctor stopped instantly. "Juan," he said coolly to one of the Mexican packers, "quit foolin' with that *riata*. You'll have that stake out and that mule loose in another minute. Come over this way!"

The Mexican turned a scared, white face to the Doctor, muttering something, and let go the deerskin hide. We all up-raised our voices with one accord, the Judge most penitently and apologetically, and implored the Doctor to go on. "I'll shoot the first man who interrupts you again," added Thornton persuasively.

But the Doctor, with his hands languidly under his head, had lost his interest. "Well, the dog ran off to the hills, and neither the threats nor cajoleries of his master could ever make him enter the cabin again. The next day the man left the camp. What time is it? Getting on to sundown, ain't it? Keep off my leg, will you, you d—d Greaser, and stop stumbling round there! Lie down."

But we knew that the Doctor had not completely finished his story, and we waited patiently for the conclusion. Meanwhile the old, gray silence of the woods again asserted itself, but shadows were now beginning to gather in the heavy beams of the roof above, and the dim aisles seemed to be narrowing and closing in around us. Presently the Doctor recommenced lazily, as if no interruption had occurred.

"As I said before, I never put much faith in that story, and shouldn't have told it, but for a rather curious experience of my own. It was in the spring of '62, and I was one of a party of four, coming up from O'Neill's, when we had been snowed up. It was awful weather; the snow had changed to sleet and rain after we crossed the divide, and the water was out everywhere; every ditch was a creek, every creek a river. We had lost two horses on the North Fork, we were dead beat, off the trail, and sloshing round, with night coming on, and the level hail like shot in our faces. Things were looking bleak and scary when, riding a little ahead of the party, I saw a light twinkling in a hollow beyond. My horse was still fresh, and calling out to the boys to follow me and bear for the light, I struck out for it. In another moment I was before a little cabin that half burrowed in the black chaparral; I dismounted and rapped at the door. There was no response. I then tried to force the door, but it was fastened securely from within. I was all the more surprised when one of the boys, who had overtaken me, told me that he had just seen through a window a man reading by the fire. Indignant at this inhospitality, we both made a resolute onset against the door, at the same time raising our angry voices to a yell. Suddenly there was a quick response, the hurried withdrawing of a bolt, and the door opened.

"The occupant was a short, thick-set man, with a pale, careworn face, whose prevailing expression was one of gentle good-humour and patient suffering. When we entered, he asked us hastily why we had not 'sung out' before.

" 'But we *knocked!*' I said impatiently, 'and almost drove your door in.'

" 'That's nothing,' he said patiently. 'I'm used to *that.*'

"I looked again at the man's patient, fateful face, and then around the cabin. In an instant the whole situation flashed before me. 'Are we not near Cave City?' I asked.

" 'Yes,' he replied, 'it's just below. You must have passed it in the storm.'

" 'I see.' I again looked around the cabin. 'Isn't this what they call the haunted house?'

"He looked at me curiously. 'It is,' he said simply.

"You can imagine my delight! Here was an opportunity to test the whole story, to work down to the bed rock, and see how it would pan out! We were too many and too well armed to fear tricks or dangers from outsiders. If—as one theory had been held—the disturbance was kept up by a band of concealed marauders or road agents, whose purpose was to preserve their haunts from intrusion, we were quite able to pay them back in kind for any assault. I need not say that the boys were delighted with this prospect when the fact was revealed to them. The only one doubtful and apathetic spirit there was our host, who quietly resumed his seat and his book, with his old expression of patient martyrdom. It would have been easy for me to have drawn him out, but I felt that I did not want to corroborate anybody else's experience; only to record my own. And I thought it better to keep the boys from any predisposing terrors.

"We ate our supper, and then sat, patiently and expectant, around the fire. An hour slipped away, but no disturbance; another hour passed as monotonously. Our host read his book; only the dash of hail against the roof broke the silence. But"——

The Doctor stopped. Since the last interruption, I noticed he had changed the easy slangy style of his story to a more perfect, artistic, and even studied manner. He dropped now suddenly into his old colloquial speech, and quietly said, "If you don't quit stumbling over those *riatas,* Juan, I'll hobble *you.* Come here, there; lie down, will you?"

We all turned fiercely on the cause of this second dangerous interruption, but a sight of the poor fellow's pale and frightened face withheld our vindictive tongues. And the Doctor, happily, of his own accord, went on:—

"But I had forgotten that it was no easy matter to keep these high-spirited boys, bent on a row, in decent subjection; and after the third hour passed without a supernatural exhibition, I observed, from certain winks and whispers, that they were determined to get up indications of their own. In a few moments violent rappings were heard from all parts of the cabin; large stones (adroitly thrown up the chimney) fell with a heavy thud on the roof. Strange groans and ominous yells seemed to come from the outside (where the interstices between the logs were wide enough). Yet, through all this uproar, our host sat still and patient, with no sign of indignation or reproach upon his good-humoured but haggard features. Before long it became evident that this exhibition was exclusively for *his* benefit. Under the thin disguise of asking him to assist them in discovering the disturbers *outside* the cabin, those inside took advantage of his absence to turn the cabin topsy-turvy.

" 'You see what the spirits have done, old man,' said the arch leader of this mischief. 'They've upset that there flour barrel while we wasn't looking, and then kicked over the water-jug and spilled all the water!'

"The patient man lifted his head and looked at the flour-strewn walls. Then he glanced down at the floor, but drew back with a slight tremor.

" 'It ain't water!' he said quietly.

" 'What is it then?'

" 'It's BLOOD! Look!'

"The nearest man gave a sudden start and sank back white as a sheet.

"For there, gentlemen, on the floor, just before the door, where the old man had seen the dog hesitate and lift his feet, there! there!— gentlemen—upon my honour, slowly widened and broadened a dark red pool of human blood! Stop him! Quick! Stop him, I say!"

There was a blinding flash that lit up the dark woods, and a sharp report! When we reached the Doctor's side he was holding the smoking pistol, just discharged, in one hand, while with the other he was pointing to the rapidly disappearing figure of Juan, our Mexican vaquero!

"Missed him! by G—d!" said the Doctor. "But did you hear him? Did you see his livid face as he rose up at the name of blood? Did you see his guilty conscience in his face. Eh? Why don't you speak? What are you staring at?"

"Was it the murdered man's ghost, Doctor?" we all panted in one quick breath.

"Ghost be d—d! No! But in that Mexican vaquero—that cursed Juan Ramirez!—I saw and shot at his murderer!"